"BRENDA JOYCE
CAPTURES YOU AND
DOESN'T LET YOU GO!"
—JOHANNA LINDSEY

PRAISE FOR HER PREVIOUS
NOVEL, *THE FINER THINGS*:

"A sophisticated, stylish reading
brimming with elegant prose."
—*Romantic Times*

"Ms. Joyce's books always flow with
richness and anticipation. This one is so
good I felt transported into the lives of
these magnificent characters. The plot is
enormously absorbing, the settings are
vibrant and the sensuality abounds
throughout. I cried and loved right along
with the characters." —*Rendezvous*

"Likeable characters... Intriguing."
—*Publishers Weekly*

"Brenda Joyce is a master storyteller."
—*CompuServe Romance Reviews*

"Very satisfying. You won't be
able to put it down...Ms. Joyce
only gets better and better."
—*The Bells & Beaux of Romance*

*St. Martin's Paperbacks Titles
by Brenda Joyce*

THE FINER THINGS
SPLENDOR

Splendor

BRENDA JOYCE

St. Martin's Paperbacks

SPLENDOR

Copyright © 1997 by Brenda Joyce.

Photograph of the author by Sigrid Estrada.

ISBN 0-312-96391-2

Printed in the United States of America

St. Martin's Paperbacks edition/December 1997

St. Martin's Paperbacks are published by St. Martin's Press, 175 Fifth Avenue, New York, NY 10010.

10 9 8 7 6 5 4 3 2 1

This one is for Jen Enderlin, my editor. For being brilliant, for being a joy to work with, and for being a true believer—and a new friend.
Jen, thanks for *everything*.

❧ PROLOGUE ❧

THEY were fighting.

Her mama and papa were fighting.

Tears slipped down her cheeks. Carolyn hugged her skinny knees to her chest, holding her breath, trembling and afraid. She could not understand what was happening. They never fought. But now they were shouting at one another and Carolyn could hear their every word from where she sat hunched over in her small bed. Their bedchamber was across the narrow hall; the bookshop her papa owned was downstairs. Carolyn's door was open because she didn't like the dark. But she almost wished that it were closed so she would not have to hear them.

Her father was shouting. Carolyn choked on a sob.

"Why won't you let me go?" Her mother was crying now. "How can it hurt to try?"

"You've written her two letters. And she did not even send a one-word reply!" Her father cried.

Carolyn's mother, Margaret, wept.

"Oh, God," George said thickly. "Please, Mag, don't cry. I love you. I hate seeing you this way."

There was silence now.

Carolyn sucked down her sobs, rising impulsively to her feet. Her heart was banging against her chest. Clutching the folds of her cotton nightgown, she crept to the door. Her feet were bare and the wood floor was icy cold—outside, it was snowing heavily, huge fat flakes sticking to the windowpanes. Surely if she went to her parents they would stop fighting and everything would be all right. Their door was ajar. Carolyn peeked around it.

Her father held her mother, who wept on his chest. He caressed her blond hair, tied into one long braid. Her parents were also dressed for bed. Carolyn felt better, seeing them in a familiar embrace, and she started forward, to join them as she so often did, but her mother started to speak and instinct made Carolyn freeze.

Margaret lifted her head. "Let me try, George, before we lose everything. She is my mother," she pleaded.

He stiffened. "I'd rather lose everything than take her charity—and her abuse."

"If she only got to know you, she would love you—the way I do," Margaret cried, gazing at his face.

"She has hated me from the moment she found out about us, and that was six years ago. Face it, Mag. Your letters have gone unanswered. She doesn't want anything to do with you or our daughter—because of me."

"The government official was serious. They're going to auction this house and shop out from under us if we do not pay our debts. And then where will we go?" Margaret cried anxiously.

"I can find work in France. Or perhaps Stockholm or Copenhagen. And there is a huge foreign community in St. Petersburg. I will tutor nobly born children again, the way I did when we first met." His smile was brief.

"France?" Margaret was horrified. "They are in the midst of a revolution! Stockholm? Russia?"

George stood. "What would you have me do if we lose our bookshop? Where would you have me go? Your mother has made it impossible for me to continue as a tutor in this country. She has not changed. There are no doors open for me here." Suddenly he sat beside her. "God, look at how I have ruined your life!"

"You have not ruined my life!" Margaret was fierce, and she hugged him, hard. "I love you. I always have, I always will. I cannot imagine life without you, and I do not care how we live, only that we are together with our daughter, with a roof over our head and warm food in our bellies.'' She smiled, her eyes glistening.

He was grim. ''We are going to have to move. Our landlord was not jesting. If we do not pay what we owe, they shall seize this house and all of our possessions.''

Margaret stood abruptly. ''You must let me go to my mother. We are blood. In six years I have never asked her for anything. Let me ask her for her help now.''

George did not move. And then he saw his daughter hovering in the doorway with wide eyes and tearstained cheeks. ''Carolyn!'' he cried. He stood and swiftly crossed the room, picking her up. She was five years old, but as light as a feather. He smiled. ''Can't sleep?'' He kissed her cheek.

Carolyn shook her head, not liking what she had heard. ''Why is Mama crying? Why are you making her cry? Why won't you let her go where she wants to go?''

George turned white. ''Darling, we are only having an argument. Sometimes people who love each other very much have different ideas and different opinions. It doesn't mean that we don't love each other. In fact, it is good for the mind and the soul. I love your mother more than I have ever loved anyone—other than you.'' He kissed her cheek again. But his tone was worried now.

Margaret had come over to them and she stroked her daughter's platinum hair. ''Your papa is right. We are only discussing a trip I wish to make.'' She looked at George with sudden determination. ''But your father is going to allow me to go to Midlands. And I will take you, Carolyn,'' she said firmly.

They had been traveling since early that morning, well before dawn. It had not stopped snowing. The entire Essex countryside was blanketed in white, the roads covered with huge drifts. Ponds and lakes were frozen over, and oaks and dogwoods bent double under the weight of their white burden. Periodically the mail coach would halt and all the passengers were required to disembark, and one and all would have to push the vehicle free of the ruts, mud, and snow. Then, cold and aching, Carolyn and her mother would clamber back to their seats atop the coach and the vehicle would set off again.

Carolyn was hungry, tired, and cold, even though she wore many layers of clothing and a heavy wool coat. She and her mother were riding with two other passengers on the outside seats behind the coachman because they could not afford the seats inside the carriage. Although they had hot bricks wrapped in towels for their feet, it was frigidly cold and Carolyn wished their journey was over. Margaret could not stop shivering.

"We are almost there." Her mother had her arm around her, holding her tightly to her side as they shared their body heat. Margaret smiled at Carolyn, but her lips were oddly blue. "This is Owl Hill. When I was a child not too much older than you, I used to ride my pony here. There is a small lake on the other side. In the summer, I used to picnic there with my sister, Georgia. It was fun." Her expression had turned wistful.

"I like Aunt Georgia," Carolyn said truthfully. "Why haven't we seen her in such a long time?"

Margaret smiled and looked away, but the smile was forced and Carolyn saw the tears shimmering in her mother's eyes. "She is married and very busy these days." Her mother's tone was flat, and Carolyn knew the subject was closed.

The mail coach, pulled by four weary bays, halted. "We are here," Margaret said.

Carolyn squinted through the snow. The side of the road boasted a wooden fence and, beyond that, nothing but snow-covered meadows and snow-clad trees. "We are? Where is Midlands?"

"At the end of the drive. We shall have to walk, I am afraid." She smiled again, encouragingly.

Carolyn waited as the coachman helped her mother to

climb down to the ground, and then he lifted her down and set her on her feet beside Margaret. A big, lanky man bundled up in a wool overcoat and a huge scarf, he eyed Margaret kindly. "I do hope you ain't got too far to go, ma'am," he said.

"We are fine, but thank you for your concern." Margaret smiled at him and Carolyn saw her press a shilling into his hand. "That is for your kindness on this journey. I'm sorry it cannot be more."

He started. "I can't take this from you, ma'am!" He was blushing as he handed the coin back to her. "Use it to feed the young one tonight."

Margaret smiled and took Carolyn's hand. They watched the coachman climb up to his seat, lift the reins, and drive the team forward. Snow blew in their faces as the mail coach hustled down the winter-white road. It grew smaller and smaller and smaller until it was a dark speck amidst the vast surrounding whiteness.

Carolyn saw the drive now, another snowy road that wound through the snow-covered fields on the other side of the fence. But she still could not see a house. "Mama?" she asked as they started walking, hand in hand. "I don't see your mother's house."

"It's about a mile from here," Margaret said. "But walking is better than sitting, don't you think? Shall we sing a song?" She was cheerful.

Carolyn did like walking better, because she was rapidly becoming less cold, although her mother's lips remained blue. "Mama, are you all right?"

"I am fine. Shall we sing 'Over the Hills and Far Away'?"

Carolyn grinned. And they started to sing.

Carolyn's eyes widened. Her grandmother's house was huge—and it seemed much more like a castle than a house. Long, relatively low and rectangular, it was built of huge slabs of pale taupe stone, with two towers forming wings on either side of the central building. In front of the entrance, which had a temple front and pediment, was a limestone water fountain. Low, sculpted hedges surrounded the fountain, now dry, and also bordered the house.

"Mama," Carolyn whispered, clutching her mother's hand. "She is rich."

"My mother is a viscountess, Carolyn." Her mother's teeth chattered as she spoke.

"But this is the kind of house the king lives in."

Margaret did manage to laugh. "It is impressive, but not that impressive, dear. It is just that you are not accustomed to the homes of society."

"But you grew up here?" Carolyn was amazed.

"We spent summers here—and Christmas."

Carolyn glanced up at her mother, whose tone had become husky. Her mother was very pale. She increased her grip on her mother's hand. Her mother seemed to be increasingly nervous—and even sad.

"Come," Margaret said. They walked past the limestone fountain, icy snow crunching under their shoes, and up the front walk, which was brick. It had been shoveled free of snow and salted. At the front door Margaret rang a bell, which resounded loudly. Behind them, the sky was already darkening. Soon night would fall.

A bald man in livery answered the door. He stared.

"Hello, Carter. Is my mother home?"

The footman blinked. His expression turned from sheer impassivity to utter surprise. "Lady Margaret?" he cried.

"Yes." Margaret smiled. "And my daughter, Carolyn." She held Carolyn's shoulder. Carolyn was incredulous—she had never heard her mother addressed as Lady Margaret before.

"Come in! Out of the cold!" He glanced past them, appearing perplexed when he did not see a coach in the drive.

"A mail coach dropped us off at the foot of the drive," Margaret explained as they entered a large, spacious foyer with marble floors.

Carolyn gaped at her surroundings, standing as close to her mother as possible now, clinging to her hand. Ahead of them was a sweeping staircase, the banister wrought iron, a red carpet runner on the steps. How could her mama have lived here? It was as if her mama had been a princess!

"You walked! In this weather?" Carter was stunned.

Another servant, in black, entered the foyer.

Now Margaret was really smiling. "Hello, Winslow."

"Lady Margaret!" The butler rushed forward, as if to embrace her, but then he skidded to a halt and dropped his arms to his sides. "How good to see you, my lady, how awfully good."

Margaret kissed his cheek. "It is awfully good to see you, too, Winslow. This is my daughter, Carolyn." Margaret pulled Carolyn forward.

Winslow beamed. "She is just like you, my lady, if you do not mind my saying so," the butler said.

"Winslow, Lady Margaret and her daughter walked all the way from the road," Carter said disapprovingly.

Winslow straightened. He was appalled. "Let me take your coats. I will bring hot tea immediately."

Margaret no longer smiled. "I think, before you bring any refreshments, that you should tell my mother that I am here," Margaret said.

Winslow stared. His expression was impossible to read. "She is in residence, is she not?"

"Yes, Her Ladyship is at home." The butler's gaze shifted. "Very well," he said. He bowed. "I will be right back." He turned and strode briskly down the corridor, past the sweeping staircase, and disappeared.

Margaret reached for and took Carolyn's hand. Carolyn looked up and saw the worry on her face. "Don't worry, Mama," she said in a whisper. "Everything will be all right." But she was still in disbelief. How could her mother have grown up here, in this castlelike place? And was she really Lady Margaret and not Mrs. Browne?

Margaret bent and kissed her daughter. "I love you," she whispered.

"I love you too, Mama," Carolyn said.

Margaret straightened just as rapid, no-nonsense footsteps could be heard approaching. She paled.

A slim, gray-haired woman with a handsome face and a set expression marched into view, her pale green gown swirling about her. She saw them and halted in her tracks. Mother and daughter stared at one another. Carolyn looked from one to the other and felt dread. The old lady was angry. Her eyes were cold. And her mother was clearly afraid.

"Hello, Mother," Margaret whispered almost inaudibly.

The viscountess came forward. "What are you doing here?" she demanded. Her gaze moved to Carolyn, swept over her, making Carolyn feel as if something were terribly wrong with her, and then it returned to Margaret. "Did you not tell me that you would never come back?"

Margaret swallowed. "That was six years ago."

"Oh? So you have changed your mind? Are you leaving him?"

Margaret's face was pinched. "My feelings have not changed. But I pray that yours have. Did you get my letters?" she asked.

"Yes." One word, harsh, uncompromising, final. Lady Stafford stared. The viscountess glanced at Carolyn, but it was impossible to decipher what she was thinking. "Did you think to soften me by bringing her here?"

"Yes, frankly, I did," Margaret said, her voice choked with tears.

"Well, such a ploy will not work," Edith Owsley stated. "You made your choice, Margaret, all those years ago. Now, if you will excuse me?"

Margaret inhaled. "Mother, we have traveled since well before dawn in order to see you, through wind and snow. Could we, at least, adjourn to a quiet, private room so we might talk? Carolyn can stay here with Winslow."

Carolyn started and immediately gripped her mother's coat. She did not want to be left behind.

"What is there to talk about?" the viscountess snapped. "Unless you have come to your senses and are coming home?"

Margaret was frozen. "I cannot come home. I am not a child anymore. I am a wife and a mother." She wet her lips. "Mother. We need your help," she whispered. "Desperately."

Carolyn pressed closer to her mother.

For one moment, as Edith Owsley, the Dowager Viscountess of Stafford, stood there, Carolyn thought she was going to relent. But her face—and eyes—hardened. "You can always come home, in spite of what you have done," she said. And she turned her back on them and marched, soldierlike, out of the foyer.

"If not for me, then for Carolyn—your granddaughter," Margaret cried.

But Lady Stafford did not falter now, and she disappeared around the corner. The tableau in the foyer was frozen, a still life. A horrendous silence hovered.

Carolyn looked up and saw her mother crying silently, wet tears streaking her frozen cheeks. She wrapped her arms around her. "Please don't cry, Mama," she pleaded, ready to cry herself.

"I know you will not believe this," Margaret said, kneeling and embracing her daughter, "but she loves us, she does." Margaret closed her eyes tightly. "She does."

Carolyn did not believe it, not for a moment. She clung to her mother, feeling safe now in her embrace in spite of the general uneasiness around them. "Are we going home?" she asked. She wanted nothing more than to leave.

Margaret straightened, sniffing. "Yes." And then she started to cry again.

PART ONE

The Prince

✒ ONE ✑

THE crowd was impatient. Women whispered to one another behind gloved hands and mock fans, diamonds glinting on their throats, dangling from their ears, woven into their coiffed hair. The men shifted, murmured, coughed, their dark evening clothes, piped with satin, shining in the light cast by thousands of candles in the dozens of huge gilt chandeliers overhead. Invitations had specified that the festivities were to begin at nine P.M. and it was now a quarter past. Fifteen hundred guests had already arrived at the prince regent's palatial London residence, and the ballroom was so crowded that it did not seem possible for there to be any dancing that night. But finally the stream of bejeweled, magnificently gowned ladies and their escorts had slowed to a trickle. From Pall Mall to St. James, the road was clogged with barouches, phaetons, and town coaches. Liveried footmen, hussars, and bewigged drivers waited with craned necks. In the courtyard outside the residence, a Royal Guard stood as still as statues, prepared to deliver a fifty-gun salute. Even the exiled royal French family, the Bourbons, waited with growing restlessness amongst the guests. The regent was intent upon making an entrance, as usual. It seemed that he would succeed.

"You are distracted, Excellency, or you are bored?" a sultry red-haired lady asked.

He turned. He was tall and golden-haired, clad in an

officer's uniform, a dark green jacket with rows of brass buttons and gold epaulets, dozens of medals pinned upon his chest, and pale dove-gray pants. Immediately the man bowed over the lady's extended gloved hand. "Lady Carradine, you have taken me by surprise," he murmured, his English flawed with the tiniest trace of some exotic foreign accent.

"Indeed?" She smiled. "I doubt anyone can take you by surprise, Prince Sverayov."

Nicholas Ivanovitch Sverayov stood a handful of inches over six feet, which meant that he now towered over the petite woman facing him. His body was not quite lean, for the fine cut of his uniform suggested a powerful physique. Clearly his shoulders were broad, his legs long. He stared at her out of compelling amber eyes. "I am as human as anyone here." His lips turned slightly. "Contrary to the recent spate of gossip in your newspapers."

"Surely you do not read the gossip columns?" She was coy, a smile on her rouged mouth.

"Only when it is unavoidable."

"Do you know Charles Copperville?" she asked, fluttering her fan. "He certainly seems to know you!"

"If we have met, he has retained his anonymity." Sverayov's cool smile did not give any sign of what he might be thinking. "I do look forward to making his acquaintance, though, as soon as possible."

"I shudder for poor Copperville," Lady Carradine said dramatically. "Perhaps he will retract the barbs he has made against you, your mission, and your country."

He chose not to respond. He was a Sverayov, and had centuries of notorious behavior to live down—not that he cared. He was used to gossip and rumors attaching themselves to him wherever he went, for whatever he did, and because of whomever he was currently associated with. Especially at home, where every word, every action, indeed, every probable thought, of a member of the Sverayov family, no matter how far removed, was constantly speculated upon. But he was in England on state business. Technically,

England and Russia were at war—and had been so ever
since the Treaty of Tilsit of 1807. His reception in London
had hardly been warm to begin with, and he did not need
a certain satirist named Copperville stirring up more hostility against him. The tsar, Alexander, desperately needed
an alliance between his empire and Britain, for Napoleon
had invaded Russia three weeks ago after much posturing.
Sverayov's command in the First Army had been turned
over to a subordinate, much to his dismay. For he was a
longtime personal friend of Alexander's, and Alexander
trusted him completely in this instance.

"Of course," the very beautiful woman continued, "I
cannot imagine you really caring about a single thing Copperville or anyone else has said about you." She stared him
in the eye.

He knew she was referring to the recent spate of gossip,
which maintained that Lord Carradine was furious at being
cuckolded by that "arrogant foreigner." Apparently some
threats, specific and drunken, had been made against his
person yesterday evening at White's. Sverayov was unruf-
fled. Lord Carradine was sixty if a day, quite obese, and
according to his wife, very impotent; he was hardly capable
of exercising an act of vengeance.

"Perhaps I am less interested in what others think of me
than what you think of me, Lady Carradine." The gallantry
was automatic. Lady Carradine was enjoyable in bed, and
he expected to be diverted by enjoyable companions in his
leisure hours. It was a fact of his existence, and had been
since he was a boy.

"Last night you were extraordinary," she said in a murmur.

He bowed slightly. "As were you." His reply was meant
to keep his options open. But the truth was, he could hardly
remember the particulars of their trysts last night or the two
evenings prior to that. What was on his mind was Castlereagh's incredibly stubborn nature, and the fact that he must
somehow break the man down. Sooner, not later, so he
could return to his command. Time was running out. The

French had taken Vilna two days ago. Alexander, who against the judgment of most of his advisors had taken command of all the armies in the field, had himself led his troops in a complete retreat. In effect, Vilna had been abandoned.

"Can I expect you later?" Lady Carradine asked, a purr.

He was undecided, and was about to put her off, when, across the numerous heads of the crowd, he saw a couple on the stairs at the entrance to the ballroom, poised to descend. He stiffened, forgetting all about Lady Carradine.

She followed his gaze. "Has the regent finally deigned to join us?" Her words died. She squinted. Her genuine smile was gone. A parody of it remained fixed on her attractive face.

Nicholas did not hear her. He stared at the exquisite, raven-haired woman still standing on top of the short flight of steps. His pulse banged wildly. He could not believe his eyes. The black-haired woman wore a bare silver gown that left little to one's imagination. She might as well have arrived naked. And although she was petite and slim, her abdomen protruded quite discernibly. He could only stare at her in dumbfounded shock.

"I see you are distracted," Lady Carradine said, quite evenly. "And I can see why. She is stunning."

Nicholas did not even look at her. She was pregnant, by God, and she had defied him blatantly by following him to London. He did not know which stunned him more.

But Lady Carradine was not to be put off. "Do you know her, Excellency?" Her smile was forced. "I have never seen her before, and I do know everyone. She must be from the country, or come from abroad." Her laughter—and the gaze she shot at him—was uneasy. "Surely she is no country mouse."

Nicholas felt as if he were wearing a stiff papier-mâché mask. "She is my wife."

Lady Carradine started. "Of course, I assumed you were married. Isn't everyone? But I did not know she had accompanied you to London."

And neither had Nicholas. "I beg your pardon," Nicholas said, bowing curtly. And then he began to make his way through the crowd.

She had seen him. She smiled, lifting one slender arm to wave a gloved hand at him. And she clung to the arm of her escort, Mikhail Fydorovski, a slim young man who was very flushed.

Nicholas paused and waited for her to come down the steps, aware of the crowd around them. Already he had been remarked, and he could feel people watching him, whispering about him. It was annoying, being in the public eye, but he was used to it. He suspected that within fifteen minutes Marie-Elena's identity would have been established, and the gossips would go wild. He would not have to be told what they were thinking and saying. Marie-Elena was commonly held to be one of the most stunning women in all of Europe, and they had been told, again and again, that together they made a striking royal couple. An image of their daughter, Katya, flitted instantly through Nicholas's mind. And with it, as always, there came a deep, profound sorrow.

"Niki, how good to see you, darling," Marie-Elena cried. She kissed his cheek, brushing her full, mostly bare breasts against his arm. Her eyes were as black as her hair, which made a startling contrast to her flawless ivory skin. She was wearing a diamond tiara in her hair, diamonds and rubies around her neck, and numerous diamond and ruby bracelets on top of her gloved wrists. "We have only just arrived," she said. Her escort had chosen to hang back, allowing them some privacy.

He stared. "Did I not leave you in St. Petersburg? Did I not make it clear that I was going abroad for the sole purpose of state affairs—not the purpose of pleasure?"

"I know what you are thinking," she said quickly, gripping his arm. "I know you decided against my accompanying you to London. But Katya has been miserable since you left," she exclaimed in her husky voice.

He started. "What do you mean, she has been miserable?'' He did not try to hide his utter concern.

"She cried all night after you left, and no one, not even Leeza, could console her!" Leeza was her old, nearly blind, nurse. "I did explain that you were not going back to the army, but I do not think she believed me. Niki, you know how smart she is. She stopped eating. I grew frightened." Marie-Elena's gaze was earnest, holding his.

But very little frightened her, and Nicholas knew it. Just as he knew that his daughter was his Achilles' heel. He could deal with any situation, any crisis, anything, by God, but not Katya distraught or suffering or in any kind of pain. And his wife knew that, as well. "How did you get here?" he asked.

Her brilliant yet oddly fragile smile flashed. "Alexander provided us with a ship."

He should have guessed. The tsar was currently as fond of Marie-Elena as he was of Nicholas, and Nicholas and Alexander had been friends since boyhood. The tsar had himself arranged their marriage with his typical enthusiasm—a blend of misplaced romantic idealism and stern political practicality. Marie-Elena was not just a German princess, she was the tsar's wife's cousin.

"He has also sent you a message, which I left on that desk in the library," Marie-Elena said. "Do not be angry with me, Niki. Perhaps I can be helpful to you here."

"Perhaps." His gaze wandered back to the crowd. The truth of the matter was that he knew his wife and she was selfish and spoiled and vastly used to getting her own way—by hook or by crook. She had desperately wanted to come to London with him, as if the trip were some Sunday picnic outing. He disliked her using Katya this way, but he had missed his daughter terribly, and did not know how long these damned talks would continue. And although he had insisted on being recalled if and when the treaty was concluded, that could be many months from now.

"Have a good evening, Niki," she said, smiling, shrugging free of his grasp. She tossed her blue-black head, pushing back hunks of hair with her satin-gloved fingertips, a sensual mannerism most men, Nicholas knew, admired. "And save me a dance, darling." She turned her back on him to join Fydorovski, and the pair glided off into the crowd.

And then the rifles outside blasted, fifty guns at once. Trumpets sounded just outside the ballroom. The prince regent had arrived.

"I'm glad you were free to come home with me," she said hoarsely.

"So am I." He did not consider his words. He did not even glance at her as he dressed. Lady Carradine remained in repose, her rose silk ballgown twisted about her torso, a collar of pearls about her throat. As he buttoned his snugly fitting pants, he heard her sit up and arrange her clothing more modestly. He was preoccupied.

The very last thing he needed right now was the distraction of Marie-Elena running all over London as if she owned it. She was not a discreet woman, it was not her nature, although too many times to count she had promised to be more careful. And while they had gone their separate ways for many years, in London it might be better to create an illusion that they shared a more conventional marriage. For the pendulum of public opinion often swung to their side when they did move together in society—the golden Russian prince, the beautiful German princess, a match made almost in heaven, if not by the tsar. It could very well help his mission if he could warm up the cold British fish he had thus far encountered. Until now, the British peerage had seemed curious but suspicious, and a few ladies and lords in his corner could definitely help him in his quest when he had so far come up against Castlereagh's very solid brick wall.

Nicholas suspected that someone inside of the government was working very hard to sabotage the talks. He had the strongest sixth sense about it. But he had yet to identify that man—or woman.

But his wife was pregnant, shockingly so. And the British were so boringly, damnably, conventional. Marie-Elena might hinder his mission far more than she might aid it. He shrugged on his jacket, adorned with a dozen rows of gold buttons and golden epaulets, rather violently.

"Nicholas? Is something wrong?" Lady Carradine moved to the side of the four-poster bed, her legs over the edge.

"I have to go. It is late." That was the truth. But it was the price paid for these kinds of encounters.

"You cannot leave now!" she exclaimed.

"It is unfortunate," he agreed, a mild lie, "but I can, and will." He reached for his ceremonial sword.

"You have been distracted all evening," she said evenly. But there was the slightest trace of hurt in her eyes.

"I am sorry." To make her feel better, he added, "I have grave matters on my mind."

She stood. "When will I . . ." She hesitated. "Now that your wife has arrived, will I see you again?"

He hated messes and scenes. He did not see the point of seeing Lady Carradine again. "I do not think so."

She nodded, pursing her mouth. Then abruptly she rose, moved to him, and put her arms around him. "Let me take care of you," she whispered. "One last time."

"It's not necessary," he said, taking her hands in his and removing them from his hips.

"Then promise me that we shall see each other again." Her brown eyes searched his face. "Or have I displeased you in some way?"

"You have not displeased me, Marcia. And I am sorry to have disappointed you. But we made one another no promises."

She sank back down on the bed, watching him stride to the door. "Then it is true. What they say—what I have heard. That you are inhuman when it comes to women— unfeeling. Incapable of love."

He paused. "If you are asking me if I am a romantic, then the answer is no," he said calmly. "I am not a poet, Marcia."

"Have you ever loved a woman, Nicholas?" she asked, her eyes glistening. "Have you ever even tried?"

The question was absurd. "What does love have to do with the few nights we shared? Did I ever speak of love? We are two adults. We have enjoyed one another's company. That is all there is to it."

"No." She smoothed her gown, as if intent on ironing out the wrinkles with her palms. "You made me no promises, but you are very compelling, Nicholas, when you wish to be. I knew I was going to fall for you—just as I knew I was going to get hurt." She blinked several times. "I have fallen in love with you."

He refrained from sighing. "I am sorry."

"Sorry," she echoed. She glanced up. "Is it because of her? Your wife? Do you love her? She is so terribly beautiful. And who was that man she was with?"

He stared. He had no intention of telling her the truth, that no, he did not love his wife and he never had, and that her escort was, probably, her latest lover. "That was a very personal question, Marcia," he said coolly.

"Do you go to her now?" Lady Carradine cried.

Nicholas bowed. "Do not disturb yourself on my account. I shall see myself out."

She rushed forward. "I apologize."

He shrugged, turned and walked across the dark room, his boots making no sound on the thick Persian rug. He unlocked the door and slipped through it. The corridor outside was lit by several wall sconces, and he walked unhurriedly downstairs, frowned upon by grim Carradine ancestors. He was feeling more than grim himself. The evening felt like a disaster, yet he hardly had cause to label it as such. And he was not a man given to premonitions.

A bleary-eyed servant snapped to attention in the foyer downstairs and let him out the front door. Nicholas's coach, black lacquer with gilt trim and a completely gilded roof, emblazoned with the Sverayov coat of arms in silver, red, and gold, was around the block, since he had no wish to blatantly advertise his presence at the Carradine residence.

But as he strode down the sidewalk, a thin, dapper form materialized from beneath a street lamp, rushing forward. Nicholas recognized his valet immediately, a Frenchman by birth, and stiffened in surprise. "Jacques!"

"My lord." The slender, mustachioed servant reached him, out of breath. "Thank God you 'ave come. I 'ave been waiting over 'alf an hour—uncertain of whether to interrupt you or not."

And Nicholas knew it was an emergency. Every fiber of his being tensed. His first thought was that it was too late—Napoleon had marched on either St. Petersburg or Moscow. "What is it?" His strides lengthened.

They hurried side by side around the corner, toward the waiting coach with its four footmen, six horses, and two drivers. "It is the princess. She 'as begun to deliver the child. Two hours ago, to be exact."

Nicholas stumbled and froze. "She cannot be due for at least four more months!"

"Yes. It was four, exactly." Jacques's brown eyes were somber. "The physician says the child is already dead—and your wife may die as well this night."

Nicholas could not move.

"Excellency, let me get you a drink. I have vodka in the carriage," Jacques said, holding his arm as if steadying him.

Nicholas looked at him. Jacques had to suspect the truth. "I am sorry the child is dead. But it was not mine." And there was no doubt—for he had not slept with Marie-Elena in five years.

Jacques nodded. "*Oui.* I thought as much, my lord."

But Nicholas did not hear him. For all her failings, and there were many, Marie-Elena might die. And she was Katya's mother—and Katya was at the house. Oh, God. Nicholas came to life. "Let's go," he said.

❧ TWO ❧

"BROWNE'S Books—Old and New, Rare Manuscripts a Specialty" was nestled amongst a series of shops in a small, pleasant alley with a dead end two blocks over from Bond Street. It was a sunny spring morning, not yet nine o'clock. The air was unusually blue, marred only by a high passing cloud or two, and a bird was singing from the shop's second-story window box. Windowsills up and down the street sported gay summer flowers; the stout lady whose husband owned the bakery was sweeping in front of their store. Carolyn waved at her and then smiled up at the bird, which had stopped singing as she stepped outside.

"Good morning, sparrow," she said cheerfully. "It is a wonderful day, is it not?"

The bird hopped about the box far above her head then froze, peering down at her expectantly.

Carolyn slipped her hand into the pocket of the apron covering the somewhat faded navy blue striped skirts of her simple gown and tossed a handful of stale bread at the base of the tree. "Enjoy your breakfast," she said.

She turned and unlatched the shutters to reveal the large window of her father's store. Two beautiful maps were on display there, one centuries old, one brand-new. Then she stepped back inside, inhaling deeply.

She loved the somewhat musty smell of the bookstore, a smell of leather bindings and old paper, just as she loved the smell of the early morning. Now sunlight filtered into the dimly illuminated two-story shop, which was lined wall-to-wall with books. The shop was Carolyn's home. She had been born in the bedroom above it.

But today she missed her father. He had been gone for almost two weeks now, and she expected him back at any moment. He was delivering a rare medieval manuscript to a client in Copenhagen. She wished he could entrust the task to a courier, but she knew the value of rare tomes, and understood why he could not and would not do so. George Browne was all the family she had. Her mother had died when she was six, and Carolyn did not count her mother's relatives as family, because they had disowned Margaret Owsley Browne many years ago, just as they had ignored the fact of Carolyn's existence, too, ever since she was born. The Dowager Viscountess of Stafford had one other grandchild, Margaret having had an older sister, but she had never forgiven her eldest for running off with a commoner. Their love, apparently, did not matter.

When George was out of the country, Carolyn was always somewhat lonely—her father and her books were her best friends. She had never had friends her own age. She had yet to meet a woman who had read David Hume or Adam Smith or who could discuss Plato intelligently. Carolyn read everything she could get her hands on, whether it was a tract on the origins of mankind by Lord Monboddo or a popular poem by Walter Scott. And she had undoubtedly become a bluestocking because of her father. George had told her, many times, that Margaret had loved to read.

As Carolyn crossed the bookshop, she smiled at the thought of their many fervent discussions, not only on the subject of books, both old and new, instructional and fictional, but on politics, philosophy, science, and even unfashionable topics such as astronomy. Then Carolyn wondered what he would think of the Russian envoy recently come to London.

But there was so much to do today, so Carolyn made sure she had plenty of coin in the cash drawer in order to make change for any customers she might have. Of course, sales were very slow, and it was possible they might not have a single one. Carolyn knew that a part of the economy's problems were caused by the war on the Continent. She sighed, picking up a duster, thinking about how lucky they were to still be in business, but before she could approach a single book, the bell over the front door tinkled as it opened. She turned with a smile. A well-clad young gentleman stood in the doorway. He smiled at her, his blue eyes intent.

"Good morning, Lord Anthony," Carolyn said, forgetting to set the duster down.

He came forward. "What a beautiful day, Miss Browne." His gaze roamed over her face.

"Do not tell me you have already read the tract on metaphysics by Sir William Hamilton which I gave you?" She thought that it was impossible. She had only sold it to him yesterday.

His smile was engaging. He was a very attractive young man of medium height and build with boyish good looks. He wore fine, expensive clothing. Earlier in the week he had let it slip that he was the youngest son of an earl. Carolyn had learned that his father, Stuart Davison, was a ranking member of the foreign ministry, working closely with Castlereagh. "Actually, I have not. But I was passing by, and thought I might pick up a gift for my sister. You see, she likes to read."

"Oh! Well, does she prefer novels or poems? Or could I interest her in something philosophical?"

He stepped closer. Since he had entered the store, his blue gaze had not moved from her face. "I think you should choose," he said. "Anything you think a young woman about your age would enjoy."

"Well, most young ladies come here for novels, my lord. I personally am rereading a tract by Jeremy Bentham, a very enlightened thinker, I should say. Of course, I do admit to occasionally enjoying a poem. Has she read *Childe*

Harold's Pilgrimage by Lord Byron? It was but published a few months ago.''

''I do not know,'' he said. ''Miss Browne. May I say something?''

But Carolyn had turned away to fetch Byron's latest work which all of society was atwitter about. In the process, she pulled a novel for Anthony Davison to also inspect. ''Of course,'' she said over her shoulder. Her platinum-blond hair was cut short, just above her shoulders, where it was a riot of waves and curls.

''You are very lovely this morning,'' the young man said.

Carolyn was climbing up on a step stool—and now she almost fell off it. She shifted so she could look at him, somewhat amazed. Was he serious? Her dress was old, faded, and entirely out of fashion. She had cut her hair herself—and continued to do so every two months. She was far too tall for a woman, and unfashionably slim. In fact, her long legs often caused her a bit of awkwardness. But he was regarding her with very serious eyes, unsmiling now.

''You have incredible green eyes,'' he said, low. And then he blushed.

''That is a very kind thing to say,'' she finally said with a quick smile. He was just being kind, and gallant, she decided. She pulled her favorite pamphlet by Bentham from the stacks for good measure. ''Here, if you don't mind.''

He took the pile, not even looking at them. ''Let me help you down, so you do not fall.''

Carolyn protested. ''This stool is my second home,'' she said, arriving with a small jump on the floor. ''Now, I do recommend Byron. I personally thought it quite vain, but it is good reading anyway.'' She smiled at him.

''If you recommend it, I shall buy it,'' Davison said.

''Don't you want to look at it?'' she asked. ''Peruse a few pages?''

''I will take everything,'' he declared.

Her green eyes widened. They were neither as dark as

emeralds nor as pale and muddy as moss. Carolyn thought
them an enigmatic shade of green, neither here nor there.

Davison followed her to the counter. As she was writing
up the sale, the bell again tinkled over the front door.
"Right with you," she called, not looking up.

"Is that my welcome home?" George Browne asked.

Carolyn turned, saw her father, and beamed. "Papa! You
are back—and all in one piece, too! How very wonderful!"
She rushed past her customer and gave him a huge hug.
Father and daughter smiled at one another. "Did all go
well?" she asked.

"Very. But I see that I am interrupting," George said,
setting his single valise down.

Anthony Davison was flushed now. "I am pleased to
meet you, sir. You must be Mr. Browne, the proprietor."

"Yes, I am, both the proprietor and Carolyn's father."
But his tone was mild. George came forward and shook the
young man's hand, his gaze twinkling. "I see you enjoy
popular fiction?" he said.

Anthony started, glanced down at the two books and
pamphlet in his hands. One novel was titled *Love Lost,
Love Won*. "Oh, no! These are for my, er, sister," he said
somewhat lamely.

George looked as if he were swallowing laughter. "I
see." He glanced fondly at his daughter. "The greatest
good for the greatest number?" he mused, referring to Bentham.

Carolyn blushed now. "I could not resist. Actually, Lord
Anthony is reading Hamilton," she said brightly. "But
maybe he will glance at Bentham next."

"I imagine he shall."

"Your daughter sold Hamilton to me, er, yesterday,"
Davison fumbled.

"Ah, yes. And you were just passing by and decided to
make another purchase—for your sister?" George asked.
He had dimples in both cheeks. He appeared amused.

"Exactly," Anthony said.

"Shall I tally those for you?" Carolyn asked.

"Please, er, do," Anthony said, following her to the money drawer.

When the transaction was completed, Carolyn carefully wrapped all the items in a single bundle and tied it with a pink ribbon. She saw her customer to the door and cheerfully bade him farewell. When he was gone, a very brief moment of silence reigned inside of Browne's Books.

"I see you have won another heart," George remarked.

"Oh, Papa, please!" Carolyn scoffed. "He was buying a gift for his sister."

"I do not think he has a sister, my dear," George said gently.

She looked at him. "Papa, you are thinking the wrong thing—again."

"Am I? And how many times has he been here to purchase books while I was gone?"

She shrugged. "I don't know. I haven't kept count. Perhaps five or six times—this past week."

George laughed loudly. "Case won, my dear. Case won. You could never be a barrister."

Carolyn sat down on the step stool. "As if any woman would even be allowed to try," she said somewhat dejectedly.

"Well, that might one day change, if there are more women in the world like you," George said affectionately. "Since when have the rules decided by my own gender ever stopped you from accomplishing your ends?"

Father and daughter shared a look. "How well you know me," she said.

"And how is Charles Copperville?" George asked.

"Very well." Carolyn grinned. She became serious. "Now tell me, what news from the Continent?"

"La Grande Armée has taken Vilna, apparently without a single shot being fired," George said as lightly as if they were discussing the weather.

"What happened?" Carolyn asked, wide-eyed.

"It seems that the Russians abandoned the city," George said, patting her back. "Tsar Alexander truly does not belong in the field at the head of his troops. How deluded he is.''

"You'd think he would have learned his lesson at Austerlitz, not to mention Eylau and Friedland," Carolyn said briskly. "He is hardly a soldier. What do you think will happen next, Papa?"

"I do not know," George said. "What news at home?"

"The usual. There have been more riots in the north—the Luddites. Wheat prices just keep rising, Papa. Everyone is hungry and afraid."

"Do you justify the destruction of private property by unruly mobs?" George asked mildly.

"Of course not. But I sympathize with those who are ill-fed and underpaid with families to house and feed."

George smiled fondly at her.

Carolyn straightened. "The regent had an outrageous fête last night. I suspect that six months from now we shall learn it cost ten thousand pounds. The Bourbons were there. He invited everyone at nine, but did not arrive himself until half past the hour. It was so crowded in the ballroom that half a dozen ladies fainted and had to be carried outside." Carolyn smiled wickedly. "Apparently quite a few young bucks were very helpful, not just in carrying the unconscious ladies out but in restoring their health by *loosening* their clothes."

George tsked.

Carolyn's chin had been on her hand, now she dropped it. "The Russian prince was there. The one who is a special envoy from the tsar. Sverayov. What do you think about him, Papa?"

"I really haven't given him much thought. They say he was an excellent commander on the battlefield. He comes from a wealthy, prominent family. He has one brother, I believe, younger than he. And that is really all that I know about him, other than that he is here to conclude an alliance between our countries."

"His morals are despicable."

George blinked at her. "Do you know the man?"

She flushed slightly. "Papa, he is jaded! He has been in town a mere fortnight and has been linked to half a dozen very prominent ladies—every one of whom, I might add, is married."

"And is his behavior any different from that of our own rakes?"

"The behavior of Darnelly and Shadow and their kind is as immoral," Carolyn said flatly. "I spare no one."

"I have a feeling your quill has found a new target," George said seriously. "Be careful, my dear. If you play with fire, you may get burned."

Carolyn stood, anticipation washing over her in a rush, and it was thrilling. "Are you suggesting I set my sights elsewhere? Lower, perhaps?"

"The prince is, by all accounts, a seasoned veteran of many wars. I do believe I have heard that he is extremely clever—and extremely heartless. He might prove dangerous, my dear."

Carolyn tossed her head. "He is interested in one thing, Papa, and it is not negotiating with Castlereagh! I suspect—no, I am certain!—he is another one of the tsar's incompetent cronies. He is probably here because he requested a leave from the field—perhaps he is even a coward! I would not be surprised. Surely, for him, this mission is all a gay pleasure trip. I mean, would you rather be in the midst of booming cannons or a gala at Carleton House?" Carolyn took a breath. "I am certain we will never sign a treaty with Russia now. And why should we? Just because they need us? Has everyone forgotten Tilsit?"

"Apparently you have not forgotten, my dear," George muttered. "Since when have you become so passionate about the subject of our relations with the Russians?"

Carolyn flushed. "If I thought we could trust him, I would not be so passionately opposed." She was already heading toward the back of the store, where the stairs leading to their private apartments were.

George regarded her thoughtfully. "My dear, do you not mean, if you thought you could trust *them*?"

She paused, one hand on the smooth, old wooden banister. Her color was high. "Of course that is what I meant."

George stared at the narrow staircase after she was gone. "I wonder," he mused aloud, "what has been going on while I was gone?"

Upstairs, she sat at her small, sturdy desk, a quill in hand. She was drawing frantically. A few deft strokes gave way to a cartoon in which two young men were rushing away with two unconscious women draped dramatically in their arms. Meanwhile two other ladies lolled on the ground, attended by two young bucks with far more lascivious expressions on their faces than their counterparts. One of the ladies was being divested of her gloves and had already had her shoes and stockings removed. Her skirts were draped above her knees, revealing ample calves and ankles. The last young lady was having her entire gown unbuttoned down the back, and her breasts appeared in dire jeopardy of being exposed at any moment.

Carolyn blew on the cartoon to dry it, then quickly scribbled a few lines of dialogue beneath. "I say," the last buck was saying. "Jolly good time. Old Prinny should be late more often!"

Carolyn smiled and shoved the cartoon aside. Her masquerade last night had already paid off well, indeed. Then her smile faded. Her brow furrowed and an unfocused golden image came to mind. She had never seen the prince, but she had heard all about him ever since he had arrived in town. Who hadn't? He had already won and broken dozens of female hearts in London and the country. They said he was as cold as ice until it suited him to be otherwise, and that when hot, he was dazzling enough to melt anyone. Apparently even the regent was fawning over him now. Perhaps the only one not yet endeared to him was Lord Castlereagh—thank God.

Carolyn had heard that he was tall, golden, handsome. She was sure the reports of his physical charms were highly exaggerated. It was always that way. For rumor held that four women had actually swooned merely upon being introduced to him. Carolyn scoffed at the idea.

But she could not caricaturize him because she had never seen him herself—and that was going to have to be rectified immediately. She smiled to herself.

She dipped her quill in the inkwell, dated the top of the page, and titled it "A Royal Sham."

Of the fifteen hundred *illustrious* guests invited to attend Prinny's latest *extravaganza*—one boasting no less than sixty-five thousand candles, one hundred and fifty supper tables, fifteen hundred chairs for fifteen hundred guests, and a staff of three thousand two hundred and eighty-three—one very illustrious *foreigner* provided a shining example of superior morality to all those present and all those not present but waiting so eagerly for this column. If the walls of Carleton House could talk! (Fortunately others can!) This particular *prince* was not French. Prince S—— arrived with his own entourage in a huge black coach with *silver, red, and gold* arms. He never goes anywhere without his *French* valet, and a troop of armed, mounted *Cossacks*. Although the festivities continued until dawn, S—— chose to leave at the unheard-of hour of one o'clock. And what could entice such an esteemed guest to quit the premises at such an extraordinary hour if not for the very lovely charms of a certain Lady C——e? Of course, Lord C——e, who was also present at Carleton House, was otherwise preoccupied with his port and cigars. Lord C——e would undoubtedly *pretend* to be preoccupied with his port and cigars even if he were not, not daring otherwise. Just another *uneventful* evening? I doubt the prince thinks so. No one, I am told, not even the prince, expected a certain *princess* to appear that evening, whom, apparently, had last been seen in St. P——. She, of course, had her own *personal* escort. Apparently the very beautiful princess has put on an extreme amount of *weight* lately. I wonder what she is expecting? Needless to say, that did not stop Lord C——e from his preoccupation with port and cigars.

Carolyn was breathless as she paused over her column. Her pulse raced, and an unfocused golden image filled up her mind. She could almost envision his face—high-cheekboned, Slavic, rough. Her father's warnings abruptly returned to her, but she shoved them aside. Society carried on as if hundreds of thousands of soldiers of all nationalities were not being slaughtered on the Continent, as if British prisoners of war were not being starved to death in French prisons, as if the dislocations here at home caused by the war were all a fairy tale! Farmers, miners, weavers, were losing everything, the poorhouses were full. God! No one seemed to care about the tremendous suffering everywhere. Carolyn could not understand it.

And she was glad that her mother had loved George enough to turn her back on such a self-absorbed society. Her father might have been common and poor, but he had ideals. Margaret had fallen in love with the man, not a title and a fortune.

Carolyn stood abruptly and walked over to the small bureau beside her bed. She picked up the miniature portrait of her mother, completed when she was just an infant. How beautiful Margaret had been, and how kind—her sensitivity was written all over her features, expressed in her green eyes.

She had died when Carolyn was five. Shortly after their return from that awful visit to Lady Stafford at Midlands. Carolyn could still remember being tucked into bed by her mother, whom she had adored. She could still see her soft smile, feel her mouth as it touched her cheek in a kiss. She could still hear her soft "I love you," words she uttered every night. And Carolyn had replied in kind. "I love you, too, Mama." Margaret had blown out the candle she was carrying. And when Carolyn had awoken the next morning, her mother had been dead.

Carolyn turned abruptly away from the portrait. She never thought about that morning, not ever. Even now, thirteen years later, it had the power to twist up her insides and form tears in her eyes. She supposed that when you truly loved someone, you never recovered from their loss.

She had died from pneumonia. They had said it was an advanced case, and that she had probably not been well for some time.

She wiped her eyes again, shoving aside the image of her stricken, bereft father, and returned to her desk. Prince Nicholas Sverayov certainly deserved her barbs. He was as bad, if not worse, than the rakes and dandies and hypocrites of her own country. If he intended to carry on openly with one woman after another, with his pregnant wife present, while on official state business, in London society, he was as much a target for her quill as anyone else. It was not personal. It was a question of principle. But Carolyn truly felt sorry for the Princess Sverayov. How could she bear being wed to such a man?

Carolyn had decided long ago that she would never wed, not unless she met a man of high principle like her father, and shared an extraordinary kind of love.

She dipped the quill one last time and signed the column "Charles Copperville" with a flourish.

❧ THREE ❧

HE knew it was a dream. He always knew, yet that did not make it seem any less real. And the first sign of the dream was the heavy sickness inside of him, a strong and overwhelming premonition of disaster, and the snow. There was so much snow. Outside the world was white, a blur, visibility reduced to nothingness.

And he knew that something terrible was going to happen if he did not wake up.

But he did not wake up, for he could not. Instead, as he stood by the window at his dacha in Tver, unmoving, staring out into the blizzard, a fire roaring at his side, he heard her voice, sharp and angry at first, then plaintive, and finally, tearful and afraid.

"Excellency." A man had spoken.

But Nicholas already knew that. And the intrusion was so outlandish he should be shocked, but he was not shocked, for he had expected it, and he turned. A young groom stood there in the doorway, tall and strapping, a determined light in his eyes. His wife stood a few feet behind him, her face as pale as moonlight, her black eyes wet with tears. "Niki," she began. "Don't listen, it is not true."

The truth. He sensed it, had sensed for some time, but did not want to know, not now, not ever. He tried to tell the groom, Piotr, to leave. But his mouth would not open to form the words, and no such command came. And he desperately wished to see Katya. Needed to hold her, as if in holding her he would not lose her.

"Excellency, there is a grave matter we must discuss." The lad shifted uneasily.

Marie-Elena cried out, turned, and fled.

A grave matter. A grave matter, indeed. The groom's ruddy face blurred as he began to talk about the greatest treasure in Nicholas's life, his daughter, Katya. His face twisted, fading, his words incoherent, incomprehensible. And Nicholas's heart was filled with a stabbing pain. His world with sheer blackness.

Katya. Where was she? Where was his daughter?

Panic replaced the pain. Panic and terror. Katya was lost, lost forever, and he could not find her, and now he was running in the snow, fighting the wind, the branches of trees, screaming her name, oblivious to the cold, desperate to find her. But she was gone. Nicholas clawed the bark of a snow-laden pine tree. The snow came up past his knees. Tears burned his eyes, freezing on his skin as they streaked down his face. "Katya!" But she was gone, gone, gone. . . .

"Excellency?"

The dream had changed. Someone was calling his name, but that was not how it ended. It ended with him shivering and afraid in the snow, his daughter lost forever, and when he awoke, he would be weeping.

"Excellency!" And there was knocking now, on the door. Loud and insistent. Nicholas did not, could not, move. Caught between sleep and waking, he was trying to recall the results of the investigation he had immediately mounted. Not to find his missing daughter, for she had not wandered out in any snowstorm, but into the activities of his wife.

"Prince Sverayov!"

Nicholas started. His eyes opened suddenly, and for a moment he was confused, not recognizing the oddly appointed room he was in. He expected to be in Tver, at his country home, but that was because of the damned dream.

He sat up, realizing in an instant that neither was he in the lavishly gilded salon of Vladchya Palace, his home in St. Petersburg, where Katya had been born; where he and his brother, Alexi, had been born. Instead, he sat on a crimson damask sofa in a small, wood-paneled library with windows that were undraped, revealing rioting gardens outside and a bright blue sky.

He was in London.

Nicholas brushed a fine film of perspiration from his brow, tears from his cheeks, his pulse pounding far too erratically. He had fallen asleep on the sofa in the library of the Mayfair town house he had leased when he had arrived in London three weeks ago. In spite of the knocking, it took him one more moment to recover from the dream. He stared toward the windows but really saw nothing in front of him. And he reminded himself that the past, as it could not be changed, was not worth dwelling upon.

As usual, cold logic, which he so often applied when he was commanding his troops, failed to satisfy him now or alleviate the lingering bitter aftertaste of the nightmare—or the daily anguish he now lived with. He could only thank God that Katya was not, and had never been, lost in any snowstorm.

And he forced Piotr's image aside. The groom now lived in Murmansk, rather comfortably, his attempt at blackmail successful.

"Excellency?" The door opened. It was Taichili, his daughter's governess. Comprehension flooded him. Marie-Elena lay upstairs with doctors and nurses, close to death. She had miscarried another man's child just before dawn. A glance at the clock showed him it was after nine. He had only fallen asleep a short while ago.

"Father?" a small, hesitant voice said.

Nicholas rose swiftly to his feet, fully returned to the present now. Katya had been asleep when he had returned home last night. And Marie-Elena had been unconscious, having lost not just the child but a tremendous amount of blood. Three physicians were doing what they could to save her life. They were not hopeful. A Russian Orthodox priest, attached to the Russian ambassador's household, had already administered the last rites.

Nicholas managed a smile as the six-year-old child hesitated on the threshold. She was so beautiful and so special that his heart twisted as it always did at the mere sight of her. "Come in," he said, his pulse accelerating.

She was a thin child with porcelain skin, black eyes, and even blacker hair—one day she would be a replica of her mother. Katya regarded him with wide eyes that were far too old for a girl of her few years.

Her governess, a tall bespectacled woman with an eternally stern countenance, stood behind her. "Excellency," she said. "I told the princess not to disturb you."

"My daughter is not disturbing me," he said. He continued to smile. "Please come in, Katrushka," he said formally, but he was trembling. He clenched his fists, shocked with the impulse he had—to run to Katya and hold her. But he didn't know how to hold her. Marie-Elena had seen to that.

Katya entered the room, closing the door behind her, Taichili waiting outside. "I hope I am not disturbing you," she said very gravely.

"I think we must talk," he said.

She nodded, her big eyes riveted on his face.

"Please, sit," he said. "Sit with me, *dushka*."

Katya, dressed in a beautiful white dress trimmed with ribbons and overlaid with lace, came forward and settled herself down in one of the two large armchairs facing his desk. Nicholas also sat back down. Katya remained impassive.

"You mother is very ill," Nicholas began.

"She is dying." Her tone was flat and without emotion.

Nicholas looked into her eyes. He hesitated. Her eyes were oddly blank. Katya's eyes always were shadowed. How had one so young learned to be so impassive? "I believe so. But there is some hope. Shall we pray for her together?"

Katya nodded, not saying a word.

Nicholas stood, as did Katya. He gestured her forward and they both knelt and bowed their heads. He felt like a hypocrite, but knew he had to do this for the child. He was not a man given to prayer, although he did, he supposed, believe in God. He had seen too many men die to think that any amount of praying might wrest a miracle from the Almighty.

"Dear Father, who art in Heaven," he began, "please spare the life of my wife, Katya's mother. Please let her live. We pray here today together, begging you to spare her life." He crossed himself. "Amen." He looked down at Katya's bent head. "Do you want to add something?"

Katya looked up at him, mouth pursed, eyes tearless, and nodded. She was very pale.

"Go ahead," Nicholas said gently, wondering how he could console Katya if Marie-Elena died. She was hardly the best mother. As often as possible she left Katya in Tver with her tutors and nannies—while she cavorted in Moscow, St. Petersburg, Vienna, Prague, and Rome. While Marie-Elena was gone, Katya eagerly awaited her return. Nicholas had caught her watching out the window for Marie-Elena too many times to count.

But she was not the worst mother, either. When she returned, she did so bearing incredible gifts, at once animated and gay, regaling her daughter with her incredible cosmopolitan adventures. Katya, Nicholas knew, worshipped her mother.

"Dear Lord," she said, hushed, "don't let my mother die. . . . Please. She is so young, so beautiful, and I know she loves me . . . and Father. I will do anything, Lord, if you let her live. Amen."

"Amen," Nicholas echoed, close to tears.

He helped her to her feet. Nicholas did not know what to do. It was so much easier to directly console a soldier dying in the mud and snow than his own tearless daughter now.

Nicholas touched Katya's thin shoulder impulsively. "Do not be afraid."

Katya started at the contact. Then she looked down, away from him, her small mouth pursed. "But maybe I will never see her again."

"If your mother does go to Heaven, one day you will see her there."

Katya stared.

He continued to grasp her thin shoulder. "We do not bargain with God, Katya. Perhaps the next time you pray, you should offer Him something whether or not your mother lives."

She nodded gravely.

He forced a smile that felt miserable. "I think we should go upstairs to see how she is doing. We will see if the doctors will allow us to visit her," Nicholas said. He knew he had to be careful. If Marie-Elena passed away, he wanted Katya left with memories of her vibrant, beautiful, and alive.

They left the room silently. Upstairs, it was deathly quiet and deathly still. The door to the sickroom was closed. He was reminded of the night when Katya had been born. "Wait here," he said.

He slipped into the room. Physicians and nurses turned. One doctor came to him immediately. "She was conscious a few moments ago, Excellency."

Nicholas froze, his regard jerking to his wife, who was as pale and lifeless as a corpse, appearing incredibly diminutive in the midst of the large four-poster bed. The sheets around her, thank God, had been constantly changed, and were currently pristinely white. "There is progress?" he asked, incredulous. She had been conscious. What if she regained consciousness again? He desperately wanted Katya to be able to say good-bye to her mother. "Is it possible that she may live?" he asked.

"We seem to have stopped the bleeding. But she has lost blood. I do not think that she will live. I am sorry, Prince Sverayov," the British physician said. "But she might awaken again, if you think to speak to her.''

"I want to bring her daughter in," Nicholas said, "but I do not want to upset the child."

"I would advise you to bring the child in now," the physician said.

But Nicholas continued to stare at Marie-Elena—and saw her lashes flicker. He did not move. And then her eyes opened slowly—and focused on him.

He went to her side. "I am sorry," he said, meaning it.

She stared at him, and then her mouth twisted slightly—into a shadow of her usual smile. "Are you sorry, Niki? Do not lie. You will be glad when I am gone," she said wearily—bitterly.

"I am very sorry," he said firmly. "I will not be glad. Katya wants to see you."

Marie-Elena made a shrugging motion, telling him that she did not care whether she ever saw her daughter again. He was shocked—and certain he had misunderstood.

"Marie-Elena, you are very ill. You may well die. Surely you want to see Katya now."

Marie-Elena's eyes opened and she gasped for breath. "You love *her*, don't you?" she finally said. "In spite of what you have feared—and been thinking—all these years. You love her—insanely—but you have never loved me."

He was so astounded by her words that he could only stare. She was dying—and admitting to a profound jealousy of her own daughter? It was impossible.

"Do you know," she said slowly, thickly, her words very low now, "how many men have loved me? Me. Completely. They still want me. Years later. Would kill to have me take them back." Her eyes, black and glittering wildly, held his.

"How could I not be aware of your conquests?" he said stiffly—thinking of the damned groom, not any of the others. Piotr, the man who was, in all likelihood, Katya's father.

"Even Alexander loves me," she whispered. "He told

me so.'' And it was suspended between them, unspoken, *But not you.*

He finally spoke. ''There is no point in discussing this now. We did not marry for love—no one does.'' He turned to leave, in order to get Katya.

''Damn you, Nicholas! Damn you to hell!'' she cried.

He froze, facing her, stunned by the anger and hatred he saw. Yet he was the one who had been betrayed, he was the one who had every right to rage and fury—not her. ''I am getting Katya,'' he said. He turned away, motioning for one of the servants to let Katya in.

And Katya came cautiously forward, her wide gaze seeking the figure in the bed. Nicholas immediately moved to her side, overwhelmed with the urge to shelter and protect her.

''Mother?'' she whispered shrilly.

Marie-Elena appeared not to hear. She seemed to be asleep. Katya cried out, rushing forward, flinging her arms around her mother, burying her face against her chest.

And Nicholas felt a tear beginning its way down his own cheek. Marie-Elena was dead—and Katya was not his daughter. Had never been his daughter, not even in those first few months after she was born, before he had learned the hideous truth.

Katya began to cry.

And so did Nicholas.

He walked her into her bedroom. ''She is very sick, Katya. We can only pray again.'' Somehow, Marie-Elena clung to life. And Nicholas felt oddly impotent, offering his daughter only prayers, when he did not believe in their power himself.

Katya faced him, tearless, expressionless, even her eyes blank. She did not speak.

''Do you want to pray with me again?'' He tried to smile, knew that this time he failed.

Katya stared.

''Katya, come, please.'' His chest ached with every

heartbeat, not for himself, and his own loss—the hope that she was truly his daughter—but solely for his daughter and her pain. "Can you speak?" he asked. Of course, Katya did not know. No one knew, not even his brother.

It was a moment before she said, "Yes. Thank you."

He was at a loss. He clenched his fists, realized he still trembled. "Your mother loves you very much," he managed. "As do I."

Katya looked at him and her face began to crumble.

To hell with prayers, he thought. He knelt, and awkwardly, he took Katya in his arms. Waiting for her to weep. But she did not cry.

As awkwardly, he touched her hair. "I know you are afraid. I wish I could take away the fear, but I cannot. I am not that powerful."

Katya pushed back and looked up at him, her face starkly white. "Do you believe in miracles?"

He lied. "Yes."

She stared. "Have you ever seen one?"

He told the truth. "No."

She nodded unblinkingly.

He stood up. "What would you like to do, today?" Wanting to caress her cheek.

He thought she would not answer. But she said, "I have my lessons, Father."

"I will speak to Signor Raffaldi. Today is not a day for lessons. You may do anything you wish. Even go to a circus," he said. Hoping to make her smile.

Katya said politely, "I think I prefer to stay in my room and read my books, Father, if you do not mind."

He stared at her, this beautiful, expressionless, sober child—this child who was not his. Why was she always so self-contained? Her mother was certainly the opposite—and he knew now that her self-control did not come from him. He could not understand it. "As you wish," he finally said. "But Katya, if you change your mind, that is fine." Yet he knew she was not going to change her mind.

Katya remained still. Nicholas finally bent and touched

her cheek with his hand. He thought he glimpsed a single tear in her eye. He went to the door, summoned Leeza, the nurse she'd had since the day of her birth—the nurse he had had, as well. The old woman was ancient, ageless, nearly blind. Yet sometimes she looked at him as if she could read his mind—as if she knew every one of his secrets.

She looked into his eyes just then with her oddly vacant silver ones. "I will take care of her, Excellency. Do not fear."

"Thank you," he said, feeling relieved.

And then she caused him to misstep. "She is sleeping, my lord, and out of danger. God has decided that she will live."

❧ FOUR ❧

CAROLYN felt uncomfortable—and it had nothing to do with her disguise.

She crouched in the shrubs outside the brick Mayfair town house which had been leased by Sverayov, her short hair slicked back behind her ears and covered with a bicorne hat, a sparse goatee pasted onto her chin. She was clad in a man's coat, waistcoat, shirtwaist, breeches, stockings, and buckled shoes. Her pulse was racing wildly. She was accustomed to wearing a disguise—how else could she discover the activities of those she wished to write about in her column for the *Morning Chronicle*? Men, unfortunately, had far better access to the news than women.

She was also accustomed to investigating those she pursued, but somehow, now, crouched outside of Sverayov's residence, two days later, she felt uncertain, uneasy, almost as if she were in danger—which was absolute nonsense. Yet she could not still her racing heart. An odd premonition haunted her, one she could not quite identify.

Carolyn did not even know if Sverayov was at home. She assumed that he was because it was only mid-morning. Perhaps, once again, he had carried on with Lady Carradine last night till dawn. The mere recollection of his flagrant illicit behavior in front of his pregnant wife was enough to disturb her pulse all over again. Two nights ago, Carolyn had been disguised as a footman so that she might ''attend''

Prinny's ball. It was amazing, truly, the gossip amongst the servants—and the actual information to be gleaned there.

Carolyn peered hard at the front door of the brick town house. Hopefully he would appear at any moment, perhaps for a ride in Hyde Park. Carolyn intended to familiarize herself with his daily routine and habits being as she was now going to include him in her columns. For he was exactly the kind of self-absorbed aristocrat she sought to expose.

She had been writing the column for a year and a half. At first, she had started her commentary strictly to amuse herself and her father. But George had thought her writing so insightful—and so witty—that Carolyn had approached several newspapers. The *Morning Chronicle* had eagerly snatched her work up, in spite of the fact that she was a woman. Her editor asked only that her gender be kept a secret, while Carolyn asked for anonymity in return.

She could not help wondering what her grandmother would think if she knew how Carolyn portrayed her class. But Carolyn did not write out of spite or malevolence. She wished to expose the utter moral corruption of those peers who thought themselves above the rest of society. Her aim was to shame those who deserved it, and perhaps, in the future, men like Sverayov and women like Lady Carradine might think less about their own pleasure and more about the misfortunes of others less mighty than they—and how to attend to those in need.

Carolyn carried a small sketchbook with her at all times, in a satchel on her back. She pulled it out and wrote down "S-routine" at the top of one clean page. Then, thinking a bit, she added "Background, personal and otherwise" to the very same page, feeling a quite delicious tingling along her spine and at the nape of her neck.

The front door opened and male voices could be heard. Carolyn stiffened with expectation as two men came into view, carrying on a conversation in low tones. And getting a clear view of them, she froze.

One of the men was Sverayov. Tall, disheveled, bronzed—it could be no one else but him.

Her heart had actually skipped an entire series of beats. She could not inhale, could not move. More frozen than a block of ice, Carolyn stared.

The prince came to a halt only a few dozen feet from her hiding place beside the walk. He was bareheaded, his hair a tawny, sun-streaked gold, worn slightly longer than the current fashion allowed. He was not in uniform. He wore a simple lawn shirt, a pale vest, and gray trousers. He was extremely tall and powerfully built, both broad-shouldered and slim of hip. His legs were very long. It was possible that his physical charms had not been exaggerated. But there was far more to the man than that. He moved like one who had been born to power and wealth. There was a sense of dominance about him, and arrogance, that no one could miss. This man had no doubt about who and what he was.

Trembling, Carolyn looked again at his impossibly arresting face. This time, she dissected his features one by one—the darker, slashing eyebrows, the high, sculpted cheekbones, his hard jaw and straight, aristocratic nose. His mouth, even at this distance, appeared somewhat cruel and blatantly sensual.

He reeked of power and sensuality. For the first time in her life, Carolyn did not have a coherent thought in her head. Briefly she closed her eyes. And when she could think, she recalled her father's warning, and wondered if, this time, she might be getting in over her head.

And when she opened her eyes, the two men were bowing. Carolyn realized she was perspiring, and now she gulped air. She had, in her amazement, dropped her pad. She picked it up and began to draw with feverish strokes.

Quickly, first the prince, a lion of a man. Her swift pen strokes were hard and slashing, and there he stood, towering over the other, smaller gentleman, but disheveled, as if from the debauchery of the last evening, his vest wrinkled, his shirt unbuttoned—Carolyn portrayed it open right down to the waistband of his trousers—his posture careless and arrogant, his mouth far too sensuous and far too bold. As she drew the other, smaller gentleman, she realized he was a physician, for he carried a doctor's bag. Out of breath, Carolyn closed the pad and slipped it into the satchel. Trembling.

Sverayov began walking with the doctor down the front walk—his strides taking him closer and closer to her as she hid. For the first time in her life, Carolyn was terrified of discovery. She did not move, did not dare to even breathe. Her eyes were wide, riveted on the two men.

Sverayov and the doctor drew abreast of her. Sverayov was saying, his voice husky, "You will be amply rewarded for all that you have done."

"Excellency, I shall send you a fair bill for my services."

"No. You will be rewarded," he said flatly, and there was little doubt that he would have his way. "Thank you for coming again."

"Thank you, Excellency," the doctor said. "I am just glad she has survived her ordeal."

The two men paused a few feet past Carolyn, now on the sidewalk. The Sverayov coach was coming round the block, obviously summoned for the doctor from the carriage house.

"As am I. I cannot thank you enough for saving her life," the prince said. Carolyn started. His expression was drawn and grim. But whose life had been in jeopardy? Surely not his wife's?

"I did little," the doctor said. He smiled. "Your wife is stronger than she appears."

Carolyn jerked. His wife had almost died? But it was very hard to focus on the questions arising from her natural curiosity, because Sverayov was almost facing her. She swallowed, unable not to admit to herself that he was the most devastating man she had ever seen. Carolyn understood now why four ladies had fainted merely upon being introduced to him.

She almost felt like fainting, too.

His gaze suddenly shifted, toward the bushes where she hid. Carolyn wanted to sink down lower, but was afraid he might detect the movement, so she held her breath and prayed.

The huge town coach halted in front of the men. A snarling red wolf crouched with bared fangs atop crossed silver swords and a gold banner which, in Latin, read "My Own." How arrogant was that motto, Carolyn thought. Footmen appeared to open the carriage door and hand the doctor in. Sverayov nodded to the pair of liveried drivers. The team of six took off. Sverayov watched for a moment, his back to Carolyn, then turned suddenly, his gaze darting over the sidewalk—and the bushes where Carolyn hid. Carolyn thought her heart had stopped, thought she had been discovered. But he ducked his head and strode decisively back up the walk, disappearing into the house. The front door closed solidly behind him.

Carolyn sank to the ground in a heap, her clothes damp with sweat, her pulse racing even more erratically than before. *Oh, God.* She closed her eyes, trying to regain her equilibrium. Nothing could have prepared her for her first glimpse of this man and her reaction to him.

Carolyn took a few deep breaths, her mind beginning to function again. She shoved her pad in the satchel, reminding herself very firmly that Sverayov was debauched, depraved, amoral—all that she despised in either a man or a woman. She began to feel better. He might look like some ancient Roman god of war come down to Earth to avenge the weak, the needy, the poor, and the abused, to right wrongs, to fight evil, to create justice, but he was no immortal. How deceiving appearances could be.

And his poor wife had almost died. Of course, she could not quit the premises now. Not without learning what, exactly, had transpired that night.

Carolyn gathered her belongings, looking now across the small garden to the house—trying to decide just how to cross those gardens without being detected by anyone, either manservant or master.

Nicholas hunched over his desk, frowning, a quill in hand. Outside his closed library doors, a courier was waiting to speed his missive to Alexander, who remained with the Russian army at their new headquarters in Drissa. Barclay was there with the Russian First Army—and Nicholas was acutely aware that, had he not been sent to London after the invasion, he would be there too with his own battalion.

He sighed, laying the quill aside. It was hard to concentrate, for many reasons, and Nicholas had no good news to relay to the tsar. He was extremely frustrated, but he would not allow Alexander to comprehend just how difficult the talks were. Castlereagh was as stubborn as his reputation made him out to be. But then, so was Nicholas. There was, possibly, some hope of a treaty that would officially end the war between the two countries—and, he hoped, grant the Russians some financial aid. Nicholas still wondered who was secretly and adamantly opposed to the alliance inside of the British government.

He finally scribbled a brief note, cautioning Alexander against hoping for an early outcome to their talks—and once again requesting he be returned to his command under Barclay. Nicholas was signing his name to the missive when the door to the library opened abruptly—the intruder had not knocked. Nicholas jerked his gaze upward, immediately furious, a reprimand forming on his lips.

The tall, disheveled, dark-haired man standing on the threshold grinned. His clothing was stained with dust and dirt from travel. "Hello, Niki. Am I interrupting?"

Nicholas stood, crossed the room with long strides, and embraced his younger brother. "Alexi! This is a surprise! I thought you were in Vienna—playing cat and mouse with the Hapsburgs."

"Cat and dog is more like it." Alexi grinned, his teeth white in his dark, swarthy face. "My job is done. We have obtained certain paltry guarantees from the Austrians. I requested a brief leave of absence. It's been a long time since I strolled down Oxford Street.''

Nicholas smiled still. ''You haven't been to London since you were a boy.''

''I am aware of that.'' Alexi sauntered into the room, tossing his narrow-brimmed hat onto the sofa. It was as dirty and dusty as the rest of him. ''Actually, I thought you might need me here.''

''What I need,'' Nicholas said, ''is to find out who is really working so furiously against this treaty inside Castlereagh's government. What guarantees did the Austrians give?''

''They will not do very much to aid Napoleon when he invades our country,'' Alexi said, plopping down on the sofa and stretching out his long, long legs. ''But they have no intention of declaring war on Bonaparte. They are as afraid of him as ever.''

Nicholas made no comment—it could have been worse. He walked to the sideboard and poured two vodkas and returned to his brother, handing him one. Alexi grunted his thanks and quaffed half of the glass. Nicholas took one sip and said, ''Marie-Elena is here. She came with Katya.''

Alexi's face changed before he could hide it. Briefly, disgust was mirrored on his unusually striking face. ''How pleased you must be—to have her here with you. I think you should know the latest gossip about your wife.''

Nicholas sipped the vodka again, its heat searing the inside of his abdomen. ''I do not pay much attention to gossips, and neither should you.''

''Usually I don't. But this is important, Niki.'' Alexi stared.

''What are they saying now?''

''That Vorontsky is the father of the child she is carrying.''

Nicholas refused to allow his shock to show. He steeled his face into an impassive mask. But he stood up, setting his glass down. "You would not tell me this if you did not believe it yourself."

"You are too kind to her."

"She has many problems."

"And Vorontsky? Our cousin and our friend? Does he have problems, too? Is that his excuse for betraying you this way?" Alexi asked savagely.

Nicholas remained stunned. He recalled too many moments shared with himself, his brother, and their cousin since they were all children running wild through the streets of St. Petersburg. And even though Sasha knew that he and Marie-Elena shared nothing but a name and a child, if this was true, it was a betrayal. Another cruel betrayal. Anger flooded him.

"Why not ask her?" Alexi said rather snidely. "Of course, she will cry, quite prettily, and deny it, while begging for your love."

"I will ask Sasha," Nicholas said tightly.

"And then?"

"I will send her to Tver for the winter. And the spring— and next summer."

"A good idea." Alexi stood. "I know that Katya loves her, but she is dangerous. I personally believe she chose Vorontsky on purpose—knowing that if you found out you would be hurt."

"Do I appear hurt?" he asked coldly. "I am angry. She can choose her lovers at will—but not from amongst my friends and family."

"She wants to hurt you, Niki. I can see it in her eyes. Send her to Siberia. Tver is too close to Moscow. And just leave her there until she is old and gray."

"Alexi, I appreciate your concern, but you are not a father. Katya worships her mother. I prefer not to hurt Katya by punishing Marie-Elena—who is really no more than a selfish, willful child herself."

"Thank God the tsar has not arranged a marriage for me," Alexi exclaimed, moving to the sideboard and refilling his glass. "If I ever take that step, I want to know that divorce is an option without my being hanged by the balls in Siberia, no less.''

''Thank you. I needed that,'' Nicholas said. But he had never considered a divorce, and why should he? On a personal level his marriage was no different from those of most of the couples he knew, while politically, it was beneficial to everyone, including himself. And unlike other men, Nicholas was not worried about a legitimate male heir. Katya was his heir. He sighed. ''She miscarried the child the night before last—and almost died herself.''

Alexi stiffened. ''Christ. Now I am sorry for running on at the mouth.''

''Do not be sorry. You have always despised her, and if I were you, I probably would, too.'' Nicholas slanted a look at him. ''She lost a tremendous amount of blood, but it seems she will live.'' He hesitated. ''Thank God.'' And he was not thinking of Marie-Elena and Sasha, but of Katya.

''Too bad,'' Alexi growled.

Nicholas paced. ''Alexi, I am worried about Katya.''

Alexi stared. He came over and placed his hand on his brother's back. ''I am sorry. I was not thinking clearly. Poor Katya. She must be distraught. Where is she? I wish to see her.''

''She is upstairs with Leeza.'' Nicholas hesitated. He wondered how much his brother really knew. Alexi had to have heard the rumors, five years ago, when Nicholas had launched a huge investigation into Marie-Elena's life, past and present, uncovering every possible stone. But Nicholas was an extremely private man, and while he had then needed, desperately, a confidant, he had not told his brother or anyone about the possibility that his daughter was not his. Even now, he could not bring himself to share the truth with anyone.

Nicholas turned and strode across the library to one of the open windows, his face grim. ''Do you think Katya is a happy child?'' he asked without turning.

Behind him, Alexi started. ''She is a very quiet child,'' he finally said. ''I don't know, Niki.''

Nicholas turned. "I don't think she is happy, but I do not know why. I try to come home as much as possible, and I am certainly more fatherly than most men I know who ignore their children—especially their daughters—entirely. And Marie-Elena is not atypical. Every woman I know is like her—more interested in galas and diamonds and lovers than in their own children. Is it possible that I am overly concerned?"

"I don't know. I am not a father. At least you really love your daughter," Alexi said.

"What does that mean?" His tone was sharp.

Alexi actually flushed. "I don't know what I meant. I am going upstairs. How about drinks later—and a little prowling about town?" He grinned, pausing at the door.

"Perhaps," Nicholas said. At that moment, he had not the slightest interest in either carousing or women, by God. And what had Alexi meant? Was he implying that Marie-Elena really did not care about her own daughter? Nicholas refused to believe it. He continued to stare outside. His gaze was searching.

"Well, enjoy the landscaping," Alexi said with a teasing tone. "Until later, big brother."

"Actually, there is a spy lurking about," Nicholas said as casually as if discussing the weather.

Alexi froze, his eyes widened. "Are you in jest?"

Nicholas turned. "A young lad. He's been snooping around for some time now. I am debating whether to end this farce now, or later. I am not in the mood for these kinds of games, not after the night and morning I have just had." He was in the mood, actually, to wring the spy's skinny neck and choke the information out of him which he wished to have. However, he was too experienced and astute to do that. He supposed he would now have to play cat and mouse himself.

Nicholas turned away from the window. "I think I shall fetch the morning journal and take some breakfast before I toy with the spy."

Alexi smiled. "You do that. I am visiting my niece." He swiftly exited the room.

Nicholas followed, more slowly. As he left the library, Jacques instantly materialized. "My lord, your breakfast is ready," the slender Frenchman said. But then, he could almost read Nicholas's mind. "I have laid out your fresh clothes. Do you wish to bathe before carrying on with your morning since it is already rather late?" He coughed slightly. "You have a luncheon with Lord Stuart Davison, Excellency."

Nicholas had not forgotten; Davison was a member of the foreign ministry and worked closely with Castlereagh. He had already met the man and while he appeared to be sympathetic to the possibility of an alliance between their two countries, Nicholas suspected there was far more to the man than met the eye. "I will bathe, but briefly," he said. "Jacques, after I have gone, I have an errand for you. I want you to purchase a kitten."

Jacques smiled. "For Princess Katrina?"

"Yes. Find her something she will adore—with a good temperament. I wish to present her with the gift this evening."

"As you command, Excellency."

Nicholas strode into the breakfast room, a small chamber with several large windows, papered in a bright floral print fabric he found far too feminine and frivolous for his personal taste. But then, he did not particularly like the town house, either. It was a far cry from the many magnificent homes he had in Russia, including the ancestral palace in St. Petersburg, a fantastical new palace he had just finished building in Moscow, and Tver, his country home, a sprawling stone mansion built hundreds of years ago and added onto numerous times.

Nicholas took his place and allowed himself to be served. All of his staff had come with him from his homeland. He would not trust a British chef *not* to poison him if the price were right. Europe was a continent at war, with ever-changing alliances, and agents operated in all of the major cities. Nicholas dug into a plate of broiled sirloin and pickled red cabbage, dismissing those thoughts while reaching for the *Morning Chronicle*. And instantly he became aware of eyes upon his back.

He stiffened, annoyed—he could not even enjoy his meal. The spy was undoubtedly outside the window that was just behind him. How tempted he was to end this moment of subterfuge.

Determined to ignore the spy, Nicholas skimmed several pages of the newspaper. Then he saw his name, and froze.

He slammed down his knife and fork, eyes wide, stared at the title atop the column, three words engraved on his mind—"A Royal Sham."

"What the hell?" he said, and then he read the article— every single blasted word.

He saw red.

Charles Copperville. The man was naïve and romantic and far too idealistic, but Nicholas was a liberal himself, and he had, until now, agreed with some of his views. He had even enjoyed some of Copperville's columns, especially the one in which he had blasted two very well-thought-of lords for their wrangling in Parliament— presenting both men as they truly were—as vain, egotistical fools. But recently, goddamn it, he had been blasting Nicholas. And that was an entirely different matter.

And an entirely unacceptable matter.

Nicholas wondered if he knew the man. If Copperville were an alias—and the man himself was an old enemy of his.

Nicholas was shaking with anger. Copperville had made him appear to be a depraved, jaded, amoral rake—while Marie-Elena had been portrayed as some kind of holy victim. *"Chort voz'mi!"* Nicholas rolled up the paper and threw it at the wall. He was standing.

And when he turned, he came face-to-face with a young man with a scraggly goatee and a bicorne hat set on a head of blond hair at an untidy angle. Only a simple windowpane of glass separated the two men.

For one instant, Nicholas was shocked. But not half as shocked as the young spy, whose eyes were bulging in a face gone frightfully white.

And then he smiled, savagely. To hell with cat and mouse. He had had enough.

The spy ducked frantically, disappearing from sight.

Cursing, Nicholas lunged forward. He was suddenly, savagely, determined.

✑ FIVE ✑

NICHOLAS shoved the window open. The spy was running pell-mell across the small garden. Nicholas put one foot over the sill and bent his body in half, trying to get outside. He cursed, following the spy with his eyes. He could not fit through the damnable window, he was too large, too tall.

He remained crunched up now, his gaze narrowing. Surely what he was thinking was impossible—was it not?

Nicholas jerked himself back into the breakfast room, rushed through the house. He exited through a back door and ran hard around the side of the house until the front sidewalk was in view. Sure enough, his quarry was across the street, still running away. His hands found his hips. He was not a fool.

The little spy, inept that he was, was no he. He was a *she.*

He began to smile. How very amusing, indeed.

And then he began to button up his jacket. An instant later he was also crossing the street—and flagging down a hansom.

Carolyn dashed inside the bookshop. She instantly saw that her father was with a customer, and she regretted her haste. George looked up and his eyes went wide. Carolyn had already recognized the customer; he was an elderly gentleman fond of Gothic novels. She sucked down her breath and gave both men her back, pretending to browse one of the stacks. With a shaking hand she pulled down *Troilus and Criseyde* by Chaucer.

What a close call!

She had yet to recover from having been face-to-face with Sverayov, a mere pane of glass separating them. His expression of fury remained engraved upon her mind. She had not a doubt that if she had not reacted immediately by fleeing, he would have broken that window and done bodily damage to her.

Carolyn was wet with sweat. She had walked a dozen blocks until she'd found a hansom to take her home. And she was still trembling.

And to make matters worse, had Sverayov caught her, he'd have been within his rights to press charges against her for trespassing. Carolyn had never precipitated such a disaster before. But never before had she tried to spy on one of her subjects in such an intimate fashion.

The bell over the front door tinkled. Carolyn turned, and trying to appear disinterested, she watched Mr. Ames leave the store. When the door was closed solidly, she faced her father, her eyes lighting up. "You will not believe what has happened!"

George came over to her. "Your goatee is askew."

Carolyn reached for her scraggly beard, and realized a part of it was hanging off. She flushed. No wonder people had been giving her odd looks.

"Perhaps you should use more glue next time," George said fondly. His eyes twinkled.

Carolyn sighed and yanked off the small beard, shoving it into the pocket of her tan coat. "His wife almost died last night."

"Whose wife?" George asked, reaching for her bicorne. He adjusted that, too.

"Sverayov's," Carolyn said impatiently. She was still stunned over what she had learned. And she could imagine the scene two evenings before—the prince arriving home, disheveled from his love affair, only to find his wife at death's door. Had he felt any remorse? How could he live with himself? And she had lost the child. *Their* child. He had not appeared to be grieving. He had been calmly dining as if nothing at all had happened. What kind of unfeeling man was he? She shuddered. His bronzed face loomed in her mind. She couldn't help wishing he were scarred or pockmarked or something.

"Is that where you were?" George frowned. "Carolyn, I don't want you pursuing the Russian. Leave him alone."

Carolyn stiffened, immediately confused. Her father's tone had been unusually sharp. And although George was her father and she was only eighteen, he had always treated her as an independent thinker—as an adult. He had never ordered her around, not even when she was a child. He had always given her choices and allowed her to make up her own mind. Yet now his words had sounded suspiciously like a command. "Why should I leave him alone? He embodies all that I stand against. Immoral extravagance, self-absorption, self-indulgence, and the tyranny of the few over the vast majority. For goodness' sake, Papa, Russia is a country of *serfs*."

George sighed. "And is that Sverayov's fault?"

"He is an accomplice," Carolyn said firmly. "And I can not respect a man who comes to this country during a time of war, on official state business, and then behaves as a carefree cad, as if nothing were wrong in the world! He should be setting an example for us, and for his own people, don't you agree? Instead he is carousing all night while his wife lies on her deathbed."

"Not everyone is as high-minded as you," George said with a smile. "I see I am going to lose this debate. I am afraid to ask how you found out about his wife. In any case, I hope you are not going to write about the princess in your column."

Carolyn sighed. "Of course not. That would be too low a blow, although I do hope that man is ashamed of himself." She started toward the stairs, her spirits quite high. "Although I doubt he has even thought twice about his behavior. . . . I am going upstairs to change clothes."

"Good idea. I have to go out for a few hours."

Carolyn nodded, flying up the stairs to her bedchamber. She hung up her hat and quickly stripped out of her clothing, hanging everything up carefully on wall hooks. She slipped on a chemise, pantalets, and a pale blue gown with a sash that tied just below her breasts. She pulled the ribbon out of her hair and quickly ran a brush through her blond curls—not that that could tame them. She could not get Sverayov out of her mind. She started to smile. Truthfully, she had had a very good morning, indeed.

And how could she leave him alone? If he continued to provide material for her column, why then, she would use it as any civic-minded journalist would. The whole point of Copperville's column was to expose any and all hypocrites to the rest of society—and maybe, just maybe, make some of them think twice about their own behavior.

Carolyn wondered if he would be at the Sheffield dinner dance a few days hence. Although it was not a ball, a hundred guests had been invited, making it a grand event—for it was to honor Lord Sheffield on his fifty-fifth birthday. Caroline had already surmised just who was on the guest list. She knew for a fact that Prinny was attending, for there was little that the prince regent did or intended to do that Caroline was not aware of, as she had excellent connections with a member of his household staff, and leading Tories had apparently been invited as well, including Liverpool. She imagined that if Sverayov had not been invited he would probably change that himself. But she knew Lady Sheffield. She would never exclude any royalty, much less a gorgeous Russian prince, from a party of her making. Caroline's diary already listed the fête as a "must-do." She had no intention of missing it.

She stared at herself in the mirror atop her small bureau and washstand, frowning at her reflection. Her cheeks remained flushed, her eyes very bright. She was seeing an interior lit up with a dozen chandeliers, couples waltzing across a parquet floor, an orchestra playing, just hidden from view, with servants rushing to and fro with refreshments. Suddenly she could see Sverayov, standing a head taller than the crowd, watching the dancers with a jaundiced eye. And she did not want to masquerade as a footman again, and be resigned to observing the dinner dance from the ranks of the servants waiting outside.

But did she dare? Could she give herself a title, gain entrée to the fête, and actually participate? Could she avoid detection—and being thrown out on her ear? Surely, once inside, no one would notice her amongst the crush.

Her pulse went wild. But how could she *not* try? There would be so much more information to glean if she were on the inside instead of the outside. And she was not taking such a risk because of Sverayov!

When Carolyn went downstairs a few minutes later, excited now at the scheme taking place in her mind, George was putting on his own frock coat and top hat. He picked up a bundle of books from the counter. "I shall be about two hours," he said.

Carolyn nodded, realizing he was meeting a client. The shop was empty, so she walked him to the door. "I am so glad you are home," she said earnestly, kissing his cheek.

George put his arm around her. "There is no place like home," he declared. "I am taking us out tonight. We'll share a pint or two."

"That will be fun," Carolyn said, hugging him again.

After he had left, Carolyn went to the money drawer to check the morning's receipts. They'd had only one sale, and her spirits sank slightly, but then she purposefully buoyed them up. Depression was not in her nature; optimism was. It had been a long winter and a slow spring, but she just knew it would be a wonderfully busy summer—it had to be. The war had hurt them as much as it had hurt anybody. Inflation, shortages of goods, lost employment, these factors impacted on all but the very rich. Although Carolyn did not want to think about it, it was getting harder and harder every month to pay the rent, and harder each year to pay the government taxes. She was very thankful that Copperville had become an instant success when he had first been published last year. She and her father desperately needed the extra income generated by the column.

The doorbell tinkled. Carolyn slipped the receipts away, smiling brightly and looking up. And her heart careened to a halt.

Prince Sverayov stood in the doorway, tall and powerful, golden and bronze, filling it up. His form actually blocked out the sunlight from outdoors.

Carolyn could not believe her eyes. And then her heart began to beat again, but hard and fast, so hard, and so fast, that she could not breathe adequately. She did not move.

He stared at her. His mouth formed a smile. And he stepped inside Browne's Books, closing the door behind him.

Carolyn began to shake. Her mind came to life. Panic filled her. *He knew.* He knew she had been disguised as a man, spying on him while he was at home.

But Sverayov did not make any such accusations. He strolled forward, a slight, very masculine swagger to his stride, his gaze sliding over Carolyn from her head of blond curls to the tips of her breasts—all that was revealed of her because she remained frozen behind the counter. "Good day," he said, the slightest Slavic accent tinging his otherwise flawless English.

Carolyn opened her mouth to speak but no words came out. He had to know. This could not be a coincidence. But she hadn't noticed anyone following her. Yet neither had she checked to see if she were being pursued.

He moved closer, his eyes now on her face, moving languidly from feature to feature. He seemed to stare longer than necessary at her mouth. Carolyn knew her cheeks were burning as her mind raced. Had he followed her? Think, she ordered herself. But her mind refused to cooperate and she could not recall a thing about her short trip home.

He smiled at her. Carolyn's heart turned over from the impact of that wolfish smile. "I have been told that this is the finest bookstore in London. That this is the place to come when one wishes to locate a rare manuscript.''

Carolyn wet her lips. She berated herself for having lost
her wits. She had no choice but to play this out. To see
where this would lead—and whether he knew about her
subterfuge or not. ''Yes. Good day. What is it that you are
looking for?'' She thought her tone sounded like a croak.

He paused very close to the counter—so only a dozen
inches separated their bodies. Carolyn was forced to crane
her head slightly to look up at him. Her pulse continued to
pound. He was wearing his military uniform, studded with
close to a dozen medals. He was intimidating. Not just because of his power, but because of his very potent, very
bold sensuality. It was there in his heated amber eyes, suggested by the bare curve of his full mouth. There was a
cleft in his chin. Carolyn told herself that she would not
faint, by God. She was not going to be affected this way
by him, she was not like those other mindless women. She
was an independent thinker—and proud of it. He was a
hedonistic tyrant. She must remain focused on that fact.

''I am looking for an original copy of Peter Abelard's
Sic et Non and an unoriginal version of Bartholomew's encyclopedia of universal knowledge,'' Sverayov said, staring
unblinkingly at her.

Carolyn jerked to attention. ''I beg your pardon?''

He began to repeat what he had said, but she interrupted.
''Abelard's original treatise is in Latin,'' she said.

He smiled slowly at her. ''I am aware of that.''

She nodded, reached for a quill and made a note. She
wished her hand would stop trembling, hoped he would not
remark it. So he read Latin? And was interested in academic dialectic thought? ''It will be extremely hard to find
such a manuscript.'' She lifted her eyes to his and felt
seared. Her heart leapt wildly. ''Abelard wrote in the elev-
enth century.''

''You are very well informed,'' the Russian said calmly.
''For a woman.''

Carolyn stiffened. Was there a double meaning to his
words? ''I have read Abelard,'' she said far more heatedly

than she wished. "I read him when I was eleven years of
age."

If he were impressed, he did not show it. "The original—or in translation?" he queried.

Her chin tilted. "The original." She did not add that she
had also read the translation.

"I am impressed," he said, something slipping into his
tone that was husky and intimate. "It is unusual, a woman
well versed in Latin."

Carolyn lost her wits again. She was riveted by his magnetic gaze. "I am also fluent in French," she managed.

His brow lifted. "The language of the Russian court.
How interesting. And you have also perused Bartholomew?" he asked.

"Yes."

He leaned on the counter, the movement bringing him
even closer to her. His face was only inches from hers, and
Carolyn could feel the heat generated by his big body.
"And who was responsible for your unusual education?"

She knew her cheeks flamed. Her gaze wandered to his
lips. Why was it so suffocating in the shop? "My father,"
she said.

"Mr. Browne?"

"Yes," she whispered.

His gaze slid slowly over her face again, down her bare
neck—Carolyn was terribly relieved that she was wearing
a high collar—and over her chest. He straightened. "When
shall I be able to meet with Mr. Browne to discuss the
probability of success in his executing my request?"

"He will be back in a few hours," Carolyn managed.
Sverayov was coming back? She felt oddly elated—yet she
also remained eerily afraid.

His hand slipped into an interior breast pocket. He
handed her a snow-white calling card. "This is where I can
be reached." He smiled slightly. "In case you have a need
to do so."

Their fingertips touched. Carolyn flinched. Was he mocking her? Was he trying to tell her that he knew all about

her escapade that morning? Surely he was not flirting with her—and intimating that she might wish to contact him for personal reasons?

"Th-thank you," Carolyn said, slipping the card into the drawer of the counter without even glancing at it. "We shall probably have some luck with Bartholomew." She had the awful feeling that he knew her every single thought.

"I am more interested in Abelard," he returned coolly.

Carolyn swallowed.

"In any case, tell Mr. Browne that I look forward to our association," Sverayov said. "If he can accomplish this mission, I shall use him again."

"Yes, of course," Carolyn said.

Sverayov's mouth curved again. Carolyn expected him to bow. Instead, he suddenly had her hand in his—and was lifting it to his lips as he bent over it.

She stared in shock. Then he straightened—a flicker of amusement in his eyes?—and he bowed briefly and strode out of the store.

Carolyn sank abruptly to the floor, her legs having turned to jelly.

❧ SIX ❧

HER father returned earlier than she expected him. He came into the bookstore appearing a bit harried. Carolyn had long since recovered from her encounter with Sverayov. She had still not decided if he had followed her from his leased town house or not. The possibility raised a portentous question. Did she dare attend the Sheffields' soirée on Tuesday next? But it was one way of finding out for certain if he knew of her masquerade or not.

Her blood pulsed. Fear mingled with exhilaration. At least Copperville was at no risk. He must remain anonymous at all costs.

She had briefly forgotten about "The Royal Sham." Now she cringed somewhat. Had he seen it? Did he even read the *Morning Chronicle*? Eventually, she knew, someone would mention it to him. Thank God he did not know she was Copperville!

"How has business been?" George asked, hanging up his coat.

"Mrs. Henson came in to buy that novel that was written anonymously," Carolyn said. "*Sense and Sensibility.*" She handed her father the note itemizing Sverayov's requests. He read it, his eyes narrowing.

"Someone wants an Abelard original? That's impossible!" George exclaimed. But he was smiling now.

"Impossible or unlikely?"

"Both." He put the note down. "Bartholomew I can find. I saw a copy in Prague at the home of a private client. If this customer wishes to pay, and dearly, I can obtain it." He studied Carolyn. "Who has made these requests?"

She smiled at him, not suspecting what his reaction would be. "You will never guess. None other than our illustrious Russian prince, Sverayov."

George stiffened. "He was here?"

"Papa." Carolyn was puzzled. "Is something amiss?"

He stared at her. "Carolyn, you write about him as Copperville, the column was published this morning, and the man suddenly appears in our store. Is that not worrisome? Only your editor and myself are aware of your real identity."

Carolyn became a bit uneasy. "We have a bookshop and he is looking for rare books," she said. "It's impossible that he has connected me to Copperville. He probably hasn't even read the column yet—or even learned of it." She hesitated. "But it's possible he followed me this morning," she confessed.

"I don't like this," George exclaimed. "You have never gone this far before!"

That was true. "Well, he did not expose me as a trespasser or worse," Carolyn said slowly. "So if he knows what I was up to, he is keeping closemouthed about it. But I cannot think of why he would do such a thing," Carolyn said, "for surely if he knew it was I who was in his gardens this morning, he would accuse me outright."

"He is here to negotiate an alliance between his country and ours, Carolyn. He is a Russian prince, a colonel, and a close personal friend of Tsar Alexander," George said quite grimly.

Carolyn frowned. "What are you trying to tell me?" she asked.

"I think you are going too far with Copperville. Until now, you have written about the wildly extravagant or illicit behavior of society—but never have you targeted such a public figure before. It is a mistake. You could get into trouble, Carolyn, for interfering with the conduct of official state business in this time of war.''

Carolyn was genuinely alarmed now as George turned and walked up the narrow staircase. It was certainly true that for several years now, the laws had become very strict about expressing one's opinions, whether written or not, especially if those opinions were at all political. But no one could accuse her of interfering in the treaty negotiations just because she had blasted Sverayov for his amoral behavior last night! Carolyn suddenly realized that George's concerns were natural—those of a worried father trying to protect his wayward daughter. Perhaps she *should* be a little bit more cautious in the future.

Carolyn felt a tad guilty. George would be distraught if he knew just what she intended to do—even though he never forbade her anything. Carolyn was certain of it. Therefore, he must not know that she would still attend the Sheffield dinner affair.

Nicholas paused on the third-floor landing of the town house, straining to hear. It was late afternoon. The nursery was on this floor, as was the schoolroom where Katya took her daily lessons with her Italian tutor, Raffaldi. Her governess had her room here, as did Leeza, but Nicholas knew for a fact that Leeza slept on a pallet in Katya's bedchamber, no matter which residence they might currently occupy.

He strained to hear and heard nothing. Disappointment claimed him. No childish giggles or laughter or soft, happy singing, not even animated reading or the strains of the harpsichord or pianoforte which Katya played so well. He sighed and walked forward.

The schoolroom was not empty. The door was open, and Nicholas saw Katya bent over a book on the table, carefully reading. Raffaldi sat at the same table, a notebook open before him, and he was correcting Katya's work, Nicholas saw. The governess, Taichili, a woman whom Nicholas found entirely lacking in warmth and compassion but whom Marie-Elena insisted was dedicated to her charge, was not present. Nicholas knocked on the door. "May I interrupt?"

Raffaldi stood while Katya straightened. "Excellency," the dark Italian said. He beamed. "I shall have you know that your daughter had only one misspelling in this entire essay!"

"That is wonderful," Nicholas said, his eyes on Katya, his heart heavy. "And what was the subject of the essay?"

"Katya, tell your father what you have written about," Raffaldi said pleasantly.

"My essay was about the Empress Catherine."

"An important topic," Nicholas said. "And what did you say about her?"

"She was a great ruler because she sought to make Russia better," Katya said seriously. "She made Russia bigger and she taught everyone to be responsible toward their serfs," Katya said. "She wanted government to come from 'Nature and Reason.'"

"I am very impressed," Nicholas said truthfully.

"Thank you, Father," she said, lowering her eyes. Was she flushing ever so slightly? With pleasure, he hoped?

"Do you wish to read it?" Raffaldi was enthusiastic.

"Yes, but later. May I speak privately with my daughter, signore?" It was not a request.

The Italian quickly left the room.

Nicholas came forward. Katya sat absolutely still, regarding him. He pulled out another child's chair and sat down opposite her, feeling terribly oversized and terribly awkward, as well. In fact, if he dared to face his innermost thoughts, he felt overwhelmed. "Did you like your gift?" he asked.

Katya nodded, eyes large, mouth pursed. "Thank you, Father."

He wished she would leap up and hug him with abandon. "Would you like to show it to me?" he asked. He glanced around the schoolroom, but saw no sign of an animal.

She nodded. "Madame Taichili said I must keep him in my room."

"You may go and fetch him," Nicholas said. "It is a boy?"

Katya nodded, and quickly left the schoolroom. A moment later she returned, a ball of white fur and blue eyes in her arms. Her expression very serious, she paused in front of Nicholas and held the kitten out. "Do you want to hold him?"

"No, thank you," Nicholas said, but he stroked the kitten between the ears. It was purring.

Katya kept her eyes glued on Nicholas's face.

"Does he have a name?"

"Yes. Alexander."

Nicholas almost laughed. "You have named him after the tsar?"

"No. After Alexi."

Nicholas wanted to hug her. "My brother must be flattered," he said, trying not to laugh.

"He said I should get Alexander's brother and name him Nicholas," Katya returned evenly.

"I think one kitten is enough," Nicholas said. "Do you want to talk about what happened this morning, Katya?"

She stroked the kitten, her eyes downcast. She did not reply.

"I spoke with the doctors just a few moments ago. Your mother is out of danger. She will live."

Katya remained silent. The kitten's purring filled the void between them.

"But she is weak," Nicholas said, oddly desperate now. "Can you wait until tomorrow to visit her?"

When Katya did not reply, he repeated the question. "Yes," she mumbled in the kitten's fur.

"Do you want me to take you to see her now?" he asked, against his better judgment.

She looked up, her nearly black eyes meeting his. "I will wait as you have asked me to do, Father," she said.

He nodded, standing. It was always this way, his words and feelings coming up against a solid wall. "I am glad you like Alexander, Katya.'' He bit back a frown as Taichili sailed into the room.

"Excellency," she said briskly. "Katya, it is time for your pianoforte lessons."

Katya's face fell. Immediately it became impassive. Had Nicholas not been so attuned to the child, or such a keen observer, he might not have noticed her disappointment. The kitten remained in her arms.

"And please, put the cat back where it belongs," Taichili said, arms folded beneath her narrow chest.

"Perhaps you should do as Madame Taichili says," Nicholas suggested. "You can play with Alexander after your lessons."

"Yes, Father." They both watched Katya exit the room, hugging the Persian kitten to her chest.

Nicholas faced the dark-haired governess. "She is more despondent than usual?"

"I do not think so," Taichili said. "Katya is a serious child, and there is no harm in that."

"Has she spoken at all about her mother?"

"No. She has not referred to the princess even once."

Nicholas hesitated. "Allow her a special dessert tonight. Tell the cook to make her favorite."

"You will spoil her by coddling her, Excellency."

Nicholas said tersely, "That is my right," and he left the room.

He strode downstairs to the second floor, grim. Katya's governess had no sensitivity because any fool could see that Katya was more remote and self-contained than usual since her mother had almost died.

His wife's door was closed. Nicholas did not bother to knock. He crossed the sitting room, ignoring two maids who blanched, and strode into the bedroom. It was brightly lit, a fire blazing in the hearth. He wasn't sure what he expected, but Marie-Elena was sitting up in the four-poster bed, leaning against several huge pillows, clad in an exquisite dressing gown of beige lace. She was extraordinarily pale herself, huge circles beneath her eyes. A tray of food,

most of it uneaten, was on the table beside the bed. A flute
of champagne was also on the tray, half full. Someone had
sent her dozens of roses and they were everywhere, on the
bedside table, on the bureau, and the windowsill—cloying
and annoying. Vorontsky remained in Russia, or so Nicholas thought, so clearly they were from another lover.

"Hello, Niki," Marie-Elena said, her tone low and weak.
"Join me for some champagne?"

His fists were clenched. He had done his best to block
out the events of that morning all day. "I am glad that you
have survived your ordeal," he said tersely. "But it is too
early for champagne."

She was regarding him searchingly. "Please, do not be
angry at me, Niki. I am so weak. But I am so glad to be
alive." Tears spilled down her cheeks. She was the only
woman he had ever seen who remained beautiful while crying.

"Perhaps you should not be drinking champagne if you
are so ill," he said flatly.

She smiled tremulously at him. "You seem very angry.
Niki, I was *dying*. I did not know what I was saying!" She
tried to sit up straighter and failed. Because he was not
heartless, he went to her and placed several pillows behind
her back and helped her to sit more fully upright. "Thank
you," she whispered, reaching for his hand. But he shifted
so she could not touch him.

He folded his arms across his chest. "The roses. Are they
from Sasha?"

Her eyes widened. She was already pale, but the last
vestiges of color seemed to drain from her face.

"Well?" he demanded unpleasantly.

"They are from an admirer—an anonymous admirer,"
she said huskily. "The card is over there."

He walked to the bureau and flipped over the small white
parchment card, which read, "To a True Beauty, Your Devoted Servant." He tossed it aside and faced her. Very,
very softly, he said, "You have gone too far."

"I don't know what you are talking about!" she cried.

He came forward and towered over her and the bed. "When you are well, you shall be escorted to Tver, under an armed guard, where you shall stay—indefinitely."

Her eyes widened. Her nostrils flared. "You cannot imprison me against my will!"

"As I have said, you have gone too far. And Katya remains here with me," he added.

"It's not true!"

"What is not true, Marie-Elena?"

She stared back at him, her breasts heaving. "What you are thinking."

"I don't think you know what I am thinking." He turned to go.

She cried out. "Niki! You are angry—but what have I done? Please! You cannot send me away!"

His striding did not cease. He reached for the door.

"Alexander will not allow it!"

He froze, then slowly turned. "The tsar is my friend, too," he said succinctly. "And even he would not approve of *all* that you have done."

She stiffened in obvious fear. "You would not tell him that—rot—about Katya?"

"I would prefer not to," he said flatly.

She stared. He could see her shrewd mind spinning. "You would never do it. You love her too much. You would never shame her publicly that way. Never."

She was right, but Alexander could be trusted to keep such a secret, and Nicholas merely smiled.

"If . . ." She struggled to speak. "Perhaps I will tell Katya, Niki. Perhaps I will tell her everything—and you will lose her forever—I shall see to it!"

"Do you really wish to do battle against me?" he asked.

Tears spilled down her face now, copiously. She collapsed against the pillows, and Nicholas walked out.

Nicholas found Alexi in the library, pouring two vodkas. He accepted one. He remained very disturbed over his wife's behavior—and her threats. He was equally distressed over his own behavior, but there had been no choice. She had gone too far in seducing Sasha; it was a blow he could not accept.

And he felt sick inside. But Sasha had always been incredibly weak when it came to women, especially beautiful, seductive women like his wife. Still, that was no excuse. In time, though, he supposed that this latest crisis would pass. Eventually Marie-Elena would be allowed to return home, a bit wiser, he hoped, and a bit more circumspect, while he and Sasha would never be close friends again. Unfortunately, he ached with the loss.

He sipped the vodka, his thoughts veering unexpectedly to one curly-haired Carolyn Browne—he had learned her name from a neighbor—and he found himself smiling ever so slightly. Did she truly think to outwit him in whatever game she was playing? And he was, suddenly, sorry she was playing games—he had enough intrigues to deal with at home. She also did not seem at all like the type to play games—either in espionage or anything else—and he was an exceedingly good judge of character.

He glanced at his brother. "Our morning spy is a woman," he remarked. "A woman and an amateur."

Alexi, poised to settle into a plush golden chintz chair, started. Then his teeth gleamed as he plopped down and stretched out his long, booted legs. "Then you have little to worry about."

Nicholas perched on the edge of the leather-inlaid desk, also stretching out his legs, as long or longer than his brother's, contemplating the enigma of Carolyn Browne. "To prowl about my house—and get caught doing so. Why didn't she wait to seduce me at a fête? And she did not even think to look over her shoulder once when I followed her from this house." He could not help his thoughts, which rushed off now into a fantasy scenario of her seducing him. He had to smile at the idea, because it would be very amusing, for she was clearly no femme fatale—yet it was also, oddly, arousing.

"Poor lamb," Alexi said with exaggerated concern. "Is she attractive, I hope?"

Nicholas eyed him. "If you like hacked-off blond curls, a tender age, and a skinny frame, why, then I suppose she is passable." He was certain that she did not know the first thing about seduction. Any fool could see that. Somehow, his judgment left him relieved, and he thought about Marie-Elena, an expert courtesan. And what woman read Abelard at the age of eleven? It was astounding.

"I prefer redheads," Alexi announced. "With big breasts."

Nicholas looked at him. Alexi's mistress was as fair as this Carolyn Browne, and rather petite.

"As a matter of principle," Alexi amended.

"I wonder why the British would send such an innocent lamb after me," Nicholas mused aloud. "I wonder if her father is also involved in these intrigues. He is a bookseller. Perhaps I shall have them both watched."

Alex crossed his ankles. "If the female spy wants state secrets that would affect our position in the talks, she will soon try to bed you. I hope you are prepared for the occasion?" Alexi was openly trying not to snicker.

"Perhaps I shall be the one to seduce state secrets from her." The concept was exceedingly tempting.

"This should be quite amusing," Alexi mused.

"Indeed." Nicholas set his drink aside. He was looking forward to their next encounter. If she were in disguise, perhaps he would strip her of her mask then. If not, perhaps he would seduce her. In any case, he realized that it had been a long time since he had so anticipated being with a woman.

Poor Carolyn Browne. She did not stand a chance.

❧ SEVEN ❧

CAROLYN had decided to forgo the goatee. Should it slip she would be unmasked immediately—and undoubtedly Sverayov would recognize her the instant he saw her if her disguise were not more elaborate.

She had darkened her face and hands, and had managed to get her hands on a reddish gentleman's wig. She wore horn-rimmed spectacles, and she had exchanged her simple tan coat for an evening coat in dark blue velvet. Carolyn was quite certain that even her own father would not recognize her now.

Her heart was beating madly. She had just stepped down from a hansom amidst dozens of coaches discharging the Sheffields' guests. Her plan was very simple. She would attach herself to a large group and enter the huge mansion with them.

Carolyn loitered on the sidewalk in front of the Sheffield residence as couples passed her, going up the stone steps to the open front doors of the house. The stone mansion was entirely lit up from within, and reminded Carolyn of an All Hallows' Eve jack-o'-lantern. Her blood was racing. And then raucous male laughter and conversation made her turn her head.

A group of five young men in tailcoats and satin knee breeches were climbing out of an open carriage. They were clearly guests, and far more than boisterous and noisy—

Carolyn thought that they were already drunk. She crossed her fingers. This was her chance. And then Sverayov's huge black coach cruised to a halt beside that of the young men.

It was unmistakable, not just because of the red wolf snarling from the side door, but because it was escorted by a dozen mounted Cossacks. Her heart seemed to be beating from the oddest location of her throat.

The rowdy men had congregated on the street, not yards from her. It sounded like two of them were arguing about a horse race. A third said, "Here comes Sverayov."

The redhead jabbed his friend in the ribs. "Did you see his wife the other night? My God. I would give my right hand to have a woman like that just for an evening."

Carolyn was much dismayed by this last comment. She continued to observe the Russian's coach as a liveried footman opened the door. Was the princess a raving beauty? She would have to do a bit more research, she decided somewhat grimly. But now that she had overheard the brief dialogue, she thought it unlikely that a man like Sverayov would wed anyone other than some exotic treasure he could show off to friends and peers.

Carolyn tensed. Two men swiftly alighted, one behind the other. Carolyn hardly saw the dark-haired one; she only had eyes for Sverayov.

Once again he was wearing his green and gray uniform with its gold epaulets and numerous medals. He was bareheaded, and the street lamps highlighted his thick golden hair and slashing cheekbones. Two women were passing Carolyn with their escorts and they faltered, craning their necks to look at him. One began fanning herself theatrically.

The Russian moved quickly by the group of loitering men. He ignored the women. And briefly, his gaze swept over Carolyn.

Carolyn could not even duck her head, and their gazes locked.

He seemed startled. Her mouth dry enough to grow cotton, Carolyn thought, he knows it's me.

But then his gaze continued on past her, his expression so filled with ennui and disdain that, as he strode up the stone steps, moving away from her, she wondered if she had mistaken his reaction. He did not cast a single glance back.

Her heart trying to defy all physical limitation, Carolyn stepped behind the young men as they bounded up the walk. One of them was asking what everyone else had thought of "The Royal Sham." Carolyn could not forget about Sverayov, but all of her attention went to the conversation taking place around her.

"A good article," the blond fellow with whiskers said. "Did you hear she lost her child that night? An omen, perhaps?"

"I heard Sverayov swore murder when he read it. If I were Copperville, I'd be in Paris right now."

"Taking potshots at Napoleon?" Someone chuckled.

Carolyn kept her head down, trailing behind the red-haired man. Copperville's columns were usually a subject of gossip. Part of her felt sorry for Sverayov, but on the other hand, his behavior had been reprehensible and she reminded herself of that. As they stepped into the foyer, it occurred to her that if Sverayov had seen through her disguise, or recognized her as the intruder from the other morning when he visited the bookshop, he would have confronted her. Wouldn't he?

Servants took their canes, walking sticks, and any hats. No one blinked at her much less pointed an accusing finger.

Quite breathless now, but filled with growing exhilaration, Carolyn ignored a member of the group of young men who was giving her an odd glance. She quickly stepped past them and down the short flight of steps into the ballroom.

She had made it.

Carolyn did not pause. She quickly disappeared into the elegant, animated crowd. No one would unmask her now.

*　　*　　*

An hour or so had passed. Carolyn was impatient. She had wandered around, admired the dozens of tables set up in the gardens for dining *en plein air*, had studied the guests, eavesdropping whenever she could, wishing she had her notebook so she could make observations and record her thoughts, but thus far, she had not found any spectacular piece of gossip or news to write about in her column. More importantly, she had not found Sverayov.

Where was he?

Carolyn sighed, filching a piece of raisin-studded bread from the buffet in the dining room. She stood staring out at the crowd of guests. Had she not been there for a specific purpose, she would be bored by such an affair. If she had been born a noblewoman, she would not bother to attend, either. She thought about her mother, who had turned her back on such a life. Margaret had always told Carolyn, before her death, that everyone had an obligation to help those less fortunate than themselves. Although they had been as poor then as she and her father were now, Margaret had always had a few coins to press into a beggar's hand. She had spent one afternoon a week tending the ill at St John's. Why did these nobles enjoy such nonsense? Why did they not devote themselves to good works and more interesting, important matters? At least the men congregated in clusters to discuss the war on the Continent and domestic politics. Carolyn had discovered that the ladies seemed only interested in discussing themselves, their clothes and jewels, and the men.

Sverayov had been a frequent topic of conversation amongst the female guests.

They adored him. Carolyn had heard enough graphic remarks to realize that many ladies present had set their sights on him—hoping to seduce him into a heated liaison. She could not help feeling quite disgusted. And Lady Carradine was present, too, looking stunning in a low-cut gown that showed off every possible inch of her bovinelike breasts. Nor did she appear to be wearing anything underneath it, and it molded her figure indecently. This, then, was his type of woman—and Carolyn was not at all surprised.

Carolyn turned and stole a pastry from the buffet, ignoring the disapproving look from a waiter who caught her in the act. It was too early for supper and she was well aware of it. She ate the fruit tart in three bites and licked her fingers. It was time to take action. She had been present at the soirée for at least an hour and had seen neither hide nor hair of Sverayov. She suspected he had taken himself off with a peer or two for private conversation. What if he had used this opportunity to closet himself with the very difficult Liverpool? How she wished she could be a fly on that wall. She studied the crowd in the ballroom and was certain he was not present. Where was he?

Vastly impatient, Carolyn left the ballroom. A group of men were playing billiards, others played whist in the game room down the hall. Across the corridor was a pair of solidly closed oak doors. She smiled at them.

The library? Carolyn thought so. It was undoubtedly the perfect place for a private conversation. Yet she could hardly press her ear to the wood. Or could she?

Carolyn darted a quick glance around, saw that no one was paying her any mind in the game room, and that the corridor was, momentarily, empty. She darted forward and leaned against the door, straining to hear. Silence greeted her efforts.

She was not prepared to give up. She retraced her steps, crossed the very crowded ballroom where the dancing had begun, and stepped onto the terrace outside. Constructed of flagstone, it ran along the length of the house. Carolyn traversed it, circling two water fountains, not even pretending to be taking air. She ignored an embracing couple. The gentleman gave her a dirty look before bending his lover over backward in his arms.

Carolyn's pace quickened. She couldn't help wondering if the gentleman would make love to the lady right there, on the terrace. Not that it was her affair. She had never understood the passionate interest both sexes had in each other. A male friend had kissed her once when she was fourteen. His lips had been wet and distinctly unpleasant.

Once near the library, her thoughts veered to the task at hand and she raced up to a window and tried to peer inside. She was instantly disappointed. The room was shrouded in blackness. No one was inside.

She scowled, shoving her hands in the pockets of her velvet coat, staring into the dark room. *Where was he?*

"I know you cannot be a burglar," a low male voice said. "Even a burglar would have more sense."

Carolyn would recognize that rough, warm voice with its faint Slavic accent anywhere and she froze in disbelief. And then she whirled.

Sverayov stood not far from her in the shadows cast by high blossoming shrubs. Behind him a crescent moon hung in the blue-black sky. His gaze steady on her face, he sipped coolly from a flute of champagne, observing her as if she were a specimen he wished to dissect.

Had he been following her? Carolyn fought to find her composure. Surely that was not the case! "I beg your pardon?"

"Perhaps it is the books that interest you?" he said, sauntering forward. He did not inflect on the word "books." His stride was long and rolling.

Did he know? Or was his comment a mere coincidence, as all libraries were filled with books? Carolyn managed to reply, her tone sounding like a croak in her own ears. "Books? Actually, there is this . . . er . . . I did wish to go inside, but not of course to burglarize . . ." She could not think clearly.

"If you are trying to gain entry into the library," he remarked, "one usually uses the doors."

She could not see his eyes. His face remained mostly in shadow. She suspected that he was mocking her, but could not be sure. "I, er, yes. I did wish to go inside."

He stared. He was close enough now for her to see the amused light in his golden eyes—or was it predatory? Carolyn stared back, trying, frantically, to find an excuse for hovering under the window outside the library. Just as fran-

tically, she was trying to determine if he had seen through
her disguise. Her efforts were abruptly interrupted. The
woman at the other end of the terrace cried out, the sound
blatantly sexual.

Carolyn whirled, eyes wide, mouth open. Heat flooded
her face.

But now the terrace was absolutely silent. Carolyn saw
no sign of the couple. Wherever they were, probably in the
maze beyond the terrace, they were out of sight.

Carolyn became aware that Sverayov was staring at her.
His eyes were piercing. Her heart felt as if it were trying
to pump its way out of her breast. She opened her mouth
to speak, but no sound came out.

Slowly, he smiled at her. "It appears that someone is
thoroughly enjoying herself."

She inhaled. This man was neither embarrassed nor
shocked. She had to say something to break the tension
stabbing knifelike between them. She could not think of a
single thing. He said, "But then, romance is so very enjoyable for all parties involved, would you not agree?"

She must agree. Thank God it was dark, so he could not
see how scarlet she was. "Of course. I . . . er . . . am a firm
believer in romance. Have you read *Sense and Sensibility*?"
And the moment she said those words, she wanted to kick
herself. She was supposed to be a he, and Sverayov would
guess who she was if she did not rectify the situation immediately.

"I'm afraid I have not even heard of the work." Laughter was evident in his tone.

"My sister adores the novel," Carolyn said quickly.

His gaze was unwavering even as he sipped from the
flute. "Romance has excited the imagination since Adam
discovered Eve."

Carolyn stopped breathing. "Yes," she finally said. "It
has."

"Shall we go inside? And leave Adam and Eve to their
earthly pleasures?" He inclined his head toward the unseen
couple, just as a man's rough groan could be heard.

"Inside, yes, that is a very good idea." Carolyn turned abruptly and almost walked into the window.

He laughed softly behind her. His hand closed on her shoulder, making Carolyn stiffen. "We are not burglars, remember? The doors are to your left."

Carolyn allowed him to turn her in the correct direction. He removed his hand, but her shoulder burned, and worse, her body was coiled up tightly with tension. She trembled. And her mind would not function as it usually did, damnation.

He moved ahead of her and swung open a door, then stood back, allowing her to precede him in. "Please," he said.

Carolyn stepped inside the unlit library, which was even blacker than the night outside. He entered the room, and she heard the door close. Her mind froze now that they were alone in the dark, silent room. It was far too intimate. Carolyn did not know what to expect. Her tension, impossibly, increased. And it flashed through her mind that if he knew she was Carolyn, he would make an improper advance to her.

He moved behind her. So softly, so stealthily, that she could hardly detect a single footstep. His arm—or thigh— brushed her hips. He smelled of rich and exotic scents, a blend of leather, tobacco, and heavy, musky spices from the East.

"I am surprised that the couple outside did not choose this room for their little tryst," he said huskily.

A tryst. Carolyn suddenly wished she were not in disguise. Or that he would confront her and accuse her of being Carolyn. She did not move. She did not have the courage.

"I happen to be a friend of Sheffield's," he said, as Carolyn's eyes began to adjust to the darkness. "Ah, here we go."

She stared through the darkness and saw him leaning over an immaculate desk, lighting the wick of a small lamp. He replaced the glass dome. The light illuminated only a small area around the desk, which he dominated. It played over his arresting features—those startling cheekbones and straight, flaring nose. He straightened and smiled at her, catching her staring. Then he leaned one hip oh-so-casually on the desk. "So, my friend, if you are not a burglar, why do you not tell me what you were doing a few moments ago?"

She leapt at the explanation he himself had provided. "I was, er . . . awaiting a friend."

He cocked his head. "Male . . . or female?"

Was he toying with her? Or was she misinterpreting his every word because of her guilt? But by now he must believe her to be a young man, or surely he would have exposed her as a fraud. "A lady friend," Carolyn answered.

"Ah yes, how foolish of me. *You* were anticipating a tryst." His golden eyes seemed to spark with amusement.

Carolyn blinked up at him. She was so warm now that her spectacles were beginning to fog up. But she did not dare remove them. "I am very disappointed," she said.

He smiled and sipped the champagne, his gaze holding hers over the rim of the flute. "You seem young—too young to have a lover," he said.

Carolyn swallowed. "I am eighteen." Here, at least, was the truth.

"You look fourteen," he said. "No insult intended. Well, eighteen is certainly old enough to be playing in haystacks with buxom dairymaids." His teeth flashed. "You have rolled in the hay?"

Carolyn nodded. "Of course."

"Is she winsome?"

"Very," Carolyn said, her chest heaving. She could not imagine where he was leading, but had little doubt that he had a goal in mind.

"Let me guess. She is blond and fair with blue eyes. No—with green eyes."

Tension pervaded every fiber of her being. Carolyn was so tense she wondered if she could turn her head to either side should she wish to do so. "She is blond—and amber-eyed."

He absorbed that. "She appears to have misled you," he finally said.

"I think so," Carolyn managed, ordering herself to un-scramble her wits immediately. He was winning every round. But it was not her fault. It was because he had taken her by surprise, because the couple outside was behaving so shamelessly, and because his gaze was so heavy and sensual, as if he wished to behave as shamelessly—now. But surely she was imagining the heat coursing below his aristocratic exterior. He thought her to be a young man. Sverayov was infamous for his numerous liaisons with beautiful women.

He stood, setting the empty flute aside. "I prefer some-thing stronger." He gave her a long look, one impossible to comprehend, and walked over to the sideboard. Carolyn watched him open a bottle of amber-colored liquor, relieved at the brief respite he was providing. She stiffened when he poured two large glasses.

"Unfortunately, Sheffield has little appreciation for good Russian vodka." He returned to the desk, handing her a glass. "Cheerio, as they say in your country."

"Cheerio," Carolyn mumbled, watching him take a draught. Having little choice in the matter, she followed suit—and instantly began coughing.

He was immediately at her side, taking the glass from her hand and pounding her back until she had ceased chok-ing. When she was breathing normally again, a tear rolling down her cheeks, she looked up, into his intent regard. It was then she realized that his palm remained splayed on her back, close to her nape, beneath her short curls. Heat unfurled all over again inside of Carolyn, but this time with shocking intensity.

And he gave her a slicing look. Penetrating, promising, and very, very male.

Carolyn's heart lurched.

He dropped his hand and moved slightly away, and when

he faced her again to return her glass to her, his expression was bland. But Carolyn remained breathless and disoriented. Had he really looked at her in such a feral, sensual manner? And what did such a look mean? Did he like boys as well as women? He did believe her to be a boy—didn't he? And if he didn't, why did he not unmask her? Carolyn had the insane urge to unmask herself.

"Eighteen? When you drink, my friend, sip with caution," he advised.

Carolyn nodded and took a careful sip. The whisky burned a hole as it trickled down her throat and settled in her abdomen.

"Very good," he said. He sat back on the edge of the desk.

The heat of the whisky seemed to have moved immediately to her brain. She glanced again at his hard thighs and the bulge that was suggested by his trousers just above them. The tension afflicting Carolyn had changed. Her body was becoming softer now, oddly warm and pleasant. But something else was burning inside of her. She took another sip to force away the image which suddenly came to her— of the couple she had witnessed so passionately entwined outside. The stranger had become Sverayov. "I don't know what happened. I must have swallowed the wrong way."

"Of course." His warm gaze slid over her face. "It is a common affliction—amongst those your age with your experience."

"Are you making fun of me?" Carolyn asked baldly.

"Do I give that impression?"

She realized that half of her drink was gone. "Yes, you do. I think you mock most people. Why is that, I wonder?"

He grinned. "I would drink a bit slower if I were you. What did you say your name was?"

She almost said "Carolyn." It was on the tip of her tongue, but in the nick of time she remembered where she was and who she was supposed to be. She smiled at him. "I am Charles Brighton."

"Brighton? Hmm, no relation to Edmond Brighton, the

sly old fox who outmaneuvered Pitt in the far east trading scheme some years ago?''

Carolyn blinked. Why could she not recall that scheme? ''He is my . . . er . . . great-uncle.''

''A useful connection,'' Sverayov said. ''Well, you must be pleased that your great-uncle is here.''

Carolyn clutched her glass. Her heart seemed to have stopped. ''My great-uncle is not well and he has been in the country these past few months.'' Which was why she thought to choose him as her relative.

Sverayov smiled slowly at her. ''I have met the man on several occasions and he is here, my friend. Apparently his health has improved since your last communication. Or are you estranged?''

Carolyn blinked. How her mind came to her rescue, she did not know. ''He has disapproved of me for several years. Actually, we have not seen one another or spoken in some time.'' She smiled brightly. ''Not since I was fifteen, actually. I doubt he will recognize me.''

''I am sure he will not.''

Carolyn wondered if she had misheard, but Sverayov was calmly sipping his whisky. ''And you, my lord? You have failed to introduce yourself.''

''Have I? But I thought you already knew who I am.'' His eyes gleamed.

''I have not the foggiest idea,'' Carolyn said a bit sharply.

He stood and bowed. ''Prince Nicholas Ivanovitch Sverayov, at your service, my young friend.'' His gaze skewered hers.

''Oh, yes. You are the Russian, the tsar's special envoy,'' Carolyn said, sipping the whisky. She was truly beginning to enjoy herself. ''So tell me, Your Excellency. Have you made any progress with Castlereagh?''

He smiled, like a wolf. ''Every exchange constitutes progress, don't you think?''

''I think,'' she said, somewhat loudly, ''that we do not trust your tsar to be a staunch ally in the present circum-

stances. I think that the moment our friendship ceases to
be a dire necessity, he will reforge an alliance with Bonaparte." She smiled sweetly at Sverayov. "I also think that
you need us far more than we need you." She did feel
somewhat smug.

He stared. "Well, you think as most of your countrymen
do." Now he smiled back at her. "And what if I tell you
that the tsar has learned from his mistakes and is absolutely
opposed to the Napoleonic Empire?"

"I would reply that the proof is in the pudding, sir,"
Carolyn said tartly, enjoying herself.

He smiled. "A true skeptic when it comes to my coun-
tryman. Yes, proof is always in the pudding. What a quaint
expression. Perhaps one needs to analyze the pudding's ingredients?" He was calm, and, perhaps, amused.

"The first ingredient is Tilsit," Carolyn rejoined evenly,
sipping her whisky.

"Yes, you Brits do have a terribly long memory. But
why exclude so many other ingredients? Erylau, Friedland,
Jena? Even Salamanca, if you will?"

"I do agree that we have a common cause in opposing
Napoleon," Carolyn said. "But once again it is a matter of
trust. Should Napoleon surrender to your tsar on the issue
of trade and tariffs, I do wonder if Alexander would not
rush to scribble his signature on a treaty with *him*." She
smiled.

His eyes widened briefly, then narrowed as he recovered
from his surprise. "Well, well," he said softly, "you are
an astute observer of international politics."

It was praise. He was complimenting her intelligence,
and there was no mistake about it. Carolyn flushed with
pleasure.

"Tell me why we should aid you in a war, Excellency,"
Carolyn said.

His gaze held hers, then moved slowly over her face.
"What is not obvious is that, when the war is over and
Napoleon is defeated, there will be much work to be done
on the Continent. And it will be done more easily if we

have built some trust between us, and have shared some of the pain as well as the glory. Otherwise the postwar years will be disastrous—nations reduced to petty bickering over the spoils like willful children fighting over spilled candies.''

Carolyn thought about what he had said. ''We do not want to fight your war,'' Carolyn said slowly. ''We have troubles enough on the Peninsula. Russia is huge, too huge a canvas for us to become embroiled there, and should Napoleon adjust your frontiers, we can survive the consequent economic and political dislocations.''

He eyed her, brows arched. But his gaze was hard and brilliant. ''There will not be any adjustments to my country's frontiers. Alexander will never make a peace with Napoleon while a single enemy soldier remains upon our soil.''

Carolyn bit her tongue. She hoped he was right, and she could see, obviously, how patriotic he was. She would not mention Vilna being abandoned in the face of an invading army—with the tsar leading the retreat. ''Of course, it would be preferable if he did not adjust your frontiers or those of any other country's.'' She sighed. ''When will this war end? We have already lost so many men. And so many boys.''

''This war will end when La Grande Armée is defeated, and not a moment sooner. And that is the crucial, overriding goal, which we share.'' His gaze softened. ''Have you lost friends and relatives . . . Charles?''

She looked up and spoke truthfully. ''I have been lucky. No. I have not. But I have witnessed firsthand the pain and suffering the war has caused here in Britain. There are so many hungry children, so many homeless families.'' She brooded. And then she saw something in his eyes. A shadow that was not amusement or mockery. ''Have you?''

''I have lost many friends and many relatives,'' he said, staring abruptly down into his drink. He quaffed it. ''Well.'' He smiled at her, reached out and clasped her shoulder. ''Shall we return to the party? Perhaps to look for your lady friend? I would be most curious to meet the lady in question. Perhaps I can even help arrange a tête-à-tête.''

Carolyn tried to recover her wits; he had changed the subject so quickly. But her mind seemed a little blurry. Slow and blurry.

He put his arm around her, hugging her to his side. ''I hope you are not cup shot, my little friend,'' he said softly, maneuvering her across the room. ''Not when the night is so young.''

''I am hardly foxed.'' Carolyn's chest was tight. His body was hard and hot against hers. As they walked, his thigh rubbed her hip repeatedly. Her loins throbbed in a way she was entirely unfamiliar with.

He smiled down at her, not letting her go. ''I would be very disappointed,'' he said. ''For I thought that you might wish to join me later for some further entertainment.'' His eyes gleamed.

Carolyn forced herself to think. She could hardly believe her ears. Their encounter was not yet over, and she could not resist him—did not even want to. ''I would love to join you later,'' she heard herself say quite breathlessly.

''Good. Let us plan to depart at midnight.'' He paused before the closed library doors. His arm was still around her and Carolyn remained glued to his side.

She stared up at him. His heat, his scent, his potent male sensuality, enveloped her, rendering further thought impossible. His smile had faded. His gaze was brilliant and intense. For one moment, Carolyn sensed that he was going to kiss her. It was a moment of suspense and anticipation that stretched on endlessly. It was a moment of insane yearning.

But he dropped his arm and opened the door. The sounds of the party crashed over them with jarring suddenness—laughter and conversation, both male and female, the rich sounds of the orchestra. The corridor, however, was strikingly empty.

"I was thinking," he said, "that we shall amuse ourselves in a brothel. What do you think, Charles?"

Carolyn met his enigmatic gaze and was instantly rendered speechless.

✒ EIGHT ✒

CAROLYN allowed herself to be guided by Sverayov down the corridor and onto the threshold of the ballroom. His words rang in her ears. Surely he had not meant what he said? She cast a stunned glance at his face.

He smiled at her. "You shall forget your lost lady love in no time."

Her pulse raced. He had not been jesting with her.

"Niki! I have been looking everywhere for you," a male voice drawled.

Carolyn recovered some of her composure just in time to see a striking dark-haired man who bore a stern resemblance to Sverayov detaching himself from a lush redhead and striding over to them. So this was the brother, she thought. And then she wondered if she dared continue her charade—and join Sverayov in a brothel. Immediately, images she had never before entertained flooded her mind.

The tall, dark-haired man blinked at Nicholas. "Where have you been?" he said, more mildly:

"I have been sharing a drink with my young friend," Sverayov said. "Alexi, meet young Brighton. Charles, this is my brother, Alexander."

Alexi was staring, making Carolyn feel awkward. She extended her hand. "A pleasure, sir," she said.

He took her palm as if reluctant to do so, shooting Nicholas a slanting glance.

Carolyn withdrew her hand. "I have enjoyed our conversation," she said to Nicholas Sverayov with a brief bow.

"As have I." He was smiling. "I will see you at midnight," he said firmly.

She felt her cheeks heat, though she nodded, and she rushed off into the crowd.

"Good God," Alexi said, staring after her. "Are you insane? Or have you recently acquired a yearning for boys?"

Nicholas started to laugh. "Brighton is a woman." He continued to chuckle.

Alexi started, and then his eyes narrowed. "Not the intruder from the other morning?"

"Yes. That is he—which is also she—and her real name, of course, is Carolyn Browne. Does she really think to fool me with that silly disguise? I am a man. I can tell the difference between a man and a woman. Besides, I saw her on the street outside the very moment I arrived." He started to laugh again.

"Well, you seem happily amused. What is she up to?"

"I have no idea. But I do intend to find out." Nicholas folded his arms, staring across the crowd, locating Carolyn with her back to a pillar, pretending to be preoccupied with watching the dancers. "Surely she wants something from me. But why masquerade as a man when she would be so much more likely to achieve her ends if she approached me as a woman?"

Before his brother could respond, Nicholas espied Lady Carradine emerging from the crowd. He prepared himself. She floated forward, her lush figure enticingly revealed. "Nicholas," she said, hand extended. "How wonderful to see you."

He took her hand, bowed over it, and voiced those same sentiments, which he did not feel.

Carolyn was waiting for Sverayov in the foyer when the clock struck midnight.

She had done little other than to think frantically about

what he intended for them to do. The more she thought about it, the more she realized that she could not refuse this golden opportunity. Or was it Sverayov whom she could not refuse?

Carolyn sought to be rational. What woman ever got a chance to see a brothel firsthand? Curiosity alone made her case overwhelming. But she had Copperville to think of now, too. Carolyn imagined that she might come up with half a dozen good pieces from this one night alone.

She was excited, exhilarated, and of course, she could not help but being afraid. Surely she would not be put in the position of having to carry on with some prostitute as if she were a man! For then she would be unmasked.

Carolyn had a simple plan. When that moment came, she would become ill—and she would make a very hasty retreat. But until that climactic ending to an extraordinary night did occur, she would keep her eyes and ears wide open.

Now Carolyn stood with her hands in the pockets of her blue velvet coat. She saw him coming toward her from the ballroom. She felt her tension increase. She stared openly, helplessly. Of course, she was not the only one doing so. Heads turned in his wake, every one of them female.

"Ahh, there you are." With long, lithe strides he bounded up the three short steps that led to the foyer. "You did not forget our little rendezvous," Sverayov said with a cool smile.

"I am looking forward to it," Carolyn said, smiling briefly. However, in spite of her anticipation, her fear seemed to be increasing.

He clapped her lightly on the back. "As am I. There is no better way to end an evening, is there?" He winked.

Carolyn did not reply because he did not remove his hand from her back as they walked outside past two unsmiling footmen. His touch was arousing. She had never had this kind of reaction to a man before. He finally dropped his palm as they trotted down the steps leading to the sidewalk. Carolyn was disappointed—she was also relieved. And had he meant what she thought he did? That an evening's best conclusion was lovemaking? Her heart beat double time now.

His magnificent coach was waiting for them on the street below. The Cossacks sat mounted behind the carriage as still as stone statues. Footmen leapt to attention, opening the door for them.

"After you, my friend," Sverayov drawled.

Carolyn stepped up into the coach, feeling his gaze on her back. Her eyes widened. The interior of the coach was well lit by sconces attached to the interior walls. The coach boasted royal blue velvet seats with trim braided in gold. A fur rug was folded in the corner of one seat. Carolyn sat down. In that moment, she thought about her mother and her grandmother. Margaret could have had all of this. But she had chosen the splendor of true love instead. Yet Carolyn could not help thinking about the obvious attractions of life in society. It was not just the fine things one might have, but the relief from the constant worry of how to make ends meet. She reached out to touch the fur.

"Russian sable," he said, low, interrupting her thoughts. His breath brushed her ear. Carolyn jerked around, only to find his face inches from hers, their gazes immediately connecting. His was bright. She plopped down backward as a result of their sudden proximity. The coach was far too small for the two of them.

"We have very long, cold winters at home." He settled on the squab facing her, stretching out his long, booted legs. Their knees brushed.

Carolyn was hot. The door had been closed and now the coach moved forward. She clasped her hands in her lap.

"Did you ever find your lady friend?" he asked, his eyes sliding over her face.

"Actually, I did."

"And what explanation did she give you for her failure to keep your tryst?" Amusement laced his tone.

"She had a change of heart," Carolyn said.

"How fickle females are." Sverayov stared. "Fickle . . . and deceitful."

"That is a vast generalization, is it not?" Carolyn said as calmly as possible. After all, Brighton, had he existed, might agree. Still, she had to defend her own sex. But his words did remind her of her own deceit.

"Not true. In the vast realm of my experience, I have found the fairer sex to be quite inconstant—and quite misleading, as in your case tonight."

Carolyn met his gaze and tried to decide if he meant what his words seemed to mean or if his remark was but another coincidence. His gaze was bland, innocent. She swallowed down a stabbing of fear and smiled—far more boldly than she felt. "Men can be as inconstant. Take myself. My heart is broken, but already I am intent on consoling myself with someone else."

He smiled at her. "So that is your intention, eh?"

She flushed. "Of course."

"I would hardly label your behavior as inconstant, nor is it deceitful," Sverayov drawled. His eyes held hers. "Would you?"

She prayed she would not flush. "In this case, no, of course not." She looked away, anywhere but at him.

"Although one might say your behavior is misleading," Sverayov said. Carolyn's pulse leapt. He smiled and added, "If one had known of your fondness for the lady in question."

"Well, I am certainly not fond of her anymore," Carolyn managed.

"That is wise. It is better to recover immediately and move on than to linger hopelessly where one is not wanted, like some foolish romantic."

Carolyn looked into his compelling golden eyes and thought of Lady Carradine, whom she had noticed fawning over him some time ago, and all the other women he must have swept off their feet. Thankfully, she was not now, and would never be, one of them.

"Absolutely," Carolyn said, glad the topic had veered

away from innuendos that seemed to strike at the very heart of her deception. But his barbs against her own sex still rankled. "Do you dislike women, Sverayov?"

He laughed. "To the contrary."

She shifted in her seat. "I know you are a ladies' man, and that was not my meaning. I have found that some men, although quite fond of, er, passion, actually are not at all fond of women. Have you not found this to be the case?"

"That is a wise observation for one as green as you," Sverayov said. He reached down and produced a leather flask from a compartment beneath the seat. "Vodka, my friend. Will you share?" He extended the flask out to her. His eyes were bright, intense. Intent.

"I . . ." Carolyn trailed off. She did not dare. She wanted her wits about her.

"I understand. Performance fears. I myself have never had to worry about that," he said, tipping his head back and taking a draught of the flask. He then slipped it into his coat pocket.

"I do not understand," Carolyn said cautiously.

He started, then smiled. "You are refusing to imbibe, are you not, because it will interfere with your ability to make love to a woman? Many men suffer from such an affliction. They drink and cannot maintain an erection. It is nothing to be ashamed of."

Carolyn knew that she turned red. She gaped, a very graphic image coming to mind—and realized what she was doing and quickly closed her mouth. If he noticed her shock, he gave no sign of it. How she wished she could fan herself with any object close at hand.

"To answer your question, I hardly dislike women. I only dislike those particular ones who are dishonest and inconstant." He smiled at her. "I am not a man who enjoys being misled."

She wet her dry lips. "I dislike dishonesty in general," she said, then wanted to kick herself. And take back her words.

"Really? Then we have a great deal in common, you and I."

Carolyn closed her eyes briefly. She could not seem to get out of the hole he was digging—with her very own help.

"Have you ever noticed," Sverayov drawled, causing Carolyn to meet his gaze, "that in the best of times, women are nearly impossible to comprehend?"

She took a deep breath. "Women can be difficult to comprehend." She had no choice now but to agree.

"They will say one thing, and do another. Or act one way, but it is sheer subterfuge."

"I am not sure I understand your meaning." Her tone was hoarse. She was so warm now she wanted to remove her coat—an impossibility.

"What I am saying is that women often give off mixed signals, making it almost impossible for a man to understand what they want—or know who they really are." He smiled at her.

Her heart beat with maddening force. If the carriage had seemed overly warm before, it was hotter than Hades now. Was he about to unmask her? But surely he would not have waited this long to do so. "That is funny. I have several sisters, and they all say the very same thing about men." How else could she respond?

"Oh? Is that what they say about *us*?" His gaze was wide, benign.

"In fact, they decry the hypocrisy of our behavior," Carolyn said rapidly. "They find *us* misleading and, to be blunt, dishonest. They think we say one thing, and mean another. After all, when a man vows undying love, and later that evening indulges himself with another woman, that is quite incomprehensible, is it not?" She could hear how her own tone was pitched too high.

He smiled slightly. "Honesty. We cannot seem to get away from the topic. Only a fool would vow undying love, or a liar, for it does not exist."

"You are a cynic."

"Precisely. And you, I am sure, are an eternal optimist."

"I am proud of it."

"I am sure that you are," he rejoined.

"Sverayov, you have been linked to several women since you have arrived in town. Is that not an example of the dishonesty typical of men?"

He regarded her, his expression impossible to read. "And why is my private life an example of dishonesty?"

"Well, you do have a wife." Carolyn began to feel uneasy. She wanted to retreat.

"My wife and I go our separate ways." He was cool. He smiled at her. It was dangerous. "Many couples do. Neither one of us expects or even wants fidelity from the other. Actually, I would describe our relationship as painfully honest. Wouldn't you?"

Carolyn squirmed. "I suppose so," she said carefully. "If I have offended you—"

"Why would such a statement offend me?" His posture was completely relaxed, his amber eyes unblinking. "My behavior is hardly uncommon. And if it is, to some degree, dishonest, than so is my wife's, and that of much of society."

"If a room is filled with people," Carolyn said quickly, "and everyone lies, that does not mean it is acceptable, nor does it mean that you should also lie."

"Are you a proponent of fidelity?"

She hesitated. "Yes. I think if two people enter the state of wedlock, fidelity is desirable."

"Spoken like a true romantic." His long fingers played over the velvet of the seat he sat upon. "Women, I find, tend to favor commitment and fidelity."

"Another vast generalization."

"How fond of your sisters you must be, to defend their gender so faithfully and repeatedly."

"Have you no sister you are as fond of?" Carolyn retorted.

"None."

"So you have never proclaimed undying love to any

woman, Sverayov?" Carolyn could not help herself.

"Never." He was adamant. And amused.

She thought about his wife, who was supposed to be stunning. She could not get her out of her mind. His wife, who had just lost a child. But if they led independent lives, had the child even been his? It was a stunning possibility. "Not even to your wife?"

His smile vanished. His eyes cooled in spite of their amber color. "I am neither a fool nor a liar, my friend. I never promised my wife anything I did not intend to give her."

She pushed herself back into the velvet seat. There was danger in his tone. "I was intrusive. I am sorry. It's just—"

He stared.

Carolyn was sorry to have even raised the topic. She cast her eyes down. Only one thing was clear. He did not seem to be in love with his wife. But he was a self-confessed cynic, with a renowned reputation for being heartless when it came to women.

Sverayov interrupted her thoughts. "Are you sure you do not wish for a sip of vodka? We are almost there."

Carolyn froze, her gaze slamming to his. "At the brothel?" Alarm was apparent in her tone.

"Was that not the plan? Are you having second thoughts? Perhaps you are pining for your lady friend?"

"I . . ." Dear God, she was having second thoughts— dozens of them. Was she really going to enter a brothel, disguised as a man? But what could possibly befall her? If she were clever and careful?

He reached out, squeezing her knee quite suddenly. "Have you ever been to a brothel before, Charles?"

She blinked. Hesitated, her mind racing, her wits once again thoroughly scrambled. She said, "No." Honesty seemed like the best recourse, now.

"I did not think so," he said, and he patted her leg. "There is nothing to be afraid of," he soothed.

"I am not afraid," she lied. And the coach halted. Her heart jumped.

"These are very beautiful women," he said, his tone

soft. "You do like women, don't you . . . Charles?"

Their gazes met. Now was the time to confess—if she were to confess at all. Carolyn almost felt like taking off her spectacles and shouting out the truth to him. Instead, she sank her fingers into the fur of the sable rug.

"Charles. Why do we not be honest with one another? And cease all foolish pretense?"

He knew. He had known all along. She hadn't fooled him, not for a moment. Carolyn's pulse thundered in her ears. She nodded slowly, eyes wide, glued to his.

He patted her knee again. "I know you have never been with a woman," he said, low. "I doubt, also, that you are eighteen. There is nothing to be ashamed of."

Carolyn was still. He continued to hold her knee. His eyes were very warm. She found it difficult to breathe. She could not utter a single word.

He smiled at her. "The first time can be frightening. Or so I have heard. I have a suggestion."

"What?" she heard herself whisper.

"Do not plan on doing anything. Instead, come with me."

"With you?" she squeaked.

"Yes." He reached for the door. "It is not uncommon, actually." And he swung it open before the footman could.

What was not uncommon? Surely he was not suggesting that something take place between the two of them? Did he know the truth—or not? Carolyn did not move. "What do you mean?"

"It is simple. I will make love to a woman . . . while you watch. It will be very instructive," he said. "I promise you that."

ৰ্ঙ NINE ৩৯

CAROLYN was reeling.

Sverayov smiled at her, as if it were settled, and stepped down from the coach. For one moment, Carolyn did not move. Watch him make love to a prostitute? Had her charade gone too far?

"Coming?" Sverayov queried coolly.

Carolyn started and eased herself out of the coach. The brothel appeared to be a nondescript brick town house. She glanced quickly around, trying to discern just where they were. It was a quiet, unlit residential neighborhood. "Is that Delancey Square over there just behind the church?" she asked. How breathless her voice sounded. But images were dancing inside her head, of Sverayov in bed with a faceless woman, Carolyn watching from nearby.

Of course, she would *never* do such a thing.

"It is," Sverayov drawled. He rapped on the door, which was immediately opened. Carolyn did not know what she was expecting, perhaps a half-nude woman, but the gentleman facing them seemed quite respectable in his waistcoat and trousers. But the usher did not bow, he seemed to bar the doorway, instead. "My lord?"

"Please tell Madam Russell that Prince Nicholas Sverayov is here to see her," Sverayov instructed.

The usher bowed and left. Carolyn glanced up at Sverayov, who caught her studying him, and he smiled at her.

Carolyn ducked her head, wondering what would happen next—wondering what Sverayov would do if she bolted and fled. But that would be ridiculous. She might never have this opportunity to see the interior of a brothel again.

The usher returned. Carolyn and Sverayov followed him inside. They paused in a pleasant if not simple foyer with parquet floors, red rugs, and walls upholstered in a multi-colored fabric. A staircase with red runners was in front of them, and Carolyn could well imagine where those stairs led.

"Madam will be right down," the usher said. "Would Your Excellency and the young gentleman care to wait in the parlor?"

"We shall wait in the other salon; I do believe the young gentleman is in need of some refreshment." Sverayov threw his arm around Carolyn and quite dragged her down the hall. They passed the parlor—the doors were open—and Carolyn craned her neck to see inside. Several gentlemen were seated there, with an equal number of attractive women. Carolyn dug in her heels. One glimpse was definitely not enough.

Sverayov's brows lifted. "You prefer the parlor?"

Carolyn did not reply. She was staring. She recognized Sir Thomas Woodhaven, an outstanding member of Parliament who was a fervent champion of all kinds of reform, especially for those who had so little. Recently he had taken up the cause of young children employed in the mines. Carolyn's eyes were popping. Woodhaven was there, in a brothel! She was incredulous, disappointed, and even angry. She had always admired him so. But he was a fraud.

Her gaze moved to the other gentlemen as Sverayov tugged on her arm, but she recognized no one. And the women were not half-dressed. Although their gowns were very revealing, they were no more daring than many of the gowns Carolyn had seen earlier at the Sheffields', including that of Lady Carradine. She was somewhat disappointed.

"Shall we?" Sverayov asked as if impatient.

Carolyn nodded and he guided her down the hall and

into the last salon, which could have been the salon of any gentleman's club. It was paneled in wood, filled with small tables, and a fire roared in a stone hearth. Carolyn sat down with the Russian prince, searching the cozy room for any other faces she might know. She stiffened. "Is that not Lord Davison? One of Castlereagh's assistant foreign ministers?"

Sverayov leaned back in his chair. "It is." He eyed her. Davison looked their way and nodded briefly at the Russian.

Carolyn wondered if Anthony knew his father frequented a brothel. And Sverayov thought women inconstant and hypocritical! "I saw Sir Thomas Woodhaven in the parlor," she said in a strained tone.

"How shocked you were."

"He has spoken more than once, with great passion I might add, about the failing morals of this country. He has taken a very strong position publicly against all vices, and that would include the vice of dallying in a brothel." Her eyes flashed. "He was a hero of sorts for me."

"I am sorry you have had to remove your rose-colored glasses," Sverayov said. "No one is perfect, Charles. And rose-colored glasses could very well become your downfall one day."

"And what is Stuart Davison doing here?" she demanded.

Sverayov signaled to a servant. "Two ports, if you please," he said. "I imagine he is doing, or shall do, almost exactly what we plan to do." He smiled.

She met his gaze and drowned there. Their eyes held. Forbidden, erotic images quickly returned to her. For a moment she was swept away, imagining Sverayov passionately involved with a woman. Then, to her amazement, the fantasy changed and the woman in his arms became herself.

"This will be an experience which you will never forget," he promised her softly.

Instantly, shaken to the quick, Carolyn forced her mental wandering aside. Carolyn did not doubt his words—except that she was not going to turn herself into a voyeur, even if she was, shockingly, tempted. Suddenly his hand covered hers. Carolyn forgot to breathe. "Sverayov," she said huskily as he oh-so-casually removed his hand, "I understand your intention and it is . . . it is interesting. But I cannot watch you while you make love to one of these women. It is sinful."

He smiled. "Surely you are not an overly moral prig? An enlightened young man like yourself?"

She bristled. "Perhaps my morals are the norm—and your vices are not."

He laughed.

"Sverayov, I am being serious. It just is not done."

He laughed again. "To the contrary, young Charles, it is done all the time. In fact, there are rooms with mirrors one can see through from an adjacent room, just for the very purpose of voyeurism."

"There are?" Carolyn gasped.

"Yes, there are." He seemed satisfied.

Carolyn's mind had become peculiarly blank. And her pulse was racing faster than ever before. But she could not, must not, do as he wished.

Suddenly Sverayov was standing. Carolyn looked up as he embraced a faded but still lovely blond woman, elegantly dressed in lavender silk. Diamonds sparkled from her ears and throat.

"Claire, how are you?" he asked, smiling.

"Niki, what a pleasure, and what a surprise," she said warmly. Her gaze immediately went to Carolyn, who looked away. "It has been more than a few years, my dear," Claire Russell said.

"Yes, it has." His gaze was steady on Claire's face. "You have remained as beautiful as ever."

She scoffed. "Please, I am ten years older, but you have hardly changed. Even had I not been told that you were here, I would have recognized you immediately."

He chuckled. "This is my young friend Charles Brighton," he said, turning. "Brighton, Madam Claire Russell."

Carolyn stood quickly, avoiding the woman's eyes, which seemed searching. "A pleasure," Carolyn muttered. The woman's eyes were far too intelligent, too probing. Carolyn was afraid that Claire Russell could see right through her disguise. And what did the apparent fondness between the Russian and the madam mean? Had they once shared a liaison? Carolyn thought it likely. She gazed from one to the other, unable not to remark that Claire Russell had a beautiful figure and those strong, striking looks that only faded but never disappeared with age. She was jealous and incapable of denying it even to herself.

But how could she be jealous of one of Sverayov's old flames?

"Charles, I am going to speak privately with Claire." Sverayov's eyes caressed her flushed face. "I shall explain our little predicament."

Carolyn took her seat, watching them from the corner of her eye. She could not catch a word being exchanged. Undoubtedly Sverayov was telling Claire that she was an inexperienced young man. Oh, Lord. He was intent upon teaching her how to make love by demonstrating his technique to her. Did she dare, just this once, allow herself to fall into the sinful jaws of voyeurism? Could she watch Sverayov perform with another woman?

Had she become mad?

A servant placed two glasses of port on the table. Carolyn quickly reached for one and took a draught of the sweet, heavy wine. She then felt eyes upon her and she glanced up, only to find Sverayov regarding her intently with his gleaming gaze even as he spoke to the blonde. Carolyn returned his stare. The port was already warming her insides and calming her pounding heart. Her shoulders, until now as stiff as two boards, had relaxed slightly. She sipped the port again. This was, she now told herself, an incredible opportunity. She was already inside a domain reserved exclusively for wealthy, powerful men. And while she knew how a man made love to a woman, she could not really imagine just what the procedure entailed—and if she were absolutely truthful with herself, she had wondered about it for some time. She was being given the chance to witness expert lovemaking. Although she was hardly a depraved voyeur, and certainly not titillated by anticipation, who could, in their right mind, pass up such a chance?

Carolyn sipped her drink, thinking about how she might never fall in love and therefore might never actually experience lovemaking herself. This might be her only opportunity to truly learn what the act was all about.

She smiled at her glass. Actually, now that she had thought things out, she was beginning to realize how very fortunate she was. She would stay, she decided, for a few minutes, just to get the gist of things.

How warm the salon had become.

Sverayov returned to the table but did not sit down. Madam Russell left. "Do you wish to finish the drink or go upstairs?" he asked. His gaze was brilliant, like yellow diamonds.

Carolyn clutched the glass, her pulse rioting in spite of the fact that she had almost finished her drink. "Go upstairs . . . now? So . . . soon?"

He seemed to bite back laughter. "Everything is arranged. Madam Russell has suggested Victoria, a young lady who enjoys the use of mirrors—and is adept at performing for outside parties. You have nothing to fear, Charles," he said softly. His eyes gleamed. Wickedly? "You are only going to watch from an adjacent room. Or would you rather leave? My coach can take you home."

Carolyn stared at him. It was hard to think. But she had made up her mind and was not about to go home. This was her golden opportunity. She stood abruptly, so abruptly that she knocked over her chair. But Sverayov righted it. "I am ready," she said thickly.

"Have you become eager?" he asked, slipping his arm around her shoulders. "Perhaps you should not have drunk the port so quickly. It is potent."

"I am as sober as you," Carolyn said, although she knew she was a bit inebriated.

He chuckled softly. "Perhaps your sobriety is just as well. Being as you are quite shy."

Maybe he was right. Carolyn walked with him into the hall and up the stairs. He did not remove his arm from her waist. It felt far more than pleasant—his arm was warm and strong around her waist, making her acutely aware of him. But he, of course, was merely being friendly, the gesture being naught but male camaraderie. As they walked her hip bumped his thigh repeatedly. His hand tightened on her waist.

Carolyn tried to clear her head, which was beginning to feel rather fuzzy. It was hard to remember that she must not be a woman, not when his body was so hard against hers. But he was convinced she was Brighton. And they were in a brothel—where he was about to make love to another woman. Carolyn realized that she was growing a bit anxious.

The second-floor corridor was lined with closed doors, except for one. They paused on the threshold. Carolyn inhaled, confronted now with what was about to happen. One of the most exquisite women she had ever seen, clad only in a pastel pink satin wrapper, was brushing her thick, blue-black hair in front of a huge mirror. She paused and faced them, her limpid gaze going from Sverayov to Carolyn. Her skin was as pale as ivory, as delicate as porcelain.

"Hello, Victoria," Sverayov said flatly. "This is my young friend Charles. You may call me Nicholas."

Carolyn's heart beat hard. Had she lost her mind? Should she leave? Now, before it was too late?

Victoria smiled at them both, coming forward, her heavy breasts swinging beneath the thin satin wrapper, her nipples visible beneath it. Carolyn was already blushing. The woman did not seem to have a stitch on underneath. But of course such a woman would not be modest.

"Good evening to you both." She spoke with a childish voice, her turquoise eyes bright and somehow innocent.

Carolyn wondered how old she was—her womanly body appeared at odds with her expression, which made her seem fifteen. "Claire said you were handsome, that I would like you very much." Her fey smile reappeared. "And she said that you are a real prince!"

Sverayov smiled with amusement. "A very real prince. Shall we show Charles to the other room?" He was no longer looking at Victoria, but at Carolyn. He still had his arm around her. "Charles?"

Carolyn began to perspire. In spite of her own tension, she managed to wonder about Victoria. What if she hated being a prostitute? What if she were fifteen? What if some of her clients abused her?

Victoria came forward, the wrapper parting to reveal that she did have something on beneath it, shockingly black, lace-trimmed stays and pantalets. If Carolyn had thought her cheeks to be aflame before, now they were positively burning. She glanced at Sverayov, only to find him watching her, Carolyn, with very calm golden eyes. Their gazes held.

And in that instant, she forgot the other woman's presence in the room. In that instant, she thought Sverayov had forgotten her, too, for his smile had vanished as he stared at her and his eyes were far too brilliant for comfort. Carolyn almost thought that he was going to reach out to her, Carolyn.

But Victoria broke the moment. "Are you sure you want to watch, Charles?" she asked with a slow, sweet smile. "I don't mind if you stay with us. I've done a threesome before." Her gaze moved to Sverayov. "Maybe the prince would like that best," she said, her tone turning husky. Her small pink tongue actually came out and touched her bottom lip.

Carolyn stared at her, fascinated. And then she looked at Sverayov, who was still not watching Victoria, oh no. He observed Carolyn very intently.

"Charles?" Sverayov asked. "Do you wish to join us?"

Carolyn wet her lips. "No! Really . . . I will watch," she managed, incapable of any other reply. But she was now having grave doubts about her courage to actually go through with this.

Victoria smiled and swished past her, out into the hallway. Carolyn was about to follow but Sverayov gripped her wrist, halting her.

His gaze was brilliant, yet odd. "Perhaps I have been remiss," he said slowly, his eyes moving over her face and lingering on her mouth. Carolyn's pulse tripled. "I feel as if I have become the Devil himself, about to corrupt the innocent. Perhaps we should leave—and find some other sport to occupy us for the rest of the evening."

Carolyn's breasts heaved. She found herself staring at his mouth, wondering what his lips would feel like, how they might taste. Dismayed at her reaction, she tried to tell herself that this was not the time or the place to desire Sverayov—who was not her type of man anyway. And surely he desired the beautiful, childish prostitute. She swallowed. "I want to leave," she said, "but I might never have this chance again." Too late, she realized she had been speaking as Carolyn.

He stared.

A hot, hard silence fell between them.

Victoria reappeared on the threshold of her room. "What are you two doing?" she said in protest.

Sverayov ignored her—perhaps he had not even heard her. "How badly," he said, his tone husky, "do you want to stay—and watch me?"

Carolyn trembled. That was a very good question. "I don't know," she whispered back, her heartbeat deafening in her own ears. "I am very . . . curious."

Sverayov did not release Carolyn's wrist. His gaze darkened. Finally he gestured at the door. "After you . . . Charles," he said.

Carolyn swallowed, her mouth completely dry now, and she followed Victoria into the adjacent room. Carolyn's eyes widened. Although the room was furnished like a bedchamber, a couch faced the wall, not the fireplace, and there was a window in it. She could see right through the window into the room where the prostitute would make love to Sverayov. She felt Sverayov come to stand directly behind her—so closely that she could feel his body's heat. Carolyn did not move.

"In her room it is the mirror," Sverayov said softly, from behind, his breath fanning her ear.

Carolyn stiffened. Shivers of delicious sensation swept over her.

His palms closed lightly on her shoulders. Carolyn found herself swaying backward, against his hard, strong body. "This is where you would watch me," he said as softly.

Carolyn trembled.

Victoria laughed. Once again, Carolyn had forgotten that she was present. "So clever, isn't it?"

Carolyn nodded, speechless. Abruptly Sverayov released her and stepped away from her. She stole a glance at him. His expression appeared strained, but she could not guess why.

And immediately Victoria moved to Sverayov and pressed against him, gazing up at him. Her wrapper had parted, revealing both bare breasts, in their entirety, which were pushed up against his arm. Carolyn bit her lip.

"Let's begin, my lord." She squirmed against him, smiling coquettishly.

Sverayov did not move. The wriggling woman did not seem to have very much of his attention. "Charles?" he asked.

Carolyn clenched her fists. She did not know what to do. She was confused, so very confused, and inexplicably aroused. Her gaze slid over his face, over his impossibly arresting features, lingering on his mouth.

"What are you both waiting for?" Victoria was cross. "Do you two even need me?" Her hand moved over Sverayov's abdomen, stroking small circles there. "If he wants to watch, let him watch. Why don't we go?" She was petulant. And her hand was sliding lower and lower down his uniform jacket. To where it parted over his trousers.

And now Carolyn could not miss the fact that a very

large, rigid line was distending his trousers. She blinked—
and stared.

"Let's go," Victoria whispered in Sverayov's ear. Her
fingers skimmed his length very blatantly—up to the tip
and back down.

Carolyn's heart went wild. She was frozen in place.

Sverayov gripped Victoria's wrist, halting her. "I am
afraid," he said evenly, "that this has gone far enough."

He was ending it. Carolyn was ready to collapse into the
closest chair. But she could not get the image of the prostitute's hand on his manhood out of her mind. She raised
a shaking hand to her eyes, briefly covering them.

Victoria began to protest. Carolyn recovered enough to
watch Sverayov hustling her from the room and into her
own room. She turned and stared at them through the window. Victoria was angry, fists clenched, and her wrapper
had opened completely. Carolyn searched Sverayov's face
desperately for a sign that he was even remotely interested
in the prostitute, but failed to find anything other than annoyance in his expression. She turned away as he left the
room, hugging herself.

She felt as if she had had a very close call.

Sverayov appeared in the doorway. "Let's go." His tone
was sharp. His jaw was tight.

Carolyn nodded grimly, thinking breathlessly that this
had been a disaster, and tried not to recall her recent ex-
periences. She sidled past him then lengthened her strides,
hurrying down the hall and downstairs. He followed her.
Unfortunately, she came face-to-face with Madam Russell
on the landing below when she was hoping to escape the
brothel without seeing a single soul.

Claire's blond brows lifted. "Charles. Is something
amiss?"

"It is late. I must go. I . . . am not well."

"You are white. You seem upset." Claire looked concerned—but then she and Sverayov shared a glance. "Can
I help? Can I get you a brandy?"

"No. Thank you."

Sverayov took her arm very firmly in his. "Thank you, Claire. I hope to see you again."

Carolyn was guided swiftly outside by the Russian. She gulped in the fresh air. Now she wondered whether he would have stayed with the prostitute if she had not come with him that evening. She flushed. Her heart hammered. The thought made her angry—an emotion she refused to entertain. And the last place she wished to be now was inside his coach. She could still feel his breath feathering her ear, his palms cupping her shoulders, and the length of his hard body against her posterior. And she kept seeing Victoria's milk-white hand teasing the length of his manhood.

"Charles?" Sverayov queried.

Carolyn met his gaze for an instant—and tore it away. "I will take a hansom."

He followed her to the curb. "You cannot find a hansom at this hour of the night." He nodded to the waiting footmen standing by the coach. The door was swung open. "After you, Charles."

Carolyn took a final deep breath of the cool night air and stepped up into his carriage. As he also stepped up, the coach dipped slightly under his weight. They settled onto opposite seats. Carolyn toyed with the soft sable rug, keeping her eyes downcast.

"Charles? You seem very . . . disturbed," he said.

She forced a smile. "I am not disturbed." Oh, but she was. Disturbed and hot and throbbing in places she was just now beginning to understand. And she looked up.

Their gazes clashed. His tone might have been odd, but his eyes were brilliant, mesmerizing. Their eyes held.

"It was a disturbing evening," he said slowly, "for me, as well."

Carolyn could not move. What did he mean? Why could he not speak directly? She could only think how much she wanted him to bend down and kiss her—how much she wanted to feel his mouth on hers, his body against hers. How much she would like to be as bold as Victoria.

His jaw flexed. The night had become hot around them. And suddenly his hand lifted.

Carolyn flinched, shocked, as he reached for her cheek to caress her. Her pulse exploded. She forgot she was masquerading as Brighton.

But his fingers did not touch her cheek. Instead, he removed her spectacles. "Your lenses are fogged up." He produced a handkerchief and cleaned them, his gaze on hers. And then he slid the spectacles back on her nose. "Let me take you home," he said.

❧ TEN ❧

"WHERE am I taking you?" Nicholas asked as the coach moved forward.

She avoided his eyes. "I am staying at an inn." She gave him an address two blocks away from her father's bookshop.

Nicholas watched her. He had only meant to amuse himself by toying with Carolyn—a just consequence of her charade. He had wanted to see how far she would go, for he had been certain she would unmask herself before they had even gone upstairs. But she hadn't. She had remained mute, playing out her hand. And he, Nicholas, had been the one to fold. Carolyn had won this round.

He wondered what she would have done if he had made love to the prostitute. He stole a glance at her flushed face. Would Carolyn have stayed? And watched? He would not be completely surprised.

Of course, he'd had no choice but to quit the game. It had been glaringly evident that Carolyn was completely innocent—as much a virgin as she was a total amateur as a spy.

"You are staring," she said abruptly. "Have I sprouted horns on my head?"

He had been staring. Because even the ugly stain on her face and hair, and the narrow horn-rimmed spectacles, could not disguise her full, ripe mouth or her perfect little nose. And her eyes remained huge and vividly green behind the lenses of her glasses. Which were fogging up again.

He was a vastly experienced man. He had been aroused in the brothel—and it had had nothing to do with the prostitute. But where did that leave him? The idea of making love to an innocent woman, even one playing games with him, was at bitter odds with his higher self. He had never even contemplated such a liaison before. But suddenly he could imagine himself and Carolyn engaged in a passionate affair. The problem was, she was far too romantic to survive its demise. He knew it, the way he knew the sun must set every night.

He shifted, acutely disturbed. "You have hardly said a word since we left Madam Russell's."

"What is there to say?" This time she held his gaze.

"Why are you so hot?" he asked, the sound softer than he had intended. As if he did not know.

She shifted uneasily now. "Perhaps we could open a window."

"Did you find the evening educational?" He could not resist.

She was still, rapidly turning crimson. And her gaze slipped over him. "Yes."

His reaction was immediate. And he thought, everyone, eventually, had to grow up. But he still did not want to be the one to shatter her romantic illusions.

"Perhaps," he said, leaning forward, "you will decide that you are ready to return to Madam Russell's—by yourself? I am sure Claire will welcome you now, anytime."

Her eyes, behind the foggy lenses, widened. "Per . . . haps."

He tried not to laugh, imagining that.

"You seem to be good friends with Madam Russell," she said suddenly.

He was bland. "I am. She used to keep an establishment in Paris, years ago. My father took myself and my brother there on several occasions when we were boys."

"You remain fond of her?"

Was she jealous? Oddly enough, the idea appealed to him. "She is a unique woman, sincere, without pretense."

Carolyn squirmed, as well she should. "You know, Sverayov, I do not think that you hold women in high esteem."

He was annoyed. "Actually, I hold very few women in high esteem, women like Claire—and can you blame me? Most women want one thing or another from me, and they are not very subtle or genuine about getting it."

She flushed. "Yes," she mumbled. "I can imagine."

He stared at her downturned face. She was so damnably naïve. She could not be a political agent, it was impossible. In that moment, he was certain of it. She had some other reason for her charade, perhaps one as simple as an overwhelming intellectual curiosity which demanded satisfaction. After all, most women were content to remain ignorant, marry designated buffoons, deliver children to their husbands, relinquish their households to a capable staff, and do nothing other than attend galas and soirées. Yet Carolyn was astoundingly intellectual, unusually educated, and obviously carelessly unconventional. She read Abelard, for God's sake. He still could not get over *that*.

"They say," she said suddenly, very softly, not glancing up, "that you leave a trail of broken hearts wherever you go."

He regarded her as she slowly lifted her eyes. His heart lurched oddly. "That is nonsense."

"Is it?"

"If any heart is broken in my wake, I am quite unaware of it."

"Yes, I imagine that would be the case," she said very somberly.

Their gazes locked. Nicholas could not look away. Suddenly she seemed so fragile and vulnerable, as well as innocent and naïve, and terribly feminine and alluring—in spite of the garish disguise. As suddenly, he had the overwhelming urge to make love to her, and to hell with the future consequences. He looked away, thinking that this momentary madness would pass. "We are here."

The coach had heaved to a halt. Booted steps sounded outside as the footmen leapt to the ground from the rear runners. The door opened.

She remained seated, her eyes holding his, the tension between them as thick as before—if not thicker. "It was a very . . . interesting evening."

He did not smile. Nor did she. "Good night, Sverayov." Pausing before stepping down, she looked back at him. And she stepped out of the coach.

"I look forward to seeing you again, Charles," he said. Meaning it.

She stared up at him from the sidewalk.

And he rapped on the roof once and the coach started forward. He did not look back. It took an immense effort. And his smile was gone. Nicholas brooded.

A few hours later, Nicholas paused outside of Browne's Books, drenched in morning sunshine. It was the next morning. He could not resist temptation. After last night, he knew Carolyn would not be expecting him.

He pushed open the door to the shop, the bell ringing overhead. A stocky man with graying hair was behind the counter, scribbling in a ledger. Carolyn was nowhere to be seen, but then, it was not yet ten o'clock. He had not dropped her off last night until almost two o'clock in the morning.

The elderly man looked up with a smile as Nicholas sauntered forward. Nicholas assumed that he was George Browne, but found little resemblance between father and daughter. He paused in front of the counter. "Good morning. George Browne, I presume?"

George snapped the ledger closed and shoved it into a drawer underneath the wooden counter. "Yes." He smiled, but it was forced and did not reach his eyes. "Do I know you, sir?"

"Prince Nicholas Ivanovitch Sverayov, at your service, sir." Nicholas bowed, remarking the frisson of alarm which sparked the other man's eyes. Why was the bookseller disturbed?

"Ah, yes. Your order was taken the other day by my daughter." George turned away quickly. When he faced Nicholas again, he had a sheaf of paper slips in hand, and he filed through them intently.

Nicholas saw the slight tremor in his hands and frowned. Something was wrong, but what? It was easy to draw the conclusion that George was involved in his daughter's intrigues, except Nicholas had decided last night that there was a sensible explanation for Carolyn's disguise which had nothing to do with spying and warfare. And George surely did not know about Nicholas's recent involvement with his daughter.

"I am interested in the original version of Abelard's *Sic et Non*," Nicholas drawled. He glanced briefly at the stairs, but there was no sign of Carolyn. He assumed both father and daughter lived in the apartment above. "And a copy of Bartholomew's encyclopedia."

"Yes, now I recall." George set the papers aside. "Abelard may be impossible to find. I am contacting my clients on the Continent, as well as here at home. I have seen Bartholomew in Prague. I do believe it can be purchased, for a dear sum."

Nicholas leaned on the counter. "How dear?"

"Perhaps a thousand pounds."

He nodded. "Notify your client of my offer. I am prepared to double that if need be."

George's eyes widened.

A noise made them both look toward the stairs. Carolyn paused halfway down them, one hand on the banister. Nicholas forgot all about George.

He turned, staring. She was clad in a pale blue muslin gown with long sleeves and a high neckline. It was simple yet so very feminine—a glaring contrast to her disguise last night. For one moment, as he stared at her, realizing that she was far more than pretty, that she was lovely, very lovely, he felt as if he had been kicked in the chest by a good-sized mule.

And then his heart resumed its normal beat again. Nicholas felt the tension riddling his body, was aware that he stared as her smile faded and she began to come down the stairs, her expression uncertain. The stain had been scrubbed from her face, which was once again as pale and delicate as the finest English porcelain. Charles was gone. In his place was a beautiful young woman with huge green eyes and golden curls.

"Carolyn, good morning," George said brusquely.

Nicholas did not even try to remove his regard as she stepped onto the landing, approaching the two men. Her eyes had locked with his and a pink flush colored her high cheekbones. Was she also remembering all that had transpired last night? He certainly was.

"Father, I am sorry I overslept." Carolyn kissed her father's cheek before facing Nicholas with a brief curtsy. "Prince Sverayov. How good to see you again." She did not smile. Anxiety seemed to fill her eyes. How vulnerable she appeared.

He bowed over her hand. "How could I stay away? I do not think the lure of rare manuscripts brought me back here today," he said softly.

Her color increased.

"We have been discussing the prince's requests," George said quickly, his gaze going back and forth between Carolyn and Nicholas. "And we have just concluded our business," he added. "I have just assured the prince that he need not pay for Bartholomew in advance."

Nicholas had no intention of taking the hint that he should leave, and he opened his wallet. "Please, do keep these funds as a deposit on the business we shall transact." He faced Carolyn, ignoring George as if the older man had left the room. "Miss Browne. Would you help me choose a book for my sister?"

She smiled in surprise. Nicholas smiled back blandly at her. He had told Charles that he did not have a sister, but

Carolyn was not supposed to be aware of that. "Of course," she finally said. "What does your *sister* enjoy reading?" Her tone was both tremulous and tart.

"She is very romantic. Perhaps poetry? Love poems? All women dream of love."

She stared at him, wetting her lips. Was she remembering their conversation last night? And as he had thought, she could not resist the bait.

"Love is an essential ingredient of life for both men and women, Your Excellency. Surely you must agree?"

"I think," he said, enjoying himself vastly, "that it is far more essential for women than for men. Is it not the rage nowadays for women to try to marry for love? An absurd notion, you must admit."

"I do not find it absurd. My parents actually married for love," she said, her chin shooting up.

"But you are a woman, Carolyn," he said.

"My father married for love." She turned to George. "Did you not, Papa?"

"Of course I loved your mother, Carolyn. That was a long time ago."

Carolyn smiled at Nicholas.

Nicholas decided not to tell her that George had not admitted to marrying for love. "And you, Miss Browne? Will you seek to marry for love?"

Her eyes widened. Before she could reply—if indeed she would—George interrupted. "Carolyn, I have an eleven-thirty appointment."

"Well, then you should run along," she said, obviously relieved. "I am, apparently, about to search for romantic poetry for the prince's *sister*."

Nicholas smiled, regarding both father and daughter, impatient for George to depart.

"I can wait a few more minutes," George said, his glance hovering on both Carolyn and Nicholas.

"Do not linger on my account," Nicholas said with a cool smile.

George did not speak, but Carolyn frowned. "Of course

he is not lingering on your account. Papa, feel free.'' She turned and walked over to a stack of books labeled ''Poetry.'' She pulled down a volume. ''This is Wordsworth.'' She smiled at Nicholas, but it was fleeting. ''We have such a vast selection. There are Thomas Moore, Lord Byron, and numerous others. Perhaps you should *describe* your sister to me.''

''What is *your* preference?'' Nicholas asked instead. ''I think my sister would enjoy anything you recommend. I know that I would.'' His smile flashed. ''You never answered my question. Will you marry for love?''

She hesitated. ''Actually, I am not sure I will ever wed.''

''Really?'' He doubted that.

''You are mocking. I am sincere.''

''You are a beautiful woman. Sensible and intelligent—although overly romantic. You will hardly live your life as a spinster.''

''I will if that is what I choose to do,'' she said firmly.

''But you just told me that love is an essential ingredient for women and men. Yet you would deny yourself?''

''One does not snap one's fingers and summon love,'' Carolyn said. ''I see no need to tie myself down to some hardheaded gentleman with a base male nature who will think to entrap me in a role I do not wish to play. I am an enlightened woman who has much to do.'' She smiled as if that explained everything.

Was she referring to his base nature last night? He could not help but think so. ''I am impressed. But what will you do if you experience *le coup de foudre*?'' He stared.

She returned his gaze, her eyes wide. ''I do not know,'' she finally said.

''I know,'' he heard himself say, his tone far lower and more intimate than before.

She inhaled, motionless.

''You will embrace this hero with all of the passion you have thus far embraced your books,'' he said firmly. And he did not have a doubt. Perhaps he was even—the slightest bit—jealous of this man who would one day enter her life and turn her head and win her heart. What wonderful debates they would have.

"I do not know what you are speaking of," she said, flushing. "Now, are we not trying to locate a volume of poetry for your sister?"

"Yes. What is your preference?"

She hesitated.

"Are you trying to hide something?" he asked, amused.

"You are a very good judge of human nature, are you not? Actually, I am particularly fond of Shakespeare's sonnets." She waited for his reaction.

He smiled, trying not to laugh. "Shakespeare? I should not be surprised. There is little predictable about you, Miss Browne. Shakespeare." He shook his head. "And this from the woman who reads Abelard and Bentham?"

"We all have multiple facets to our natures, Excellency," Carolyn said pointedly.

He leaned one shoulder on the shelf of books. Images from last night flitted through his mind. He knew she was also recalling it. "Find me Shakespeare," he said abruptly.

She nodded, returned Wordsworth to its place, and extracted a volume of sonnets. She handed it to him. "I think your sister will enjoy this."

Their gazes collided. "Actually," he said, "I am going to read it myself." He stared at her.

She did not look away.

A cough sounded behind them. Carolyn started. Nicholas turned slowly. George stood there, having donned his coat and hat. "I must go," he said very grimly. Clearly he did not want to leave them alone. "Shall I give you a receipt for your purchase?" he asked Nicholas.

Nicholas smiled slowly. "I am not finished."

George nodded with dismay. "I will return within an hour and a half," he told Carolyn anxiously.

"Do not worry so, Papa." She kissed his cheek. Reluctantly, George turned and left the store.

Nicholas studied Carolyn, who stared after her father.

She tore her gaze from the closed door, wet her lips, smiled briefly. "What else would you like?"

"Actually," he said, low, "what I would like has little to do with poetry or books."

She was motionless.

He smiled. "I know you must tend the store now. But perhaps, later, I can take you for a drive in the park? Say, tomorrow at three?"

Her eyes were wide. Surprised. "I . . . I don't know."

He smiled slightly, his gaze intent, and touched his heart very briefly with his right hand. "You cannot disappoint me," he said.

She swallowed. "I do not understand this. Your intentions . . ."

"It is really quite simple. I wish to further our friendship, that is all."

She stared. "Perhaps your wife might object."

"To an innocent acquaintance?" he asked. "I think not. Surely you are not afraid?"

Her chin tilted. "I am no meek mouse, Excellency."

His mouth curved. "Good, then I shall not be denied."

"Have you ever been denied, Excellency?"

"No."

She smiled. "I did not think so. Perhaps this shall be the first time."

"But we can debate Bentham, if you wish."

And she laughed.

He laid his hand on his heart. "As an officer and a gentleman, I promise to return you home untouched and unhurt. If that is what you are afraid of?" he challenged her.

And her eyes flashed. "Did I say I was afraid, Excellency?"

"But it was a natural assumption," he rebutted.

"Well. It has been some time since I have driven in the park." She smiled slightly. "At three then, Excellency, on the morrow."

He bowed. "I look forward to it," he said softly.

⊰ ELEVEN ⊱

"Lost Ladies of the Night." Just how popular is the bordello amongst today's most fashionable set? Why, the answer is, quite popular, for on an early weekday night there were no less than a dozen gentlemen present at one very nondescript brick town house not far from Delancey Square whose female proprietor proved most eager to please her clients. (Lady loves are hand-chosen to meet a gentleman's specific requirements.) And these dozen gentlemen were the ones in the public rooms; this reporter has no idea of how many more gentlemen were behind closed doors with their lady friends. But how does one justify the presence of a certain member of the Commons, Sir T——s W——n? Perhaps Sir W——n was also investigating the popularity of illicit love in order to render a more fervent speech in the Commons on one of his favorite subjects, the evils inherent in today's society. Or should we recall the old adage that "he who protests overmuch . . . ?" Unfortunately, this illustrious member of Parliament was not the only renowned nobleman and member of our government who was present. A certain member of Liverpool's cabinet is clearly not the type to linger at home in the wee hours of the morning. Or is Madam's establishment a particularly fashionable gathering place for the more renowned (or should I say infamous) members of our society? For even a certain visiting foreign dignitary was seen entering one of the rooms upstairs, this man a prince no less.

Nicholas stared down at Copperville's article in shock. He had just returned home to change after a late lunch, before leaving to pick up Carolyn for a jaunt in the park. His mind spun, his pulse raced. Was it possible? Was Carolyn Browne, who was Charles Brighton, also Charles Copperville?

It was absurd.

It made perfect sense.

But that would mean that she had frantically written the column and delivered it to the *Chronicle*'s offices sometime yesterday. Perhaps she had even penned the satire the evening of their visit to Claire's. His jaw tightened, ground down. He stood up, staring down at his desk. He did not believe in coincidence. What were the odds of Copperville just happening to be at Claire's while he and Carolyn were there? It was possible—but not likely.

What was likely was that little Carolyn Browne was Charles Copperville.

And then he began to laugh. Hard. Until tears streamed down his face. Good God! He should have guessed from the beginning that Copperville was a woman, but he had assigned the satirist's naïveté and romanticism to youth, not the female gender. Well, now he knew it was due to both youth and femininity. He shook his head, amazed. And suddenly he understood Carolyn's disguise—it was a strategy for her to gather news for Copperville's column. Of course she was not a political spy. How else would she gather news when she was no peer? His smile widened. Of course Carolyn was Copperville—they shared the exact same views!

Complete comprehension struck him then. To have expected Carolyn, who posed as Brighton, to be anything less than a satirist like Copperville would be absurd. She was too clever, too well read, too enthusiastic, romantic, and optimistic not to challenge society and attempt to turn it on its head. His admiration for her knew no bounds.

And now her disguise made as much sense as her prowling about his house. She had been spying on him not because he was a Russian envoy sent by the tsar to negotiate an important treaty, but because she needed grist for her mill.

Of course, that still did not explain what her father was hiding. He was up to his ears in something unpleasant, and something far less innocent than Carolyn's charade. Nicholas had no doubt.

Nicholas paced the library, hands clasped behind his back. How stealthy and clever she was.

But not, he decided, as clever as this one visiting foreign dignitary.

Carolyn told herself that she must not change into a nicer dress, put a ribbon in her hair, or even, God forbid, rouge her lips. She was not a silly, vain, besotted nitwit, and she was not going to act that way.

Anticipation filled her. Why had he invited her to drive in the park?

This was the man who had taken her to a brothel the other night—one he was no stranger to. It was the same man who had carried on with the equally ravishing Lady Carradine. He was married, or so it was said, to one of the most beautiful women in the world. What could his invitation mean?

There was an obvious conclusion. He was a rake. She was a woman. In spite of his promise to return her home unharmed, he wished to amuse himself at her expense. She was courting jeopardy by driving with him in the park. Any sane person could see that.

Her pulse was pounding wildly. Carolyn glanced at the small clock in her room; it was already three. She took her blue shawl from the wall hook and went downstairs. She could not refuse this challenge; she was not like the other women he usually pursued, and he was about to find that out.

She had already told George she had some things to do in the afternoon. He was sitting behind the counter, reading. A novel Carolyn recognized as being by William Cobbett was beside his elbow, but her heart skipped when she saw the *Morning Chronicle* open on the countertop before him. She had taken a risk in writing about the brothel, but she had been unable to resist—there had just been too much to write about to pass up the opportunity. She was prepared, too, for the next time she encountered Sverayov as Brighton. He would probably assume that Brighton was Copperville, but she would deny it, maintaining that Copperville must have, coincidentally, been present that evening as well. He could be as suspicious as he wished; Carolyn would not ever confess to Brighton's other identity. And she smiled to herself, a small thrill of excitement rushing over her. Sverayov was clever and he knew it—but she was very clever, too.

George looked up and stared gravely at her. "How on earth did you write this, Carolyn?"

Carolyn gave a worried glance at the door. But Sverayov was not in sight. "I have my sources, Papa." She managed a bright smile.

His scrutiny was intense. "If you went into that kind of establishment in your disguise, then I must put my foot down," he finally said.

Carolyn hurried behind the counter and put her arm around him. "Papa, you know that no journalist can reveal his or her sources!"

He was very grim. "You were there, were you not? Carolyn, you have gone too far."

She felt her cheeks heating. "Papa, did you not enjoy the column?"

He finally sighed. "Was Woodhaven really there?"

Carolyn nodded, mouth pursed.

"I cannot believe it! What hypocrisy! And who, might I ask, was the other gentleman—the member of Liverpool's cabinet?"

Carolyn's eyes sparked and danced. "Perhaps that is for

me to know and you to wonder about," she said happily.

George sighed with mock exasperation, putting his arm around her. "You are not being careful, Carolyn."

Carolyn glanced again nervously at the doorway, but no tall, tawny form loomed there. "Actually," she said in a hushed tone, "it was the elder Davison."

"Really? Well, one never truly knows what goes on in a man's mind, now does one?"

Carolyn agreed. "It is amazing."

George shook his head, smiled. "It's a perfect day to go out. Where are you going, my dear? And do not tell me you are doing more investigative work."

Carolyn hesitated. "Actually, I am going for a drive in the park," she said carefully.

George's eyes twinkled. "With *young* Davison?" The bell over the front door was tinkling.

Carolyn's heart leapt as she turned. She started upon seeing Anthony Davison strolling into the store. "Er, no," she said quickly to her father.

"I do not understand," George said.

Carolyn hesitated. "I am going with Sverayov."

George's eyes widened and Carolyn knew he disapproved and was about to protest. But she turned her back on him—something she never did—as Davison came forward, smiling. Carolyn saw that he held a bouquet of flowers in his hand. Her eyes widened, but she was already smiling. "Hello, Lord Anthony."

"Miss Browne." He bowed over her hand. "Mister Browne. I brought you these," he said, his blue eyes holding hers.

Carolyn hadn't expected flowers, but was hardly amazed. In fact, she was rather preoccupied with her pending outing in the park. "Why, thank you," she said, taking the lilies. "How very thoughtful. Let me get a vase and put them in some water."

The bell over the door sounded again.

Carolyn tensed as Prince Sverayov strode into the bookstore. Behind him, she glimpsed a small cabriolet, a vehicle which seated two. She had expected to see his black lacquer town coach emblazoned with the snarling red wolf atop the crossed swords, and his mounted armed guard of a dozen Cossacks behind. The cabriolet seemed remarkably small—and remarkably intimate.

She thought about that night again. Specifically, she recalled the incredible tension she had felt all during the evening. But as she had been in disguise, she assumed that she had been the only one to experience it.

Sverayov approached. Her heart tightened because even casually dressed in a riding jacket, breeches, and high Hessian boots, he was too striking for comfort. "Good afternoon, Miss Browne." He bowed briefly, did not take her hand. His eyes seemed to sparkle, as if he knew something amusing which he was keeping to himself. "Mister Browne." His gaze settled briefly on Anthony Davison before returning to Carolyn. "If you hold that bouquet any tighter, you shall strangle the flowers," he said.

Carolyn felt herself turning red. "I was just about to get a vase," she said. Her glance went from Sverayov to Anthony. The younger man was also flushed, and quite obviously dismayed.

"A nice gesture," the prince said easily to Anthony. "I do not believe that we have had the pleasure. Prince Nicholas Ivanovitch Sverayov, at your service."

"Anthony Davison," Anthony replied with a bow. "I have seen you at several gatherings, Excellency, but we were not introduced."

"I am flattered," Sverayov said, his smile both cool and amused. It was definitely superior.

Carolyn felt awkward and uncomfortable. The men gave off the impression that they were rivals—which was absolutely ludicrous. "I'll be right back," she said, fleeing into the kitchen behind the shop. She quickly pumped water into a porcelain vase and slipped in the bouquet of lilies. Her heart felt as if it were staging a riot inside of her chest. "Do calm down," she gritted to herself. "He is only a man, even if he is gorgeous, and he is a rotten one at that! With no morals. He frequents brothels!'' she reminded herself.

George entered the kitchen. "Are you talking to yourself?" he asked, his expression somber.

Carolyn faced him. "Caught in the act," she said brightly.

"You are driving with him?"

She paused. "Yes."

"Carolyn. I do not approve."

She was very still, holding the vase of flowers in her hands. "Why?"

"He is only toying with you. As you yourself have said, he is immoral, a rake. He wants only to use you. You will be hurt."

Carolyn stared. Had she not already drawn precisely the same conclusion? The prince had no honest intentions toward her. Not that she would even define what honest intentions meant! He was a cad, he used women, frequented harlots, ignored his wife. Her father had been terribly blunt. But not as blunt as the thoughts Carolyn was now entertaining. Sverayov undoubtedly wished to make love to her once or twice—the way he had carried on with Victoria.

Caroline's lungs somehow lacked air. She got a grip on herself. She was an enlightened thinker—but not that enlightened. Because for one astounding moment, the notion of accepting his advances had flashed through her mind. Carolyn sighed and turned to George. "You are right, of course," she said slowly. She reminded herself that she had no interest in passion. She had never had any interest in passion. She did not even understand it. Not even now. She believed in true love—the kind of love that had existed between her mother and her father—the kind of love that was so rare.

"Good," George said flatly. "I am glad you have come to your senses. If you wish, I can tell Sverayov that you are too busy to accompany him this afternoon."

"Papa, that would be rude. I have already committed myself. Besides, I am hoping to learn something useful for a future column."

George flinched. "Carolyn, I have never forbidden you anything before."

She lifted her chin. "Then do not start now. I am eighteen. Legally I may be under age, but we both know I am an adult woman and an enlightened thinker. Surely you trust my judgment. And if he tries something wicked, I will resist." She smiled. "He is not one of those cads renowned for forcing women against their will, Papa."

George was clearly torn. "I do trust your judgment, I always have, but it is the prince's intentions which I do not trust—and his powers of persuasion."

"Bah!" Carolyn scoffed, waving her hand. "You have nothing to worry about." And at that moment, she meant it.

Sverayov handed Carolyn up into the cabriolet, his grip firm on her elbow. Carolyn wished she were not so excruciatingly aware of him. He settled on the seat beside her, his hard thigh against hers. He shot her a smile and lifted the reins.

Trying to move over and put some distance between them, thinking about her father's warnings and her own fears, Carolyn saw Anthony Davison regarding them from the doorway of the bookstore. His expression was one of dismay. Feeling badly for him, Carolyn sent him a smile and a parting wave. The cabriolet jolted forward. She tumbled against Sverayov.

"Poor chap. Your admirer is not pleased to see you driving with me," Sverayov remarked.

"He is hardly my admirer," Carolyn said. She gave up trying to keep an inch between their thighs.

Sverayov leaned back against the seat, as if driving were effortless for him. He had one leg stretched casually out. That leg brushed against her. "No? Does your average customer bring you flowers?"

Carolyn flushed. "I seem to have a lot of customers who are buying books for their sister," she said, giving him a sideways glance.

"How odd," Sverayov remarked.

Carolyn started. She had just glimpsed a newspaper rolled up in the corner of the seat. Briefly, he followed her glance. Then he turned the single gelding around the corner. Hyde Park was across the street.

"I imagine you keep abreast of the news," Sverayov said.

Carolyn hoped, fervently, that the journal was not the *Morning Chronicle*. Her heart thrummed against her ribs. But she would deny, to her dying breath, that Brighton was Copperville. And then she grimaced, almost exclaiming out loud. She was Carolyn—not Brighton. There would be no disclaimers to make today.

"I try," she said, a fib. She read at least one paper every day. It was her responsibility to herself. How else could she remain an enlightened thinker?

"Hmm. And which paper do you prefer?"

She hesitated. "The *Times*."

He swiveled his head, eyes wide. "Really!" he exclaimed. "I would have never guessed. The *Times* is a very conservative journal. Run by Tories, you know. Written for Tories, too. I assumed you were a Whig."

Of course she was a Whig. "Actually," Carolyn said, "I read the *Times* because it is crucial to know what the opposition is thinking and saying and hoping to do."

He gave her a glance that might have been admiring— except that Carolyn had the strongest sense that she was being toyed with. "Very clever," he said.

Carolyn's heart did an odd flop as their gazes connected and held. In spite of her suspicions, she did seem to see admiration in his gaze, but there was that infernal mockery, too. What did he know, or what was he thinking, that he was not sharing with her? She glanced away as they entered the park. In truth, she hated the *Times,* and most of its editorials made her see red.

"I prefer the *Morning Chronicle*," he said abruptly.

Her heart lurched as they turned down a wide dirt path. Carriages, barouches, landaus, and phaetons were ahead of them, as were pairs of riders or individuals astride their hacks. The oaks lining the path were tall and leafy, the grounds beyond the path verdantly green. Daisies flowered randomly amongst the trees.

He was not trying to tell her something. He could not possibly connect her to Copperville—not unless he knew she was Brighton. But he would have never taken her to the brothel if he had known of her charade—no man could be so reckless, amoral, reprehensible.

"I would imagine," Carolyn said slowly, "that you preferred the *Times*." Had he read "Lost Ladies of the Night"?

"I find the *Chronicle* amusing," he said. "In fact, I have a copy with me—if you care to borrow it."

Carolyn stiffened. "When do you have time to read?" she asked very carefully—breathlessly. "Surely your schedule as an envoy of the tsar keeps you extraordinarily occupied."

He gave her a wolfish smile. "I am one of those men who sleep very little—and do very well in spite of that. I am up before six every morning—no matter my activities of the night before. I browse the papers briefly while I sip a cup of tea, but it is after my morning ride that I read far more thoroughly while I enjoy a leisurely breakfast." His eyes gleamed.

Now she was certain that he had read Copperville's article in that day's *Chronicle*. She managed to smile up at him. "How I envy you your stamina," she remarked.

He slanted a glance at her. "An interesting choice of words."

"I do not understand."

He smiled at her but was saved from having to reply because they were being greeted by an oncoming rider.

"Excellency, good afternoon," the passing gentleman said, tipping his hat. Stout and elderly, he peered long and hard at Carolyn, who immediately decided to seize upon the new topic being provided.

"Good afternoon," Sverayov said affably.

"He cannot decide who I am," Carolyn said.

"And it is killing him," Sverayov murmured with obvious amusement.

Her gaze shot to his strong, perfect profile, and she saw the laughter in his eyes. It struck her then that he was amused by some of society's foibles, just as she was.

A open barouche was behind the rider, driven by a coachman and containing two well-dressed, attractive ladies. The two women looked from Sverayov to Carolyn and back again. "Good afternoon, Your Excellency," they said with wide smiles as their gig passed. One of the ladies wiggled her gloved fingertips at the Russian.

"Good afternoon," Sverayov returned, smiling.

The other lady, a pretty but plump brunette, giggled, red-faced. The first one kept regarding Carolyn, even craning her neck to do so when their rig was past.

"Everyone is wondering who I am," Carolyn remarked.

"Ummm," Sverayov said. "It shall be the rage of gossip this evening, I imagine, who I was driving with."

"I suppose that the peerage is always gossiping about the . . . er . . . entanglements of its members."

He eyed her. "You do have a way with words."

"What do you mean?"

He did not answer her. "Actually, it is far worse for royalty. I cannot sleep late without some nosey columnist writing the world that I am at death's door."

Carolyn did feel guilty. "Surely it is not that bad."

"It is worse. But we Sverayovs are used to being remarked on, approached, followed, hounded, and forever gossiped about. It is a fact of royal life. One must remain amused. I suppose most people have little to do in their own lives or they would not take such a huge interest in mine."

Carolyn felt far more guilty than before, and immediately had to protest the concept—for she herself had a full life, did she not? And was not hounding him out of boredom—was she? "It is natural for the average person to put someone as noble as you up on a pedestal. That hardly means that we do not have full, interesting lives. It means we cannot help ourselves when it comes to being curious about you.''

''Really? And are you curious about me, Carolyn?'' His tone was silky.

She knew she flushed. She clasped her gloved hands in her lap. And avoided his penetrating amber eyes. ''How could I not be curious? I have never met, face-to-face, a prince before, much less a Russian one, and here we are, driving in the park as if we are old friends.''

He was silent.

She stole a glance at him and found him watching her. ''Well, perhaps not as if we are old friends, perhaps as if we are new friends.''

It was a moment before he spoke. ''In my experience, I have found it unusual for a friendship to form between the genders.''

''That has not been my experience,'' she said quickly, wetting her lips.

He smiled. ''And I am sure you have had a great deal of experience. Do you have many male friends, Carolyn? And I do mean platonic ones.''

Her face fell. ''Actually, I have few friends. My father is my best friend.''

He nodded. ''I see. Point conceded?''

''No.'' She was firm, and he laughed, the sound warm and rich. ''Excellency,'' she said, when his laughter had faded into the pleasant afternoon, and she now felt somewhat relaxed and was truly enjoying his company. ''Don't you think people will find it odd that you took a bookseller's daughter driving in the park?''

He shrugged. ''I imagine they shall, but I have always done as I please.''

How arrogant his words sounded. Carolyn twisted to gaze up at his profile. It was easy to see why women fell all over him. He was a foreigner, which was exotic, he was royalty, which was intriguing, and in sum, he was powerful, arrogant about it, and blatantly sensual as well. But she was not going to become one of his brokenhearted victims. It was too bad, though, that he had such a charming, enjoyable side.

"Today's *Chronicle* was particularly interesting," Sverayov said, out of the blue. "Have you had a chance to read it?"

Carolyn gulped air. Her tension returned, magnified a hundredfold. "No."

"No? Did you oversleep this morning?" He slanted her a look. "Then you have missed some very amusing columns."

He could not know, she reminded herself, that she was Copperville. Even though his look and remarks were so damnably pointed.

"Miss Browne?"

Carolyn looked up at him, struggling for composure.

"You are white. Is something wrong?" When Carolyn did not answer, he veered the cabriolet off the track, between two oaks. He proceeded to a grassy glade some distance from the track and halted the gelding. "Carolyn?"

"I'm fine," she said sharply, breathing again. But now she was more anxious than before, because they were no longer on the riding path—they were alone.

He wrapped the reins around the brake and put his arm around her. "You do not look fine. You appear shocked. Is it something I said?" His golden eyes held hers. As enigmatic as could be.

Carolyn was now pressed against his side. Her mind was assimilating many things at once, including how strong the arm around her shoulders was, the scent he wore, which she could just detect, one of both earth and spices, perhaps containing cinnabar, and the fact that his face, turned down toward hers, was but inches away. His eyes were very golden, very bright. Her father's harsh warnings—and her own assessment of his intentions—returned forcefully to mind.

"Have I alarmed you?" he asked softly, his arm remaining firmly around her.

Her pulse raced. Her body temperature was soaring. Her wits were becoming scrambled. She knew she should accuse him of foul play, demand he remove his arm, and return to the track. But would it be so terrible if he kissed her? Just once? She had only been kissed that one single, unappetizing time.

Carolyn wet her lips, and when she spoke, her tone seemed odd. "No. I am not alarmed. It is just that I have entirely forgotten to eat today." Now, she knew, she should ask him to return her home.

His gaze held hers. It was brilliant, intense. He did not speak.

Carolyn swallowed. She was not an idiot—she knew he was going to kiss her—unless she stopped him. But just now she could not bring herself to care about his many previous conquests, or if she were behaving like one of his lackwit paramours.

"I would regret very much ending our afternoon so quickly," he said.

His words did sound dangerous but Carolyn did not move.

His gaze caressed her face. "But, in spite of the defamatory remarks made about me by those who do not know me, I am not an unfeeling cad." He removed his arm and unwrapped the reins from the brake. He gave her a sidelong glance and urged the gelding back toward the track.

Carolyn hugged herself, hardly breathing more easily now, stunned by the depth of her disappointment. He had not kissed her. His behavior had been honorable. And she fully comprehended that his last barb was aimed at Copperville and his kin.

Suddenly Carolyn felt miserable. It had felt good being hugged to his side. She wanted him to touch her again. Never in her life had she had an outing with a man like this—much less a caress or a kiss. Images from the brothel flashed through her mind, along with her father's warnings. But George was wrong. Because Sverayov had just had the perfect opportunity to take advantage of her—and he had not even tried. The track was just ahead, through the line of trees.

"Wait," she heard herself say.

He immediately halted the cabriolet and faced her, holding the reins lightly. His expression was not grave—it was strained.

And Carolyn thought she understood—he felt the tension, too. She looked up into his eyes, filled with reckless desire. She knew she was asking for trouble. But she could not seem to help herself.

Besides, she could not rendezvous with him now as Brighton. Who knew when—if ever—she would see him again?

"What are you thinking, Carolyn?" he asked very softly.

She wet her lips. What would he do if she told him the truth? She opened her mouth, shut it, then opened it again. Her heart was slamming with alarming strength against her breast. "I was kissed, once, when I was fourteen," she said slowly. "It was awful."

His eyes widened, he did not move.

Carolyn prayed she was not making a fool of herself. "Since then, kisses have not interested me." She fell silent. Now she could not met his probing gaze.

"But now?" he prompted, his eyes searching her face.

"Now I . . ." She inhaled, staring at her hands, clenched in her lap. "Now I find myself interested," she finally said, and she dared to look up at him.

Their gazes locked. But he was not smiling—all the amusement and mockery she had thus far seen that day were gone without a trace. Carolyn did not know if she could continue to breathe.

"I am flattered," he finally said, and then he turned slightly and slowly looped the reins back around the brake—as if he had all the time in the world to do so. Clearly he was not in a hurry.

Carolyn watched his long fingers, his powerful hands. Her pulse drummed and raced. In her mind's eye, she saw the beautiful prostitute's hands, sculpting his hardened manhood through his clothes.

"Carolyn?" His tone was gentle.

Carolyn met his gaze, which was brilliant. She could not speak.

He reached out and tipped up her chin. "I find it amazing," he said, his head lowering, "that a woman as beautiful and curious as you has never experimented since with kissing—to say the least." His mouth hovered just an inch or two from hers. His breath, sweet and clean, feathered her lips.

"I thought it all ridiculous," she said huskily.

A smile flashed. "Indeed? I hope you do not still think 'it' ridiculous when we have finished our experiment." His gaze pierced right through her.

Oh, God, Carolyn thought, stiffening.

His hands cupped her shoulders and he pulled her forward, his mouth touching hers. The brief brushing of their lips lasted but a second, and then his mouth was on hers, demanding but not hard or hurtful, urging her lips open, wide and wider still, molding them as he chose. Carolyn was crushed against his hard, powerful frame. One of his hands cupped her hips. And his mouth, insatiable, expert, continued to devour her lips.

And now Carolyn understood passion; it was a raging conflagration of the body and the soul. She found his shoulders, clung to them with all her strength. She began kissing him back, at first tentatively, then with increasing boldness. Suddenly their tongues entwined.

Carolyn found herself in his lap, her hip on top of something brutally hard, her shoulders pressed down into the firm leather seat. His mouth moved feverishly over her throat—and then returned to her lips. Carolyn moaned.

Eyes closed, Carolyn lost herself in the hot, hot passion. She felt him pushing aside her shawl, felt his hands caressing her breasts through her muslin dress.

Carolyn gasped with pleasure as her nipples stiffened beneath his fingertips. "Oh, God," she thought, then realized, too late, she had cried out aloud.

He froze. She heard him breathing harshly, his face against her cheek. And then he lifted his head.

Carolyn opened her eyes and their gazes met. He stared. And she could not read his feelings, not a single one, as he continued to regard her.

Carolyn began to flush. Overhead, through the treetops, she saw a bright blue sky, and, in fact, a striped balloon containing several occupants. Good God. She was in Sverayov's carriage, flat on her back, in a public park. And she did not want their encounter to end.

Passion was hardly ridiculous.

He sat up slowly, running one hand through his thick golden hair. Then he helped her upright, too. He did not say a word, but reached for the reins and picked them up.

Carolyn, having recovered her shawl, hugged herself as he clucked to the gelding. What was she supposed to do now? When her body was burning in anticipation of a consummation which could not, must not, take place? Why didn't he say something? But what was there to say? Especially as she had instigated the entire episode? Especially when she had behaved as badly as any of his other lady loves?

The cabriolet merged onto the track, which was, fortunately, empty.

"Well," Carolyn said brightly, "that was not ridiculous."

His jaw flexed. He finally cast a sidelong glance at her. He seemed flustered, angry. "No," he said. "That was not ridiculous."

❧ TWELVE ❧

NOT only was she feeling somewhat better, she was starting to look like herself again.

Marie-Elena smiled at her reflection in the mirror, studying herself critically—looking for wrinkles or other signs of illness or aging which hadn't been present before the miscarriage. She remained pale, and she was still weak, but her beauty was unmarred. A collar of pearls and diamonds glinted on her throat and it was only dinnertime. Being the niece of the crown prince of Baden-Baden, and the wife of Prince Sverayov, she could flaunt convention when she wished.

She left her bedroom where two maids were putting a dozen dresses away—the gowns she had decided after much nerve-wracking hysteria not to wear that day. Marie-Elena could hear her daughter reciting Latin as she approached the nursery.

Smiling, she walked into the schoolroom.

Katya, in the midst of reciting verbs, stopped, gaping. Signor Raffaldi, holding a book open, somehow dropped it, and it crashed on the floor. Taichili, who had been sitting at the children's table, making notes, slammed her small notebook closed, sitting up as straight as any soldier. Her eyes were also wide.

"Good morning," Marie-Elena cried with enthusiasm. "Signore." She smiled at the tutor, who turned red. "Madame Taichili." She inclined her head. "You are all acting as if I have never been in the nursery before!" she exclaimed. Before anyone could respond, she faced her daughter, who was motionless. "Darling! Come give Maman a hug and a kiss."

Katya obeyed, walking quickly forward to wrap her thin arms around her mother. Marie-Elena bent so the small child could kiss her cheek. Then she beamed at her again. "How beautifully you recite your Latin, dear. Is she not a premier student, signore?"

Still flushed, he came forward. "Katya excels in every subject, Princess." He bowed.

"I am so proud of you," Marie-Elena said to Katya.

The child's eyes were glued on her mother's face. "Thank you, Maman," she said, two bright pink spots on her cheeks.

"I have a wonderful idea," Marie-Elena said. "Why don't you join me this afternoon for a drive in the park? Wouldn't that be fun, Katya?"

Katya stared, her eyes huge. Silence filled the classroom. "Yes," she finally said, shooting a glance at her governess and tutor.

Taichili cleared her throat. "Katya has her dance instruction after dinner, Princess."

"Tell her dance instructor that Katya will miss today's lesson," Marie-Elena said airily. "You, Taichili, will accompany us, of course."

Taichili inclined her head.

"I will see you at three o'clock," Marie-Elena told Katya.

Katya nodded, smiling slightly. "I will be ready, Maman. I promise."

Marie-Elena whirled and left the room. She no longer smiled as she hurried downstairs. Her pulse was racing. How she wished that she had not lost her wits when she had thought herself to be dying.

In the hallway on the ground floor she paused before a mirror, to pinch her cheeks and adjust the low neckline of her gown. She patted her curls and tested a smile, and somehow appeared both uncertain and vulnerable. Then she took a breath for courage. Nicholas was never easy. But that was why he had remained exciting after all these years—that was why he was still one of the most attractive men she had ever known. But he was also, at times, the most despicable.

The library door was open. Marie-Elena saw him sitting behind the desk, and Alexi was with him. The younger brother had one hip carelessly on the edge of the desk as the two men spoke in quiet tones. Marie-Elena's heart pounded far more swiftly now. Nicholas saw her and ceased speaking.

Marie-Elena smiled slightly. "May I speak with you for a moment, Niki?" She ignored Alexi.

His expression was impossible to read. He sat back in his chair, arms folded, his golden eyes steady upon her. "Do come in."

Marie-Elena came forward, glancing quickly at Alexi, once. He did not even try to hide his dislike of her. The once-over he gave her was disdainful—as if her charms were not enough to ever interest a man like himself. Marie-Elena knew he found her attractive. All men did.

"I shall take my leave," Alexi said, not even bothering to greet her. "Good day, Niki."

Alexi sauntered from the room. Nicholas slowly stood and strolled past Marie-Elena, who waited in front of his desk, not sitting down. She wanted him to have a clear view of her nearly translucent dress. Like the most fashionable women in society, she wore nothing beneath but a fine chemise. The apricot silk caressed every curve of her body, and then some.

Marie-Elena watched him close the door and turn to face her. "What is it you wish to speak about?" he asked quietly.

She inhaled, which accentuated her mostly bare bosom. "Nicholas. You seem angry. Surely you have had some time to realize that these silly rumors are all untrue?"

He did not respond. His golden gaze was cool, unfathomable.

She smiled briefly, touched his arm. "I would never do such a thing—I would never take your best friend as a lover."

He shook her hand off. "You are hardly convincing."

"That is not fair," Marie-Elena said with indignation. "The rumors are lies. How can you not believe me?"

"Is this why you came to see me? To convince me that you are innocent of seducing my cousin?" He shook his head. "Please. I am very busy today. Is there anything else?" His eyes were hard.

Her temper flared. Marie-Elena fought it. "You are so angry." She stepped closer and touched him again. "I do not blame you. To have to hear such horrid nonsense. Niki, do you know what it is like to face death?"

"Your theatrics will not work with me, Marie-Elena," he said warningly.

"I am not being theatrical. It was terrifying." Tears filled her eyes. "I am young, I had no wish to die. And I was afraid to pray to God, for surely he knows the sinner I have been. Niki, I must try to make amends. I do not want to go to hell!" she cried.

He stared. "Then maybe you should have stayed away from Sasha."

Her heart lurched. "Niki, how many times must I tell you that Sasha is merely a friend—and more your friend than mine. Niki, we cannot go on this way." She gripped his arms. "Do you know that I regret the past—all of it?"

He calmly removed her hands. "As do I. Which is why you are going to Tver."

"No!" she cried. "You cannot send me away! I despise the country!"

"I have allowed you to live your life as you chose, but you have not been discreet. I cannot allow it." He turned away.

Marie-Elena's mind raced. She took a breath, touched

him again. "What about Katya? How will you explain to her what you are doing?"

"That is my affair." He did not even glance over his shoulder at her.

"I am her mother. It is my affair, too. Perhaps I will explain," she said carefully.

He folded his arms, facing her. "Is that a threat?"

"Of course it is not!" she cried. "Niki, I almost died! I am not the same woman! I love Katya and . . . I miss you."

He stiffened immediately. "What do you really want, Marie-Elena? Spit it out."

"Why won't you believe me? I was dying, for God's sakes!" She placed one small hand flat on his chest, on top of his waistcoat. "I have thought about little else but you and her, Niki. Not since I regained consciousness after losing the baby," she breathed, her black gaze holding his.

His jaw was tight. "I hope so. And you can continue to contemplate your past—and your future—at Tver. Now, if you will excuse me." He turned away.

She was breathless. "Do not be cold and cruel now!" she shouted. "Not after how sick I have been! I promise to behave myself. I promise to be a good mother to Katya." She rushed around him and barred his way, standing between him and his desk. "And I can even be a good wife to you, if you will let me."

He started to smile. "I do see. You have finally realized that I have no tolerance left for your behavior—and you are scared. Scared enough to throw yourself at me. It will not work. I have not the slightest interest in sharing your bed, Marie-Elena."

She stared, trying to control herself, trembling. It was a moment before she could speak. She licked her lips; he watched her tongue. "Please, Niki," she said, her tone low and husky. "I beg you. I want to start over."

His eyes narrowed.

"Please." She pressed against him, her full breasts crushed by his arm, and on tiptoe, pressed her soft, wet mouth to his cheek. "I want you back. We were so good together, once," she breathed.

Immediately he seized her wrist, and yanked her back to her feet and away from him. "Do not even try," he said harshly. "I am not Sasha." He had not released her wrist.

He was hurting her. And her body was pressed against his, the many buttons of his uniform abrading her nipples, which were hard and erect. "You are hurting me, Niki," she whispered. She shifted slightly so that her sex brushed his thighs.

He released her, turning away, picking up a folder from his desk. He opened it. "I have appointments today."

She could not believe he was dismissing her this way. "You are lying to yourself. I see the way you look at me. You want me. Still. After all these years—in spite of everything!"

He did not respond, immersed in what he was reading.

Her temper exploded. "Katya will be upset if you send me away. And how will she feel when she learns that you have imprisoned me?"

"Good day, Marie-Elena." He walked away.

Carolyn had not slept a wink all night because she had been unable to forget the earth-shattering kiss she had shared with Sverayov in the park. Bleary-eyed and preoccupied, she went downstairs. The bookshop was dimly lit, pale morning sunlight escaping through the cracks in the shutters and the parted shades. She found her father in the kitchen, hovering over the stove. He had already put a kettle to boil for their tea and was slicing a thick loaf of warm, crusty bread. Three newspapers awaited them on the kitchen table.

"I overslept again. I'm sorry, Papa," Carolyn said.

He handed her a cup of black tea. "I am worried about you." His gaze searched her face.

"There is nothing to worry about." Carolyn went to their icebox and removed some leftover roast chicken, which she began to slice.

"What is bothering you?" George asked, carrying plates to the table.

Carolyn set the chicken and a crock of butter down as well. She sat, forced a smile. "Absolutely nothing."

"It is Sverayov."

She froze.

"You refused to say a word when you came back from the park yesterday," George accused. "I know you better than I know anyone. There is something you are not telling me."

"There is nothing to tell," Carolyn said neutrally. Oh, but there was. Against her will, against all common sense, she was suffering from a case of severe infatuation. Sverayov was a self-absorbed aristocrat, and he stood for all she wished to correct. Worse, she was appalled by her own unenlightened behavior, by her own desire. She was agonizingly attracted to him, and damnation, he was even charming company. How could she put him out of her mind?

But she knew better than to tell George any of this. He would only worry—with just cause. He must not know.

Carolyn sighed, not certain she had ever felt this confused. She reached for the *Morning Chronicle*. Sipping her tea, she began browsing through it. Her father was eating and reading the front page of the *Herald*. Carolyn turned the first page and almost fell off her seat.

She must have gasped, because George faced her. "What is it? You look as if you have seen a ghost!"

Carolyn did not answer, staring down at the column, for she could not be seeing what she thought she was seeing—she could not. But the column was titled "Public Trysts and Other Nonsense—or Private Royal Affairs." And it had been written by Charles Copperville.

She could hardly breathe. She had not written this column—someone had usurped her column and her name!

Carolyn focused, still shocked, and began to read.

"How odd it is that the rules of decorum and etiquette escape the attention of those who need to attend to such dictates the most. Once again, a certain visiting foreign dignitary has seen fit to use our world as his public stage, as if completely careless of any and all morality! And who was the beneficiary of this particular royal personage's attentions? Speculation has been running rampant since the prince was seen in a most intimate position in a very public place yesterday afternoon with a young woman of indecipherable identity. Numerous witnesses to the event describe the young lady as both blond and lovely, but to wit, no one has ever seen her anywhere before. Is the prince now a magician? Summoning up beautiful blondes at whim? One rumor suggests that this very well read young lady is not a member of the ton, leading one to ask the inevitable: where did he find her?''

''Carolyn?'' George's voice cut through her shock. ''What are you reading? What is wrong?''

Carolyn blinked, unable to concentrate on what her father was asking. Someone had stolen her column. Someone had written about her and Sverayov. But this made no sense!

''Carolyn?''

Carolyn snapped the paper closed. She smiled at her father, her heart banging against her chest. The column even sounded a bit like hers, damn it. Who had stolen her column and her name? Who?

Surely not Sverayov.

Surely not.

Because if he had, then it meant that he knew she was Copperville, and that was impossible. Because of ''Lost Ladies,'' he thought Brighton was Copperville, not she herself, not Carolyn.

Carolyn did not know what to think. But she had to tell George something. ''I just realized,'' she said quickly, ''that I promised my editor a new column for tomorrow.''

''But you've already given him two columns this week,'' George said.

''He has said that he will publish Copperville as frequently as possible.''

''That is wonderful news. You didn't tell me. Carolyn,

do sit down. Finish your breakfast and then go upstairs and write.''

She clenched the newspaper in her hand. ''I can't eat. I'll eat after I come up with something.'' She smiled far too brightly again, dashed over to George and kissed his cheek, then fled from the kitchen—the *Chronicle* in hand.

George stared after her, unsmiling.

Some time later, Carolyn was downstairs in the store, feeling as if she had survived, and just barely, a very close call. She had hidden the newspaper in her bedchamber, and hoped George, who at times could be absentminded, would forget that he had not read that day's *Chronicle*. Now she had a mystery to solve. Her first step would be to contact her editor and ask him who had delivered the article. She already expected the courier to have been a paid lackey.

In the future, she would tell Mr. Taft that he should not accept any pieces not hand-delivered by herself.

Her heart skipped. It was absurd for her to suspect Sverayov. Absurd.

Except that he was very clever.

But if he had written that column, then he knew all about her and he was playing cat and mouse with her, by God.

A chill, half fear, half thrill, swept through Carolyn.

Carolyn tried to turn her attention to the store, for she was supposed to be taking inventory, but her mind was not on the task. Did Sverayov suspect, or know, that Carolyn, Brighton, and Copperville were all one and the same? She shivered. It seemed to be the only possibility. But why had he gone along with her charade? Could some third party have written the column?

Carolyn had the impulse to confront Sverayov, but she did not want to completely reveal her hand—in case there was some other explanation for the column. But surely she could test him just a bit? She only needed an excuse to seek him out. And then she smiled. What if she called on him at his town house, ostensibly with another book for his sister?

The doorbell tinkled and Carolyn quite jumped out of her skin, expecting to see Sverayov. But Anthony Davison entered the store, smiling at her. This time he was not carrying a bouquet.

Suddenly Carolyn flushed. She hoped, fervently, that Anthony had not read Copperville's column that morning. Not that it was really Copperville's column! But even if he had, surely no one would suspect that she was the woman in the prince's arms!

"Good day, Miss Browne. You look as lovely as ever." He smiled earnestly at her.

Carolyn relaxed slightly. "Thank you. Surely you have not read all that you have purchased here in the past few days?" Carolyn smiled, teasing him just a bit.

He blushed. "No, I have not, actually. Er . . ." His color deepened. He took a breath. "There is a wonderful opera tonight, and I happen to have a box. Would you care to join me?"

Carolyn blinked. First an invitation to drive in the park— from a Russian prince—and now an invitation to the opera from a peer? "This is so odd," she mused aloud.

"It is?" He appeared disconcerted.

She shook herself free of her amazement. "I beg your pardon. Actually, I would love to attend the opera," she said. She had only been to an opera once, on her thirteenth birthday, with George, of course. And that had been a very long time ago. But how she had enjoyed it.

"Then I shall pick you up here at half past seven," Anthony said, smiling.

"That is fine." Carolyn hoped she had a serviceable evening gown and doubted it. She glanced up as the doorbell sounded again, and she froze.

Her cousin Thomas Owsley strolled into the store.

She had not seen him in over a year. Her pulse raced and her stomach lurched with dread. But she should have expected this—his annual call. For next week was their grandmother's birthday—not that he had come to invite her to the fête. Carolyn had never been invited to Midlands, neither before or after Margaret's untimely death.

Carolyn tried to smile as he sauntered toward her. He was half a dozen years older than she, a husky man of medium build who was quite dandified and even more pleased about it. Thomas was always at the forefront of fashion, and Carolyn's glance slid over him, remarking the dark wine-colored jacket with velvet lapels, the gold foulard cravat, a silver and gold waistcoat, and pale tan trousers. He wore a wide-brimmed top hat and carried a walking stick with a mother-of-pearl nob. He wore several rings. He smiled at her, but it did not reach his dark eyes. "Hello, Carolyn."

He was her mother's older sister's only child, the heir to the entire estate. Carolyn did not know him well, for their paths rarely crossed. A few times before her mother had died, the sisters had gotten together secretly, in defiance of Edith Owsley, with their two children. Even as a child, Thomas had been snooty and rude, pulling Carolyn's hair when he could, slipping worms into her tea, and reminding her incessantly that she lived in an attic atop a simple bookstore—reminding her that her father was a commoner. In the ensuing years, Carolyn had seen no sign that he had changed. She was tense.

"Good day, Thomas," Carolyn said without her usual animation. She became aware of Anthony's curiosity, and perhaps his dismay. She certainly did not want him to think her loutish, self-centered cousin a suitor, so she introduced the two men. "Anthony, this is my cousin Thomas Owsley, Lord Stafford. Thomas, this is the Honorable Anthony Davison."

Thomas bowed, but so cursorily that it was rude. But Anthony was only the youngest son of an earl, and Thomas outranked him.

Anthony gaped. "You are an Owsley?"

Thomas laughed. "She is a Browne, Davison."

Anthony stiffened. Carolyn plucked his sleeve. "Our mothers were sisters."

"Then"—Anthony's brow furrowed—"you are Lady Edith Owsley's granddaughter!"

"That is true," Carolyn said, not smiling.

Now Thomas swaggered closer. "It is her birthday—her seventy-fifth. We are having quite a celebration at Midlands." He smiled.

Carolyn ducked her head. "Yes, I am well aware that it is our grandmother's seventy-fifth birthday. I have never missed the occasion, now have I?" Her tone was bitter and tart.

"I think I shall buy her a book. Do you have a gift you wish me to send on for you?" He smiled at her widely.

"No, thank you. I shall post her a gift, as I always do." Not that her grandmother ever acknowledged the receipt of Carolyn's gifts, not even with a simple thank-you note. "Now, what kind of book do you wish to buy?" She was brisk.

"I shall look around," Thomas said, smiling as if pleased with himself.

Carolyn ignored him as he began his inspection of their books. She knew from experience that he would make a big show of not liking anything, and would only very reluctantly make a purchase in the end.

"I shall see you at half past seven," Anthony said softly.

Carolyn looked up, into his sympathetic blue eyes. "Yes, without fail."

He tipped his hat and left the store. Thomas turned and strode back to her. "Is he courting you?" he asked loudly, brows furrowed. "I cannot believe it!"

"You may believe whatever you like," Carolyn answered calmly.

Inwardly she did not feel calm at all.

He glared. "You are just like your father. That must be it," he declared.

"And what does that mean?" Carolyn asked stiffly. "My father is a wonderful man."

"Your father seduced your mother and eloped with her—

thinking to win himself a fortune.'' Thomas was exasperated.

"That is not true, and I will not even dignify that comment with an answer. If you wish to make a purchase, please do so. If not, please leave.'' Carolyn fought hard to keep her tone level, but her fists were clenched in the folds of her skirts.

His brows lifted. "Well, so be it,'' he said. "If you do not want my business, I shall not give it.'' Thomas turned and strode out of the store.

Carolyn gave in to her childish self, and stuck her tongue out at his departing back. But she felt like crying. She had never been able to understand why her grandmother hated her so.

❧ THIRTEEN ❧

CAROLYN'S heart was racing, and she could not control it. She paused in front of Sverayov's brick town house, aware that he might not even be home. She crossed the fingers of her right hand—she carried a gift-wrapped book in her left. And she started up the short walk.

It was just now dawning on her that while he might not be in, his wife might very well be at home. Carolyn was torn, worried about confronting the other woman, yet intensely curious to glimpse her after having heard so much about her. Very bravely, she lifted the heavy brass door knocker.

A liveried footman immediately appeared. Carolyn introduced herself, asking for Sverayov. She felt as if she were attempting to bait the lion in his lair.

"I am afraid His Excellency is not in," the footman said firmly.

Carolyn was dismayed, but in a way, she was also relieved. She debated leaving the book with the footman, accompanied by a note. It flashed through her mind that in all likelihood, he would thank her in person for her thoughtfulness. But suddenly a dark-haired man entered the foyer, shrugging on an exquisitely tailored jacket. Carolyn immediately recognized Sverayov's brother from the night of the Sheffields' dinner-dance. Of course, Alexi could not know her. He had been introduced to Brighton.

But he paused in the midst of settling his fine royal-blue wool jacket about his shoulders, his long strides slowing. His gaze narrowed, intent on Carolyn. Carolyn recognized that he was another dangerous rake. And Alexi flashed his white teeth at her.

"Good afternoon," he said, his smile somehow predatory as he bowed. "As I do not know you, you must be calling on my brother." His words were silky and soft.

He knew. He knew she was a besotted female idiot. Carolyn flushed. "Actually, I have brought a book for his sister." The moment the words were out she turned red. Sverayov did not have a sister—as his brother undoubtedly knew.

Alexi's slashing black brows shot up. "I see. Please, do come in," he said. And he reached past the footman to shut the door solidly behind Carolyn.

Carolyn's adrenaline rushed. "Sverayov...I mean, Nicholas...I mean, His Highness was in the bookshop shopping for a gift for his sister." She lifted her gaze to Alexi's, challenging him to refute his brother's behavior. "He purchased a volume of poetry as well as a novel. I recalled another perfect gift for her just this morning. I have it here with me." She held it up. "Sir Walter Scott's *Marmion*. It is not new, it was published several years ago, but it is a good and lively adventure."

Alexi smiled at her. Slowly. "How very kind of you to come all the way over here to personally deliver it. Our sister shall be thrilled, Miss...?" He trailed off.

"Carolyn Browne," she said, swallowing.

"Do come inside for some refreshments. If you do not mind waiting, I am certain that my brother shall be home at any moment." Alexi took her arm, quite firmly, and propelled Carolyn down the hall. In another moment she found herself inside an elegant salon. "Actually, Niki told me all about your father's shop."

"He did?"

Alexi's wolfish smile reappeared. "He was very impressed with all that he saw,'' he said pointedly. His amber eyes danced.

Carolyn stared. Was the younger brother also toying with her? He was making it sound as if Sverayov had been impressed with her.

A sudden movement in the doorway made Carolyn turn. A streak of white fur flashed by and disappeared. Alexi had also seen the ball of fluff, and he chuckled. ''Taichili must be apoplectic.''

Carolyn wanted to know who Taichili was, but did not ask. ''Is that a kitten? A Persian, in fact?''

''I believe so,'' Alexi said.

Carolyn did not hesitate. She moved toward the sofa where the cat had last disappeared, and stooped down. ''Here, kitty, kitty,'' she said softly. ''Ppst, ppst, ppst,'' she said.

A small white head, dominated by huge blue eyes and big ears, appeared from beneath the sofa. Carolyn smiled at the cat while a male cough sounded from behind her.

The cat vanished. Instinct made Carolyn stop breathing, made her heart slam with alarming strength. She quickly stood, losing her balance as she did so. Nicholas Sverayov reached out to steady her, staring down at her with his gleaming golden eyes.

Carolyn felt faint.

And he smiled. Far more wolfishly than his brother. ''Miss Browne. What an unexpected pleasure.''

She knew she flushed. She stared at him, unable to look away. But if he knew she was both Brighton and Copperville, he gave none of his thoughts away. Carolyn wet her lips. ''I brought your sister another book.''

''I see.'' He continued to stare, his expression not quite enigmatic. Caroline thought he was both pleased to see her and amused by her call.

Carolyn tore her glance from his. It was clear to her that he had been riding in the park. He wore snug doeskin breeches and high riding boots, a ruffled silk shirt and a tweed hacking coat left carelessly open. In fact, his ruffled shirt was open, too, several buttons below his collarbone. Carolyn had glimpsed the dark gold hair that dusted his broad, hard chest. She had glimpsed his hard thighs. Even the breeches could not disguise the corded muscles there.

Carolyn recalled their long heated kiss, remembering vividly how his body had felt against hers, impossibly hard and strong, and how his mouth had tasted.

"Sir Walter Scott," Alexi drawled. "*Marmion*, I believe."

"How thoughtful," Sverayov murmured.

His tone was so blatantly sensual that Carolyn's gaze shot back to his. "Is your sister here? I should so love to meet her," she dared huskily.

He smiled slowly. "I am afraid that my sister is in St. Petersburg. But I am sure you shall meet some other time."

Carolyn felt like scoffing, but refrained. "I doubt I shall be journeying to Russia at any time in the near future. It might prove a difficult feat for an Englishwoman, don't you think?"

"I do not think that any feat would prove too daunting for an original thinker like yourself. And if I succeed in my negotiations, why, there shall be no trouble at all." Sverayov came forward and he gestured magnanimously at the sofa. "Please, make yourself comfortable. I hope you did not walk all the way here from your father's shop?"

Carolyn had little choice but to sink into the very soft sofa. Sverayov loomed over her. "I took a hansom. I only walked a few blocks." Did he really mean what he had said? Was it possible that he understood her originality and admired her mind? Carolyn was bewildered. Such a possibility meant that she might have to reassess her judgment of him entirely. And that she was not prepared to do.

At that moment, Alexi caught her eye and winked at her. "I have an affair to attend to," he said, and he strode from the room.

"My brother enjoys choosing his words with utter carelessness," Sverayov remarked, still standing.

"Either that, or he chooses them with utter care," Carolyn returned.

He inclined his head. "You have not lost your keen powers of verbal repartee or astute observation since we last spoke."

Carolyn did not mean to be coy. "Are you flattering me?" She wished he would not continue to unnerve her so. "I do not know how keen my powers are, but I do think that your brother enjoys being observed."

"He does, and I am."

She lifted her chin and held his eye. "Is such a penchant another male Sverayov trait?"

He smiled. "Like that of our passionate nature?"

Her heart skipped a number of beats. Her smile faded.

"Are we speaking now of flattery—or flamboyance?" he asked.

"I think we are speaking of both," Carolyn returned slowly, every fiber of her being attuned to this man.

"Yes," he said softly, not waiting for her to reply. "Sverayov men quite enjoy flattering those women they wish to pursue—and they are renowned for their flamboyance."

Was he serious? Was he pursuing her? "We have our flamboyant royalty here," she said huskily. "Royalty, given its very nature, must always be excessively arrogant and prone to posturing."

"I agree," he said, surprising her. "But did you really come here to discuss family traits and characteristics with me, Carolyn?"

Carolyn swallowed. Her name had rolled off his tongue like the softest strains of a lute. And she had come to find out if he knew the truth about her. "I came in order to bring you the book." Her heart hammered incessantly against her ribs. "Actually, I was reading this morning's papers when I was struck by the thought that I should have given you *Marmion* yesterday," she said, regarding him closely.

His expression did not change. And he did not take the bait. "So I was on your mind this morning," he said softly, and he did not pose his remark as a question.

Carolyn opened her mouth to reply, and found she did not know what to say.

He did not smile at her. "But it was my sister you were thinking of. Not our small experiment."

She could not speak.

He was also silent.

Carolyn fought for her wits. She felt her cheeks burning. "Your Excellency, you must think me shameless," she began, but he cut her off.

"I do not think you shameless." His hands went into the pockets of his jacket. And he stared at her with intense amber eyes.

Carolyn stood up. She could not believe her audacity. "Then what do you think?"

"I think you are extremely intelligent, quick-witted, curious, without guile or pretense. I think," and he paused, his gaze direct, "that you could not lie well if your life depended on it."

Her heart thrust against her chest again. Hard and fast. Was he referring to her deception, which was immense? Or did he believe what he was saying—and had no clue as to her charade? Carolyn watched him walk away from her. She had come here to test him, but she was at a loss. She did not know what to conclude. Except that he did not seem to think badly of her for her terribly forward behavior yesterday. To the contrary.

He faced her abruptly. "What would you do, or say, if I said that I intend to drive you home when you leave here today?"

She was at a loss. Did she dare accept his offer? Did he think, this time, to seduce her? Could she resist him if she truly wanted to? When, if she were daringly honest with herself, she knew she did not want to refuse him at all?

"Katya," Sverayov suddenly said, an unfamiliar tension in his tone.

Carolyn tensed, following his gaze. Her own widened as it settled on a small child with startlingly fair skin and jet-black hair. The little girl stood hesitantly in the doorway, her expression far too severe for such a young child. She did not smile. Carolyn suddenly sensed that she was afraid.

She turned to look at Sverayov and her gaze widened yet again. He was smiling—but it was a far different smile than the one he had directed toward her. "Katya, do come in. I'm sorry, I did not see you there. Please meet Miss Carolyn Browne."

Carolyn waited as the child obeyed, coming forward and curtsying, keeping her dark eyes lowered.

"Katya is my daughter," Sverayov said.

Carolyn started, her gaze flying to his. Then she regarded the child, who was truly beautiful—and did not resemble Sverayov in the least.

"You seem surprised." He shrugged. "Why should it be surprising that I have a daughter?"

"I . . . I have never thought about you in that role," Carolyn said, faltering. She looked from the prince to his daughter again. Clearly the little girl took after her mother, and Carolyn was dismayed to finally be faced with some evidence of just how beautiful the other woman was. But why was this child afraid? Was she afraid of her own father? Instantly Carolyn's heart went out to the little girl. And even though Sverayov was a prince and a libertine, she did not think that he would be a poor father. Oddly enough, she thought quite the opposite.

"Hello." She smiled at Katya. "You may call me Carolyn if you wish. All my friends do."

The girl nodded, not answering.

Carolyn bent down, still smiling, so their faces were almost level. "Are you looking for your kitten?" she asked in a conspiratorial tone.

Katya's eyes flashed with sudden enthusiasm. "Have you seen him?"

"I most certainly have. He is very beautiful. What is his name?"

"Alexander."

"You named him after the tsar?" Carolyn asked, without amusement.

Katya shook her head, her expression again blank. "I named him after Alexi."

"I see. What a splendid honor for your uncle." Carolyn winked at Katya. "He is under the sofa, or that is where he was when I last saw him." She turned, in order to glance at Sverayov, and then her smile died. He was staring at both her and his daughter with an oddly intense expression she did not, could not, understand. But the moment he saw her regarding him he smiled, all charming pretense.

Shaken, Carolyn knelt beside Katya, on her knees, confused, her pulse pounding. Something was terribly wrong, and it was disturbing her mightily. "I see him," she said cheerfully.

"Alexi," Katya called. "Alexi, come here."

"Try this trick. Cats love soft, funny sounds. Ppst, ppst, ppst," Carolyn said.

Katya looked at her as if she had lost her mind.

"It usually works," Carolyn told her.

Katya looked over her shoulder at her father. Carolyn also glanced back, suddenly aware of just how undignified she must appear, on her hands and knees, peering under the sofa. She smiled sheepishly.

"It is all right," Sverayov said softly to his daughter.

"What, may I ask, is going on here?" a woman exclaimed.

Carolyn stiffened, expecting Marie-Elena, the wife. But the moment she espied a tall, thin middle-aged woman in spectacles standing in the doorway, her entire demeanor reeking of disapproval, she knew that this was not Katya's mother.

"Excellency," the woman cried. "Katya has her arithmetic lessons to do—but when I turned around, she was nowhere to be seen!"

"Well, Taichili," Sverayov said carelessly, "as you can see, Katya is looking for her cat."

"That cat can wait," Taichili sniffed. "Signor Raffaldi is having an apoplexy."

Carolyn looked from the stern woman who must be the child's tutor or governess to Sverayov, who appeared annoyed, and then at Katya. The little girl had tensed. Tears had filled her eyes, but no one could see them except Carolyn, as they both remained on the floor. Carolyn's heart broke. Katya began calling frantically to the kitten. "Kitty, kitty," she cried.

Carolyn laid her hand on her thin shoulder. "Don't worry," she said soothingly. "We will find Alexander and put him back where he belongs."

Katya gave her a beseeching look and shoved her face closer to the floor. "Kitty!" She was desperate.

And Carolyn was angry. She did not understand what was going on, but knew the child was in pain—and it was far more complicated than a mere hiding cat.

"Excellency, Katya finishes her lessons at four. Surely she can look for the cat then." Taichili spoke shrewishly, with bitter authority. Carolyn despised her.

"The cat is under the sofa," Sverayov said flatly. "A few more minutes will not hurt anyone."

Taichili huffed with displeasure.

Carolyn climbed to her feet, brushing off her skirts. The sofa was up against the wall. She bent and pushed at it, moving it forward an inch.

"Stop. I will do that," Sverayov said sharply. He had moved beside her before she could try to budge the furniture again. "Ladies do not push sofas about," he said, sending her a sidelong glance.

"This lady does," Carolyn returned.

He said, under his breath, "Why should I be surprised?"

They pushed the sofa forward. It screeched against the floor. Katya gasped as the kitten darted out from underneath it and flew across the room. She stood, gave both Nicholas and her governess a frightened look, before racing after the kitten.

Nicholas watched as the Persian leapt onto a chair and

from the chair onto a table boasting numerous items, most of them exceedingly fragile porcelain vases and plates. He smiled, remarking Carolyn's alarm. Taichili harrumphed as it rushed past a vase and a snuffbox. As usual, the governess annoyed him.

Miraculously nothing crashed to the floor. And then Katya claimed the cat, scooping it up into her arms and holding it tightly to her chest. She buried her face against its fur.

Nicholas hated seeing Katya so distraught, but before he could speak, Carolyn had swiftly crossed the salon. She smiled at Katya, who did not look up, and patted her back. Nicholas found himself staring once again. "I imagine it must be quite frightening when you lose your kitten in a house that is so big," she said.

That got Katya's attention. "He is my best friend," she whispered. There was a sheen in her eyes.

"I am sure that he is. But cats are very smart. He won't get lost. Where do you feed him?"

Katya hesitated. "He eats in the kitchens."

"Do you want me to tell you a secret way to make sure that, even if he gets lost, he always comes back to you?"

Katya nodded eagerly.

Carolyn put her hand on her head, stroking her hair unthinkingly. Nicholas continued to watch his daughter and Carolyn, tension riddling his body. "From now on, feed him in your room. And that will be his home."

Katya stared up at Carolyn. "They won't let me."

Carolyn turned to regard Nicholas. "I'm sure that if you ask your father, he will give you permission to feed Alexander in your room. It is a very small request." She smiled sweetly at him.

Nicholas managed to remove his gaze from its intense focus upon Carolyn. But he could not smile. Carolyn was so genuinely kind, so impossibly compassionate. He would have never guessed that this master of wit and disguise would be so wonderful with children.

Katya did not make her request.

"Excellency?" Carolyn prompted.

"I heard," Nicholas said slowly. An idea, one both absurd and astounding, had suddenly taken hold of him. "Of course you can feed the cat in your room, Katya," he said, shocked by his thoughts.

Katya's eyes brightened. And for the first time since entering the salon, she smiled. Nicholas was motionless, his gaze glued to his daughter's face. She was hugging the kitten, hard.

"That is absurd." Taichili came forward. "Excellency, there will be food all over the floor—and insects! I must insist, Excellency—"

"We have a house filled with maids," Nicholas said flatly. "Alexander eats in Katya's room—if that is what Katya wants."

Taichili was furious, her face red, but she said not a word.

"Perhaps you should return to your lessons, now, Katya," he said kindly.

She nodded. "Thank you, Father." Suddenly she faced Carolyn. She smiled shyly. "Thank you, Miss Browne, for helping me find Alexi."

"It was my pleasure," Carolyn said sincerely. She reached out to rub the kitten behind its ears. "You have a beautiful friend, Katya," she said.

Katya beamed.

"Miss Katya?" Taichili intoned.

Katya's smile vanished. She followed Taichili from the salon, not looking back a single time. The room was achingly silent when they were gone.

Nicholas studied Carolyn. How full of surprises she was. But now, suddenly, the stakes had changed. And he was so uneasy.

"She is a beautiful child," she said hesitantly. It was obvious that she wished to say more, but did not.

"Yes," Nicholas returned. He met her gaze. "You were very kind to her. Thank you."

Carolyn was startled. "There is no need to thank me."

His lashes lowered. "To the contrary," he said. If only she knew how affected he was by this brief encounter.

"I don't understand."

"I am sure that you do not." His lashes lifted. He hesitated. "It is getting late. Let me see that you get home safely."

Carolyn flushed. "I can take a hansom."

"No." He was firm. "I will send you home in my coach. It is still out front." He met her gaze. "I would see you home myself, but I forgot about a late appointment that I have to keep." It was a lie. But he needed time now, to think carefully about what he intended to do—and how it would bode for everyone.

And Carolyn seemed disappointed. Her smile was forced. "That is unnecessary in any case."

He did not reply. Staring, he could only think that Carolyn would make the perfect companion for his daughter, the absolutely perfect companion.

But did he need such a complication in his own life?

❧ FOURTEEN ❧

"I do not understand," James Taft said. He sat at his desk in the bustling ground-floor office of the *Morning Chronicle*. The room was filled with desks and printing equipment, the latest technology just imported from Germany. One of the new steam presses was even now rolling, and in spite of the importance of her visit, Carolyn could not help watching with fascination. Thank God, she thought, for both the steam press and another new invention which allowed paper to be machine-made.

Carolyn faced Taft, a short, plump man with a face full of gray whiskers. "I want to know who brought in the last Copperville column."

Taft blinked. "That is an odd request. Some young boy. He said you were in a hurry and could not deliver it yourself." Taft leaned back in his solid oak chair. "What is wrong, Carolyn? It was a good column. My readers enjoyed it immensely. Prince Sverayov is an engaging topic, because he is foreign royalty. I want more columns about him."

Carolyn forced a smile. Inwardly she was dismayed. She did not, suddenly, want to write about Sverayov. Not now. Not anymore. "Did you notice anything unusual about the boy? Did he come on foot? Was there a town coach outside?" The office had huge glass windows, and usually the shades were up. Currently Carolyn had a perfectly unfet-

tered view of the bustling street outside. Pedestrians
thronged the sidewalks, and vehicles of all kinds, carriages
and phaetons, mail coaches and heavy drays, were driving
by.

"How would I know if he came on foot?" Taft frowned.

Carolyn swallowed, certain she was chasing a wild
goose. "Perhaps there was a huge black lacquer coach outside, drawn by six blacks, with a snarling red wolf emblazoned on the door?" Surely it was a wild-goose chase—
but Carolyn could not shake her feeling of uneasiness.

"A black coach drawn by a team of six blacks?" Taft
chortled. "Please, Carolyn, some waif delivered the column. Now, unless you wish to tell me what this is about,
I have work to do."

"Thank you, Mr. Taft. I will see you in a few days."
Carolyn started to leave. "But in future, I shall not entrust
any articles to anyone, so please do not accept my column
unless I deliver it myself."

Taft laid down his quill and the article he was editing.
He squinted at her. "I think I finally understand. Are you
suggesting that the column was not yours?"

"Of course not!" Carolyn cried.

Carolyn was wearing her most elegant gown, a white muslin dress flecked with small sea-green flowers, and a green
sash tied beneath her breasts. As it was short sleeved and
had a scooped neckline, she wore a pale cashmere mantle
over it, which had belonged to her mother. She had added
a darker green satin ribbon to her hair, and was wearing a
pearl necklace and earbobs which had also been Margaret's.
Anthony had been giving her numerous admiring glances
since picking her up at the bookstore.

His carriage was queued up in front of the opera house
as they waited their turn to disembark. Carolyn was not
thinking about Anthony now, even though he sat across
from her in the small space, for she was watching couples
and parties in their splendid evening wear descending from
one coach after another, only to congregate briefly on the

sidewalk to greet one another before going up the sweeping
stone steps of the opera house. She was itching to take up
a quill and open a notebook. Of course, she had neither
accoutrement with her—neither an inkwell nor a notebook
would fit inside her small reticule, another possession
which had been Margaret's.

"Is that Lord William Darrow?" she asked.

Anthony peered out of the window. "Yes, it is. Why do
you ask?"

"Who is that with him?" The elderly Darrow was with
a much younger man, someone not much older than Carolyn.

"That is his son."

"That's not Fred Darrow, Anthony." Darrow's heir and
only child was at least thirty-five.

Anthony colored. "That is John Lewis."

Carolyn turned to gaze at Anthony. "An illegitimate
child?"

Anthony nodded sharply. Clearly he was uncomfortable
with the subject. Carolyn asked a few more questions and
learned that Darrow had three children out of wedlock. Of
course, it was hardly uncommon amongst the peerage.

"It is our turn," Anthony said, relieved.

Carolyn allowed him to help her out, feeling somewhat
guilty for embarrassing him. She couldn't help comparing
Anthony to Sverayov. The Russian would have been
amused by her curiosity and would have supplied her with
all the information she wished to have—if he had known
it. Carolyn had no doubt.

They ascended the many front steps of the wide, granite
building. Carolyn was somber now, recalling her visit to
Sverayov's town house earlier that day. She thought about
him, his child, the kitten, and that grim, nasty Taichili.
Mostly, she thought about him and his daughter. She felt
so sorry for them both. She had the instinctive urge to med-
dle in their private lives and somehow correct whatever it
was that was wrong.

The foyer of the opera house was white marble, filled

with columns, and so crowded with chatting guests that it was hard to maneuver through them. Anthony kept a firm grip on her elbow, and every minute or two they paused to greet lords and ladies whom he was acquainted with. Carolyn was introduced, and was aware of a few mildly curious gazes turned her way, but she herself was more interested in observing the crowd than in noting their reactions to her. As Anthony led her through the throngs, she craned her neck, watching everyone, enjoying herself. She saw half a dozen noblemen and women whom she recognized. More than a few had made an appearance in a Copperville column. She saw Anthony's father in quiet conversation with a leading Whig, and she wondered what that was about. She saw the very notorious Lady Hampton, the mother of six children, none of whom had the same father, or so it was said, flirting outrageously with the very young, very dashing Lord Monroe.

And then she glimpsed Sverayov.

Carolyn halted without knowing it, turning, straining to glimpse him again to make sure it had not been an illusion. But he stood a head taller than most of the crowd, and she saw his perfect profile and crown of tawny hair as clear as day. It was too crowded for her to see whom he was speaking with. Anthony was tugging on her elbow so she turned reluctantly, and followed him into the theater.

They took their seats in his box, which he was sharing with three other couples. Everyone was politely introduced, but, like Carolyn, more interested in who was flocking to their seats than in each other.

"You shall enjoy this performance," Anthony whispered in her ear. "They say Giuseppe Maione is excellent."

Carolyn did not nod. Sverayov had entered his box, not far from where she and Anthony sat. He paused, nodding at the box's other occupants, before taking his seat. Unlike everyone surrounding him, he did not seem to care who was present in the audience that night. And he was alone. She was, insanely, relieved.

"Sverayov," Anthony said matter-of-factly.

Carolyn realized that she was staring, and that he was aware of her interest. She blushed. "He is very tall. He is easy to notice, impossible to miss."

"Does he shop in your store frequently?" Anthony asked.

"No." Carolyn's reply was hasty. Her gaze remained on Sverayov as he chatted with a gentleman, although she did so out of the corner of her eye. She had never seen him in a tailcoat before. He was breathtaking. "He has asked my father to locate two rare manuscripts." She faced Anthony.

"I see." Anthony did not sound happy.

Suddenly a woman appeared in the box, a flash of silver, equally impossible to miss. Carolyn stared openly. Sverayov stood. She held on to his arm and kissed his cheek very intimately, pressing her body familiarly against his. Carolyn froze. The woman was magnificent, surely the most exotic, sensual creature Carolyn had ever seen, with thick blue-black hair and pale ivory skin, and although she was petite, her body was lush, and she was wearing the kind of gown made fashionable so recently by les merveilleuses, a nearly transparent silvery-white silk that skimmed every curve of her body, leaving nothing to the imagination. She wore a huge necklace of sapphires and diamonds, the kind of jewelry that only royalty could afford. Carolyn could only guess who this woman was. Pain seemed to lance through her breast. She watched Sverayov bow over her hand. "Is that his wife?" Carolyn heard herself ask breathlessly—bitterly.

"I don't know," Anthony said, his tone strange.

Carolyn's gaze flew to his face. She caught him staring at the woman. Immediately he looked away. Carolyn quickly glanced around and saw that every man in the vicinity had eyes only for the princess. When she regarded Anthony again he was blushing, and looking everywhere but at Marie-Elena.

"She is ravishing," Carolyn said thickly. But it was more than that. It was her blatant sensuality, perhaps, that drew every eye to her. Why was she so dismayed? Carolyn was not competing with the other woman, not for anything, and she had never believed that beauty was relevant or important. And beauty was in the eye of the beholder. But God, Marie-Elena and Sverayov suited one another perfectly, for they were both incredible, superlative shining examples of their gender.

Anthony did not answer.

Carolyn watched Marie-Elena detach herself from Sverayov and leave his box. A moment later she had entered another box, the silver gown shimmering as she sat. Carolyn thought she could see right through the silvery fabric and glimpse the woman's actual skin. At least, she thought dismally, the princess had an entourage separate from Sverayov's.

Carolyn looked away, sorry now that she had come to the opera, for suddenly the day seemed burdensome, overwhelming. And when she glanced up again, it was not to watch the stage curtains parting, it was to find Sverayov.

He remained seated in his box. It was full. And one of the occupants, newly arrived, was Lady Carradine.

During the intermission everyone descended to the lobby to chat and mingle, the gentlemen with a glass of cognac and, occasionally, a lady with a sherry. Carolyn found herself face-to-face with Anthony's father, Lord Davison, a prominent member of Castlereagh's foreign ministry. She kept recalling the fact that Lord Davison had been in Madam Russell's brothel that night she had gone there with Sverayov.

"Father, I wish to introduce Miss Carolyn Browne," Anthony was saying.

"How do you do?" Carolyn said politely.

Stuart Davison gave her an odd glance and a stiff bow. "A pleasure," he said, turning a dark look on his son. Clearly it was not a pleasure, quite the opposite. "I will see you later," he said to Anthony, a warning in his tone. And then he turned abruptly and began chatting, quite animatedly, with a group of gentlemen.

Anthony was red-faced.

"I am afraid your father does not approve of your choice of guest," Carolyn said flatly. She could not help being angry. Davison had no right to judge her, none at all.

"I apologize. He will come around. He will change his tune when he finds out that you are Lady Stafford's granddaughter."

Carolyn opened her mouth to tell Anthony to please not bother to relay that information, then saw Sverayov staring at her. She felt herself flush and she said nothing.

"Would you like a glass of sherry?" Anthony asked.

Carolyn nodded. Anthony disappeared. Sverayov shot her a look from across the crowd, nodded to something a woman Carolyn did not recognize was saying, and began, quite deliberately, making his way over to her. Carolyn did not move.

At least, she thought, he was not with the voluptuous Lady Carradine.

He reached her and bowed. "Miss Browne."

"Your Excellency."

His gaze slid over her face, as if memorizing every feature, and then over her décolletage, her waist, and her legs. He was very obvious, and she was both flattered and amused. Carolyn felt like lifting up one foot and asking him if he liked her slippers. She remained silent.

"Once again, this is an unexpected pleasure," he said. "I did not think to find you here." He smiled. "You do have the habit of turning up in the most extraordinary places."

Carolyn wondered if he referred to her masquerade as Brighton. "One could say that about you, Excellency. Are you enjoying Maione?" she asked politely. Thinking about him, his wife, his daughter—and his mistress.

Sverayov shrugged. "I am not an opera lover. I prefer the theater."

Carolyn hesitated, for his gaze was piercing. "There is much theater here."

He smiled, the expression genuine. "There most certainly is."

Carolyn also smiled, and for one moment it was as if they understood one another perfectly. It was a stunning, beautiful moment.

And then his expression changed. His glance had moved beyond Carolyn—behind her.

Carolyn shifted—and saw Marie-Elena staring at them both. For some unfathomable reason, a chill swept over her.

"My wife," he said, unnecessarily.

"I guessed as much." Carolyn gave the other woman her back, although Marie-Elena still stared, but not before she had seen how cold and malevolent the princess's regard was. Carolyn was unnerved. "She is extraordinarily beautiful. Your daughter resembles her."

"Yes, Katya does." He hesitated. "I am afraid I have decided not to stay for the second half of the opera. I have work to attend to tonight."

"I am sorry," Carolyn said. "Maione is superb."

He held her gaze. "You are superb this evening, Carolyn. Evening wear suits you."

She was stunned.

He bowed briefly, with his customary arrogance, wheeled, and disappeared into the crowd.

Carolyn stared after him, aware now of her thundering heart. Such a simple piece of flattery—and she was bowled over. But she was intelligent enough to know that no good could come of her feelings and his sudden interest in her.

And when Carolyn turned, looking for Anthony, she came face-to-face with his wife.

Marie-Elena smiled at her, very coldly. "And whom do I have the pleasure of meeting?" she said, her tone dripping with condescension.

Carolyn's heart had slammed to a halt. Now it beat with frightening force. She managed a smile and a curtsy. "Carolyn Browne, Princess."

Marie-Elena stared. "And just how do you know my husband?" she asked imperiously.

Carolyn felt her cheeks flaming. "He, er, my father sells books. He specializes in locating rare manuscripts. The prince has asked him to locate a copy of Bartholomew and the original *Sic et Non* by Abelard." Carolyn's face continued to burn. Now shame and guilt afflicted her. It was one thing to know by hearsay that Sverayov had a wife from whom he was estranged. It was another to be confronted by the woman after having shared even the briefest passionate encounter with her husband. But Marie-Elena could not know. Carolyn was not soothed.

Marie-Elena tossed back her head, exposing the lovely column of her throat, and she laughed. "A bookseller's daughter?" She was incredulous. Carolyn might as well have claimed that she was an odd species of animal from Africa. "A bookseller's daughter!" She laughed again, and shook her head. "My, Niki has lost his head, indeed, he has. Whatever can he be thinking!"

Carolyn was frozen, shocked by Marie-Elena's rude response, incapable of finding her tongue. The other woman turned abruptly, still chuckling, and melted into the crowd.

Carolyn hugged herself. Oh, dear. Whatever had she done?

And what, pray tell, should she do now?

❧ FIFTEEN ❧

MIDLANDS was a wide, rectangular manor built of pale stone earlier in the reign of the mad King George III. Spacious green lawns swept up to it, rioting gardens encroached upon the house, and rolling green hills, dotted with sheep, surrounded it. The air was fresh and clean. The sky overhead was as blue as any robin's egg. Today was Edith Owsley's seventy-fifth birthday. Midlands was her favorite home, and these past ten years she had spent more time there than anywhere, by choice. But today she felt no peace, no serenity, no happiness. She could not find beauty in the environs. She was depressed.

The old lady tossed her London newspaper aside. Not even the witty Copperville, whom she so enjoyed, could lift her spirits today. She sat outside in the gardens which were to the back of the house, wrapped in a light shawl, thinking grimly about her life—thinking about how short it had been. How fast it had gone by. And what, pray tell, did she have to show for it all?

One day, sooner or later, she would die—and that vain idiot Thomas would inherit everything.

Margaret's image flitted through her mind, as she had been when Edith had last seen her, thirteen years ago on a cold, snowy day. Pale and blond, with a beauty that went far deeper than the skin. Edith closed her eyes. She lived with regret every day of her life. If only Margaret had not run away with that fool, Browne. Dammit.

She sighed. But she was a survivor and a warrior, however unfashionable those traits might be. She had survived Margaret's betrayal, and her death. Just as she had survived the death of her husband, Seymour, another male fool, thirty years ago. Edith had chosen not to remarry, although, being a handsome woman, and a wealthy one, she had had many suitors. Edith had rejected them all. She had enjoyed the absoluteness of her newfound freedom, not that she had really allowed Seymour to fetter her in any way when he was alive. Seymour had always thought he knew best, but in truth, he had been susceptible to suggestion and quite pliable, indeed. It hadn't hurt to let him think he was running everything! And Edith *had* been fond of him, she supposed, in her own way, for he had been gentle and kind and besotted with her from the first.

Edith hated dwelling on the past. But her birthdays always did this to her. Soon Thomas and his nitwit wife, his spoiled sons, would arrive to celebrate her birthday—when Edith had told him years ago that she hated celebrating the passage of another year. Against her will, she thought about Margaret again, and this time, about Margaret's daughter, who was now, Edith knew, eighteen.

Eighteen and unwed. Eighteen and living atop a bookshop, with her imbecile father—the man who had ruined Margaret's life.

Edith leaned forward and picked up the beautifully bound leather volume which was comprised of the best essays of Edmund Burke. That was Carolyn's gift to her and it had arrived earlier that day in the post. Margaret must have told her daughter before she died just how much Edith loved to read—but not nonsense, mind you, only intelligent, thought-provoking essays and such. She read half a dozen books every week—not to mention reviews, journals, periodicals, and newspapers. Edith was very fond of Burke.

Carolyn never forgot a single birthday. But neither had Margaret, before her death.

Edith squinted, noticing the dark carriage rolling through the hills on the dirt road that would eventually turn into Midlands. That would be Thomas, his spectacularly unintelligent wife, Dorothea, and their two little boys, who, so far, appeared to take after their father exactly. She sighed and got to her feet. The two cocker spaniels which had been sleeping by her chair immediately awoke, and began dancing around her skirts, tails wagging. Three servants appeared at her side, almost materializing from the air itself. Her butler asked her if there was anything she wished. Edith waved him away. "Unless you can make me sixty-five, Winslow, the answer is no. Got to greet my birthday guests." She gave Winslow a glare. He was as old as she was—if not more so.

Her strides were brisk for a woman her age, but Edith thought that was because she rode twice a day every day, rain or snow. She skirted the house, not entering it, even though it would have been faster to go through it. But she also liked walking, and she rarely used a cane.

But the past was on her mind now, dammit. She hated thinking about it. It was too painful. Still, every time she did, the thought planted itself in her head: if only she could have kept George Browne and her daughter apart. It had been one of the few failures in her life.

Edith Owsley planted herself on the front steps and waited with vast patience for the brown carriage to finish its approach. It finally halted in the drive in front of her and the door was swung open. Foolish Dorothea stepped down first, for Thomas had no manners, he never had, and clearly did not think to help his own wife down. But he took after his mother, Georgia, who hadn't a brain in her silly head, either. Georgia was not coming to the fête. She was one of those women who were constantly ill with one malady after another. Actually, Edith knew the truth. Georgia was afraid of her mother, and preferred staying as far away as possible from her. Edith did not mind.

Margaret had had all the brains in the family—or so Edith had thought until the fateful day of her elopement.

Edith scowled now as Thomas alighted, the carriage dipping a bit under his weight. He was stouter than ever, Edith saw. She had little use for fools who could not discipline themselves, who could not even say no to a mere piece of bread. She herself was as slim as the day she'd gotten married. She wondered what Thomas would do when she told him how she intended to dispose of her personal fortune.

She smiled.

"Grandmother," Thomas cried, beaming. He threw his arms around her. "Happy seventy-fifth!"

Edith glared until he released her. "Do you have to remind me of my age?"

"I'm sorry. But you look wonderful." He backed up and pulled his wife forward. "Kiss Grandmother, Dottie."

"Stop fawning," Edith said irritably. Edith allowed the timid bird to peck her cheek. Than she ignored her. "Let me see the boys," she demanded.

Thomas pulled his two squirming sons forward. They were six and seven, and already showing signs that they would one day be as stout as their father. "Congratulate your great-grandmother on her birthday," he said firmly.

Henry bowed over her hand. "Happy birthday, madam."

Tom did the same. "All the best, madam."

Edith studied them, but they were unable to meet her gaze. They were flushed and perspiring. The younger one had chocolate all over his shirt. "What have you done to them? Why are they twitching? Why is Henry fat? Why won't they look me in the eye? What does Tom have in his pocket? Is that leftover cake?"

"Stop twitching," Thomas growled. "Henry has been eating too many desserts. Tom, what is in your pocket? Good God! Get rid of that moldy thing. Look at Lady Stafford, boys!"

The boys straightened and met Edith's gaze. She saw no sign of remarkable character or intelligence in their eyes. She already knew from their tutors, whom she had interviewed both privately and secretly, that the boys were not good students. They were more than lazy, they were spoiled, demanding, boisterous, and filled with uppity airs. Even had they better comportment, their tutors despaired of them ever being more than competent in the pursuit of an education. Edith had been horrified by their report. As she paid for Thomas's entire life until three years ago when he'd come of age, including the education of his sons, it was quite depressing.

Yes, she had made the right decision—because Thomas would merely fritter away the fortune she had acquired over the years—and if he did not, then his sons would after him.

They adjourned to the house. To Edith's relief, Dorothea pleaded a headache and retired instantly to her rooms, while the boys ran outside with the spaniels in spite of their tutor's protests. Thomas beamed at Edith and handed her a small gift-wrapped parcel. "May I give you your present now?" he asked.

"It does not matter to me," Edith returned. She weighed the object in her hand. "This feels like jewelry."

"Open it, Grandmother," he said.

She did as he asked and held up a double strand of black pearls, which were quite beautiful. Of course, Edith was well aware of the fact that she had actually paid for the gift herself—since Thomas had never made a single penny on his own and the Owsley estates were very profitable only because of all that she had done, these past thirty years. "Thank you," she said, thinking about Carolyn, who received nothing from her and still sent her a gift. "You are very thoughtful," she said, knowing he would not understand her sarcasm.

"You know how I try," he said. "You know how much we all try to make you happy."

She made a sound, one that came out as disdainful as she felt.

"How are you these days, Grandmother?"

They entered the smaller of Midlands's three salons. Edith smiled. "I have never been better," she said. It was the truth. She had been ill during Easter, the last time she had seen her grandson and his brood. Now she saw Thomas's dismay, which he tried to hide.

"That is wonderful," he lied.

He was just itching to get his hands on her money, by God. The oaf.

"By the by," he said, "when I was in town to purchase your gift, I stopped by at Browne's."

Edith froze. She rearranged her face before facing her grandson. "And?" she demanded. "Did you see her? Your cousin?"

Thomas was taken aback. "Grandmother, you are shouting. Am I upsetting you?"

"Thomas, you upset me every time you enter this house. She sent me a book, you know. A wonderful collection of essays." Edith smiled.

Thomas stared. "But I gave you very rare pearls."

"Hmmph. And what did Carolyn do and say?"

"She was very rude. She actually ordered me out of the store."

"Really?" Thomas was not fooling Edith. She knew that he had probably been so obnoxious that Carolyn had had every reason to demand he leave. "What does she look like?" Edith asked, aware of an eagerness she refused to entertain.

He scowled. "Odd, I'd say. She has a funny haircut, far too short, as if she took scissors to it herself. And she is tall and thin. Of course, she was wearing some horrible dress, a real rag, if you ask me." Thomas smiled. "Yes, that is how I would describe her, as odd."

Edith knew better than to trust his judgment. It crossed her mind that she was old, and getting older every day, and that as she had not glimpsed Carolyn since the funeral, she might go to town and take a look for herself. Secretively, of course.

The idea stimulated her as nothing else had recently.

"Thomas, sit down," she said. "I wish to speak to you."

He seemed pleased with himself as he settled his bulk into a heavy brocade chair. Edith did not sit. She settled her hands on her slim hips and anticipated his reaction to her next words. "Thomas, I have changed my will. You will, of course, retain the Owsley estates and all the titles, but I have decided to give my fortune away."

Thomas turned white.

Carolyn was alone in the bookshop. Three days had passed since the opera. Carolyn was restless, could not concentrate, and knew precisely why. Every time a carriage passed by the shop on the street outside, or the doorbell sounded, she looked up, filled with sudden anticipation. And every time the coach turned out to be the mail, or a brougham or landau filled with gay, well-dressed ladies, or the door opened and a stranger appeared, her disappointment was overwhelming. Sverayov, it seemed, had forgotten all about her.

She had not forgotten about him.

How could she? She was highly disturbed by their last two encounters and all that she had learned about him and his family. It was clear to her now that he was a man with hidden facets—facets he had no wish to reveal. He was not the superficial rendering she had expected to see. There was a great problem between him and his daughter, and he seemed to be harboring sorrow and grief. And Carolyn's heart also went out to the little girl. The child was unnaturally quiet, and Carolyn was quite certain that she was sad. None of this was her affair. Yet she could not stop thinking about them—about him.

And to make matters far worse, her interest and memories were hardly noble. They were hardly moral. She was not ever going to forget his embrace, his touch, his kiss. She had discovered passion, at long last—in the arms of a notorious womanizer.

And he was a married man, even if he and his wife went their separate ways. Carolyn wished she had not met his ravishing yet cruel wife. And while Carolyn did not approve of adultery, she thought it unfair to criticize arrangements like Sverayov's. It was undoubtedly for the best that he had forgotten all about her, Carolyn. While she had become a stupidly besotted lackwit like half of the ladies in society who pined after him.

Now she sat at the counter, rather glumly, bathed in warm summer sunshine. All of the shutters were wide open, as were the windows. On the countertop in front of her was a beautifully bound volume containing Burke's most brilliant works—identical to the one she had sent to her grandmother. Thomas had not needed to remind her of the old lady's birthday.

The doorbell tinkled. Carolyn started but it was only George. Her father entered the shop, perspiring, removing his hat and mopping his brow. "It's going to be a hot summer," he announced.

Carolyn managed what she hoped was a cheerful smile. She did not reply.

"What are you doing?" he asked, removing his jacket and loosening his stock. He walked over to the counter to peer down at one of Burke's essays. "Ahh, wonderful reading. But you've already read most of Burke's work, haven't you, dear?"

Carolyn nodded. "I sent my grandmother this for her birthday."

George was still. "I see. Well, that explains your unhappy face."

Carolyn closed the thick book and ran her hand across the leather cover, which was engraved with scalloped borders and lettering in gold. "It would be nice if once, just once, she acknowledged a gift from me."

"She's too old to change her ways."

"Perhaps I should say, it would be nice if just once she acknowledged me." Carolyn looked up. "She must have hated my mother."

"She loved Margaret. Everyone did. No one was more sincere or more kindhearted. Old Owsley despised me. And still does." He was grim.

Carolyn had heard all of this before. She knew the entire story. But today it was depressing. Today was her grandmother's actual birthday. "It is just not fair," she heard herself whisper.

"Carolyn, you are not a child. Life is rarely fair. Why are you dwelling on all of this now?" George asked suddenly. "We do not need her. We never have." He became silent.

Carolyn could imagine he was thinking of the past, of all those times when there had been bills to pay and mouths to feed but not the wherewithal to do so. She was also silent.

"Let's talk about something else. Today they hanged a Luddite, Carolyn. They hanged a man for the crime of rioting when he had just cause."

"I know," she said somberly. But she was not in the mood to discuss the very harsh laws against workers associating much less protesting or destroying property. Sverayov's image came to mind. She wondered how many serfs were tied to his estates. Hundreds if not thousands. Her mood became even gloomier.

"Are you going to see Anthony Davison again?" George smiled at her. "He is a nice young man. And a good catch."

Carolyn shrugged. "He is just a friend, Papa, and I am not the kind of woman to catch a husband—as you of all people should know."

"I was merely using a figure of speech," George said lightly, "and trying to cheer you up. Actually, he would be very lucky if he could catch you."

"We are from different worlds," Carolyn pointed out, thinking more about Sverayov now than Anthony, "and I hardly think the son of a peer would condescend to marry a bookseller's daughter."

George sighed. "Carolyn, you cannot change your grandmother's feelings. I know how much her exclusion has cost you."

"I just do not understand and I never have!" Carolyn exclaimed in frustration. "She is my grandmother. We are the same blood. Next fall I will be nineteen. She may be dead. And we will have never spoken. I almost feel as if she is blaming me for my mother's choice. Or does she despise me because I am a reminder of that choice?''

"I am certain that both explanations are correct." George suddenly put his arm around her and hugged her briefly. "You cannot make anyone think or do what they do not wish to think or do for themselves. *That* is life, Carolyn."

With that, he smiled and went up the stairs.

Carolyn watched him until he had disappeared from view. She knew her father was right, and there was no point in thinking about her grandmother until next year, when she was faced with another birthday. Her pulse began to race. She reached beneath the counter and removed a sheaf of handsome ivory stationery. She picked up a quill and dated the top of the page, "July 13, 1812."

And she was not penning a column for Copperville. "My dear Sverayov," she wrote, her hands shaking, "several days have elapsed since we met at the Sheffields'. Tomorrow is the event of the season, one of the last, the Roundtree Stakes at Newmarket. If you wish to join me, I shall be in box 102." She hesitated and added, "I do hope we meet again." And she signed the brief note "Charles Brighton."

Carolyn closed her eyes. Since she could not forget about him, she would play her charade one more time. She prayed he would join her—and wondered what their next encounter would bring.

Alexi entered the library, narrowing his eyes. "Why are you sitting there in the gloom?"

Nicholas looked up. It was growing late and twilight shadows had filtered into the room, but he had not thought to light any lamps. "I am thinking. What does it seem that I am doing?"

Alexi smiled and struck a match, lighting the lamp on Nicholas's desk. "Brooding, perhaps?"

Nicholas smiled. "I am doing that, too."

"Care to tell me what is on your mind? Other than your

daughter and the oh-so-unique Miss Browne?''

Nicholas eyed him as Alexi sprawled in a chair. ''Do you now read minds like a gypsy fortune-teller?''

''Not at all. I saw the way you looked at her last night.''

''Really?'' He hoped his tone sounded far cooler than he himself felt.

''I think you have been struck by Cupid's arrow, big brother.'' Alexi grinned widely.

''You are quite mad—as mad as our dear departed father was.''

Alexi's smile faded.

''I am sorry,'' Nicholas said, instantly contrite. Rumor had held for too many years to count that Ivan Sverayov was not Alexi's father. And that did seem likely, as the brothers' mother, both beautiful and despotic, had had numerous lovers, both during and after her marriage.

Alexi shrugged. ''No harm,'' he said, his teeth flashing. His smile did not reach his eyes, and Nicholas knew he had opened up an old wound, and inwardly, he cursed himself. ''Actually, I have been contemplating hiring a companion for Katya.''

Alexi was surprised. ''Katya has a governess.''

''Taichili is hardly kind or caring. And when Marie-Elena is sent to Tver, in the very near future, Katya will need someone about her, someone kind and caring, witty and instructive. Someone who will be intelligent, resourceful, and unquestionably loyal to my daughter. In fact, as I shall rejoin my command, this person shall in effect be my daughter's supervisor—a substitute parent, or a guardian, if you will.''

Alexi blinked. And then his gaze narrowed. ''I take it you have someone in mind for the role?'' He began to smile. ''Dare I guess the identity of this superlative woman? It is a she, is it not?''

''I see that you have already surmised that I intend to approach Carolyn Browne regarding the position.'' His pulse raced, competing with his myriad, spinning thoughts.

Alexi chortled and produced an envelope from an interior

pocket. "And speaking of the original lady herself, this just arrived. Apparently it is from Charles Brighton." And he started to laugh.

Nicholas took one look at his smug, know-it-all face and all of his previous sympathy vanished. He broke the wax seal and read.

"Well?" Alexi asked, laughter lingering in his tone. "What does he want? Or should I say *she*?"

"He—that is, Carolyn—has invited me to the races tomorrow at three." His jaw flexed. And his heart beat a bit faster than it had.

"And? Will you go?"

"How could I resist—much less refuse?" And Nicholas began to smile. "I think the time has come to unmask Charles Brighton, wouldn't you agree?"

✒ SIXTEEN ✑

CAROLYN fidgeted, barely able to watch the horses racing across the turf on the course below the bandstands. Almost as one, the field took the first hurdle, a high hedge jump. The only other fans present in her box were strangers to her. And the races had started forty minutes ago; she was vastly disappointed. Sverayov was not going to appear.

She should be relieved. Maybe Sverayov knew that she was really Charles Brighton, anyway, even though he had not given a sign or a clue of his suspicions if that were the case.

But she was not relieved. Her spirits were vastly low, and it was not like her. She was thinking about how she had to shake off her infatuation, for it was not serving any purpose in her life, and where could her passion lead anyway? He was married, and even though he had an understanding with his wife, Carolyn knew she was not capable of having an affair with him. And even if he had been a bachelor, he was a foreigner and a prince—he was not for her. And then Carolyn realized the direction which her thoughts had taken, and she was appalled with herself.

Shaken, she watched the field from the fourth race take a brick wall. He said, from behind her, "I have bet a hundred pounds on Topper to win."

Carolyn whirled. Sverayov stood in the aisle, his gaze narrowed, amber eyes gleaming, impeccably clad in a dark blue tailcoat and pale beige trousers. Flushing she stood. "Sverayov. I am pleased to see you." She bowed, reaching for her spectacles as they slipped down the bridge of her nose.

He entered the box. "Your invitation was a pleasant surprise, young Charles." He smiled benignly at her.

Carolyn stared at him, searching his eyes for a hint of what he was really thinking. He must certainly know that Brighton was Copperville, but his smile was friendly, nothing more. Her color, unfortunately, increased. "Is Topper in the next race?"

He handed her a program. "He's handicapped at seven to one."

Carolyn glanced at the program, having no real interest in it. She had only decided to attend the races in the hopes of luring him there. All gentlemen, it seemed, liked horse racing. She wondered if she should confess.

"You seem disturbed." Sverayov raised his looking glasses and studied the racing field. "Number six is down at the last water jump."

Carolyn glanced up and saw another Thoroughbred go down because of the first fallen steed. She winced. But the rest of the field was thundering toward them into the flat homestretch. "Are you a racing fan?"

He smiled at her. And his gaze slipped from her face to her cravat, and down her waistcoat. "Of course. I have racing stables in Tver. That is one of my country homes. I have one of the best studs on the Continent, and in all of Russia."

"What is it like? Tver?" She had, she hoped, avoided his question.

He started, holding her gaze. "Tver itself is rather provincial. It is somewhat like a smaller version of St. Petersburg." He smiled briefly. "Although at one time hundreds of years ago it was a very unruly state and one of Moscow's chief rivals." His smile widened. "It has been ravaged throughout its history, including by the Mongol Tartars, and was destroyed by a fire in 1763. However, it is quiet and picturesque. The city is situated on the Volga, one of our largest rivers, and it is a land of contrasts—winding rivers and flower-filled meadows, pine forests and ice-cold lakes. At night the sky is so clear that it seems one can see every single star—and there are hundreds of thousands. It is a good place to be able to hear oneself think.''

Carolyn studied his handsome face as he turned his gaze back to the track. A dozen horses were lining up for the start of the fifth race. ''I should like to see such a place sometime,'' she heard herself say.

His head swiveled. ''Perhaps, one day, you will.'' His gaze connected with hers.

Shivers swept up and down Carolyn's spine, and for one moment, she had the oddest premonition that she would visit Tver, and far sooner than seemed possible. But she shrugged the notion aside as mere fantasy.

But he said, ''When I intend to be at Tver, I shall send you an invitation, Charles.''

She started. Had he pronounced her alias with the faintest touch of mockery? But his gaze was steady on hers.

''Why are you disturbed today, Charles?'' he asked suddenly—softly. His tone had become too sensual for comfort.

She tensed. ''I thought perhaps . . . that I had offended you and you might not accept my invitation.''

He was amused. ''And how did you offend me, my young friend?''

She swallowed. And tugged at her collar, which was too tight. ''I'm not sure. Have I offended your sensibilities in any way?'' she asked carefully.

He sent her a sidelong glance, which made Carolyn begin to shake, and handed her his looking glasses. ''They're off.'' The field thundered past them, toward the first jump.

Carolyn wet her lips, raised the glasses, but could not concentrate. In truth, she no longer wanted to play this charade. She wanted to be with him as Carolyn. ''Where is Topper?'' she asked.

''He is about fifth from last.''

They watched the field in silence as horse after horse took the first hedge and galloped around the first turn. Another hedge followed. Topper remained in the cluster of horses to the rear of the galloping pack.

"He will make his move after the brick wall," Sverayov said very calmly. For one instant, his gaze found and held hers, his eyes bright, but also languid. Carolyn was tense. She could not look away. He had the most sensual manner about him, and she wondered if he regarded all women in the same way, with smoky golden eyes. Maybe she was imagining the sensuality in his gaze. But if she was not, why did he not just come out with it and accuse her of treachery?

The brick wall was ahead. Topper had inched ahead of the lagging horses now. Horse after horse cleared the fence, landing and stretching out. "Go," Sverayov said very firmly.

Carolyn raised the glasses and saw Topper's jockey using his crop. The bay crept away from the lagging horses, now coming abreast of five horses racing in the middle of the field. All the horses easily cleared a box hedge. Topper was leading the middle of the field now.

Sverayov smiled at her.

Carolyn watched, growing amazed, as the bay drew abreast of the two horses just behind the leader, which was a gray. The four racers took the final water jump almost as one. And then Topper was alongside the gray, nose for nose with him.

Sverayov was standing, everyone was standing, the crowd was roaring. Carolyn felt her heart pounding and she, too, was on her feet. "Go!" she couldn't help crying.

Nose and nose, gray and bay, the two horses battled down the final turn and into the stretch, coming back toward the stands. And then the bay's dark nose was ahead. He was ahead. By a neck, a length, two lengths. And Topper flashed under the finish wire, followed by the gray, the crowd going wild.

Carolyn covered her racing heart with her hand, and realized Sverayov was staring. "That was incredible," she said. "How did you know that he would win?"

He continued to stare, smiling slightly, not answering her. And then he threw his arm around her shoulders and pulled her tight and hard against him. For one moment, Carolyn forgot that she was supposed to be Brighton and thought he was going to kiss her. But he only embraced her.

And when he released her, leaving her breathless, her pulse pounding, desire rising like fire in her body, he said, "Because I bred Topper."

The country inn was halfway to London from Newmarket. Carolyn had not minded when Sverayov had insisted they stop for supper—and it was suppertime. She was barely hungry, but she was in no rush to end their outing. He had insisted on a private dining room. And he was still calling her Charles.

Carolyn had taken a seat at the table, watching a fire dancing in the brick hearth, while Sverayov ordered them a meal that the two of them could not possibly finish. He also ordered them two bottles of French red wine, which caused Carolyn's brows to lift questioningly. The proprietor was waiting on them himself—no one could mistake Sverayov's coach for anything other than what it was, a vehicle belonging to a very prominent, powerful, and wealthy nobleman, and Carolyn had overheard one of Sverayov's servants, a slim man with an accent that was suspiciously French, whispering to the proprietor's wife. Undoubtedly he had been informing the inn's owners just who was dining at their establishment that night.

A serving maid was lighting the table's candles, her eyes continually drifting toward the Russian. He sprawled indolently in his chair, staring at Carolyn. He appeared relaxed in a way that Carolyn had never really seen him be before—but then, she had never been alone with him like this before, either. He also appeared quite satisfied, for he had won several thousand pounds that day at the track.

Clearly, he was no amateur when it came to gambling. Carolyn had been encouraged to place a few bets herself, which she had done, rather reluctantly. She had no money to lose.

But she had also won—fifty pounds. Of course, she had followed Sverayov's suggestions when placing her wagers.

"Shall I pour the wine, Your Highness?" the proprietor asked.

"Please," Sverayov said with a slight inclination of his golden head.

Carolyn watched first Sverayov's and then her own goblet being filled. The balding innkeeper left, shutting the door behind him. Sverayov lifted his glass. "To an entertaining afternoon."

Carolyn raised her own wine glass. "To my fifty pounds—and your several thousand."

He chuckled warmly and sipped his wine.

Carolyn felt absurdly pleased that she had made him laugh, and she also took a generous sip. "This is wonderful," she said, setting her glass down.

"We are drinking Burgundy," he announced. "I prefer Bordeaux, but in this time of war, one cannot have everything."

Carolyn drank again. "May I ask how we came to have a French wine, Sverayov? This is in direct violation of the Orders in Council."

He laughed, amused. "Do you think Englishmen will stop drinking fine wines just because of a governmental decree? Have Englishwomen stopped wearing French fashions?"

"We are aiding smugglers," Carolyn said glumly. "And putting our pounds into Napoleon's coffers."

"Someone always gets rich during wars, Charles." His eyes gleamed. "And do not fear. There are British goods in France and all of the countries Napoleon controls."

She felt her insides warming considerably. Her false name had rolled off his tongue like thick, molten honey. Sverayov, she decided, was inherently sensual, and did not mean to provoke the disturbing thoughts and sensations in her which he did. "You are very quiet," he said suddenly. "A tuppence for your thoughts."

She met his smoldering gaze. "I was recalling how enjoyable this day was for me, as well."

"Let us toast our new friendship." He raised his glass, waiting for Carolyn to imitate him, which she did. "To fine friends," he said softly.

Carolyn echoed him. "To fine friends." Her pulse was racing now as she quickly drank. The wine was making her light-headed, and she knew she should be cautious, but the effect was wonderful. She was used to wine in any case, for she and her father often shared a bottle with their supper. But indulging with George was one thing, with Sverayov, another. Carolyn had the uncanny feeling that she was courting danger. But she had no urge to stop herself.

Carolyn smiled widely at him.

He was startled, and his glance pierced hers. Abruptly he stood, shrugging off his dark blue tailcoat and loosening his paisley cravat. His fitted brocade waistcoat left little to Carolyn's imagination, nor did his perfectly tailored trousers. Then he stepped around the table. Carolyn's heart rate increased as he paused beside her, his thigh brushing against her arm. But he only reached for the bottle and filled her wine glass before returning to his chair.

"Have you read anything interesting lately, Charles?" Sverayov drawled as Carolyn was reaching for her glass.

She had sensed that this was coming all day. Carolyn froze, but only for an instant, then she quaffed half of her wine. "I happen to enjoy reading. I am rereading some of Burke's better works."

"Burke?" His brows slashed upward. "I grant that I do not know you well, but oddly enough, I am surprised to find you reading Edmund Burke when he is so conservative."

"I read from a wide range of authors." Carolyn reached for her wine again. "You are familiar with Burke?"

"Of course. I also read avidly." He sipped, peering at

her from over the rim of the goblet. "Did you not tell me the other day that you enjoy the *Times*?"

She swallowed. "I believe I said I liked to know what the opposition is thinking."

"Ahh, yes. So you prefer a liberal journal like the *Chronicle*." His smile was wide.

Carolyn felt like a mouse being pawed by a big lazy golden cat. "Sometimes."

"I wonder why, recently, my name comes up so frequently in that Copperville column." He stared.

Carolyn forced a smile, clutching her wine glass. "You are the kind of man to attract attention and speculation."

He laughed. "I am flattered that you think so." His gaze slid over her face.

Carolyn forgot to breathe. She was not imagining the smoke in his eyes. His thoughts were as illicit as hers. He knew. But why did he not say something? Surely he did not, also, like boys!

"I have enjoyed Copperville for the most part. In spite of his naïveté. Until recently, that is. And you?" Sverayov asked.

She was frozen. "You think him naïve?" She was not going to answer that damning question.

"Don't you? Or perhaps you agree with his fervent idealism. After all, you must be of the same age." He smiled.

"I have no idea if we are the same age. Why is he naïve?"

"He wishes to reform society, does he not?"

"He appears intent upon exposing its flaws and excesses," Carolyn said carefully.

"But that implies that society could be golden, without flaws, without excess. He wishes to reform society, in favor of the working man."

She inhaled. "And what is so very wrong with that?"

"Do you approve of the anarchy we have seen in the past two decades in France? Do you approve of mobs stabbing peers to death—merely because they do not have calluses on their hands? Of noble children being torn apart only because of their blue blood?'' He stared.

''Of course not. But the anarchy that occurred in France was the result of a revolution—not of reform.''

''It began as reform.''

''So you defend the status quo. Tell me, Sverayov, how many serfs are tied to your lands?'' She also stared.

''Ahh, I was wondering when the attack upon society would turn personal—against myself.'' He lifted his glass and saluted her. ''Hundreds are bonded to my lands. Thousands.''

''Are they starving? Do they die at the age of twenty-five?'' Carolyn could not help herself. She had to know.

''My people are well fed, their homes have solid roofs and floors, and I would hazard to say that the average life expectancy is about fifty years of age.'' His eyes had become distinctly cool.

''I apologize,'' Carolyn said, ''for being so rude to you when I invited you to the races today as my guest.''

''But you still despise the institutions of my country— when you have never even been there.''

She inhaled. ''I despise the fact that your class attends balls in the midst of winter, while the serfs freeze in their wretched huts. I also despise the fact that here the peerage carries on with complete indifference to the suffering of commoners. Do you know that most of these people couldn't care less about the war? Couldn't care less if it never ends?''

''That is because most of the upper class here in Britain are wealthy enough not to feel the war's effects. You expect too much from mankind, my friend.''

''Without expectation, there cannot be achievement. Without dreams, there is no hope.''

Sverayov laughed softly. ''You are a hopeless romantic, Charles.''

''And proud of it.''

''I imagine Copperville feels exactly the same way.'' Their gazes met.

She hesitated. "Why don't you just come out and say what is on your mind?"

Sverayov slowly smiled at her. "And what," he said, "do you think it is that I wish to say?"

Carolyn tensed. A confession was on the tip of her tongue. But at that moment the door to their dining room opened, and two servants entered carrying platters of food, followed by the balding proprietor. Sverayov met her regard, with a bigger grin.

"Ahh, Your Highness, we have a feast here fit for a king—or should I say a prince?" The innkeeper beamed as the platters were set down and uncovered. He reached for the wine bottle, emptying it into Sverayov's glass. Carolyn looked at it, then at the remaining bottle, and thought, one down, one to go. She glanced up, caught Sverayov staring with his intense eyes, and felt her heart turn over.

"Oh, dear," Carolyn said, and she heard herself giggle. In the process of standing up, she had somehow lost her balance and crashed her hip into the table.

Sverayov was at her side, smiling benevolently down at her, his eyes gleaming. His arm locked itself firmly around her waist. "Disguised, Charles?" he purred.

Carolyn blinked up at his handsome face. "I have somehow had too much to drink." She was pleased, though, because her words did not sound slurred.

He continued to hold her upright—and pressed tightly against his strong, warm side. "You have only drunk the equivalent of a bottle of wine, and of course, the two glasses of port you consumed afterward." He smiled, like a well-fed lion. Or one about to become well fed, Carolyn managed to think.

"I am afraid it all went right to my head," Carolyn apologized.

"You have the constitution of a woman," he remarked, steering her to the door. One tawny brow lifted. "No slur intended."

Carolyn gazed up at him, enjoying the sight of every

feature of his spectacular face, thinking, but I am a woman. But no, that was not right, he was calling her Charles. Had she told him she was Brighton? Copperville? Blast, but she could not remember.

"Having trouble talking?" he asked, guiding her through the public rooms.

"O' course not." She was indignant. "I was just thinking. Actually, I was trying to remember something."

"May I be of service?" he drawled, pausing on the threshold of the front room of the inn.

"You do have a way with words, Sve-Sve-Sverayov," she said. His name came out scrambled on her tongue.

"My close friends," he said softly, watching her closely, "call me Niki."

She liked the way he rolled the common nickname off his golden tongue, making it sound exotic and frankly sexual. "Niki," she tried. "I see your coach."

"It is rather hard to miss," he intoned as the six blacks were driven around to the front of the inn. "Shall we?" His grip tightened on her waist.

Carolyn leaned into him with a sigh. How she liked his body. How she wished to touch him as boldly as that beautiful prostitute had. She tried to remember the raven-haired woman's name.

"Charles?" Sverayov's low tone intruded on her thoughts.

"Victoria," she said, pleased that she had remembered after all.

His eyes widened. "Do you wish to pay another visit to her? Tonight? Are you, perhaps, feeling randy, my fine young friend?"

She stiffened because his words were so very explicit, the kind of comment neither she nor any woman would ever be the recipient of. But, by God, even though she was a woman, she was feeling extremely passionate. "I . . ." She paused. Too well, she recalled Sverayov's passionate kiss.

He smiled, his eyes trained upon her face. "Your spectacles," he said softly, "are steaming. Are you, perhaps, warm?" He removed them before she could protest.

"Yes." In fact, she was spectacularly hot, and the front room must be what the tropics, which she had only read about, were like.

He pocketed her spectacles and propelled her through the front door. "I don't think you need these," he said. "Are we paying the lovely Victoria a visit? Perhaps you are brave enough to make love for the first time?"

Carolyn felt numb. He could not mean what it felt like he meant, what it sounded like he meant. He knew, did he not, the truth? But she did feel brave enough to make love for the first time—with him. She closed her eyes, knowing she was far more inebriated than she had thought—or than she had ever been in her life. She managed to recall that he had a wife. A very beautiful wife. A wife from whom he was estranged.

"Are you ill? Or dismayed?" he whispered in her ear.

"Dismayed," she heard herself say.

She thought she felt his mouth touch her ear as he spoke again. "Do not be dismayed by desire. It is natural and healthy . . . Charles."

She opened her eyes and saw his face close to hers. His mouth inches from hers. "I don't . . ." She hesitated, afraid of what she could not refrain from saying. Her words came forth in a rush. "I don't want to make love to Victoria."

"I know you don't." Their gazes locked.

Carolyn felt the heat seething between them, smoldering inside of her. All she could think was, Oh, God.

He broke the moment by moving her forward and handing her up into the coach, climbing in behind her. The footman outside closed the door. How resounding and final it seemed. Carolyn somehow found herself seated. The interior of the coach seemed very small. Sverayov filled up that interior space as he stood between the two seats, staring down at her, his gaze brilliant. Carolyn found it difficult to breathe.

And then he sat, but not across from her. His big body

settled onto the velvet squabs beside her. Carolyn faced him, unmoving. Her heart raced.

"And I do not want to make love to Victoria, either," he said, low and husky. "I never have."

Carolyn could not believe what was happening. All thoughts slammed to a halt inside of her head.

His big hand cupped her chin. "I have become extremely fond of you—in a very short period of time," he said in his liquid tone.

Carolyn opened her mouth, closed it. She could not think of what to say, much less what to do. "Niki," she finally whispered.

"How do you feel about me?" he asked.

"I . . ." She swallowed. "I am also very fond of you." She wet her lips.

His eyes turned fierce. And his fingers tightened briefly on her chin. Before Carolyn could protest, his mouth claimed hers. Hard and hot and hungry.

⊷ SEVENTEEN ⊷

CAROLYN forgot everything, including who she was. Sverayov's mouth was impossibly demanding—and impossible to get enough of. She clung to his broad shoulders as he pressed her down into the seat. He urged her lips to open and suddenly their tongues met.

Carolyn thought, This is heaven. He is heaven. And her hands slid over his broad shoulders, down his muscular back. Niki, she thought.

His mouth paused against hers. His hand was anchored in her curls. His breathing was somewhat labored against her ear. "I am so very tempted," he said.

She tried to think. Her wits were fuzzy, scattered. Her body was feverish, and nothing had ever felt this right. He was tempted—and so was she. Agonizingly so. But he was married. Married, a Russian and a prince. While she was mere Carolyn Browne. Which he knew, of course. She turned her face so she could blink at him.

His golden eyes were brilliant—yet somehow calm, too. "You have had too much to drink, Charles," he said.

She started. "But . . ."

His mouth crooked into a smile, at odds with the blazing light of his golden eyes. "Do you wish to confess?" he asked, his tone strangely tender. One of his strong arms slipped beneath her, forming a pillow for her neck.

"I . . ." Carolyn hesitated.

"Charles?" he purred, his eyes dancing. "Your goatee is askew."

She began to smile at him, her heart impossibly warm, bursting with the power of her emotions. And in that moment, as intoxicated as she was, she felt it—*le coup de foudre*. The bolt of lightning. Cupid's arrow. She stared into his golden eyes, at his stunning face, immersed in his powerful, sensual aura, and her heart flipped wildly. Oh, dear God, I am in love, she thought inanely, aghast.

His hand stroked through her blond curls. "Have you seen a ghost?"

She shook her head slightly, trying to put aside her stunning realization for the moment. "How long have you known?"

"How long have I known what?" he asked with too much innocence.

"How long have you known the truth about me?" she asked huskily.

He chuckled. "From the first." Gently, he removed the goatee.

"From the first?" she echoed. "Surely not—surely you are exaggerating!"

He was smiling. "Carolyn, you are every inch a woman. That absurd disguise was just that—absurd. I understood you were a woman when you were spying outside of my house."

Because of Copperville. She swallowed. "Oh." And then she struggled to sit up. "You knew I was a woman when we went to the brothel?" she asked incredulously.

He also sat up. And he had the grace to flush. But he did not look away from her, to the contrary, he held her gaze. "I did. I thought you would turn tail and flee long before anything of consequence happened."

"And . . . I almost did."

He stared. "Fortunately, I came to my senses." Silence fell. Hot, heavy, knifelike.

She wet her lips. What would he have done if she had stayed? Her gaze fell to his arrogant, sensual mouth. She gripped the velvet seat, clawing it, and wished she had not drunk so much wine. "But when did you know that Brighton was Carolyn?"

His mouth curled. "Immediately." And then his smile faded.

Carolyn did not speak.

He hesitated, reached out, lifted her chin. But made no move to kiss her.

"What else do you know?" she whispered, trembling, barely able to think.

He leaned toward her. "What else is it that you wish for me to say?" he asked, low, his mouth very close to hers.

"Do not play any more games," she said, inhaling. His mouth brushed hers. His eyes were fire.

His smile was brief. "Does this seem like a game?" His lips feathered hers again.

Against them, her heart expanding impossibly, she said, "No." Love was not a game. Oh, God. She was doomed.

"I did not think so," he murmured, and he kissed her again, openmouthed, at once firm and possessive, sensual and tender.

Carolyn grasped his shoulders, straining for him. He wrapped her in his arms and pressed her against the seat. The kiss went on and on, increasing in its fervor.

"Carolyn."

She met his eyes, hearing the command in his tone, and with it, the question. "Don't."

His jaw flexed. "Don't what?"

"Don't ask me to make such a monumental decision—when I am as drunk as any soused lout."

His temples throbbed visibly.

"Do you read minds—as well as write columns?"

She shook her head. But what he wanted—what she wanted—was obvious. Just as the impossibility of a liaison was also obvious.

"I am taking you home," he said flatly.

She nodded, eyes wide and glued to his face, beginning to ache now, in her heart, only then realizing that the carriage was not even moving. He rapped on the ceiling, barking out an order to go to Browne's Books in London. And then he faced her, his expression very grim. "We shall talk in the morning," he said carefully.

Carolyn did not reply. She watched him as he carefully moved from her seat to the one opposite. She remained silent, aware of her pounding pulse, her heated loins, and worse, all the mixed-up, confused emotions in her heart. The joy had given way to wretched misery. Just as sanity had given over to madness. She kept thinking about Marie-Elena now.

"Go to sleep," he said, his eyes hard, his tone soft. "Everything will be all right."

His tone had a hypnotic effect when combined with all the red wine and port she had thus far consumed. And closing her eyes in the hope that she might sleep for the duration of the trip back to town was a relief. Carolyn obeyed, but not before doubting the veracity of his words. It was not going to be all right. How could it be?

Nicholas had knocked, somewhat unsuccessfully, upon the door of the bookshop. The maneuver was awkward because he held the sleeping Carolyn in his arms. There was no response.

But he could see a light flickering at the far end of the shop, perhaps from another room. "Damnation," he said, a growl, and he managed to turn the knob and push open the door, vaguely surprised that it was not bolted at this time of night.

But he had hardly stepped inside when he heard raised voices, both male, and realized that George was not alone. He used his hip to push the door closed. Why was George Browne so upset—and whom could he be entertaining at this hour?

The stairs were just ahead. Nicholas knew Carolyn's chamber was on the upper floor. Instead, he strode into the shop, rather soundlessly. Carolyn did not stir. He was very aware of her cheek resting against his shoulder, her curls feathering his face.

"But I am pleased with you, Browne, very pleased. Your next destination is Calais."

Nicholas stiffened.

"I have had enough," George cried, in a pleading tone. "I cannot sleep at night anymore, for fear of the authorities discovering my deceptions!"

"You should have thought of that eight years ago," a cool yet quite familiar voice returned. "Surely you do not think to ask for more money?"

"Carolyn will become suspicious. I am traveling every month now." There was a pause. "I do not wish to hang! Please, my lord, I have had enough."

"You are in far too deeply, my friend, to get out now. I cannot allow it—you are too useful. You make sure this *manuscript* is delivered to your contact in Calais. It is urgent, my friend. Very urgent."

Nicholas turned and strode back out of the shop. He grappled with the doorknob, Carolyn lolling in his arms, cursing inwardly. His pulse was racing with alarming speed. Good God. Browne was a courier—and if he had understood correctly, he was a traitor to his own country.

And Nicholas was also quite sure he knew the identity of the nobleman Browne had been closeted with.

Once outside, he shifted Carolyn to a more comfortable position, and banged very loudly on the door, shouting Browne's name. But he was thinking that George Browne was a fool. Did the man wish to hang? And what if his daughter ever found out the truth?

"My God!" George cried, swinging the door open. "Is she ill?"

Nicholas entered the bookstore, barely recovering from what he had just discovered. "She is not ill," he answered George, carrying his burden toward the stairs. "She is drunk." He was very angry.

"Drunk!" George raced after him. "What in bloody hell have you done to her?"

Nicholas started up the stairs and did not answer until he stood on the small landing between two open doors. "Dear

Browne," he said coolly, "I have done nothing but accept her invitation. I did not force her to imbibe."

George was red-faced. "If you have touched her . . ." he cried, trailing off.

Nicholas smiled coldly at him. Then he turned and shouldered open the door that let onto a small chamber with a pretty floral bedspread and equally feminine curtains. He deposited Carolyn carefully on her bed. Her eyelids did not even flicker. He watched her roll over and curl up. And an oddly tender sensation warmed his heart. And then he frowned. She would be devastated if she ever learned the truth about her father.

He could not shake his thoughts. Turning, he faced George. "And what will you do," he said coldly, "if I have touched your daughter? Shall we duel at dawn?"

George became pale. He was silent, anxiety written all over his face.

Nicholas stalked from the room, and when he and George stood once more upon the landing, he closed her bedchamber door. He smiled coolly at her father. "Do you approve of your daughter's exploits, my friend?"

George inhaled. "I do not know what you are talking about."

"Really?"

"Carolyn is strong-willed, Excellency. What have you done to her?" George clenched his fists.

"I repeat—nothing."

"I want you to stay away . from her," George said, breathing harshly.

"Or what?" Nicholas queried innocently. "Perhaps you should have thought to be less approving of your daughter's iron will, my friend, that and her ever-ready quill."

"What does that mean?" George cried. Then he accused, "You wrote that last column, did you not? That was your idea of revenge—as is this, this, seduction?"

"If you choose to think I would seduce a young woman as an act of revenge for the crime of satire, then I will hardly try to dissuade you." Nicholas smiled unpleasantly at him again and started down the stairs. When he was at the front door he turned, and smiled at George, who remained on the landing. "Or are you afraid she is my target for other reasons? Good night, my friend." He smiled again. "Or should I say *bonne nuit*?"

"You cannot go."

Carolyn held an invitation to tea from Sverayov in her hand. She had only just awoken. Behind her, on the stove, a kettle was beginning to boil. "You opened my invitation?" she asked, aghast.

He flushed. "He brought you home last night. You were sleeping off the effects of too much wine!" he accused.

Carolyn also flushed. She had definitely imbibed far too much last night, but this morning, she could recall most of the evening with utter clarity—including her stunning realization that she was far more than attracted to Sverayov. "I did have too much to drink. For that, I apologize."

George stared, incredulous. "Is that what you have to say for yourself? That you are sorry for becoming soused? When that rake carried you in here in his arms?"

"He did?" She could not help but enjoy the idea.

"Yes, he did." George walked past her to remove the kettle from the fire, for it was singing. "Enough. Sverayov is a rake—you know that as well as I do, for God's sake. You yourself have been reporting his behavior in your columns. Do you want to be used and then tossed aside like cold, leftover meat?"

"That was a horrible thing to say," Carolyn said tersely.

"Sometimes the truth is horrible."

Carolyn stared. She knew that George was right. Which was why she felt so sick inside her heart, as if sensing impending doom. On the other hand, Sverayov had not had a normal relationship with his wife in years. That left certain possibilities open—although Carolyn knew she must not consider them. She decided that all the wine had befuddled her usually sharp mind.

"Tell me that you do not agree with me," George said.

Carolyn did sigh. "I know you are right. But Sverayov is very intelligent—he is extremely good company. I have enjoyed all of our outings."

George stared at her as if she had grown two heads. "Who are you fooling?" he asked very sharply.

Carolyn faced him, hands on her hips. "Father, I am not quite up to this conversation today. But since when have you told me what I could and could not do? Whom I could and could not see? You have always trusted my judgment implicitly."

George stared unhappily. "I do not want you getting hurt," he said finally.

Carolyn rubbed her temples. "I am an adult. I have the right to make my own choices, and my own mistakes."

"You are going to see him again?" He was aghast.

Carolyn recalled their devastating kiss. She also remembered his parting words to her—that they would discuss everything the next day. "We actually have some business to conclude," she said, a half lie.

"I beg you, Carolyn, stay away from Sverayov."

Carolyn looked into her father's anxious eyes. "What is it that you're not telling me?" she asked.

George returned her gaze, hesitating. "Carolyn, he said something about Copperville. I think he intends to seduce you in revenge for your columns."

She somehow smiled. But her pulse raced. "That is absurd," she said, her smile plastered in place. But God, it made perfect sense. Why else would he wish to dally with her? When he could have the most beautiful, sophisticated women in the world? Carolyn did not want to believe it. But now she did not know what to believe.

"So you will refuse his invitation?" George asked.

Carolyn lied. "Yes." And she turned away, because now she had to go.

Carolyn was ushered into the foyer. A butler materialized. "Madame," he said, indicating that he wished Carolyn to follow him.

Carolyn trailed after him. She had been preoccupied all day, not merely with her latest encounter with Sverayov, but now, with her father's accusations as well. In all likelihood George was right, which meant that Sverayov was not even basely attracted to her. It was the perfect explanation for his interest in her. Yet she kept recalling the heat in his eyes, the passion in his kiss, and his strangely gentle tenderness.

"Madame." The butler gestured for her to go through a pair of wide-open doors.

Carolyn saw him at the exact same moment that he saw her. Their gazes met and locked. He was not smiling. Her heart, briefly, lost its momentum. And then it resumed its normal pace.

But she could not smile either as she entered the salon, that very same room where she had first met his daughter. He stared, coming forward. Katya was seated on the sofa beside her uncle Alexi. The Persian kitten was between them, enjoying a vast amount of petting. His purring was the only sound in the room.

Carolyn wished, desperately now, that she were a better actress, one who could hide all her feelings. Surely her current confusion and apprehension were written all over her face. "Your Excellency," she said huskily. And, to make matters worse, he looked so good.

He bowed, taking her hand, for one moment holding it tightly. Then he lifted it to his lips. "Thank you for joining us, Miss Browne." He did not smile. But his eyes were hardly cold, and Carolyn was almost certain that he was remembering their last encounter, too. He turned. "Katya."

The child came forward, curtsying. "Thank you for coming, Miss Browne." She echoed her father exactly.

Carolyn smiled down at her, forgetting all about her father. She stooped slightly. "Did I not say that you could call me Carolyn, as all my friends do? And how is that clever kitten today? Have you tried my suggestions?"

Katya nodded. "He eats in my room. Taichili doesn't

like it at all. But yesterday he got out and I thought he was lost again. But he came back.'' She smiled.

Carolyn also smiled. ''He also came back because he loves you and is learning that you are his mistress,'' she said.

Katya pursed her lips as she thought about that, and finally, she nodded.

Carolyn looked up to find Alexi standing beside Sverayov, and both men were staring at her. Her smile faded. Had she been transformed into an insect that lay beneath a microscope? Their gazes made her feel as if she were being dissected and thoroughly studied.

Alexi came forward with an exaggerated bow, smiling, a twinkle in his eye. ''Miss Browne, I am terribly pleased to see you again. I think you are mending my broken heart.''

Carolyn almost laughed. ''Thank you,'' Carolyn said. ''It is a pleasure to see you, too. I did not know that you have a broken heart—I am so sorry.''

Alexi's grin widened. ''Not as sorry as I.'' He briefly slid his arm around her. ''Come, sit next to me, and give me advice on the fairer sex. It seems I never learn and am destined to repeat my past mistakes again and yet again.''

Carolyn had to laugh. ''I wish I could help,'' she said, aware that Sverayov appeared annoyed with his brother's bold flirting, ''but I am not very educated when it comes to romance.''

''No? Why ever not?'' Alexi asked, offering Carolyn a seat. As he did so, he gave his brother a sidelong glance.

She accepted. Katya came with the Persian to take a chair in the grouping, her eyes upon Carolyn. Sverayov also wandered over, but he did not sit. ''I fear it never entered my head to study the subject, not when there is so much else to concentrate on.''

''Spoken like a true bluestocking,'' Alexi said pleasantly. ''Niki tells me you are extremely intelligent and fabulously well read. I am impressed.''

Carolyn pinkened, wondering if Sverayov really discussed her with his brother, and in such glowing terms. "I enjoy reading. How could I not? Being the daughter of a man who owns a bookshop?"

"Your father owns a bookshop?" Katya asked suddenly.

Both brothers turned to stare at her as if such a statement were extremely out of place. Carolyn looked from Nicholas to Alexi and realized they were supremely surprised. She reached forward and patted the girl's hand. "Yes, he does. And I help him manage the shop. It is one of my favorite places in the world. Do you like to read?"

Katya nodded, wide-eyed.

"Katya is an excellent reader," Nicholas said, moving around her chair. He still did not sit, towering over everyone present.

"Katya, what is your favorite story?" Carolyn asked.

She hesitated. "The history of Peter the Great."

Carolyn's eyes went wide. "Dear, I meant, what is your favorite tale? Or do you so adore history that you would rather read about Peter the Great than *La Belle au Bois Dormant*?"

Katya was silent. "I don't know," she finally said.

Carolyn looked up at Nicholas, understanding in that instant that Katya had never been exposed to fairy tales. "Can I bring her some storybooks? There are a few very nice ones for children."

"Of course," he said automatically.

"Taichili won't like this." Alexi chuckled.

Carolyn turned to look at him. "Why not?" Her dislike for Taichili had grown.

"I do believe Katya's program is rather rigid."

"There is nothing wrong with a structured education, and I believe everyone, including children, should read from a wide range of subject matter. But fiction is particularly suitable for a child. I do not have to be a wizard to know that. Children have great imaginations, far greater than ours. It is a blessing, and should be cultivated and encouraged—not stifled and repressed."

Nicholas and his brother stared at her as if she had indeed

become an insect, but with a good dozen legs and at least two heads.

Carolyn blushed. "I am sorry to be so fervent. I cannot help myself," she said. "I do apologize. But it is unfair that girls—and women—are not allowed to fully cultivate their minds."

Sverayov did not speak. After a silent moment, Alexi smiled at her. "My brother's tongue is, apparently, tied. How unusual. Do not apologize. How refreshing you are—in this household, my dear."

"Yes." A silky female voice sounded, making them all look toward the threshold of the salon. "How very refreshing." Marie-Elena whirled into the room, her dark hair swirling about very bare shoulders. She wore a pale pink gown that was low-cut and short-sleeved. A strand of sapphires circled her neck. She was smiling, and far too widely. She halted in front of the group, directing her smile at Carolyn. "What a quaint concept. Cultivating one's mind—as one would a garden."

Carolyn found herself standing. She made no reply, but fought hard to remain composed, confronted again by Sverayov's wife. Many volatile emotions swept over her, including, Carolyn thought, dismayed, actual jealousy. And she also felt guilty. Last night, she had been in her husband's arms when she should have known better. But it was too late for regrets.

Marie-Elena turned. "Niki, darling." She kissed his cheek, ignoring Alexi, clinging to Sverayov as if she were a besotted newlywed. Then she smiled at her daughter. "Katya, baby, come give Maman a kiss."

Carolyn's pulse was swift. She watched Katya obey. Like a little soldier, she quickly got up, allowing the kitten to race away, and walked over to Marie-Elena, who bent. Katya pressed a kiss to her mother's cheek. Before she could return to her chair, Marie-Elena put her hand on the child's shoulder, forestalling her. She turned her gypsy-black gaze and wide smile on Carolyn.

"I did not know that you were entertaining . . . Niki," Marie-Elena said very sweetly.

Sverayov stepped forward, his expression impossible to read. "Miss Carolyn Browne, may I introduce my wife." He stared coldly at Marie-Elena. "You have finished your shopping early, have you not? Or were you lunching in town?"

"A little bit of both." Marie-Elena was gay. She laughed. "And how lucky I am to be home in time for tea." She faced Carolyn. "I believe we have already made one another's acquaintance, have we not, Miss Browne? Hmm, let me see, your father is a bookseller?" Her tone was decidedly innocent, as was her expression.

Carolyn kept a firm grip on her temper. "Your memory serves you well, Princess. My father's bookshop is one of the finest in London, indeed, in the world."

"How proud you are," Marie-Elena said. "And are you also an expert on children and their education? Are you a schoolmistress, perhaps? Or a tutor?"

Carolyn paused. "I do not consider myself an expert on any topic, my lady. And no, I am neither a schoolmistress nor a tutor."

"Oh. That is odd. For I could not help hearing your fervent opinions on the subject of what children should read. I had assumed you were well informed on the subject." She smiled widely.

Carolyn could not summon a smile in return. "I have passionate opinions about many subjects, especially the subjects of reading and education. And I am well informed on those many topics which I study—especially the subject of the education of our gender. Princess."

Sverayov stepped between them. "Are you intending to join us for tea, madame?" he asked his wife.

"However could I refuse such a gracious invitation?" She stroked Katya's hair. "Come, baby, sit with Maman." And she took a seat on the sofa, Katya beside her.

The tea was already ruined for Carolyn. Her nerves felt stretched tight. Carolyn wished she could smile, and as she took a seat, she met Alexi's dark eyes. His gaze was genuinely sympathetic, and he gave her an encouraging smile which made Carolyn feel only slightly better.

Sverayov turned and it was as if he had pulled a bell cord, for servants materialized, wheeling in a tea cart which also contained numerous pastries and cakes. He took a seat facing his daughter and his wife—diagonally across from Carolyn.

Marie-Elena kept one arm around Katya, who had not said a word since her mother entered the room. "Ah, now I recall. I saw you at the opera the other night, Miss Browne."

"Yes, you did."

Marie-Elena studied Carolyn, and although her expression remained fixedly pleasant, Carolyn was reduced to feeling very young, impossibly thin and unattractive, and very gauche. "I think I recognized that pleasant young man you were with. Hmmm—I just cannot recall his name."

Carolyn's reply was automatic. "Anthony Davison, my lady."

Marie-Elena's eyes widened. "No relation to Lord Stuart Davison—that so very prominent member of Castlereagh's government?"

"He is his youngest son," Carolyn said. She shot a glance at Sverayov, who sat with one leg crossed, looking rather annoyed now.

"You are doing very well for yourself, Miss Browne," Marie-Elena remarked. "My, what a catch for yourself—should you succeed."

"We are friends," Carolyn returned somewhat defensively. "And I am not interested in catching anyone."

"Every woman wants to snare a rich, handsome husband," Marie-Elena laughed.

Carolyn decided not to respond, and she merely forced a smile. Inwardly she seethed. It was impossible to feel very guilty now about her behavior of the night before.

"And since when have you become so knowledgeable

about the British government?'' Sverayov drawled, the question directed at his wife.

Marie-Elena had been stroking Katya's hair. Now she smiled at her husband—a smile brilliant enough to melt the coldest of male hearts. ''Darling, you are here on a very important mission. Surely it is my responsibility to understand the situation—and to be as helpful as I can.'' Her smile faded and her gaze held his, wide, dark, earnest. ''You know how much I want to help, Niki.''

Carolyn felt ill. Sverayov had said that he and his wife were estranged. But it did not seem that way, and was certainly not that way for Marie-Elena. Had he lied?

Sverayov's smile flashed, without mirth. ''Helpful. What an unusual concept.''

Marie-Elena's hand fell to her side. And for a moment, silence fell between the pair as they stared at one another. Suddenly Marie-Elena faced Carolyn.

''Recently, I lost a child,'' she said, her tone high.

Carolyn hardly knew what to make of such a comment. ''I am sorry.''

Marie-Elena nodded. ''I almost died. Now, having recovered, I do not feel like I am the same woman. There is so much that I have done that I regret.''

Why was she telling Carolyn this? ''I am sure it was an overwhelming experience.'' How she wished to leave. She stole a glance at Sverayov, and saw that he was extremely annoyed now. But it was clear to Carolyn that Marie-Elena was having regrets about her relationship with her husband. Surely she—or any woman—would regret breaking it off with a man like Sverayov.

Alexi stretched out his legs. ''How easy it is to have regrets—and how convenient. How difficult, though, it is to make amends.'' He smiled at the assembly.

Marie-Elena stared at him, her eyes cold, not saying a word.

Sverayov stood, his temper obvious, but he spoke calmly enough. ''Katya, why do you not choose a piece of pastry for yourself and pass the platter to Miss Browne?'' He smiled at his daughter, then met Carolyn's gaze, his smile vanishing.

Her heart beat hard. She was just now, finally, realizing how impossible the situation was. Marie-Elena regretted the past, was impossibly beautiful, and would surely win back Sverayov's heart. As she should. She was, after all, both his wife and the mother of his child.

While she, Carolyn, was an interloper, and if events continued as they had thus far developed, she would also become the other woman—an intolerable circumstance. Carolyn looked down at her hands, clasped in her lap. Tears burned her eyes.

But it was a good thing that she had come to tea. To see him and his family. Finally she had been confronted with the truth of his life.

Alexi stood and bowed at Carolyn. "I am afraid I cannot linger, as I have other engagements. As always, Miss Browne, it is a great pleasure to be in your company." His smile was wide, but it reached his eyes, and Carolyn knew she had somehow made a new friend. He then stooped low and kissed Katya. "Later, *dushka,*" he said.

She nodded, her expression remaining somber.

Ignoring Marie-Elena, he strode from the room.

Marie-Elena's eyes sparked with anger, but her tone was languid. "He is such a boor." Then she turned to face Carolyn. "So you decided to call upon my husband?" She smiled.

"Actually," Sverayov said, "I invited her to tea."

"How kind of you," Marie-Elena said. She faced Carolyn. "How atwitter you must be, to have the attention of a man like my husband."

Carolyn could not smile. "I do not twitter. Especially over men. I am an enlightened woman." How she wished to brush any obvious moisture from her eyes.

Marie-Elena's eyes widened. "Oh, I do beg your pardon."

"Miss Browne's passions are reserved solely for her books and the many causes she espouses," Sverayov interjected in a tone of authority. But there was also an oddly gentle pitch to his voice.

Carolyn started, grateful for such high praise at that moment. He smiled faintly at her.

Marie-Elena looked from one to the other. "So she is an expert on children and books, and you are an expert on her?" she asked, her tone high and fixedly sweet.

"I doubt any man could be an expert on the subject of Miss Browne."

Carolyn flushed with pleasure, looking away.

Marie-Elena's black brows lifted. "Well, well, my husband so rarely dispenses praise, Miss Browne. You have accomplished an impossible feat in winning his admiration."

"Madame, you may pour," Sverayov said flatly.

Marie-Elena smiled quickly at him and began to pour the tea into fine, gilt-rimmed porcelain cups. Her slim, elegant hands were steady. She wore a huge yellow diamond on her left hand. "So Niki invited you to tea. I suppose it was to discuss books?" She offered Carolyn a cup.

"I invited Miss Browne to take tea with myself and Katya because Katya enjoys Miss Browne's company," Sverayov said, smiling at his daughter.

Her brows shot up. "And how is that? When did you meet my daughter? I do not understand."

"They met the other day." Sverayov's gaze softened as it settled on Katya again—before he looked directly at Carolyn. "Miss Browne helped us with the cat."

And in that moment, Carolyn glimpsed Marie-Elena staring at Sverayov with hostile eyes. An instant later, her angelic mask was back in place. It had happened so quickly that Carolyn wondered if she had imagined it. Her temples throbbed now. How she wanted to escape the room, the house, the family. She would seize the first acceptable moment. Carolyn intended to go home and cry. How foolish she had been.

"She helped with the cat," Marie-Elena repeated. "How wonderful. How kind." She faced her daughter, smiling brightly. "Katya, darling, do you know that you have yet to show me your new cat?"

Katya's gaze was fastened on her mother. "You did not ask to see him," she said in a low, cautious voice.

"I am asking now." Marie-Elena was gay. "We shall go see your cat directly after tea. Perhaps we shall go out together and buy him a pretty collar." She turned suddenly to Carolyn. "You are not enjoying your tea. Is something amiss?"

This was the opportunity she had been hoping for. "My head aches," Carolyn said. "I am sorry to be rude, but I do think I must go." She stood, avoiding Sverayov's eyes. One quick glimpse told her they were searching.

Sverayov stepped forward. "I wish to speak privately with you, before you go."

Carolyn froze, her gaze lifting to his. She was in disbelief. How could he suggest a private meeting now? In front of his wife? But he had said yesterday that they would discuss what had happened. She trembled, truly wanting to flee. "Perhaps we can discuss whatever it is you wish at a later date?"

"I think not." He was firm.

Marie-Elena also stood and smiled at Carolyn. "I do hope we have the pleasure again."

Carolyn could only nod. "Do hug to Alexander for me," she whispered to Katya, "and I will drop those storybooks by."

Katya smiled. "Thank you, Miss Browne." She hesitated. "Perhaps, if Father allows it, you could come to tea again."

Never, Carolyn thought. "Perhaps," she said. Impulsively she bent and hugged the child hard, in spite of her mother, whom Carolyn could feel stiffening behind them.

"Let us go to the library," Sverayov said. He gestured for her to precede him, which Carolyn did. She could feel Marie-Elena's eyes burning on her back until they rounded the corner. Once inside the book-lined room, Sverayov closed the door. Carolyn walked over to the empty hearth and stared into it. She felt him come up behind her.

"Are you all right?" he asked.

She did not turn. "I am fine."

"You are not fine. You are upset. Please look at me, Carolyn."

She flinched at his use of her name. She turned. The intensity of his gaze took her breath away. "Yesterday . . . was a mistake."

He stared and said softly, "Was it?"

"Yes." She meant to be firm, but heard the quaver in her own tone.

His jaw tightened. "Perhaps it was a mistake. But not for the reason you are thinking."

She could not help herself. "So you do read minds?"

He smiled. "Perhaps I read yours."

Her smile faded. She stared. His golden gaze was mesmerizing. And it was there again, between them, inexorable, intolerable, a force that seemed determined to pull her toward him.

"You are upset," he said softly, "because Marie-Elena is a superb dramatist. You have been taken in by her theatrics."

Carolyn could hardly breathe. "She is your wife, the mother of your child, she has the face of an angel, and she loves you."

For one moment, he was silent. "I beg to differ with you. She loves no one but herself."

"I do not know why you are so set against her, but it is clear to me, an outsider, that she wishes to win back your heart." Carolyn studied him carefully.

But his expression remained serious, dangerously so. "She has never had my heart, so she could not possibly win it back." He suddenly tilted up her chin with two long fingers, then dropped his hand to his side. "A vain, empty-minded woman could never hold my affection," he said.

Carolyn inhaled. She must not, she knew, take his meaning literally—or any other way. She must not.

"You have read Adam Smith, the economist?"

Carolyn started. "Of course."

"You undervalue yourself," he said softly.

She could only stare. Her heartbeat had become thunderous.

His expression changed. "I did not ask you here to discuss my wife. I have something else on my mind."

Carolyn tensed. Surely he would not refer to their passion of the other day. It had been a mistake, and she was convinced of that. Of course, it was easy to be rational, but how to convince her heart to follow suit? She was heartsick.

"I have a business proposition for you."

Instantly Carolyn became alert. She had not expected this. "You wish to discuss business with me? I do not understand." What did business have to do with the passion they had shared?

"You will." He paced a few steps away from her, then back. "You are very good for Katya." He was blunt. "I wish to offer you a position here, in my household, as her companion and supervisor, if you will."

Carolyn gaped.

✿ EIGHTEEN ✿

SVERAYOV smiled at her. "You appear stunned," he said.

"I am stunned." Carolyn turned and walked toward a group of chairs, running her palm along the high wooden back of one. Her mind raced, spun. This was the very last thing she had expected. And why was she not refusing, immediately?

Katya's image was there in her mind, that of a lonely, needy child. Sverayov's child. Carolyn slowly turned to find him watching her with his brilliant eyes. "This is very complicated."

"It is only complicated if you allow it to be," he said flatly.

Their gazes met. Carolyn did not look away, but she was thinking, trying desperately to identify her many roiling emotions. She was compelled by this man. She liked him, admired him even, and found him insanely attractive. She was jealous of his wife. There, she had admitted it. Even though he was not for her, a mere bookseller's daughter, an exceedingly romantic part of her yearned for a Cinderella storybook ending. Carolyn rubbed her temples. This was not going to work. It would be an impossible situation. The two of them, together in the very same house.

He smiled, and the corners of his eyes crinkled in a very attractive manner. "Say yes," he said. "I shall pay you handsomely, you need only name your price."

Carolyn froze. She and her father desperately needed funds. They teetered on the brink of severe impoverishment. But that, of course, should not sway her. "Excellency," she said slowly, "I love working with my father in the store. I love books." She wanted to confront him directly—and ask him, what about last night? And tomorrow and the day after that? What about us?

"I know. You are perfect for her, Carolyn."

She tensed. The way her name rolled off his tongue was enough to make her recall every moment of passion shared between them. She suspected he was now attempting to seduce her to his cause. "What about your wife?"

He made a dismissive gesture. "My wife does not run this household. I do not think I have been clear. My wife is returning home in another week or so, as soon as the physician says she is rested enough to travel. My wife will reside at Tver—indefinitely. Katya will remain here with me, but once my job in England is done, she will return to St. Petersburg. I, of course, will resume my command in the First Army."

Carolyn blinked. She was trying, desperately, to understand what was happening. "Tver is your country home," she said cautiously. "Why is Katya not going there with her mother?"

His regard remained steady, but enigmatic. "I have personal reasons. But I shall try to elaborate. Marie-Elena does not wish to go to Tver. I am . . . insisting."

Carolyn's eyes widened. She could read between the lines. He was forcing his wife to go to the country—to remain there. It was not unheard of. Unwanted wives were often shunted aside in such a fashion. But what, exactly, did this mean?

And although Carolyn did not like Marie-Elena, she could not help but be disturbed by Sverayov's arrogant, high-handed, dictatorial behavior. No woman should be sent away as if she were a mere unfeeling object.

Carolyn's mind raced. In another week or so, Marie-Elena was leaving—for Tver. He and Katya would stay in

London, until the treaty was signed, or the peace effort given up. If she dared accept his offer—which she must not—she would take up a place in his household now, and she would see him on a daily basis. Eventually she would go to St. Petersburg with Katya, while he rejoined his command.

Carolyn could not help being torn and dismayed, but she was also intrigued—and excited. She had never been abroad. The war had seen to that.

Carolyn tried to rein herself in, with some difficulty. She could not help being concerned about Marie-Elena's situation and her feelings. She wished she knew more, but did not dare intrude. And she was certain that she had nothing to do with his decision—she would never assign such importance to her place in his affairs. And she must not even contemplate the fact that his wife would shortly be leaving town. That was dangerous—and wrong.

She tore her gaze from his and walked across the large salon. She should not accept the post of companion to Katya. Even though the little girl desperately needed her, or someone like her. But she was so tempted. And was it because she genuinely liked Katya, and wanted to help her? Or because she was so damnably attracted to the girl's father? To the point of following him shamelessly back to his homeland?

"Katya needs you. You are bright and bold, well educated, opinionated, articulate. And most importantly, you are kind. Kind and caring. I saw how Katya reacted to you, both the other day and a few moments ago. Already she likes you very much," Sverayov said. "She especially needs you because her mother will be absent."

Carolyn chose her words with care. "Excellency, considering what happened in the park the other day, and last night in the carriage, do you think this would, truly, be a good idea?"

His easy expression vanished. His eyes were piercing. "Yes, I do. I have given this tremendous thought. My daughter needs someone exactly like you."

Carolyn sat down abruptly. "If I refuse, who will be in charge when you return to Russia?" That worried Carolyn.

"Taichili," he said.

Carolyn grimaced. But she was even more worried about residing in his home with him present.

"I see that you are anxious," he said. "Why do you not speak freely, Carolyn?"

"I do not think your wife would like it if I took up this position now."

"She will not like it, either now or if you start at a later date. But is that what is really on your mind?"

She flushed.

"And I do not think you are afraid of living in a foreign country," he said softly.

"No. I am not." Carolyn imagined herself in some palatial Russian home, a mansion built of stone, crowned by gold Byzantine onion domes, with gilded interior rooms, red and royal-blue runners on the floors, and a staff of hundreds. She thought the house would feel empty, for it would be just she and Katya residing there with the other servants. But she could imagine Sverayov's sudden arrival home—the flurry of the staff, the eagerness of his daughter, and the tension she herself would feel. He would appear on the threshold in his immaculate uniform, a greatcoat swinging about him, dripping snow. She closed her eyes.

What about accompanying his daughter now? They would see one another every day. No. This would never work.

"Do you doubt that I can comport myself correctly if I so choose?" He interrupted her thoughts.

She started and breathed, "Can you deny that there has been a certain illicit attraction between us?"

"I am not inviting you into my home to mistreat you, Carolyn," he said far too sharply. "I am not inviting you to be Katya's companion so that I can take advantage of you."

Foolishly, her heart and spirits sank.

"Nor do I regret anything that we have shared. But I

have received the feeling that you think I should. Why?''

She was incredulous. ''I can give you two very good reasons. Your wife—and your daughter.''

His eyes hardened. ''Did I not explain to you, once before, that Marie-Elena and I are estranged?'' His voice was cold. ''I do not like to repeat myself—and I like defending myself even less.''

Carolyn flinched.

''Have I suggested that you enter my home in order to become my mistress?'' He was angrier now. ''We are discussing your position as my daughter's companion—nothing more.''

Carolyn was shaken to the quick. She had never seen him in a temper before, and did not know what she had done to cause it. And she was also hurt. For she did understand one thing. If she took this post, there would not be any more moments shared between them—not of passion or anything else. He had just made that clear. And that, of course, was as it should be.

She was heartsick. For now she knew the extent of his feelings for her. It was minimal, or else they could not be so easily shut off and denied.

''You seem dismayed,'' he said harshly. ''Why?''

She shook her head. ''I need time to think this through.''

''I assumed that would be your answer.'' He swiftly strode to her, gripped her arms. ''Katya needs you, Carolyn. You are far too intelligent not to see that.''

She knew she must not accept. But he was right, that little child needed her. Oh, God. For even now, his palms cupping her elbows, her skirts brushing his boots, she was agonizingly aware of him in ways she did not want to be. ''I cannot,'' she whispered. For instinct told her where such entanglement would lead.

''Carolyn,'' he said. ''I suggest you accept the post here and now. You will have time, then, to decide if you will return to Russia with Katya.'' His gaze held hers. ''Which I urge you to do.''

She could not move. With her every instinct, she knew

that to become more enmeshed in his life was the biggest mistake she could ever make.

"If you wish, you could consider it a temporary position. Until you feel reassured about it," he said.

She met his golden eyes. Felt her heart race. And she heard herself say, her tone husky, "Very well. I accept. For the time being." There was no harm in that.

And slowly, he smiled.

Or was there?

Marie-Elena had changed her plans for the evening. She studied herself in the standing full-length mirror in her dressing room. She had never looked better and she was fully aware of it. She had always had a superb body, even while enceinte, but her recent encounter with death had taken another inch off her waist, accentuating the fullness of her bust and the pleasing curve of her hips. The pale ivory chiffon gown she wore floated over her body, outlining every curve. There was no possible way, she decided, that Nicholas could remain immune to the vision she had created for that evening.

Her pulse rioted and anger overcame her. Thank God she had eavesdropped on Nicholas's business proposition. And she had been right to suspect his interest in that skinny commoner. Just what had occurred thus far between her husband and the bookseller's daughter? Just what, exactly, had happened in the park? What had happened last night? And how dare he tell that plebeian outsider that he was exiling her to Tver!

Marie-Elena swept from the room and down the hall, fighting her rage and fear. It was unbelievable. Nicholas enamored of a peasant girl like that, when he had his choice of the most beautiful women in the world. When he could have her.

He hadn't touched her in five and a half years.

On the landing she paused, taking a deep breath, adjusting her décolletage, thinking about Carolyn Browne actually taking up a position in her house. She would not allow it. He could, of course, have his affairs as he chose, as he had done, these many years, but not with that overeducated, opinionated shrew. Oh, no. She just could not allow it—even though she told herself that Carolyn Browne could not possibly be any threat to her.

But she was grim. Niki's affairs were always very brief and very impersonal. In fact, he was usually bored by women, even in the company of those stunning enough to rival Marie-Elena, and once or twice Marie-Elena had seen him with a woman reputed to be his latest liaison, and still his ennui had been obvious. He had not seemed at all bored this afternoon while in Miss Browne's company, or that other evening at the opera.

She did not understand what, exactly, was happening, but it had to be stopped. And Carolyn Browne was not returning to Russia with them, by God!

Marie-Elena entered the salon. Nicholas and Katya were watching the kitten chasing a ball of yarn. Katya was smiling, and so was her father. "Hello," Marie-Elena said brightly.

Katya's smile disappeared, but her gaze fastened on her mother unblinkingly. Marie-Elena swept forward and put her arm around her daughter. "Did you show your father the cat's beautiful collar?" she asked, turning to Nicholas.

He recrossed his legs. He was sprawled now negligently on the sofa. But there was nothing negligent about his regard. Marie-Elena knew him well; he was not a man to miss a trick. Yet if he noticed how alluring she looked, he gave no sign of it. "Do you think a sapphire-studded collar appropriate for the cat of a child of six?" he asked.

"You have never questioned my spending before."

He turned his attention to Katya. "Shall we put Alexander away so we may eat?"

"Yes, Father." Katya slipped off the sofa and scooped up the kitten. She waited for permission to leave, which came when her father nodded. She hurried out of the salon.

"It is not your spending I question," he said flatly, once their daughter was gone. Nicholas stood, but before he could walk anywhere, Marie-Elena came up behind him. "I am sorry if I was too extravagant. Please, Niki, do not be mad. Katya and I had such a marvelous time shopping together!"

"Really?" One tawny brow lifted. "I hope that was the case." He started to move away again, but she caught his arm.

"How was your afternoon?" she purred.

He eyed her. "Since when do you care about my afternoons—or mornings or evenings, for that matter?"

She smiled archly. "I assume your little bookseller friend returned home safely?"

"Yes, Miss Browne did."

"You are losing your superb taste, darling. She is hardly worth your attention."

"Your spiteful nature is showing, Marie-Elena. I have no intention of discussing Miss Browne with you. But I did offer her the post of companion to our daughter."

Marie-Elena did not bother to feign surprise. "Absolutely not."

"I beg your pardon?" he asked, his eyes turning to steel.

She regrouped. "I do not want that commoner around my daughter, and Katya has Taichili, she does not need a companion." She smiled brightly.

His smile was ice. "My dear wife. I am not asking your opinion, or advice. This is my household—of which you are only one part." She stiffened and he smiled. "I have hired Miss Browne as Katya's companion, and that is that."

Marie-Elena could not believe her ears. Although they fought over Katya periodically, she had long learned how to use her power as the child's mother to win most of the arguments, and it had been years since the present household arrangements were formed. Never had she dreamed he might suddenly think to change the staff—upsetting what worked so very well for Marie-Elena. "Over my wishes?" she cried.

"Yes."

"But there is nothing wrong with the staff we now have!"

"I do not want Taichili in charge while you are at Tver," he returned coolly.

Marie-Elena's heart beat hard. "What do I have to do to get you to change your mind? Niki, I hate the country!"

He gave her a disdainful look, not answering her, moving toward his desk.

Marie-Elena wet her lips and spoke in a rush. "We did have a wonderful afternoon, ask Katya." It was a lie. She had hated the two hours they had spent together. Katya never spoke unless spoken to, and when Marie-Elena had lost her temper, Katya's silence had become even worse. At one point Marie-Elena had been afraid that her daughter was going to cry—and she had really lost her temper then. And all for a damned cat.

"In fact," she continued brightly, just now deciding to accept an invitation she had received earlier, "tomorrow I am taking her to tea with the Duchess of Hartford. She shall so enjoy herself!"

"Really?" He slowly looked up. "You can spend every minute between now and when you leave London for Tver with our daughter, but that will not change my decision; it is final."

Marie-Elena stared. "I sent a letter to the tsar today. And another one to my father."

"Well," he said, smiling, "unless they plan to send a liberating army to the countryside, you will remain at Tver."

Marie-Elena stared at his hard, set face—and burst into tears. "Niki, why are we fighting?" she whispered. She stepped close to him, clasping one of his hands with both of hers and holding it to her breasts. "I am begging for forgiveness."

"Please." He was disgusted, shifting away from her. "Save your theatrics for someone else."

"I want to start over," Marie-Elena said frankly. Their

gazes met, locked. Her tone was husky. "I keep thinking about you, really, I do. I miss you."

"Just stop," he said tiredly. "And even if you were telling me the truth—this time—I do not think about you. Except for the fact that you bear my name, our marriage ended five years ago—and that is the truth."

She stiffened. She had never in her life been rejected like this. She could hardly believe it was happening—he must be lying to her—he must. "Is it that little commoner?" It was hard to breathe. "Are you smitten? That is why you want her here—that is why you want her to return to Russia with Katya."

He shook his head. "Only you, my dear, would think such a thing."

Marie-Elena clenched her fists. Trembling. "I don't believe you."

He shrugged dismissively. "I am going out. Good day, madame," he said, and he strode from the room, leaving her standing there in its center, alone, clad in her stunning, nearly translucent chiffon gown.

She took a deep breath, but failed to find any composure. Nicholas could not treat her this way and get away with it. Oh, no. She had some serious thinking to do.

But one thing was clear, Marie-Elena thought grimly. She would not allow that common tart into her home. And she would not allow Carolyn Browne to seduce Nicholas away from her. For, as ludicrous as it seemed, Marie-Elena had seen them together, and she knew with every fiber of her being that the bookseller's daughter was, somehow, a threat. She would do whatever she had to do to make sure that Carolyn Browne stayed out of their lives.

PART TWO

The Companion

⇜ NINETEEN ⇝

GEORGE was seated at the kitchen table, sipping tea and reading a newspaper when Carolyn entered the room that next morning. She was filled with tension and had hardly slept that night, tossing and turning and thinking about what she was going to do—knowing she was entering extremely dangerous territory, yet trying to tell herself that she was merely becoming a small child's companion. And she worried about her father. She knew exactly how he was going to react to the news of her new employment.

The moment she entered the room, he looked up, shoving the journal aside. They had hardly spoken at all last night when Carolyn had returned from Sverayov's. He could not have made his disapproval of her taking tea with the Russian more clear. She had been hurt. She had also been angry.

She tried to smile at him. "Good morning." She bent and kissed his cheek and quickly poured herself a cup of the freshly brewed tea. She hesitated, sucked up her courage, and sat down next to him. "Papa, we must talk."

He regarded her. "What is on your mind?"

She wet her lips. "Sverayov offered me a position—and I have accepted it."

George gaped. "He what! He offered you what position? Are you mad? This is a ruse," he finally shouted.

Carolyn stood up, alarmed. "He has a terribly neglected

child. A child I feel strongly for. Her name is Katya and she is six years old. I am now her companion.''

George also stood, seriously flushed. "I do not believe what I am hearing," he said tersely. "You—a child's companion?''

"He told me I can name my price." Carolyn tried to appease him. "I was asking for a modest salary, but he is paying me five times the usual rate! In advance!''

George stared. "We do not need the income that badly. And who will watch the store when I am away? I have to go to the Continent again, very shortly.''

"We can arrange for temporary help," Carolyn said.

"Have you truly made up your mind? You will go against my wishes?" George asked. "Because I am opposed to this. Nothing will change my mind.''

Carolyn nodded. "I am sorry, Papa.''

He was breathing harshly. "And what happens, when he seeks you out—when his daughter is not present?''

Carolyn stiffened. She felt her cheeks turning red. "He has not invited me into his home to take advantage of me," she said, mimicking the prince's exact words.

"Please! This is not about his daughter. It is about his seduction of you.''

"Oh, God, Papa, you are so wrong," Carolyn cried.

"You are so innocent! So gullible! You are no match for a man like him.''

Carolyn did not know what to say, because in spite of all of her resolutions, in spite of his adamant claims, she suspected that George was right.

"He intends to use you, Carolyn," George said with anger. "I am certain of it.''

"No. He is an honorable man," Carolyn said firmly—yet with a twinge of dismay she could not deny. But she was going to have to accept reality, and she did not quite know how she had strayed so far from it. She was now his daughter's companion, period. And he had never been eligible for any other relationship. Not from the very first moment she had laid her eyes upon him.

"You are falling in love with him, aren't you?" George asked accusingly.

Carolyn was silent. She knew she must not respond.

"Can you deny that you have feelings for him?"

"No. I cannot. You are right." She turned away. "Even though I know it is wrong—and hopeless."

George looked at her.

Carolyn reached for her coat. "I am going, Papa. I will be back later to get more of my things." She picked up a small valise. "Please don't worry. And I am only going across town." Now was not the time to tell him that she might depart with the family to Russia.

"Oh, God," was all her father said.

He held his head in his hands, worrying about his daughter, feeling as sick as if he had lost her, and perhaps he had. They had never had this kind of disagreement before, but it was far more than that. He knew Carolyn was being used, and he knew she was going to get hurt. Just as he also knew that he was poised on the edge of a cliff, and it would not take much for someone to push him over. Someone— Sverayov.

Damn him, he thought. And in the next breath, he almost choked on a sob, thinking, Please, Carolyn, please.

He remained in the kitchen, even though it was now almost nine and he had a bookstore to open. His temples had begun to throb with a headache that was afflicting him far too often recently. How he hated the war.

He became aware of someone rapping on the front door of the store, perhaps with the head of a walking stick. George sighed. He could not refuse to open up, not when every single sale was so important to them. Slowly, he stood, feeling every one of his forty-eight years.

Whoever was at the front door began banging now, loudly and obnoxiously. George's stride increased as he left the kitchen. "Hold on," he shouted somewhat irritably. "Good God, you'd think someone has died."

George squinted, approaching the door. But he could see nothing, because the shades were drawn.

"Is someone at home?" a woman demanded huskily from outside. "Open up, I say! Open up!" She was an old woman—her voice was raspy from age and use.

Perplexed, George threw the bolt and pulled the door open, and came face-to-face with an elderly, gray-haired noblewoman clad in a simple yet elegant navy-blue ensemble. There was something familiar about her, yet he was sure they had never met before. And then he saw the carriage parked on the street. His heart slammed to a stop. He stared, stunned, at the blue and silver crest. The Stafford coat of arms.

"Took you long enough, Browne," Edith Owsley snapped. Without a hello, she strode past him and entered the store, not using the cane she had been banging on his door.

Tension filled him. And with it, anger. So much anger—dozens of years of it. He stalked after her. "You are not welcome here."

She faced him, after having looked all around the shop. "So this is it. The place where you sell your books—where you and Margaret lived."

"Do not mention my wife to me."

"Please. She was my daughter for more years than she was your wife." The old lady stared at him.

"Get out."

"Not until I've seen her."

He stiffened. "Seen who?" But dear God, he had an inkling. Could his life get worse?

"Her. Carolyn. My granddaughter."

He wet his lips. His mind raced. His reflexive reply would have been to tell her to go to hell, where she would one day go anyway, he was quite certain. But he could not comprehend why, after all these years, she wished to finally meet her granddaughter. Dammit. He didn't want to think about her money, but he could not help it. They were so poor. He could barely support himself and Carolyn. And it was Carolyn he worried about, especially as he was not sure she would ever marry. In spite of his better intentions, he could not help thinking that if Edith Owsley suddenly took an interest in her granddaughter, their problems might be over.

Carolyn would not have to work for Sverayov.

He would not have to go back and forth to the Continent—not ever again.

He wet his lips. Cautiously, fighting the urge to grab her and drag her from the store in spite of her age, he said, "She is not here."

Lady Stafford's hands found her hips. Her green eyes, hardly clouded by age, pierced right through him. "Where is she?"

"At her place of employment," he said.

She stared. "I was led to understand that she worked here, with you, selling books."

"She did." Now he was perspiring. "Until recently. She has become a companion to Prince Sverayov's daughter."

"A companion?" The old lady's brows lifted. "Are the two of you so poorly off that she has been reduced to becoming a governess?"

He fought his temper. "Carolyn has always done as she pleases. I believe this post interests her for many reasons."

"Such as?" The old lady was not mocking, but forthright.

"I think she sees it as both a challenge and an opportunity."

"Explain," Edith Owsley demanded.

He only did so because he knew he should not throw her out on her ear. "Carolyn believes education needs to be reformed. Especially the education of her own gender."

The Dowager Viscountess of Stafford stared, wide-eyed. And then she laughed. "Really? How unusual." She pulled on her gloves. "Good day, Browne."

He blinked as she strode past him. And then, before he could even reply, she was marching out of the door.

* * *

Upon arriving at Sverayov's residence, Carolyn was shown to her room, which was on the fourth floor where the nursery, the classroom, and the rest of the household staff's bedchambers were. She was very surprised by how pleasant and spacious her bedroom was. In fact, this room with its eastern rug, chintz draperies, armoire, and chest made her own attic bedroom seem miserable in comparison.

She thought about her father and hoped, very much, that he was not as unhappy as he had been when she had left a short while ago.

"If there is anything that you need, His Excellency has instructed me to see to it," Whitehead droned. The butler was expressionless.

Carolyn smiled. "Thank you, but I believe that I am fine. Is Katya in the schoolroom?"

The butler confirmed the fact. And he had hardly exited the chamber when Carolyn spied a ball of white fur racing past the door, left ajar, and into her new room. Carolyn eyed the kitten, now perched on a beautiful pink and white chair, licking one of its paws. "Are you here to welcome me?" she asked with a laugh.

Carolyn walked over to the blue-eyed kitten and scooped it up. "Let us go find your mistress, Alexander," she said, leaving the chamber. Voices could be heard coming from what must be the classroom. Carolyn paused on the threshold.

Katya sat at the small table, her head bent studiously over her task, a pencil in her hand. A small, dark-skinned dapper man was seated at a different desk, thumbing through a sheaf of papers, speaking to the room at large about Peter the Great. The tall, no-nonsense Taichili sat at another table, hands clasped, her spectacles sliding down her long nose. Everyone looked toward Carolyn at the exact same time.

"Hello," Carolyn said cheerfully. She entered the room. "I am sorry to interrupt."

Katya stared.

"Your kitten wandered into my bedchamber," Carolyn told the little girl. "How are you today?"

"Fine, thank you, Miss Browne," Katya said, glancing somewhat nervously at Taichili.

Carolyn let the kitten go, and it immediately raced to Katya, but the little girl did not stoop to pet it. She remained still.

The Russian woman was standing, scowling. "Katya is in the midst of her history essay, Miss Browne."

"I am terribly sorry," Carolyn said, sincerely. "I will come back later. When will she be through?"

Taichili seemed smugly pleased, but Raffaldi had shot out of his seat and grabbed Carolyn's hand, preventing her from leaving. "His Excellency told us about you, Miss Browne, and may I welcome you into his employ?" Raffaldi was smiling and affable. "As the princess is a stellar student, a small interruption does no harm. I am Signor Raffaldi, Katya's tutor."

"Thank you," Carolyn said. She ignored Taichili, who made no effort to hide her displeasure, and faced Katya. "Katya, your father has asked me to be your companion, and I have agreed. I hope you do not mind."

Katya lifted her eyes to Carolyn's, but before she could speak, Taichili marched forward and interrupted. "Surely you do not ask a child for her opinion?"

Carolyn straightened. "I most certainly do."

"That is not how we do things here, Miss Browne."

"It is how I do things," Carolyn said calmly.

"A child is not entitled to an opinion," Taichili said fiercely.

"Every human being, man or woman, child or adult, free or slave, is entitled to think independently and form opinions," Carolyn said, as fiercely.

Raffaldi's eyes were wide—but he hid a smile. Katya was also wide-eyed.

"Does the prince know that you hold to such a position?" Taichili cried, aghast.

Carolyn smiled. "He most certainly does." She turned

her back on Taichili. "Katya, do you mind that I have been appointed your companion?"

Wide-eyed, Katya shook her head.

Carolyn touched her hair. "Good. That pleases me. Now, as soon as I learn the details of your schedule, I shall find out what times we have together, and we shall begin our explorations."

Katya did not speak, but Taichili choked, "Your explorations?"

"Yes." Carolyn faced her, smiling. "Katya and I have so very much to explore. Since she is a foreigner, I thought an exploration of London the first order of business. That and an exploration of fictional reading material."

"Fiction?"

Carolyn's smile widened. "Fiction." From the corner of her eye, she saw that Raffaldi was trying not to laugh. At least she had one ally up here in the nursery.

Taichili recovered. "Well," she huffed, "Katya's schedule has no time for explorations. She has lessons from the morning until tea." She glared.

"Then I shall have a discussion with His Excellency—because Katya's schedule must be entirely rearranged."

Sverayov had already left. Carolyn refused to feel even faintly disappointed—she had not taken up this position in order to pine after him. Carolyn had no chance to see Katya again until lunchtime. Katya took her dinner with Taichili in the nursery. When Carolyn entered, she was witness to a very somber scene: the child eating as silently as the governess.

Carolyn smiled brightly, swiftly approaching. "May I join you?" As she had anticipated Taichili's glare, she addressed only Katya, and sat down when the child nodded hesitantly. "I have asked Whitehead if I may eat with you. He is bringing me up a table setting and a light meal."

Katya glanced briefly at Taichili before smiling slightly at Carolyn. Carolyn only had to look at her face to know that she was bursting to speak. "What is it?" she asked gently.

"Can we really explore London?" Katya asked breathlessly.

"I do not say what I do not mean," Carolyn responded.

Taichili snorted and stood. "I have lost my appetite." She walked away from the table, only to stare with folded arms out of one of the windows.

Carolyn sighed. "I only have to discuss your new schedule with your father, but I am sure he will not be a bother."

Katya stared at her as if she could not believe what was happening.

"Are you afraid to smile? Are not smiles allowed?" Carolyn asked gently. She squeezed the child's hand.

Katya smiled reluctantly.

"That is much better. What is black and white and red all over?"

Katya blinked. "I beg your pardon?"

"I am asking you a riddle. Can you guess the answer?"

Katya eyes brightened. She glanced over her shoulder at Taichili. "Black and white and red all over?" she asked breathlessly.

Smiling, Carolyn nodded.

"Is it an animal?"

"No. But I'll give you a hint. It involves my previous profession."

Katya's brow screwed up. From her position by the window, Taichili turned. "This is absurd," she said. "Why the prince employed you, I cannot imagine."

Carolyn felt like telling her that was exactly why the prince had hired her, because of the lack of imagination and inventiveness in his household, but she smiled and held her tongue. "Give up?" she asked.

Katya nodded, her gaze glued to Carolyn's face.

"A newspaper," she said.

Katya's eyes widened and then she laughed. Merrily. It was a beautiful sound, Carolyn thought with real satisfaction.

"What is going on in here?" a woman cried.

Carolyn had been seated with her back to the doorway. Never mind, she would recognize that sultry voice anywhere, for it belonged to Sverayov's wife. Her spine stiffening, dismay unavoidably overcoming her, Carolyn turned.

"Hello, Maman," Katya said shyly.

Marie-Elena stood angrily in the doorway, her hands fisted on her hips, which were frothed in pink pleated chiffon. "What is going on in here in the middle of Katya's lessons?" she demanded. Her black eyes were ice cold. If she had heard her daughter she gave no sign of it.

Taichili sailed forward, a dangerous light in her eyes. "His Excellency has employed Miss Browne as the princess's companion, Your Highness. Miss Browne was asking Katya a riddle."

Marie-Elena swept past Taichili to stand in front of Carolyn and Katya. "A riddle? Is that what you intend? To amuse my daughter with foolish jests?"

Very uneasy, but prepared to stand her ground, Carolyn stood. "There is no harm in a riddle," she began slowly. "To the contrary."

"There is every harm," Marie-Elena cried.

Carolyn instantly knew that the other woman was not reasonable. The other woman hated her—with good cause. She could probably sense how drawn Carolyn was to her husband. Guilt consumed Carolyn. Yet nothing, really, had happened between her and Sverayov, and her intentions were honorable. Carolyn spoke with care. "Laughter is an important part of childhood, Your Highness. Especially, I think, for your daughter."

"My daughter is extremely intelligent, too intelligent to be amused by your nonsense." Marie-Elena's eyes were black flashing orbs, but suddenly they leveled on Katya and she smiled. How eerie it was, that brilliant, dazzling smile and those dangerous black eyes. "Katya, baby, am I not right?"

Katya nodded, biting her lip.

Marie-Elena swung her head and stared at Carolyn. Even though she was a couple of inches shorter than Carolyn, she somehow managed to look down her nose at her. "You are the last person to tell me what is good for my own daughter. Do you understand?"

Carolyn stiffened. "I apologize if I have overstepped my bounds," she began, "but my job is to nourish your daughter, intellectually and emotionally. I—"

"Nourish my daughter!" Marie-Elena was sarcastic. "My daughter is not a plant in your garden, Miss Browne. I don't want you here. I will not allow you to be here, Miss Browne—and I intend to do whatever I have to, to see that you are dismissed."

For one moment, Carolyn remained silent, her pulse pounding, in shock. Even Taichili was pale. No threat could have been more clear. "Your Highness, I am only here as a companion to your daughter. I wish only to help Katya." But she was thinking, this is far worse than she had anticipated. How could she remain? If Marie-Elena would act like this? Attacking her so bluntly?

Marie-Elena flashed a cold smile and reached down and took Katya's hand. "I know exactly why you are here, Miss Browne, and it has nothing to do with my daughter."

Carolyn was taken aback.

"Come, baby. We had such a good time the other day that I have decided you can go out with me again. Your lessons can wait." Marie-Elena continued to smile coldly.

Katya's eyes widened. Carolyn immediately saw that she was torn, at once wanting to go with her mother and wanting to stay. "My lady," she said quickly, "Katya is about to begin an essay. Perhaps she could step out with you another time?"

"Do not tell me when I can and cannot see my own daughter." Marie-Elena pulled Katya forward. "Taichili, she will be back for tea." And the pair disappeared through the door—but not before Katya flung one last look at Carolyn over her shoulder. Was it a silent plea for help?

Carolyn was trembling and damp with perspiration. She was shocked over what had transpired.

"You!" Taichili whirled. "I hope you are happy with the chaos you have wrought!" Grimly, she pushed past Carolyn.

And Carolyn found herself standing alone in the classroom, aching not for herself, but for the child.

Clad in a black tailcoat, pale satin breeches and stockings, and an exquisite white shirt, Nicholas knotted his cravat, facing the mirror over a side table in the library. Not turning, his eyes met Carolyn's in the looking glass. "You wished to see me?" he asked.

She hesitated on the room's threshold, clearly surprised and discomfited to find him finishing his toilette in the library rather than upstairs. But his wife was upstairs, pacing her bedroom in a fit of pique. Nicholas had no wish to learn what was bothering Marie-Elena, not that he could not guess, and he had decided to finish his preparations for a night about town downstairs. He watched her blush, and slowly, he turned. Not for the first time, he wondered if hiring her as Katya's companion was a mistake.

He faced her, their gazes locking.

"Yes," she said huskily.

"Do come in. Close the door if you wish." She did as he asked and came forward. "You seem disturbed, Miss Browne." It was not a question. He would have been surprised if she had not been disturbed after her first day in his employ.

"I am very disturbed." But her gaze held his unflinchingly.

"What has happened?" He was quiet, but alarm bells were ringing inside his head.

Carolyn worried her hands. "I have met extreme opposition from Taichili—and from your wife."

He nodded, not relieved, even though he had been anticipating this, and motioned her to take a seat. When she had settled on the sofa, he sat down facing her. He saw now how still her small hands were on her skirts. "I will deal with Taichili immediately. I will also deal with my wife."

Her color increased. "I do not want to cause a problem between you and her."

He eyed her. "I have no intention of responding to that remark and thereby discussing my marriage with you."

"I realize that. I apologize. I . . . I am very fond of your daughter, Your Excellency. But I question my ability to be helpful, given the circumstances."

He stood. Thinking of the circumstances—precisely. That is, he was thinking of her going upstairs to her bed-chamber to spend the night—a thought he refused to en-tertain no matter that it would not leave his mind. But she was there in his house. This was not going to be as simple as he had thought. He had been distracted all day. Hoping for a glimpse of her, a word, a smile. It was insane.

"You cannot run out now, at the very first sign of dif-ficulty. I give you far more credit than that, Carolyn. I know you are a woman of strength and courage."

Carolyn stared, her cheeks pinker than before. "I did, for a moment, think of leaving. But Katya is the reason I shall stay on. At least"—her color increased—"until she departs for Russia."

He was relieved. "I have spoken to the physicians. I am told my wife can travel in another seven days. I am making arrangements as we speak for her to return home." His gaze found and held hers again.

And he did not want to even think about it, but how could he not? It was going to be very different when Marie-Elena was gone, and Carolyn continued on in his house-hold. He knew of several men, in his position, who had had liaisons with the governesses of their children.

From his point of view, it was not wrong. But he knew Carolyn could not be happy in such an arrangement.

She took him by surprise. "You seem morose tonight, Excellency. Is something amiss?"

He started, smiling faintly. "I have much on my mind."

She might have guessed just what was on his mind, because her high color did not fade. She wet her lips. "Can I be of any help?"

Instantly, an image flashed through his thoughts, of her and him, entwined in his bed. He became furious with himself. "No." His tone was harsh.

She stared.

He paced. "How can I be of help to you regarding my daughter?" he asked, purposefully steering the conversation back where it belonged.

She worried her hands. "We must discuss Katya's schedule."

"Is there something wrong with it?"

"Yes. It must be rearranged." She hesitated. "In fact, I would like to rearrange her schedule—and program—entirely."

He began to smile. "Oh, really?"

Carolyn nodded. "There is much she should be learning, Excellency. I understand that Russian history and the social graces are rather, er, important, but what about anthropology? For example?"

He slowly smiled. "Anthropology. Is that not the study of foreign cultures?"

She stepped forward eagerly. "It is. I thought we could start with the study of Egypt—as the war has made that country so popular recently."

"I see. I imagine you have other ideas on the subject of my daughter's education?"

She hesitated. "First tell me how you feel if I add the subject of anthropology?"

He laughed outright. "I applaud it."

"You do?" She gasped.

"Yes." He relaxed. Realizing now that he had been anxious, thinking she might leave her post. And in spite of how complicated her being in his household had become, he wanted her here—it was right. "I am giving you complete authority over my daughter. Did I not make that clear when I hired you? Raffaldi and Taichili report to you. You shall manage my daughter's entire care, and that includes her education.''

Carolyn gasped again. She cried, ''Are you sincere?''

He smiled. ''I thought you were about to say, 'Are you mad?' ''

And she smiled, sharing his amusement. ''That was my next question,'' she admitted.

He sobered. ''I am sincere. And if Taichili does not like the situation, she may leave. I can replace her easily enough—there are many Taichilis here and at home.''

''I agree,'' Carolyn said.

''Raffaldi will not mind. He is quite genial. So, now you have the scope of your authority. Devise a new schedule and, with it, an entire new program. Present it to me when it is complete. I will study it, make my additions or deletions as need be, but I feel assured your program will remain mostly intact.'' He had to smile at her stunned expression. Her eyes had turned a brilliant shade of green, mirroring her excitement. He could not catch himself in time to prevent his next words. ''I am certain you have heard this many times, but your eyes are extraordinary,'' he heard himself say.

She inhaled. One sharp rise and fall of her bosom beneath her sprigged day dress. ''No.'' She was frank, hoarse. ''No. I have never heard such a compliment before.''

''Then the men you associate with are fools.'' He abruptly turned away from her, annoyed with himself. He was crossing a very fine line. When he had employed her, he had committed himself to a restriction of his interest in her. For there were many women in London for him to dally with, but not the companion of his daughter—not given the nature of these circumstances.

Nicholas did not look at her as he walked to his desk, where he feigned an interest in what lay atop it. ''Is there anything else?'' he asked.

There was no answer.

He glanced up, and saw that she was gone. He cursed.

* * *

Carolyn was exhilarated.

She would spend the evening devising Katya's new program, and a new schedule to accompany it. There was no desk in her bedchamber where she might work, and Carolyn intended to use the classroom—until she arrived there and found Taichili seated at one of the desks, apparently penning letters. The governess stopped what she was doing, looking up, her expression unpleasant. Carolyn stared back at her, dismayed. There was no possible way she could revamp Katya's program in front of the governess. She had no idea if Taichili even knew yet that her authority had been subverted. She did not look forward to resolving the crisis that would surely ensue.

Carolyn smiled. "I meant to go the other way down the hall—I am looking for something to read. Good night."

Taichili barely replied.

Carolyn hurried back down the hall, clutching a notebook in one hand, thinking, why not? Both Sverayov and his wife were on the town for the evening, and she knew firsthand how late the aristocrats stayed out. Surely no one would mind if she worked in the library—least of all the master of the house.

The ground floor of the town house was dark and silent. Carolyn did not see a soul as she traversed a corridor and slipped into the library, which was unlit and filled with shadows. She made her way carefully to Sverayov's desk, lighting a lamp. Carolyn sat down in his chair and opened her notebook, all thoughts of Sverayov gone, immersed now in speculation, brimming with ideas. She intended to reduce the importance of certain studies in Katya's life, such as dance, floral arrangement, and watercolors, while increasing the amount of time spent on other, more worthy pursuits. And of course, she would add certain exciting new subjects as well. Carolyn realized she was being given an incredible opportunity to mold and develop a bright little girl's mind, in defiance of the current mode of conventional education, which seemed structured only to fetter a woman's mind to the will of pompous men.

Carolyn was not aware of the passing of time until she heard voices in the hall, one male, one female. She froze. She had left the library door open, and there was no mistaking who had returned home—both Sverayov and Marie-Elena. Her heart lurched. She could only assume that they had gone somewhere together. And why shouldn't they? They might be estranged, but they were man and wife.

Their voices were becoming louder—they were approaching the library.

Carolyn heard Sverayov saying, with anger and annoyance, "Is this why you chose to leave the fête with me?"

"I am not allowed to ride home with my husband?" Marie-Elena replied in her husky tone.

Carolyn was standing, her heart pounding with explosive force—and she did not think twice but snuffed the lamp's wick as Sverayov retorted, "You have not returned home with me in many years, my dear. And frankly, I am in no mood to discuss anything with you tonight." He had barely finished his second sentence when he appeared on the library's threshold, but Carolyn was already under the desk where she crouched, shaking and breathless.

"But I am in the mood for a discussion," Marie-Elena said, apparently following him into the library.

The library was suddenly cast in light as Sverayov lit a large table lamp. His buckled patent shoes passed closely by the desk. Carolyn could also see the hem of Marie-Elena's ball gown, which was red and trimmed with black lace. She hugged her knees, wishing she had made herself known instead of hiding—and eavesdropping. For if she were discovered now, she would be accused of just that. And then she recalled the fact that she had left her notebook open on the table and her heart, literally, stopped.

"I want to discuss that commoner—that bookseller's daughter," Marie-Elena said petulantly.

Carolyn grimaced. Even though Marie-Elena's words should not hurt, they did.

"I do not wish to discuss Miss Browne."

"Have you taken her to bed yet, Niki?"

Silence filled the room.

Carolyn forgot to breathe. Appalled.

"Marie-Elena, my private affairs are exactly that. Private," Sverayov finally ground out.

Carolyn could not believe it. Why didn't he deny it?

"What can you possibly see in her!" Marie-Elena cried.

"I see a wonderful companion for Katya," he said flatly. "Now, why don't you leave—or shall I?"

Her dress swished as she moved. Carolyn could not help but lower herself to peer out from under the desk—and she saw Marie-Elena's red hem swirling about his polished patent shoes.

"I do not like her, nor do I like her ideas," Marie-Elena cried. "And it is unacceptable for you to bring your current *affaire de coeur* into this house."

"I refuse to defend myself against your accusations. Miss Browne stays. She is good for Katya, and I would hope that even you have enough maternal instinct to agree with me." Sverayov's tone was dire.

"Do not cast stones at me," Marie-Elena cried. She paced, her gown swishing, swirling, exposing beautifully beaded red satin slippers. "I am Katya's mother. Surely I have some rights!"

"You seem determined to do all that you can do, my dear, to incite me to take away those rights," Sverayov said.

Marie-Elena said, viciously, "I am her mother, Niki! And I do not wish to discuss that nasty gossip about myself and Sasha another time!"

Suddenly he said, as viciously, "Perhaps, if your prior behavior had been more honorable, I might not be inclined to heed the gossips. You may lie until you are blue in the face, claiming that Sasha was not the father of the child you just lost, but I will not believe it."

His words were angry, but they were also bitter, and Carolyn sensed that he had been deeply hurt by this last betrayal.

"Stop throwing the past in my face!" Marie-Elena cried.

"I am sorry! So sorry!" Her tone dropped dramatically, and she whispered, "I *swear,* I am so sorry about all of the past." Now she was bitter. "But you will never forgive me, will you?"

There was a long, heavy silence. Sverayov finally said, "How can I forgive you for taking away the one thing in this world that I cherished more than anything else?"

Marie-Elena answered after a pause, her tone terse. "We can never know for certain that Katya is not your daughter, Niki."

His laughter was harsh. "It is highly unlikely," he said.

Carolyn was frozen, shocked. She could not have heard what she thought she had just heard!

And Marie-Elena was silent.

So was Sverayov.

And Carolyn, crouched beneath the desk, was panting— terrified now that they would hear her labored breathing or her deafening heartbeat.

"Damn you!" It was an explosion. Marie-Elena left the room, slamming the door behind her.

Another brief, tense moment of silence reigned. Sweat streamed down Carolyn's body beneath her clothes.

And Sverayov said, coolly, "You may come out from under the desk now, Miss Browne."

❧ TWENTY ❧

CAROLYN prayed she had misheard, better yet, imagined his words.

"Miss Browne?"

Her heart sank like a rock, then began to beat with frightening force. Carolyn crawled out from under the desk, feeling like a very guilty child caught with her hand in the cookie jar, or worse. His black buckled shoes were beneath her nose. She started to stand and hit her head on the desk and winced. Aware that her cheeks were burning, Carolyn crawled another two paces and glanced gingerly up. Sverayov stared down at her.

Taking a deep breath for courage, Carolyn rose to her feet. It crossed her mind that he was going to dismiss her on the spot—and she suddenly had no wish to lose her newfound post. To the contrary. She could not leave his household now—for many, many reasons.

"Are you in the habit of spying, Miss Browne?"

She found his choice of words unnerving. "No. I am not. I am terribly sorry."

"Then you must be in the habit of crouching under desks," he said coldly.

She met his golden gaze and tried to decide just how angry he was. "Actually, I don't know why I hid under the desk when I heard you and your wife in the hall."

"People usually hide when they are up to no good," he stated flatly.

Carolyn swallowed. "I was working on Katya's new program. I had intended to work in the nursery classroom, but Taichili was already there, penning letters, and I did not think it a good idea for me to revise the schedule in front of her."

He stepped past her and picked up the notebook, glancing at it. "You have only allotted two hours a week for watercolors and dance," he said. "An hour each on Tuesday and Thursday."

Carolyn was relieved that they were on firmer territory. "Yes, Your Excellency. I think that too much emphasis is given to those pursuits in a female child's education. Watercolors are a relaxing pursuit, and dance an important social skill for Katya, but neither will broaden her mind."

His gaze held hers. Then it moved back to the notebook. "Astronomy? You wish for my daughter to study the stars?" One brow slashed upward and he slanted his gaze at her. "And what is this? Taxonomy? Drama?"

Carolyn became nervous. "I wish to open up her mind to the world, Your Excellency, and there are so many possibilities when it comes to learning."

"Such as anthropology." He faced her.

Carolyn thought he was upset, but it was very hard to read his expression. "Yes." She swallowed. "Just as anthropology is the study of different people and different cultures, taxonomy is the study of different classifications. Both give one a broad mind and a broader view of life. As far as astronomy is concerned, the Greeks studied the galaxy—and the Egyptians did, as well. Did you know that?" She could not help smiling. She was trembling, her hands damp.

"Ptolemy," he said.

Her eyes widened. "And Copernicus. Yes, well, I wish for Katya to become aware of the vaster scope of nature, as well. And astronomy is a science, but of course, you must know that if you are familiar with Ptolemy. Sciences are very precise, logical ways of studying things and ideas. Science will teach Katya how to think in a specific, structured, analytical fashion. Actually, the same is true for taxonomy.'' Carolyn smiled.

''I am surprised you are not a scientist instead of a bookseller,'' Sverayov said.

She thought he was joking—but could not be sure. She said in a rush, ''She will learn how to look at the world and classify its elements—and thus obtain a far better understanding. Like science, taxonomy will teach Katya how to think objectively.''

''And drama? Will the study of the theater also teach her how to think objectively?''

She was riveted by his golden gaze—and his eyes were gleaming. ''Are you amused?''

His brows arched and his eyes widened. ''Absolutely not.''

She did not believe him and she folded her arms. ''Objective thinking is precisely one half of what an education should be comprised of.''

''I am afraid to ask what the other half must be.''

''The other half must be subjective thinking. The other half must be filled with the exploration of ideas that are creative, imaginative, and bold,'' Carolyn said earnestly.

He stared. ''Then you are clearly the perfect person to revamp Katya's program,'' he finally said.

She flushed. ''I believe you are complimenting me.''

''I am.''

Briefly, Carolyn was flustered. She struggled to continue in a logical fashion. ''We will attend the theater, and afterward we can discuss the merits of what we have seen. Katya can write essays espousing her point of view. Perhaps, together, we shall write a Christmas skit. Did you notice that I also want her to keep a journal? This is all the subjective part of the program.''

''No.'' His gaze remained on her face. ''I did not notice that.''

''I think that keeping a journal will do far more than

develop Katya's mind—it will expand her ability to express herself.'' Carolyn stared back at him. "You hate it. It is too liberal."

" 'Liberal' is hardly the word I would choose to describe this program, Miss Browne."

"Am I dismissed?" she heard herself say.

"No. Your ideas are extraordinary. I do not object at all to the revisions you have made to Katya's program—as long as she continues to learn the classic subjects as well." He snapped the notebook shut. "For example, I insist that she continue to learn Latin."

Carolyn began to breathe more easily. "I am in agreement with you. There is wonderful literature, essays and poems, for her to read when she is fluent in the language, Excellency." She could not help but be enthusiastic.

He smiled, slightly. "Perhaps my daughter will also read *Sic et Non* at the age of eleven."

Carolyn also smiled, and for a moment, their eyes held. But suddenly his expression changed drastically, a cloud covering his face, shadows filling his eyes. In that instant, Carolyn knew he was recalling his wife's recent words—as was Carolyn. Dear God, was it true? That Katya was not his daughter? But he had always referred to her as "my daughter."

He handed the notebook to her and paced across the room. Carolyn watched him pour vodka into a glass. She took the time now to notice how good he looked in his beautifully tailored tailcoat and satin breeches. But of course, he had the kind of physique that would look good in just about anything, including a Roman toga. Carolyn quickly averted her eyes as he glanced over his shoulder at her. She was Katya's companion; Katya must be her only concern. And then she thought, just whom was she fooling?

"Would you care to join me?" he asked.

She stiffened with surprise, knew she must, of course, refuse. "Yes, please." Her wayward self was once again ruling her better self.

He poured a second glass and returned to her, handing

it to her. "What you have heard tonight in this room cannot ever go any further."

Carolyn nodded. She wanted to ask if it was true—but his words seemed to indicate that it was, and the question would be prying. "I am very sorry I overheard such a private conversation between you and your wife, Your Excellency."

He did not answer, sipping his vodka and staring over the rim of his short glass at her.

Carolyn swigged her drink. "I suppose I should go." She started to set the glass down on a side table but he said, "No. Don't go."

She froze, then straightened, facing him.

"It's the truth," he said.

Carolyn stared at him, but he looked away, gazing instead, she thought, at some distant object—or into the distant past. "But you love her," she finally whispered.

"I fell in love with her the moment she was born," he said, and he smiled, meeting her gaze. "She was the most beautiful sight I have ever beheld. So precious, a tiny, priceless treasure."

Carolyn was motionless. Her heart beat hard. Why was he exposing himself this way to her?

He drank. "Of course, I did not learn until six months later that Katya was not mine, and by then, it was far too late." He set his empty glass down and it thudded loudly in the silent room. He did not have to explain what it was too late for—for it was obvious. It had been too late to take back his love. Carolyn ached for him.

"Of course it was too late," she whispered.

It was as if he did not hear her. "I banished mother and child to my estate in Tver, what else could I do? But I was tortured by what I had done. And I missed Katya. And surely an innocent infant was not to blame for the sins of her mother. After a few months I allowed them to return home." He stared at Carolyn. "No one knows the truth. Until now."

Carolyn could only nod. She wanted to go to him and

hold him. How inappropriate that would be. Yet how right it would feel. "Katya needs you desperately, Excellency."

"Yes." He drank. His regard was piercing. "And you?"

She started.

He stared.

She inhaled, trembling. Suddenly the night became a force enveloping them—one capable of extending the intimacy already formed. For the first time that evening, Carolyn became aware of the late hour, the sleeping, silent household, and how alone the two of them were. She did not want to recall their encounter after the races at Newmarket. "I am Katya's companion," she finally said, managing a small smile. "I thought we had formed a . . . an understanding."

"Do you think I have forgotten? For even a single moment?" He walked away to refill his glass. Then he held it up and stared at it.

Carolyn knew that she must leave. Being alone with him now, at this late hour, was too dangerous. But she did not move.

Then, "And why did you hide under the desk, Carolyn?" he said, interrupting her thoughts.

"I don't know. I reacted, I did not think."

His expression suddenly softened. "Only you would hide under my desk rather than revealing yourself." He stepped closer to her. He tilted up her chin; his hand was very warm. "Only you would instruct my daughter in taxonomy and astronomy—with such enthusiasm."

His fingers seared her skin. It was hard to think. Her knees seemed weak. "Your Excellency, I forgot to mention philosophy. She must read Plato and Socrates—"

"Nicholas," he said softly, not removing his hand.

Her heart had never beat this swiftly before. Carolyn felt faint. She knew he must not try to kiss her. For she did not think she could resist his advances. Not now, not tonight. "I must go upstairs."

He had not removed his fingers from her chin. "Why are you so very intriguing?"

She managed to open her mouth and form words. "I am not trying to be intriguing."

"I know. Women who try inevitably fail." His gaze moved to her mouth. He dropped his hand. His golden eyes were searing. Carolyn understood.

He said, "In the future, if you are going to be working late, in the library, please inform me of the fact."

Carolyn wanted to make her feet move, but couldn't. She understood his meaning. In the future he would not be up and about if she were present downstairs. Somehow, she was dismayed. But it was only proper. It was only right. Carolyn closed her eyes, thinking of Marie-Elena and Katya upstairs. She had known it would be this way if she took the position. She had known that temptation would be there forever in her face. Temptation—enticing, alluring, seductive. Temptation—in the form of a golden Russian prince. "Perhaps"—her tone was husky as she opened her eyes— "you could put a small desk in my room?"

He hardly smiled. "An excellent idea." He did not sound very pleased.

"Good night."

He saluted her with his glass.

Carolyn tensed. There was one more thing, and she could not leave without speaking of it. "Nicholas, I am sorry about tonight. So terribly sorry."

Their gazes locked. She referred not to their desire but to the tragedy of Katya's paternity. His jaw flexed. "Good night," he said firmly.

Carolyn turned, stumbling as she did so, and somehow crossed the library. She felt his gaze on her back. She could not help wondering as she hurried from the room what would have happened if she had stayed. And then she chastised herself for being a fool. Of course she knew.

"How morose you are, Niki," Alexi said.

Nicholas was trying to read the *Times*, a plate of untouched food in front of him. He did not acknowledge his brother, having just passed a night from hell.

"No good morning, tsk, tsk." Alexi slipped into a seat. "And last night at the ball you glowered at everyone—even that incredibly beautiful red-haired Lady Danziger." Alexi smiled.

"I have no idea what—and whom—you are discussing," he said, rattling his paper.

"I was just up in the nursery," Alexi said casually, reaching for a croissant.

Nicholas lowered his journal.

Alexi grinned. "I thought that would get your attention. My God, what have you done?"

His jaw flexed, his pulse raced. "What, precisely, are you referring to?"

"It was chaos in the classroom. Taichili was apoplectic. Katya and Miss Browne were discussing theater. I do believe Miss Browne is taking your daughter to a play tonight."

He found himself smiling. "Indeed."

Alexi lifted a brow. "How interesting. I now have your undivided attention."

He gave his brother an annoyed look. "She is very good for Katya."

"I agree. She is also, quite possibly, very good for you. You are in a bind."

He raised his paper, shielding his face—and hiding his expression. "I have no idea what you are talking about."

Alexi made a scoffing sound. "You want to bed the little lady—but cannot, now that you have employed her in your home. Niki, as soon as you send Marie-Elena back to Tver, you can dally where you will."

Oddly enough, Nicholas was angered by Alexi making light of Carolyn. "She is not a tart like the red-haired Faye Danziger."

"Oh-ho. So you did notice her."

"She has nothing that could possibly interest me," Nicholas said truthfully. "I am bored with the type."

"I realize that. So what are you going to do about Miss Browne?"

His heart skipped. What he was not going to do was to have an affair with her, no matter how much, and how often, he was thinking about it. "I am going to allow her to broaden my daughter's mind with astronomy, taxonomy, Greek, and theater." He had to smile to himself.

"What?" Alexi said.

Nicholas merely shook his head and resumed reading.

"Your Excellency," Whitehead said, appearing in the doorway. "A Mr. Browne to see you."

Nicholas lowered his paper, met Alexi's eyes. An unspoken communication passed between them, and he was grim, unable not to think about the effect that George's treachery would have on Carolyn should she ever learn about it. "Ask him to wait in the library, Whitehead," Nicholas said.

"Yes, Your Excellency. You also have a missive." Whitehead extended a large, sealed envelope. Nicholas recognized the royal seal instantly and stood.

He accepted the envelope. "Is the courier outside?"

"We are feeding him in the kitchen, Excellency."

"Very well. I shall undoubtedly have a message for him to take with him when he leaves," Nicholas said.

Whitehead bowed and left.

Nicholas went to the door and closed it.

Alexi was also standing, his amber eyes alert. He had recognized the seal as well, how could they not? For it belonged to Alexander.

Nicholas tore open the envelope and extracted a single-page letter with beautiful penmanship. He read it quickly, his pulse accelerating. *"Chort voz'mi,"* he cursed.

"Tell me," Alexi said.

Nicholas stared. "Davout has taken Minsk."

Alexi also cursed.

Nicholas left the dining room, his feelings about the war masked. Soon the fall of Minsk would become general knowledge, but he thought that he had a few days left in which to push hard for the conclusion of an alliance—before the British learned of Russia's ever-worsening fortunes. Would Napoleon turn his armies north, and march on St. Petersburg? Or continue east, toward Moscow? How he wished to return home and take up his old command.

His grim thoughts were interrupted. Browne was already in the library when he entered, the bald spot on his head shining. Nicholas smiled. "Good morning, Mr. Browne. This is a pleasure." He shut the door solidly behind them.

George faced him with his hands in his pockets, unsmiling. "This is an outrage," he said.

"Indeed?"

"Only too well, I can imagine how you cajoled my daughter into accepting employment in your house."

"I care little for your imaginings," Nicholas said, with a smile cooler than before, "but I am happy to inform you that Carolyn is an excellent companion."

George stared. "Have you ruined her?"

"I do take offense at your question, but I will answer it anyway. No, I have not ruined her," Nicholas said quite calmly. "Perhaps you wish to see her in order to calm yourself."

"I do." George inhaled. "What do I have to do in order to get you to dismiss her?"

Nicholas froze. And he was rarely taken by surprise. "What do you offer me?" he asked softly.

George was pale. "I do not want her hurt."

"Nor do I. But you hardly addressed the issue," Nicholas said. "I understand you are on your way to the Continent?"

"Tomorrow," George said.

"And with Stuart Davison's blessings, I presume?"

George stiffened, wide-eyed. "How much do you know?"

So he had been right. It had been Lord Davison with Browne that night in the bookshop. "Enough. Precisely where are you going?"

George stared. "Stockholm," he finally said. Sweden was not in Napoleon's back pocket, yet Nicholas knew he lied, for his destination was Calais, France. "I think I have located a copy of Abelard there," he continued. "The copy. I might forward it to your relatives in Russia if you wish."

Nicholas stared, smiling but inwardly grim. "And the price is that I dismiss your daughter?"

George nodded, using a handkerchief to mop his brow.

"This copy. It is rare and valuable, I presume?"

"Yes."

Nicholas leaned his hip against his desk. When he looked up, his eyes were hard. "I have no intention of dismissing your daughter, Mr. Browne. None whatsoever."

George cried out.

"You should not dabble in what you do not understand," Nicholas said harshly. He was angry, angry because George was a traitor to his country and traitors were hanged. "Do not play games too advanced for your level of skill," he said. "For you can only lose."

"Damn you," George cried.

"No, I think it is you who shall be damned." Nicholas stalked forward. "And you will deliver the copy of Abelard, my friend, to relatives of mine who reside in Kiev. I shall give you all the necessary information."

"You are mad." George backed up. "Absolutely not," he almost shouted.

Nicholas smiled ruthlessly. "If you do not," he said, very, very low, "I shall inform both your daughter and the British authorities of your activities . . . my friend."

George blanched.

Nicholas returned to his desk and wrote down an address and the name used by the Russian agent there. He handed it to George, who stared at the piece of vellum as if stupefied. Then Nicholas walked to the door. "Mr. Whitehead, if you please. Summon Miss Browne," he said. He turned and smiled benignly at George. "Do have a seat."

George did not move.

Nicholas meandered over to his desk, feeling no guilt whatsoever for his ruthless lie—for he had no intention of ever allowing Carolyn to learn the unsavory truth about her father, much less turn him in so he could be hanged. But whatever was important enough for Davison to send on to the French was important enough to be transferred to the Russian agent in Kiev, as well. Then he heard a soft footfall and he looked up.

Carolyn stood in the doorway, wearing a simple pale blue dress, her pale blond curls rioting around her small face. Her huge emerald-green eyes, filled with intelligence, dominated her face. Nicholas felt his heart turn over, hard. God. George Browne was such a fool—and that scared Nicholas.

"Papa!" Carolyn said in surprise.

Nicholas watched her rush toward her father. He forgot about himself and his odd feelings. He watched father and daughter embrace. He could see—and sense—that something was wrong. There was a tension present between them which he had never before seen.

"What are you doing here?" Carolyn asked.

"My plans have changed and I am leaving tomorrow. I came to say good-bye," George said too rapidly, and he shot a glance at Nicholas.

Carolyn also glanced his way, and their eyes connected. She flushed. "Papa, I am so happy to see you." She smiled at him. "I have revised Katya's education completely. This is a dream come true! I am teaching her astronomy, philosophy, taxonomy, mathematics—it is the most wonderful opportunity!" she cried. "I do want you to be pleased for me," she added.

"Then I suppose I do not have to ask if you are happy here, working for the prince," he said quite forlornly.

Her smile faded. She did not look toward Nicholas again. "Yes, I am happy here. Did you hire someone to watch the store while you are away?"

George nodded. Then he handed Carolyn a sealed envelope. "Young Davison delivered this earlier in the morning. He was very disappointed that you were not in, and I did not tell him that you have decided to take up employment here. I did not think that a good idea."

Carolyn glanced at Nicholas as she tore open the envelope. "Oh, my," she said. "He has invited me to a ball at his father's house—and it is three days from now."

"You must go," George said abruptly.

Nicholas smiled coldly at George, aware of a jealousy he had no right to feel.

Carolyn looked from her father to Nicholas. "How can I? I don't own a ball gown and I have responsibilities here."

Nicholas turned away, his jaw tight. Davison was pursuing her. With honorable intentions? He was a good judge of character, and he thought that was the case. Nicholas raked a hand through his hair. *Chort voz'mi,* he thought silently. "You must go," he said abruptly.

Carolyn stared at him, and he wondered if she was remembering last night—the intimacy and the tension. She walked toward him, holding the invitation. "That is very generous of you," she said slowly.

"I do not own your time in the evening, Carolyn. You do not need my permission to attend, not this event or any other one." He gazed into her confused and cautious green eyes. "I am confident that Katya will not suffer because of a fête or two. I have full faith in you."

She hesitated. "Thank you. And you are right. My attending will not interfere with my employment, I assure you of that. But perhaps you will be there. Or your wife. I am your daughter's companion. It could be awkward for you and the princess."

He shrugged. "I happen to be attending, but I have never given a damn about convention. And do not worry about my wife." He did not smile. "The decision is, of course, yours."

Her gaze held his for an instant longer, still somewhat bewildered by his encouragement, and then she turned to her father. "Let me walk you to the door, and then I must return to my student." She beamed, taking his arm. "She was fascinated to learn that the earth revolves around the sun, Papa. She asked me half a dozen questions!'' They paused at the door.

George faltered. ''Good day, Your Excellency.''

Carolyn continued to smile.

''Good day, Browne,'' Nicholas returned, quite politely. ''I do look forward to hearing all about your trip. And to receiving my copy of Abelard.''

George stiffened, while Carolyn looked from one man to the other.

❧ TWENTY-ONE ❧

CAROLYN was nervous. She had never attended a ball before, not even as Charles Brighton. She stood beside Anthony on the edge of the vast room. Huge chandeliers, boasting thousands of dripping candles, cast a mellow light upon the glittering throngs. Already, Carolyn thought, there were hundreds of guests present. An orchestra of string and percussion instruments was playing, concealed behind a latticework partition made of papier-mâché, but no one was dancing as yet. The atmosphere was gay, festive. The crowd was animated; the conversation was punctuated with frequent laughter. Champagne flutes sparkled in the candlelight.

"I feel like such a hedonist," she mumbled more to herself than to Anthony. She wanted to keep her head on straight, and reminded herself of how much this extravaganza cost, while men were dying daily in battles being waged just across the Channel. But with the music, the food, the crowd, it was awfully hard to remember the war, poverty, suffering, and injustice. She sighed. Worse, she felt beautiful in her pale chiffon gown and her mother's strand of pearls, and at some point in the evening she was sure to stumble across Sverayov.

"I beg your pardon?"

Carolyn flushed. "I feel so . . . different tonight."

He smiled at her. "You are very beautiful tonight, Miss Browne." His blue eyes were earnest.

"I am hardly beautiful," she demurred.

"You are very beautiful," he said firmly, "and I have always thought so."

She glanced away, thinking that he must be mad. And then, through the crowd, she saw Marie-Elena and she froze.

Of course, she had been certain the other woman would attend the ball, so she should not be surprised. But for one moment, Carolyn stared at her. She was so stunning. Her skin was flawless and ivory, her hair thick and blue-black, her features perfect. She was clad in a wisp of gold chiffon, her extremely bare, translucent gown leaving very little to the imagination, her every curve obvious, and no woman, it seemed, could have a more perfect body. Carolyn considered that she was Sverayov's wife. In spite of how strained their relationship was, and Carolyn had witnessed it firsthand, surely he found her incredibly attractive. Carolyn no longer felt very beautiful.

And Marie-Elena, who had been holding the arm of a handsome young man, had seen Carolyn. Her laughter died abruptly and her eyes widened, turning hard and cold.

Carolyn shifted. But not before noticing that Anthony had espied Marie-Elena, too. He cleared his throat. "Shall I get us some ratafia?"

"That would be wonderful," Carolyn said grimly.

"Miss Browne," he said, his tone changing, "is that not your grandmother?"

Carolyn stiffened, her gaze moving in the direction he stared. She saw a small, handsome white-haired woman simply dressed in an expensive dark blue brocade gown and a matching plumed turban, speaking with two other couples, standing not far from her and Anthony. And although Carolyn had not seen her grandmother since she was a small child, specifically not since she and her mother had not been allowed past the foyer of Midlands, she recognized

Edith Owsley instantly. Her heart, already racing, beat so hard now that Carolyn was left breathless.

"That is Lady Stafford," Anthony said firmly. "I haven't seen her in a year or two, but I am certain of it."

Carolyn could not speak. Her grandmother was listening intently, with dissatisfaction, to a younger woman. She frowned and began to speak rapidly. Carolyn could not move. Lady Stafford was lecturing upon some subject dear to her, that was clear. She was speaking with passionate conviction.

And so many thoughts tumbled through Carolyn's mind that she was almost incoherent. She hated her grandmother, she did. Her grandmother had turned her and her mother away, both literally and figuratively, in a time of dire need. And her grandmother hated her.

"Shall we go and say hello?" Anthony asked.

Carolyn started, about to protest. And as she did so, her grandmother suddenly turned and met her gaze. Her expression changed immediately—her eyes widened in shock and recognition.

Carolyn tensed. George had always told her that she was very much the image of her mother. She turned her back on Edith Owsley, her pulse roaring in her ears. She was incapacitated. "Anthony," she said huskily, "I have no wish to speak with my grandmother. Could we get that ratafia now if you do not mind?" She was shaking.

Anthony gave her a queer look. "Of course." He tucked her arm in his and they moved deeper into the crowd. "Are you all right, Miss Browne?"

Carolyn could feel her grandmother's eyes following them—following her. She wished she hadn't come. But then she refused to be cowed by Edith Owsley's appearance at the ball—she would enjoy herself. She was determined. "I am fine." She paused by a marble column, beneath a portrait of some dandified Davison ancestor, perspiring. She managed a smile, making it firm.

"I will be right back," Anthony promised, but he looked alarmed.

Carolyn nodded, grateful to have a moment alone. When he was gone, she leaned against the pillar. What should she do if her grandmother approached her? Be polite, she decided. But that would be awfully hard when she would want to scream at her, Why? Why? Why?

"I do not believe it," a woman said tightly.

Carolyn was swept with dismay. This was not what she wished to deal with now. She turned to face Marie-Elena, marshaling her defenses. "Hello." She nodded politely.

"What are you doing here?" Marie-Elena exclaimed, her black eyes filled with anger and hate.

Carolyn wet her lips, once again taken aback by the other woman. "I was invited—exactly as you were."

Marie-Elena's hands found her lips. Her full bosom heaved, threatening to overflow her extremely low-cut gown. "Who would invite you? Surely not—Niki?"

Carolyn felt like saying yes. "Is it really your affair?"

"Are you not in my employ?" Marie-Elena demanded.

"I am employed by your husband."

"Yes, and I suppose he pays you handsomely—for *all* that you do." Her eyes glittered.

Carolyn fought to hold on to her temper and succeeded. "If you wish to question my wages, I suggest you discuss it with him."

"I shall. Does Niki know you are here?"

Carolyn hesitated. She almost told the other woman that Nicholas had encouraged her to come. "He knows. I thought it his business to know of the invitation."

"I see!" She was trembling. "He has lost his mind—somehow you have bewitched him—but I cannot imagine how!" She raked Carolyn with a condescending regard. Her meaning was clear. Carolyn was a cow—who could not possibly interest Sverayov.

"I have not bewitched your husband," Carolyn said quietly. "I doubt any woman could bewitch him. He obviously has a strong mind of his own."

"So now you are an expert on Niki—as well as my child's education?"

Carolyn shrugged, having already protested her expertise to this woman before. "Think as you will."

Marie-Elena stared. "This is disgusting," she finally said. "You in my home, and now, here. I will not put up with it. Your days are numbered, my dear."

Shivers swept up and down Carolyn's spine. "Are you threatening me?"

Marie-Elena laughed, tossing her head of thick, blue-black hair. "Yes. I am threatening you. If you do not leave of your own accord, I shall make sure I arrange your dismissal, one way or the other, myself."

Carolyn was afraid. She had not a doubt that Marie-Elena had no morals, and no compunction about doing whatever she had to do to accomplish her own selfish aims. But she said, stiffly, "I care about your daughter and I am not abandoning her now. In spite of your threats."

"You care about *my* daughter?" Marie-Elena was aghast, appalled, furious. "She is my daughter. Mine. And I will not have you poison her against me!"

Carolyn was in disbelief. "Princess, I have no interest in poisoning Katya, not in any way."

"You are such a liar. I know what you want. Do you think me stupid? You want my husband, my daughter, my home. In short, you think, idiotically, to take my place. You must be insane. Niki will never divorce me in order to marry you." And Marie-Elena's smile was at once bitter and triumphant. "You are a nobody!"

Carolyn was so shocked that she could only stare.

And then, in a split second, Marie-Elena's expression changed. She smiled, becoming radiant and beautiful. "Hello, my lord. I do not believe we have had the pleasure."

Carolyn shifted and saw Anthony holding two glasses of ratafia. Two spots of pink colored his cheeks. He handed Carolyn a glass and bowed. "Anthony Davison. It is a pleasure, Princess Sverayov. I am at your service."

The gesture sensual and elegant, Marie-Elena extended her slim arm and small hand. Anthony took it, kissing it.

She gave him an artful, promising look. "Hmm. You are Lord Davison's son?"

"Yes. The youngest, I am afraid." Anthony straightened. He was trying very hard, Carolyn thought, not to look down at Marie-Elena's revealing gown. His eyes were glued on her face.

"I met your father at the opera. I can see the resemblance. I am very pleased to meet you. Perhaps later you might wish to share a dance with me?"

Anthony's eyes widened.

Carolyn felt herself flushing as well. She did not have to be a genius to understand what Marie-Elena was doing—wooing Anthony right out from under her very nose while in front of her. Proving that her feminine power was far superior to Carolyn's.

"I shall save you the last dance," Marie-Elena purred. She did not even bother to look at Carolyn as she slithered away, her gold gown dripping like fluid over her high buttocks. Carolyn gazed down at her drink. She had felt beautiful a few moments ago. Now she felt downright ugly.

"Well," Anthony said, too loudly. "Shall we find a quiet corner?"

Carolyn managed both a nod and a smile.

Nicholas arrived at the ball late. But it took him only a matter of minutes to learn that Davison was closeted in the library with both Castlereagh and another member of the foreign ministry and the ambassador from Sweden. The Swedes had reached a rather loose arrangement with the Russians, which in actuality promised little and satisfied no one, and Sverayov would have loved to know what was being discussed inside the library.

"How long have they been inside?" Nicholas asked his brother who had provided him with the news.

"Half an hour. Why are you so late?"

"I had some correspondence to catch up on," Nicholas said as he and his brother paused on the threshold of the ballroom. He regarded the festively attired crowd with great interest. He estimated that there were a hundred couples on the dance floor. But there was no sign of Carolyn. He continued to search the crowd, and was disappointed.

"She is here with young Davison," Alexi remarked, obviously attuned to his thoughts. "I saw them earlier. But I do not think she is enjoying herself."

"That can be changed," Nicholas muttered, more to himself.

"Has George left the country?"

"Yes. With an escort—unbeknownst to him."

Alexi shook his head. "Why do I suspect that you are following him not just to make certain that he fulfills all of his newfound obligations?"

Nicholas tore his gaze from Carolyn. "I have no idea what you are talking about."

Alexi chuckled. "How you lie when it suits you! I have the strongest feeling that his escort is under orders to protect him—at all costs."

"You are mad," Nicholas said.

Alexi grinned. Then he gripped Nicholas's sleeve. "Your quarry arrives."

Nicholas had already seen Carolyn pausing on the outskirts of the ballroom on its other side. She was alone. "I shall see you later," Nicholas said.

"Do you wish to dance?" Anthony asked.

Carolyn had not the slightest desire to join the dancers on the dance floor. "Would you be terribly affronted if I declined?" she asked.

"Hardly." Anthony smiled at her. "I am not particularly fond of dancing myself. Shall I fetch us some supper?"

Carolyn smiled. "That would be wonderful."

Anthony left, and Carolyn sipped her ratafia, watching the dancers, relieved that she had not been forced to take to the floor, where she would have performed abysmally, for she did not know how to dance except in theory. She thought about Sverayov. She had yet to see him tonight, and she was very disappointed even though she was trying to feign indifference, even to herself. And she brooded about Marie-Elena.

His wife was a problem. Carolyn was now certain of it. At first, she had been fooled by the other woman's demeanor and appearance—or as Sverayov would say, by her theatrics. But her angelic façade was only that, a façade. That was now very clear.

And she could not entirely blame Marie-Elena for feeling threatened and being nasty earlier, but the fact that she had so thoroughly cuckolded Sverayov had confused Carolyn completely. Or was she confused because he was hurt and angry, and that was making her hurt and angry? But the fact did remain that Marie-Elena was his wife. Nothing was ever going to change that.

And, thinking of the devil, it was as if she had summoned him up. Carolyn saw him pause on the short flight of steps on the opposite threshold of the room. She stiffened, clutching her glass. He stood above the crowd. How her heart raced. How magnificent he was. No one could mistake him for anything other than royalty, Carolyn thought, and then she was angry with herself for being so affected by him that she was now becoming impressed even by his lineage.

He was regarding the crowd. He seemed to be gazing out over the dancers, searching for someone. But surely not for her. The entire ballroom separated them. As Carolyn stood alone, near a column, in spite of being five feet six inches tall, she was certain she could not be seen by him. She wondered if she should attempt to work her way through the dancers and wander over to him. Better yet, she should leave and pretend she had never seen him. She was Katya's companion and she was at the ball with Anthony—there was no point in pursuing an encounter.

But suddenly he seemed to be gazing in her direction. Carolyn tensed, as, across the entire ballroom, and the hundreds of guests, the impossible happened. Their gazes met.

And then he smiled. Although quite a distance separated them, there was no mistaking the flash of white teeth in his tanned skin. Abruptly Sverayov descended the short flight of steps and entered the ballroom. Even though he was a head taller than most of the guests, the crowd quickly swallowed him up.

Carolyn did not move, stiff with expectation, certain he was coming to seek her out. Her gaze was glued on the crowd, and then he materialized from amongst them, his strides long and swift.

"Are you enjoying yourself, Carolyn?" he asked, bowing briefly.

Carolyn returned his smile. "You have taken me by surprise."

"A common military maneuver," he said, and his eyes seemed to dance.

It took Carolyn a moment to realize that he was jesting with her. She smiled. "Good evening, Your Excellency. Do you have battles on your mind?"

His own smile, brief as it was, disappeared. "Frankly, I do."

Her intuition screamed at her and she plucked his sleeve. "What has happened?"

He regarded her steadily. "Unfortunately, I am not at liberty to divulge that information to you."

"You seem disturbed. The news is not good, then?"

"Do not jump to conclusions," he chided gently. "We are not here to discuss war, but to enjoy ourselves."

She nodded. "I am sorry."

"Are you?" His gaze was probing. "Enjoying yourself, that is?"

Carolyn hesitated, lowering her eyes. "How can I not? I am lucky to even be here."

"Perhaps young Davison is the lucky one."

His soft tone made her look up, only to meet his brilliant regard. She had to admit it. When he spoke to her in such a manner, he seemed sincere. Not at all like a rogue—or a man bent on an odd kind of revenge. "I am the fortunate one," she said firmly.

He laughed and shook his head. "Well, there is another

side to all of this. Copperville can surely enrich his column after this night."

She grinned. "Did you know that several high-ranking diplomats, including our very own Castlereagh, were ensconced in the library for over half an hour?"

His eyes widened. "No," he exclaimed.

She eyed him. "And Lady Carradine is here. I think she has mended her broken heart—quite swiftly, too."

He smiled back at her. "Whom is she with?"

"His name is William O'Connell, he has no title, but he is the second son of an earl. He is also tall and blond, like you." Carolyn smiled, enjoying herself.

"Will Lady Carradine suffer the same blows as one particular visiting foreign dignitary?"

"How would I know?" Carolyn laughed, shrugging widely.

"You could always write about young Davison and his new *affaire de coeur,*" Sverayov said, their gazes holding. "Where is he, by the way?"

"He went off to fetch us some refreshments. I think you are exaggerating my relationship with Anthony," she said.

He only smiled.

But Carolyn stared at him, for the question had immediately formed in her mind, one she knew she had to ask. She screwed up her courage. "You wrote 'Private Royal Affairs,' did you not?"

His gaze was wide and innocent. Smiling, he shrugged. "I have not a clue as to what you are speaking about."

Carolyn harrumphed. "You wanted to make me know what it felt like, precisely, to be on the other end of the stick." She was smiling.

"And how did it feel?"

"Not very good," she had to admit.

His smile faded. Carolyn realized his gaze had fallen to her breasts, and she flushed. "It doesn't matter," she said weakly.

He met her gaze. He did not reply.

But Carolyn was shaken by the light she had seen in

his eyes. Had she imagined it? She tried to think of something witty and clever to say, managing to tear her gaze away. And then she stiffened, as her eyes locked with her grandmother's.

Edith Owsley stood directly behind Sverayov, and now she moved purposefully forward, her gaze intent upon Carolyn. Carolyn could only stare, quite certain all the color in her face had drained away. From the corner of her eye, she saw Sverayov look from one to the other, perplexed.

"We have not been formally introduced," the old lady said.

Carolyn fought for the ability to speak. "We have met. Or do you not recall one snowy winter day, thirteen years ago?" Her tone was pitched too high.

"Margaret failed to introduce us even then," her grandmother said. "I never expected to find you here. You may call me Lady Stafford, or Grandmother if you wish."

Carolyn squared her shoulders, aware of Sverayov's shock. She said, slowly, "Perhaps I do not wish to address you at all."

Edith's eyes widened. "You are abominably rude."

Carolyn ground her jaw down and bit back an even hotter reply.

"But at least you have a spine, unlike that nitwit Thomas," Edith said, shocking Carolyn yet again.

Sverayov stepped between them. "Excuse me," he said, his tone polite. "I have not had the pleasure." He smiled at Edith. "Lady Stafford, may I?" He did not wait for a reply and he bowed. "Prince Nicholas Ivanovitch Sverayov, at your service."

"And I am the Dowager Viscountess of Stafford." She smiled faintly at him before narrowing her green eyes. "I know who you are. Who doesn't? Did you bring her here?"

"No. I did not. Is this a family reunion?" he asked, as politely as before.

"One might say that." Edith looked at Carolyn. "You look exactly like Margaret."

Carolyn wet her lips. "Did you receive your birthday present?" It was hard to moderate her tone.

Edith nodded, appearing almost pleased. "Burke is one of my favorite authors, I have been enjoying rereading him immensely."

Carolyn started, and was unable to deny the pleasure her grandmother's words had induced—even though she was determined not to give a damn about what the older woman felt, not about anything—including Carolyn herself.

"So who brought you here?" Edith pried. "Surely not your father?"

"My escort is Anthony Davison," Carolyn said stiffly.

"Young Davison!" Edith appeared surprised. "You are doing very well for yourself. He is a good, solid chap even if rather penniless."

"He is a mere friend," Carolyn retorted.

"Hmm." Edith squinted at Sverayov, who was regarding them both. "And the prince? How does he fit into this equation? I thought you were his daughter's companion."

Carolyn swallowed. She had no idea how to reply. And how did her grandmother know so much?

But Sverayov stepped gracefully into the breach. Smoothly, he said, "Miss Browne is my daughter's companion. But surely that does not preclude her attending a ball with young Davison."

"Oh, really?" Edith looked from Sverayov to Carolyn.

Carolyn remained silent, fingers digging into her own palms. She was perspiring. What did her grandmother want?

"She is one of the most original and well-educated women I know," Sverayov said. "The perfect companion to my daughter."

Edith regarded him closely, and then gave Carolyn the same scrutiny. "This is amazing," she finally said. "An amazing turn of events." She seemed pleased. "So. Where did you get this wonderful education?"

Carolyn lifted her chin. "From my father. And books. Lots of books," she said succinctly.

Edith stared. And muttered, "I suppose George was good for something after all."

Carolyn stepped forward, furious. But Sverayov gripped her arm, pulling her back, his gaze commanding hers. She swallowed an enraged reply.

Edith watched them both, her sharp green gaze moving between them. She said to Sverayov, "You are awfully protective of your daughter's companion, Your Excellency."

"I am," he said calmly. "Carolyn is in my employ— dependent upon me, as are all my staff. Thus my loyalty knows no bounds."

Edith nodded. "I am forewarned," she said. But the old witch was actually smiling.

Bewildered, Carolyn studied her grandmother and then the Russian. "Sverayov understands diplomacy, my lady, that is all."

"As well he should. Just what is your tsar up to, Your Excellency?" Edith demanded.

His brows lifted. "I beg your pardon?"

"How serious is this situation in your country? Will you lose the war?"

He actually laughed. "I cannot give away military secrets, Lady Stafford."

She made a scoffing sound. "Are we still technically at war?"

He laughed again. "To the best of my knowledge," he said.

She waved at him dismissively, then skewered Carolyn with a look. "I imagine that my party is searching for me," she said. "Whom else do you read, other than Burke?"

Carolyn did not want to answer. "I read everything."

"Whom are you most fond of?"

Carolyn lifted her chin. "Bentham."

"So you are a liberal?"

"Vehemently so," Carolyn said heatedly.

"But Burke is archly conservative."

"Obviously I am aware of that. But only a fool reads

one point of view—especially a self-serving point of view.''

"This has been very interesting," Edith mused.

Carolyn's chin remained high. "So I have amused you. How nice."

Edith paused in mid-stride. "Did I say you amused me, my girl? I said no such thing. But you are not what I expected. Not at all." And she marched off.

Carolyn stared after her, hugging herself, shaken and close to tears.

"Here," Sverayov said very kindly, and he handed her an embroidered handkerchief.

Carolyn dabbed at her eyes.

"Shall we dance?" he asked suddenly.

Carolyn started.

He smiled at her, taking her arm. "Perhaps you should release that glass. Before you break it from clutching it so tightly."

"I . . . Your Excellency. I cannot dance."

"Nicholas," he said. "We are quite alone, Carolyn."

"Nicholas," she whispered.

"Why can't you dance? Because you do not know how?"

"I understand the principle," she began. "I have read about it."

He laughed. "But not the act? Then I shall have to teach you." His expression sobered. "Carolyn. Are you all right?"

Carolyn flushed and nodded but she was not all right, she was miserable and blue.

"I imagine you do not wish to discuss your mysterious ancestor?"

"There is nothing to discuss." She dabbed at her eyes again. "My mother was her daughter, my father, a tutor. They fell in love and ran off. Lady Stafford never forgave my mother, who died when I was six. And she has never acknowledged me—until now, that is." She pursed her mouth tightly, because she could feel several tears trickling down her cheeks.

"I think the old shrew liked you," he said.

She shook her head. "She hates me—and I hate her."

He stared. "Let's walk outside," he said. "I need air and I imagine that you do, too. I will also fetch us some punch."

She would never have imagined him being so compassionate and sensitive. Carolyn could only stare up at him, beginning to forget her grandmother. How wonderful it would be to seek sanctuary in his arms, to be smothered by his kisses. She would surely forget all about that horrid Edith Owsley then.

She had not even thanked her for the Burke book.

But then her sanity returned, full force. An encounter with her grandmother, no matter how horrid, was no excuse to throw herself at Sverayov. No excuse at all.

Sverayov suddenly sighed. His eyes had moved past her. "In fact, your lucky escort has arrived. Unlucky me. Good evening, Davison."

Anthony appeared, balancing two very full plates. He looked from Sverayov to Carolyn and back again. "Your Excellency. I am pleased to see you again. Forgive me for not bowing," he said. He was flushing.

"You are forgiven," Sverayov said, bowing abruptly. And then he plucked Carolyn's glass from her numb fingers. "I suppose my suggestion was not the best of ideas, in any case. But I shall refill this for you anyway." And he was gone.

Numbly, Carolyn stared after him.

❧ TWENTY-TWO ❧

"ANTHONY, thank you so much for a wonderful evening," Carolyn said. She stood in the doorway of the bookstore, holding the door ajar. Anthony stood on the front step outside.

"Are you certain that you are feeling all right?" Anthony asked with real concern.

Carolyn smiled, but felt miserable. She had not been a very good companion during the past few hours, picking at her meal, unable to concentrate on Anthony. Instead, her eyes repeatedly wandered around the crowd. But Sverayov, after returning to hand her a glass of punch, had disappeared as effectively as any ghost. And she had seen her grandmother leaving early with her friends, as indifferent to her presence at the ball as she was indifferent to her complete existence. "I do have the slightest headache," she said: "I'm sorry if I was poor company."

Anthony smiled at her. "How could you ever be poor company?" His smile vanished, his eyes were intent. "Thank you for joining me. I'll come by tomorrow, if you don't mind."

Carolyn hesitated, her mind racing. Anthony did not know that she had taken a position in Sverayov's household. Although that was not the reason she had decided to return home instead of to Sverayov's. And she did not believe in lying, and an omission of this nature seemed to qualify as exactly that. "Anthony, I won't be here tomorrow. Although my father is away, he has hired someone to look after the store temporarily."

Anthony regarded her with mild bewilderment.

Carolyn felt her cheeks heat. "Actually, I have taken a position—one that is most likely temporary."

"Really? But you so love books!" he burst out.

Carolyn somehow kept smiling. "I am a companion for Sverayov's daughter. He has a daughter, you know," she rushed on, "a wonderful child who is six years old. He is allowing me to totally revise her program of education. It is a golden opportunity!"

Anthony said not a word, staring at her in obvious horror and shock.

And oddly enough, Carolyn felt terrible. She plucked his sleeve, sighing. "It is actually rather complicated. The child is very lonely. She needs me."

"I see," he finally said. He was clearly unhappy. "You would rescue an unhappy princess, Carolyn."

Anthony finally bid her good night and left. Carolyn closed the door and bolted it. She was distraught. Her life had suddenly become so very complicated. Sverayov's allure was too powerful—and it was clearly growing. He had become an obsession, haunting all her thoughts. How could she continue on as Katya's companion now that she had realized this? Especially when she had also realized precisely how estranged he was from his wife?

But mostly, she was shaken by her encounter with her grandmother. Why had the old lady sought her out—after all these years? To amuse herself, at Carolyn's expense? And what had all her glances and remarks meant?

As Carolyn slipped off her lightweight shawl she thought about Edith Owsley's comment that Thomas was a nitwit and she had to smile. The old lady might be a witch, but she was no fool.

Heavyhearted, Carolyn made her way through the silent bookshop with a candle in one hand. She was weary, but knew that tonight sleep would be impossible. For, on top of everything, her temples did throb painfully. In the kitchen she set the candle down, lighting two lamps. She would make herself some tea and a light snack, and for a while, she would work. That had always been a cure-all. And Copperville had a column due. Perhaps she would write about the Dowager Viscountess Stafford. Why not?

"She is not home, Your Excellency," Jacques said, holding Nicholas's ceremonial sword in one hand.

Nicholas paused in the act of unbuttoning his jacket. "But she left the ball some time ago." They were in the master suite.

"Are you certain?" Jacques asked. The valet regarded him shrewdly. "Perhaps the couple left to take a stroll."

Nicholas felt his jaw tighten. He was not discussing his wife—he did not give a damn if she had returned home or not—but Carolyn. And he had watched her exit the house with Anthony—they had left through the front door—not a pair of terrace doors as his cheeky valet was suggesting. Why was Carolyn not at home?

"Shall I bring you something to drink?" his valet asked, correctly assessing his temper, which was not good.

Had she had second thoughts about her position? Or was her absence an indication of something else. "No." He rebuttoned his jacket, heading toward the door. Perhaps she had gone home to the bookshop, but that would only mean that she was so shaken from the evening that she was quitting his employ. Or was she out and about with Davison? *That,* he reminded himself, was not his concern.

"Your Excellency!" Jacques ran after him. "Are you going out?"

Nicholas flung a glance over his shoulder at him, his strides eating up the carpeted corridor. "What do you think, *mon ami*?"

Jacques finally halted, watching him hurrying down the stairs. "I think that this is long overdue," he muttered to no one in particular.

* * *

A Ball and Ancient Crimes Revisited—or an Unusual Family Reunion. At least five hundred of *la crème de la crème* of the London *haut monde* chose to attend the ball given by our very esteemed public-serving Lord D——n last night. Surely not a thought was given to the incongruity of such a festive occasion; no one seemed to be thinking of poor Wellington, up to his Hessians in mud and blood. Not only did the prince regent attend with his usual cronies in tow, and they were quite lively, I might add, but so did most of the members of Liverpool's government, not to mention our favorite foreign prince and an especially slippery ambassador. What schemes were hatched behind closed library doors?

But the best of the evening was to be found in the most odd and fateful encounter. A certain elderly Dowager Viscountess S——d had finally left her home, M——s in the Essex countryside, where she had spent most of the past two years in utter seclusion (to repent her sins?) in order to attend the *grande soirée.* O ye ancient gods! For surely that was what *la grande dame* was thinking when she encountered not the fawning of her diamond-studded friends whom she surrounds herself with, but a long-lost relative, a granddaughter no less, whom she had disowned upon birth for the crime of being fathered by a plebeian, yes—a plebeian and a bookseller! Were swords drawn? Did blood flow? Apparently, as *la grande dame* is archly conservative, her young relative passionately enamored of Bentham and company, and sharp words were exchanged. Poor Lady S——! Now the ancient crime is revisited for all the world to see. Now the evidence of the heinous crime dares to step out in society! Can *la grande dame* survive the embarrassment? Only this reporter dares to hazard a guess, and his guess is no.

A loud knocking sounded from the front of the store,

making Carolyn start. She had just been finishing the column, and her quill slipped, dragging a jagged line across the bottom margin of the page. Carolyn froze, filled with sudden fear.

She did not know what time it was, but it was several hours past midnight. Perhaps she had misheard? No one could be outside the door to the bookstore at this hour? Her heart hammering, a lump in her throat, she was motionless. The banging began anew.

Oh, God. Carolyn dropped the quill, standing, and instantly doused both lamps. The single burning candle she held aloft. What should she do? Surely an intruder with vile intentions would not knock on the front door. But that thought hardly calmed her, because the hour was too odd. Should she answer the door? Perhaps it was a neighbor, perhaps someone was dying. Or should she sneak upstairs and hide?

"Carolyn!"

She faltered, certain she had heard her name, but the sound had been muffled. Every fiber of her being tensed and alert, she cautiously peeked through the kitchen doorway into the dark, unlit bookstore. She strained to see the front door, but could barely make out its outline. The street outside was pitch-black.

"*Chort voz'mi,*" a man said—or so she thought.

Carolyn straightened, incredulous. Muffled though the voice had been, it had sounded like Sverayov using a Russian expletive. But that was impossible—was it not? As she stood there, undecided, she saw a match flaring outside. And she glimpsed a large, towering form. It was Sverayov. Incredulous, for an instant she just stood there.

"Carolyn," Sverayov commanded, pounding two more times on the door.

Carolyn came to life. She turned and lit the lamps before going to the door. What did he want? She lifted the bolt and pulled the door wide open. Her intention was not to invite Sverayov in. Definitely not. But he gave her an enigmatic look and casually walked past her and inside.

"Is something wrong?" Carolyn asked, shutting the door and facing him, holding the one taper aloft. Trepidation filled her, but it had little to do with her question. "Is Katya all right?"

The candlelight flickered over his high cheekbones and straight, aristocratic nose. He stared at her. "Katya is fine."

Carolyn realized why he was regarding her so intently. She was in her cotton nightgown and wrapper, her feet bare. She quickly tightened the belt, flushing, wishing it were winter and she were clad in heavier garments. "What are you doing here?"

He smiled faintly. "You left the ball so suddenly." He gazed past her. "You are still up. What are you doing?"

She followed his glance to the lamps burning in the kitchen. "I was working."

"Copperville?" His eyes gleamed.

"Yes."

He faced her. "I would have thought you to be asleep by now."

She became aware of her heart, beating heavily and erratically. Now it was her turn to stare. "I have a small headache."

"I cannot say that I blame you."

Carolyn thought of all that had occurred that night at the ball, and of the fact that her father was traveling, which meant that they were alone in the bookshop. She was tense. "I do not understand why you are here—at this hour."

He shoved his hands into his pockets. "Do you want the truth?"

She stiffened. "I am not sure."

His smile flickered. "I thought you might be here—but I also thought you might still be out and about with young Davison."

"Well, now you know," Carolyn said with a levity she did not feel. She clasped her hands. "It is very late—" she began.

He interrupted. "Why did you come here tonight, Carolyn?" His gaze was direct.

She turned away. "I needed to think." She wondered what he would say, how he would react, if he knew just how often she thought about him.

He was silent. She assumed he was accepting her statement. But he said suddenly, "I have not eaten tonight. I am famished."

Carolyn started. "I was going to take a snack myself, but I got carried away with my column and forgot," she said truthfully. Her heart was fluttering.

He smiled. "Perhaps we can share a light supper." His gaze was penetrating.

She knew she flushed. She thought about the icebox in the kitchen. Her mind screamed at her to refuse him, and certainly not to invite him in. But she said, low, "Actually, I could probably fix us some bread and cheese. Would that be enough?"

"Only if you have some wine to go with it," he said.

Their gazes locked.

Her pulse was pounding. Why was she tempting fate? Carolyn started for the kitchen, aware of him following her. In the kitchen she lit the stove in case he wanted tea. Her hands were trembling ever so slightly.

"There." Carolyn turned, only to find herself practically in his embrace. "You may look for the wine in the pantry. Although I doubt it is from Burgundy or Bordeaux."

"I can settle for less," he said, laughter in his eyes. "God forbid we should find smuggled wine here."

"I could not live with myself," she admitted, their eyes holding. Nor could she live with herself if their relationship took a fateful turn.

"You are dismayed," he said softly. "Disturbed."

"You are my employer." Shaken, she reached for the bread box. His hand caught her wrist, stilling hers.

"Perhaps tonight, we are just friends."

She met his intent gaze. "The pantry. There should be wine in the pantry," she said.

"As you wish," he returned evenly. He released her. Carolyn found a loaf of bread while he stepped into the pantry.

"We have half a bottle of port," he said, returning to the kitchen.

Carolyn was placing a wedge of Stilton on a plate. "I think we shall have to replace it."

"I will buy your father an entire case," Sverayov said.

He was a prince, she was a commoner. He was her employer. Carolyn reached up to a shelf for two glasses. Her pulse continued to race. What was she doing? Was she insane? To put them both in such an intimate situation? What good could possibly come of this? She was so acutely aware of him. She was, by God, in love.

Sverayov was opening the port. Carolyn carried the wine glasses over, then two plates and flatware. Sverayov brought the plate of cheese and bread. "I did not know princes set tables—much less ate in kitchens," she remarked, unable to smile.

"This prince has eaten snakes, my dear, outside of a field tent in the mud and the rain—in full sight of Turks bent on murder and mayhem." He pulled out her chair for her. "Although I do confess," he said as she sat down, "that I have never actually dined in a kitchen before—much less with a woman in cotton nightclothes."

Carolyn froze. She had somehow forgotten about her nightclothes. "I will change."

"There is no need. You are quite decent, I assure you," he said, taking his own seat. But his eyes were bright. "Until now, I have preferred lace."

Carolyn did not believe for an instant that he had changed his preferences in ladies' nightclothes.

"What is this?" He pulled the sheet of vellum forward which contained her new Copperville column. And as he did so, he exposed a cartoon she had drawn before writing the article. It was a caricature of Sverayov, one impossible to mistake.

Carolyn flushed.

Sverayov stared down at the picture of himself, poised on top of the steps leading down to the ballroom. He was in his uniform and ceremonial sword, numerous medals decorating his chest. Not only was his uniform a dead give-away, she had drawn his face with remarkable accuracy. His expression was at once amused and indifferent, arrogant and bored.

He looked up at Carolyn. "Do I truly wear such an expression?"

She nodded. "Tonight you did." She added, "At that moment."

He glanced back at the cartoon. "Is this for publication?" She had roughly sketched in the crowd below him and one huge chandelier overhead.

"No."

He met her gaze. "Then I am flattered."

Carolyn did not look away. She did not know what to say. The darkness outside, the intimacy and warmth within the kitchen, her nightclothes, his uniform, it was all adding up to roiling desire. "You are an unusual subject," she finally said.

"Is that all?" he asked very quietly, not smiling.

Carolyn gripped the edge of the table. She knew she must not answer him.

He finally inclined his head and reached for the written column. Carolyn had never let anyone read her column before it was published. She busied herself with cutting two generous wedges of cheese and serving them. "You may read it if you wish," she offered.

"Thank you."

Carolyn sliced the bread, watching him as he read the column. She was aware of becoming anxious—she wanted to know what he thought of it. But more importantly, she was acutely aware of all the currents ebbing and flowing around them. She set her plate aside. This was a mistake. It could only lead one place. Her feelings for him had not been contained by any of the obstacles in her path. To the contrary. Impossibly, they had grown.

She should not have gone to the ball, accepted the post as Katya's mistress, or let him inside, now.

He set the page carefully aside. "An interesting choice of topic."

She could not help herself. "Is that all you . . . have to say?"

He took a bit of cheese and bread and slowly chewed. "God, this is good." He reached for the port. "You are upset."

Carolyn looked down. "How can I not be?"

"Do you want to talk about it?"

"What more is there to say? They eloped. My grandmother never forgave my mother, and has hated my father from that very day." Carolyn stared at the table. "She refused to help us when I was very young, when we were in dire need. My mother begged her and she refused us. Because of her, my mother is dead." Carolyn realized what she had said, thoughts she had never dared admit to herself much less verbalize, and she was aghast.

"I am very sorry. How did your mother die?" Sverayov asked.

Carolyn refused to cry. But she told Sverayov exactly what had happened. "I do not know why I am telling you this." She managed a wan smile. "You must be very bored."

"You could never bore me. Perhaps your grandmother has as many regrets as you do."

"I doubt it. How can you say that? When she has ignored me my entire life?"

"I can say that because I am a very good judge of character," he said calmly, "and I saw just how interested in you she was."

"Yes. Interested. The way I am interested in the pygmies of Africa!"

Sverayov smiled, then reached for and covered her hand. "She does not hate you. She may hate your father, but you are her flesh and blood. Trust me," he said.

She looked from his warm, amber eyes to his full, sensual mouth and then to his large, tanned hand on top of hers. So many thoughts and feelings tumbled through her, too swiftly for her to sort out or identify. "I don't think trusting you is a good idea."

"I did not mean it that way," he said tersely, removing his hand.

"I am sorry," Carolyn whispered. "It is just . . ."

"What?"

And the silence was unnerving, as was the night. She shook her head. He was unnerving. "I am very tired. I must go to bed." She started to stand.

He caught her hand, restraining her. She froze. She looked at him and met his brilliant amber eyes. And then he lifted her hand and pressed it hard to his mouth, still holding her gaze.

Her only coherent thought was that she had known that it would come to this.

"Carolyn," he said harshly, standing. "I knew I should not have come here tonight." He did not release her hand.

She wet her lips. "But you did."

"Yes." He stared, not offering any explanation.

"We should say good night."

"Yes, we should. Why are your eyes tearing?"

"I suppose I am feeling sorry for myself," she whispered.

"Don't cry. There is no reason to cry."

And there wasn't—not from his point of view. After all, he did not love her. Carolyn pulled her hand free of his and wiped her eyes with her fingertips. "You must think me as childish as Katya."

"No. There is nothing childish about you. Will you come to work tomorrow?"

She watched him, not wanting him to leave, which was absurd. She felt paralyzed. "Yes."

He nodded, hesitated. "And Davison?"

"I don't understand."

"He is pursuing you."

"I don't think so."

He did not smile, his hands gripping the back of his chair. "Your grandmother was right about Davison. He is a solid young man. His intentions, Carolyn, are legitimate.

I do believe that he is in love with you and that, in time, he will offer for you.''

Carolyn's disbelief was vaster than before. ''I do not think so. You are wrong. Why are you telling me this?''

''I feel obliged to do so,'' he said. ''If he offers for you, you should seriously consider him.''

Carolyn was taken aback. Was he encouraging her to marry Anthony? She felt crushed. ''We are just friends, and,'' she added carefully, ''I do not think it could ever be anything more.''

''But if he offered for you?'' he pressed.

''I do not love him.''

''Ah, yes, you are a romantic—and proud of it.'' His tone became oddly gentle. ''Carolyn, could you not marry a good young man—without love?''

Her mouth pursed as she shook her head. ''No, I could not.'' She looked away, thinking not about standing in a quaint Norman church with Anthony, but in a magnificent, soaring cathedral with him. Oh, God.

Sverayov suddenly leaned forward. Before Carolyn knew it, she was in his powerful arms. His mouth touched hers. Brief and butterfly-soft. Carolyn moaned.

And then his lips were hot and hard on hers. Demanding that she open to him, for him, with him. Carolyn found herself clinging to his uniform, the dozens of gold buttons hurting her breasts, her body crushed by his. She forgot to protest, forgot to care. Carolyn kissed him back with all the desire she had been trying to deny since they had first met. Carolyn kissed him back hungrily, aching with her love.

It was an endless kiss, there in the dimly lit kitchen, the flickering candlelight playing over them, the night around them black and still and silent.

It was Sverayov who finally broke away, tearing his mouth from hers. Carolyn took one look at his fierce eyes, and buried her face against his chest. Now what? He would walk out of the shop—and tomorrow she would return to her position as Katya's companion, as if nothing had ever happened, as if this powerful bond did not exist.

His arms remained around her, hard and possessive, powerful and unyielding, like the man himself. And Carolyn held on to him, as tightly. A part of her yearned to be held by him like this forever. But it was only going to last for another instant, and she knew she must relish this brief moment, hold on to it for as long as she could.

"I must go," he whispered. "I did not come here to make love to you—no matter how I want to."

"Yes," she said hoarsely, "you must go." Married, she told herself. He is married. And suddenly she hated Marie-Elena.

Sverayov stepped back. His gaze held hers, with a promise that was powerful and male—one they were both determined to deny. And then he was gone.

Carolyn sat down at the kitchen table and cried.

❧ TWENTY-THREE ❧

IN spite of having passed a sleepless night, Carolyn arrived at Sverayov's town house at eight, in time to take breakfast with Katya. Katya brightened when Carolyn entered the small, brightly lit breakfast room. The governess glanced up once from her plate of cold meats and sausages, glared briefly, and resumed eating. Raffaldi was not present.

"Good morning," Carolyn said cheerfully. She was exhausted. She had spent most of the prior evening thinking about the impossibility of her predicament—and the impossibility of continuing this way when she had such powerful feelings for an unattainable man. She had been reduced to feeling hatred for another woman. What was happening to herself? How could she have become so base?

Carolyn knew that if she dared to continue on as Katya's companion, she must get an iron rein on her heart. She must gain control of her feelings, for they were forbidden, illicit, wrong. And she and Sverayov must never allow themselves an intimate moment again. Not in any way, shape, or form. Never.

"Good morning," Taichili returned grudgingly.

Katya smiled. "Good morning, Miss Browne."

Carolyn took her seat. "Where is Signor Raffaldi?" She hoped he was not sulking because of Katya's new program.

"He is taking a cup of cocoa in his room," Taichili answered without looking up.

Carolyn smiled at Katya. "It is a beautiful day. Perfect for an excursion to a museum this afternoon."

Taichili glowered again. This time she did not look away.

Carolyn smiled, trying to remain friendly. "Did you have a chance to study Katya's new schedule?"

"I certainly did," she said harshly. "It is absurd. I have never heard of teaching a little girl or any woman, for that matter, astronomy and philosophy. How will that prepare her for her life as a princess and a wife?"

"I do believe it shall prepare her very well," Carolyn said blandly. "So, you can see that two hours twice a week in the afternoon are cleared for educational excursions."

"Educational excursions," Taichili huffed.

"We are going to a museum?" Katya asked with wide eyes. "I have never been to a museum."

"This one is rather new and quite extraordinary. It has a wonderful exhibit on ancient Egypt. Whom do we know who was an Egyptian?"

Katya's brow furrowed. "Ptolemy?"

"You are right," Carolyn cried, delighted. "Before we go, we shall briefly discuss the pharaohs."

"What are pharaohs?"

"They are the rulers of Egypt, descended from an ancient royal family."

"Like my father," Katya said.

"Yes, like your father," Carolyn agreed, her smile fading. She was going to try to be far more compassionate toward Marie-Elena in the future. She would never allow herself to feel even a moment of jealousy or bitterness as far as the other woman was concerned. After all, were there not always two sides to every story? Perhaps she would even try to befriend the other woman!

"I would not mind studying the pharaohs, either," Sverayov said, breaking into her thoughts.

Carolyn almost fell off her seat as she twisted to look at him standing in the doorway. He filled it up. There were shadows beneath his eyes, as if he, too, had passed a restless night.

She gripped the table. If he had passed a sleepless night, undoubtedly it was not because of herself.

His gaze held hers. "Good morning," he said, apparently to the room at large. But his words were directed to her and her alone.

Katya smiled slightly and briefly. "Good morning, Father."

He walked over to his daughter and kissed the top of her head. He nodded at Taichili, who was seated as ramrod straight as any soldier now, and he slowly faced Carolyn.

She, of course, was helplessly absorbed in her recollections of the evening before. She was afraid that everyone present would guess that there was something between them. But she could not look away from his magnetic gaze no matter how much she wished to.

"Good morning, Miss Browne," he said.

"Good morning," she managed.

"Do you mind if I join you?" He was speaking to everyone, but continued to regard only Carolyn. His golden eyes were smoke. "The dining room is distinctly unappealing."

Carolyn knew he never ate in the breakfast room with his daughter. She shot a glance at Katya and saw her wide surprise. Even Taichili's normally taciturn expression was gone.

"Please," Carolyn said, since no one else spoke. "Did you enjoy your morning ride?"

"Actually, I did not ride today." His gaze was probing as he sat down at the head of the table, Carolyn on his right. "Does the visit to the museum today fit into your anthropological program?" he asked Carolyn.

She wondered why he had changed his daily routine. "Actually, it does. Egypt seemed the perfect place to start, because of the recent rage for its fashion and culture. Of course, we have Napoleon to thank for that." Carolyn finally smiled.

"Yes, we do," Sverayov said, his eyes still glued upon her.

Carolyn fell silent, wishing Sverayov would stop looking

at her in such a penetrating manner. Then she noticed that Katya was regarding him with worry. "Katya," she asked gently, "what is wrong?"

Katya looked down.

"Katya," Sverayov said, "is something amiss?"

Katya hesitated. Her cheeks were flushed. "Are you going to tell Miss Browne that we cannot go to the museum?" she asked in a strained, low voice.

"Absolutely not. I think it is a wonderful idea. In fact, I wish I were free this morning, for then I would join you." He smiled at his daughter.

Carolyn was amazed. She caught herself gaping and slammed her mouth shut.

"Hello," Alexi said from the doorway. He sauntered into the room. "What a cozy scene." He smiled widely at Carolyn and bent and scooped Katya up into his arms. She giggled as he hugged her hard before depositing her back in her chair. He slanted a look at his brother. "Might I take it that your interest this morning does not include a late gallop in the park?"

Sverayov's expression was bland. "It does not," he said. A servant had placed a plate of chops and broiled kidneys in front of him. He eyed Carolyn. "For some odd reason, I am ravenous."

Carolyn quickly looked away. She did not reply, knowing he referred to their encounter last night, which had ended so suddenly.

"Perhaps," Alexi slid into a seat, "you would not be so ravenous if you had not been out gallivanting last evening. Where did you go after the ball, big brother?" He was smug.

"I came home and went to bed," Nicholas said flatly.

Carolyn peeked first at him and then at his brother. Alexi was enjoying the moment, as if he knew all that had transpired. He, too, was served.

"Are you not eating?" Sverayov asked Carolyn.

She had not been served, but she was staff, and there

was a buffet on the sideboard. Carolyn began to stand.
"Yes."

His hand clamped down on her shoulder and he pushed
her gently back into her chair. "Please," he said. He transferred his plate to her place setting. Carolyn stared at the
food, then peeked at the raptly attentive faces around her—
even the two serving men were staring. But then, she was
the companion, and a prince had just served her. "My good
fellow." Sverayov addressed one of the staff, whose name
he obviously did not know. "Kindly bring me another
plate, exactly the same as the one Miss Browne is about to
enjoy."

The servants scurried to the sideboard.

Carolyn swallowed and met Sverayov's golden eyes.
"Thank you," she said.

"Ladies first," he replied politely. "Do not wait for me,
Miss Browne."

Carolyn picked up her fork, aware of Alexi, Katya, and
Taichili regarding her and Sverayov. Good God, she
thought, torn between despair and hope, they all think
something is going on between us. In the next breath, she
thought, And they are all correct.

At the last minute, Raffaldi had asked if he could join them,
a pleasant surprise. It was not quite three that afternoon
when the trio arrived at the museum.

"Why, look at that, Katya," Carolyn exclaimed, pointing
toward a small fresco of pyramids. "Do you remember
what we learned this morning about the pyramids?"

Katya nodded, barely looking at the artwork, around
which many visitors to the museum were oohing and aah-
ing. Carolyn and Raffaldi exchanged glances.

"The Egyptians were brilliant engineers in their time,"
Raffaldi told Katya.

Katya shuffled her feet, staring at the cool marble floor.

Carolyn was holding Katya's hand. "What is wrong,
dear?" she asked. "I thought you were looking forward to
our excursion."

Katya flushed. "My father said he wished he could come with us. He has never said that before."

"And he meant it." Carolyn squeezed her hand. "We shall invite your father to join us another time."

"Will he really come?" Katya asked with transparent hope.

"I believe so," Carolyn said firmly.

Katya looked up at Carolyn. "But he's so busy."

Carolyn frowned. She was going to make certain that they had an outing with Sverayov in the very near future. "I do not think he is too busy for you."

"What is that?" Katya asked suddenly, pointing across the cool, dimly illuminated room.

Carolyn turned, and as she did so, she saw a shadow out of the corner of her eye. Not for the first time since they had entered the museum. Carolyn shifted, not certain why, to glance around, but no one was standing behind her. She felt slightly uneasy, but dismissed it as nonsensical. "That is a mummy," Carolyn replied.

"What is a mummy?"

Carolyn began to explain, but instantly felt eyes upon her—or them—again. This time she whirled. But no one stood anywhere in the vicinity, staring at her back. Carolyn wondered at herself. Was she having an attack of overeager imagination? "Come. Let's take a closer look."

As the trio crossed the room to study the mummy, which was cordoned off, Raffaldi took her aside. "Is something wrong, Miss Browne?" he asked.

"No." Carolyn smiled. "Nothing is wrong. I had a poor night's rest and I am merely fatigued."

Raffaldi smiled. "Katya, let me tell you how they make mummys," he said.

Carolyn listened with half an ear, while her gaze kept wandering around the room.

An hour later, Carolyn, Katya, and Raffaldi stepped out of the museum and walked down the wide front steps of the Greco-Roman building. Carolyn and Katya were holding hands, and they paused in the cobbled courtyard, looking for their carriage. "There it is," Katya said, pointing down the street, which was very congested with traffic. Their phaeton was momentarily blocked by a huge dray, drawn by draft horses, which was attempting to turn onto the street, but had to cross through the oncoming traffic to do so.

"Stupid driver." Raffaldi shook his head. Other coachmen and hansom drivers were shouting at the driver of the dray.

"We can wait," Carolyn said. "It will not be more than a few minutes."

Pedestrians, many of them museum visitors, were hurrying to and fro all around them. Most of the passing crowd were well-dressed ladies and gentlemen. Carolyn continued to hold Katya's hand. Two ragged boys were rolling a ball in the gutter of the street. Katya smiled at their antics.

Suddenly one of the boys turned and kicked the ball hard, away from the sidewalk, into the traffic of the street. Carolyn could not imagine why he would do such a thing, but was not given even a moment to contemplate it, for the two boys were suddenly on the sidewalk, racing up it furiously. Carolyn and her entourage stood directly in their path. She suddenly realized they were all about to be barreled over and she stiffened, gripping Katya's hand more tightly, beginning to drag her away.

But it was too late. The bigger boy barreled his body between Carolyn and the child, severing their grip. Carolyn cried out, "Katya!" But she saw, with relief, that Raffaldi had grabbed her and jerked her aside safely. And then she felt her reticule being torn out of her other hand. She cried out again, in protest, comprehending what was happening, yet now she was shoved hard to her knees. Carolyn gasped as she hit the stone sidewalk, the cutpurse fleeing with her bag.

It had all happened so quickly and Carolyn was briefly dazed. Then the anger began. As a gentleman offered to help her stand, his lady friend crying out in concern, Carolyn glanced around with worry, trying to locate her charge and the Italian. She espied them standing on the steps of the museum with sheer relief. She had been thoroughly separated from Katya and Raffaldi, however. Carolyn had been pushed to the curb. "I'm fine," Carolyn muttered.

But no harm was done. She'd had little of value in her reticule, and Katya was all right. Carolyn supposed that she had two bruised knees. It could have been worse.

"Are you all right, Miss Browne?" Raffaldi called over to her.

Carolyn was about to reply, the stranger helping her up. And suddenly Raffaldi screamed to her in warning—just as someone slammed into her, hard, from behind. Carolyn was shoved violently forward—into the street. She landed on her hands and knees and then her face. Her cheek and temple burned, a pain shot through her side, and the wind was knocked completely out of her. For one instant, blackness enveloped Carolyn.

"Carolyn!" It was Raffaldi, screaming. "The dray!"

The cloud of blackness lifted. Carolyn was seized with comprehension. She twisted to her hands and knees, glancing up. Horror immobilized her. The dray being pulled by the huge draft horses was bearing down upon her. And it was obvious that, the horses being so huge, the driver could not see Carolyn, prone in its path.

Katya screamed, shrill and high. Strangers also cried out.

Carolyn rolled. Hard and fast, to the side. And as she lay there, she watched, in disbelief, huge hooves pounding down by her head, her shoulder, her hip. Narrowly missing her. In fact, Carolyn could feel the draft caused by each hoof. Then the oversized wheels rolled by. And the dray was gone.

Carolyn lay in the street, unmoving. Sweat streamed down her body. Her heart beat with frantic urgency. And then she began to shake.

Katya flew off the museum steps, followed by the Italian, and knelt beside Carolyn. "Miss Browne, Miss Browne!" she sobbed. "Don't be dead, please!"

Carolyn inhaled, trembling. *She had almost been run*

over. "I'm not dead, Katya." Sweat continued to pour down her body. She tested her arms and legs, gingerly, and found that she could move. But pain lanced through her side. "Oh, God," she said, sitting up slowly.

Raffaldi squatted beside them, his swarthy face filled with concern. Bystanders had formed a half circle around them. Carolyn heard several ladies chatting rapid-fire, in- dignation in their tones. Someone cried, "Did you see that? She was *pushed*!"

"Miss Browne, dear God, let me help you up. Are you hurt?" Raffaldi asked, wide-eyed.

"I think I am fine. Except for my side, which may be strained." Carolyn's shock was severe. It was hard to think of anything other than that she had almost been run over by the draft horses. But how had she fallen into the street?

An image of the two boys, playing with the ball, seared her mind, as did the bigger boy barreling through her and Katya, in order to steal her purse.

"You are bleeding," Katya cried. "Your face is all scraped!"

Carolyn touched her cheek and found her fingertips stained with blood and dirt.

"Let me help you up," Raffaldi said, putting his arm around her. "We should get out of this street."

As Carolyn stood, the pain renewed itself in her left side, and she bit off a gasp. Her knees refused to hold her up. She had fallen into the street, hadn't she? The exact se- quence of events was scrambled in her mind.

"She was pushed!"

The woman's shocked statement echoed in Carolyn's mind. Had she been pushed? Carolyn touched her throbbing temples. But why? Why would someone push her into the street—and into the path of the oncoming dray?

"Miss Browne, you need a physician," Katya said, her voice choked.

Carolyn looked down at her, saw she was close to tears

and terribly frightened. "I am fine, Katya." She hugged the child only to wince with pain again. Then she looked up and met Raffaldi's eyes. "It was just an accident."

His expression was severe. And doubtful.

❧ TWENTY-FOUR ❧

NICHOLAS hesitated on the threshold of the nursery class-room, but it was vacant. Of course, it was past teatime, and he had not really expected to find either his daughter or Carolyn in the schoolroom at this hour. Nicholas turned and walked down the corridor toward his daughter's rooms. He heard Katya's voice, followed by Taichili's firmer tones. He knocked upon the door. It was promptly opened by the governess. "Good afternoon," Nicholas said to her. He smiled at Katya, but quickly saw that Carolyn was not present in the room. He was disappointed, undeniably so. "How was your outing, Katya?"

She looked at him and said not a word.

Nicholas entered the room. "Did you enjoy the museum?"

Katya remained silent.

"Surely you have some wonderful anecdotes to share, perhaps about the pharaohs?" he prompted. He was becoming concerned.

Katya finally said, reluctantly, "We saw a mummy."

Nicholas was somewhat alarmed now, and he glanced at Taichili, who was suddenly very busy in the corner of the bedroom, folding clothing—which the maids usually did. He faced his daughter. "Katya, clearly something is amiss. What?"

She appeared ready to burst into tears.

Nicholas wheeled. "Taichili. Do you know what is wrong?"

Taichili faced him with maddening slowness. "Apparently there was some, er, trouble on the, er, excursion, Your Excellency."

He was on alert. "What kind of trouble?"

Taichili said, "There was a mishap. The, uh, companion was robbed."

He stared. "Miss Browne was robbed? Where is she? Is she all right?" He was more than alarmed—and stunned by the intensity of his concern for Carolyn. He turned to gaze at his daughter again. "You are all right, Katya?"

She nodded, eyes wide.

"Where is Miss Browne?" he demanded.

"In her room, I suppose," Taichili sniffed. Then she said, under her breath but loud enough for him to hear, "An excursion, hmph. Taking a small child out on the streets was asking for trouble, I say." She glared at the floor.

Nicholas strode from the room. Carolyn's door was closed. He rapped smartly on it, but there was no answer, and he knocked again. "Miss Browne?"

When there was no response, he opened the door. The room was empty. It quickly occurred to him that she must be downstairs, taking her supper with the staff. Nicholas strode down the hall, pounded down the stairs, reminding himself that she was not harmed. As he approached the kitchens, which he had never entered before, he could hear the uproar and clamor from within—pots and pans clanging, knives chopping and thudding on cutting boards, and quiet conversation punctuated by someone's—the chef's, he assumed—near-hysterical directives. He stepped inside. Cooks and their helpers were in the midst of supper preparations—chopping and slicing, mixing and baking, stirring heavy iron cauldrons. Other servants were scurrying about with pots and pans, while others were scrubbing them. The room was resonant with chatter, gossip, and even chuckles and laughter. But suddenly someone, a maid, saw him and cried out. Everyone turned—and froze. A dozen pairs of eyes riveted upon him. The silence was so absolute that he could hear his own breathing.

Nicholas ignored everyone. Carolyn stood with Raffaldi by the huge iron sink, her back to him. His coachman, he realized, was also with them—which made little sense. "Miss Browne?"

Her shoulders stiffened. Both Raffaldi and the coachman, whose name he did not know, faced him immediately. Raffaldi smiled obsequiously, but was pale beneath his swarthy coloring. His coachman's smile was frozen in place. And finally, Carolyn also turned.

He was shocked. One side of her face was scraped raw. Her dress was torn on the same shoulder, and rudely stained everywhere else. He cursed. "*Chort voz'mi*! What happened?" he cried, striding forward.

She was pale. "My lord, your daughter is unharmed."

"I know that," he said furiously. "Are you hurt?"

"No."

"I want to know what the hell happened," he demanded.

She blanched even more. "A cutpurse stole my reticule—and I fell into the street."

His active mind absorbed that instantly. He knew she was not telling him everything—he saw it in her green eyes. "And?"

She forced a smile. "And that is all."

"Carolyn." He tilted up her chin. "There is more."

She shook her head, avoiding his eyes.

He glanced at Raffaldi, who also avoided his gaze, and cursed again. "You need a physician."

"No. I am fine."

He looked at the coachman. "Bring a physician to the house immediately."

"Yes, Your Excellency." The coachman bowed and ran from the kitchens.

"Come with me," Nicholas ordered. He stepped back and waited for Carolyn to precede him. He followed her into the corridor, his booted steps sounding briskly on the parquet floors. "To the library," he instructed.

She turned down another corridor and they entered the room, where a small fire had been set in the tawny marble hearth. Nicholas went to the sideboard and poured a large glass of vodka.

"I am beyond needing that," she said quietly.

He ignored her, removed a handkerchief from his breast pocket, and dipped it into the liquid. "This will sting, but it will help to avoid infection—and scarring."

She met his gaze. Their eyes held. "I can do that," she said slowly.

Nicholas did not respond. He dipped the kerchief in the alcohol and gently washed the abrasion on her cheek, noting that Carolyn neither gasped nor flinched. Their gazes met again. Where her sleeve was hanging off her shoulder the skin had also been bruised, and he applied alcohol to that scrape too. "Is there more?" he asked.

"No."

He planted his hands on his hips. "Now," he said, "why don't you tell me what really happened?"

She hesitated. "I have already told you. It was a boy. I'm sure he did not mean to hurt me, and that he is tremendously disappointed with the meager contents of my purse."

"I will replace those contents," he said automatically. "You are dissembling."

She stiffened.

"I am adept at reading people, Carolyn." His tone was low.

Her jaw flexed. Her gaze wandered. "Very well. I may have been pushed."

His brow lifted. "You said you fell."

"I'm not sure."

Nicholas studied her silently. "The cutpurse pushed you? Accidentally?"

"I assume so," she said.

"I am glad it was not worse." But his mind was racing. "You are upset."

"A little," she admitted. She lowered her gaze. "It was terrifying. Almost being run over by that dray. And I feel that I have let down my charge. If I cannot take Katya on a simple excursion—"

"You were almost run over!" He was aghast.

She looked up. "Yes."

He stared, his heart pounding, sweat upon his brow. "God," he finally said, and reflexively, he reached out and cupped her cheek. Immediately their gazes met.

And he thought about last night, in the kitchen behind the bookshop. Nicholas dropped his hand and paced away from her, disturbed both by what had happened and what seemed to be happening now. Controlling his feelings for Carolyn no longer seemed quite so simple.

Finally he faced her, only to find her regarding him intently. "This was not your fault. Next time you will have a pair of brawny footmen as an escort."

"Most people do not need an escort to go to the museum, Your Excellency."

Again he thought about last night—about how Carolyn had looked in her cotton nightclothes, about how she had felt in his arms. "Nicholas," he said softly.

She was still.

"Carolyn." He hesitated. "There is something I must discuss with you." His business in London had been concluded that afternoon. A treaty had been signed between their respective countries. He had, obviously, been right. Davison had been the last obstacle to the conclusion of the alliance. In the very near future not only would Marie-Elena be returning home, but so would Katya, and so would he.

"What is it?" she asked, her tone strained.

"We signed the treaty this afternoon."

Her eyes widened.

"I have already sent a courier home with the good news."

Carolyn had turned white.

But before he could ask her if she would be returning with them, his wife burst into the room. She saw them and froze on the threshold. Nicholas felt a twinge of guilt when he saw her, in spite of all that she had done. Being estranged was one thing, but having strong feelings for another woman was quite different.

Marie-Elena's smile was brittle. "I do hope I am not intruding," she said, entering the room.

Nicholas eyed her. "If I had wished to be left alone, the door would have been closed." His gaze met his wife's.

She looked at Carolyn. "Oh, my. What happened to you, Miss Browne?"

Carolyn was staring at Marie-Elena with obvious dismay. "I . . . have had an accident."

"Oh, really? What kind of accident?" Marie-Elena asked with blatantly feigned concern. Clearly she did not care.

Carolyn said, unsmiling, "I had a minor run-in with a cutpurse, Your Highness. Now, if you will both excuse me, I am very tired."

"Oh, but you must tell us the details," Marie-Elena said. "How upset you must be. Are you hurt?"

"That is enough," Nicholas said flatly, furious. "If you cannot muster up any genuine compassion for Miss Browne, perhaps you should leave us."

Marie-Elena's eyes widened. "But I do feel terrible about Miss Browne's accident. And I only came to ask if it was true. The rumor is all over the city. I've also heard that the treaty was signed this afternoon. Is it true, Niki?" Marie-Elena asked.

For one moment, Nicholas met Carolyn's eyes. What if she did not return to Russia with them? He realized that he would miss her terribly. And that his interest in her returning with his household had become personal, not professional.

"Niki?" Anger was in her tone as she jerked on his arm. "It is true. That is why you were gone the entire day. Isn't it?"

He tore his gaze from Carolyn. "Yes. It is true. I signed in lieu of the tsar, and the prince regent also signed. Our countries are no longer at war."

"That is wonderful," Marie-Elena cried. She smiled at Carolyn. "Isn't that wonderful? Now we can go home *together*, Niki." Her eyes glittered. "When do we leave?" she asked Nicholas.

He hesitated, his gaze locking with Carolyn's. He did not look at Marie-Elena. "As soon as possible."

She laughed, looking from Carolyn to Nicholas and back again. She touched her heart theatrically. "This is wonderful. I cannot wait. I have missed my homeland so." She was smiling.

Carolyn had remained motionless. But she looked at him, blinking furiously, the tip of her nose turning red. And she turned, rushing from the room.

"Carolyn!" he cried.

Marie-Elena took his arm. "Let her go. Just let her go. She is not for you, Niki, and you know it."

Nicholas met her gaze and did not reply.

"Signor Raffaldi, please take a seat." Nicholas regarded the Italian through shrewd eyes. Raffaldi was as pale beneath his natural olive coloring as he had been in the kitchen a few minutes ago.

The tutor did as he was asked, sitting stiffly, his gaze upon Nicholas.

"I am very concerned about what happened this afternoon," Nicholas said, standing in front of his desk.

"I am so sorry, Your Excellency, and I swear we shall never allow any bandits to ever come so near the princess again!"

Nicholas sighed. "Neither you nor Miss Browne could help the fact that a cutpurse singled your group out as a target for himself. That is not what I am concerned about. I want to know exactly what happened this afternoon. Miss Browne is not being cooperative."

Raffaldi nodded, leaning forward eagerly. "She was robbed by a boy, perhaps one thirteen years old."

"And?"

Raffaldi shook his head. "It was terrible, Excellency.

The cutpurse ran away, but a man was standing behind her, clad as a gentleman, although he was hardly that! I thought he was moving to help her, as the cutpurse had knocked her to her knees. Instead, Excellency, he pushed Miss Browne from behind, not only into the street, but right into the path of an oncoming dray.''

Nicholas stared. "He pushed her? Not the cutpurse?"

"No, Excellency. It was the gentleman."

"Surely he bumped into her accidentally," Nicholas said.

"It was not an accident. I saw the entire incident!" Raffaldi cried.

Nicholas thought that he could feel the blood draining from his face. But who would push Carolyn into the street—and into the path of an oncoming dray? Had the intent been to cause an accident—or worse?

What immediately went through his mind was that her father was involved in espionage and treason, and that through Carolyn, he could be manipulated. But he also could not help suspecting his wife. She was thoughtless and spoiled and terribly vain, and she sensed how involved he was becoming. Could she go so far?

He did not think it likely. But he did not think it a possibility he could dismiss.

And if he ever found out it was Marie-Elena, he would exile her to Siberia.

"Thank God she is not hurt. Or dead," the tutor said dramatically.

"Yes. Thank God," Nicholas said.

Carolyn lay on her bed, in her cotton nightgown and robe, unable to sleep. She had finally given in to the urge to cry. She felt crushed, devastated. The treaty had been signed and Sverayov was going to leave as soon as was possible. He would return to Russia, and she would never see him again.

Unless she went with him.

She closed her eyes, one arm flung over her forehead,

imagining a battlefield filled with soldiers and horses, muskets firing, sabers rattling, cannons booming, smoke mushrooming in the air. He would rejoin his command, she had not a doubt. What if he were killed?

She hugged her pillow. She was so very tempted to go with him, and she was not thinking now of Katya's needs. She had fallen in love, and while Nicholas was, superficially, the antithesis of all she believed in, a man who represented a class system founded on privilege not merit, on autocracy not democracy, in truth, he was no jaded, self-centered aristocrat. He was a caring father, a powerful leader, a nobleman and a patriot. He was even a gentleman, for God's sake, he had proven that time and again since they had met. He was a man motivated by honor and by duty. How could she not love him?

But he was going home, and he was married. Carolyn wiped her eyes. She would be insane to return to Russia with him and his household. Insane. For being Katya's companion—and being around him this way—was actually hurtful. No, she must be strong. She would spend whatever time she had left with Katya, and then she would return to Browne's Books, Old and New, and she would forget that Nicholas Ivanovitch Sverayov even existed.

Her bedchamber was dark. The candle had burned out hours ago. Carolyn did not care. She kept recalling the way he had been looking at her while his wife rattled on about their returning home. Carolyn did not think it was her imagination, but he had not been happy, either. He had seemed very grim.

If only they could talk about it.

Carolyn sat up, hugging her knees now. But that would be a mistake. For she imagined that he was downstairs at this hour in the library, brooding and alone. And Marie-Elena had gone out for the evening.

Carolyn tried to imagine his departure—and the days and weeks and months that would ensue. She would never see him again—she would be heartbroken. But did they not say that time healed all wounds? Even a broken heart?

But he was waiting for her reply. She had not told him that she could not go to Russia with him. Carolyn slipped from the bed, retying her wrapper very firmly. Her heart was wedged in her throat and she was grim. The damnable truth was, she wanted to go with him, she did.

She left her bedroom. The hall was unlit, black with shadow. Attempting to be soundless, she tiptoed to the stairs. And as she went down them, each step seemed to creak with deafening loudness.

The library door was open. Carolyn saw that the fire was blazing in the hearth. She swallowed, moving closer to the open doorway—close enough to peer around the corner and gaze into the room. Her heart slammed to a halt.

Sverayov lay on the sofa, but he was not asleep. He was staring, morosely, she thought, into the dancing flames of the fire.

She summoned up all of her courage. "Nicholas."

He started, sliding his legs immediately over the sofa's edge, standing. Their gazes locked.

"I know it is late, but I was hoping to speak to you," she said nervously.

"You have been reading my mind," he said harshly. "For I have been willing you to come downstairs."

She stared. These were not the kind of words she wanted to hear—it would make what she had to say so much more difficult.

He moved toward her and shut the door firmly behind her. "Carolyn." His face was taut. "I am sorry about Marie-Elena's behavior this afternoon, and even sorrier that you had to learn about the treaty the way that you did."

"I was shocked," she admitted, trembling.

"I know you were," he said simply.

"When do you think you will be leaving?"

His gaze moved over her face. "I hope within a week. Davout has taken Minsk. I must rejoin Barclay, who guards the road to Moscow. It is my duty. There is no choice."

Carolyn tried to control her trembling. "Within a week," Carolyn echoed.

"Are you coming with us?"

Carolyn hesitated. "I cannot."

His eyes were intense. "I want you to come with us."

She closed her eyes, her heart hammering. When she opened them, she tried to choose her words with care—hoping he would not try to exercise his powers of persuasion on her. "My life is here. My father is here."

His nostrils flared. The firelight played off one side of his face, highlighting his Slavic cheekbones. "Katya needs you. You could try the position—say, for six months. And if you are unhappy, then I shall not try to convince you to stay."

She was tempted. Terribly so. And a part of her wanted him to acknowledge the real problem, their desire for one another—their feelings for one another—and the fact of his wife. "No."

But he said, harshly, "It will not be dangerous. I would never put you in any danger. I will leave my household in St. Petersburg. It will be completely safe. If it becomes apparent that Napoleon will march on the north instead of Moscow, there will be plenty of time for everyone to be evacuated. I would not allow Katya—or you—to be jeopardized." His eyes were fierce.

Carolyn stared. "No."

His golden eyes were piercing. "You are resolved."

Suddenly tears filled her eyes. She nodded.

"I cannot bear your tears," he whispered, and his hand was cupping the back of her neck, beneath the curling tendrils of her hair. "Do not cry. Why are you crying?"

"I am crying because I am a fool," she whispered.

"There is nothing foolish about you, Carolyn," he said.

"Then this is good-bye." But he spoke as if it were a question.

She nodded again, incapable of speech. And it would be a final parting—within a week. How her heart hurt her now.

He stared as if undecided. And his eyes blazed. Before Carolyn could blink or protest, he pulled her forward. Carolyn found herself in his arms, and then his mouth was on hers, and all resolutions and protestations died. Their mouths locked. Carolyn pressed against him, open for him, clinging, praying he would not die when he went to war, praying he would one day return, and praying she might forget him—while praying that she never would.

He tore his mouth from hers. "I am not good at games," he said. "I want you, Carolyn."

"I want you, too," she whispered, her palms flat on his chest.

He lifted her in his arms, carrying her to the rug in front of the fire. He laid her down on her back, one hand on each side of her shoulders. Carolyn was faint with the immensity of the feelings exploding from within. She had never dreamed that love and desire, blended together, could be so potent, so powerful, so overwhelming, so terrifying—so real. She felt more tears. She had this moment, this one single moment to love him and be loved by him, and she knew that it was going to be over and that it would never happen again. There was no way she could deny herself.

For one more moment, they looked into each other's eyes, and Carolyn felt as if she were being stripped bare to her very soul. And then he bent his head and kissed her.

He kissed her deeply. She reached up and found his hard, broad shoulders, aching to explore him. While he kissed her, she slid her palms down his arms, which were taut and bulging with muscle. She touched his flat, concave abdomen.

His mouth moved over her face, down her throat. Carolyn gripped his wrists, eyes closed, aching to be joined with him—never had she wanted anything more. He covered one of her breasts with his hand. The thin cotton of her nightclothes might as well have been nonexistent. Carolyn inhaled. "I think I might die from pleasure," she whispered impulsively.

"Many times, I hope, before the night is through," he whispered back. "I will try very hard not to hurt you," he said. He slipped her nightgown down to her waist and caressed her breasts, his palms brushing over her nipples.

Carolyn gasped, unable to reply. And then his mouth was on hers again, hungrily, his hands on her breasts, then delving between her legs. Carolyn tensed briefly, shocked, as he stroked the folds there, generating a wet heat that left her dizzy, clinging, and breathless.

Carolyn cried out. She stroked his hair and back while he kissed her neck and throat. She managed to slide her hands into his shirt, across his chest and down his hard, flat belly. She felt him tense. How she needed him. How she wanted to explore every single inch of him.

He rose up over her, eyes hot, straddling her and ripping off his shirt. Carolyn was mesmerized, hardly able to breathe. Her gaze took in every inch of his broad, muscular shoulders, the hard slabs of his chest, the bulge of his biceps, and the flat planes of his abdomen. Tawny hair swirled just above the narrow waistband of his dove-gray pants. Her eyes froze. There was no mistaking the long, hard line pressing up against his wool trousers.

"I am very excited," he said, watching her.

Her gaze flew to his. "You are beautiful."

He smiled slightly. "As are you, dushka." He bent and tongued one of her nipples very languidly, a shocking contrast to the way he had just been kissing her. Carolyn closed her eyes, heard herself groan helplessly.

He stood.

Carolyn's eyes flew open but she did not move. His hands were on the flap of his trousers, his long, nimble fingers unbuttoning it. Her mouth became dry. She stared, watching the fabric covering his groin parting into a vee. His manhood was visible, bursting the wool seams.

Carolyn had never felt more exquisite, more desirable, or more feminine than she did in that moment.

He slid his trousers down his long, muscular legs and kicked them aside.

Carolyn looked up. He towered over her. Allowing her, she thought, to satisfy her curiosity—but it was far more than that.

He knelt over her, unsmiling, his expression strained. She

tensed as his hands slid over her, pulling the wrapper from her body. Her heart hammered now with lightning speed. She clenched her fists as he slowly drew the cotton night-gown up over her head, tossing it aside.

He smiled very slightly, his gaze moving over her breasts, down her torso, and to the vee of her sex. One of his hands ran down her slim thighs. Brushing the vee there.

Carolyn felt her nails digging into her palms. Desperately, she wanted him to touch her, take her, now.

His gaze on her face, he slid his hand between her thighs and palmed her sex. Carolyn began to die, bit by bit, piece by piece, as his slow, gentle exploration began. "Oh, God," she heard herself say.

He found her and rubbed.

She gasped.

He slid over her. "You are beautiful, Caro."

Carolyn could not reply. She was rapidly losing the last of her sanity. It had never occurred to her that a man might touch a woman this way, and that it might provoke such heated, intense, feverish longing. And then she felt something else, stroking over her, wet and soft and greedy.

She cried out, for he was there between her legs, and it was his tongue now touching her, tasting her, laving up her essence. Exploring every nook and cranny, parting the thick folds, licking the tiny apex hidden there.

Carolyn gasped, gripping his shoulders. "Oh, please!"

He lifted his head and briefly, their eyes met. He bent again, holding her thighs wide apart. All rational thought fled her mind. Carolyn cried out.

She could not stand it. Carolyn sat up, reaching for him, on the verge of whirling away into the heavens far above. He did not stop what he was doing no matter that she tugged on his bulging arms. "Nicholas," she cried.

He lifted his face and she found his mouth, kissing him frantically. He moved over her. His arms encircled her and his knees kept her legs spread wide. And his huge, rock-hard manhood pushed into her.

He thrust into her. Carolyn gasped, stunned by the pleasure, the beauty, the completion. Their gazes met once, briefly, and she saw the shock in his eyes, too. And then he was thrusting, hard and fast, while raining kisses on her mouth and neck. Carolyn held on to him and managed to think, I will love him forever. And then the pressure that was rapidly building within her, one which, she knew, promised eternity and paradise, crested. She heard herself calling his name.

The explosion came. Vaster than anything she had imagined, and it took Carolyn completely by surprise. Hurling her far away, into the throes of the universe. Eventually the stars and lights faded, and she was drifting somewhere, outside of her body. She became aware of him arching over her, caught in the throes of his own climax. Carolyn returned to earth, smiling as she held him.

For a long moment they just lay there together, regaining their breathing. Carolyn decided that the aftermath was as wonderful as everything else. She remained somewhat dazed, very awed. He kissed her shoulder once and rolled to his side, still holding her in his arms.

And then it all clicked—the past, the present, and the oh, so horrible future. A future apart, a future without him. Carolyn stiffened.

"Do not have regrets now," he said harshly.

She pushed herself out of his arms and sat up. He also sat, regarding her silently. Then Carolyn thought about the fact that they could be discovered at any moment, and she looked fearfully toward the door. Now guilt overwhelmed her. Guilt because of his wife.

He was grim as he stood and, starkly, beautifully naked, went to the door and locked it. He returned and stared down at her. "Now you are unhappy," he said. "Now I have hurt you."

Carolyn turned away, groping for her nightgown. She quickly slipped it over her head and pulled it on. "I do not know how I feel," she said as harshly, reaching for her wrapper. "But adultery is wrong."

He stood and pulled on his trousers, his gaze on her. "I

have not slept with my wife in five and a half years, Carolyn. I will never sleep with her again. I tolerate her presence in my life only for Katya's sake."

Carolyn stared, stunned. "I did not know."

"I mentioned more than once that we are estranged."

"I did not know that you do not have any . . . intimacy with her."

"How could I? After all that she has done." He regarded her. "Does that change anything?"

Carolyn bit her lip. "It does not make what we did right."

He shrugged on his shirt, his movements filled with anger. "Life is rarely fair, Carolyn, or easy or simple." His fingers moved swiftly over the pearl buttons. "I did not expect this, either."

She was silent. It was hard to think rationally, for her heart was begging her not to be a fool. Not to throw this away. To take a lover's crumbs. "Should I remain here as Katya's companion until you leave?"

He came to her and, before she knew it, he had lifted her to her feet and was holding her hard and firm against his body. "What would you say, and do, if I said I still want you to come to Russia with us?"

She pulled away. "That is impossible." It had never been more impossible—except her heart yearned for him, even now, and she missed him when he had yet to go.

He stared. "I knew you would say that." His eyes were dark. "Well, you are far more noble than I. I suppose you think I should live as a monk?"

Carolyn looked away. "I did not say that."

"What if I asked you to come to St. Petersburg independently—in order to be my mistress," he said.

Carolyn gasped.

His jaw flexed. His eyes blazed. "It is not an insult. It is done all the time when a married man, in a position such as mine, cares for a woman. If you asked me to, I would build you a palace."

"No," Carolyn said, far closer to tears now than before—and for a very different reason. "No." She shook her head. "How many mistresses have you built palaces for, Nicholas?" she asked, quavering.

"None."

She turned away, hugging herself.

"But I see that does not console you."

She closed her eyes. The only real solution to what she was feeling was to stop loving him.

"Will you be here tomorrow?" he asked harshly, interrupting her thoughts.

Carolyn looked at him. "I shall be leaving in the morning, Nicholas."

He stared grimly at her.

"I cannot continue here. It is the worst idea," she managed. She was perilously close to tears. "I will make up some excuse for Katya. Perhaps I will tell her that my father is ill. But I will promise to write her frequently," Carolyn said. She felt that she was babbling. She also felt tears on her cheeks.

"And will you write to me, as well?"

She pursed her mouth, about to weep.

"Well?" he demanded.

"If you wish," she gasped. "Good-bye, Nicholas." She turned blindly away, stumbled to the door.

"Wait!" he cried. He strode to her. "Do not leave like this. Surely you can work for the rest of the week—and we can use the time to think."

"Good-bye." She did not face him, holding on to the brass door handle as if for her life. She wept silently now. "You are . . . the most . . . extraordinary man," she somehow managed, choked, and then she flung the door open.

"Carolyn," he cried.

Carolyn ran barefoot down the hall.

He did not follow her.

PART THREE

Embers

❦ TWENTY-FIVE ❦

IT was a propitious day, but it did not begin that way. Carolyn sat alone at the counter in Browne's Books, staring at the four walls. It was almost closing time. It had been pouring since noon, the perfect accompaniment to her mood, and she had not had a single customer all day. Not a single customer, not a single sale. And George was still away.

She rubbed her eyes. As she did so, visions of bloody battles danced in her head. Soldiers on foot, screaming and wounded, guns firing, cannons booming, flames licking the sky. Sverayov and his family had left almost a month ago. He had not remained in London for another week. Exactly three days after that fateful, terrible night of misspent passion, the Sverayovs had departed England on a Russian military transport ship, bound by sea for St. Petersburg. Carolyn knew, having done a bit of investigative work, that by ship, they would have arrived at their destination within ten days to two weeks. Assuming they had not been caught in the cross fire of the war.

Carolyn cradled her head in her hands. The war. Suddenly it loomed in front of her as if it were taking place in her backyard. She had not heard of any engagements taking place at sea, but she guessed they must, at least a broadside here and there, surely, considering the British and the French blockades, but such incidents must not be significant enough to be reported in the papers. Wellington had recently taken Salamanca, and that had taken up days and days of the news, with most of London jubilant and celebrating, already expecting him to enter and take Madrid. But there was very little news from the Russian front, dear God. There had been a battle at Ostrowo in July, but no one seemed to know where that even was! And there had been another small battle recently at Kubrin, which Carolyn had learned was near Brest. It had been a small Russian victory, one of their first. But it was clearly peripheral to what was happening—yet what was happening? Napoleon's army seemed to be forging deeper and deeper into the Russian countryside without resistance. Rumors held that La Grande Armée was approaching Smolensk. But were these mere rumors—or the truth? Carolyn had immediately rushed to an atlas, and had been horrified to learn just how close Moscow and Smolensk were to one another. Only one hundred and fifty miles or so. If it was true, did that mean that Sverayov was there, in the vicinity of Smolensk? Carolyn knew—or assumed—that Sverayov had rejoined his command in the First Army. And now she was beating herself over the head for not finding out, before he left, exactly where he was going, and which army he would be with. But then, she had been in pain, and had never dreamed he would leave so swiftly—without even a goodbye.

A tear slipped down her cheek.

At least, she thought glumly, Katya was safe in St. Petersburg. At least she knew where to find the child if she ever wanted to. She would be at his ancestral home, the Vladchya Palace. Then Carolyn realized where her thoughts were leading. Absurd! As if she would ever have the need to go and locate Katya there.

She fought hard not to cry. She was brokenhearted, and she had never imagined it would be this way. But there was no alternative. She must forget him. She must redirect her heart. What they had done was wrong, nothing could ever make it right, even if it had been glorious at the time, even if it had felt so absolutely right. But how was she going to forget him when he now haunted her thoughts even more incessantly than he had before he left? When she was so worried about him and his welfare? When, being in damned London, she could not find out anything about him, his country, or the damnable war?

At moments like these, Carolyn felt like going to Russia herself, just to find out what was happening. Hopefully, when George returned, he would have some news.

The bell over the door tinkled. Carolyn started, realizing that it was twilight now, still pouring outside, and she was sitting at the counter in absolute darkness. She stared through the gloom, trying to make out her visitor. Knowing she was being very foolish, not to mention a bit rude, she said, "I am afraid we are closed for the day." They could not afford to lose a sale, but she was too despondent to care.

"That is not what the sign on the door says," the old lady said tartly.

Carolyn started again.

Her grandmother approached. "Why are you sitting in the dark? Are you blue? My God, you look as if you have been crying," Edith Owsley said, not mincing words.

Carolyn could not believe her misfortune. She hardly needed a confrontation with her grandmother at this moment. She stood up. "I most certainly have not been crying," she lied, chin up. "I have a head cold."

"Hmm," the old lady said, clearly skeptical. "And why are you sitting in the dark?"

"I was thinking," Carolyn said.

The old lady was close enough to give her a penetrating look. "Do you mind if we light a lamp? My eyes are not quite what they used to be."

It was hardly a request. Reluctantly Carolyn removed a glass dome and lit an oil wick. She replaced the dome. Her pulse was racing. What did her grandmother want now? Slowly, she turned. How could she maneuver the old witch into leaving? Already she had a headache.

Her grandmother thrust something at her, an old, worn book. Carolyn relaxed slightly. So her grandmother was there on business. "Do you wish to sell me an old tome?" Carolyn asked, not taking the book.

The old lady laughed. "No, I do not. This is the family Bible. It's been in the family for two hundred and twenty-eight years. I've decided you should have it."

Carolyn blinked at her in shock.

"Cat got your tongue?" Edith said, amused.

It seemed to be a challenge. "Why?" Carolyn was blunt.

The old lady's smile was cagey. "Why not? I don't feel like giving it to the lout. And his mother's no different, not a brain in *her* head. If Margaret were alive, I might be giving it to her. But maybe not. Let's just say this is an even exchange, because I so enjoyed Burke."

Carolyn was in shock. It was hardly an even exchange. Burke could be purchased easily enough. A two-hundred-year-old family Bible was priceless. "I don't want it," she heard herself say stiffly. Oh, but she was lying. She did want it!

Edith shrugged. "Then throw it out." She smiled.

Carolyn felt like telling her that she was a witch, no ifs, ands, or buts about it. But that would be going too far. She found herself staring at the Bible as Edith placed it on the counter. "I took the liberty of adding your name and birth date. Every single blasted Owsley is in there. Or, at least two centuries' worth."

Carolyn felt faint. She was trembling. She managed a negligent shrug.

"So why were you crying?" Edith demanded, peering far too closely at her.

"I told you. I have a head cold," Carolyn managed. She tore her gaze from the Bible with difficulty.

"Hmm. And I'm forty-two. I imagine you're pining after that fascinating foreigner." Edith smiled at her.

Carolyn gasped, imagining that all of the color was leaving her face.

"Well, that was a reaction if I ever saw one! What happened? I thought you were his daughter's companion. Why didn't you go back to Russia with them?''

Carolyn stared, having no intention of explaining one single thing to her feisty, witchlike grandmother. But how had she guessed the truth? How? ''Why would I go to Russia?'' she asked carefully. ''That would be absurd.''

''Really? Many Europeans have flocked to St. Petersburg over the years,'' a man drawled casually from the doorway.

Carolyn cried out, for the accent was impossible not to recognize, slightly coarse, Slavic, and so very exotic.

Alexi sauntered forward, dripping water off the brim of his hat and down his broad, mantle-cloaked shoulders. Disappointment immobilized Carolyn. For one stunning instant, she had thought it was Nicholas.

''You seem dismayed,'' Alexi said with a smile. ''But then, I am only six feet three, and my hair is black, not blond.'' He grinned.

Carolyn hugged herself, her heart pounding, knowing that her grandmother was staring closely at her. ''This is a surprise,'' she managed almost inaudibly.

''Yes, I think, for a moment, you thought you were seeing a ghost.'' He laughed.

''What are you doing here?'' Carolyn asked—when she wanted to run to him, grab him, shake him, and demand to know if Nicholas was all right.

''I am here on business, of course. It seems I am forever ordered back and forth between various governments.'' He removed his hat. ''I am dripping all over your floor.'' He faced Edith Owsley. ''Good day, madame.'' He bowed.

''You are the brother,'' Edith said flatly.

''Yes. I take it you were discussing Niki?'' He shot an amused glance at Carolyn, who flushed.

''She is brooding. I imagine she yearns to go to Russia, to be with her charge.'' The old lady was also amused. ''Has he packed that miserable wife of his off to wherever it is that you royalty send the misbegotten?''

Alexi grinned. ''Unfortunately, he has not packed the princess off to Siberia—my choice for an extended exile, I might add. But he has sent her to the country, which she truly hates. I imagine in time he might be persuaded to send her farther east, perhaps as far east as the Kamchatka Peninsula.''

"How is Katya?" Carolyn interrupted, having gotten the definite feeling that the Kamchatka Peninsula was so far east it was probably in the Pacific Ocean.

Alexi reached inside the pocket of his coat. "Actually, the reason I am here is to deliver this." He held out a sealed letter.

Carolyn's heart turned over and she met his eyes.

His smile was gone. Their gazes held. "No," he said softly, "it is from Katya."

For one more moment she continued to stare at Alexi, waiting for him to hand her another letter, dear God, or even a note, from Nicholas. But he did not. And she realized that no such personal missive was coming.

Tears shamelessly filling her eyes, Carolyn accepted the child's letter and held it to her breast. She was going to lose control, break down and weep. Had he already dismissed her from his mind? From whatever small place she had managed to claim in his heart? Had he even forgotten her very existence? If not, why would he not have sent her a letter, too?

Her grandmother interrupted her thoughts. "Sometimes life is full of surprises, and that is what makes it worth living." She smiled at Carolyn, who remained paralyzed with grief. "If you decide to travel, Carolyn, do come and say good-bye." She saluted Alexi. "An interesting development, I would say. Oh, by the by. Shall you win or lose the war?"

"Win, madame. We shall win. For no Russian will ever lay down his arms while there is a single foreign soldier on Russian soil. In this, peasant and peer, serf and clergyman, are united."

"Hmm. Perhaps your tsar should stop leading his armies in retreat, then," the old lady had the nerve to say. "Eventually he must stand firm. Good day, Your Highness."

Alexi bowed as the old lady swept past him as if she were the royal personage present.

Carolyn's temples were throbbing. She slowly met Alexi's gaze. "I am being terribly rude," she finally said. "You are wet and cold, probably hungry, too. Come inside. There's a fire in the kitchen, and I can feed you supper if you will."

"I thought you would never ask," he said, following her through the store and into the kitchen.

As Carolyn lit the stove, her hands trembled and she was swept forcefully into the not so distant past. How painful it was. But it was not so long ago that she and Nicholas had actually been together in the kitchen almost like this, after the Davison ball. Oh, God. Had it been a dream? "I only have port," she said, pouring him a glass of the aged wine. She handed it to him. "Is he all right?"

He no longer smiled. "He is fine."

"Where is he?" she asked, not even trying to hide her concern.

"Smolensk."

So the rumors were true. "That is where the First Army is?"

He nodded. "And Bagration's army, too. The Second."

She wet her lips. "Will there be fighting?"

"I can only hazard a guess," he said carefully.

"Please," Carolyn whispered.

"Yes," Alexi said. "Yes, I believe that this time, there will be a battle. Napoleon has pressed too far east. There is no way the high command can allow him to continue. No way."

Carolyn sat down abruptly, her heart sinking.

Alexi did not linger, but he promised he would call on her again in the morning. Apparently he intended to conclude his business that night, if he could, and his intention was to leave the following day.

Carolyn was torn when he left. He was her last solid link to Nicholas, or that was how it seemed, but she was also desperate to read Katya's letter. The moment he was gone, she bolted the door, and ran back into the kitchen where she had left the letter and her grandmother's Bible. The latter she ignored. With a pounding heart, she tore the seal and removed a single page of parchment.

Dear Miss Browne,
When my uncle told me he was returning to London, I asked him if he would forward a letter to you. He agreed, of course. I wish you were here.

    Father is back with the army, and soon there is going to be a huge war, or so everyone says. I know they try to hide it from me, but all the servants talk of little else. It is so strange. The house is dark and quiet. But so is the city. It used to be so gay, with pretty ladies in the streets, gentlemen on their hacks, and servants rushing to and fro. But not now. We have gone out every day to ride in the park, but even that is empty. Because of the war, I think, everyone is afraid and sad and chooses to stay home. At night, there are no lights. I did not understand, but Taichili told me the war has cost so much money that candles and oil are dear. Even for us. We have never worried about candles and oil or anything else before.

    Mother isn't here. Father sent her away. He sent her to Tver. I wanted to go with her, but he explained to me that my mother needs some time alone in the country. I wish I could go to Tver. I love it there. I used to love St. Petersburg even more, but not now. Not when it is so quiet and dark, not when everyone talks in whispers, even here in the house. I hope Father changes his mind and lets my mother come home. I know the truth. And I miss her.

    Miss Browne. I wish you had come home with us. I think you would like St. Petersburg. Not the way it is now, but the way it was before Napoleon invaded our land. I miss our talks, and I keep remembering our single outing. The accident was horrid, but the

*museum was so much fun. Taichili doesn't let me
study astronomy or philosophy anymore.*

*I must say good-bye. I have embroidery to finish.
I hope you are well. And just to let you know, Alex-
ander misses you, too. I can tell.*
Your Friend, Katrina Elenovna Sverayov.

Carolyn put the letter down, laid her head on her arms,
and wept. She wept the way she had not done since her
mother had died. It was hard to even understand why she
was crying. At first, she thought it was for Katya, who was
alone, lonely, sad, and afraid. But she realized she also wept
for herself. Because she was hopelessly in love with an
unattainable man—one who did not, she was sure, return
the least of her feelings.

And when Carolyn finally stopped crying, it was only to
fall asleep there at the kitchen table, her head on her arms.
And she dreamed of gilded palaces, sable rugs, a red snarling wolf, and muskets firing. And blood. There was so
much blood.

Carolyn awoke, and the first thing she thought about was
blood. For a moment she did not move, lying in her bed,
remembering horrible dreams. And then two thoughts
flashed through her mind. Alexi might leave today, and her
father had returned home last night. Or had his waking her
up gently, and telling her to go up to bed, been a dream,
too? Carolyn jumped up, splashed water on her face from
the washstand, and threw on a robe. She flew across the
hall, found his bedroom door open, and sure enough, his
bed was mussed—he had come home. She rushed down
the stairs, almost falling in her haste. He was making notes
at the counter. ''Papa!''

. He looked up and smiled. Carolyn flew toward him to
embrace him. But the simple hug became much more;
George held her very hard and for far longer than usual.
Instantly Carolyn sensed that something was wrong. She
broke the embrace and peered up at his face.

"Papa. What has happened?"

He forced a smile. "I am merely very glad to see you, my dear. I have missed you."

He was not telling her something. He seemed distraught. She smiled at him. "I missed you, too. Did your trip go well? All manuscripts delivered safe and sound?"

He looked away. "Yes." Then he smiled at her. "So you are not still employed by the Russian."

"Papa, he went back to Russia. I am sure you heard about the treaty that was concluded July twelfth. He left with his family just a few days later."

George smiled, clearly relieved. "That was for the best. Of course I know the treaty was signed. This is where you belong, dear, here in the bookshop with me."

Carolyn hesitated, eyes downcast, pulse thudding. He would rant and rave if he knew what she was thinking of doing. No. If he knew what she intended to do. She had not a doubt.

"How is young Davison, by the way?" George asked.

Carolyn sighed. "I suppose that he is fine."

"Have you seen him since the ball?"

"He came by the store several times, but . . . I was not feeling well." Poor Anthony. Carolyn had pleaded illness but the truth was that she had been too heartbroken to accept any of his invitations, of which there had been many.

"And how is Copperville?" George asked.

Carolyn glanced away. "Copperville has had a mental block. He has turned in only one column since the Sheffield affair—and Taft rejected it."

George stared. "Carolyn, is something wrong?"

She no longer attempted to lie. She hugged her cotton wrapper tighter to her body. "I received a letter from Katya last night. She is frightened and alone in a country that is at war. Her mother has been sent to the country, her father is with his troops, and she is in the care of a grim, bespectacled monster named Taichili. She is sad. Not only did she write so directly, it was obvious by the tone of her letter."

"I am very sorry for her," George said far too brusquely.

"But Sverayov's daughter is not your concern. It is his concern—and his *wife's*."

Carolyn regarded him with dismay. As she did so, someone banged on the front door. George looked up. "It is only eight o'clock. Whoever would come by at this hour?" He started forward to open the door, then halted in midstride. "Dear, go upstairs and dress."

But Carolyn already knew who their caller was, without having to look, and she turned, and through a crack in the shade, saw a part of what could only be Alexi's tall, arrogant form. "It is Sverayov's brother," she said, hurrying for the stairs. "I will be right down. Do not let him leave, Papa!"

She heard George opening the door as she reached the landing and raced into her bedroom. Never had she donned underclothes and a dress more swiftly. To hide the fact that she was too agitated, and in too much of a rush, to fasten up the back of the dress, she threw a shawl over her shoulders, and, in her stocking feet, she raced back downstairs.

The two men were quietly discussing Salamanca. They both ceased conversing and turned to regard her. Carolyn smiled nervously. "Good morning," she said to Alexi.

He returned her smile with one of his own, one that lit up his topaz eyes, eyes that were almost exactly like Nicholas's. He bowed, the gesture grand. "Good morning, Miss Browne."

"Did you have a restful night?" she asked, although she was dying to get to the point she wished to make—and desperately wishing that her father would leave them alone for a moment or two.

"Hardly." His grin flashed, reckless and suggestive. "And I am departing for St. Petersburg this morning."

Her heart did stop. Oh, God. He was going to St. Petersburg. Oh, God. Carolyn crossed the fingers of both her hands and hid them in the folds of her skirt. She could not speak.

"Well," George said. "Then we both wish you bon voyage."

Alexi inclined his head, and now, regarding Carolyn, his gaze had become eerily intense—and too reminiscent of the way his brother had so often looked at her. "Did you have a chance to read Katya's letter?" he asked.

Her cheeks were hot, burning. "Yes." Her tone was a croak, worse than a frog's. She cleared her throat.

"Do you have a reply that you wish me to take back?" he asked.

Carolyn shook her head.

"Shall I wait for you to pen a response?"

She wet her lips. Then she darted a glance at her father. "Papa, I am stepping outside with His Excellency. I wish to discuss something with him."

George stared, jaw tight. "What could you possibly wish to speak to him about?"

Carolyn took Alexi's arm. She did not answer her father, but began steering him from the store.

"Carolyn!" George cried.

Carolyn ignored him, her pulse roaring in her ears, her steps fast now, and she swung open the front door. Outside, the air was wet and fresh, and raindrops sparkled with the dew on the flowers in the windowsill boxes. Carolyn inhaled as the door swung shut behind them. The stone pavement was cold beneath her stocking feet, and she hopped a bit on her toes.

Alexi stared at her, looked down, and smiled. "You have forgotten your shoes," he said in an oddly tender tone.

Carolyn froze. His voice had sounded just like Nicholas's in an unguarded moment. "Yes. I have." She clutched her shawl more tightly.

"I will wait if you wish to go and put them on," he said, smiling.

She shook her head and blurted, "You don't have a message for me, do you?"

He hesitated. "I did not see Nicholas before I left. He is in the interior. I never left St. Petersburg. I doubt he even knew I was there, as we did not leave London together."

"I see." She was only partially relieved. She needed courage if she were really going to do this.

"Miss Browne?"

She met his gaze.

"Do you need help with the back of your dress?" His eyes sparkled.

Carolyn realized that she was in such a state that she had pulled her shawl around her neck. "I am not usually so absentminded," she whispered, pulling the shawl back down over her shoulders. "Katya sounded so sad and so lonely."

He nodded somberly. "She is not happy. The house has become a mausoleum. Taichili does her best, but she is a cold fish."

Carolyn wet her lips. "Take me with you."

Alexi stared.

Carolyn stared back.

And slowly, he smiled. "Can you be ready in two hours?"

"I am ready now," Carolyn said.

Alexi left. Carolyn slipped back into the bookshop, and heard George in the kitchen, slamming a pot on the stove. She walked slowly through the store, dreading their encounter.

She paused on the threshold. George did not face her. She watched him for a moment as he searched through the canisters on the counter for the tea he was so especially fond of. "Papa."

He whirled. "What are you hiding from me?"

"When I took up employment with Sverayov, he asked me to return to Russia with Katya," Carolyn began.

George turned white. "No."

"It is my decision to make. And I have decided to leave with Alexi. This morning."

George stared at her, blanching impossibly more. "You have lost your mind!" he finally cried. "Carolyn, I forbid it!"

"You cannot forbid it, because I am not asking your permission," she said, dismay beginning to overwhelm her. "Papa. I have to go. The child needs me."

"This is not about the child. This is about that rogue. He is married, Carolyn. Or have you forgotten?"

She flushed, and felt like screaming, how can I forget? When it is his wife who is keeping me from my dreams? But that wasn't fair, it wasn't just Marie-Elena who stood in their way, it was the difference in their stations, and it was also him. Because surely if he loved her, he would find a way—a legitimate way for them to be together, properly.

And Carolyn was aghast for daring to wish for the impossible—a marriage between them.

Carolyn felt tears burning her eyes. "I have to go."

"Go? Go?" he asked, but it was a roar. "Go and do what?"

"I am going to be Katya's companion," Carolyn cried.

"Her companion—or his?" George cried back.

Carolyn was so taken aback that she froze. And then she was hurt—and she was angry. "You should know me better than that."

"I do know you. And every time I saw you with him, I saw the stars in your eyes. He is married. And Russian princes do not divorce their wives—and they only *carry on* with commoners—and for him, it will merely be a passing fancy, but for you? You will never recover, Carolyn."

Oh, God, he was right. He was right, but she could not turn back from what she intended to do. From what she had to do. "I am going to St. Petersburg with Alexi. And I do not intend to warm his bed. I intend to care for his child, Papa. He is with the army, near Moscow. Katya is in St. Petersburg, hundreds of miles away."

"And if Napoleon changes course? And marches on St. Petersburg instead? Then what? You shall be trapped in a city under invasion, by God!"

"If Napoleon decides to march on St. Petersburg instead than I shall be glad to be there to take care of one small lonely child. Katya will need me more than ever," Carolyn said evenly. But inside, she felt as if she were breaking into millions of tiny, shardlike pieces. "Don't do this, Papa. I must go. I need your blessing."

"You are not going to get it," George said harshly.

Carolyn was stunned and mute. Silence fell between them, hot and hard, bitter and angry. "I am going, Papa," Carolyn said. "With or without your blessing." She turned away to go upstairs to pack a small valise.

"He is using you," George cried. "And he will destroy you, mark my words!"

Carolyn left the kitchen, aching.

"Has he slept with you?" George cried, following her. "He has, hasn't he!"

She faltered, reaching for the banister. And she bit down hard on a reply, starting up the stairs, her shoulders ramrod straight.

"Carolyn!" her father cried. "Please, do not go. I beg you!"

She paused but did not turn. "Perhaps I am making a mistake. But that is my right. I love you, Papa. I will write." Her voice broke. Carolyn broke into a run, dashing upstairs as fast as her legs would carry her.

Behind her, George sat down and started to cry.

❧ TWENTY-SIX ❧

IT was cold. Carolyn huddled in her wool winter coat, thankful she had had the common sense to bring it with her. The carriage Alexi had hired at the docks just a few moments ago hurled down a wide commercial street that in no way resembled any London thoroughfare. For one, there were many trees lining the street, mostly birches and firs. It was impossible for Carolyn not to be aware of just how far north she was. And the sky overhead was gray, but not a London gray, which was dense with fog. It was crisp and clear, suggesting rain or even snow, the same iron color as the water she could periodically glimpse through the clustered, mostly two-story stone buildings on the streets. Alexi had already told her that St. Petersburg was Russia's gateway to Europe, that it was built around the Neva River, on a gulf of the Baltic Sea, and that numerous rivers and canals ran through it. Their ship had docked on Vasilevsky Island, which lay in two arms of the Neva, and explained why, no matter where she looked, she could see water.

Her heart felt lodged in her throat.

Now they were passing numerous low buildings which seemed to be warehouses, and behind them, docks. Some of the buildings had once been painted in gay, bright rainbow colors, and patches of those colors clung to the stones and bricks like forgotten quilting rags—testimony to the fact that the city had once been Swedish. There was little pedestrian activity. Most of the other vehicles on the streets were drays loaded with various merchandise, bound for the city markets. But here and there a solid woman heavily clad would attempt to navigate through the traffic, laden with baskets or satchels.

Their carriage took a corner so abruptly that Carolyn slammed into Alexi, who shouted at the driver in his native language. The carriage tilted precariously to one side, almost overturning, or so it seemed to Carolyn. It was an open vehicle, and they were lucky they were not flung into the damp street. However, it was quickly righted as they flew over a narrow stone bridge.

Carolyn sat up straighter. Ahead of her, on the opposite side of the bridge, through a cloud of fir trees, was a series of incredible buildings.

"Dvortsovaya ploschad," Alexi said with a bemused smile. "The Palace Square. The long building with all the columns and the gold spire is the Admiralty. It is still in the process of reconstruction."

There was a huge garden in front of it, still colorful and blooming in spite of the autumn chill, and several limestone water fountains. But Carolyn's gaze moved to the left, where a violent rococo profusion of columns and windows, painted in brilliant shades of green, white, and gold, faced her. Huge statues, far larger than life-sized, graced the top of the sprawling palace. And it had to be the palace for which the square was named.

"The Winter Palace, a favorite retreat of the tsars," Alexi said, having followed her glance. "Beside it is the Hermitage, built for Catherine the Great as a retreat." He smiled wryly. "She also used it to house her art collection, one begun by Peter. It is still there."

Carolyn inhaled. "It is magnificent." But the words were barely out of her mouth when the carriage suddenly hit a huge rut and Carolyn was thrown out of her seat, as was Alexi. Carolyn crashed into the back of the driver's box. Alexi shouted at the driver again. This time, Carolyn gripped the cracked leather seat. "We have made it this far, without incident," she said, thinking of the two-legged voyage from London. They had changed ships at Riga.

"Only to die because of one mad Russian driver?" Alexi chuckled. "He is eager to get home. He is expecting a big tip for having taken us out of his way when his supper is waiting."

The carriage careened off the bridge. Carolyn's heart stopped and started again as they veered past another oncoming coach, also containing passengers. How had they managed to avoid a head-on collision?

"We are not noted for our careful driving," Alexi said.

"That I believe." She swallowed, her mind filling with Sverayov. She shoved his image aside, forcing herself to focus on Katya instead, the reason she had come all the way across Europe. "I cannot believe I am here," she said, more to herself than to Alexi.

Alexi shot her a glance. "You are not the only one who will be surprised."

Carolyn's heart raced. "He will not know." Then she flushed, feeling that she was far too transparent. She had just spent eleven days in his company, and she found him every bit as astute as his brother. He was not a man to miss a trick.

Alexi eyed her. "He will, because I intend to make a short trip to Smolensk—or wherever the First Army is now."

Carolyn swallowed. Their carriage was now hurling down a wide, fir-lined boulevard, having left the Winter Palace and the Hermitage behind. Elegant stone mansions, most of which were square and three- or four-story, bordered it. Many had been built in a beautiful crimson stone. A canal loomed ahead of them, and there were numerous gardens and parks on both sides of the street. A cathedral with a gilded dome and steeple appeared on her left, soaring into the clear, chilly sky.

Alexi patted her knee. "He will be pleased. I know my brother, and he is very concerned with Katya's welfare, especially now, with his responsibilities keeping him so far away, and with Marie-Elena at Tver. Do not fear.''

Carolyn remained silent. Oddly enough, she felt terrified. What if Nicholas thought she had chased him to Russia? For that was *not* the case, and she was adamant about that. She had not come to St. Petersburg to renew her relationship with him, she had not. No matter the yearning that remained in her heart.

''We are on the Nevsky Prospekt,'' Alexi murmured. ''That is the Kazan Cathedral we have just passed. The house is but a few minutes from here.''

Carolyn's heart pounded harder and faster than before. But he would not be at the house. He was with the army, guarding the road to Moscow, or so she had inferred from her many conversations with Alexi. Carolyn lapsed into silence, regarding the city now as they turned up a street filled with shops and stores no different from the ones at home, aware of being filled with a combination of exhilaration and dread.

And then she realized why St. Petersburg seemed so different from London. It was not the fir trees, the crisp cold, the odd yet beautiful red stone that abounded, or the Neva which snaked all around them. ''The city is so quiet,'' Carolyn said, watching a single noblewoman and her maid exiting a shop that appeared to be filled with ladies' toiletries. Theirs was the only vehicle on the road except for one parked carriage which they had just passed. Far in the distance, she saw a horse-drawn trolley crossing an intersection. Where were the coaches and carriages, the hansoms, the riders? ''Where is everyone?''

Alexi faced her. ''It is odd, is it not? The city used to be so busy, and so gay. Normally, at this time of the day, the traffic is impossible—and we might sit here at a standstill for a quarter hour or more. We are at war, Carolyn. Napoleon continues to push deep into our countryside, and thus far, he has not been decisively stopped. In fact, there has not yet been a major encounter between the two countries. Most nobles have not fled the city, but it is not a time to shop, stroll, dine, attend parties, give balls. And there is a shortage of goods.''

The city appeared deserted. Carolyn was now acutely aware of how depressing it felt. And the silence, when one was used to the shouts of hansom drivers, the clang of trolley bells, the hoofbeats of horses, and the sound of human voices, was unnerving. She glanced past a deep puddle at rusted iron gates in front of a silent stone church. The only thing moving in the courtyard were pigeons.

''It has also been expensive maintaining a huge army in a time of war.'' Alexi was grim. ''Taxes have been very high. We are all feeling the pinch.'' He shot her a rueful smile and held up one arm. Carolyn saw how threadbare the wool on the elbow of his jacket was. He shrugged. ''Eventually, this will pass.''

They turned another corner. And Carolyn sat up, eyes wide.

They had just left a retail neighborhood filled with stores, some fancy and exclusive, others as simple as bakeries and butcher shops. But there it was, directly ahead of them, sitting on a huge rise which was undoubtedly man-made. ''That's it, isn't it? The . . . er . . . house?''

Alexi nodded. ''Our family home.''

It was not a house. Hardly a family home. It was, Carolyn decided, swiftly counting the sections, the equivalent of five mansions put together, at least. Carolyn stared.

The palace marked the end of the street, and sat crosswise to it. An iron fence that was probably waist high on the average person ran the length of the street in front of the palace. The railing was decorated with gold figurines. Carolyn had no doubt that it was solid, real gold. The posts holding up the railing were painted black and white. Two sets of wide, sweeping staircases, extravagantly adorned with more gilded figurines and colorful railings, and black and white posts, were parallel to one another and led up to the house. In between them was a stone courtyard and a huge water fountain. The statue atop the fountain was also gold—a man stood victorious atop a hill, two of his victims fallen at his feet. Five stone arches at the far end of the courtyard indicated that there was more to be seen on the other side of it.

The house was huge, long, vast, and built of stone, painted a pink-beige, in the classical style. White moldings surrounded the many oversized, arched windows. It was six or seven stories high. There were wrought-iron balconies over one central section, and Carolyn could imagine Sverayov and his wife standing there to greet guests or to preside over a gathering of the hoi polloi on the grounds below. Temple pediments adorned the final floor. The roof was pale slate, gently sloping and rounded, and atop the very central portion was another gold statue, which Carolyn could not make out. But she thought it might be a motif from the coat of arms.

"It is spectacular," Carolyn said hoarsely.

Alexi shrugged as the carriage paused before a gate Carolyn had not thus far noticed. It was flung open by two liveried guards. The carriage moved into the courtyard, past the fountain, and through a vaulted stone arch. Carolyn found herself on a graveled drive in front of the palace, green lawns spreading out from either side of them. Superbly cut hedges bordered the house.

Alexi jumped down and helped Carolyn out. The driver was hauling out their two small bags when servants appeared, bowing before Alexi. As they spoke, Carolyn continued to study the house and grounds, for she did not understand a word being said, of course.

"Come." Alexi took her arm and they walked up more steps, past the huge double doors, which had been left open. Carolyn by now expected grandeur, and was not disappointed. She was in a dimly illuminated but huge foyer, the ceiling with its gilt moldings many floors above, a vast crystal chandelier hanging there above their heads. The floors were a tawny, gold-flecked marble. There were statues, busts, and artwork everywhere.

"The house is large, and most of it is not used. The staff has separate quarters in the back, the family lives in the east wing. Because Marie-Elena is not in residence, I will give you a room near Katya's.''

"That would be wonderful," Carolyn said, following Alexi. They exited the foyer, going left, down an endless corridor with gleaming wood floors. Carolyn passed salon after salon, managing a hurried peek into each one, as the doors were open. She could only glimpse for an instant the huge Persian rugs and wall-sized tapestries, gold and crystal chandeliers, the portraits 'and landscapes, and the clusters of magnificent furniture upholstered in brocades, velvets, and damasks, all in strong, vibrant colors of royal-blues and purples, reds and golds—all now faded with time and use. The palace was clearly royal, and as clearly, it was ancestral; many generations had lived in it.

They turned down hall after hall. Carolyn was lost. But Alexi finally pushed open a pair of gleaming wood doors and announced that they were in the east wing. "The public rooms are on the ground floor—the salons, the music room, and so on. The family rooms are on the first story, the master suites on the second, as are the guest rooms. Katya sleeps on the third story. I believe Taichili does as well. Signor Raffaldi has his own rooms in the city.''

"I am lost," Carolyn said sheepishly.

Alexi's smile was warm. "Never mind. Katya knows the palace—all of it, I think—like the back of her hand. You know, when she is angry, she will disappear for hours at a time.''

Carolyn's smile faded. "I did not know," she said, as they went upstairs.

They found Katya and Taichili in a lush, overly appointed salon, one that was large but, in comparison with what Carolyn had just seen, seemed intimate and cozy now. A fire roared in the beautifully carved wood hearth, Katya was curled up in a huge crimson chair, a book on her lap. The kitten, now grown into a small cat, played with a ball of yarn at her feet. Taichili sat on a sofa, and Raffaldi was nowhere to be seen. Carolyn felt a surge of joy at seeing the child again, and so comfortably occupied.

"Katya," she said.

Katya looked up, eyes wide, and shrieked. She jumped out of the huge chair and flew across the many overlapping oriental rugs in the salon. And she flung her arms around Carolyn.

Carolyn stooped, hugging her, tears filling her own eyes. She had never expected such an emotional display, and she was more than pleased. She had worried endlessly about the little girl. She knelt. "I am so happy to see you," she whispered.

Katya was flushed. "Miss Browne! I did not know you were coming. I am . . . speechless."

Carolyn laughed, and from the corner of her eye, she saw Taichili, who looked stunned, and distinctly displeased. "I received your letter. I had to come. I have missed you."

Taichili sniffed.

Alexi stepped forward. "What kind of greeting is this, *dushka*? Have you forgotten me?"

Katya smiled. "I'm sorry," she said, as her uncle scooped her up into his arms and then high into the air. She laughed as he set her down.

Carolyn nodded at the governess. "How are you, Taichili?"

"Browne." The governess inclined her head. "His Excellency did not inform me of your arrival."

Carolyn knew the governess meant to put her on the spot, and she was not in the mood. "His Excellency does not know I have come," she said too sweetly.

"But that is neither here nor there," Alexi intervened. "Miss Browne has so kindly agreed to return to Russia with me, and I am placing her in charge of Katya, Taichili, as was done by my brother when we were last in London."

Taichili bowed her head. "Yes, Your Highness, you are making yourself very clear. May I write to His Excellency?" She looked up, glowering.

"By all means. I am leaving tomorrow, and it is my intention to speak with my brother myself. I shall convey your letter to him.'' Alexi smiled. "Do you know where he is, by the by?''

Taichili's expression changed, and briefly, Carolyn saw anxiety cross her features, and perhaps with it, fear. Carolyn was instantly uneasy. But instead of answering Alexi, she glanced with worry at Katya.

Carolyn stepped forward and took Katya's hand. "Katya, would you show me to a guest room? Alexi says I should have a room on your floor. And perhaps, while you are at it, you can show me your room?'' She smiled brightly.

Alexi turned. "That is a good idea,'' he said evenly, without a hint of any emotion. "I wish a private word with your governess in any case. Shall we all plan on an early supper together? It is almost that time, and I intend to go out this evening. There are affairs I must attend to.''

Katya nodded. "Come, Miss Browne, do come,'' she said, smiling and tugging on Carolyn's hand.

Carolyn laughed, allowing the little girl to pull her from the room, the Persian cat following. But the moment they were in the hall, she turned and saw Alexi's expression as he closed the door behind them. It was more than grim. Her heart sank.

"This is your room?'' Carolyn asked, forgetting about her concern over the conversation which was now taking place in the cozy family salon.

Katya nodded proudly. She had a bedchamber grand enough for a queen, but then, she was a princess, and it was possible if she married well that she might very well become a queen one day. It was a state bed, floor to ceiling in height, and the hangings of the canopy could be drawn at night to entirely enclose the person inside. There were two vast marble fireplaces and two seating arrangements. The entire room was done in shades of blue, green, and gold. The walls were a gold silk fabric. Katya had her own water closet, with running water, and her own sitting room—and a dressing closet. "Do you like it?'' the child asked.

"Of course," Carolyn lied. It was so . . . adult. So . . . grim. So . . . formal. That was it. It was not a child's pretty room, but the room for an esteemed personage. It was so . . . mature. "Where are your toys?"

Katya led Carolyn over to a dollhouse. It was not very miniature. It took up an entire table and was fabulously constructed, each detail precise. It was, in fact, a replica of the palace they were now in. And the tiny dolls were exquisite—princes and princesses, children and servants and guests.

"My God," Carolyn said. The dollhouse was almost as big as Katya.

"It was my birthday present when I was four," Katya said modestly.

Carolyn looked at her. What four-year-old received a gift like this? "And your other toys?"

Katya hesitated. "I don't have toys, not really."

"What did you receive for your last birthday, dear?"

Katya beamed, went to a beautiful bureau with gilded knobs, and opened a top drawer. Carolyn blinked when she produced an exquisite strand of small pearls with a diamond clasp. "I have the earrings to match," Katya said shyly.

"That is beautiful," Carolyn said honestly. But it was a gift for a debutante. Where were the toys? "Surely you have some toys, Katya?"

"I have a pony. His name is Anton. He was my birthday present when I was five. He's out back in the stables. Do you want to see him?" She was eager and hopeful and Carolyn's heart went out to her.

"Perhaps later." Carolyn wondered how she could purchase or otherwise procure some real toys for Katya. How *pinched* were the Sverayovs?

"I have books," Katya said helpfully.

"Well, that is wonderful," Carolyn said. "Do you want to show me to my room?" Her heart dipped a bit. She hoped it was . . . normal.

Katya led her from her bedroom and opened a door that was adjacent. "Don't you think this will do?"

And Carolyn fell in love. The room was a quarter of the size—though it was still vast—the walls were simply whitewashed, the fireplace was limestone, and it was done in shades of red, blue, and white. It was airy and fresh. The bed was a simple—in comparison—canopied affair. Carolyn walked over to the pale blue muslin draperies and pulled them open, tying them back with red tasseled cords. She smiled as the Neva River greeted her. A small dhorry was sailing past the palace at that exact moment, a gull wheeling overhead.

She blinked. On the opposite bank was another palace—or building—painted red and green, with gold domes and spires. ".What a view to wake up to," she said, thinking about her small attic bedchamber at home. And then she felt a tiny pang of homesickness and regret, her father's image coming to mind. She sighed. She would write to him immediately.

"What is it, Miss Browne? Don't you like your room? If not, you may have another one. In fact, you may choose any one you want." Katya smiled encouragingly.

Carolyn walked over to her and stroked her hair as Alexi appeared on the threshold. "I love this room. It is perfect for me, not too large, not too spectacular, I just love it." She smiled at Katya's uncle.

"Then it is yours," he said. "And if there is anything you need"—and he looked around—"such as a *secrétaire*, just ask any of the servants. The upper servants are all fluent in French, the language we use at court, and German."

Carolyn nodded, thinking that at least there would not be any real language barrier.

He smiled and turned his attention to Katya. "Katya, why do you not tell Taichili to inform the kitchen staff of the arrival of myself and Miss Browne?"

Katya nodded and ran off, but not before scooping up the cat.

"So you are set," Alexi remarked. "And you seem pleased. I am glad."

Carolyn faced him, her heart slamming now, thinking of Nicholas. "Why is Taichili so worried? What has happened?"

Alexi hesitated.

"Is Nicholas all right?" she cried.

He held up a hand. "Whoa. Of course Niki is fine."

She swallowed, faint with relief. Carolyn turned and sat down in a pretty red and white chair. She rubbed her temples. "What has happened? Do not keep me in the dark, Alexi. I am a foreigner in a foreign country. I need to know."

"That is fair. But I do not want to alarm you. You are not in any danger. You will never be in any danger. Neither Niki nor myself would ever allow that."

Carolyn, of course, grew more alarmed. "What has happened?"

"Smolensk has been burned to the ground, and they have taken Vyazma."

"Vyazma?" Carolyn asked fearfully. "Where is that?"

"Perhaps a hundred and fifty miles from Moscow, no farther."

Carolyn stood. "Where is Nicholas? Precisely?"

"With the First Army. Which, I assume, is somewhere between Vyazma and Moscow."

"Oh, God. Napoleon cannot be stopped!"

"Do not say that," Alexi snapped. "That is absurd. He will be stopped."

Carolyn nodded. "I am sorry. I am just . . . afraid."

Alexi stared. "We are all afraid," he finally said, softly. "But for very different reasons."

❧ TWENTY-SEVEN ❧

ALEXI was leaving. Carolyn had been up before dawn, not wanting to miss his departure. She hurried downstairs, a shawl around her shoulders, her dress far too lightweight for the Russian climate. It was exceedingly chilly out, but Carolyn had already learned that it could snow as early as October in this northern clime. As she passed through the house, the east wing was silent, all of its inhabitants still asleep. Or so Carolyn thought, until she approached the dining room. She heard Alexi's soft, masculine chuckle and Katya's higher, childish voice as well as the crackling of a cheerful fire.

Carolyn smiled. So she was not the only one who wished to say good-bye to the all-too-charming prince. She paused on the threshold. A fire blazed in the hearth, making the wood-paneled room with its intricate, exotic carvings far more than warm, but inviting and intimate. Katya, in her lawn nightclothes, was poking the fire with a stick. How pretty she was, with her dark hair in one long braid, in her beribboned nightgown. And then Alexi moved into Carolyn's view, to stand beside the child. Carolyn froze—and cried out.

He turned, his smile remaining in place. "Is something amiss?" he asked very casually.

Carolyn gaped. Alexi was not dressed in his usual trousers and tailcoat. Oh, no. He was wearing a crimson uniform. Gold-tasseled epaulets adorned his shoulders, gold cording and buttons his jacket. His breeches were also crimson, tucked into high, gleaming black boots. Gilded spurs winked there. "You have joined the army," she whispered, aghast and accusing.

"Actually, the cavalry," he said. "I volunteered my services last night." His smile was as easy as his tone.

"He is so handsome, is he not?" Katya cried, beaming.

Alexi knelt beside her, throwing one arm around her. "As handsome as your papa?"

Katya nodded. "More so, I think."

Alexi stood and laughed. "I think my niece has an infatuation for me." He winked at Carolyn.

But Carolyn could not smile. Not if her life depended on it. "Why?" she whispered deploringly. "Why would you do such a thing?"

"I suppose I am irresistible to the fairer sex."

"No. Why would you go and join the army, for God's sake? Is it not enough that Nicholas already serves your country?"

His smile, finally, faded. "Perhaps I have grown tired of playing shadowy games these past eight years with an elusive enemy."

"Perhaps you are a fool," Carolyn cried, unable to deny her fears now. What if they *both* died?

"Perhaps," he continued, eyes flashing. "I have also become tired of these damned Frenchmen on my land. What has happened to this city? To the people? To *my* people? You do not know the difference, Carolyn. This is your first time here. But I know the difference, and I am sick and tired of seeing nothing but fear on the faces of everyone I meet, fear and sadness, and worse, shame." He stared. "I am ready to drive the enemy away with my own hand. I wish to fight the damned, bloody, accursed French."

Carolyn could not help understanding, in spite of her fear. She felt her eyes growing moist. "I have become fond of you, Alexi. I do not want you to get hurt."

He softened, moving to her, and throwing an arm around

her the very same way he had with Katya, except that he only had to stoop halfway down in order to do so. "I have become as fond of you as if you were my sister," he said, smiling and releasing her. "You have nothing to fear. I like life too much to allow myself to be killed by some ill-bred French peasant. Besides, I have bought myself the rank of colonel."

"Colonel. The same rank as Nicholas," Carolyn said. "And do colonels stay to the rear of their troops when the fighting begins? Do the cavalry not lead the charge?" Her tone rose to a precariously high pitch.

"Some colonels choose to remain behind," Alexi said very calmly.

"The cowards," Carolyn returned, not calm at all.

Alexi smiled at her. "I must go. I am late. I am joining the First Army."

"So you will see Nicholas," Carolyn said, her heart now wedged in her throat and pounding very swiftly there.

"I am making a point of it. Do you wish to quickly write him a note? I will wait a few more minutes."

Carolyn shook her head. She walked over to Katya and took the child's hand, to comfort herself, not Katya. "Just tell him . . ." She hesitated. "I pray for him, and his men, and for a speedy end to this war." She paused, choking on her own words. "And tell him that I will do my utmost to take care of his daughter."

Alexi smiled at her. "I shall tell him exactly what you have said. Good-bye, Carolyn. Katya, one more kiss."

The little girl broke free of Carolyn, rushing to her uncle to obey. He swept her up into his arms, spinning her around as he hugged her and held her hard. And Carolyn thought she saw moisture sheening his eyes for one brief moment, before he put her down. She turned away. Ordering herself not to let the fear control her mind, not yet, anyway.

Supper was a somber affair. Katya played with her food, pushing it back and forth around her plate. Taichili ate with mechanical determination. Raffaldi had gone home to his city flat, so only Carolyn sat with them at the table in the family dining room, and she herself had no appetite. Just as the table, which could seat two dozen, was far too big for the three of them, so too was the palace. Especially with the city in such a state of silence and sobriety. The city, the palace, this room, had become oppressive. And so disturbing.

She wondered when she would learn if Nicholas was all right. And she imagined his reaction when Alexi appeared in his uniform—and then told him that she was in St. Petersburg.

Carolyn forced her imagination aside, folding her hands in her lap. She looked around, saw that Taichili had also finished, as had Katya. She summoned a smile. "Shall we have dessert? I think I saw a tart in the kitchen this afternoon."

Katya brightened. But then she sobered. "Why didn't he come?" she asked.

Carolyn hesitated. By now, rumor held that the tsar was in the city. That afternoon, most of St. Petersburg, Carolyn and her charge included, had turned out to witness the spectacle of his arrival at the Hermitage after a mission in Abö. The parade had been spectacular, with hundreds of white cavalry chargers bearing crimson-clad officers in their plumed helmets, followed by regiment upon regiment of foot soldiers and marching bands. But the tsar had never appeared.

And the crowd, tense, silent, and grim to begin with, had finally given over to boos and hisses, overwhelmed by their disappointment. Carolyn herself had remarked just how confused and bewildered her own entourage was by the tsar's failure to appear. Apparently, Alexander had waited until after the parade was over to be taken incognito to the Winter Palace. Had he been afraid to face his own people after the constant humiliation his armies had suffered at Napoleon's hands?

"He was probably tired, Katya," Carolyn said. "After all, he is human, like you and I. I think he wished to please the people by giving them the parade, but needed some privacy for himself.''

Katya seemed to accept that, but Taichili did not. In her usual brisk manner, she said, ''Royals are not entitled to privacy.'' And she made a harrumphing sound.

For once, Carolyn was in agreement with her.

Footsteps had sounded in the corridor, and Carolyn assumed it was a servant. But now she heard Nicholas say, ''That is vastly unfair.''

Carolyn's gaze flew to the doorway, where he stood in a caped gray-green greatcoat over a similar uniform, smiling ever so slightly. Her heart stopped alarmingly, then beat with maddening force. But he was not looking at her, he was smiling tiredly at Katya. Had he even seen her?

''Father.'' Slowly Katya stood up, her eyes wide with surprise and excitement, belying her controlled tone.

''Come here,'' Nicholas said, squatting. But his jaw was flexed tight.

Katya quickly obeyed, walking into her father's arms. He held her briefly, then straightened, nodding at Taichili, and finally looking at Carolyn.

She knew she was red-faced. She could not speak. Their gazes connected then, in that stunning instant, and held.

And if he were surprised—or glad—to see her, he gave no sign of it. She looked him over again. His gray-green greatcoat was streaked with mud, as were his knee-high boots and pale, dove-colored breeches. ''Miss Browne,'' he said. ''I did not expect to find you here.'' Did his temples throb?

Carolyn stood up. After what they had shared during their last encounter, he seemed so formal, so remote. Images flashed through her mind, graphic and intense, accompanied by sweet, then bitter, sensations. ''Excellency,'' she said, and she was aware that she had never before addressed him that way. ''We did not expect to see *you* here.''

He smiled faintly at her repartee, his gaze still locked on her face. ''My presence was requested by the tsar.''

''I see.'' But she did not. What was he thinking and

feeling? Was he thrilled—and frightened—to see her, as she was to see him? And why, why was he so obviously exhausted? "Have you traveled far?"

"Yes. About seven hundred kilometers—in four full days."

"That is nearly impossible," Carolyn said, wide-eyed. Wanting to rush to him and relieve him of the burden of his wet, dirty greatcoat, and then take him in her arms. But that was not why she was here, in his palace, in St. Petersburg. The fact that he was married, and out of her reach, had not changed. Nothing had changed—not even her feelings. Impossibly, they seemed to be far greater than before. Carolyn looked down at her plate.

"Little is impossible," Nicholas returned.

"Excellency, are you hungry?" Taichili asked, standing, as a servant suddenly appeared, only to see the prince and gape. "Fyodor. Another place and more food. His Excellency is famished."

Nicholas's smile was wry. He removed his coat and flung it over the back of a chair, then took a seat—between Carolyn and Katya. Carolyn now became aware of the tension pervading every fiber of her being. He had come to meet Alexander. How long would he stay? She was certain that it would not be for very long. Her heart sank. He would probably leave in the morning!

She stole a quick glance at him. Was he acting as if they were total strangers? Did he now regret his invitation to her to come to Russia to care for Katya?

Silence reigned as Nicholas was served. Carolyn watched him as he attacked his plate with the gusto of a man who has not eaten in a long time. No one spoke until he had finished every morsel and quaffed the last of a second glass of red wine. Carolyn had seen the bottle. It was not French.

"Is there anything else I may get you, Excellency?" a servant asked.

Nicholas declined. "No. Katya, is it not time for your bed?"

''Can I not stay up just a little bit longer?'' Katya asked breathlessly.

Nicholas smiled slightly. ''For a few minutes, then. For I must leave to attend my meeting.''

''With the tsar?'' Katya asked.

Nicholas nodded.

Katya glanced at Carolyn, who realized she was clutching the table, so great was her tension. He was going out. She was dismayed. Weren't they going to have even the slightest chance to speak together? Alone?

She closed her eyes. But that would be asking for trouble, would it not? But perhaps he no longer felt for her as she did for him. He certainly did not seem to care that she was present in his home—so very far away from hers.

''Are you unwell, Miss Browne?''

She opened her eyes to find him watching her with his steady golden ones. ''Not really,'' she managed. She forced a smile, thought she failed. ''We went to watch the tsar's arrival today,'' she said, hoping to sound lighthearted.

He raised a brow.

''But we only saw a wonderful parade.''

''He did not come,'' Katya said.

Nicholas's jaw flexed. ''Alexander has a way of avoiding unpleasantness,'' he murmured. Suddenly he was on his feet, not looking at Carolyn. ''Excuse me. I am going to be late if I do not go now. Katya, we will share breakfast in the morning.''

Katya smiled.

And Carolyn thought, so he will not leave before that, while we are all asleep. She found herself standing as well, and when she realized she still clutched the table, she forced herself to open her hands and shove them down at her sides.

The huge greatcoat was swirling about his shoulders as he settled it on. He strode to the door. Carolyn, Taichili, and Katya all stared after him, Carolyn with growing despair. He is leaving, she thought. Only half an hour after he has arrived. And he has not given a single indication that he still feels at all fondly toward me. Oh, God. I am such a fool.

But at the door his purposeful strides faltered. And suddenly, slowly, he turned.

His piercing gaze went right through Carolyn, striking away any and all doubt. For it was filled with desire—and there was no mistaking it.

The household was asleep. Carolyn sat in the salon on a leather couch, not far from the hearth, where a fire danced and leapt. A cashmere throw was across her legs, a book, which she had no intention of reading, in her hands. The tall ornate grandfather clock in the corner of the room chimed the passage of another hour.

It was eleven o'clock.

Nicholas had been gone for three hours. But he was in a meeting with the tsar, and it could go on for many more hours, if Alexander so wished it.

Her heart went out to him, for she recalled his fatigue. It was impossible for her to deny the urge she now had to be with him, to offer him comfort and solace and some respite from the very real, harsh world. She bit her lower lip.

It was too late to decide that coming to Russia was a mistake. Now she must make sure that it did not become a bigger mistake. And that was not going to be an easy task, because she loved him more than ever, and had finally faced the dire truth. She was *always* going to love him, even if she returned to London and married someone like Anthony and had her own children. He was, simply, an unforgettable man.

And she did not even want to forget him, not when he meant so much to her. But in time, she was going to leave Russia, and she would have to make some kind of complete life for herself, she must, because he would stay here—with his wife. She, Carolyn, would become someone else's wife, or remain unwed, but she was never going to become *his* wife. There. The truth was out, her secret, insane desire, to be his partner, helpmate, and wife, she had finally admitted it to herself.

She wiped her eyes. She fought the urge to cry. Why was she so emotional? When he returned from his meeting, she did not want to break down and weep in front of him. That would not do. Oh, no.

But why did she have to want the impossible? Why? The boyars did not divorce. As unacceptable as divorce was at home, here, in Russia, it was not even an option. Men like Nicholas might eventually separate from their wives, and keep a mistress or two. Period.

In any case, Carolyn knew she could not live with her conscience if he could, and would, divorce Marie-Elena. Thus her choice was clear. She could take whatever crumbs he tossed her way, becoming his lover, or not. She was certainly damned if she did, and damned in this life if she did not.

The tears came. Carolyn laid the book on the floor and sank down deeper on the couch, hugging the throw and herself.

Nicholas walked his mount through the dark, sleeping streets of St. Petersburg. The horse did not object to the sedate pace. His hooves rang loudly on the cobblestones, which were damp from an evening mist, and echoed in the silence of the night. Above Nicholas's head, several lonely stars blinked through the cloudy night sky beyond the steeple of a cathedral. A sliver of moon was just visible.

How dark the unlit city was, he mused. Dark, dreary, depressed. Not too many months ago one could ride home at night after a reception or a ball, and every mansion would be completely lit up, carriages would be racing down the streets, and drunken rakes would be staggering from one party to the next. Laughter would fill the air.

Ahead lay the ghostly stone form of Vladchya Palace. Carolyn's image instantly filled his mind.

His grip on the reins tightened, making his horse prance and snort in protest. Immediately Nicholas relaxed his hands, but his heart raced uncomfortably now. In a way, he had not been surprised to find her at his home when he had arrived there. Oh, God.

The recent past had taught him a monumental lesson. From the very moment when she had walked out of the library after they had made love, refusing to return to Russia with him, he had been a man with a broken heart. And for a heart to be broken, it first had to love. But Nicholas did not have to be rational and analytical to realize that, somehow, somewhere, sometime, he had fallen in love with a mere slip of a girl—a bookseller's daughter with a penchant for charades and debate.

His heart was tight now, and aching. He was so damned glad that she had come, yet he was filled with dread, too, and resignation. He'd had more than enough time in the past month to think about their situation. For him, a liaison with Carolyn would be enough. He could build her a palace, anywhere she chose, and if she wished to reside in England, he would spend as much time there as possible in order to be with her. He could escort her to dinners, dances, and balls—if that is what she wished. And if she preferred intimate evenings spent in philosophical debate? Why, that would please him, too.

He was grim. For him, such a liaison would be enough, for he had no other choice. But it was not enough for her, and he knew it with every bit of rationality he possessed. He knew it with every fiber of his being. He knew it with his very soul.

She deserved more. She deserved a husband, a title, and a name. She deserved legitimacy. And he could not give her any of those things. Not now, not ever, or at least, not until his wife died.

Nicholas dismounted in the courtyard. His entire chest was tight. Up until that evening, whenever he thought about her, whenever he picked up a quill to pen her a missive, which was frequently, he stopped himself, reminding himself that her decision to remain in London was the right one. But now she was here. And although he was determined to be honorable, to resist temptation, god*damn* it. He had missed her so much that it had been painful.

He supposed he should consider himself lucky. He had finally discovered what love was like. And as he left his horse with a groom, walking up the steps to the front door, his laughter rang out in the night, harsh and grim. Love was hell.

He stomped through the front door, nodding at the footmen, and down the corridor that led to the east wing. He was sorry now that he was not drunk. He had shared a bottle of wine and several cognacs with Alexander, but had declined when Alexander had offered vodka. And Alexander, clearly in need of company, had been very persuasive. It had not been easy to take his leave.

Of course, now all he had to do was go to his room, for she would be asleep in hers—wherever that might be. And then, tomorrow, he would take breakfast with his daughter, trying with all of his soul to pretend that Carolyn was a mere companion, a servant in his employ like any other. And he would leave. How simple it seemed, on the surface; how complex, in reality.

But then Nicholas saw her. In the salon, asleep on the sofa, a fire dying in the hearth. He found himself standing on the threshold, shocked, dismayed . . . excited.

He ordered himself to continue on down the hall and to the master suite.

His legs carried him inside the salon instead.

Nicholas walked to the sofa and stared down at her face, which he had come to love. And then he realized that she had been crying, for the tears had not yet dried on her cheeks, and anguish seemed to bubble up inside of his chest. He knew he must go. But he knelt at her side, laying a hand on her shoulder.

Would it be so terrible to speak to her, just for a while? Tomorrow he would return to his command. In a few days, if he did not miss his guess, there would be a major battle, the very first of the war. "Carolyn?" he said softly.

Immediately her lashes, which were the color of honey, lifted. And her green eyes met his.

He found himself smiling, then realized he must be wearing his heart on his sleeve, and he quickly erased his expression. But she was already smiling back at him.

He stood. "You fell asleep."

She sat up, covering a yawn with her hand. "I was . . . reading."

He glanced at the book by her feet. And then he had to smile, widely, as he bent to retrieve it. "I did not know that you read Russian."

She blinked, glanced at the book, and turned an adorable shade of pink. "I don't," she said sheepishly. "I must have not been thinking clearly when I grabbed the book."

"Obviously." His smile faded.

Hers also died. She clasped her hands in her lap. "Your meeting? Was it satisfactory?"

He nodded, hesitating, then pulled an ottoman over and sat down on it, taking off his coat as he did so. He draped it on an adjacent chair. "How did you get here?"

"Alexi. He brought me a letter from Katya. I realized"— her tone became cautious—"that she needed me, she sounded so lonely, so I returned with your brother." She avoided his eyes.

"I am relieved. It would have been madness—and dangerous—for you to travel any other way." He stared, and as she stared at her hands, he took in every inch of her, wanting to hold her, touch her, kiss her—and tell her just how he felt. But he did none of those things.

She glanced up. "How have you been? I have been . . . worried."

His jaw flexed. He had to ask, when he was not sure how personal he wanted the conversation to become. "About me?"

She nodded. "Yes."

He inhaled, a steady, persistent aching in his chest. "I have been fine. There has been no fighting as of yet. Kutuzov has replaced Barclay as commander of all the armies, although Barclay retains command of the First Army. It is a good choice, I think. He is a veteran of Austerlitz. I have confidence in him. But until now, we have been withdrawing, allowing Napoleon to advance freely.''

She stared searchingly at him. ''You are worried. I see it in your eyes.''

''I would be a fool not to worry,'' he said. ''Napoleon's army has been invincible for many years. We cannot afford to lose more than a battle or two—or we shall lose the war—and our country. Withdrawing is actually very strategic. When we fight, we must win.''

Carolyn nodded. ''I understand.'' Suddenly she reached out and laid her hand on his arm. ''Nicholas. Do not worry about Katya. I will take care of her as if she were my own daughter.''

He fell in love all over again. ''I know you will,'' he said hoarsely.

And suddenly she was crying.

''Don't cry,'' he said, taking her hand in both of his. ''Why are you crying?''

She shook her head wordlessly, tears streaming down her face. ''How can I not cry? I have missed you so!'' she finally blurted out.

He inhaled, fighting himself and his inclinations, trying to be noble. He said, stiffly, ''I have missed you, too.'' He added, ''Terribly.''

She regarded him through her tears, her mouth trembling. ''But we must be fr-friends, no-nothing more. Life is so unfair!'' She pulled her hand from his, covered her eyes, and wept again.

He watched her. ''Yes,'' he whispered. ''Life is unbearably unfair.'' And then he could not stand it. It was one thing to be honorable, to deny himself of her, but it was another to watch her suffer so. He slid to his knees and put his arms around her and pulled her off the sofa into his embrace. And he held her, hard, against his chest, while she wept.

She cried for a long time. Nicholas stroked her hair and

her back and finally said, "Please, Carolyn. Your tears could kill a man."

She sniffed, her sobs subsiding. "I am sorry," she whispered, her breath feathering his neck.

Instantly he stiffened. His hand no longer caressed the length of her spine. Now, he knew, was the time to release her and stand up. He did not move.

She was also motionless. Her cheek pressed to his shoulder, her breasts crushed against his chest, their thighs melded. Her hips were firm against his loins. Suddenly his arms tightened. He closed his eyes. "Carolyn." And he felt his heart, trying to drum its way out of his chest. It was so loud that he was certain she could hear it, too.

"Nicholas," she whispered.

Their eyes met. His hand cupped her cheek. He refused to think. Not now, not anymore. And he bent, lowering his mouth to hers.

✖ TWENTY-EIGHT ✖

THE kiss deepened.

Nicholas's mouth became urgent, insistent, plying hers with something akin to frantic determination. Carolyn clung to his shoulders, responding with the same urgency and desperation. She shut down her mind. Except for one resonating thought—this was as it should be. This was so right.

He tore his lips from hers, held her face in his hands. His golden gaze was searching, the lines on his face harsh.

Carolyn touched his mouth. ''There will be no regrets,'' she said, understanding him completely—and yet she was not certain that she was not lying to them both.

His smile failed. He stood, lifting her to her feet. ''Last time,'' he said unsteadily, ''I made love to you on the library floor. This time, I want it to be in my bed.''

Carolyn managed a smile. Her heart seemed to want to explode with so many different emotions, not the least of which was her love.

He put his arm around her and they left the room, hips bumping together, torsos in firm contact. Carolyn's heart beat hard with expectation and the ever-present force of her feelings for him. She must not, she knew, give in to rationality now. Instead, she must allow anticipation to rule the day. And God, there was so much of it.

They climbed the stairs and hurried down the dark cor-

ridor, under, Carolyn thought, the watchful, sometimes bemused stares of numerous Sverayov ancestors. Sverayov's
door was open and they entered a candlelit room. Carolyn
paid no attention to the rich, heavy red and gold fabrics or
the equally heavy wood furnishings, her gaze flying to the
huge, fabulously carved canopied bed. The wood was
painted ebony. Nicholas closed and locked the door behind
them.

She watched him approach, suddenly, foolishly, nervous.
She wanted to blurt out her feelings. She wanted to tell him
that she loved him, more than she had ever dreamed it
possible to love anyone or anything. But she just stood
there silently in the center of the huge, overappointed room
with its exotic overtones, clutching the folds of her pale
blue gown so tightly that it was a miracle the fabric did
not rip.

He reached her, smiled tenderly, then took her hands in
his. "I think I knew that I would find you here when I
came today," he said, feathering her mouth with a series
of tender, sensual kisses.

Her heart leapt. Her body tightened. Her nipples became
erect, straining against her chemise and gown. "No wonder," she managed, "you seemed so very complacent about
it."

He removed his mouth from hers and laughed harshly,
his fingertips fluttering over the tops of her breasts, left bare
by the low round neckline of her gown, causing Carolyn
to gasp. And then they slipped down her nape, and began
to unbutton the back of her dress. "I was hardly complacent, love," he said.

Carolyn tensed as he slid her gown down her shoulders,
her arms, to her waist. Her chemise was transparent. Carolyn watched him stare at her breasts, which she knew
heaved. He then pushed the gown directly to her feet. Carolyn stepped out of it.

He slid one arm behind her, gave her a shockingly intense look, bent, and nudged her breasts with his face. His

dexterous fingers pushed her chemise down, and his mouth brushed one aching nipple.

Carolyn bit off a gasp as he tugged, very gently, on that oh, so attentive part of her anatomy through her fine chemise.

She clutched his hair.

He continued to tease her breasts with his tongue and mouth as he finally relieved her of the sheer garment. It fluttered across the floor. He bent lower, pressing a kiss to her midsection, and pulled off one white kid slipper after another. Carolyn's heart now beat with frightening force.

And he kissed the side of her knee.

Hot chills swept over Carolyn. And out of the corner of her eye, she saw the bed. "Nicholas," she whispered, about to suggest moving to it.

But he had reached up beneath her chemise and was divesting her of both pantalets and stockings in one single fluid motion. Carolyn tensed.

He straightened and looked at her.

Carolyn had never felt more vulnerable—or more seductive and beautiful. His eyes were male, bold, promising.

His strong hand clasped her knee, slid up her thigh, paused, slid up higher still. He began to caress the inside of her thigh, his gaze on hers, still filled with heat and promises. He was not smiling. But then, neither was she.

The back of his hand brushed her sex.

Carolyn gasped.

His jaw flexed. His gaze was blazingly hot. The *chamber* was hot. And he began to force her to step backward.

"Where?" Carolyn cried, but then her buttocks hit the edge of his bed. It was so high that she could not sit down, but remained pressed there against the mattress instead.

"Trust me," he said—the way the devil might speak to a saint.

Carolyn could not reply, because he was on his knees, kissing *her* knees, and then he was kissing her thighs, his mouth moving steadily upward. Carolyn closed her eyes. She sensed his intention, could not bring herself to protest, delicious shivers sweeping all over her body. His lips found and caressed the inside of her thigh where his hands had so recently been. Carolyn gripped the back of the bed, afraid she could no longer stand upright. Thinking, please.

And then his mouth found her. Carolyn cried out as his fingers spread her lips and his tongue swept over her, again and again. The death came suddenly, instantly, taking her by complete surprise. She cried out repeatedly, her body wracked with impossible ecstasy.

Carolyn returned to earth from God only knew where and looked down. Nicholas remained kneeling, his face pressed to that juncture where he had so recently wreaked such havoc. He lifted his head. The light in his eyes was nothing like the light she had seen before, it was like looking into a volcano about to erupt, and desire began to rear itself all over again.

Swiftly, he stood. He lifted her and deposited her on the center of the bed. Carolyn sat up on her elbows as one boot after another thudded to the floor. She watched him rapidly unbutton his military jacket, his expression fierce, intent—savage. But as he tossed it aside, he caught her watching him, and he smiled at her.

Carolyn smiled back, her heart turning over many times, overwhelmed with far more than mere physical yearning. She whispered, "I need you, Nicholas. I love you." So much, she added silently.

His smile faded. "I need you, too." His tone was hoarse. "I need to be joined with you, Carolyn. I need to be inside you." His eyes, piercing, held hers.

It wasn't what she had wanted to hear—she had wanted to hear, I love you, too, but she thought that he had been trying to say those very words. She hoped that was what he had meant.

He moved to the bed, splendidly nude and spectacularly aroused. Carolyn blushed.

He laughed, moving over her, and then his laughter died abruptly as his mouth claimed hers, hotter, harder, more insistently than before. Their tongues entwined in a complete act of possession.

He broke the searing kiss. "I cannot wait. God, I have missed you," he cried.

Carolyn held him tightly. "Don't wait. I have missed you, too," she began, but then she felt him, huge and hard, entering her, and she gasped.

"Don't tense," he whispered, slowly, very, very slowly, sliding himself inch by agonizing inch inside of her. He was wide and thick and he was long and the pressure was exquisite. Their eyes met and held.

And Carolyn knew that she had found heaven on earth. To be joined with the one she loved. To become one with him.

Carolyn woke up when she rolled over and was drenched by a surprisingly bright light. She blinked, finding herself hugging a crimson pillow, in a huge bed with dark red hangings and darker red covers. And then she recalled all of last night. She was in Nicholas's bed. They had made love—not once, but several glorious times.

She started to smile. Her body was sated, and so was her heart and her soul. But then her smile faded as full comprehension began to intrude and she sat up, holding the sheets up over her breasts. Where was Nicholas? She looked toward the windows. The curtains were drawn, but not fully, and bright sunlight was pouring through the six-inch opening left by the drapes. Oh, God! It must be mid-morning! It was so late!

For one instant, Carolyn tried to comprehend what waking up alone in Nicholas's bed, at this hour, meant. She looked across the room. There was a door on the other side; she assumed it led to a sitting or a dressing room. Abruptly, Carolyn flung off the covers and leapt to the floor.

She cursed, searching for her clothes. Her pantalets and chemise were on the floor scattered about the foot of the bed. She struggled into them. Her dress lay in a pile on the floor in the middle of the room, and she rushed to retrieve it, coloring, finally recalling all of last night in exquisite detail. She felt her cheeks heat. No one had ever told her that passion could be so fine, so grand, so absolutely astounding.

Carolyn pulled her dress over her head, turned it backward, and did up all of the buttons before twisting it back around so that it was properly in place. She could only find one stocking, so she slid her slippers onto her bare feet. And she ran to the closed door on the far side of the room.

She flung it open. "Nicholas?"

Her smile faded. It was a fabulous sitting room, for it would qualify as a salon for most people, but it was empty, Nicholas was not there. The thought crossed her mind that he had already left St. Petersburg. Her heart went wild. That was, she told herself furiously, impossible. He would not leave without saying good-bye. Whatever had made her even think of such a thing?

She crossed the sitting room and found a dressing room adjacent to it, but it was also empty. Immediately she saw his dirty uniform lying in a pile on the floor. Her heart lurched with sickening force.

Had he left?

Carolyn left the suite, fighting nausea now. She hurried down the hall, ignoring his ancestors, who seemed to be glaring this morning and hardly as benevolent as they had been last evening. He would not leave without a good-bye. But now she had the folly of remembering that he had a wife, even if they were estranged, and she did not want to think of Marie-Elena at all. Not now, dear God, not now.

She had promised him that she would not have regrets. But now, close to tears, Carolyn did not know what she was feeling. She supposed the only emotion that she could identify was fear. No—it was more like terror combined with dread.

Carolyn stumbled down the two flights of stairs, and rushed toward the salon where she had fallen asleep last night. It was vacant, not even a small fire stoked in the hearth. The dining room was also empty, but the buffet on the sideboard and the used place settings told her that breakfast had already been served.

She could not have missed him.

Carolyn turned, panting, and ran down the hall to the stairs, flying down the steps to the ground-floor landing. A servant was approaching. Carolyn grabbed the maid's arm, aware that she was frightening her but helplessly out of control. "Nicholas—Sverayov! Where is he?" she cried wildly.

The maid blinked at her and responded in Russian, not a word of which Carolyn understood.

"The prince! His Excellency! Nicholas Sverayov! Where?" She gestured urgently, shrugging her shoulders, hands lifted, imploring the heavens, it seemed. "Where is he? He did not leave?"

The maid pointed toward the central wing of the palace, eyes wide.

Carolyn released her wrist and lifted her skirts and ran as fast as she could through the rest of the east wing. And in the foyer she skidded to an abrupt halt. Clad in a clean uniform, his greatcoat swinging from his shoulders, Nicholas squatted there, hugging his daughter. Taichili looked on from a short distance away.

He was leaving? Without a good-bye? Carolyn was stricken.

He released Katya, looked up, saw her, and slowly rose to his full height. Not a trace of emotion showed on the mask of his face.

Carolyn started forward quickly. "Nicholas! It's late and—" She darted a glance at Taichili, saw the other woman's mottled face and dark glare, and thought, Oh, God, she knows. She glanced at Katya, who was regarding her innocently and felt instant relief—the child did not know. She turned her eyes back to Nicholas. "Excellency," she said, panting. "It's late and you're leaving? So soon?" Her words came out with a hysterical pitch.

He inclined his head. "Good morning, Miss Browne. I am afraid I have a seven-hundred-kilometer ride ahead of me. In fact, my departure is already somewhat tardy.'' His gaze was remote, and what? Disdainful? Heartless? Thoroughly detached? Chillingly cold?

Carolyn stared. It was hard to breathe. Her mind raced, spun dizzily. This could not be happening. She glanced once more at Taichili and Katya; the governess was glowering. Desperate, she turned to Nicholas. ''May I walk outside with you, Your Excellency?'' She forced a too-bright smile. Surely he wished a private word with her. A private good-bye.

One brow lifted. ''I am behind schedule, Miss Browne. Is there something you wish to ask of me?''

Carolyn stared, shocked, for he was as cold as ice, as if she were a mere member of his staff, dear God, not as if he had made love to her last night with unimaginable passion, with love and devotion. But surely she was wrong. Surely he was only acting this way because Taichili was present. ''I hoped to briefly discuss a matter with you that relates to your daughter,'' Carolyn said huskily. Do not cry now, she told herself. This is not happening. This is a performance, for the sake of Taichili—it must be.

He shrugged. ''Very well.'' He faced his daughter. ''Write me, *dushka,* and I will write you, too.'' And then he wheeled, his coat swirling about his shoulders. Without waiting for Carolyn to follow, he strode quickly from the house.

Carolyn lifted her skirts and ran after him, stumbling down the front steps. A groom was holding Nicholas's horse, a huge chestnut with a white blaze, while two footmen remained at the front door. Carolyn's heart, sick with dread, sank.

She reached Nicholas as he took the reins from the groom and swung up into the saddle.

Oh, God! How could he leave her like this?

He stared down at her. ''Yes?''

''Nicholas,'' she began.

His nostrils flared and he cut her off. ''I am pleased that you have come to take care of my daughter after all. I am sure she shall be well cared for while in your capable hands. Is there something of importance that you wish to discuss with me?''

She stared up at his beloved face, his words a knife blade dragged through her from neck to groin. Clearly he was telling her that he wished only to be formal. Why did he not dismiss the groom? She shot a glance at the servant, but Nicholas did not order the fellow away. ''Nicholas. What have I done? How can you leave me like this?'' she asked desperately.

He tightened his reins; his horse pranced impatiently. ''I do not understand you, Miss Browne. To my knowledge, you have done nothing but perform your duties with excellence and dedication, which is no more than I or anyone could ask. As for my hasty departure, I do believe I mentioned last night that I would leave first thing in the morning.'' He inclined his head. ''Adieu, Miss Browne.''

''Adieu?'' She was in disbelief.

He wheeled the horse and, without a single backward glance, cantered across the short drive, through the courtyard, and onto the cobbled street. A moment later he turned a corner and was swallowed up by the city, disappearing from sight.

Carolyn thought she would die. She staggered, losing the ability to stand upright. Her world darkened, turning black. And as the blackness overcame her, she was vaguely aware of being caught by the groom. Her last coherent thought was, Why?

This would not do.

Carolyn sat upright, her face wet with tears, gulping air. She was in her bedchamber, where she had fled after regaining consciousness from the very first swoon of her life. She used the sheets to wipe her eyes, then burst into tears all over again.

It had not been an act. No one could be so cold, so cruel, as to perform in such a manner. And what did a Russian prince care if his child's governess or even if his entire household staff knew of his affair? Had Sverayov not said, time and again, that he was used to doing as he pleased, that the Sverayovs were notorious for their flamboyance and disregard of convention? It had not been an act. She was the idiot. For clearly she had imagined that his interest in her was anything other than mere lust.

She moaned, covering her face with her hands, while a little voice inside of her head berated her, trying to whisper in her ear that she was not a fool, that he loved her, he did, how could she doubt it even for an instant? Trust your heart, the voice said. There is an explanation. There is!

Carolyn managed to stop crying. She knew she must not listen to her overly imaginative, romantic self. Logic must rule the day. She must listen only to her head. And her mind was convinced that she had been foully abused—that she had been an utter idiot.

She slipped from the bed, to splash water on her face. She regarded herself dismally in the looking glass. It was obvious that she was devastated, and that she had been weeping. Either that, or she was ill.

She felt as if she were going to die.

She dried her face and hands and left her room. She was heartsick, heartbroken, in a world of shadows and darkness, but she had a job to perform, and it was far too late for regrets now. Katya needed her. Maybe this war would finally end. In which case, Carolyn would return home. Sverayov would have to find someone else to take on the role of companion and supervisor of his daughter.

She paused before entering the classroom. Raffaldi was drilling Katya on her spelling. The language they were speaking was French. Taichili was not present. For that, Carolyn was thankful.

But the moment she stepped inside, both student and tutor saw her, and faltered. Raffaldi turned red and avoided her eyes even while bowing and murmuring, "Good day."

Carolyn was too despondent to blush, but it was obvious that he knew of her fall from grace, and if he knew, surely the entire staff knew as well. "Good morning. It is twelve. Time for Katya's half hour of philosophy."

Katya brightened, but then said, "Miss Browne? Have you been weeping?"

Carolyn had the urge to cry all over again; Nicholas's cold expression was engraved on her mind, as he sat his mount, preparing to leave, gazing down at her as if she were of no consequence at all. "I am slightly ill," she said.

That seemed to satisfy Katya. Carolyn walked over to the table and sat down beside Katya, clasping her hands in front of her. "Did you write the essay about Socrates that I assigned to you?" Carolyn asked.

Katya nodded, reaching for the sheet of vellum in her desk drawer. Suddenly Taichili strode briskly into the room—ignoring Carolyn. "Katya. Come immediately. Your mother is here."

Carolyn's heart skipped numerous beats. She stared in alarm.

Katya was standing, eyes wide. "My mother? But . . . she is at Tver!"

"The princess is here, downstairs, she has just arrived." Taichili's tone was urgent. She still refused to look at Carolyn. "And as she has come with several trunks, I think she intends to stay. We must go down and greet her."

Carolyn was light-headed. How could this be happening? First Nicholas's cruel rejection, and now this, Marie-Elena's arrival. How could she manage? How? The other woman was going to take one look at her and sense her vulnerability and attack. Carolyn had never been more sure of anything.

Katya turned. "Miss Browne?" Her expression was eager. "I must go down and greet Maman. May I?"

Carolyn stood; how weak her knees felt. She forced a smile. "Of course, dear. We will continue tomorrow."

Taichili gripped Katya's arm, steering her toward the door, when brisk slippered footsteps sounded in the corridor outside, swiftly approaching. Carolyn tensed. Marie-Elena swept into the classroom, exquisitely dressed in a high-necked silvery-gray silk gown and a matching fur-lined cape. Her gaze immediately settled on Carolyn, and it was piercing. "You! I just learned that you were here!" she cried, gloved hands on her hips.

Carolyn did not move. But then, neither did the tutor, Taichili, or poor Katya, who gazed at her mother expectantly. "Good day, Princess," Carolyn said huskily.

"Maman," Katya began eagerly.

But Marie-Elena stepped forward, apparently not having heard her daughter. "What are *you* doing here? You are too bold, following my husband all the way to Russia! How dare you!"

Carolyn was aghast, and she shot a horrified look at Katya, who was regarding them both, distraught. "Your Highness, I beg you, if you wish a word with me, may we do so privately? And do you not wish to greet your daughter?"

"If I wished to speak to you privately, I would," Marie-Elena said harshly. Then she glanced at her daughter. "Katya is a very grown-up child. Aren't you, baby?"

Katya nodded uncertainly.

"She need not be left in ignorance of her father's outrageous behavior. Niki has gone too far." Marie-Elena marched forward to stand face-to-face with Carolyn. She stared at her and said triumphantly, "You have been crying!"

Carolyn kept her shoulders squared, her head high, and her tone very even. "Actually, I am ill."

"You have been crying." It was an accusation. Her smile was cold, her eyes black and hostile. "So he has tired of you already."

Carolyn trembled. Marie-Elena had just struck at the very heart of the matter, and she was opening up a wound that Carolyn had not even begun to heal. Had she taken a knife and twisted it in that wound, she could not have done a better job of ripping it open again. Carolyn told herself she would not cry, not now, not in front of this horrid woman, whom she thoroughly despised. "I do not feel well," she said, but her tone was hoarse and almost inaudible.

Marie-Elena laughed.

Carolyn knew that she would leave. Not the palace, but Russia. Tomorrow. Sverayov would have to find someone else to care for his daughter. The situation had become intolerable.

"That is what you get for daring to reach above yourself," Marie-Elena said. And she turned her back on Carolyn, facing Taichili, Raffaldi, and Katya. She smiled. "It is so good to be back in the city! How I have missed the gay life! It has already snowed in the country, my dears. In any case, the tsar is having a very small, intimate reception tonight. The Grand Duchess Catherine insisted I attend. And how could I refuse? I traveled with her, you know." She bent and ruffled Katya's hair. "I have so much to do! I must decide what gown to wear, and I think I need new shoes." With that, she rushed from the room.

Leaving its occupants in absolute silence.

Carolyn looked at Katya. Her face was set, but moisture was sheening her eyes, and the tip of her nose was turning red. And Carolyn felt a surge of hatred for the callous, shallow woman who could be so cruel to her own daughter. Tears threatened to choke her again as she stepped forward, reaching out to Katya, intending to take her hand. "There, there," she whispered. "You must forgive your mother, for she is like a butterfly, a very beautiful, gay butterfly, who must flit from leaf to leaf. She knows no other way, my dear," Carolyn said softly.

Katya's mouth trembled.

It was too much. Carolyn bent and opened her arms and the small child flung herself against Carolyn, sobbing. Carolyn was shocked, for she had never seen Katya shed a tear, much less display a hair of emotion—and now this. She held her, hard. Wanting to cry, herself, for them both.

"Why?" Katya wept. "Why? Why?"

Carolyn finally felt tears, hot and wet, streaking down her own cheeks. Nicholas's image seared her mind. She tried to force it aside, and failed. She stroked Katya's hair as she rocked her. "Why what, dear?" she choked.

"What did I do?" Katya cried, clinging to Carolyn. "Why doesn't she love me?"

The pain went through Carolyn like a knife. She buried her face against the child's, and finally, allowed herself to vent her own grief. And as Katya sobbed out years and years of anguish, Carolyn thought, What did I do? Why doesn't he love me?

What did I do?

✒ TWENTY-NINE ✒

THEY were in the midst of their midday dinner the following afternoon when Marie-Elena returned from the reception. Carolyn had not, after all, left the country. Not only would it have been extremely difficult to navigate her way home, she could not abandon Katya now, for she had become terribly silent ever since her mother's appearance in St. Petersburg the day before. She had also become a reluctant student, refusing to perform in any way. In a way, Carolyn thought it was very positive that Katya had wept so hard, and was now showing her unhappiness so openly. She was not the same child she had been several months ago when Carolyn had first met her.

But Carolyn was not prepared for the sight of Marie-Elena in a stunning ice-blue chiffon ball gown, one cut almost as low in the front as it was in the back, a diamond tiara on her blue-black head, a triple-tiered diamond rope about her throat. It was one in the afternoon. And Marie-Elena, standing there on the threshold of the dining room, was smiling cheerfully at the assembly as if it were hardly extraordinary for her to return home from an evening affair at this particular hour. Carolyn actually dropped her fork to the floor.

"Good morning," Marie-Elena cried. Her cheeks were flushed. In her hand she held a sable pelisse.

Katya sat stiffly, staring not at her mother but at the

opposite wall, her expression impossible to decipher. She might have been a beautiful, inanimate porcelain doll.

"Baby, what is wrong? Is it not a beautiful morning? I have had such a wonderful time!" Marie-Elena swept into the room and hugged Katya even while she sat there at the table, unmoving. Then she straightened. "Taichili," she said, "see to it that I am not disturbed until six this afternoon. I intend to take a nap. I may be awoken then with tea and chocolates. You know the kind I adore, the ones filled with raspberry cream."

"Yes, Princess," Taichili said, expressionless herself.

Marie-Elena's gaze slid over Carolyn with utter condescension. "What? You are still here? I am surprised." With that, she turned and sailed from the room, dragging her sable on the floor after her.

It was odd, Carolyn thought, picking at her salmon fillet and potatoes, how a tension-laden silence was the immediate consequence of Marie-Elena's visits. She glanced up, saw Katya stirring her salmon about her plate, and summoned a smile. "Do eat, dear. It is very good, and God only knows when we shall have salmon again."

"I am not hungry," Katya said, staring determinedly at the salmon as if she expected it to swim off her plate.

"But you did not eat last night—not a single bite."

Katya stood, shocking everyone, for she had not asked permission to rise. "I am sick," she announced. "I wish to go to bed."

Carolyn gaped. Taichili was standing. "Young lady, you may be ill, but that is no excuse for forgetting your manners."

Katya stared at Taichili, and did the unthinkable. She turned abruptly and flew from the room.

Carolyn turned to look at Taichili, who was in danger of having an apoplexy. Raffaldi's brows were raised. And then, slowly, Carolyn smiled, and a giggle escaped her.

Taichili whirled. For the first time since Sverayov had left the day before, she looked directly at Carolyn. "You would find such behavior amusing!" she cried.

Carolyn bit off another giggle. "Taichili. Surely you must see that this kind of behavior is far more natural than soldierly obedience to your every command. We are not an army, thank God."

Taichili stared. "Perhaps it is more natural, but something is happening here, and I am not sure what!"

Carolyn blinked, for the governess had never before revealed herself this way, and her frustration was obvious. "I am sorry if you are confused." She hesitated. "I think we are all confused, and the prince's absence does not help." Immediately her heart turned over, stabbed with pain.

Taichili sank back into her seat, glowering at her plate.

Raffaldi said, in his usual amiable manner, "The prince is always absent, dear Miss Browne. He is a military man. His stays home are brief and infrequent."

Carolyn nodded. It crossed her mind that if Marie-Elena were not so horrid, his stays home might be less brief and less infrequent. But she kept the thought, which was so disturbing, to herself. She hesitated. "The princess." Her tone was low. "Does she always. . . . stay out so late?"

Raffaldi ducked his head, choosing not to answer. It was Taichili who met her gaze. "She is the princess. She can do as she wishes, when she wishes, and no one can say a word against her. That is the way of it."

"I see," Carolyn said, thinking it was intolerable to flaunt one's dissolute way of life before an impressionable child.

But then Taichili said, "Yes. She is always this way. Except when His Excellency is at home."

The princess had a visitor two times that afternoon while she napped, a gentleman who was turned away. The third time Carolyn stood at a window looking out on the lawns and drive in front of the house from a ground-floor room in the central wing. The window was open, for the breeze was fresh and crisp. She watched a handsome, swarthy man in uniform leave the house, trotting toward his black steed, held by a groom. She could not help being curious. Was this one of Marie-Elena's lovers? Had this man been the one to keep her out so late the night before? He was certainly darkly handsome and dashing in his white uniform.

"That is Prince Vorontsky," Taichili said behind her.

Carolyn whirled. "He must be amongst the tsar's advisors, or he would not be here in St. Petersburg."

"No," Taichili said firmly. Her cheeks were flushed. "He serves in the Second Army, which we know is to the south, guarding the road to Moscow."

"Well, apparently the princess has an admirer," Carolyn said lightly.

Taichili was silent.

"What is wrong?" Carolyn asked.

Taichili turned away. "He is the Prince's cousin. He is just a family friend."

"I see," Carolyn said. She continued to stand at the window after Taichili was gone, then realized that Vorontsky was not leaving. The groom was taking his horse and leading it toward the stables. A moment later someone flew across the lawns toward Vorontsky, having come from another part of the house in the east wing. It was a woman. It was Marie-Elena.

Carolyn watched, unable not to. Marie-Elena paused before the prince, and he reached for her hand and kissed it. Did he hold it to his lips far longer than necessary? Carolyn was not sure. But Marie-Elena seemed terribly arrogant as she stood there before him in a pale white muslin dress. She had no wrap and she began to shiver as they exchanged words. Vorontsky took his short fur-lined coat off his shoulder where it had been fashionably draped and settled it over her shoulders.

Carolyn knew that to eavesdrop was wrong. But she pushed the window open further and strained to hear. Not a sound came to her ears. She was disappointed.

They were walking away, alongside the house—in her direction. Their voices could finally be heard, his low and masculine, hers higher-pitched. Carolyn slipped behind the draperies, her pulse pounding, imagining Marie-Elena's fury should she be discovered spying. There was no mistaking the tone of the prince's voice. He was upset and angry.

"Why?" she finally heard him say, demandingly. "Why? You ignored me last night. Dammit, what are you doing?"

"Sasha, we are through," Marie-Elena said in a silken voice. "I am so very sorry."

"And when were you going to tell me about the child? I had to see for myself that you lost it!" he said harshly.

Carolyn could not believe her ears. The father of the child Marie-Elena had lost was Nicholas's own cousin! She peeked out from behind the draperies. They had halted not far from where she stood, and Vorontsky was gripping both of Marie-Elena's arms. Now she could see his features, and hers. He was flushed. Marie-Elena was disdainful.

"Sasha, please. That is old news. I thought by now you would have heard," Marie-Elena said dismissively. "By the by, he knows."

Sasha turned white beneath his dark skin. "Not . . . Niki?"

"Yes." She smiled.

"Good God! You told him!"

"Sasha, I am not so stupid—he found out. It was Alexi. He will probably insist on a duel, you know." She smiled as if pleased with the notion.

"Are you enjoying this?" Sasha said furiously. "Do you wish him to die—or myself?"

"Can I help it if the two of you fight over me?" She shrugged.

"Perhaps we will decide that you are not worth fighting over, my dear," he said coldly.

Her slap rang out, cracking loudly across his cheek.

Carolyn gasped, almost as loudly, but they were too caught up in their own drama to hear. Sasha had grabbed both of her wrists, wrenching her forward, and she fell completely against him.

"Did you sleep with him?"

"It is not your business," she hissed. "Let me go!" She struggled against him but it was futile.

"You did. You bitch. You slept with Anatole. Did he make you happy, *chérie*? Did he make you happy the way I have made you happy?"

"Yes!" she spat at him. "Yes! Yes! Yes!"

He stared at her, his handsome face enraged, and then he jerked her, viciously, Carolyn thought, unsure of whether to run for help or not. Yet she was mesmerized. And Sasha locked Marie-Elena in an embrace and bent her over backward as if he meant to break her in two—except that his mouth was on hers.

Carolyn stared as the violent kiss went on and on—watching as Marie-Elena visibly melted, her hands coming up to clutch his shoulders, her body melding to his.

She inhaled, her pulse pounding. Stunned with what she was witnessing, stunned with what she had learned. Sasha Vorontsky was Nicholas's cousin—and the father of the child Marie-Elena had lost. Oh, God. Surely he was as shocked and offended as she was. And surely, he was terribly hurt.

The lovers broke apart. Sasha stared at her. "I am leaving in an hour."

"Leaving?" she cried, dismayed. "But, how can you go now? You cannot go now!"

"I can, and I shall." He was grim. "There is going to be a battle, Marie. At a tiny village, one hundred and thirty kilometers from Moscow, which no one has ever heard of. Not myself, not the tsar. It is called Borodino. I do not intend to miss the first major engagement of the war. We expect our armies to meet as early as the day after tomorrow—unless there is a miraculous change of heart on either the tsar's part or Napoleon's."

Marie-Elena was staring at him. So was Carolyn, her heart trying to beat its way out of her breast. A battle. No, he had called it a major engagement. The first of the war. And Nicholas's words returned to her, full force. They could not afford to lose more than a battle or two or they would lose the war and their country.

She closed her eyes, gripping the windowsill. Nicholas was going to be there. Carolyn had no doubt. And so would Alexi. She was afraid.

"Stay at least for a few hours," Marie-Elena was pleading. "Sasha, darling, stay."

Carolyn glanced up through blurry eyes to see Marie-Elena in his arms. Their kiss was long and hungry.

He broke away. "I cannot. But I will come to see you as soon as is possible. In the meanwhile"—he gave her a piercing look—"stay away from Anatole, and if you communicate with Niki, do not discuss me. God knows he must be furious, and as much as I need you, I do love him. I will speak to him myself."

He turned away.

Marie-Elena stomped her foot. "Do not think to come back and visit me, Sasha, if you are leaving now, like this!"

He did not reply.

Carolyn watched him stride across the lawn, toward the front of the house, not really seeing him, stunned by the entire episode and the thought of the pending battle—and startled to realize that, in spite of what Nicholas had done, she was so very afraid for him. But surely he would survive this battle. Surely he would.

And she was so engrossed that she failed to move back behind the draperies. Marie-Elena turned to go back to the east wing of the house. She saw Carolyn in the window and cried out.

Carolyn's instinct was to seek sanctuary in the classroom, even though it was not the time for her to instruct Katya, but on second thought, she knew that would not be wise. She did not want Katya to witness her mother's temper, or hear anything Marie-Elena might say. She walked slowly back to the east wing, and found herself correct. Marie-Elena appeared, her strides hard and swift, approaching her. Her face was dangerously flushed.

She stopped in front of Carolyn, her hands on her hips. "And just what do you think you were doing?" she demanded. Her dark eyes glittered.

Carolyn remained as calm as was possible—outwardly. "I was taking some air."

"You were spying!"

"No. I was taking air."

"What did you see, exactly? How long were you standing there?"

"I was there but a moment. I saw nothing," Carolyn lied. She felt her own cheeks heating.

"Good." Marie-Elena was vicious. "I suggest that you hold to that denial, dear Miss Browne. I will not have you reporting my activities to anyone!"

Carolyn might hold to her denial, but she could not hold her tongue. "And to whom would I report your activities, Princess?"

Marie-Elena's hand flashed out. Carolyn realized the woman's intention to strike her, but was so shocked that she did not move. And just as she had slapped Sasha Vorontsky, her palm cut sharply across Carolyn's face. It stung.

Carolyn backed up a step. "How dare you," she said low, trembling. How she wanted to attack the other woman. But she managed to control herself, thinking of Katya. Because of the child, she must not reduce herself to such outrageous, despicable behavior.

"How dare I? I am not the one who has gained employment in this house—only to pursue another woman's husband."

Carolyn inhaled. "I will not even respond to that." But she was guilty, at least to some degree, and she knew it, just as Marie-Elena must have sensed it.

"You slept with him!" she cried. "Do you think I am a fool? I have maids here who report directly to me. Everyone knows you spent the other night in his bed, Miss Browne. So cease your innocent behavior. You are not better than me. If one would discount the difference in our stations, I would say that we are the same.''

For Carolyn, the truth was a blow. And it hit her like cold water in the face. And she groped for a response, for a defense, and said, unthinkingly, ''I am sorry. I am truly sorry. But I fell in love with Nicholas. I did not mean for anything to happen. I am not that kind of woman.'' How pitiful she sounded!

Marie-Elena's glance was disparaging. ''Please! Hundreds of women, like yourself, have fallen in love with him . . . and into his bed.'' She turned on her heel and walked away, then paused. ''I am summoning all of the staff to a meeting in the grand salon in a quarter of an hour.'' She disappeared down the hallway.

Carolyn stared after her, continuing to shake. Marie-Elena's words cut her to the quick, hurting far more than the unkind slap. Was she merely another conquest? Another victim of his stunning looks, his station, and charm? For that would explain his coldness to her the following morning, the way nothing else could.

Her temples throbbed now, along with the side of her face. Carolyn was not going to join the staff in the grand salon, but on her way upstairs she encountered Taichili, Raffaldi, and Katya, all descending. ''Miss Browne, everyone is summoned to the grand salon,'' Raffaldi said pleasantly. And then his eyes narrowed. ''Are you ill?''

''I suppose,'' Carolyn said, changing direction. Katya reached for and took her hand. Carolyn smiled at her as they made their way through the house.

Carolyn had not realized the staff was so large. Perhaps sixty servants had gathered in the huge room, everyone silent with expectation. Ten more minutes passed after the designated quarter hour before Marie-Elena entered the salon. She clapped her hands, perhaps for silence, but everyone was already hushed, their attention focused on the princess. Carolyn had a sense of dread.

''We are going to Moscow,'' Marie-Elena cried enthusiastically. ''And I wish to leave in two hours, no later. That means that one and all must begin packing up our belongings immediately. Wagons and coaches must be readied. I think we shall drive through the nights, so that we may reach Moscow as soon as possible. Is that clear?''

Carolyn stared at her, wondering if she was demented. There was going to be a battle not far from Moscow. Whatever could Marie-Elena be thinking? And then it flashed through her mind that Sasha Vorontsky was going to be quite close to the city.

"Very good," Marie-Elena said, satisfied. "In two hours, then, we shall leave. I suggest that everyone get to work immediately.''

The staff dispersed, rushing from the room. Carolyn found herself standing there holding Katya's hand, Taichili beside her, and Raffaldi. Marie-Elena began to leave. Carolyn glanced at Taichili, but the other woman's mouth was pursed. Wasn't anyone going to object? "Princess!"

Marie-Elena turned, her expression cool. "I suppose you wish to tell me that you are terminating your employment?''

Carolyn's pulse raced. "Your Highness. I mean no disrespect. But the prince ordered us to remain here, for safety's sake.''

She smiled thinly. "Niki is not here. But I am. And we are going to Moscow.''

Carolyn stared, and said harshly, "Rumor holds that there will be a major battle on the morrow, Your Highness. Surely it will not be safe to travel anywhere even remotely close to the fighting.''

Marie-Elena smiled, her eyes brightening. She sailed forward and took Katya's hand from Carolyn's. "That is just it. Tomorrow, or shortly after, there will be a battle, and afterward, Moscow will be gay and festive like before the war! It is going to be wonderful! There is no city like Moscow when it is the season. After tomorrow, when we will have our first victory of the war, the city will be filled with revelers, to celebrate what may very well be the end of the war! It will be so exciting! We cannot possibly stay here and miss all the fun.''

"Will the war really be over?" Katya asked.

"I think so," Marie-Elena cried. "Our soldiers are far superior to Napoleon's, everyone knows that, and now we shall finally have the chance to prove it to the world. Come. Come help me choose which gowns to bring. There are going to be so many parties." Marie-Elena whirled, taking Katya with her. And when the pair was gone, the salon was silent.

Absolutely astounded, Carolyn faced Taichili and the tutor. "This is madness! The prince will be furious when he finds out. And this could be dangerous—or am I mistaken?" How she wanted to be told that she was mistaken!

"What do you know of this battle?" Raffaldi asked, yet he did not seem very perturbed. He seemed, crazily, as excited as Marie-Elena.

Quickly, Carolyn told them what she had overheard, although she did not tell them from whom the information came.

"It will not be dangerous," Raffaldi said, patting her shoulder. "By the time we reach Moscow, the battle will be long over, dear Miss Browne. For even if we travel through the nights, it takes at least a week to make the journey. And we are not going to drive into the midst of a battle! The princess is very clever. Moscow will be in the mood to celebrate. Have you ever been to Moscow, Miss Browne? It is an engaging city, truly."

Carolyn stared at him as if he had grown horns. "And if the battle is lost? What if Napoleon wins—and proceeds to march on Moscow, Signore? Would it be safe for us to be there, then?"

"You exaggerate. He cannot win. We have never chosen to engage him yet. He shall soon see how fierce the Russians are." He grinned. "And I am an outsider, telling you this. I am going to my flat to pack. I suggest you do the same, unless you are returning to London?" With that, he left the room, smiling.

Carolyn confronted Taichili. "And you? Have you been

seized with this madness, too? Is the air suddenly foul? I do not understand!''

But Taichili was not smiling. ''Miss Browne, I do hope the princess and Raffaldi are right in their predictions of victory and success. But that is neither here nor there. The prince is absent, the princess is present. She has ordered the household to Moscow. And to Moscow we shall go.''

Carolyn stared, her heart sinking. Of course, she did not have to go. But she thought of Katya in her mother's care, so close to the fighting, and she shuddered. She knew that Taichili was right. There was no choice.

⊷ THIRTY ⊷

THEY had traveled for six entire days, obtaining fresh horses in the small villages they had passed through, leaving behind forests of firs and pine and spruce. They had crossed too many rivers to count, and the surrounding countryside now consisted of flat hills, barren and faded because of the autumn chill. Firs still appeared from time to time, but silver birch trees dotted the land. As it had not rained in over a week, they had made good time, and would hopefully arrive in Moscow the following day before nightfall.

It was almost evening. Their entourage consisted of five horse-drawn wagons, one of which contained the dozen servants chosen to accompany them to Moscow, the others laden with trunks of personal belongings and supplies of food. A single covered carriage led the convoy. Carolyn sat in it with the princess, Taichili, Raffaldi, Katya, and Marie-Elena's favorite maid, a fair young woman in her thirties who had accompanied her mistress from Baden almost a decade ago.

Carolyn was awake, everyone else had fallen asleep. A riverbank had appeared in her view on the carriage's right, and she stared at the slow, muddy waters, watching what appeared to be a lynx slinking along the far side. She had been determined to put her anxiety aside, and thus far, there had not appeared to be any cause for concern. They had hardly passed a soul on the road from St. Petersburg. The villages were sleepy and quiet, as villages should be. But the faces in them, mostly the old and the young except for the women, had been friendly and curious. One would hardly think that the land was at war; in every village where they stopped they had asked about a recent battle but no one had heard of Borodino or any other engagement. Perhaps Sasha Vorontsky had been wrong.

Carolyn hoped so. And she could not help thinking about Nicholas. In Moscow, they would not be very far from him. Just before leaving, she had managed to send a brief message to him, explaining that his wife had ordered their departure for Moscow. Surely, once he learned of their whereabouts, he would come to visit his family. And then what? Carolyn's stomach curdled with dread. She could not bear to be confronted by his coldness again.

Inwardly, she still cried. And she thought of his lovemaking, of every single instance of it, both the frantic passion and the tenderness, and she thought, surely she was mistaken, surely there was an explanation, there just had to be.

Suddenly the carriage halted.

Carolyn tensed, as the coach's other occupants began to awaken. She leaned across Katya, to stare out of the window, but she saw nothing but bright blue sky. Katya also gazed outside. "Why have we stopped?" the child asked.

"I'm not certain," Carolyn began, and then she stiffened.

Hoofbeats had suddenly sounded. Loudly, rapidly approaching, and it could not be one rider, but half a dozen or more. Carolyn stiffened, glancing around the carriage at everyone else, and saw that one and all were as anxious as she. Quickly she stuck her head through the window and her heart plummeted. Perhaps a dozen soldiers were cantering in their direction.

Carolyn jerked back inside. "Soldiers," she said tersely.

Marie-Elena was white. "Ours, I hope?"

"I have no idea, they are still too far away to tell." Six pairs of eyes met and held.

Katya broke the tension filling the coach. "If they are French, what will happen to us?"

Carolyn took her hand again. "Nothing, dear," she said with a cheerful smile. "We are ladies, and we shall be allowed to pass on." But her heart beat hard with dread. All she could think of was how ladies could so easily be overpowered by enemy soldiers. She shuddered to think of what her and the other women's fates would then be. And then their carriage halted.

Horses and uniforms surrounded them, sending up huge, enveloping clouds of dust. And when the dust settled, Carolyn glimpsed familiar green and gray, and she slumped against her seat. The soldiers were Russian, thank God. And in her next breath, she prayed, God, she did, to see a familiar face—Alexi or even Nicholas. But the young man's face that was peering through the window, a dark plumed helmet atop his head, his brass buttons glinting on his chest, was not familiar. His tone was crisp as he addressed them in French, swinging open the door. He bowed briefly, his gaze immediately finding Marie-Elena.

"Madame, I am Major Verenko," he said crisply. "I must ask you what you are doing on this road."

Marie-Elena extended her hand. "Major, I am Princess Sverayov, and we are on our way to Moscow."

"Princess, I am terribly sorry, but you cannot continue on this road. Why are you traveling to Moscow? The city has been evacuated. You must change your course," the flushed, begrimed officer said.

"Moscow has been evacuated?" Marie-Elena exclaimed. "But why? Surely Napoleon is not advancing undeterred upon her?"

Carolyn reached for and held Katya's hand, her mouth dry.

"I am not here to discuss the war or the evacuation, Princess," he said. "But the city's residents were ordered to leave by the authorities."

"But we must reach Moscow!" Marie-Elena cried. "My poor mother is there, and she is dying."

Carolyn gasped, wanting to strangle Marie-Elena. And she was afraid. Why had Moscow been abandoned? Was Napoleon advancing upon her? Would not the Russians resist?

But Marie-Elena did not hesitate. "Perhaps you can escort us to the city, Major?" she asked with a seductive smile.

He was grim. "I am very sorry, but I am on state business, and I cannot escort you to Moscow, although I wish I could. If it is dire, you must detour. At the next village, there is an old bridge where you can cross the river. There is another road, slightly longer, and not as convenient or well kept, that will take you to the city."

"Must we detour?" Marie-Elena asked, pouting. Making Carolyn want to reach out and shake her, hard.

Verenko was flushed. "Princess, if you continue as you are, you might very well ride into a battalion of Napoleon's soldiers," he said flatly. "And I cannot allow that to happen."

He swung the door closed. Abruptly ending the conversation.

Carolyn had not been able to believe her ears, in truth, she was appalled with Marie-Elena's selfishness, and now she flung open the carriage door and stumbled outside, reaching the major from behind. "Major! I beg your pardon," she said in a rush as he turned. "Please. Borodino. What news? Was there a battle?"

He faced her. "The battle is over, my lady. We continue to guard the road to Moscow. We have won."

But his expression was so severe that Carolyn again detained him as he began to mount his sweaty steed. "Why are you so grim? And if we have won, why has Moscow been abandoned?"

"The French are also claiming a victory, my lady. Truthfully, I do not think either side has won." He swung up into the saddle. "Many died in the battle. Many." He gathered up the reins, causing his horse to snort and dance. "Look behind me," he said.

Carolyn did. And she saw a large blur on the horizon, one she did not understand. But it was colorful, and it was approaching them. Slowly the forms began to take shape. Carolyn realized it was a mass of slowly moving wagons and people.

"Those are the wounded," Verenko said grimly. "The wounded and some of Moscow's citizens. Refugees, all of them." Suddenly his eyes were sheened. "Thousands have died on both sides, my lady, and never in my life did I dream I would ever see such a thing."

It took them another full day to reach Moscow, which they did at mid-afternoon. They had taken the detour, which proved to be a narrow, terribly rutted road, but before doing so they had seen firsthand some of the devastation wrought by the war. Hundreds of wagons filled with bandaged soldiers had passed them, many of the wounded more dead than alive. Other soldiers, vacant-eyed, had hobbled by with the help of crutches or their comrades, their uniforms stained with dried blood. And of course, wagons filled with household possessions, with chairs and pianofortes, with old men, grim matrons, and young children, with maids and grooms, as Moscow's residents also ran away from the war.

They were the only ones going against the human tide. There was no changing Marie-Elena's mind. Carolyn damned her selfish stupidity.

The sun was still high when their group of wagons and the single carriage plodded across a canal bridge and through the city's outskirts. Carolyn's eyes were wide. While she almost expected to see French soldiers bearing down upon them at any moment, she could not help but be seized by the exotic appearance of the city. Moscow in no way resembled St. Petersburg or any other city she had ever seen. Churches were everywhere, with distinctly Russian motifs engraved upon the stone walls, the woodwork more often than not brilliantly painted, with high, ornate bell towers and tent-shaped steeples. And of course, buildings with those odd, onion-shaped domes abounded. Now Carolyn

glimpsed a huge Gothic cathedral with numerous bell towers and needlelike spires, in the distance, toward what had
to be the heart of the city.

And the city was vacant.

"There is no one here," Carolyn whispered fearfully,
holding Katya's hand. She did not see another carriage in
the street, or any pedestrians on the sidewalks. Her heart
beat hard. "Princess, it is not too late to turn back." Her
tone sounded desperate even to her own ears. She did not
like being here. She was clammy with sweat; she was
dread-filled, afraid.

Marie-Elena glared. "We are not far from the house."

In the neighborhood they now traversed, huge stone
mansions lined the street, all of which were barred from
the public by high iron gates, through which cobbled court-
yards could be seen. Many of the mansions boasted columns and pediments, having been done in the Classical
style, while others seemed very Russian with odd, nearly
flat or sloping roofs, some with upwardly pitched ends or
even statuary carvings. This second style of home was,
more often than not, as gaily painted as the most ornate
and colorful churches.

And Carolyn saw several mansions that were not yet
abandoned, with relief. Across the street, in front of one
palatial home, servants were rushing to and fro from the
house to the street. Belongings were being taken outside
and loaded up onto a dozen waiting wagons. Carolyn espied
every manner of thing, from trunks that surely contained
clothing to Venetian mirrors and mahogany *secrétaires*.

Smug, Marie-Elena smiled at Carolyn. "Not everyone
has left."

Carolyn did not reply. She looked at Taichili and Raffaldi, but neither one of them seemed to wish to reply,
either, and pretended not to hear. "We have nothing to gain
by staying here," she began.

Marie-Elena's gaze swung to Carolyn. "Enough! Do not
tell me that everyone has run away from Moscow! We won,
did you not hear that young major? No one is leaving the

city, Miss Browne. That was an ugly, vicious rumor!''

They drove through a set of open iron gates and a stone archway that soared many meters into the sky, boasting minarets and domes and steeples, finally pausing in a square cobblestone courtyard. Carolyn remained in the carriage staring out at Nicholas's Moscow palace while the rest of her party alighted. With its many gilded domes and spires, its ornate moldings, its heavily tiered blue bell towers, and fabulously engraved and decorated stone walls, painted blue and gold, it was as different from the Vladchya Palace as night was from day. Gone was any trace of European influence. She felt as if she had stepped either through time or backward in it, only to arrive at some exotic oriental place. Carolyn sighed and stepped out of the carriage, following the group to the pitch-black front doors. One of the servants was banging on it, announcing Marie-Elena's arrival.

The house had not seemed deserted, and a bewigged, liveried servant appeared. He gaped at Marie-Elena then bowed. ''Princess! We did not expect you.'' He was flushed.

''Obviously not,'' Marie-Elena said, shoving past him and inside.

Carolyn followed alongside Katya, and found herself standing in a huge foyer painted pale blue and white with fabulously carved, whitewashed wood moldings. Round white plaster columns, carved in upwardly ascending spirals, supported the ceiling overhead. It was painted with a fresco in the rococo style. The sight of angels and trumpets above her head in such a frankly Muscovite setting made Carolyn smile despite her tension.

''Princess, forgive us, we thought you were at Tver,'' the fellow continued.

''Kerinsky, we have five wagons to unload.''

His heels snapped together. ''Yes, Your Excellency. But Princess, most of our neighbors have left.'' His color deepened.

''And why is that?'' Marie-Elena's tone dripped ice.

"Did we not win at that nameless village no one has ever heard about until a day or two ago?"

"Yes. We have claimed a victory, Princess. But we have been told to leave the city. An official proclamation was issued. Those who remain do so at their own jeopardy. Everyone has gone except for Kazan across the street, and he is leaving now."

Marie-Elena stared. As did Carolyn.

"This must be rubbish, a misunderstanding," she finally said, stamping one foot. "What does the army intend? To flee Moscow—abandon it for Napoleon?"

"I am afraid I do not know," the servant said uneasily. "But we have been preparing the house the best we can to obey the proclamation."

Marie-Elena whirled and scowled at Carolyn. "Do not say I told you so!"

Wisely, Carolyn held her tongue. Please, she thought, let her be sane. Obviously they must return to the carriage and depart Moscow. Immediately.

"Very well," Marie-Elena said. "I shall get to the bottom of this. Only unload what we need for a brief stay. If we must leave, we will go to Tver, which is less than a day from here. In the meantime, I am going out. I shall find out exactly what is happening." She smiled. "After I bathe and dress, of course."

Another evening had fallen. Twilight was becoming to the countryside, casting a pale, mellow glow in the encroaching darkness over the many canvas tents and camp fires spread across the rolling land. The birches whispered in a night breeze, and not too far away, a wolf howled. From a distance, the scene was serene and peaceful. No one would ever guess at the bloodshed, the mutilation, the death, which had transpired just six days ago.

Nicholas stood outside of his tent, listening to the hushed whispers of the weary, frightened voices of the First Army. He had only to look across the small distance separating his quarters from those soldiers in his command, to begin to make out the individual faces of the men he was responsible for. Their expressions were far more weary than their voices, and worse even than that. No one, he knew, had recovered from the shock of Borodino. He had not recovered from the shock.

His stomach turned over and he had the urge to vomit, but as he had eaten nothing since the morning, it would be impossible. Nicholas turned and paced away, to stare out now toward Moscow, which could not be seen. More hills, jagged and dark, met his gaze, along with the very first few winking stars. Kutuzov had ordered the First and Second Armies to withdraw another sixty miles to the east. Moscow herself lay a day's ride away.

He closed his eyes. There had been so much death. Never in his life had he thought an engagement could be so monumental and so indecisive. Estimates of the dead were just coming in. Perhaps one-third of the entire Russian force had been decimated, and the French had not fared much better. *One-third.* By God, that was about forty thousand men.

The field hospital lay two dozen miles to the north, in a safer band of territory. The wounded kept staggering in. Nicholas was afraid to learn just what that tally was, and knew very well that many if not most of those injured in battle would also succumb to death.

The high command was claiming a victory, because they still barred Napoleon's path to Moscow. Nicholas was disgusted. That might be true, but he was quite sure that Kutuzov did not intend to make a stand before Moscow, and it sickened him, while the French had captured the Russian positions at Borodino, and they too were claiming a victory. The brutal truth was that both sides were the loser, and for what possible reason? Because of one man's determination to conquer half of the world.

"Colonel Sverayov?"

Nicholas turned at the sound of his aide-de-camp's voice. "Yes, Andrei, what is it?" he asked quietly.

"Sir." The young major saluted smartly. "A messenger has arrived from St. Petersburg."

Instantly, Nicholas thought of the two people in the world most dear to him—his daughter and Carolyn. His pulse thundered and he strode past the aide, wondering if he dared hope for a letter from Carolyn. But he kept recalling Carolyn's shock and hurt when he had so coldly left her standing in front of the house, and anguish filled his own breast. He had done what he had thought was right. Now, surrounded by agony and death, he knew he should have discussed the future with her instead of trying to force it on her, his way. He had already written her a letter of explanation, but knew it was too soon to expect a reply.

What if she did not understand? Did not accept his explanation? What if he had succeeded far too well in what had first seemed to be the only possible solution to their passion and their dilemma? He had known she would never be happy with a liaison, that it would ultimately destroy her and her feelings for him. He had thought about it all that night, and knew he could not be a party to such an erosion in her feelings. He had realized that he must give her up, maintaining a course of honor, rather than indulge in an affair that would inevitably break her heart. But he did not think Carolyn would, or could, accept a mere goodbye, or a falling back to the position of friendship. So he had played the cad.

Nicholas recognized the courier as one of his grooms. He was eating a hunk of bread and a bowl of watery soup ravenously, but he immediately leapt to his feet and saluted Nicholas smartly. "Excellency. I have been sent by Miss Browne."

His heart slammed. Carolyn had sent him a letter? He was afraid to see what she must have written him, not having yet received his own apology. Slowly, Nicholas tore open the missive—and stared in utter horror at the single scripted line.

"Your wife has ordered our departure to Moscow and

we are leaving as I write this.'' It was signed ''Carolyn Browne,'' and dated September the fifth.

And Nicholas felt all of the blood draining from his face.

Carolyn paced, furious and frantic. Where was Marie-Elena?

An entire day had passed since they had arrived in Moscow. That morning, their neighbors across the street, the Kazans, had also left. Carolyn had awoken only to walk outside and watch their neighbors loading up the last of their possessions, climbing aboard their wagons, and driving away. The courtyard outside of Nicholas's palace had been filled with birdsong and silence. Carolyn had stood there for a long time, shivering in her thin dress and shawl, staring down the block. No one stirred, not a single soul, not behind the draperies of the adjoining mansions or on the wide, cobbled street. Only a stray mongrel trotted by. She realized that they alone remained in residence. The neighborhood was deserted.

Where was Marie-Elena? Carolyn's fists were clenched. She had left yesterday evening, dressed as if she planned on attending a ball, and had not returned.

She heard racing footsteps and turned from where she paced in the foyer, desperate for the princess's return, and saw Taichili hurrying down the wide, dark wooden stairs. The governess's expression fell. ''She hasn't come home yet?'' Her tone was no longer brisk and pointed. It was aghast.

''She has not,'' Carolyn said grimly. ''I think we are the last ones left in the city.''

Taichili wet her lips.

Katya was currently with Raffaldi, in the midst of a lesson. What if Marie-Elena did not return? Carolyn could certainly make excuses for the princess, but her senses were screaming at her that they must leave the city—immediately. To remain was insane. And Carolyn's first responsibility was to her charge. Not to anyone else.

''This is appalling,'' Carolyn said tersely to Taichili.

Taichili hesitated. "Maybe something has happened to her."

Carolyn gave her a glowering look. "I can imagine what has happened to her, Taichili. She has rendezvoused with the very dashing Vorontsky, and the two have found it impossible to get out of bed!"

Taichili gasped, but seemed to agree, for she did not even cast a single reproving glance Carolyn's way. "What are we going to do?"

Carolyn thought of Nicholas. He trusted her to care for his daughter, and in spite of what had happened between them, she could never let him down. "We are leaving. Now. Tell the staff we depart in two hours for Tver."

"Without the princess?"

Carolyn inhaled, aware of how monumental her decision was. "Yes. Without the princess. She will have to make her way to Tver herself."

"We cannot leave without Maman," Katya said shrilly from above them.

Carolyn whirled and saw Katya standing on the landing above, pale and distressed. "I thought you were having your lessons, darling," she said cheerfully.

"It is time for astronomy, and I came to get you." Katya glared, coming down the stairs. "We cannot leave without Maman."

"Katya, I am sorry. I know how worried you are about your mother, but she is an adult, and capable of taking care of herself. Everyone has been ordered to leave the city. All of our neighbors are gone. Napoleon may very well ride into Moscow at any moment. We must go."

"No," Katya said. "I am not going without Maman."

Carolyn started, and Taichili stepped forward. "Your mother will meet us at Tver, Katya. And what is happening here? You used to be such a well-mannered girl. Curtsy and apologize to Miss Browne."

Katya stared belligerently, and suddenly darted past them, racing across the foyer and out the front door. Carolyn exchanged a concerned look with Taichili, and both women hurried after her. They exited the palace just in time to see her flying through the entry tower and out onto the public street. Carolyn then realized that Katya's intentions were genuine. That Katya was running away.

"Katya!" she screamed.

But the child's speed increased as she ran down the street, darting around a corner. Horrified, Carolyn snapped, "Get help!" And she lifted her skirts and ran after the child, across the cobbled courtyard, through the tower's vaulted arch, and out into the street. She rushed down it and around the same corner Katya had turned and stopped short. Panting, and out of breath. Katya was nowhere to be seen.

It was a few hours later; mid-afternoon. Carolyn's white muslin dress, sprigged with yellow and green, was gray. She sank down on the front steps of the palace, tears filling her eyes. Her limbs were shaking.

In the courtyard, the five wagons were loaded with all of their possessions, including Marie-Elena's. They were ready to leave. They had been ready to leave since half past nine that morning. But Katya was still missing. Carolyn told herself that she must not cry—but she was exhausted and never had she been more worried in her life. More worried—and more frightened.

What if Katya was lost? What if something had happened to her? What if the French had entered the city—and stumbled across her? Perhaps she was hiding from the soldiers!

Taichili suddenly sank onto the top step beside her, handing her a shawl. "You will catch an ague," she said. The governess was clad in a wool coat with a fur collar and fur cuffs. Then she said, "Most of the servants are leaving, on foot, and I cannot stop them."

Carolyn accepted the shawl, but she did not feel the cold. The servants were fleeing and she and Taichili were alone in the courtyard with the loaded wagons. The horses slept in the traces. Occasionally one would snort or flick its tail. Beyond the courtyard, the street was deserted, still, silent. "We cannot leave without her," Carolyn said heavily.

Thinking in despair, How? How could she run away now? When every minute counted? When the French might be descending upon the city as they sat there?

"Of course not," Taichili agreed.

Raffaldi appeared from the house. "Ladies, we must go. We cannot stay in the city another moment. Good God, we are the only ones left! What if the French come? And there are rumors that they are coming, ladies."

Carolyn looked up at him in real shock. "We cannot leave without Katya, signore."

Raffaldi stared. "I am as upset as you that the child has run away. But I have no wish to die. Good day, ladies." He stepped past them and down the stairs. Carolyn watched him climb into one of the wagons and lift the reins; she was absolutely dumbfounded. Taichili also stared as the Italian tutor drove horse and wagon through the iron gates and down the street. A moment later he was gone.

"Traitor," Carolyn said hoarsely.

Taichili laid a hand on her knee. "Perhaps we should let the rest of the staff go, as well. We could keep two horses here, and when we find Katya, we will catch up to them."

Carolyn stared. "Taichili, I cannot ride."

Taichili looked at her.

Carolyn stood. "But I suppose I can learn. Let's tell the remaining staff they can—and must—go."

But before Carolyn could move, a carriage came hurtling down the street, a riderless horse tied to it, and into the courtyard. Carolyn saw khaki and gray and thought, Nicholas! But as the dust settled it was Sasha Vorontsky who held the reins in the driver's seat, and Marie-Elena was huddled up in a fur-lined cape beside him.

Carolyn itched to strangle the other woman. No, she itched to strangle them both. Sasha leapt down, then helped Marie-Elena climb out more sedately. Marie-Elena brushed the dust from her skirts, and sashayed forward. "We must leave immediately. Napoleon's army is advancing."

Carolyn inhaled, fought for self-control. "Princess. Your daughter is missing. She has run away."

Marie-Elena paused in mid-stride, about to enter the house. "Katya is missing?"

Sasha's face was grave. He spoke to Carolyn. "Madame, the child must be found instantly. There is no time to waste."

Carolyn held his gaze. "Excellency, I wish you to know that I was personally hired by Prince Sverayov to care for his daughter. I gave him my word that I would do so to the best of my ability. We came to Moscow against his express orders—because of the princess's countermand. I have spent six hours in the streets of this city, looking for Katya. I will gladly spend another six searching for her now. But we could use your help." She stared.

He also stared. "So you are the famous Miss Browne."

Carolyn glanced at Marie-Elena briefly. "Yes, I am Carolyn Browne. You can cover more territory on your horse than I can on foot. And no, sir, I cannot ride."

He nodded. "Marie-Elena, make sure the household is ready to go at a moment's notice."

"The household is ready." Carolyn could not help either herself or her acerbic tone. "What is left of it. We have been ready for two full days."

Vorontsky looked at her with a small smile. "Touché, madame, touché." He strode to the back of the carriage and untied his horse, swinging into the saddle.

Marie-Elena cried out. "Where are you going?" She was shrill.

Sasha rode over to the steps. "I am going to find Katya, Marie. Where do you think I am going?"

Marie-Elena burst into tears, tears which Carolyn thought were real. "How could she run away now? I will beat her when she returns, I will! Napoleon is coming. You said so yourself. Our stupid army is fleeing once again. Cowards! They are all cowards, every single one of them!" Marie-Elena sobbed.

Sasha's face was tight, his jaw flexed. He looked at Carolyn. "Let us plan to meet back here every second hour.

It is my guess that she is hiding close by. If you happen to find her, leave and I will catch up.''

Carolyn nodded. ''I think she must be close by, too. Perhaps we should let the staff go, Excellency. And when we find Katya we can meet them at Tver. There is no need for everyone to stay.''

''A capital idea. But if you do not ride?'' He let the question hang.

''I suppose I am going to learn,'' Carolyn said for the second time that day.

''Marie-Elena,'' Sasha barked. ''Order the last of the staff to depart. Detach that last horse and put him in the stable. The wagon will not go.'' A groom materialized, taking one of the horses from its traces.

Marie-Elena was staring at him with growing excitement. ''I will go with them,'' she suddenly said, her expression eager. ''For there is no reason for *me* to stay here now. And when *you* find Katya, you shall all rendezvous with us at Tver.''

Carolyn was numb. She clenched her fists, angry and hurting all at once. Then she stole a glance at Marie-Elena's lover. His expression was one of sheer disbelief.

''You would abandon your daughter, Marie?'' he asked quietly.

She stiffened. ''How am I abandoning her? You are going to find her, you and Miss Browne. It is perfect. She herself said there is no need for everyone to wait here. On horseback the two of you can catch up to us, for we shall progress at a much slower pace in the wagons. Kerinsky!'' she called. ''Summon everyone! We are leaving for Tver this instant!''

Seven servants suddenly came rushing from the house. It was a whirlwind, the staff climbing onto the wagons, Marie-Elena being helped back into the carriage. Carolyn felt ill. Worse, as she watched Sasha staring at Marie-Elena, now cozily ensconced in the carriage, she felt for him, in spite of his betrayal of Nicholas. His expression was not merely bleak. It suggested that he too was feeling an illness that went to his very soul.

And abruptly, without another word, he wheeled his bay charger and trotted out of the courtyard.

"Sasha!" Marie-Elena called. "Until Tver!"

He did not answer. He did not look back.

Marie-Elena's smile faded. But she tapped her coachman on the shoulder and her carriage moved forward, the three remaining wagons beginning to follow.

Carolyn did not move. She clutched her skirts. Taichili came to stand beside her. They watched the small caravan leave the courtyard, rumbling slowly down the street. By now, Sasha was out of sight.

Carolyn trembled. Too late, it occurred to her that they were not only alone in the deserted city, they did not even possess a weapon. "Shall we?" she asked. Her tone was a whisper.

Taichili nodded, and the two women set off to find the missing child.

❧ THIRTY-ONE ❧

UNDER the light of a full moon, Nicholas galloped into the courtyard of his Moscow home. He sawed on the reins, his horse rearing in protest. Nicholas did not notice, his gaze sweeping past a wagon which had been left in the courtyard, settling on the palace. It was dark and silent, as if deserted and abandoned the way the city had been deserted and abandoned. His heart pounding, he swung from the charger, strides hard, and pounded up the front steps. The door had been left unbolted and it swung open. He still did not hear a single sound. His pulse raced far more swiftly than before.

"Carolyn! Katya! Kerinsky!" But as he stood in the dark, shadowy foyer, he was certain the house was empty, not asleep, and he was swamped with relief. They had fled Moscow, as well they should. Thank God. He turned to leave.

But someone was standing on the threshold, a man, and immediately Nicholas cocked and pointed his pistol. "Who goes there?" he demanded.

"Niki," a painfully familiar voice said.

His heart turned over hard, with pain and disbelief. Nicholas released the trigger and walked forward, until he and his cousin stood outside in the moonlight. He stared at his dark face. Hating him . . . loving him.

"I am very glad to see you," Sasha said intensely.

Nicholas's mouth curled. "I cannot say the same." He had spent many nights debating whether to challenge Sasha to a duel. But why should one of them die over Marie-Elena? Still, his pride and his male nature warred with common sense. What Sasha, his cousin and dear friend since childhood, had done was unforgivable. Nicholas shoved past him, reaching for the reins of his mount. He was afraid of what he might do if he continued to linger there with him.

From behind, Sasha gripped his arm, forestalling him. "Niki. Stop."

Nicholas turned slowly. "Do not press your luck. And if you think to throw excuses at me, or confessions, I am not in the mood. Napoleon's army is on the march, and I have a command to return to."

"I neither wish to excuse my behavior, or confess. Although, at a later date, I wish to beg your understanding, if not your forgiveness." Sasha's gaze was penetrating.

Nicholas started to turn away. Never, he thought. Never.

"You cannot leave," Sasha said, his tone odd. "Nicholas. Wait."

Nicholas swung into the saddle. "And will you dare to stop me?"

"Katya is missing."

Nicholas's heart slammed to a stop—he had to have misheard.

Quickly, Sasha said, "This morning she ran away from the house. Your wife and staff only left for Tver this afternoon. I have been searching high and low for her all day, with no luck whatsoever. And Miss Browne and Taichili are also searching for her, on foot, though."

Nicholas recovered from shock and fear with great difficulty. His daughter was missing. His little girl. Defenseless, innocent, only six years of age. "Oh, my God," he breathed.

Mounted French soldiers trotted down the boulevard. Carolyn and Taichili pressed their backs into the wall of a stone-and-timber building, praying that the night shadows cast there would hide them. But Carolyn could hear her own harsh breathing, it was so terribly loud. She could hear Taichili's breathing as well, as harsh and frightened as her own. Fear almost paralyzed her. She expected the soldiers to remark them at any moment.

Carolyn trembled, clawing the stone at her back. Had she somehow stepped into some horrific, monstrous, impossible nightmare? How had she arrived at this time and place? They were two women, alone in a foreign city, a city in the midst of an invasion by enemy troops—with Nicholas's child still missing. In that moment, not for the first time, Carolyn prayed fervently that they would find Katya, or that Sasha already had found her.

The French were boisterous and noisy. Their ribald conversation echoed loudly in the silent night. But the small cavalcade continued past the two women without anyone ever seeing them, finally disappearing down another street.

Carolyn slowly slumped to the ground. She wanted to cry. In frustration, in fear, and in despair. "They have come," she said hoarsely. "They have come and we do not even have a weapon, dear God."

Taichili sat heavily on the sidewalk beside her. She lifted up her skirts. High and higher still. Tucked into her garter above her knee was a small pistol.

"Is it loaded?" Carolyn asked, staring at the incongruous sight.

Taichili nodded, dropping her skirts. "What are we going to do?"

Carolyn brushed her eyes. "There is nothing we can do, except to continue searching. If Katya is not lost, she must be somewhere back at the house."

"We have covered every street in a twenty-block grid," Taichili said grimly. "If she does not wish to be found, she will never be found."

Carolyn was feeling the same way. Worse, she was almost certain now that this was no longer a matter of Katya hiding. Something must have happened to her. Carolyn could only hope that she had been seized by Russian refugees and taken away from Moscow. "Surely the French would not harm a little girl."

Taichili looked at her. "She is a very pretty little girl."

Carolyn felt sick. "I will beat her myself if I do find her," she said tersely, her tone choked with tears, and she stood. But an instant later singing voices came to her ears, drunken ones, and the lyrics were Russian.

She sank back to the ground, huddling against Taichili, her heart in her throat, as several men suddenly ran past them, brandishing flaming torches. They were Russians, but not soldiers, and they were peasants. Carolyn's eyes widened as the three men halted on the opposite side of the street. And then approaching horses could be heard. The men exclaimed loudly, proceeded to hastily set fire to the buildings around them. One of those buildings was a stable. Flames danced along the wooden timbers. Watching, Carolyn found herself holding Taichili's hand. Whoosh! Suddenly the hay inside the stable had caught fire, and the entire building became a blazing inferno.

And the men were gone. A dozen mounted French soldiers galloped down the street, ignoring the fire, pursuing the Russians who were torching their own city.

Carolyn leapt to her feet. "Damn them!" she shouted, shaking her fist at them all, the French and the Russians.

Taichili grabbed her wrist, dragging it down. "It must be midnight. Maybe Prince Vorontsky has found her."

Carolyn nodded. They raced down the street, leaving the flaming buildings and barn behind. Carolyn's legs felt as heavy as dead pieces of wood. She had never been so exhausted, so utterly weary, but somehow, she managed to force her legs to obey her brain, to keep running. The palace loomed ahead, tall, silent, a jumble of shadowy domes, gables, and towers. Nothing seemed to have changed. The wagon remained in the courtyard, the traces lying empty on the ground. And then Carolyn gripped Taichili's arm. "Someone was—or is—here!" she cried in a whisper. For the front door was wide and starkly open.

The two women exchanged a frightened look. Carolyn's pulse pounded. She was breathless with far more than lack of air. They did not move to the house. "Prince Vorontsky!" Carolyn called in a whisper, panting. "Prince Vorontsky?"

"Excellency?" Taichili tried.

There was no response.

Behind them, there was a loud whooshing sound in the night, one frightening and familiar.

In unison, the women turned, and saw that a neighbor's house had burst into flames. Fire danced along the wood moldings, the window encasements, the roof. And they could hear the voices of the men who had undoubtedly started the fire, somewhere in the street. "Quick!" Carolyn and Taichili raced across the courtyard and darted into the house. Carolyn threw the bolt. They panted, leaning on the door.

"What if they set fire to this house?" Taichili asked grimly.

"We will have to escape through a back window," Carolyn said as grimly, already calculating the best escape route. And then, from above them, there was a sudden and loud thump.

Carolyn froze. The governess was also motionless. Carolyn lifted her finger to her lips, seized again with fear. Taichili lifted her skirts and removed the pistol. The two women melted against one of the round white columns. Fortunately, the entire foyer was cast in dark midnight blackness. Carolyn knew she had not imagined the noise. Someone was inside the house—upstairs.

A step creaked. And another. Carolyn's heart was slamming painfully against her breast. Taichili pointed and cocked the gun. That sound was horrendously loud, echoing in the spacious, high-ceilinged room.

"Is anyone there?" Katya whispered.

And Carolyn cried out. She rushed forward as the child slowly came down the stairs. Her face was pale and blotchy with tears. "It is I! Carolyn!" she cried, wrapping the child in a fierce embrace. Katya clung to her.

Taichili intruded, pulling Katya from Carolyn and likewise clasping her to her breast.

Then Caroline wanted to strangle the child. "Where have you been?" she almost screamed. She fought the urge to shake her. "We have been looking everywhere for you!"

Katya began to cry. "I was sleeping in my room. I came home and everybody was gone. I thought I'd never see you or Taichili or Maman or Father again!" she sobbed.

Carolyn stared, and realizing how terrible it must have been for her to return home and find the house deserted and everyone gone, she hugged her again, this time rocking her and making soothing sounds. "It's all right. You are not alone, and we are going to Tver to find your mother. It's all right. Sshh, dear." She looked up, no longer able to contain her own tears, which threatened to choke her. She saw that Taichili was also crying, although attempting staunchly not to.

And in that split instant, she heard voices in the courtyard.

The trio froze. Horses clattered on the cobblestones. Through the windows, hand-held torches flared, this time wielded by French soldiers. Carolyn put her hand over Katya's mouth, her pulse slamming in her throat. She and Taichili looked at one another, silently communicating. Their dilemma was clear. Should they hide in the house, and wait for the soldiers to leave? What if the soldiers did not leave? What if they torched the house? Should they try to run away instead? But what if, in an attempt to flee, they were pursued—and captured?

And then someone was trying to open the front door.

The looter said, "*Ça va ici?*! It's locked from the inside. Do you think someone could be at home, *mes amis*?"

Taichili and Carolyn moved at once. With Katya, they raced across the foyer and into the adjoining salon, shutting the doors and pressing against the wall there. They heard glass from the windows in the foyer breaking.

Carolyn looked across the huge room at the windows on the salon's other side. As she did so, she could hear the Frenchmen again, talking now excitedly as they smashed more windows in the front of the house. She measured the distance to the far side of the room, wishing it were a small, cozy parlor, wondering when and if they should make a run for it, aware that the Frenchmen were now clambering through the windows that let onto the foyer. She could hear them milling about the front hall in their heavy riding boots.

Taichili shoved Carolyn hard in the direction she had been gazing.

Carolyn looked at her, saw she held the pistol, which was cocked. Taichili mouthed, Go! Take Katya and go!

Carolyn did not want to leave her alone in the house. She shook her head—and heard one of the muffled voices suggesting a search of the entire house. Her heart rioted.

Go! Taichili mouthed.

There was no choice. Carolyn gripped Katya's hand, met her gaze, and the child seemed to understand. Together they ducked low and began sneaking across the huge room, as silently as possible, hand in hand. As they did so, the salon doors were flung open. The torches the men had brought into the foyer cast a dim, flickering light into the salon. Carolyn and Katya froze, on all fours.

"We need more torches," someone said, slowly entering the room. Carolyn tensed in anticipation of being discovered. "I can hardly see."

A gun fired—it was Taichili's pistol. A man cried out in pain and hit the floor with a rock-hard thump.

Carolyn and Katya raced across the salon for their very lives.

"It's a woman!" someone shouted angrily.

Carolyn flung Katya ahead of her against the far wall. She heard another gunshot, the sound deeper, obviously from a different weapon, as she flung her elbow against the glass windowpane. The window broke, shattering loudly. Carolyn ignored the pain as shards of glass cut into her skin. She heard the men shouting, heard scuffling, heard

Taichili scream. But she was already lifting Katya and throwing her out of the window, scrambling up and out behind her. They fell together onto the stone terrace below, and crouched there underneath the broken window, listening to the sounds of the fighting.

Nicholas saw the other rider as he came around one city corner at a canter. He reined his horse in abruptly, preparing to flee in another direction. In the next instant, he realized that it was Sasha. He spurred his mount forward. Sasha galloped toward him.

They pulled up in the center of the black, deserted street, facing one another. "Any luck?" Nicholas asked grimly, already knowing what the answer was. He could see it on Sasha's face, which was dark and grim.

"No. Let's go back to the palace. Maybe the ladies are there with Katya."

Nicholas was ill with anguish. His daughter remained missing. He wheeled his black and they cantered toward his home in silence, only their horses' hooves making a rhythmic thudding noise on the dirt road—a noise that seemed frighteningly loud given the silence of the abandoned city. Of course, he was well aware that the French had already entered Moscow. He had almost crossed the path of several French soldiers on two occasions. Fortunately, he had seen them before they had seen him. He knew he would be shot on sight if he was espied first.

"Niki. I am so sorry," Sasha said.

Nicholas took one long glance at his hard face. He knew his cousin referred to the fact that Katya was missing, not to the fact that he had cuckolded him. He no longer cared about Sasha's affair with Marie-Elena. He only cared to find his daughter, and Carolyn, and get everyone safely out of the city.

Ahead of them, they saw five buildings being devoured by a roaring fire.

Far grimmer than before, Nicholas motioned to his cousin with a nod and they swung their horses hard to the right, detouring through an alleyway. His home was not too far in the distance.

Their mounts thundered down the narrow passage. Tall buildings and a fence hemmed them in on both sides. And as they turned onto a popular shopping avenue, they rode into the midst of a dozen French cavalry.

"Arrêtez-vous!" an officer shouted.

Nicholas almost broke his horse's neck as he whirled him around in such a tight turn that the steed's hind hooves never moved a centimeter. And as he leaned low over the black's neck, spurring him into a gallop, muskets began firing. Sasha was just slightly behind him. Nicholas thought he heard him grunt.

Nicholas whipped his horse with his reins, urging the tired animal to even greater speed. He could hear the thundering hoofbeats of the French, and estimated they were not many meters behind them. A bullet whistled past his ear.

"Sasha!" he shouted, aiming his horse toward the conflagration that they had just veered away from. More muskets fired.

Nicholas did not look behind him to see if his cousin was following—but thought he could feel his presence on his flank.

His horse did not hesitate. As one, the man drove the beast into the inferno.

The horse screamed. A falling timber, on fire, caused the stallion to bolt to the side. Other falling timbers narrowly missed them, and even so, Nicholas felt one side of his leg burning painfully. With one gloved hand he beat out the flames. He gave the animal the spurs again. A flaming cart blocked their way. Savagely determined, Nicholas drove the black forward. The charger hurled over the cart. And they were through the building, and in the street on the other side, where the air was sweet and cool and clean.

Nicholas pulled up as Sasha's horse erupted from between the blazing buildings. Neither man nor animal, Nicholas saw with relief, was on fire. With one hand he stroked his mount's sweat-soaked neck. He knew the French would not risk their lives to follow them through that living version of hell.

Sasha pulled up alongside him. His face was starkly white. And Nicholas saw the blood pouring over the right side of his chest and arm.

"How bad is it?" he demanded, stabbed with real concern.

"I will live," Sasha said harshly. "It is my shoulder. The back."

Nicholas nodded grimly, but he had seen more men die than not from musket-ball wounds. He wheeled his mount, and they galloped away from the fire, down the empty street. He glimpsed the tall tiered towers and domes of his home ahead of them. And in the courtyard—in his courtyard—he saw the riderless horses, and he also saw the lights coming from inside the house. Adrenaline coursed through him.

And a woman screamed.

Nicholas did not hesitate. He cocked his pistol, whipped his horse, and galloped through the open iron gates, thundering across the courtyard—and up the front steps and into the foyer.

Carolyn heard Taichili scream, horses thundering inside the house, another gunshot, and a man's scream of agony. Katya began to cry.

Carolyn held her, hard, tears streaking her own face, knowing that now was not the time to break down, but also knowing her stamina was at an end. She heard another cry of pain and anguish, harsh, uncompromising—final. Katya was hiding her face with her hands and shaking—but Carolyn was also trembling uncontrollably.

They still crouched outside the salon on the terrace. Her pulse roaring in her ears, Carolyn released the little girl, cautiously straightened, and peered through the broken window. Her eyes went wide. Shock filled her.

Torches blazed inside of the foyer and salon, lighting

both rooms completely. Nicholas was mounted on top of a sweat-soaked black charger which was dancing in the foyer between the huge plaster columns on the blue and white floors. In one hand he swung a saber. Carolyn watched his horse rearing, saw him drive the animal forward—toward two French soldiers who were rushing at him with their sabers drawn. His horse clattering on the stone floor, Nicholas struck, instantly decapitating one man. A blow wielded by the other soldier glanced off his prancing mount's flank. Nicholas parried the other attacker and stabbed him viciously in the chest, killing him almost instantly.

Fighting the urge to vomit, Carolyn realized that Sasha was also in the foyer, astride his rearing bay, and fighting as viciously with two other enemy soldiers. As he fatally wounded one below the breastbone, hope seized Carolyn. She averted her eyes, not wanting to see him running his other opponent through with his blade.

And then she saw the two soldiers standing in the shadows of the salon, as yet unnoticed by Nicholas. One of them was raising a pistol, aiming it carefully—directly at him.

"Nicholas!" Carolyn screamed.

Too late. The shot sounded loudly. But Carolyn could not tell if Nicholas had been hit, for his horse was screaming, rearing high into the air. Sasha was thundering past him and into the salon, saber aloft. Carolyn winced and looked away as, with one stroke of his saber, he severed the soldier's arm from his body. The Frenchman screamed, falling.

And Nicholas was now riding recklessly into the salon, behind his cousin. Only one other Frenchman remained. And suddenly the tableau was frozen. Nicholas and Sasha faced the last Frenchman, their horses absolutely still, blood and foam dripping from the bits, both men holding their bloody sabers high, their expression identically savage. The Frenchman stood as still, his own saber aloft, clearly wanting to flee. No one moved. No one breathed. Suddenly a pendulum clock could be heard ticking.

And there was so much blood, everywhere, and so much

death. Carolyn suddenly prayed for Nicholas to have mercy.

And, as if he had somehow heard her prayer, he dropped his arm and nodded. The Frenchman bolted, racing past the two Russian princes, out of the salon, through the foyer, and from the house.

Carolyn sagged against the terrace post, her cheek against the outside of the house, suddenly crying. And she thanked God for His deliverance.

"Carolyn," Nicholas said tersely.

So he had heard her. Carolyn looked up and through the broken window to see him staring at her from the center of the salon where he sat his trembling, blowing charger. Relief covered his features. It filled his golden eyes.

"Katya," Carolyn choked, unable to tear her regard from his. He was here. He was alive. Dear God, they were all alive. It was a miracle. "Your father is here. Come, darling, come."

And Nicholas closed his eyes, his nostrils flaring—his nose turning red.

Carolyn was exhausted, but she somehow lifted Katya up and through the window. Katya scrambled through with the vigor of youth. "Father! Father!"

Nicholas rode forward, seizing Katya from the sill and lifting her into his saddle. He held her hard against his chest. His face was buried in her hair. As Carolyn climbed through the window very slowly, like a very old, decrepit woman, she saw his shoulders heaving. She did not blame him for crying.

She slid off the sill and landed in the salon. Her knees threatened to give way and she staggered to the closest chair. Nicholas looked up. Their gazes locked again. Thank you, God, she thought, and it was a litany, there in her mind.

"You are hurt!" he said roughly, Katya in his arms.

Carolyn shook her head. Was she hurt? She glanced down at her dress, which was spotted with blood. "It is only my arm, cut from breaking the window." That seemed to be the truth. Her forearm had been cut in many places, her sleeve hanging in tatters from her arm.

"You have a gash over your eye," Nicholas said.

Carolyn lifted her hand, which was shaking terribly, and realized that he was right, she was bleeding from the right temple. "It is nothing."

"Father," Katya suddenly said. "You are bleeding all over the floor!"

Carolyn's gaze flew over Nicholas, but he sat his horse with only his right side visible to her, and she saw nothing on him other than dirt and grime and the blood of the enemy—and then she saw the blood pooling on the floor on the charger's left. She stiffened, met his eyes, and saw how starkly white he was.

Carolyn was on her feet. She rushed around the horse and cried out. The lower half of Nicholas's left leg was covered with blood. The portion of trouser covering his knee was soaked through and through. "Nicholas?"

"I have been shot," he said.

She stared at him, her heart stopping, terror seizing her—afraid he was going to die. "I must stop the bleeding," she cried shrilly. She reached down and ripped off half of her skirt with superhuman strength.

"Is Taichili dead?" Katya asked tremulously.

Carolyn paused. Nicholas also turned. They both followed the child's gaze. Carolyn choked. Taichili lay sprawled face up on the floor near the salon doors. There was a bright red hole in the center of her chest.

"Oh, God," Carolyn said. "Oh, God," she cried, slipping to the floor. "Oh, God!"

Nicholas slid Katya to the floor. He dismounted awkwardly, hanging on to his saddle for support. "Yes," he said somberly. "She is dead. She died instantly. She did not feel a thing, Katya."

Carolyn closed her eyes, hugging her knees, tears burning her lids. Taichili had died in order that they might escape the French. And suddenly she was seized with a murderous hatred. Look at what the bastards had done! How she hated them all!

"I think she died to save us, Father," Katya said in a choked tone.

"I am sure that she did. She was very brave. Carolyn. You must pull yourself together."

Carolyn heard him and managed to open her eyes. She felt tears rolling down her cheeks, then realized the pain he was in. His cheeks were flushed, the rest of his face ghostly white, and he was using all of his strength to stand upright, clinging to the pommel of his saddle. "I'm sorry," she whispered. Nicholas needed her. She had to bandage his knee and stop the bleeding. Carolyn forced herself to her feet. Her mind began to function. "Katya. Quickly. Go upstairs and fetch me sheets." Katya raced away.

"We must leave Moscow. Unfortunately, I am going to need your help," Nicholas said grimly.

Carolyn nodded, dismay overcoming her as comprehension struck her hard. Flee Moscow. With Nicholas wounded, and God only knew how many French troops in the vicinity. This nightmare was not over yet.

But she forced a smile. "Very well. But first let me take care of your wound."

Nicholas opened his mouth to reply when a loud thud sounded.

She started, her gaze flying now to the far side of the salon. Nicholas managed to crook his head around. In the melee and the ensuing reunion, they had all forgotten about Sasha. But where was he? His dark bay horse stood by the salon doors, its head hanging low, in exhaustion—and he was riderless.

And Sasha lay on the floor by his hooves, as pale and still and lifeless as Taichili's corpse.

❦ THIRTY-TWO ❦

SASHA was alive. Carolyn knelt beside him, looking up at Nicholas, who leaned heavily on his horse, having hobbled precariously as far as he could across the salon. "He is alive, Nicholas," she whispered in relief.

Nicholas nodded, but he was even whiter than before. "Carolyn," he said, and he could not hide the urgency in his tone. "We must get him into the wagon outside. We have to hurry."

Carolyn stared at him. The depth of the dilemma now facing them hit her hard, terrifying her. They were going to flee Moscow, she, the child, and the two wounded men, one of whom was unconscious and perhaps close to death. Forget the fact that she had never driven a wagon in her life. How was she going to get both men into the back of it? And what if, while they were trying to leave, more soldiers overcame them? It quickly crossed her mind that the single soldier they had let flee might come back with friends. Her gaze locked with Nicholas's penetrating one. She knew he had already thought of the dangers facing them. Her insides curdled as Katya ran back into the room with an armful of sheets.

"Katya, put out all of the torches. Light one candle," Nicholas ordered hoarsely. As Katya ran to obey, Nicholas looked at Carolyn. "We'll tie him to his horse and drag him," he gritted. Sweat streaked his brow. As Katya put out the three torches left behind by the soldiers, the entry hall was cast into dark, menacing shadows. The child held a single taper aloft, gazing from her father to Carolyn.

"I want to bind his shoulder first," Carolyn said.

"No. Use his belt, or the cords from the draperies, and tie him to the horse. Katya will help, I will try to help as well." His knuckles were white even in the dark from the force he was exerting to hold on to the saddle of his horse. Periodically, he swayed ever so slightly.

Katya came forward. "I am strong for a child," she said to Carolyn. She was also pale and wide-eyed with fear.

"I know you are," Carolyn said softly, standing. She gave her a quick hug. "And you are very brave—like your father."

"Are the French soldiers coming back?" Katya asked anxiously.

"Probably not," Nicholas interjected calmly.

Carolyn met his gaze, recognized the lie, grabbed a sheet, and hurried to his side. She began ripping the linen into strips.

"What are you doing?" he ground out. "Carolyn, we do not have time."

"You are not going to die, Nicholas!" Carolyn flared, losing her temper. She could handle anything, including this night of hell, but not losing Nicholas. Then she realized what she had said and she glanced at Katya, who was motionless. "If you will not let me bandage Vorontsky, let me at least take care of you." She knelt.

"We have to get out of here," he gritted. "Dammit."

"Is my father going to die?" Katya whispered.

"No, Katya." Nicholas was firm. "Carolyn has a tendency to exaggerate."

Carolyn did not respond, concentrating on the task at hand. Her jaw set, she wrapped the torn piece of linen around his knee, causing him to gasp and flinch. She did not look up, refusing to think of the pain he must be in, winding it around the shattered joint many times, as tightly as she could. Katya hovered behind her. "Katya, get me the cord from the draperies,'' she said. ''In fact, get all four of them.''

Nicholas stared down at her. ''I did not know you were medically inclined as well,'' he said.

She glanced up. ''I read a medical encyclopedia when I was ten.'' It was a monstrous fib.

He smiled, slightly, the curve of his mouth twisted with pain.

Katya had obeyed. Carolyn used one of the cords to secure the bandage as tightly as possible to his leg. As she did so, she tried to remain clear-headed, no easy task. What if they could not find a physician to care for the two wounded men? Nicholas had lost so much blood. She had never seen so much blood before. She wondered if sheer force of will were keeping him conscious and upright. As she finished her task, she thought about God, praying to Him for his blessing again and again. ''Where are we going to find a doctor?'' she asked, low.

''An army field hospital. Not far from Kutuzov's camp.''

Carolyn absorbed the implications of that. ''There.'' She stood, and laid her palms on his chest. ''Can you get back on your horse?''

He nodded, his gaze locked with hers. Suddenly he bent and pressed a kiss to her cheek. Carolyn's heart turned over. She saw immense gratitude in his eyes, and perhaps even a far greater emotion. Yet she did not want to delude herself. She watched him face the mount, which was motionless, from sheer exhaustion. He tried to lift his wounded leg and cried out harshly.

Carolyn pressed her shoulder against his hips. With a cry of anguish, Nicholas somehow settled his thigh across the saddle and then his entire body followed. He slumped against the black's neck, panting, shudders wracking him from head to toe.

''Don't pass out now,'' Carolyn heard herself beg. ''Please.''

He lifted his head. ''Sasha,'' he gasped.

Carolyn whirled, racing to Vorontsky, dragging one of

the small oriental rugs with her. "Katya, help me roll the prince over onto the rug," she cried.

Katya flew to her side. As the child and Carolyn bent over the unmoving, almost lifeless prince, an odd, cracking noise sounded, almost over their heads. And then something heavy crashed, either in the back of the house or above.

Everyone flinched, before becoming still and breathless at once. Katya was so white that Carolyn reached out and hugged her to her side. And she heard a dreaded sound. The ominously merry crackling of fire.

"Hurry," Nicholas said fiercely, moving his horse across the salon.

"Come," Carolyn whispered hoarsely to Katya, kneeling over the prone Vorontsky. She was scared to check if he was still alive. Just as she was scared to decipher where the fire was. But even if it were outside, she imagined the house would soon go up in flames. "This way," Carolyn said, panting. "Push." Katya knelt beside her and grabbed his good shoulder. Huffing and puffing they managed to push and pull Vorontsky onto the rug. Carolyn had not realized how difficult it was to move a man when he was a dead weight—or perhaps merely dead. She snaked both cords under the rug and around him, in effect tying him to the makeshift sled. Another crash sounded, and this time it was definitely over their heads.

Carolyn froze, glancing up at the ceiling. Nicholas also looked up, grimly. "It's upstairs," he said.

"But how?" Carolyn did not even bother to finish her question. She wondered if French soldiers were near—intent upon burning them alive in retribution.

"Does it matter?" He rode the black past them and halted. "Give me the cord," he demanded.

Carolyn obeyed. She had left two long ends of cordage, and she handed both to Nicholas. He urged his mount out of the salon, pulling Sasha behind him. In the foyer the going was made easier because of the slick stone floors. Carolyn and Katya followed, leading Sasha's bay horse.

The sound of the upstairs fire was louder now. Carolyn was drenched with perspiration.

"Katya," Nicholas called.

Katya understood and ran ahead of him to the front door and pushed it open. Carolyn cried out.

For through the open door, the street beyond the courtyard was visible—and it was entirely aflame. Mansion after mansion was ablaze, turning the night sky an unholy shade of orange.

Nicholas's horse screamed. But Nicholas spurred the animal forward ruthlessly, dragging his cousin behind him, shouting for them to follow. Carolyn winced, hands over her breast, as Sasha went down the steps like a sack of potatoes. Her hand firm on the bridle of the bay, which was snorting in protest now, and on the verge of balking, Carolyn ran out of the house with the horse. It screamed and reared.

"Katya, show Carolyn how to hitch Sasha's horse to the wagon," Nicholas ordered.

The bay, acting up, was forced between the traces. Somewhere high up, glass shattered loudly as they buckled up the final pieces of the harness. Carolyn looked up. Flames were shooting out of several third-story windows. The palace was going to become an inferno just like the homes across the street in a matter of minutes. She glanced at Nicholas, but he was not looking at his home. She knew it would be too painful for him to do so. "Hurry," he said, sliding off his horse.

Carolyn ran to him and grabbed him as he staggered against the black's side. "What are you doing?" she cried.

"How do you think Sasha is getting in that wagon?" he gritted. "Katya, tie my horse to the rear!" He shoved Carolyn from him and bent for his cousin. Having no choice, Carolyn also reached for Sasha. "Lift," Nicholas cried.

Carolyn put every last ounce of strength she had, and then some, into heaving up his cousin. Nicholas groaned. They managed to get his upper body onto the edge of the wagon bed, his lower body dangling to the ground.

"Push," Nicholas shouted hoarsely. Carolyn obeyed, pushing him upward, as pieces of slate from the roof began to rain down into the courtyard. Suddenly Katya was there, helping them, and Sasha was heaved into the wagon.

And Nicholas, who was so tall, sank down heavily on the back of the wagon, the last of the color draining from his face. He flopped onto his back, gasping for breath.

Carolyn leapt onto the wagon bed, crawled past him, and seized his shoulders. She dragged him so that he was entirely in the cart. "Nicholas. I don't know where we are going. You must stay awake!"

He nodded, but his skin was taking on an odd green color. "Southwest," he said.

"Katya, get in the front and show me how to drive this thing," Carolyn cried, on her feet and climbing into the driver's seat.

Katya ran around the wagon and scrambled up beside Carolyn, who had taken up the reins. She glanced up at the palace. The roof was in flames. Flaming pieces of slate were falling freely to the ground. Fire licked the magnificently ornate walls. It was sad, and she was, finally, angry. So very, very angry.

"Miss Browne, look," Katya whispered.

Carolyn looked. The tower ahead of them was also on fire, flames licking the gables and domes atop the arched entryway. Carolyn lifted the reins, Katya clutching her tightly, and cried out at the horse. The animal reared. Carolyn lashed it with the whip. Screaming, it moved forward, toward the stone archway. The animal reared. Carolyn lashed it with the whip again. Carolyn lifted the reins again, hard. The bay broke into a canter, and the wagon rumbled through the vaulted arch and out of the courtyard, leaving the flaming palace and tower behind. "Faster," Carolyn shouted at the horse, whipping it again. The bay broke into a gallop, and they careened down the street, leaving the flaming block behind. And ahead of her, on the horizon, opalescent and pale gray, dawn was just breaking.

* * *

Three days later, Carolyn sat on a small wooden crate beside a pallet inside of the large canvas tent where Nicholas lay, unconscious. She held his hand tightly, her gaze on his face.

They had arrived at the army field hospital two days ago. In the course of fleeing Moscow, they had encountered other refugees, both soldiers and civilians. A pair of those refugees had been wounded, young infantrymen also needing medical attention. Carolyn had allowed the two to join Nicholas and Sasha in the back of the wagon. With their help, she had found the field hospital around mid-morning of the next day. But Nicholas had fallen into a state of unconsciousness shortly after leaving Moscow.

He had been unconscious ever since. A high fever had set in. But last night, thank God, it had broken. Carolyn had only left his side to check on Katya, who had become a benevolent little angel to the less seriously wounded soldiers outside. She spent most of her time bringing the men water, or reading old, faded letters to them. They called her "Princess," and fought for her attention. She no longer seemed six years of age. It was as if she had grown up overnight.

Carolyn touched Nicholas's brow. These past two days had been endless and terrifying. When he had been wracked with fever, she had been terrified that he would die. As it was, he was never going to walk without a significant limp again. But she did not care. She only cared that he was alive. Nothing, it seemed, had changed for her as far as her feelings for him went.

His lashes seemed to flutter. Her heart stopped and started wildly again. "Nicholas?" Hope left her breath suspended.

Again, she saw the barest fluttering of his lashes in response to his name.

She leaned over him. Praying. "Nicholas? It is I. Carolyn. Can you hear me?"

His eyes slowly opened.

And Carolyn felt tears gathering in her own eyes. She smiled at him tremulously, holding tightly to one of his hands. Secretly, she had harbored a deep fear that he would never wake up—that the doctors were all wrong.

"Carolyn," he breathed. And then his expression changed, brows furrowing his forehead.

"Katya is fine," she said quickly, immediately sensing what was bothering him. "She is outside. In a little while, when the doctors will allow it, I will bring her to you," she said tenderly. And her heart was bursting with relief and joy and so much feeling that she did not know if she could contain herself.

He smiled at her. Then, again, his face stiffened. "Sasha?"

She hesitated. "He is very ill, Nicholas. He is with fever. They do not know if he can survive. Katya and I have been taking turns sitting with him, begging him to fight for his life."

Tears slipped down Nicholas's cheeks.

Carolyn could not stand it. She laid her head in the crook of his neck, her own tears sliding freely down her face. "I am sorry, Nicholas."

His hand stroked her hair. "It is not your fault. God. I am weak."

She laughed a little, kissed his jaw, and lifted her head. "You were also very ill. You are lucky, Nicholas, to be alive."

"I owe you my life," he said simply.

She froze. And when she breathed again, it was with fear and hope, so much hope, hope she really had no right to, but damn it all, after this, she could not care anymore that he had a wife. She only cared that she loved him, and she hoped, and thought, that he loved her, and they were both alive, as was Katya. "You do not owe me anything," she whispered, laying her palm against his cheek.

He turn his face and kissed it. "Not true. I owe you, for my life, and Katya's."

Carolyn smiled at him through an even thicker haze of tears.

"How shall I repay you, Caro?" he asked.

She shook her head, unable to speak.

He closed his eyes then opened them. "I love you," he said. "Can I repay you with my love?"

She did not move. "Yes," she said, thinking of his behavior that morning in St. Petersburg when he had left her so coldly and cruelly.

And, as if reading her mind, he said, "I loved you then, too. But I was trying to push you away, so we could both be honorable. I thought a liaison would only make you unhappy."

And she understood. And hadn't she known, with her heart, that there would be an explanation? "I do not want to be honorable anymore. Life is far too precious—as is our love."

And he smiled, lifting one hand, curling it around her neck. He pulled her down, and their lips finally met.

"Excellency, it is too soon for you to be up and about."

"Nonsense," Nicholas said, leaning heavily on crutches.

"Your cousin can wait." The physician implored him. "Please, Excellency, a few more days of complete bed rest."

Nicholas stared. "Sasha is conscious and his fever has finally broken. He is so weak that neither you nor anyone else can tell me whether he will live or not. I am going to see him." With that, Nicholas hobbled past the disapproving army doctor and through the open tent flap. He paused briefly once outside, his eyes adjusting to the bright sunlight. How good it was to be alive—alive and with both his daughter and Carolyn.

Nicholas started forward, hopping on the crutches, paying no attention to the panorama of thousands of soldiers spread out on pallets on the plain that was the active army hospital. He had been told Sasha was in the third adjoining tent, where the very serious cases were. He ducked in order to enter it and paused, his eyes again adjusting to the change in lighting. Although there were a dozen men in this tent, he saw him immediately, thin covers pulled to his waist, his entire upper body bandaged, his face, usually swarthy, tinged green and cast in sickly pallor. Nicholas hobbled forward until he stood over him. "Sasha?"

Sasha's eyes opened. He saw Nicholas but did not smile. Nicholas knew he was too weak.

"You are very ill," Nicholas said. "But goddamn it, I expect you to fight to live."

Sasha seemed to smile. "N-Niki." His voice was hardly audible.

"Do not talk. We will have our entire lives to talk after we have both recovered fully from our wounds. You shall have a long convalescence. You are a lucky dog. By the time you are well, I imagine the war will be over."

Sasha stared, a question in his eyes. "N-Nap . . . ?"

"Napoleon is in Moscow. He seems to think Alexander will sue for peace." Nicholas smiled at the absurdity of that. "I have heard tell that Alexander's response has been 'Peace? We have yet to make war!' "

And Sasha did smile, although feebly.

Nicholas sobered. "Kutuzov awaits reinforcements, supplies and horses, and a more opportune moment to attack. I think I am beginning to understand the method to his madness. If we are very lucky, there will be early snows— and Napoleon is deeply in our territory, his supply lines stretched thin. I do sense that this winter will be crucial for us." He smiled. "And Alexi is well. I received a message from him yesterday. He joined the army, you know, and survived his first engagement at Borodino. But enough of the war. For us, it is most likely over. I shall convalesce in St. Petersburg." He hesitated. Sasha continued to stare closely at him. Nicholas cleared his throat. "I forgive you, Sasha, because she is not worth any grudge. And because you risked your life for my daughter, and because, mostly, you are like a brother to me." He was choked up.

Sasha's mouth tightened. "Niki. I was—"

"Do not talk now. Save your strength, my cousin, to get well." The two men's gazes held. And again, Sasha seemed to smile.

Nicholas finally turned and hopped from the tent. Outside, he took a deep breath of air. And that was when he saw Carolyn, weaving her way through the many wounded soldiers, and he became absolutely still.

But his heart sang a little, and danced in joy.

He watched her. Sunlight turned her pale curls an impossible color, almost silver. She was so beautiful. But more than that, she was the bravest woman he had ever met. He was never going to forget her courage that night in Moscow. Her courage, her loyalty, and her determination.

She had seen him and she waved, smiling, a smile that made his heart turn over again and again. She was right. Life was so fragile and so precious, as was a love like theirs. He would not ever let it go again. He would build her a palace, probably in St. Petersburg, where he would reside with her. He would also buy her a mansion in London, and anything else she wished, including an entire block of bookstores, if that is what she preferred. He intended to shower her with furs and jewels, even though he imagined she would prefer her own newspaper, but he might buy that for her, too. And he would also declare her to the entire world as his mistress. As his love. Marie-Elena could complain or not.

Carolyn reached him. "Nicholas, you will not believe who is here. Raffaldi!" Her eyes were worried.

He was surprised. "He has left Tver?" And even as he asked the question, he recalled Carolyn's description of his selfish cowardice when he had abandoned everyone in Moscow.

"Obviously." Her anxious gaze held his.

"Is Marie-Elena with him?" Nicholas asked, with some regret. He could not help but hope that she remained in the country.

Carolyn shook her head. "He is alone."

With his right hand, Nicholas reached out awkwardly and touched her shoulder. "You have nothing to be afraid of."

Carolyn smiled at him, but behind the smile, he saw her dread and her fear. "Come," he said. He hobbled back to the tent where his pallet was, and saw the Italian tutor outside, chatting with Katya. Katya giggled at something he said, then waved at Nicholas. "Father!"

Raffaldi turned and bowed. "Excellency." His smile was gone. He was very grim.

And Nicholas knew he was not the bearer of good tidings. "Signore. How are you?"

"I am fine, thank you, Excellency. And I have heard you are recovering from a terrible wound. I am so relieved!" Raffaldi cried with his usual theatrical air.

"Shall we step inside?"

"Yes."

"Katya and I will wait here," Carolyn said, holding the child's hand.

Nicholas nodded and preceded the tutor into his tent. He sat down on the cot, carefully placing his crutches where he could easily reach them. "Why are you not at Tver?"

Raffaldi was pale. "Excellency, I have terrible news."

His jaw flexed, his heart raced. "My wife?"

Raffaldi hesitated, and nodded. "Prepare yourself."

"Spit it out."

"She is dead."

Nicholas stared. And his first thought was of Katya, who loved her mother, and asked when she would see her every single day. He was grim, anguished. "What has happened?"

"Bandits, Excellency, a dozen of them. They forced their way into the house, killing many of the servants. I myself feigned being dead, which is the only reason I am alive." Raffaldi stopped. "The house has been razed, Excellency. Nothing stands except for stone."

His temples throbbed. Katya. How would he comfort her? How? But Carolyn would help him, and she was a woman, and she loved his daughter, too. He looked up. "How did she die?"

Raffaldi took a deep breath. "Unpleasantly, Excellency."

He stared. "How unpleasantly?"

"They used her first."

He was ill. She had suffered, and he had not been there to protect her, no matter that he despised her—for she was his wife, and the mother of his child. "Are you certain?"

"I heard her screams, Excellency," Raffaldi said, causing Nicholas to stare at him. He rushed on. "And then they set the fire. As I have said, nothing is left except for stone. I did find this." He opened his palm, revealing a huge yellow diamond ring. Nicholas recognized it instantly. Raffaldi handed it to him. "I am sorry, Excellency."

Nicholas closed his fingers around the ring, which he would give to Katya. "You are dismissed, signore," he said coldly.

Raffaldi nodded, turning to leave.

"No. I mean, you are dismissed from my employ."

Raffaldi whirled. "Excellency!" he cried. "What have I done to deserve—"

Nicholas cut him off. "You deserted Miss Browne and my daughter in Moscow. And far more importantly, you did not help my wife when she was being savagely attacked. Get out."

Raffaldi was white. He turned and stumbled from the tent.

And Nicholas opened his palm. For a long time, he sat there staring at the flawless diamond ring, all that was left of Marie-Elena.

Carolyn knew that something was terribly wrong as she watched Raffaldi stride from the tent, not even pausing to say good-bye to her or Katya. He mounted his horse, his face mottled with temper, and spurred it into a canter. She had the feeling she would never see him again, and could not have cared less.

"Katya, can you stay here with Major Rostov and Lieutenant Kahady?" Carolyn asked, gazing anxiously toward
Nicholas's tent.

Katya was already seated between the two wounded veterans, both young, amiable men, not much older than Carolyn, both of whom had their arms in slings. Katya had
been playing dice with them as it was. They had been
teaching her how to gamble.

Carolyn left the trio to their devices, rapidly approaching
the tent. She slipped inside and found Nicholas sitting on
the cot, his expression odd. It was grim, she decided, very,
very grim. "What is wrong?" She did not move from the
doorway.

He looked up. "Where is Katya?"

"Outside with two of the wounded." Carolyn realized
he was holding an extraordinary diamond ring in his hand.

Nicholas stared at her. "Her mother is dead."

Carolyn stared back, her mind becoming strangely frozen, while Nicholas related to her what had happened. She
thought about Katya. Katya would be bereft. And then she
remembered waking up one morning to find her own dear
mother dead. Carolyn trembled. As she well knew, one
never recovered from the loss of one's mother. Oh, God.
Never.

"Carolyn. Do not cry," Nicholas said harshly.

She hadn't realized that she was crying, and she turned
as she wiped her eyes, gazing out of the tent. Katya was
laughing, apparently having won a round of the game of
dice. "I lost my mother when I was about her age," she
said unevenly. "There is no one I loved more."

"I know," Nicholas said softly. "And only you would
be so selflessly moved by Marie-Elena's death," Nicholas
returned.

She met his gaze and suddenly understood. Suddenly
there was far more than hope for the two of them, there
was freedom. Carolyn's heart beat hard and she was paralyzed.

He reached for his crutches and stood. Hobbling over to her, he paused. "I am sending for the priest," he said.

She started. "Nicholas!"

His jaw flexed. His eyes blazed. "We are both lucky to be alive. Give me one good reason to wait."

"What are you saying?" she cried. But she knew, oh, she knew.

"I want to marry you today. And do not tell me I must wait and mourn an entire year for a woman I despised."

"But she was Katya's mother. And what will Katya say?"

"Somehow, I will explain it to her," he said. He tossed away his right crutch and reached out, pulling Carolyn against him. She clung to his shoulders, stunned, yet dismayed because she could no longer mourn for Marie-Elena, not when her death was bringing such a love and such a future. She had never wanted her own happiness to be founded on the death of someone else. But God had directed Marie-Elena's fate—or had it been the other woman's own selfishness? Through hot, thick tears, Carolyn looked up.

Nicholas met her gaze for a single instant, breathed, "I have waited for this my entire life," and crushed her hard, his mouth seeking and finding hers.

ST. PETERSBURG

"Princess Sverayov. May I?"

Carolyn paused on the stairs. Alexi was bowing with great deference, but when he straightened, he was grinning at her, and he was terribly dashing in his crimson and gold uniform. "Alexi!" she cried, lifting her silk shirts and racing down the last steps and into the huge hall. She managed to halt at the last possible moment, for she had intended to embrace him in a bear hug. Instead, out of breath, she curtsied. The diamond tiara she was wearing felt as if it were beginning to slip.

He took her hand and held her at a short distance. "My

God,'' he said, low. ''Being married to my brother suits
you.''

Carolyn knew she blushed. It had been three weeks since
they were married by the priest who had been there at the
field hospital to perform last rites for the dying soldiers.
They had only just arrived at the Vladchya Palace a few
days ago, for the doctors had not wanted Nicholas to travel
until then. Carolyn remained stunned by the turn of events.
Stunned and . . . uneasy.

''What are you doing here?'' she asked Alexi.

''Is the tsar not having a small reception tonight in your
and Niki's honor? How could I miss it?''

Carolyn smiled as they walked down the corridor.
''Nicholas is in the library. It has been a big scandal, you
know.''

''Ah, but the world is used to our scandals, and expects
no less than blatant disregard for convention from a Sverayov.''

She laughed. ''Nicholas said the exact same thing.''

They paused outside the library door. ''And how is Katya?'' Alexi asked seriously.

Carolyn's smile faded. She thought of dear Taichili,
whom she still grieved for. ''She is distraught. Her mother
is dead, and she not only knows what that means, she saw
death herself in Moscow. But I am doing my best to be a
good stepmother to her. For example, I have encouraged
her to come into our bed at night when she has a bad
dream.''

''I see. Niki must love that,'' Alexi said, hiding a smile.

''Actually, he does,'' Carolyn said seriously, pushing
open the library doors.

Nicholas was in conversation with an estate steward, the
man having arrived only that morning. But he froze when
he saw Carolyn, slowly rising from behind his desk. His
gaze slid over her. Appreciation warmed his golden eyes.

Carolyn felt her cheeks heat again. She had never in her
life been clad in such finery, and the pale silver ball gown
she wore did incredible things to both her complexion and

her figure. To hide her embarrassment and pleasure, she gave him a small, teasing curtsy.

He bit off a smile and bowed with the utmost severity. Then he dismissed the steward and strode forward, clasping Alexi warmly to his chest. The brothers drew apart with smiles. "I am glad you are here," Nicholas said.

"Nothing could keep me away. Congratulations, Niki. You have done exceedingly well for yourself."

Nicholas sent Carolyn a promising look. "Indeed."

"I am going to visit my niece. And by the by, Sasha is doing quite well. Six months from now, he will undoubtedly be as good as new." Alexi turned and strode from the room.

Nicholas shut the library doors, and slowly turned to face Carolyn. "You are exquisite," he said softly.

"I am nervous," she returned.

"It is only a small reception," he said, walking to her.

"Held in our honor—by the tsar!"

He took her hands, pulled her close, and began to kiss her. But Carolyn drew back. "What is wrong?" he asked.

She hesitated. "I don't know."

"Something has been bothering you, ever since we arrived here yesterday."

"You're right." She grimaced, then reached up to touch his cheek. "It is not about us, Nicholas. It is just—"

"Just what?"

"This is a dream come true. And it seems too good to be true," Carolyn said urgently. "I cannot explain this feeling I have. But . . . I am afraid. Afraid this will not last."

His jaw was flexed. "That is absurd. This will last. We are wed. This will last a lifetime."

But Carolyn was afraid, and her fear tainted her happiness. Somehow, for some reason she could not fathom, she expected the world to blow up in her face. Perhaps it was just her overly active imagination, hard at work because she had never had such happiness before, and there was so much to lose, but maybe it was her sixth sense, a premonition of sorts. "I just keep thinking that something is going to happen, something terrible for you and me."

He stared at her. "Carolyn, what could possibly happen?" And then he pulled her forward, this time finding her lips with his and finishing the kiss he had intended to begin just a moment before.

And then they heard a woman screaming incoherently in the corridor. Her voice was not distinct. But Nicholas jerked away from her; Carolyn froze. "No," she whispered. "Absolutely not." *It could not be Marie-Elena.*

But the woman's hysterical voice grew louder and louder as she approached. Carolyn's heart had never, not even in Moscow, beaten like this. With such commanding force. Nicholas had lost all of his color. And the doors slammed abruptly open, crashing against the library walls—revealing Marie-Elena.

"I am not dead!" she screamed. "I am hardly dead, you whore! Get away from my husband!"

Carolyn pulled her hands free from Nicholas, the numbness beginning, replacing the sick dread. She had known it. Known that this was coming. That was all she could think.

And Marie-Elena was a sight, as thin as a scarecrow, her hair hacked off above the shoulders, her face gaunt, a red, raw scar running from her temple to her jaw. One of her arms was bandaged from fingertips to shoulder and lashed to her body, her other hand was also completely bandaged. "Niki!" She hurled herself at him and collapsed on his chest, sobbing hysterically.

Carolyn began backing away. Step by unfeeling step. There was no pain. There was only nothingness.

There were only shadows and darkness.

"I almost died! That fire, it was hell, I was so weak, what those men did to me, I could hardly drag myself from the house!" Marie-Elena wept. "My hands, my beautiful hands, are burned beyond recognition. And my face! Did you see my face! God! They cut me, Niki, how they cut me!"

Unfeeling. Emotionless. How odd. It was like being a voyeur, observing a bizarre drama which left one entirely unaffected. Another step. And another one. And soon the drama would end. Soon there would be peace.

Peace . . . and nothingness.

Light, racing footsteps sounded in the hallway, and then Katya appeared as she raced around the door, her face alight. "Maman!" she cried. "Maman! Maman!"

But if Marie-Elena heard her daughter she gave no sign, continuing to weep on Nicholas's chest. Carolyn looked at him, the golden Russian prince. He was more than pale, he was greenish in coloring, his expression one of horror. Sheer, utter horror.

Katya ran forward, eager and joyful. "Maman! Maman! We thought you died! Maman!"

"Caro," Nicholas said hoarsely. "Don't go. We will work this out."

He had become a stranger, she did not know him, there was no reason to obey. But she watched the beautiful child cling to her mother's skirts—her mother, who convulsively gripped her husband's lapels as if thoroughly unaware of her own child.

A voyeur. An observer. Of an odd drama. That was what she was supposed to be. So why were there tears streaking down her cheeks? "Tell her," Carolyn said harshly, "that she must love her daughter." And she turned, stumbling from the room, and from his life.

PART FOUR

The Phoenix

❧ THIRTY-THREE ❧

SHE dipped the quill and wrote, "*The Refugees,* Chapter XIII." Carolyn paused, and wrote,

> For Sarah, it was a night without end. The fire had spread and it was everywhere, but then, through the tide of flames, she saw it, a shadow, a specter, and it was her beloved William, there at the last possible moment, but not too late, she prayed, for them to escape the conflagration together.

"Carolyn? Still working on the new novel?" George asked from the kitchen doorway.

Carolyn started, poised over the foolscap, not daring to look up. Hot, bitter tears had gathered behind her eyelids, and she needed a moment to compose herself. "Yes," she finally said, laying the quill aside. And she managed a smile for her father's sake.

He entered the kitchen, his expression grim. "I have just locked up for the night," he said, his buoyant tone at odds with the concern in his eyes. "And I do have an idea. Why don't we go to the Gray Wolf to dine? I think we both deserve a few good pints."

Carolyn gazed at her clasped hands, thinking of the red wine she had shared so often with Nicholas. "I am afraid I am not very hungry, Papa," she said. "And I do have this chapter to finish."

George hesitated, and sat down at the table across from her. "Dear, please tell me what is bothering you. Please tell me what happened while you were in Russia."

Carolyn avoided his eyes. "There is nothing to tell." Oh, but there was, and she was writing a romantic novel in consequence. Except her novel would not have a happy ending. She would leave the happy endings to novelists like the anonymous author of *Sense and Sensibility*. Her readers would weep and mourn for the heroine's sad and tragic fate, for the loss of the hero and his love.

Carolyn had never felt so alone in her life.

George reached for and held her hand. "Sometimes I feel like throttling that Sverayov. I know he is behind your melancholy."

Carolyn pulled her hand away. "Never say such a thing to me again!" she cried furiously. "He is the most honorable man I have ever known—will ever know—Papa!"

George stared. "If he is so honorable, then why is your heart so broken?"

Carolyn stood. She had no intention of telling him what had happened, none. And then she thought about Marie-Elena, brutally attacked and disfigured from the fire and the knife one of her assailants had wielded, and her heart shattered over and over again. Nicholas was a man of honor, and no matter how terrible his wife's behavior had been, no woman should ever have to suffer as she had suffered, and he would not turn his back on her now. Nor did Carolyn expect him to.

It was over.

But this dream had been impossible from the very start.

"I only want to help," George said softly.

Carolyn met his gaze. "No one can help."

George stood. "This is breaking my heart!" he cried.

"Then that makes two of us," Carolyn said grimly, turning away from him. "Now, I do have a novel to finish."

"And what about Copperville? Your editor has sent three couriers over here in the last week, begging you for a column."

Carolyn sat back down at the table, thinking not about Charles Copperville, but about Sarah and William. "Copperville is dead. He died in Moscow."

George was frozen. Then, "Before you start, this came a short while ago. It is from your grandmother," he said, holding out a sealed letter.

Carolyn put down her quill and took the parchment with no real interest in the missive, breaking the seal and unfolding it. "It is another invitation to Midlands."

"This is amazing," George said frankly. "First her appearing at the store after you had left, demanding your whereabouts, and now this—the fourth invitation. Will you go? You know, Carolyn, you should go. You have always pretended not to care about her, but I know how much her disinterest has hurt you. I do believe she wishes a relationship with you."

Carolyn shook her head, reaching for a fresh sheet of vellum and quickly penning the same polite two-line refusal she had already penned three previous times. "No. I am not going to Midlands. Why should I? The past is the past. I am living in the present." She dipped her quill and wrote,

Sarah rushed toward William as he galloped through the flames, tripping in her haste.

"And what about the future?" George demanded, laying both of his hands hard on the kitchen table.

"The future does not interest me," Carolyn said thickly, trying to keep her breathing low and even.

George cursed.

Carolyn started. His use of foul language was far more than rare. Their gazes collided and clashed.

But fortunately, there was a loud knocking on the door, interrupting any further words they might exchange. George turned, grumbling about being closed, but he stalked to the doorway and stared across the shop at the front door. When he faced Carolyn, he was exuberant. "It is young Davison!" he cried. "I shall let him in!"

Carolyn's heart sank. "Papa, wait."

George whirled. "If you send him away one more time, he will never come round again. I am warning you, Carolyn. He is a good young man, his intentions are clear, and he is head over heels in love with you. Do not send him away!"

"But I don't love him," Carolyn whispered, her mouth quivering. But George had already turned and was striding through the shop to let him in.

Carolyn fought an impending flood of tears, thinking, Oh, Nicholas. Will I miss you forever? How shall I live? From novel to novel? But I wish to die!

And it was true. She had no urge to live. Her heart was more than broken, her soul was broken, too. She had not known love could bring so much pain. If she had known, she would have avoided it—and him—from the very start, at all costs.

It had been so much easier when she had fled St. Petersburg, once again with Alexi's help. In her shock, survival had seemed possible. But during the two-week journey home, the shock had dissipated, leaving a nightmare in its place.

Anthony Davison entered the kitchen, a smile on his face, a small wrapped parcel in his hand. Carolyn stood and smiled back at him. It was not an easy task.

His own smile faded slightly as he bowed. "Miss Browne. I do hope I am not intruding. I had meant to stop by before the shop closed, but the traffic on Pall Mall was horrendous."

"Of course you are not intruding," Carolyn said politely, but her mind was filled with William, who was tall and golden, and so very much like Nicholas. She ached to get back to her writing.

"This is a gift for you," Anthony said, handing her the parcel.

"Thank you." The moment Carolyn received it, she knew it was a book. She could not feel any enthusiasm as she tore off the plain wrapper.

He blushed. "It is a book. I decided Sir Walter Scott would interest you far more than posies."

Carolyn gazed down at it. "*The Lady of the Lake*. How wonderful," she said softly.

"I do hope you will enjoy it," he said awkwardly.

"Of course I shall," Carolyn said, holding the volume tightly. But she was thinking about the next scene she intended to write, the lovers' flight from Moscow—and their passionate, long-delayed reunion. "Thank you."

"Miss Browne. There is a dinner dance tomorrow night. Might you accompany me?" Anthony asked, his color high.

Carolyn hesitated. "Anthony, I do appreciate the invitation, but I have not been feeling very well. I am sorry," she said softly.

His face fell, but then he regained his composure and bowed. "Very well. Please. Do have a pleasant evening."

Carolyn nodded. "And you," she said.

He whirled and strode from the kitchen, past her father, across the store and out the door. The doorbell tinkled loudly.

George moved into the kitchen doorway. "He will never return! That is the fourth time you have sent him away."

Carolyn was on the verge of tears, yet she was angry, and she flung the book at her father's feet. "I will never love him!" she shouted. "My love belongs to another!"

George looked at the book lying open at his feet, turning white with shock at her behavior.

Nor could Carolyn quite believe what she had done, and she covered her face with her hands. "All I want," she whispered, "is to be left alone."

And as if that were a cue, the doorbell tinkled again. Carolyn was afraid that it was Anthony, coming back for one last try. She turned away, wiping her eyes, while George muttered about "after hours." And then he cried out.

"Good evening, Browne," a very cultured voice said.

Carolyn recognized the voice, but could not identify it, and she turned around to glimpse the newcomer. Her eyes widened slightly, for it was Stuart Davison, Anthony's father. But that did not make any sense.

"My lord," George cried. "This is a, er, surprise! Do you wish to purchase a book?"

Carolyn stared at her father, who was whiter than he had been when she'd thrown the Scott novel at him, for his voice was filled with fear. Slowly, she came forward, and curtsied. "My lord."

"Ah, hello, Miss Browne. And have you recovered from your travels?" Stuart Davison smiled at her, and the effect was chilling, because there was no warmth whatsoever in his eyes.

George immediately rushed to Carolyn's side, his arm around her. "My daughter is not well. Now, if you wish to make a purchase, we are open tomorrow at nine o'clock."

"But I do not wish to buy a book," Stuart Davison said, and he walked past father and daughter, right into their kitchen, as if it were his home, not theirs, and he pulled out first one chair, then another. He was no longer smiling. "Sit down."

Carolyn tensed, shooting her father a glance. Something was terribly wrong. "My lord," she asked, coming forward, "is something amiss?"

"Please," he said, his lips curling, his voice hard. "Sit."

Carolyn glanced at her father, who was sweating. "Do as he says, Carolyn," George said. But then he gave Davison a frankly pleading look. "Not in front of my daughter," he begged.

Davison did not reply. Frightened now, Carolyn sat, staring at the peer. When her father was also seated, he said, "I need Miss Browne's unique talents."

"No!" George cried, on his feet. "Absolutely not!"

Davison slammed his hand on the table, and George sank back into his seat. Carolyn's pulse raced. Bewildered, she met Davison's cool blue eyes. "What is this about?" she asked hoarsely.

"It is about the fact that your father is a traitor to his

country," Davison said. "And only you can prevent his hanging."

Carolyn gripped the table. "Do not be absurd," she began, but then she saw George, covering his face with his hands, his shoulders shaking—as if he were weeping. Briefly, she was speechless, frozen. "Papa?"

He did not respond.

Davison explained. "Your father has been a courier for the British for eight years, Miss Browne, since shortly after Amiens. Come. Surely you did not think he traveled so frequently back and forth to and from the Continent merely to locate or deliver rare books?"

Carolyn stared. "A courier. But that is not a traitor. Papa?" Her pulse had accelerated.

He looked at her, wiping his eyes, saying not a word.

"Papa?" Carolyn cried, on her feet.

"Yes! I have been a courier!" George shouted. And tears spilled down his face.

"But not a traitor." Carolyn remained standing. "I know my father, Lord Davison. And he loves his country. He would never betray England, not in a time of war, not in a time of peace."

Davison's laughter was soft and amused. "But he has. He has been selling information to French agents for eight long years. And that is a hanging offense."

Carolyn stared, first at Davison, then at her father, in absolute disbelief. "No," she said. Shocked and frightened. But Davison was lying. He had to be.

"Tell her," Davison said.

Carolyn turned to George, who could barely meet her eyes. "Papa?" She was hoarse. This couldn't be happening. It was not true. Her world had already collapsed. But not her father, not this.

"Carolyn, I did it for you," he said thickly.

She cried out. Feeling her legs buckling, Carolyn clung to the back of her chair.

"Carolyn!" He grabbed both of her hands. "I love you so! You are my life! We have desperately needed the funds. We sell no books! We would be homeless vagrants if it were not for what I have done. Oh, God forgive me!'' he cried.

Carolyn wept, soundlessly. ''Oh, Papa. How? How could you? Anything, but not this,'' she whispered. She hugged herself. It was hard to breathe. The very air burned her lungs. Her father was a traitor. She had already lost Nicholas. How could her father be a traitor? He had said he had done it for her. But she would rather be a homeless beggar. Oh, God.

''Which brings us to you, Miss Browne.''

''No,'' George said weakly. ''Whatever you are thinking, no, please, do not involve her.''

Davison eyed him as if he were a speck of annoying dirt on his shirtsleeve. ''Browne, if your daughter does not cooperate, I shall see to it that you hang. My own tracks, dear fellow, have been thoroughly covered, for I have no intention of going down with you.''

Carolyn stiffened. ''You are guilty, too?''

''Cease your plotting, Miss Browne. There is not a trace of evidence, but I have kept files on your father's activities. I have hard proof, enough for him to hang tomorrow.'' He smiled. ''Unless you do as I ask.''

Carolyn was numb. ''What is it that you want from me?'' she heard herself ask.

He did smile. ''Sverayov arrived in London yesterday. He has certain information, and I believe you have the allure to get it from him.''

Carolyn felt it then, the shadows and darkness, threatening to overtake her mind. Threatening to make her snap.

Carolyn retreated to her bedchamber, where she curled up on her bed, hugging a pillow, desperately fighting tears. Her heart sounded like a hollow drum in her own ears. Nicholas was in London. Her father was a traitor. And if she did not spy on Nicholas, George was going to hang.

She hugged the pillow harder. She could not guess why Nicholas was in London, but it had nothing to do with herself, she was certain of that. He had to have come to town on a mission for his country. Davison wanted her to find out if a certain rumor was true: were the Russians concluding a secret alliance with Prussia, one that would join both nations in an aggressive war against Napoleon? When the peer had told her that, Carolyn had looked at him as if he had lost his mind. How, she had asked, did he expect her to find that out?

He had been explicit. He expected her to resume her love affair with Nicholas in order to gain the information—and he was giving her exactly one week in which to produce details of the alliance if there was one. And, he had already heard that Nicholas's next stop might be Breslau. If that were the case, he wanted Carolyn to go there with him— and relay further reports back to him.

Carolyn could not let her father hang. But the very idea of spying on Nicholas, of using and betraying him, was violently repulsive to her. She closed her eyes. How was she going to do what must be done?

"Carolyn?" George entered the room. His tone was bleak. "There is someone downstairs who wishes to speak with you."

Carolyn did not look at him. She loved him so much. What if she failed to find out anything? And she did not trust Davison. What if he had her father hanged anyway? "Whoever it is, tell him to go away."

"It is your grandmother, and she is adamant. She said she has come all the way to town just to see you."

Carolyn sat up, brushing her hair out of her eyes. It was far too long for her taste now, for she had not cut it in months, having no use for her old disguise anymore. "Just hand her that letter I wrote earlier in the evening." Old Lady Stafford was the very last person she wished to see.

"You have been crying. Carolyn, I am so sorry," George said heavily.

Carolyn bit her lip to keep it from collapsing. She could not speak.

George sat down beside her. "Do you hate me?" he asked tremulously.

Carolyn shook her head, very close to tears. "I could never hate you. I just wish . . ." She trailed off.

"Carolyn, I love you so. You are all that I have, with Margaret gone. I was at a loss. You know I have no head for figures, and we have no income—we hardly sell any books!" he cried.

Carolyn gripped his hand. "I know. I guess I closed my eyes and pretended not to realize that there was no way this shop paid our rent."

"I did it for you. To keep you in a proper home, to keep you well fed," George said desperately. "Please, please, forgive me."

Carolyn embraced her father. "How could I not forgive you? I love you, Papa. If only there had been another way!" she cried.

"Don't you know how many times I have wished that, myself?" George said heavily. "And now, dear, dear God, I have involved you in my deceptions. I am so afraid—for us both!"

"You will not hang," Carolyn said fiercely. "I promise you that. We shall both be fine." But her pulse raced hard enough to make her feel faint. Nicholas. She must use and betray Nicholas, when she loved him so much.

"I do not want you playing games with Sverayov—I do not want you using yourself in order to help me," George cried, gripping her shoulders.

Carolyn stepped back from him, about to tell him that she had no choice, when she saw Lady Stafford standing in her doorway, leaning on a walking stick. Carolyn's heart sank.

The old lady marched forward. "I have sent you four invitations to Midlands, three of which you have refused," she declared, her gaze sharp. "I decided, after posting the fourth, that I should come to invite you myself—or at least to learn the real reason for your refusal."

Carolyn felt hopeful—Edith had not understood or even

heard what they had been discussing. "You are in my bed-chamber," she pointed out, a rebuke.

"I know where I am," the elderly woman snapped. "What games do you intend to play with that handsome Russian prince? And why has he returned to London? Is he chasing after you? Are the two of you carrying on?"

Carolyn felt her cheeks turning red. While George moaned and sat down hard on her bed, hanging his head, she said, "You have been listening to a very private conversation, Lady Stafford."

The old lady came closer, using the gold-headed cane to emphasize her each and every step. "Yes, I have. And I am concerned. Has someone died? You are both extremely distraught. And you," she said to Carolyn, "have been crying."

"I'm ill," Carolyn said, becoming angry.

"When are you coming to Midlands?" the old lady returned.

"I am not. I am busy," Carolyn snapped.

"Busy doing what? Playing games with the prince?"

Carolyn flushed. "I am writing a novel."

The old lady stared. "What kind of novel?"

"A romantic one," Carolyn said, quite tense.

"Balderdash! And this from the brilliant Copperville? What's happened to you, girl?"

Carolyn was frozen. Even George glanced up in shock.

The old lady came forward and sat down on the bed beside her son-in-law. Carolyn blinked at the incongruous sight.

"I know," Edith said with a slight smirk. "I have enjoyed Copperville immensely. He is truly clever and amusing, my dear girl. But I decided something about him was not quite right when he blasted you and me just before you took off for Russia. I was, really, quite piqued by that column and I marched right over to the *Chronicle*'s offices and demanded to know who had dared attack me and my granddaughter. Your editor was quite reluctant to divulge that information—until I mentioned your name." Suddenly

Edith laughed. "He was so shocked, Carolyn, to find out that you were the one in that column and that you were my long-lost granddaughter."

Carolyn could only stare. "I suppose I shall have words with Taft."

"Hmm. Copperville has not written a thing since you have come back. Instead, you are writing romantic tripe. What is wrong? Did the prince break your heart?" She peered closely at Carolyn, who remained standing. "You look brokenhearted, my dear."

Carolyn folded her arms tightly beneath her breasts. "If I am brokenhearted, it is not your affair."

The old lady planted her cane loudly on the floor and stood. "I want to help," she said without aspersion. "How can I if I do not know what is ailing the two of you?"

Carolyn gazed at her as her grandmother gazed back. She had no intention of trusting her now, none, yet it would be so comforting to have someone strong to turn to and share her burden with. But bygones were not bygones. Carolyn had never forgotten the past. And she said, "Don't you think it's a bit late to be offering to help us now?"

Edith tensed. "And what do you mean by that?" she asked very quietly—as if she knew exactly what was coming.

Carolyn dropped her hands, advanced a pace. "You turned me and my mother away on a freezing, snowy day. We were desperate! Because you did not help us then, we lost our home and our store. And my mother died shortly after. But was it from pneumonia?"

Edith had turned white.

"How could you turn us away?" Carolyn cried. "How?"

"Maybe," Edith said hoarsely, "I was a stubborn, stupid, proud, and lonely fool."

Carolyn turned her back on her, marching toward the door, intending to leave the room.

"Maybe," Edith called after her, "I wish to make amends now for such a terrible mistake."

Carolyn faltered. And then she flung herself through the doorway and into the corridor outside.

❧ THIRTY-FOUR ❧

THIS time, Nicholas was staying at the St. James Hotel, where he had taken an entire upper floor, the space required for him, his staff, his daughter, and her new governess, an impoverished and widowed Russian noblewoman. He had rented the rooms for a fortnight. He intended to conclude his business within that amount of time, before he left for Breslau.

His business, which was Carolyn.

Nicholas sat at the delicate Louis Seize desk in the luxuriously appointed sitting room attached to the master bedchamber, a quill in hand. How did a man express himself in such a situation? Did one begin a letter like this with an apology? Should he begin with a confession of feelings? He had never missed anyone or anything the way he had missed Carolyn these past two and a half months. Or should he start with a declaration of love—and intentions? But he was afraid. It had been one matter for Carolyn to declare their love too precious to be denied on that terrifying night in Moscow with the city aflame and French soldiers lurking everywhere. But her heart had been broken, that day when Marie-Elena returned from the dead. As had his.

Marie-Elena was dead. The greatest scars of all had been the ones left on Marie-Elena's mind, not those upon her body. She had gone into seclusion, retiring to the countryside, not to Tver, of course, but to a small dacha in an isolated area near the Barents Sea. One night, a month after she had appeared in St. Petersburg, in the midst of a blizzard, she had wandered outside in her nightgown. Her body had been found four days later.

Had it been suicide? Or had she become completely deranged? Nicholas laid his quill down. He stared across the blue and gold room without seeing a single piece of furniture, a single painting, a single bust. Nicholas decided that it did not matter. What mattered was that he could not bear to live without Carolyn Browne. And surely she felt the same way.

But he thought of young Davison, and all that she had thus far suffered, and he was uneasy.

A soft knock sounded on the door and his valet entered the room. "Excellency, you have a caller. The Dowager Viscountess of Stafford."

Nicholas stood, reaching for a silver-knobbed cane. His pulse had accelerated. "Show her in," he said.

Lady Stafford walked past his valet, using a walking stick. Nicholas recalled that she had not needed a cane the last time he had seen her; nevertheless, she looked well for her age—which he estimated to be at least seventy-five. "Good day, Excellency," she said.

He approached her, limping, and bowed. "Lady Stafford. It is a pleasure to see you again. Please, do sit down."

"Thank you," She took an imposing chair—the grandest in the room. Thronelike, it dwarfed her. Nicholas sat on a small bergère, hiding his amusement at her choice. She said, "I am sorry to see that you are injured, Your Excellency. Is it from battle?"

"One might call you impertinent, Lady Stafford," Nicholas said, but he was not offended.

"At my age, I say what I wish to say. I do not have time to beat around the bush," she declared.

"Yes. It is a wound from the war. I am afraid I shall limp for the rest of my life," Nicholas said flatly, without any bitterness. "I consider myself lucky to be alive."

"I am very sorry that you have a slight infirmity, Excellency, but I must admit, the limp is rather becoming on a man like yourself.''

Nicholas laughed.

Edith Owsley's smile faded and she leaned forward. ''Carolyn Browne is in trouble, Excellency.''

Nicholas's brief bout of good humor vanished. He stiffened. ''What kind of trouble?''

''I do not know. She has not forgiven me for the past, and has no intention of confiding in me now, although I think it is severe. I think her foolish, incompetent father has gotten into something dangerous, Excellency. But what could that be?'' Edith Owsley blinked at him as if she were a very innocent-minded creature, indeed.

''I do not know,'' Nicholas said, but he was grim and dismayed. What had George Browne gotten himself into now? Damn the man!

''And Carolyn is being called upon to compromise herself—or so I believe.''

He was motionless. But his mind raced. Carolyn had many talents; he could see how someone like Davison might wish for her to hone those talents and use them to his advantage. And right now, the stakes were so very high. Napoleon had abandoned his own army in order to flee back to Paris, where he now remained. The French troops had been chased across Russia, harried not just by Kutuzov, but by Cossacks and partisans, suffering because of the early snows, the lack of food and ammunition, horses and supplies, until a mere ragtag remnant of La Grande Armée had finally managed to recross the Neimen and fall back on safe Prussian territory. The tides of war had changed. Finally, Napoleon's defeat had become a possibility.

Nicholas would never allow Carolyn to enter the murky world of espionage. Not now, not ever. He wanted her safe, he wanted her out of it. Damn her father, he thought savagely.

''Excellency, are you unwell? You have lost some of that stunning coloring you possess,'' Edith Owsley remarked, her glance shrewd.

He smiled at her. "I am fine, Lady Stafford, and thank you for your concern. More importantly, thank you for alerting me to the fact that Carolyn is in some danger."

Edith smiled. "So it is Carolyn, eh? And how does your wife fit into the scheme of things?"

Slowly, he stood, leaning on the cane, towering over the small old lady. "Lady Stafford, your granddaughter saved the life of my own daughter in Moscow, on the eve of Napoleon's invasion. She also saved my life, and that of my cousin. She is the bravest woman I have ever known, and given those circumstances, I do not think we need to stand on ceremony." He paused. "And my wife is dead."

"I am sorry, Your Excellency." Edith Owsley's cane thumped on the rug as she stood up. "One day you must tell me that story. I should be fascinated to hear it. And of course, I have never stood on ceremony myself." She was smiling.

"And I shall." He inclined his head.

At the door she paused. "When will you call on her, Excellency?"

He chuckled. He could surmise when another person was thinking almost exactly as he was. Lady Stafford, he decided, was a useful and enchanting ally. "Within the hour," he said.

Satisfied, she left the room, her cane thumping down the hall.

"Carolyn. He's here."

Carolyn froze. Ostensibly she was helping her father in the bookshop. She had taken down an entire shelf of books in order to dust. But her mind was thoroughly preoccupied with what she must soon do. It seemed that she could hear the pendulum clock in the corner of the store ticking off every single second. Her heart was filled with dread.

"Sverayov. Oh, God. Carolyn!" George cried anxiously.

Feather duster in hand, an apron covering her dark gray dress, Carolyn stepped down from the stool. Now her heart was slamming with frightening force, making her feel ill and faint.

Through the windows, she saw him approaching the store. His strides were long and filled with purpose, in spite of his uneven gait. A huge dark brown Russian fur coat swung about him as he approached.

Carolyn inhaled, seized with memories, too precious and painful to count.

"Should I leave the two of you alone?" George asked with worry.

Carolyn did not have a chance to answer. The doorbell tinkled as it opened. Nicholas stepped into the shop. His gaze found her instantly, and for a moment, they were both motionless.

Carolyn had known how much she missed him, had known how much she loved him, but had never imagined what it would feel like to see him again, after so briefly having attained her most fantastical dreams, and then having lost everything. She wanted to run to him, lose herself in his embrace, and stay in that sanctuary forever. Instead, she did not move, incapable of doing more in that instant other than stare.

George bowed. He was sweating. His bald spot glistened. "Excellency. How good to see you."

Amusement appeared in Nicholas's eyes, but he only spared George a brief glance, his attention immediately back on Carolyn. "Good afternoon, Browne. I am glad you have become so fond of me in my absence."

George looked nervously from Nicholas to Carolyn, and strode through the shop and into the kitchen, closing the door behind him.

They were alone. A vast and terrible silence surrounded them. It seemed to throb and undulate. It was painful. And Nicholas continued to stare. Carolyn realized she was perspiring, and she wiped her damp palms on her apron. She managed a feeble smile, setting the duster down. "Nicholas. I heard you were in town. This is a surprise."

He bowed, his gaze piercing. "How could my appearance in London—and in your life—be a surprise?'' He came forward, his regard intent.

She found herself breathless, exhilarated, and frightened all at once. For even as she faced him, wanting him so badly that it hurt, in one corner of her mind she was aware of Davison's threats and what she must do. But he was implying that it should have been obvious to her that he would seek her out. Carolyn knew she must retreat from this topic, yet a part of her eagerly went forward. ''I assumed your many affairs would keep you in your homeland for some time.'' His many affairs—his daughter and his wife.

''You assumed erroneously,'' he said.

''Apparently,'' she said dryly. ''But then, life is so full of surprises.'' And she thought, with real bitterness, of Marie-Elena's return from the dead.

''Surprises, and challenges, and change,'' Nicholas returned evenly.

She stared at him. He reached for and grasped both of her hands. ''You look very well,'' he said, whisper-soft.

Carolyn pulled her hands away from his, and saw him start—and then disappointment flitted through his eyes. Mentally she berated herself: what was she doing? She was supposed to be a seductress, luring him forward—not pushing him away. She wet her lips. ''I think I have had all the challenges a human being would ever need.''

''Yes, you have.'' He set his cane against the counter, shrugged off his coat and laid it on the counter beside the duster. He leaned on the walking stick. ''But you are strong. One of the strongest people I have ever known. If life deals you another rotten hand, you will still triumph. Of that, I have no doubt.'' His gaze was penetrating.

Carolyn met his eyes and wanted to cry. ''You are wrong. I am beaten, Nicholas. Beaten down into the dust.''

''I do not believe it,'' he said harshly.

She shrugged. ''How is Katya?''

''Katya is here. We are staying at the St. James for a fortnight, and then we are on to Breslau. Will you come and see her? And will you dine with me tonight?''

She should be saying no. But she must not refuse. Oh, God, this was happening too fast. He was on his way to Breslau, a Prussian city. Carolyn was speechless, struggling for control and a strength she no longer had.

He took her hands in his again, his palms large and strong, dwarfing hers. "Carolyn. I have missed you so. You should not have run away like that—and then refused to even speak with me before you left." He hesitated. "Marie-Elena is dead."

Carolyn's eyes widened. Before she could speak, he said, "This time there is no doubt. One night she left the house in her nightclothes. It was snowing heavily. Her body was discovered four days later. We buried her in St. Petersburg."

Carolyn was shocked. "Did . . . did she want to die?" She was recalling Marie-Elena's terrible vanity, and the bandages she had been wearing the last time she had seen her.

"I do not know," he said. Their gazes locked.

And images flitted through her head, wild but focused, of her and Nicholas, together, man and woman, man and wife. And then she thought about her father, and Davison's threats. "How is Katya?" she asked huskily, torn now, her emotions rioting.

"Sad. She is very sad, but somehow, oddly resigned. Before her death, Marie-Elena would see no one, not even her own daughter." Nicholas was grave.

Carolyn stared. "That is terrible."

"Yes, it is," Nicholas agreed, his gaze trained upon her face. "Katya talks about you. She misses you. As do I."

Carolyn found it hard to breathe. She was motionless, her heart beating hard and fast.

"Once, you told me our love was too precious to deny," Nicholas said.

Carolyn felt two tears rolling down her cheeks. "It is too precious," she whispered.

"I want you to be my wife, Carolyn," Nicholas said.

Carolyn tried to pull away, but he still held her hands, and it was an instant before he released them. Even if she did accept now, he would withdraw his proposal after she betrayed him. Carolyn was sure of it.

Unless he never found out.

"Carolyn." Nicholas's somber tone broke into her thoughts. "I need you. Katya needs you. We both miss you terribly."

Carolyn hugged herself, swallowing thick, hot tears. Cursing Stuart Davison. Their love was too precious to deny. Damn Davison. If only she could share her agony with Nicholas. And then she found herself on the verge of cursing her own father. Carolyn was shocked.

He laid both hands on her shoulders, and when he spoke, his voice feathered her ears. "Come back to the hotel with me. At the least, let us dine tonight and spend the evening together. Do not refuse me outright. You may have all the time you need to think about my proposal. I am prepared to wait."

Carolyn closed her eyes, breathing hard, seared with anguish. If only she could think clearly. But she could not. She did know, though, that she must at least accept this invitation. "Yes. I will spend the evening with you, Nicholas." And she was thinking not of the pleasure of having his company, nor of marriage, she was thinking of seduction and subterfuge.

Carolyn saw Katya, and a real gladness, one unblemished by the guilt Davison's threats had fostered within her, overwhelmed her. For one moment, as Carolyn stood with Nicholas silently in the doorway of the chamber Katya slept in, she watched the child as she read aloud to her governess by the windowsill. Katya had not seen her. How beautiful, how precious, she was. Carolyn realized she had come to love her as she would a little sister or her very own child.

And then she realized Nicholas was watching her intensely.

Carolyn took a breath and entered the room. "Katya, sweetheart," she said huskily.

Katya dropped the book to the floor as she leapt to her feet with a small but potent, and very happy, cry. She rushed to Carolyn, flinging her thin arms around her. Carolyn held her hard.

"I have missed you, I have missed you so," Carolyn whispered above the child's head. Words she was not free to utter to Nicholas.

"And I have missed you too, Miss Browne. Terribly. It has been so lonely without you!" Katya cried, looking up yet still gripping Carolyn.

Carolyn smiled fondly at her. "Well, then we are of accord," she said.

"And poor Father," Katya said, shooting a swift glance in Nicholas's direction. "He has been so sore of heart, Miss Browne, mourning your leaving us. Why did you leave us?"

Carolyn wet her lips. She did not know how to respond. She chose her words with care. "Perhaps because I loved you both so much."

"But that does not make sense. It was because of my mother, was it not? Because she was not dead, and you could not be my father's wife?" Katya's brown eyes were wide, but not accusing.

"Oh, God," Carolyn said, sinking to her knees and holding the child's hands. "I'm sorry about your mother," she whispered to the child.

Nicholas limped forward, nodding at the governess, who quickly left the room. "Yes, Katya, how clever you are, how astute. That is exactly why Carolyn left us."

Carolyn wasn't sure he should be telling his daughter the truth. But before she could speak, even though she had not the foggiest notion what she should say, Katya said grimly, "Maman was very ill. She refused to see anyone." Her mouth trembled as she formed an odd, heart-wrenching smile. "But she never loved me anyway."

"Oh, dear, she did, she truly did, but in her own way," Carolyn cried.

"It's all right," Katya said. "Please come home with us, Miss Browne. Please."

Carolyn hesitated, and did not dare look at Nicholas, wanting so much to tell the child yes. "I will try."

Katya nodded, mouth pursed. And then Nicholas helped Carolyn to her feet.

They dined in splendor, amongst silver and crystal, gold and china, a snowy white tablecloth covering the long dining table, which could seat sixteen guests. But there was only Carolyn and Nicholas, each at their own respective places—Nicholas at the table's head, Carolyn at its foot. Katya had gone to bed.

French wine was poured. Nicholas watched her intently as she sipped. Carolyn knew her anxiety was transparent. She was afraid she would blurt out the truth to him if he asked her what was wrong. "This is delicious," she said, stabbed with bittersweet memories.

He must have had the same recollections in the same instant, because his smile was brief and twisted. "It is. A Médoc. Carolyn, how is Copperville?"

Carolyn stiffened. "I have laid Copperville to rest."

Nicholas stared. "Why?" He was grave.

Carolyn stabbed her salad of pickled vegetables. Finally she looked up. "Writing about the extravagant behavior of the rich and titled no longer amuses me."

"I see." He sipped his wine. "That is a shame. Because your barbs were usually well placed and well timed, and I believe more than amusing to your readers. Social satire has an important place in our culture."

Carolyn laid down her fork more sharply than she had intended. It clattered on the porcelain plate. "This satirist no longer exists."

He stared. "You have been terribly wounded, have you not? I am so sorry."

Carolyn stared down at her plate. When she could speak

in a calm tone, she said, "I am writing a romantic novel."

His brows lifted. "Indeed?"

"It is titled *The Refugees*, and is about the adventures of a young Englishwoman who has the misfortune to be in Russia during Napoleon's invasion." Carolyn thought her tone had become belligerent. And she almost regretted telling him about the novel.

A silence reigned at the table as their plates were removed to make way for another course. Nicholas said, "And this young woman, she must fall in love, for it is a romance."

Carolyn nodded.

"And she lives happily ever after, I suppose?" But he did not smile.

"No," Carolyn said, staring down the table at him. "The novel has a tragic ending. She returns to London, where she spends the rest of her life a lonely spinster, refusing all other suitors."

Nicholas stood abruptly. A servant rushed forward to hand him his cane, which he accepted. "I am afraid I do not like your novel," he said harshly.

"I am enjoying writing it," Carolyn cried, also on her feet.

He thumped and limped around the table. "You are angry," he ground out, his eyes flashing. "I do not blame you for being angry for all that has happened." He paused in front of her, his cane thudding on the rug. "But you have no reason to be angry at me."

He was right. But she was angry, furiously so, at life, at Marie-Elena, at her father, at herself, and dammit, at him. "I did not ask for any of this!" she cried, covering her heart with both hands. "None of it!" She was shouting.

He threw the cane aside, staggered slightly, and grabbed both of her hands, holding them far too tightly. "And did I ask for this? Did I ask to fall in love? You've changed my entire life! Did I ask for anything other than to serve my country in a time of war and to be a responsible and caring father?"

Carolyn tried to jerk her hands free of his. "As neither of us has asked for anything, perhaps I should go home?" Her voice was insultingly sweet.

"Like hell." He jerked her forward and she fell against his chest, and as she did so he tipped up her chin and seized her mouth with his.

For one instant, as he kissed her with a strength and determination that was almost brutal, Carolyn was stiff, and filled with anger and resistance, ready to fight him physically if need be. But then her mind snapped. She *was* angry, but not at him. She was angry at fate, and God, and just about everyone, but she loved Nicholas, and soon he would leave, betrayed by her—and she would never see him again. Her eyes closed. Her mouth softened. She melted against him.

He moaned and released her wrist and chin, sliding his powerful arms around her, kissing her face now, her cheeks and eyes, her forehead, temples, and chin. Carolyn strained to find his lips. Kissing him. Desire began, incipient and tingling, but swiftly becoming demanding and urgent. And she felt his manhood, huge and hard, pressing against her hip.

Neither one of them had seen the servants disappearing, but when Nicholas broke the embrace, the dining room was empty. Candlelight flickered over them. Their shadows danced on the walls.

He took her hand and clasped it. "If I could, I would sweep you up in my arms and carry you into my bedchamber."

She smiled. "I prefer to walk there side by side, hand in hand," she whispered, her heart singing, her body trembling.

"Only you, Carolyn, could make the perfect reply."

Carolyn bit her lip. "Only you, Nicholas, could be so perfect yourself." How she meant her every word.

"I am hardly perfect," he whispered, his golden eyes on her face.

"There is no one I admire more," she said truthfully.

His nostrils turned red. "But I feel the same way."

Carolyn smiled, perilously close to tears, and bent to retrieve his cane. She handed it to him, their gazes locked.

The covers and sheets strewn about the foot of the bed, Carolyn lay in Nicholas's arms, her cheek on his chest. But the utter relaxation and satiation she had been experiencing was fading swiftly. Tension rose in its stead. Damn Davison. And George. For ruining her life.

He rolled onto his side, propping himself up on one elbow, to gaze down at her. "You are such a beautiful woman," he said, his gaze sliding over her body, as naked as his. "And I confess. I like your hair now that it almost reaches your shoulders." His fingertips caught a platinum curl.

Carolyn could not smile. "Shall I grow it?"

"But I also like it when you are playing at charades," Nicholas said. His smile faded. "Something is bothering you. Is it the decision you must make? I do not want you to think about it now, if that is the case. You have plenty of time to decide whether to accept my suit or not."

Carolyn swallowed with great difficulty. "Yes," she lied. "It is the decision I must make which is overwhelming me." She shut her eyes, hiding her face against his bare chest so he would not see the lie in her eyes.

He stroked her hair.

Carolyn finally said, "You mentioned you are off to Breslau in a fortnight."

"Yes. I have some business to conclude there."

"Matters of state, I presume?" She kept her tone as light as possible, no easy task.

"I am afraid so. But do not ask me anything else, my dear, for my mission is confidential." His fingers continued to thread through her hair. "And do not mention to anyone, including your father, where I am off to when I leave town."

Her heart drummed, hurting her with its every beat. He was off to Breslau, undoubtedly to negotiate an alliance with the Prussians, and she must find out the details. "But why is it such a secret?" she asked.

His hand stopped. For a moment he did not answer. "I did not say it was a secret, merely confidential."

He was suspicious. She could sense it. Carolyn made herself look up. She smiled. "Will you return to London afterward?"

He met her gaze, not returning her smile. "Only if you do not come to Breslau with me."

She stared. This was what Davison wanted. Her to accompany him as a lover, while playing the spy. She could not do it. Never. She must find out what she could now, pray it was enough to free her father from the hangman's noose, and walk out of his life.

"What is wrong, Carolyn?"

She sat up, shaking her head. "I am overwrought. It has been a trying day. You will not be in danger, will you, Nicholas?"

"No."

She smiled, and kissed his cheek. "Shall we go to sleep?" she asked, her mind racing. There was a desk in the adjoining room. Clearly he was not going to tell her anything. But if he were on official business, might there not be some instructions, or notes, lying about somewhere? The sooner she did what had to be done, the better. Because she could no longer stand herself, and already wished to be alone to mourn their love.

"Very well," he said, turning to snuff out the candles. He pulled the heavy covers up over them and reached for her, pulling her into his arms. Carolyn could no longer relish the feel of him. She could not relax at all. She could only listen to his breathing, waiting for it to deepen, and become steady, slow, and even, as she clung to the present and dreaded the future.

If only time could be made to stand still.

He was asleep. She was certain of it. And time was not frozen, to the contrary. Carolyn remained unmoving for a few more minutes, just to err on the side of caution. Then she slipped from his arms. He did not move.

She slid out of the bed, shivering as the cold night air struck her naked body. Not daring to light a taper, she searched the floor for her clothes and pulled on her chemise and petticoats. The fabric rustled far too loudly in the silent night, making Carolyn pause every few seconds, waiting for Nicholas to ask her what she was about. But the only sounds she heard other than that of her underclothes was his steady, deep breathing.

I am so sorry, she thought. So terribly sorry.

She hurried across the bedchamber, carefully twisting the knob on the door that opened to the parlor where she had seen the desk. It rattled. She froze. Nicholas did not jerk upright, accusing her of betrayal and disloyalty. Carolyn pulled the door open a few inches, enough for her to slip her slender body through. Then she shut the door behind her as firmly as possible, not daring to pull it all the way closed, afraid of the noise it could make.

She paused, her back against the wall, breathing harshly, hating herself even more than she hated Davison. How could she do this? How could she not? She could not let her father die. That would be even worse.

Carolyn summoned up her determination, which had been wavering. The room was cast in darkness, but she knew where the desk was. Carolyn launched herself off the wall, telling herself not to think about Nicholas now. Now she must only concentrate on the task at hand, and on not being discovered performing this abysmal, foul deed.

At the desk she found and lit a taper. Holding it aloft, she began a methodical search of the papers organized neatly on the desktop. Every page, and there were many, was written in Russian. She was dismayed. She had hoped for correspondence written in French, the official language of the Russian court. She opened the top drawer, recognized Alexander's seal instantly; it was broken, but again, the letter was in Russian. She was stumped. Tears filled her eyes as she imagined her father hanging from a rope, his body dangling and lifeless, his neck bruised and broken.

Light filled the room.

Carolyn cried out, whirling. Nicholas stood in the doorway, holding up a taper. His expression was savagely furious . . . and filled with pain.

And their gazes locked.

Carolyn knew her horror had to be obvious, as was her guilt. Her heart threatened to burst from her chest. She clutched the tabletop, watching his anger change to a far more frightening emotion—watching it change to sheer and utter revulsion.

Without a word, Nicholas turned his back on her, to exit the salon.

"Nicholas!" Carolyn shouted.

He limped back into the bedchamber.

And she knew he was walking out of her life—forever. And in that instant, nothing else mattered. Carolyn ran after him. *"Nicholas!"*

♔ THIRTY-FIVE ♔

NICHOLAS was pulling on his breeches from the evening before. His movements were fierce and impatient, turning the endeavor into a struggle when there should not have been even the slightest contest. Carolyn paused on the threshold, gasping for air. He did not look up.

"Nicholas, I am sorry, I had no choice!" she cried desperately.

He jerked his pants closed with a violent motion, and finally looked at her. "This is how precious our love is. Precious enough for you to betray me." His eyes were dark with pain and his voice eerily quiet.

She had mortally wounded him. And she had never loved anyone more. "I had no choice," she whispered, terrified now that it was too late, that she had, finally, irrevocably, lost him—when she had never truly had him in the first place.

"I would never have thought this of you. Not this," he said, turning his back to her, his shoulders sagging.

She ran to him, clutching his back from behind. "Nicholas, my father is going to die." She began to cry, and her tears were real. "I had no choice, damn them all for doing this to me, to us!" She wrapped her arms around him, her face pressed to his back, feeling every piece of her world splintering apart, turning into dust and shadows, and she could not bear it. It almost felt as if, having endured so much, her mind could endure no more, and was about to snap.

He had stiffened and was motionless, now he turned. He set her away. "What in God's name are you talking about?" he asked very grimly.

"My father has committed treason," she almost screamed. She gripped his hands. "Nicholas, he is going to hang. I was supposed to find out about the alliance with Prussia. But I have failed, and now he will die, and I have lost you, too, I have lost everything in the world that matters to me." She choked. Carolyn turned away, sinking onto the settee at the foot of the huge bed. She slumped in utter defeat, covering her face with her hands. How could she go on? How?

He knelt before her. "Why didn't you come to me first?" he demanded.

She started, dropping her hands. "How could I come to you? Should I ask you to betray your country? How would I feel then? It is far better for me to betray us, than to force you to commit such a heinous act."

He stared into her eyes, his jaw flexed, and then he stood up. "Your father is not going to hang, Carolyn, nor am I going to betray my country. You may rest assured on both points."

Carolyn could only stare, hope beginning to rise within her breast, yet she was afraid to hope, dear God, she was, as Nicholas buttoned his shirt rapidly, reaching for his stock. "What are you going to do?" she whispered.

Tying the stock, he stared at her, his thoughts impossible to read. "Trust me," he said.

It was the middle of the night when he was ushered into Stuart Davison's town house by a bleary-eyed servant. As Nicholas had banged the knocker quite aggressively, he was only in the midst of demanding that he must see His Lordship at that moment when Davison himself appeared on the stairs, clad in his nightclothes and stocking cap, a taper in hand. But he was not sleepy-eyed, and the instant he saw

Nicholas, his entire posture changed as he became absolutely alert.

Nicholas was enraged, but knew he must not show it. Yet never had his blood boiled as it now did. Instead of strangling the man, Nicholas smiled. His bow was civil. "How sorry I am to intrude at such an ungodly hour, but there are urgent matters we must discuss, my lord, matters which cannot wait." His tone was equally restrained.

Davison's smile was as cool as Nicholas's had been. He came down the stairs. "Thank you, Giles, you may go back to bed. Follow me, Excellency."

Nicholas followed him down the corridor and into a small salon. Davison shut the door firmly and offered him a seat. Nicholas declined. He continued to struggle with his temper as he faced the other man. "So you intend to hang George Browne," he said without preamble. His eyes were hard.

Davison stared. "I have no idea what you are speaking about, Excellency."

"Really? Then how is this for news. Good news, I hope you will agree. Carolyn Browne has agreed to marry me."

Davison finally, slowly, smiled. "I had heard this rumor that the Princess Marie-Elena died. Congratulations, Excellency. But how does that affect me?"

Nicholas stepped forward. Davison, to his credit, did not back away. "Let us cease all pretense. You are a French agent, my lord, and we both know it. It was one thing for you to threaten a weak man like Browne, another to threaten and attempt to use his daughter. Now you must deal with me. And I am not an adversary you should wish to have, my lord, I promise you that."

Davison said, "You are mad."

"I have agents in London. When I left for Russia in July, they remained. Amongst their orders they were told to keep a watchful eye upon both you and Browne. I myself have an extensive log of your activities, my lord." Nicholas smiled.

Davison stared. "I think you are blustering, sir."

"Should you think to even take such a chance? Do you not think, with my heart so involved in this particular matter, that I would make sure that you hang one way or the other if Browne is even harmed?" Nicholas asked coldly.

"There is no file, no proof," Davison said flatly after a moment.

Nicholas laughed. "You are dead wrong," he said. "For example. At midnight on August the third, a Sunday, I do believe, when I was halfway to Riga, you spent three hours at Claire Russell's. The following afternoon you and Browne met at the Three Dog Inn, where you discussed his trip to Prague. A 'manuscript' passed from your hands to his. From the Three Dog, you returned directly to Whitehall. Two days later, George Browne left England. He arrived in Prague ten days later."

Davison had, finally, turned white. "It would all be hearsay."

"I have made copies of this file," Nicholas said. "And the files are in the hands of Lieven, our new ambassador—with very specific instructions."

Davison sat down in a heavy brocade chair. "You are clever, Sverayov, very clever. Very well. Browne is out of jeopardy. He was hardly worth anything, anyway."

"Of course not, as couriers are a penny a bushel. Browne is retired, my lord," Nicholas said firmly. But you are not forgiven, he thought, for how you tried to use Carolyn. And the game was hardly over—it had only just begun.

Davison shrugged. "He was inept. A fool." His gaze met Nicholas's. "But you are off to Breslau, are you not?"

Nicholas did not let his exasperation show, but he was furious that his destination was familiar. "I am on my way home," he said, a lie. "My only current interests now being the closure of my personal affairs." He bowed briefly. "As it is late, I will not intrude any longer."

Davison said nothing, but his expression was clearly dubious. Nicholas hoped his own parting smile was genteel, and not as savage with intention as it felt. He limped decisively from the room.

And once in the corridor, he could hear Davison swear, a very ungentlemanly oath.

"What do you think he intended to do?" George asked anxiously, not for the first time.

It was early morning. They sat at the kitchen table in the bookshop, Carolyn having decided to go home after Nicholas had left in the middle of the night. Her father had been up, unable to sleep even a wink, at once relieved and dismayed to see her. His reaction had been as confused when she had told him everything that had happened. Neither one of them had even attempted to go to bed.

Carolyn stared out of the kitchen window. It was raining lightly. "I don't know. But he seemed very confident," Carolyn said, probably for the hundredth time. She stood. "I cannot stand this suspense. And I cannot stand myself, for betraying Nicholas, when he has asked me to be his wife."

George also stood and walked to her, laying his hand on her shoulder. "This is all my fault. Maybe we should both flee the country."

It was so very tempting. But then she would certainly never see Nicholas again—unless they fled to Russia. The idea gave Carolyn an odd hope. But he could not possibly forgive her for her treachery, and what would be the point of residing in the same country with him? Eventually he would find someone else to wed. The thought was brutally painful. Carolyn could not stand it. Surely it would be most sensible to live as far from him as possible. Perhaps China would do. Or America.

"Someone is at the door," George cried in a low, strained voice.

Carolyn whirled, knowing it must be Nicholas, for who else would call at this hour? It was not even eight o'clock yet. She flew to the kitchen doorway, as someone rapped lightly on the front door. Her heart fell. Nicholas's knock was far more aggressive. She crossed the store and lifted the shade a hair. Her gaze met that of her grandmother. She glanced over her shoulder, releasing the shade. "It is Lady Stafford. What could she want at this hour?" She was dismayed.

"Are you going to let me in, granddaughter?" the old lady called through the door.

Carolyn sighed, unbolting and opening the door. As her grandmother marched in, raindrops on her hat and coat, she could not help peering down the street—but other than for her grandmother's barouche, it was deserted and silent, and there was no sign of Nicholas. She shut the door with a heavy sigh. Perhaps she should have stayed at the hotel. But she had been too ashamed, too filled with guilt, and surely he never wanted to lay eyes upon her again. Carolyn could not blame him. Carolyn had never in her life been at such a loss.

"Are you expecting someone?" Edith asked sharply. "Good morning, Browne."

"Good morning, my lady," George said with a bow.

"No. Maybe," Carolyn answered.

"Child, you look like death warmed over." The old lady's voice was unusually kind. She laid a hand on Carolyn's shoulder. "And you are trembling. I do not know what ails you, as you have refused to say a word, when God only knows I am clever enough, not to mention seventy-five years of age, a true fountain of experience, to help and advise you. Granddaughter, I am very glad I paid a visit to your handsome prince yesterday."

Carolyn gaped. "You what!"

Edith smiled. "I called on Prince Sverayov to inform him that you were in trouble and most definitely needed his help, as you would not accept mine."

Carolyn felt as if she were losing her wits. "But why would you do such a thing?" she asked, not accusingly, but with utter bewilderment.

"Why? Because you're my granddaughter, and clearly you and your foolish father are in trouble, and Sverayov is as much in love with you as you are with him. And he is no fool." Edith Owsley smiled with satisfaction.

Carolyn felt as if her head were spinning. "I don't know whether to be dismayed by your interference or not," she said slowly. "I am so tired. Everything is all muddled in my head. I cannot think clearly."

"There, there," Edith said. "You are a strong girl, stronger even than your mother. You shall come out on top, I have no doubt."

Carolyn swallowed. "I suppose I should thank you for your faith."

Edith shrugged. "That would be nice. After all, it could be a beginning. A truce, of sorts."

Carolyn stared. A beginning? A truce? Was she so tired that she was hearing things? But no, she had not imagined all of the invitations to Midlands. And maybe Midlands would be the perfect place to go and hide, until the pain and sorrow and regret filling her broken heart became bearable enough to live with.

The doorbell tinkled and Nicholas limped into the store, his fur swinging about him as it was only draped upon his shoulders. Carolyn froze.

Lady Stafford marched toward him. "Good morning, Excellency. I think we have all been expecting you."

His gaze was on Carolyn and no one else. Not even looking at Edith, he bowed slightly, murmuring, "Good morning."

Carolyn gripped her hands. She did not know what to say, or where to start. "Nicholas."

"Come with me into the kitchen," he said.

Carolyn turned. "Please excuse us."

"Oh, such impropriety," Lady Stafford remarked, but with unconcealed humor, not censure, as Carolyn preceded Nicholas into the other room. She shut the door firmly after him as he limped past her, and then, slowly, both terrified and hopeful, she faced him. In the folds of her skirts, she could not help crossing the fingers of both hands.

And outside the kitchen, two pairs of ears were glued shamelessly to the other side of the door.

"It is done," Nicholas said. "For now, Davison will

never dare to threaten you or your father again."

Carolyn clasped her hands to her bosom. "For now?" Her gaze was ensnared by his.

"He is a dangerous man, and a traitor, and is harmful to the interests of your country and mine. We shall send your father to St. Petersburg as soon as is possible, within a day or two at most, I hope. Once he is safely out of the country, I am bringing Davison's crimes to light. He must be prosecuted, Carolyn. I have evidence against him. I am certain we can attain a pardon for your father in return for his testimony at the trial."

"And if not?" Carolyn whispered.

"If not, he will be safe at Vladchya Palace. Or anywhere else that he chooses to live. I will take care of it," Nicholas said firmly.

Carolyn felt her knees beginning to buckle. She could not tear her eyes from his. It was difficult to breathe, to think, but not to feel. Oh, God. The hope was explosive inside of her breast. The hope, the yearning, the love. "Why are you doing this? Why? When I have behaved so abominably in betraying you and our love?"

He limped forward and clasped her shoulders firmly. "Because I love you. Because I understand."

Two such simple statements. So simple—and so powerful. Carolyn's breasts heaved. The very air seemed to burn her lungs. "You still love me?" she whispered.

"I could never stop loving you, not as long as I am alive. Carolyn, I do not want to lose you. Not now, not ever."

"You can never lose my love," she said, beginning to cry.

"But you? I want you at my side, now and always. I want your promise, now, that you will marry me. I want you to accompany me to Breslau, and then home to St. Petersburg. As my wife. Carolyn." Tears had appeared in his own eyes. "Dear God, I do not think I should wish to live without you."

She collapsed against his chest. And so many memories flooded her, good and bad, happy and not, memories of the first time he had walked into the bookstore, impossibly handsome, arrogant, and royal, filling it up, turning her heart over, and memories of Charles Brighton's charade, of the ball and the races, and then there was Nicholas's flirtation with her. She thought of her first glimpse of Katya, so melancholy, and she thought of Katya now, a child no longer afraid to express joy and pain, fear and hope. She closed her eyes, remembering the sea voyage to St. Petersburg with his impossibly charming brother as she actually dared to follow him back to his homeland. And of course, she recalled his sudden, unexpected appearance at Vladchya Palace, and the stunning night of love and passion which had ensued. The following morning of devastation, betrayal, cruelty, and loss. And then Moscow, aflame, Katya lost, and their flight from the city with Nicholas and Sasha wounded and unconscious in the back of the wagon, afraid of French soldiers on their heels. A tear slid from her eye as Carolyn remembered their being married in the army field hospital—and as she remembered Marie-Elena walking back into their lives on the eve of the tsar's reception. She clung to him. Tightly, so tightly, overwhelmed and afraid to ever let go.

"We have lived and shared and loved and suffered so very much," she whispered against his chest. "I love you more than is humanly possible, and I could not live even passably without you. Nicholas, I will return to Russia with you. I will be your wife. And I will cherish every moment of every day that we spend together, from this moment on. But I think I am always going to be afraid of having our love, one day, taken away from us."

He tilted up her face. She sensed he wished to reply, but instead, his mouth found hers. Carolyn melted against him as his mouth became hungry, when behind them, the kitchen door burst open.

"Enough of that until the wedding night," Edith Owsley stated.

Carolyn and Nicholas broke apart. Carolyn knew she was blushing, but they shared an amused smile nevertheless. "I

lo beg your pardon,'' Nicholas said very formally to the
ıld lady.

She rapped her cane on the floor. "I have an announcement to make."

Everyone turned. Nicholas reached for and held Caro-
yn's hand. Carolyn smiled up at him. She could not believe
hat this was happening. Not when they had gone through
o much, starting out so shakily, she just could not. Her
ıand tightened on his. In spite of her fear that one day their
ove would be suddenly taken away, as it had almost been,
he was not just stunned, but so deliriously happy. The
ossibility that she and Nicholas could have a glorious life-
ıme together was worth any and all risks.

"I was leaving my monetary fortune to charities. In fact,
had already informed that, buffoon, Thomas, of it." Edith
miled. "But I have changed my mind. It shall be my wed-
ing gift to the two of you. Provided, of course, that you
gree to be married at Midlands."

Carolyn froze. Not because of the incredible, generous
ift—and all that it signified—but because suddenly she
aw herself and Nicholas being crowned man and wife at
er grandmother's estate, and she had never wanted any-
ıing more.

"Well?" Edith Owsley demanded. "Aren't you going to
least say thank you, child?"

Carolyn wiped away more tears. "My lady, I—"

"Isn't it time you called me grandmother?" she inter-
ıpted.

Carolyn swallowed. "My lady . . . Grandmother . . . I am
verwhelmed." She shot a glance at Nicholas, whose heart
as there in his eyes, his happiness for her apparent. "The
ırtune I too shall give entirely away to good causes. But
Nicholas would agree," and she faced him, wide-eyed,
there is nothing I want more than to be married at Mid-
nds."

"It is done," Nicholas said softly. "It is done."

Their gazes held. Carolyn was in a state of disbelief. Her

entire world was being righted, all at once. She could not move.

"No one deserves this more than you, Carolyn," Nicholas said softly.

And then her father was embracing her, and wishing her good luck. Edith was demanding that Nicholas kiss her on both cheeks, insisting that she had known from the moment she had seen them together at the Davisons' ball that their fate was this union, and then George was shaking Nicholas's hand and apologizing for their past differences. Carolyn stepped away, watching her family with Nicholas.

Her family. Suddenly her mother's image was there in her mind, crystal clear, the way it had not been clear in years, and Margaret was smiling with happiness and forgiveness. She reached out, and Carolyn felt her hair being smoothed over. And finally, Carolyn knew she was at peace.

Nicholas moved to her side. "Are you all right?"

The image had blurred in her mind's eye. The sensation of having someone touch her hair was gone—but that had only been her imagination. Carolyn leaned against Nicholas as he put his arm around her. "I have never been better," she said. And already, the heavy pain of loss and sorrow in her chest, carried there for so long, was easing, lightening, beginning to fade away.

"I am afraid, too, Carolyn," Nicholas said gravely.

Carolyn looked up at him. "Maybe, when love is like this, so profound and precious, maybe, when two people have endured what we have, it is natural to be afraid."

"It is." He smiled, and in spite of the fact that her father and grandmother were watching them and listening to their every word, he pressed his mouth to her cheek. "Time heals all wounds, Carolyn, and it shall heal ours, as well."

Carolyn hesitated. As much as she believed him, he was in error. "No, Nicholas, I must disagree."

His eyes widened and he paused, about to press a kiss to her temple. "You wish to debate with me now?" His rich laughter warmed his tone.

She had to nod, smiling. "*Love* heals all wounds, Nicholas, and it will surely heal ours as well."

He laughed, hugging her. "Forgive me, darling, for being such a confounded realist."

"Only if you forgive me for being the eternal romantic," she whispered, hugging him back.

"I would not have it any other way," he said.

And Edith Owsley laughed and clapped her hands. "Bravo!" she said. But tears were in the old harridan's eyes.

An orphan from London's East End, Violet Cooper was tired of being hungry and cold. But she dared to enter a world forbidden to her and her kind...

He was a man of the world. The rules of Victorian society did not interest him. Yet Theodore Blake was immediately compelled by Violet——and soon found himself defending the vulnerable young widow in the face of a murder investigation...

Two people from different worlds were brought together by passion, bound together by whispered accusations, and torn apart by scandal and misfortune. The world claimed they should never love each other. Their hearts claimed otherwise.

BRENDA JOYCE

The Finer Things

THE FINER THINGS

Brenda Joyce

_____ 96391-2 $6.99 U.S. / $8.99 Can.

THE RIVAL

A spellbinding historical romance
about two lovers who discover
forbidden passion, family secrets,
and a legacy of desire . . .

Coming from bestselling author
BRENDA JOYCE and St. Martin's
Paperbacks in August 1998

Antoinette Stockenberg's
Bestselling Novels:

A Charmed Place

"Award-winning author Antoinette Stockenberg takes a dramatic turn in her new mainstream release. Passion, love, hatred and deceit all collide with unexpected force in the powerful and expressive A CHARMED PLACE."

—*Romantic Times*

"Ms. Stockenberg writes with the wisdom and grace of the ageless to create a beautiful story in this intricately woven suspense. I love everything she creates."

—*Bell, Book, and Candle*

"Well written . . . Every sentence builds the tension as the protagonists try to find their way back to each other and Maddie tries to protect her daughter. Ms. Stockenberg's passion for writing pulses through this superb story."

—*Rendezvous*

"Ms. Stockenberg has a very witty writing style and wonderfully drawn characters."

—*Old Book Barn Gazette*

"Antoinette Stockenberg has crafted an insightful novel of lost love, hidden secrets and smoldering passions, one with intriguing plot twists and well-developed secondary characters . . . Stockenberg has incorporated suspense, romance and a touch of the paranormal to bring readers a satisfying story of true love conquering all."

—*Telegraph Herald*

"Buy this book! A truly fantastic summer read!"
—*Gulf Coast Woman*

"A CHARMED PLACE is a great read, filled with extraordinary characters, compelling subplots, long-buried secrets, and a hero who is strong, tender, and irresistible."
—B. Dalton's *Heart to Heart*

"A CHARMED PLACE is a captivating mix of mystery and romance with characters so real they jump off the pages. Stockenberg is adept at capturing family relationships and conveying a real sense of the characters' feelings and motivations. An intriguing and passionate tale which will have readers longing for the next Stockenberg novel."
—Writers Write website

"With each book she writes, [Stockenberg's] style and writing become even more gripping, her characters more complex . . . A CHARMED PLACE has easily earned a place on my keeper shelf. Do yourself a favor—read A CHARMED PLACE."
—One Magical Kiss (Daphne's Dream) website

Dream a Little Dream

"DREAM A LITTLE DREAM is a delightful blend of goosebumps, passion and treachery that combine to make this novel a truly exhilarating read. Ms. Stockenberg delivers once again!"
—*Romantic Times*

"DREAM A LITTLE DREAM is a wonderful modern fairy tale—complete with meddlesome ghosts, an enchanted castle, and a knight in shining armor. DREAM A LITTLE DREAM casts a powerful romantic spell. If you like modern fairy tales, you'll love DREAM A LITTLE DREAM. Run, don't walk to your local bookstore to purchase a copy of this magical romance."
—Kristin Hannah

"Ms. Stockenberg writes with a lively and humorous wit that makes her characters three-dimensional and unforgettable, and had me smiling throughout. It didn't take long for me to become caught in the magic web of the castle and the undercurrent of the mystery."

—*Old Book Barn Gazette*

Beyond Midnight

"Stockenberg's special talent is blending the realistic details of contemporary women's fiction with the spooky elements of paranormal romance. So believable are her characters, so well-drawn her setting, so subtle her introduction of the paranormal twist, that you buy into the experience completely . . . BEYOND MIDNIGHT has a terrific plot, a wicked villain and a sexy hero. But the novel ventures beyond sheer entertainment and it is easy to see why Stockenberg's work has won such acclaim."

—*Milwaukee Journal-Sentinel*

"Full of charm and wit, Stockenberg's latest paranormal romance is truly enthralling."

—*Publishers Weekly*

"Antoinette Stockenberg creates another winner with this fast-paced and lively contemporary romance with a touch of the supernatural. A definite award-winner . . . contemporary romance at its best!"

—*Affaire de Coeur*

"When it comes to unique, eerie and engrossing tales of supernatural suspense, Antoinette Stockenberg is in a league of her own. BEYOND MIDNIGHT is a gripping and chilling page-turner . . . outstanding reading!"

—*Romantic Times*

"Spectacular! A terrific story that had me anxiously turning the well-written pages."

—*The Literary Times*

"Ms. Stockenberg does it again! She's written a story that keeps you so involved, you can't put it down."

—*Bell, Book and Candle*

"Ultimately satisfying, mystically entertaining, and a perfect book to take to the beach."

—*The Time Machine*

"If you are in the mood for a little spine-tingling, this is for you."

—*The Belles & Beaux of Romance*

Time After Time

"A richly rewarding novel filled with wrenching loss, timeless passion and eerie suspense. A novel to be savored."

—*Romantic Times*

"As hilarious as it is heart-tugging . . . Once again, Antoinette Stockenberg has done a magnificent job."

—*I'll Take Romance* magazine

"Antoinette Stockenberg is a superb contemporary writer . . . TIME AFTER TIME is that rarest of works—a satisfying treasure for a vast variety of palates."

—*Affaire de Coeur*

Embers

"Stockenberg cements her reputation for fine storytelling with this deft blend of mystery and romance . . . Sure to win more kudos."

—*Publishers Weekly*

"A moving work involving obsession, betrayal, and thwarted passions . . . A book that has 'classic' written all over it."

—*Affaire de Coeur*

"Terrific!"

—*Romantic Times*

Beloved

"BELOVED has charm, romance and a delicious hint of the supernatural. If you loved the film *Somewhere in Time*, don't miss this book."

—LaVyrle Spencer

"A delightfully different romance with a ghost story—a great combination that was impossible to put down."

—Johanna Lindsey

"BELOVED is great . . . A lively, engaging, thoroughly enchanting tale. Ms. Stockenberg is a fresh, exciting voice in the romance genre. Her writing is delicious. I savored every morsel of BELOVED."

—Jayne Ann Krentz

"The talented Antoinette Stockenberg continues to demonstrate her talent for delivering unique tales of romance and danger with tantalizing supernatural overtones."

—*Romantic Times*

Emily's Ghost

"A witty, entertaining romantic read that has everything— a lively ghost, an old murder mystery and a charming romance."

—Jayne Ann Krentz

"I loved EMILY'S GHOST. It's an exciting story with a surprise plot twist."

—Jude Devereaux

"Highly original and emotionally rich reading . . . Pure and unadulterated reading pleasure . . . This outstanding contemporary novel is a veritable feast for the senses."

—*Romantic Times*

St. Martin's Paperbacks Titles
by Antoinette Stockenberg

BEYOND MIDNIGHT
DREAM A LITTLE DREAM
A CHARMED PLACE
KEEPSAKE

Keepsake

ANTOINETTE
STOCKENBERG

St. Martin's Paperbacks

KEEPSAKE

ISBN: 0-312-96975-9

Printed in the United States of America

St. Martin's Paperbacks edition / April 1999

St. Martin's Paperbacks are published by St. Martin's Press, 175 Fifth Avenue, New York, NY 10010.

10 9 8 7 6 5 4 3 2 1

For Christine and Janine

Keepsake

Prologue

The women of Keepsake were afraid.

Young mothers moved cribs into their bedrooms for the night, and grandmothers jammed kitchen chairs against their back doors. Teenage girls agog with terror talked late on the phone with their very best friends, while their older sisters who lived alone made their boyfriends promise to stay over. The news that morning had sent shock waves of anxiety from Elm to upper Main: Alison Bennett's death was no suicide at all, but cold-blooded murder.

If Alison wasn't safe, who was? Her father was strict, her uncle was rich. She was the last girl in Connecticut anyone would have expected to find hanging from a rope above a quarry on a cold October night. That was the consensus as people turned off fewer lights than usual and tried to sleep.

No one wanted to believe that the murderer was one of Keepsake's own—but everyone knew which way the investigation was heading. Only one man in town had been questioned twice by the police about Alison, and that was her uncle's gardener.

As Keepsake tossed and turned, Francis Leary scanned the single shelf in his bedroom in the gardener's cottage at the foot of the Bennett estate, trying to decide which books to pack. It was an impossible dilemma, like choosing which of a litter of kittens not to drown. Tired, confused, overwhelmed by events, the gardener reached for his Gertrude

Jekyll, a signed first edition, and then wondered: Could he fit the Olmsted, too?

His son suffered no such agonies of indecision. With a lightly packed duffel bag slung over his shoulder, Quinn Leary poked his head into his father's room and said, ''Dad, let's *go*.'' He was seventeen and more decisive than his father would ever be.

Francis Leary fully understood his own weaknesses and his son's strengths, but he dreaded the thought of what lay ahead: a stolen truck, a bus ride to nowhere, a life on the run. ''Quinn, I know this is my idea, but . . . now I'm not so sure.''

His son felt a surge of hope, tempered by exasperation. ''You want to stay and take your chances? Fine with me. But the police will be here by morning. You won't have time to change your mind again, Dad. Understand that.''

Put that way, the plan to run became more compelling. The gardener took a last look around and said nervously, ''Let's go.''

They locked up the cottage and waded through a sea of unraked leaves to the pickup truck, registered in the name of Alison's uncle up the hill.

Up the hill, in a bedroom with high ceilings and a marble fireplace, the dead girl's seventeen-year-old cousin and classmate lay awake in her four-poster bed as she listened to the trees bend to the moaning wind. Olivia Bennett was despondent over the loss of her cousin and shocked at the news of her cousin's pregnancy—but Olivia, who lived closer than anyone to the suspect, had no fear of him. Francis Leary had been her parents' gardener for ten years, and Olivia was convinced that she knew him well: Good men didn't kill.

At seven-thirty, Keepsake dragged itself out of bed after a night of no sleep, only to find that the man it feared had fled in the night with his son. Part of Keepsake was relieved; but the other part, the bigger part, spent the next seventeen years sleeping with one eye on the bedroom door.

One

The reindeer were a bigger hit than Santa, no doubt about it. Trekking through falling snow and fading light up the far side of Town Hill, Quinn could see a moblet of small children pressing up against a temporary pen and pitching kernels awkwardly to a pair of tame deer within.

Borrowed from a petting zoo, he figured. Leave it to Keepsake to do Christmas proud. He got a clearer view of the town's copper-roofed gazebo at the top of the hill and saw that Santa, holding court inside, had a fair-sized crowd of his own: The line of kids waiting to read him their lists was impressive for a town so small.

From his vantage on the hill, Quinn studied the intersection—controlled by a traffic light now—that was the center of Keepsake, quintessential New England town. The four corners were anchored by the same historic white-steepled church, granite town hall, one-story library and sturdy brick-front bank as before. Quinn searched for, and found, the little drugstore where he'd hung out during his high school years. It was a CVS now, which meant the soda fountain would be long gone. He could almost taste the strawberry shakes that were the old place's specialty; it hurt to think that they were no more.

He scanned for more landmarks and was jolted by the perky pink-and-white logo of a Dunkin' Donuts. Like the CVS, it was a jarring reminder that time had passed. He was thirty-four now, not seventeen, and on a quest more grim than hopeful. He sighed heavily, then surveyed the crowd gathered to light the town tree.

Plunge right in, or hang around the edges?

Plunge.

The crowd was thickest near the unlit tree. Several hundred citizens were drinking hot chocolate while they waited, as they did every December, for the mayor to plug in the cord and kick off the holiday. The first familiar face Quinn saw belonged to a beefy citizen wearing a jacket in the town's high-school colors. The man had been there awhile: his green cap was white with snow. When he saw Quinn, he did a double take.

"Leary? What the *hell* are you doing here?"

"Coach," Quinn said, greeting him with a wary nod. "It's been a long time." He held out his hand.

Coach Bronsky stared at it as if it were a bloody stump. "You've gotta be kidding," he said with loathing. He swivelled his head left and right. "Where's your old man?"

"Beyond your reach now," Quinn shot back. "He died last month." He had wondered how he'd break that news to Keepsake. Now he knew.

"Dead!" The coach's face congealed into a dark pudding of anger and resentment. "You have a hell of a nerve, in that case. You think you can stroll up here . . . announce that he's kicked the bucket . . . and what? Have us carry you around on our shoulders again? You ran, Leary! You left us in the lurch. Left your team . . . your town . . . everyone. The two of you ran like a couple of scared dogs."

Quinn stood ramrod stiff under the attack, as if he were still a quarterback in the locker room after a so-so half. He didn't have to ask whether Keepsake High had won the state championship that year. The answer was a bitter, resounding no.

Offering no excuses, he said, "I'm not here either to apologize or to explain. I'm sure not here to gloat."

"Oh yeah? Then what *are* you here for?"

Quinn's response was a snort. *To find out who killed Alison. Shouldn't that be obvious?*

"To look up old friends," he said after a deadly pause.

"You won't find any in Keepsake. Get the hell out. Now."

"Thanks for the advice—but I think I'll stick around."

With a snarl the coach said, "Vickers may have other ideas," and brushed past Quinn with the force of a fullback.

Caught off balance by the shove, Quinn staggered, but he managed to say cheerfully, "Sergeant Vickers! He's still around?"

"*Chief* Vickers now, pal." The coach muscled his way into the crowd, undoubtedly to spread the word.

Not exactly the welcome wagon, but it was about what Quinn had expected. He brushed heavy snow from his bound hair and the back of his neck and wished he'd bought a hat. Too many years in La-La Land, he realized. He'd forgotten what a New England winter was like.

The cold wet snow set the mood for his next three encounters, the first of which was with the assistant librarian. When Quinn last saw her, she had been a thirty-year-old single woman who always had enthusiastic words of praise for a quarterback who actually read the novels and not the Cliffs Notes. The lady whom he approached was easily recognized as a grayer version of herself, but any enthusiasm was in short supply.

Quinn gave her a tentative smile anyway. "Hi, Miss Damian. Read any good books lately?" It used to be a standard greeting between them.

The librarian stared over the rim of her uplifted paper cup. Her eyes got wide and she choked on her hot chocolate, then recovered enough to gasp, "It's you! My God, how did you get here?"

"American Airlines and Hertz," he quipped.

Her voice dropped a scandalized octave. "So your father's turned himself in! All these years people have been waiting, and now—"

"They'll have to keep waiting, I'm afraid. My father passed away last month."

She stared at him. Her distress seemed to increase. "Oh,

but ... but how can we be sure?" she blurted out. "He could be a fugitive still!"

Quinn blinked. He hadn't anticipated that one. "Trust me," he said dryly. "He died in my arms on November twelfth."

"Yes ... yes, I'm sure you're right," she stammered. Then she threw down her cup and hurried away.

Quinn indulged in a wry smile. Freddy Krueger couldn't have frightened her more.

He reached down to the brown stain on the fresh-fallen snow and picked up the paper cup. Come the January thaw, he wouldn't want litter popping up all over the quaint town green. He was a gardener's son, and he'd been trained well.

He was at a loss during the next encounter. The woman clearly knew him—she was sneaking looks from the edge of the crowd—but he wasn't at all sure about her.

Finally he turned directly to her, a matronly woman whose apple-cheeked face was tightly wreathed in fake fur. "Myra? Myra Lupidnick?" he ventured.

"Myra Lancaster now," she said, coming forward with a nervous smile to shake his hand. "I thought it was you. How are you, Quinn?"

"Not bad. It's good to see you, Myra," he said with nostalgic affection. "Really."

Myra was the first person in Keepsake to befriend Quinn after he and his dad moved into the gardener's cottage on the Bennett estate. Quinn had just turned eight. He had made out with Myra under the bleachers shortly afterward; it was Myra who had taught him how to French kiss. For at least a year after the Frenching episode, he'd convinced himself that he wasn't a virgin anymore.

"You settled in Keepsake, then?" he asked. She had always gone on about moving up and out of it.

"Sure! I got married—George Lancaster, remember him?"

"Tall guy, red hair?"

"He's a plumber now, and doing really good. We have

four kids. And a four-bedroom house in Greenwood Estates.''

''Hey, that's great,'' he offered gallantly.

She didn't ask Quinn what he had been up to all those years, which was hardly surprising. He could see the struggle in her face as she debated what to say. Suddenly she seemed to give up the effort. She shrugged and murmured, ''Well, I've got to go. The kids'll be wondering where I got lost. I . . . See you,'' she said.

She fled from him as well, with only slightly less panic than Miss Damian, the librarian.

Shit. At the rate he was alienating people, he wouldn't find a friendly ear in the entire town. He had based his whole mission on the belief that after seventeen years, the citizens of Keepsake would have let their guard down about the scandal that had rocked the town like a West Coast earthquake; that they'd be mellowed to the point of apathy. So far, apathy was the only response he *hadn't* got.

He made his way through more of the crowd, searching for people he'd known. Near the cocoa-and-cookies table were stationed half a dozen carollers wearing Victorian capes and top hats. They had been alternating between Santa songs and Christmas hymns and at the moment were belting out a peppy rendition of ''Let It Snow.'' As they sang, Quinn circled behind the listening audience, scanning their faces, looking for anyone who might be sympathetic to his side.

Instead he found the barber. Quinn practically knocked him over as he was making his way toward the gazebo. Tony something? Tony Assorio, that was it. The man looked the same, exactly the same: small, gray, and contained, like one of the bottles of mystery liquid that he kept lined up in front of the mirror on the narrow marble counter in his one-chair shop.

''Mr. Assorio—Quinn Leary,'' he said, shaking his hand. ''You used to cut my hair when I lived in Keepsake.'' Why Quinn expected the barber to remember him as a customer rather than as the son of a fugitive wasn't clear, even to him.

The barber scrutinized him, then said, "I remember. You always did have a good head of hair. Looks like you could use a trimmin' up," he added, eyeing Quinn's ponytail. "Come in tomorrow. Two-thirty. I have an opening."

"Uhh . . . yeah, well—thanks. I may do that."

The barber moved on, greeting people like a Rhode Island politician. Quinn made a mental note to drop in on him the next day. No one had his fingers on the pulse of a town more often than a barber.

Quinn paused where he was, not at all surprised that furtive glances were beginning to be cast his way. He had wanted people to know he was back, and he was succeeding; but he was surprised at how alienated he felt from them all. By the light of the nearby gas lamp, he was able to make out the time: four-seventeen. Soon the tree would be lit and people would begin to disperse. He was, he had to admit, disappointed. He'd hoped to meet a friendly face before then. Any friendly face.

The snow was falling now in big, paper cutouts that lay on his jacket for a mere twinkling before melting into oblivion. Quinn held up a sleeve and marvelled at the sheer magic that was coming and going there. Whether it was the carollers or the children, the deer or the snowflakes—for an instant Quinn was a kid again, in harmony with the universe around him. God, how he'd missed New England.

He felt a tug on his jacket and, still smiling, turned to see a small boy looking up at him.

"Mister? Did your daddy really kill a girl in school?"

Quinn gazed down at the kid. He was six, maybe seven. What kind of parents talked about stuff like that in front of a six-year-old? Jesus.

"My dad didn't hurt anyone, sport," he said as gently as he knew how. "That was just a rumor."

"What's a roomer?"

"It's when someone tells stories that might not be—"

"Andrew!" a woman said shrilly behind the child. "Get over here right now. *Right* now!"

She rushed up to the boy and hauled him off with a brutal yank on his parka. For the first time since he'd stepped into the Currier and Ives scene, Quinn felt some of his resolve falter. If every citizen in Keepsake was going to treat him like a leper . . .

"Quinn, dear! Quinn! Yoo-hoo!"

Surprised at the enthusiasm in the voice, he turned in time to behold a petite, elderly woman angling a four-legged walker before her as she made her way by lamplight across the snow-covered grass. She wore a black wool coat and was muffled under several circuits of a fluffy red scarf; her red knit hat covered all but a few white curls. Only her eyes showed, and that was all he needed to see.

"Mrs. Dewsbury!"

It was his old English teacher, the first and only mentor he'd ever had. He'd had her for homeroom once and for English twice. Quinn had always known he was a natural athlete, but it was Mrs. Dewsbury who had convinced him that he could compete in the classroom as well.

She had to be eighty by now. He didn't like seeing her using a walker; but he liked the fact that she was still out and about.

"Mrs. Dewsbury, it really is you," he said, grinning as he approached her.

She lifted a welcoming arm for his embrace. He hugged her gently and kissed her cheek and said, "You look great. No kidding; you look great."

"Oh, tish! I'm old and decrepit and I've got two new knees that I don't trust a damn. And speaking of bones, I have one to pick with you, young man. Where have you been hiding for the last seventeen years? You might have let me know."

"Right. I'm sorry about that. We, uh, took up residence in California."

She cocked her head thoughtfully and said, "You know,

I'm not surprised. They hired your father, no questions asked out there, am I right?''

"Californians tend to do that," he agreed. "They get lots of practice with illegals."

"Hmph. Well, Frank Leary was a wonderful gardener, and the Bennett estate hasn't looked as good since. Just last fall—*early* fall, mind you!—their latest gardener went and flat-topped every rhododendron he could reach. The things looked grotesque, and after the inevitable winterkill, they looked even worse. Well, never mind. How have you been, dear? How have you *been*?" she demanded, squeezing his forearm through his thin jacket. "Oh, my," she added after she did it. "Do you still play?"

"Football? No, I left that all behind me."

"I always watch for you during the Superbowl."

He laughed and said, "I have a masonry business. I do a lot of stonework. I guess that's what's kept me in shape."

She pulled her scarf away from her face and snugged it under her chin. "And your father I just heard has passed on?"

Quinn nodded. "Last month," he said quietly. "Of a stroke. He didn't linger long . . . two and a half weeks."

"I'm sorry, dear. I know how close you must have been to him."

Somehow Quinn didn't want to talk about it, despite— maybe because of—the sympathy he heard in her voice. He said, "Can I get you something? Hot chocolate?"

"Actually, I've brought my own refreshment." She reached into the leather handbag that was hooked on her walker and came up with a silver hip flask. "Blackberry brandy is what warms me these long, cold nights."

She tipped it in Quinn's direction. Startled, he shook his head. "Thanks, but I'm driving," he said, wondering about her own ability to operate a walker while under the influence. His old teacher and mentor had always been a free spirit. Obviously that hadn't changed. "How did you get here?" he asked. He wouldn't have been surprised if she'd told him on a Harley.

"The senior citizens' van," she said with a sigh of disgust. "I flunked my driver's test last year. Macular degeneration in my left eye. And the right one's fading fast," she added. "I can barely read large-print books with a magnifying glass anymore, but I keep trying." Lifting the flask, she glanced around, then took a single prim sip, screwed the cap back on, and tucked the silver container snugly in her purse. "Well, my dear! How long will you be staying?"

He wished he knew. He had a business to run back in California. "That's up in the air. I've just paid a visit to an uncle in Old Saybrook. He's my father's brother and is ailing himself. While I was in your neck of the woods, I thought I'd drop in just to . . . to . . ."

"To see who got rich, who got fat, and who got out?"

"All those things," he said, smiling. She was making it so easy for him to lie. "And I wanted Keepsake to know that at least one chapter in their history had ended."

"And a sorry chapter it was, condemning your father without a trial! I hope you don't think we were all so foolish," she said, straightening her tiny frame behind the walker.

His response to that was drowned out by the amplified thumps on a microphone being tested for sound. Mrs. Dewsbury explained that the thumper was Keepsake's current mayor, Mike Macoun. Quinn had a vague memory of the man, a restaurateur who was undoubtedly well connected both then and now.

After a pretty little speech in favor of Christmas, the portly mayor took one cord and plugged it into another cord, and the twenty-five-foot balsam fir lit up to happy *ooh*s and *ah*s from the crowd. It was a tree for kids, not grown-ups, all buried in red bows and gaudy colored lights and topped with a giant, lopsided star. There was nothing chic or understated about it, which pleased Quinn. He was tired of the white lights his upscale clients favored.

Someone shot off a cannon and the mayor declared that Keepsake's holiday season had officially begun. Almost immediately, the crowd began thinning. The snow was beginning to pile up, and people were anxious to get on with their chores.

"Where are you staying, Quinn?" the elderly woman asked.

"Let me think, it's newish . . . the Acorn Motel."

"Heavens, don't be silly. You're not staying at any motel. You'll take me home and stay at my house while you're in Keepsake."

He protested, but she wouldn't hear of it, and soon it was settled. He would stay in her overly large and virtually unoccupied Victorian home for the duration, whatever it ended up being. Quinn liked the idea of having daily access to someone who could fill him in on seventeen years of comings and goings in Keepsake. He tried to insist on paying for his stay, but Mrs. Dewsbury wouldn't hear of that, either. They ended with a compromise: he would do a few odd jobs around the house, and they would call it even.

After giving the driver of the senior citizens' van a heads-up, they left Town Hill together to scandalized looks and some sly greetings, although no one approached them to chat. Caught up in conversation with Mrs. Dewsbury, Quinn had little opportunity to look around him, but the one time he did, he saw a man whose face he could hardly forget: his father's employer and the richest man for miles around, Owen Randall Bennett. The textile mill owner was deep in conversation with two other men and didn't notice—or pretended not to notice—Quinn, who instinctively altered course away from him. He wasn't ready to deal with the town's patriarch yet, not by a long shot.

"That way's closer to the car," he said to Mrs. Dewsbury, pointing off in another direction. As they shifted course, he found himself wondering where the rest of the Bennetts were. Owen was around. Was his wife? What about their two kids? Had Princess Olivia married and moved on? And her brother, the Prince? Knowing Rand as well as he did, Quinn guessed that he'd been given an empty title and a corner office by his father.

But it was Rand's twin sister Olivia who came more vividly to mind. Skinny, brainy, infuriatingly competitive—Quinn and the Princess had butted heads over every academic award the school had offered. He half expected her to tap him on his shoulder and challenge him then and there to a spelling bee.

Olivia Bennett. He'd never forgotten her. How could he, when they'd grown up side by side on the same estate, she in the big house, he in the cottage?

He drove Mrs. Dewsbury home with extra caution—the last thing he needed was to smash up a kindly old widow who'd taken pity on him—and then he hovered solicitously as she plowed in her fur-topped galoshes behind the walker through several inches of unshoveled snow on the walk.

Her all-white Queen Anne house was enormous; he was surprised she still lived in it by herself. But her grandparents had built it, and four successive generations had lived in it. It wasn't easy to abandon so much history. The trouble was, her son was settled in a lucrative career as a financial planner in Boston, and her divorced and childless daughter lived out west. Mrs. Dewsbury had dreams—but no real hopes—that after she was gone, one of them would somehow return to live in the family homestead.

"In the meantime," she said, handing Quinn her walker and brushing snow from the banister as she ascended the ambling, wraparound porch, "my daughter wants me to move to a retirement community nearer to where she lives. But I'd be miserable living somewhere else. I wouldn't know a soul and the food would taste different. No, the only way I'm leaving this house is feet first."

She pointed to an exterior light fixture hanging by its tattered fabric cord from the porch ceiling. "One thing you might do for me, dear, is tuck that thing back into its hole sometime. I got on a stepladder the other day, but I was still too short."

Aghast at the thought of her teetering on a ladder in her new knees and poking at a frayed cord, Quinn assured her that the job was as good as done.

They went inside to a house that was cavernous and yet

cozy in a varnished, dark-wood way. The ceilings were easily ten feet high, but the arched doorways somehow whittled the rooms back down to size. God knew, there were enough of them: twin parlors, a breakfast room, a music room, a cozy area, a game room, a reading room, a writing room— Quinn got lost just looking for the phone.

But he found it at last, an old black one being used to weigh down a slew of papers and magazines on a cluttered desk in a book-filled nook that smelled of fireplace ashes and potpourri. If rooms had personalities, then this one was smart, interesting, and heedless of other people's opinions. Quinn liked it as much as he liked its owner.

He looked up the number of the Acorn Motel and canceled his reservation there, then meandered back to the kitchen to reminisce with his old teacher over a pot of spiked tea. The second pot was steeping when they heard a sudden, sickening sound of shattering glass from in front of the house.

An accident, was Quinn's first thought; the street was still unplowed. He ran to the front door and flipped on the porch light, which, not surprisingly, didn't work. The wide street was dark, but he could see no cars embraced in a fender-bender on it. All he saw was his rented brown pickup, parked the way he'd left it in front of the house.

Actually, not quite the way he'd left it. The front windshield had been smashed to smithereens.

More surprised than angry, Quinn ran out to the now-deserted street. Hard to believe, but someone must have followed him to Mrs. Dewsbury's house. He peered inside the truck. The front seat was buried under a blanket of broken glass. His camera and suitcase were where he'd left them, but the caller had left a welcoming bouquet: red carnations, strewn all over the broken glass.

Somehow they didn't look right. Quinn reached inside and picked up a couple of them.

What the hell? He fingered the blooms. Wet. He looked at his hand. Red.

A clutch of carnations, dipped in blood.

Two

"*Any sign of* them?" Mrs. Dewsbury called out.

Quinn turned to see his elderly hostess standing in the doorway, her small frame silhouetted in the soft glow of the parlor lamps. "Nah," he said. "They're gone."

He tossed the flowers back on the seat and wiped his fingers on a floor mat, then took a closer look around. He could see evidence in the snow where someone had jumped out of a car, scrambled over to the rental, done the deed, and escaped. The depressions were already filling in with newly fallen snow; no clues there. He scanned the other homes on the street. All were large with lots of windows, but all were dark. No doubt everyone was off doing Christmas errands. Shit.

He went back to the house, brushing the snow from his sweater before he rejoined Mrs. Dewsbury in the more formal of her two parlors. He expected to find a frightened, agitated little old lady. He was wrong. Old and little she might have been, but the lady was clearly pissed.

"I have lived in this house for eighty-one years and I have never—*never*—seen such a thing," she said in a shaking voice. "What will you do? How will you drive?"

Quinn shrugged reassuringly and said, "It's no big deal. I'll have the car towed and rent another if I have to."

"Too bad I sold the Buick to my nephew last year. Really, it's just too *bad*!" Her hands were trembling as she moved from armchair to drum table to davenport to the walker that she'd left in the archway between the two parlors. With white-knuckled fury she reclaimed the walker and began marching out ahead of him.

"We'll just see what Chief Vickers has to say about *this*," she huffed. "Use the phone in the kitchen to call him. It's a speakerphone."

Oh, perfect. "Y'know, Mrs. Dewsbury," Quinn suggested, "Chief Vickers may not be the most sympathetic man in Keepsake."

"Sympathy has nothing to do with this! Someone just broke the *law*, and it's his job to uphold the *law*."

Law, shmaw. Quinn was a lot more worried about staying on in the woman's house and putting her at risk. "Okay, look. I'll call and report this, but under the circumstances I think the best thing would be for me to—"

"Don't even *think* it!" she said in her best schoolmarm's voice. "You're staying here, as we agreed. This mess has gone on seventeen years too long as it is. I blame your father for running away, and I blame this town for hounding him into it. But Frank Leary is dead and gone now. There's no reason why the sins of the father have to be visited on the son."

"There was no sin, Mrs. Dewsbury. My father didn't murder Alison." Quinn had to force himself even to say the words; they caught in his throat like barbed wire. *"He did not murder Alison."*

In her anger the old woman was candid, and in her candor she was brutal. "Some people in Keepsake will never believe he didn't hang her at the quarry, Quinn. Or that he wasn't the one who got her pregnant. I'm sure you know that."

Wincing at the all-too-familiar vision of his classmate twisting from a rope, and unnerved by the ease with which his old teacher alluded to his father as a suspected murderer, Quinn said fiercely, "He was innocent, goddammit!"

Immediately Mrs. Dewsbury's expression softened, and she became everyone's favorite grandmother again. "For what it's worth, I don't believe—I never believed—that your father did it, Quinn. He was far too kind, much too gentle. But he kept to himself, and you know how everyone always thinks that still water runs deep. It was much easier to accuse him than to search for some vagrant—or look closer to home.''

Quinn gave her a sharp look. *Closer to home.* So he wasn't the only one who had glanced in that direction.

She lifted the cordless phone from its base and held it out to him. "Now, call."

Olivia Bennett was in her shop, Miracourt, turning a bolt of satin in mistletoe green, when the bells above the door jangled in another cheerful *br-r-ring.* Two snowy children came charging inside, shepherded by Olivia's twin brother and his wife Eileen. The kids should've been droopy after their long day in New York, but they'd reached the stage of unfocused energy that comes from being overtired. Besides, Christmas was coming. Who had time to droop?

"Hey, look who's here," Olivia said cheerfully to her niece and nephew. "Two melting snowmen."

"*We're* not snowmen," said the very literal five-year-old. "We're just all *covered* with snow." The child stomped her boots on the floor, then began brushing the snow from the sleeves of her red woolen coat.

Her mother stopped her. "Careful, honey, you don't want to ruin Aunt Livvy's fabrics. That's a gorgeous color, Liv," she added, pointing to the satin. "It'd look fabulous on you. You should make something for yourself out of it."

Olivia laughed out loud at the notion, then tucked a dark curl behind her ear and began feeding the fabric through her Measuregraph. "Who has time to sew anymore, much less to design?"

Owen Randall Bennett, Jr., her handsome twin brother who was as fair as she was dark, grinned and said, "Oh, come on, Livvy, we all know you could design a dress in your sleep, weave the fabric before lunch, and sew it together by cocktails."

"Wow. Am I really that talented?" she said, giving him a mild look.

Still smiling, Rand said, "No-o; but you *are* an annoying workaholic."

"Oh, dear. I keep forgetting that I have an affliction. How was *The Nutcracker*, Zack?" she asked her nephew.

Zack, who at nine had reached the age of feeling obliged to seem bored about life in general and Nutcrackers in particular, said, "Fine."

His little sister had been turning an endearingly awkward pirouette. Suddenly she stopped and exclaimed, "The Nutcracker was big. He was *huge*."

Zack stuck his ungloved hands in his pockets and shrugged. "Not that huge."

"Yes he was!"

"Wasn't."

"Mom! He was, wasn't he? He *was*," Kristin insisted, dropping into a sudden, pitiable whine.

"Everyone's pooped," Eileen explained as she pulled off her daughter's red-and-white knitted snowflake cap. She ran her hand through the child's blond curls, blonder even than her father's, in an effort to restore some order there. "It's too bad we couldn't catch an earlier train. How did the tree lighting go?"

Liv made an initial snip in the satin, then took up the fabric on each side of the cut, tearing the yardage away from the rest of the bolt. "Don't know," she said as she folded the rich, drapey fabric into a square. "My help's out sick and I've been stuck here since nine. But I assume it went as usual."

She turned to the customer who'd been fingering various bolts of silk bouclé and said, "That was five yards of the floral tapestry, Sue?"

Measure twice, cut once; it was the creed Olivia lived by.

The customer came back to the cutting table, pursed her lips and said, "How much did you say it was a yard?"

"A hundred eighty-nine."

"Hmm. Better make that four-and-a-half yards. I'll make the underside of the cushion out of a plain fabric."

"Are you sure? You won't be able to flip the cushion,

in that case. After all that effort, it'd be a shame—''

"You're right, you're right. Add a yard.''

"It's really more cost-effective in the long run.''

"Oh! Black thread!'' The customer hurried over to the wall display.

"Did Dad drop by after the tree lighting?'' Rand asked his sister.

Carefully feeding the heavy fabric through the measuring device, Olivia shook her head and said, "I expect he's off politicking. He's trying to move up the vote on the tax relief proposal; did you know that?''

"Are you kidding?'' Rand whispered, amazed. "I'm going to need time to lobby the council for that. What the hell is he thinking?''

Olivia shrugged. "He says he's losing his shirt. Poke your nose in Jasper's. He's probably at the bar with the mayor.''

"You bet I will.'' He gave his wife a quick buss on the cheek and said, "Wait here with the kids, honey. I'll pop in, see if he's there, and then bring the car around for you. Toodle-doo,'' he said to his daughter, mussing her curls on his way out.

"Daddy, wait,'' Kristin said in a stage whisper. "Are we going shopping for Mommy's presents now?''

"No, that's tomorrow, remember?''

"Oh, good, 'cuz I don't have my money.''

"No problemo.''

Rand left, maneuvering his way around an incoming customer laden with boxes and bags bearing the imprints of the town's small but charming shops: the Kitchen Gallery, the Owl and the Pussycat, Cheap Thrills, Best Foot Forward. The lady was not only a shopper, but a local one, and that was the very best kind.

"Hi, I was in here earlier,'' the woman explained. "I bought a pair of silk tassels? Anyway, somewhere in my wanderings I lost an earring. It's a gold twist, like this one,'' she said, holding out the mate.

No one had turned in an earring, Liv told her, but she

asked for a phone number, just in case. While she rang up her latest sale, the woman scribbled the information on a Post-it Note.

"Isn't that something, about Quinn Leary?" she remarked as she handed the note over to Olivia. "He was before my time, but—"

Olivia's head came up. "Quinn? What about him?" she asked. She hadn't heard his name mentioned in years. She had a sudden, awful fear that he'd robbed a bank and killed all the customers and had made the six o'clock news.

"He's back, apparently."

"Back," Olivia repeated in a blank tone. "Back where? In jail?"

"Back here! In Keepsake!" The shopper shifted her bags to get more comfortable, thrilled that they hadn't yet heard. "During the tree lighting he was roaming all over Town Hill as if he owned the place. People were shocked," she said with a certain amount of glee. "I wish I'd taken the time to attend, but I wasn't wearing boots."

"But why?"

"Well, they weren't forecasting more than a dusting."

Eileen smiled and said, "I think she means, why would he come back now, after all these years?"

"His father died, they say, so I guess there's nothing to stop him. Not that people didn't try. Someone called the police, but their hands are tied. Quinn Leary's not a fugitive, and his father was never officially arrested, so Quinn never technically aided and abetted a fugitive, so—"

"He's back." Olivia had listened, dumbfounded, to the news. "Good God."

Her reaction took the smug woman down a notch. Nervous now, she whispered, "Do you suppose we'll have to start locking our doors during the day?"

Olivia stared at her. "Why would you do that? Quinn didn't do it. He was at a party with dozens of classmates when it happened. I know; I was there."

"Maybe so, but that kind of thing runs in families."

"What kind of thing?"

"You know—the killer instinct."

"That's ridiculous!"

Eileen jumped in to keep the peace. "Olivia went to high school with Quinn Leary," she explained. "They were on the student council together. They were friends, they—"

"No, we weren't," Olivia cut in. "We were rivals."

"But friendly rivals."

"Hardly. Oh, what does it matter! This is awful!"

"I knew it," the frightened customer said in an undertone. "He *is* dangerous."

Ignoring her, Olivia said to her sister-in-law, "My parents will be outraged. Rand, too. Oh—and my aunt! My *uncle*!"

When they were roommates in college, Olivia had told Eileen the whole shocking story of the fugitive and his son: how the gardener had been seen staring at Liv's cousin Alison on more than one occasion. How the hanging had been staged to look like a suicide, except that the rope had come from the gardener's shed. How the police had been on the brink of arresting Francis Leary when he ran off, accompanied by his son Quinn. And how Olivia's parents—the suspect's employers—had been left to fend off a nosy press and negative publicity.

Olivia had always insisted to Eileen that what little evidence the police had was circumstantial, and that she herself did not believe Francis Leary had murdered her cousin Alison. But then Eileen had begun to date Olivia's brother Rand and discovered that the rest of Olivia's family was convinced that the gardener was guilty.

And now, seventeen years later, Olivia could see that her open-minded sister-in-law was still trying hard to stay that way about the whole affair, but not succeeding. Eileen looked doubtful and troubled as she said to her little girl, "Come over here, Kristin. Let's get your hat on. Daddy's going to be bringing the car by any minute."

An impromptu game of hide-and-seek between Olivia's niece and nephew came to a sudden end when Zack knocked over a bolt of ivory *fleur de soie* onto the parquet floor and into a puddle left by someone's boots. The accident brought an accusing shriek from Kristin, mortifying her older brother and prompting a sharp reprimand from their mother.

"Okay, that's it! Let's go, you two, before you wreck the whole place," she said, picking up the soiled bolt. "Livvy, I'm so sorry. Bill me for this, would you?"

Olivia had two customers waiting with questions and another with a bolt of Ultrasuede in her arms. "Sure, okay," she said, still reeling from the news of Quinn's return.

Eileen apologized again for the silk as she rebuttoned her daughter's coat. A silver Lexus pulled up in front of the shop. Rand leaned on the horn, and his family hurried to the summons.

For the next two hours Olivia did the job of three assistants, which was the number that should've been at her shop in the course of the twelve-hour day. But two were sick and one had asked for the evening off to attend a wedding rehearsal; Olivia couldn't very well flog them into coming in. Still, it *was* the Christmas rush, and they'd put her in a bind.

And now this. Good grief—Quinn Leary. What was he thinking, strolling onto Town Hill in the middle of the tree lighting? It was the most celebrated event in Keepsake, attended by everyone who was anyone. Her father must have seen him. Had they exchanged words? What could you say at a time like that? *Gee, Quinn, the sight of you sure brings back memories of the good old days: reporters peering through our first-floor windows, police rummaging through our garbage cans, neighbors staring over the hedges to see if anyone was coming out in a body bag.*

Olivia's parents had felt utterly betrayed when they learned that their gardener was under suspicion for murder. They'd given Quinn's father a dream job, after all, with a charming cottage for him and his son to live in, good benefits, and frequent raises. Frank Leary himself had once told Olivia that her mother was the best employer he'd ever had.

To be fair, it was also true that the man was a wizard as a groundskeeper: The extensive grounds on the Bennett estate were the envy of the county and had been photographed for *House and Garden* a few months before Frank Leary and his son took off in the night. Naturally the *HG* piece never went to press—one more reason, Olivia supposed, for her father to resent them.

Him.

Damn.

They were going to have to relive the murder all again— the discovery, the shock, the publicity, the depressing realization that Alison would never be a bridesmaid at Olivia's wedding and that Olivia would never be a bridesmaid at her cousin's.

She remembered a Saturday in her junior year when Alison's father was out of town and Olivia's mother had taken Alison and her to New York on a clandestine shopping spree. Olivia had prepared for the day by reading a book on dressing for success, and then had headed straight for the racks of career clothing. Alison, on the other hand, had gravitated toward more feminine, sexier things: V necks that dipped low, and tops with front zippers.

"You'll never get a job wearing something like that," Olivia had chided. She had been young and stupid then; what did she know?

"I don't want a job," Alison had answered. "I want a husband. I want to get out of my house and away from my father. He won't let me go away to a four-year college; I'm going to have to commute to ECCC. No thanks. You pick your clothes, Livvy, and I'll pick mine."

When they found Alison at the quarry she was wearing one of those V-necked sweaters that she so preferred. She had put on weight because of the pregnancy: Her breasts were fuller than ever.

Olivia sighed, then flipped the card that hung by a silken cord in the door window to its CLOSED side. She turned down the lights in the shop and dimmed the recessed halogen lights that hovered over the window display. The holiday window was always her favorite of the year, and this December was no exception. She had draped elegant fabrics—bolts of taffeta, brocade, and tissue in glittering silver

and gold—to flow like sparkling streams and tumbling waterfalls into pools of shimmery opulence on the floor of the
display window. With the lights dimmed low, the effect was
of a winter scene at twilight: pure magic, if only you paused
long enough to take it all in.

And she did. Despite the unnerving news about Quinn's
return, despite the surge of seventeen-year-old melancholy
at thoughts of her murdered cousin, despite her dread that
her family was about to be put through the wringer all over
again—despite all those things, Olivia found herself responding to the exquisite beauty before her. It appealed to
the artistic side of her in a way that gross receipts and profit
margins never could.

Once upon a time, she had hoped to design her own
fabrics. But somehow the business side of her had taken
precedence, and this was where she ended up: buying and
selling textiles designed by people other than her. Ah, well.
Miracourt was a financial success, and so was the mill-end
outlet she'd opened six months ago to handle remnants and
misprints she was able to buy dirt-cheap from her father's
textile mill. For now, a life in commerce would have to do.

She sighed again, not so cheerful as she had been before,
and then she closed up the shop, dreading the slippery drive
to her townhouse perched on a steep hill outside of town.
She'd been too busy to go car-shopping for that four-wheel
drive—or even to have the snow tires put on her minivan—
and now she was kicking herself.

*I'm either at Miracourt or at Run of the Mill seven days
a week. I don't have time to buy a TV dinner, much less an
automobile. Rand is right. I'm out of control.*

But then, wasn't that what lazy Rand would think?

She sprinted across the snowy street rutted with tire
tracks, just two steps ahead of the *sluk-sluk-sluk* of a Jeep
Cherokee bearing down on her. After a last look at the softly
lit window in all of its holiday charm, she flipped up the
hood of her coat and hurried through falling snow to her
van.

Three

"*Glad you could* squeeze me in, Tony."

"Ah, don't worry about it," said the barber, shaking out the folds of a white linen smock with a snap, then circling it around Quinn's neck and jamming it inside his collar. "To tell the truth, business ain't been so brisk. I'm losing customers to that . . . that *franchise* down the street. Aagh! Don't get me started. So. How you want it? Short?" he asked hopefully.

"Maybe take an inch off the bottom."

Tony gave Quinn a dry look in the mirror they faced. "And the other twelve?"

"I'll keep a rubber band around it for now."

The gray-haired barber sighed and, with a look of exquisite distaste, rolled down the band from Quinn's ponytail.

"Why you want to look like this?" he couldn't help saying as he took up a comb and a small pair of shears. "You're a good-looking guy. Still in good shape. Why you wanna go around like some hippie?"

"You think this is bad, you should've seen me with the full beard," Quinn said with a smile.

"Aagh."

Quinn didn't bother to explain that the beard and long hair were part of an effort to disguise himself during those first years in hiding. Eventually he had felt secure enough to lose the beard, but the ponytail stayed. He still liked to believe that with his hazel eyes, hawk nose, and ever-present tan, he could dye his sunstreaked hair black and pass for a Native American if he had to.

In the thoughtful pause that hangs between threads of conversation, the barber ran a comb to the bottom of Quinn's hair and began, under Quinn's watchful eye, to cut it back the inch.

"I hear you had a little trouble last night."

Ah. Same old Keepsake. Thank God he hadn't mentioned the bloodied carnations to Vickers.

"Yeah, some jerk bashed in the windshield," he said. "Do you get a lot of that nowadays?"

"Never. Mailboxes, yes. Not windshields. Windshields are in the city."

Quinn grunted, the way men do in barbershops, and then he took a flyer and said, "This guy was driving a pickup."

There was an infinitesimal break in the rhythm between snips. "That so? What color?"

"Couldn't say. I'm figuring a truck by the look of the wide tire tracks."

A much more pronounced gap between snips now. Thinking . . . what?

"Aw, you can't go by tire tracks. That could be anything. SUV, souped-up Camaro, an old clunker Caddy, even. What, uh, did Vickers have to say?"

So he knew that, too. "He didn't offer an opinion," Quinn said. "Just took down the details and warned me to keep my insurance up to date."

"Always good advice."

A dozen snips later, Tony was done. He took a soft bristled brush to the back of Quinn's neck, removed the smock, and after Quinn got out of the chair, spun a push-broom flattened with wear in a quick circuit around the chair's pedestal.

Quinn fished out a ten and a five, then waved away the attempt to make change.

"You're doing all right with that landscaping business, then," Tony said, pocketing the cash.

Quinn had the presence of mind not to show surprise that

the barber knew he had a business. Instead he merely said, "Actually, my father worked the landscaping side of it; I work mostly with stone. You'd be surprised what Californians will pay for an old-looking New England wall."

"I heard millions for the fancier ones," said Tony, fishing for confirmation.

Quinn merely smiled and said, "I'll be selling off the landscaping part."

"Oh?"

"I'm tired of California." Quinn wanted that word out. This was the perfect place to launch the rumor.

"Never been there myself. Took the wife to Vegas once, though."

"How'd you do?"

"Aagh."

Quinn laughed and said, "I've lost my shirt there once or twice myself."

They had something in common, it seemed. The barber warmed to Quinn a little. He cocked his head over his sloping shoulder and said, "So you're thinking of pulling up stakes. Any idea where you'll put 'em back down?"

"I imagine somewhere around here," Quinn said equably. "Know any houses for sale?"

"You're looking for—what? New construction? Because there's a new subdivision going in at the west end that might suit."

Quinn seesawed the palm of his hand in the air. "Something with more character, I think."

Rubbing his cheek thoughtfully with the tips of his fingers, Tony said, "You know what I'd do? I'd go on the Candlelight Tour of upper Main. The houses are open tonight through Tuesday. Check out Hastings House; it's been on the market for a while. The place is maybe older than you're looking for, but it's a local landmark—well, I don't need to tell you that—and it could go cheap. It needs some structural work. Big bucks."

"Thanks for the tip," Quinn said as he shrugged into his

jacket and plucked a brand new ski cap from one of the pockets. "Maybe I'll check it out."

He hiked his knapsack over his shoulder and let himself out of the tiny one-chair shop, stopping to admire the ancient barber pole out front. It was so much a part of the establishment that he'd hardly noticed it on his way inside. The red-and-white-striped icon looked exactly the same as seventeen years earlier, spinning slowly in its glass housing, its motor still whirring along. A barber pole in working order was a rarity; it was probably worth more than the business itself.

Quinn felt yet another twinge of regret. Tony Assorio, no-nonsense barber . . . the shoemaker languishing around the corner . . . the watch repairman, struggling in the shop next to him—all of the shopkeepers were old and gray and all of them were doomed to become mere memories, like the soda fountain that once had served cherry cokes, and the elegant Art Deco theater that someone had hacked into a four-screen multiplex. Throwaway goods and volume discounts, that was the name of the game nowadays. How could the little guy hope to compete?

Maybe Keepsake would be able to hold on to its unique, small-town feel—hadn't Mrs. Dewsbury boasted that they'd recently beat back a Wal-Mart?—but probably it wouldn't. Christ, someone was cramming a subdivision into the west end. Quinn never thought he'd see the day. What next? A theme park?

"Oh, no," said Mrs. Dewsbury later when he mused aloud to her. "We won't get a theme park here. Someone's already beat us to the punch on that one—thank goodness. Can you imagine the traffic?"

Quinn reached down to the top of the ladder for the wire crimper, but, like a surgical nurse in mittens, Mrs. Dewsbury insisted on handing it to him.

"Are you really planning to come back here for good?" she asked as she watched him crimp two wires together in a plastic sleeve.

It was awkward, working with short wires in the small

hole cut into the porch ceiling. And it was finger-freezing cold; he'd hardly had time to adjust to New England's weather. But Quinn's first order of business, cold or no cold, was to get light on the porch. If someone was going to come after him, he was going to have to do it someplace other than at Mrs. Dewsbury's house.

He had to think about how candid he could afford to be with the elderly widow. She was shrewd and she was fearless, but could she hold her tongue?

He decided she could.

"You want the God's honest truth?" he said, gently easing the wires back into the hole ahead of the light fixture. He glanced down at her. She was supporting the back of her neck with gray-mittened hands while she watched him work. Her face had the charming pinkness to it that fair-skinned Yankees, young and old, got when they stood too long on their porches in fifteen-degree temperatures. She looked pleased and satisfied and curious and, yes, she clearly wanted the God's honest truth.

Quinn flattened the collar of the light fixture against the sky-blue tongue-and-groove planks of the porch ceiling. He jammed a fastener into the wood to make it stay, then began screwing it tight. "I have no intention of moving back east," he said simply. "I'm just putting out rumors. I want to see if I can stir things up a little, make people a little nervous."

"Oh. Well . . . pooh, that's disappointing," he heard her say.

"If my father didn't murder Alison," he continued, "then someone else did. I doubt that it was a vagrant. It's too coincidental that some homeless character would have stolen the rope from the potting shed, conveniently implicating a man who happened not to have an alibi for the time of the murder."

He took another screw from his pocket and repeated the routine. "No, I see a deliberate frame-up here. I see someone who knew that my dad always spent Saturday night alone, reading. Someone who knew what he did for a living, and where his tools were stored. Someone local.''

He looked down again. Mrs. Dewsbury was still watching him, still holding the back of her neck with her mittened hands, but her eyes had narrowed in an appraising squint.

"So you think this was all planned beforehand?"

"That's one possibility," he said. "Another is that it was a crime of passion and the murderer was a damned good improviser."

"It's true, you know. Some people are very good under stress," she said in droll agreement.

After a pause, she said, "Tell me. Don't you think Chief Vickers knows more than he was letting on?"

"About . . . ?"

"The windshield, of course. I've been thinking about it, and you're right. He can't be happy that you're back. It always rankled that your father slipped through his fingers; he told me so himself once. It wouldn't surprise me to learn that the chief had someone smash in your windshield."

Quinn was thinking more of the bloodied flowers. "I dunno."

"You need to watch out for him."

Quinn smiled grimly and said, "Okay, I'll bump Vickers up a few slots on the list of Those Who Wish to See Me Dead. How's that?"

"It's not funny."

"No, ma'am."

The last screw slipped through Quinn's numb fingers. He began to climb down the stepladder to retrieve it, but Mrs. Dewsbury insisted on getting it herself. Quinn made himself wait patiently on a rung while she moved the walker to the side, removed a mitten, very slowly got down into a crouch, picked up the screw with an arthritic hand, pulled the walker back to her, and then stood up again.

"Here you are, dear."

He finished the job and they went inside. One chore down, thirty-seven to go, according to the list that Quinn had put together so far. He had no doubt that the list would get longer before it got shorter. The house was falling apart in a thousand little ways, some of which could lead to disaster. An electrical short and a subsequent fire, a pitch-dark porch and a nimble arsonist. The combinations were endless.

Olivia Bennett had small, slender feet—she was pretty proud of them—but this was ridiculous. There wasn't a foot on the planet that could comfortably fit into the Victorian French-heeled shoe she was trying to wear. The handmade shoe was just one of a vast array of historically accurate reproductions that made up the evening ensemble she had committed to wear in her stint as guide on the Candlelight Tour.

"I feel like Cinderella's evil stepsister," she growled, jamming her foot into the narrow shoe. Which wasn't a shoe anyway—it was an instrument of torture, tight and stiff and with an outrageous tip that surged a good three inches past her big toe.

She threw up her hands in frustration and collapsed back on her white slipcovered tub chair. "I can't do this."

Eileen was standing over her like a maid-in-waiting who wasn't quite sure of her job description. "Maybe you'll get used to them. Try standing up."

"It's this *stupid* corset!" Olivia said suddenly, grabbing at the stiff, steel-boned vise that was responsible for her current Barbie-doll look. "What was I *thinking*?"

"What did you expect? It's French."

"Well, screw the French! I'm not wearing it!" She began tearing at the half-dozen front hooks with a viciousness that she normally reserved for pickle jars.

"Hold it right there, *mademoiselle. You're* the one who talked all the guides into wearing period getups."

Olivia sighed and tucked one of the wandering bust enhancers back into place. Her wool drawers itched. Her chemise was too tight. The petticoats were heavy. But Eileen was right—dressing for the period had been her idea.

"Bustle, please," she said grimly.

Eileen let out a little sigh of sympathy.

After some fumbling, they belted the elaborate wire

framework onto Olivia's behind. Feeling like a bronco saddled for the first time, she resisted the urge to try to kick the thing off and said through gritted teeth, "Okay—the gown."

Eileen's response was a radiant smile. "This will make it all worthwhile." She fished the padded hanger out of the taffeta gown and slipped the dress over Olivia's upraised arms. Olivia disappeared in a swishy cloud of scarlet iridescence, then emerged from a low-cut bodice that was unquestionably more European than American.

The color scheme was as bold as the plunge of the neckline: a swath of bright scarlet draped up toward the outlandish bustle to reveal a purple skirt beneath, with silver-gray passementerie looped around the cuffs, the bodice, and the hem. The heavily beaded braid caught and refracted the light from the recessed spotlight above, rimming Olivia in glittering highlights.

Eileen stepped back with a startled look. "My goodness, that's daring."

"Oh, I don't know. The only thing daring about this outfit is the crotchless drawers," Olivia said, squirming in annoyance. "It's December, for pity's sake. These damn things give a whole new meaning to the expression 'freezing your buns off.' "

Laughing, Eileen said, "Well, think about it. How on earth would anyone go potty, once she was rigged in that getup?"

"Trust me, I don't intend to find out. Start buttoning; I've got to be there in half an hour. Thank God women from that era didn't go in for makeup. I'd be pummeling herbal extracts into a pot of rouge about now."

"All right, here we go. Suck it in, Miss Bennett."

Several painful moments later, Olivia was tightly skinned in scarlet. She had achieved the desired hourglass shape at last. The curves she exhibited, though not her own, were definitely spectacular.

She said in a breathless gasp, "I think I'm going to pass out."

"The things we do for love," Eileen said, amused. "Honestly, I wish we'd featured you like that on the flyers we posted around town. The Keepsake Preservation Society would be rolling in dough after this fund-raiser."

"Shoes! What do I do about shoes? Even assuming I could take more pain, I'd fall and break my neck if I went wearing these in the snow." Olivia kicked them off, furious for ever agreeing to be part of the Candlelight Tour. It would have been better to write out a check. She had inventory to stock, she had orders to place—what was she doing pointing out crown moldings and fruitwood étagères to the hoi polloi?

Volunteering seemed like *such* a better idea at the time.

Swishing over to her closet, she yanked open a white louvred door and pointed to the shoerack on the floor. "Take out the black Reeboks for me, would you?"

Eileen was scandalized, but she did as she was commanded, even tying the laces for her immobilized sister-in-law.

"All right, let's see what it all looks like," said Olivia, striding over to the full-length mirror.

"Smaller steps! Smaller steps! Your sneakers show."

They stood together in front of the mirror, these two best friends turned relatives: Eileen, tall and thin and blond and oh-so-Connecticut; and Olivia, shorter, darker, and somehow, despite the elegance of her wardrobe, just a little bit gypsy. Olivia was very conscious of the contrast. She wasn't especially bothered by it—she looked vaguely like her mother, whom she had always considered truly beautiful—but she was definitely aware that she did not have "the look."

She shrugged and said, "I guess I'll do."

"Do? You look fabulous," Eileen insisted. "That creamy skin, those natural curls, those bedroom eyes—what man could resist you?"

"Apparently they make the effort," Olivia said dryly.

"It's your fault. Why do you go everywhere with Eric on your arm?"

"Eric is very presentable."

"Eric is gay!"

"My mother likes Eric."

"What mother wouldn't? But it's keeping you from meeting the man of your dreams."

"I don't dream about men, I dream about fabric." Olivia frowned in the mirror, then grabbed a tube of lipstick from her dresser and ran it lightly across her lips.

"Okay, I'm ready," she declared. "Point me to the drawing room."

Four

Hastings House was built in high Victorian style for a man who, quite simply, loved wood. In 1882, Mr. Latimer Hastings bought a lumberyard just to have first crack at the boards, then spent the next two years in close company with an architect and a construction crew, milling, shaping, and carving those boards for his house on upper Main. The house became an obsession, and more: It became his reason to exist. It wrecked his marriage, it alienated the neighbors, and ultimately it became a bone of contention between his heirs.

It was a nightmare to maintain, with its curved piazza and its multigabled roofline, but it was something, really something, to see. Keepsake was nearly as proud of Hastings House as it was of the Bennett estate, higher up the hill. Most people knew they'd never get the chance to poke their noses in the Bennetts' dining room; but this year they could get a fairly good idea, for a mere four dollars, of how the Bennetts' dinner guests lived.

So they paid and they poked. Despite the biting cold and windy weather, the Candlelight Tour was enjoying an excellent turnout. Keepsake was a historic town with an active Historical Society backed by a mayor who understood the dollar value of tourism. Besides, the cause was worthy: The proceeds of the Candlelight Tour were split between St. Swithin's soup kitchen and free art courses for Keepsake's children.

Olivia felt at home in the heavily carved, overly ornate drawing room of Hastings House; when she was growing up she'd been a guest there many times. Standing straight as a board (she had no choice) near a crackling fire, she greeted each new visitor on the tour as graciously as Mrs. Hastings herself might have done before dumping her husband for another man with a simpler house.

It was fun. Olivia hadn't expected to enjoy playing the part of a Victorian socialite, and yet here she was, flirting and having a great time. *Playing* at flirting, anyway. The pain of being laced into a state of dizziness had ebbed, replaced by the novelty of being the object of men's gapes and women's furtive looks. It was definitely a first for her.

"Either I've just discovered my true calling as an actress, or there's something to this corset business," she said, laughing, after two women she knew well expressed open amazement at the difference in her demeanor.

The women wandered out and another group wandered in: Eric and several of his pals, all of them history and architecture buffs. Olivia knew that one of them was an actor, so she poured it on, hamming it up outrageously until the men moved on, still laughing, to the next room.

And then there was a lull.

Quinn had heard voices in the room ahead of him—several men and a woman—who sounded as if they were having a damn good time. He was jealous; it had been a while since he'd laughed out loud. But by the time he escaped the clutches of the Victorian gentleman whose job it was to explain the Victorian library, the group had left the drawing room, taking their raucous laughter with them.

They left behind them a woman.

Her back was to Quinn, whose first impression was of a mountain of scarlet material bunched on top of a purple skirt. He saw that she wasn't tall, and yet her posture somehow made her seem so. She had dark hair, tied in a knot at the nape of her neck—without much success, Quinn could see; ringlets seemed to be escaping even as he stood unnoticed behind her.

She was standing in front of the fire with her hands extended to catch its warmth. He couldn't blame her for feeling cold: Her back and shoulders were as bare as any red-blooded man could hope for. The sight of her had sent his genitals lurching beneath his corduroys, and almost immediately he realized why.

She had the most impossibly beautiful figure he'd ever seen. He had no idea that in an age of protein and aerobics, women could still look like that: beautiful back and shoulders, tiny, *tiny* waist, flared and intriguing hips. It was an old-fashioned fantasy, a heart-wrecking dream—and it was as erotic as all hell. He might have stood gazing at that hourglass shape forever if she hadn't turned around with a start.

"Oh, I'm sorry; I didn't hear anyone come—Quinn?"

He blinked. He knew the voice, knew the eyes, he definitely knew the voice . . . He blinked again in disbelief. In a moment of complete, humiliating weakness his let his gaze drop down to her cleavage. Was it possible?

"Liv?"

"Who else?" she said, with a wary smile. "You look the same."

"You don't," he said, stunned.

A couple walked in just then with questions poised: Was the price firm? Would the owner take financing? Had he had any offers? Olivia explained with dazzling grace that she was not the realtor—Jesus, did she *look* like a realtor?—and then the couple left.

Olivia turned her dark-eyed gaze back to Quinn. "I heard you were back. Somehow I didn't expect to run into you here, though."

He took it possibly the wrong way. "Yeah, well, you know how it is when you throw an open house. Riffraff's bound to get in."

"Oh no! Is *he* here?" she said, rolling her eyes.

He chuckled. "Okay, I suppose I deserved that."

She shook her head. "You *haven't* changed, have you? I'm . . . I'm sorry about your father," she added. "I know how close you were."

Sympathy from a Bennett? No thanks; it felt too much like pity. "We did all right," he said, "once we got out of Keepsake. We had a good life."

"Yours isn't over."

"His is."

"Yes, but you said . . . Well, I'm glad it worked out. It was an awkward time."

"Awkward?"

"That's the wrong word," she said quickly. "It was . . . horrible, I guess I mean. For everyone."

"So people keep telling me. A girl is killed, my father is blamed, our lives are upended, and what do I hear? I'm the Grinch Who Stole Homecoming."

"Well, in all honesty, we haven't come even *close* to a championship since," she said with a bland look.

He snorted. He remembered that about her now—her irreverent sense of humor. She was much less straightlaced than the rest of her clan, and that always had made her an interesting opponent. He jammed his hands in his parka pockets and rocked back on his heels. "So. Which of the Ivy League schools ended up rolling out the thickest red carpet?"

Smiling at the compliment, she said, "I decided to go with Harvard."

He waved a hand airily at her getup. "And this would be—what? A part-time job to pay off your student loans?" he quipped, fighting hard not to resent her. *Harvard.*

He watched her flinch and then recover. "As it turns out, my dad was able to scrape together the tuition. But I did borrow money to get my MBA. Is that any comfort?"

"Not much," he said through a tight smile. "So what *do* you do to pay the mortgage?"

"I own a shop in town, Miracourt . . . on York Street? I sell high-end fabrics—interior, and some apparel."

He nodded. "Oh, well sure, a fabric store. It's logical,

with your father owning a textile mill and all."

"My father has nothing to with Miracourt!" she said sharply. "It's entirely mine, bought and paid for with my own money."

How wearying, he thought: an heiress who insisted on making her own way. Not him. If someone had been willing to hand him a fortune, he'd have been more than willing to spend it.

In the next breath she confessed, "I do have another, larger store—a mill-end outlet—that my father *is* involved with."

Even more wearying: an heiress who was conflicted about her family's wealth.

A new batch of visitors, awed and deferential, tiptoed in behind him and began to ask questions in hushed, respectful voices.

It's someone's front room, folks, not the Vatican, Quinn wanted to say, but he, too, was affected by the somber personality of the place, so he took himself over to the balsam Christmas tree that presided over the other end of the room and spent some time inhaling its fragrance while Olivia fielded inquiries.

He overheard all kinds of illuminating tidbits from her about pocket doors, Austrian chandeliers, coffered ceilings, and imported delft tiles, but mostly it was the sound of her voice that kept him rooted to the spot. He loved hearing it, loved the way it spoke in whole sentences free of Valley-speak and New Age clichés. It had an old-fashioned, finishing-school ring to it that blended perfectly with the scarlet gown.

And her laugh! It was the burbling of a brook, flowing and tinkling along its banks but never overrunning them. All in all, he was mesmerized. He felt like some lowborn character—who was it, Heathcliff?—in an English novel. He wasn't sure if he had the era or even the character right, but he damn well had the mood right. He felt . . . unequal, to all this. As if he were there, cap in hand, to announce to madame that her carriage was ready.

And, boy, it pissed him off.

The visitors moved on and he moved back in, reclaiming his right to converse with the Princess. He'd paid his four bucks. He was entitled.

"What about you, Quinn?" she said, turning her attention right back to him. "Where did you end up getting your degree?"

If he'd needed a splash of cold water, that was it. "A degree?" He said wryly, "I decided to pass."

Clearly she didn't get it. "Are you serious? You could've pursued any kind of scholarship you wanted. Academic, athletic . . . *Notre Dame* came looking for you!"

"Did they? Well, they never found me and neither did anyone else. But then, that would be the whole point of living in hiding, wouldn't it?"

Chastised, she lowered her gaze from his and said simply, "Yes."

He felt like a shit, beating her over the head with his unrealized promise. He was doing it because he knew that, more than anyone else, she would feel the waste of it.

Apparently he was right. Her head came back up and she looked him in the eye and said, "You didn't *have* to run, Quinn. You ended up throwing it all away, didn't you? College, a career, inevitable prestige. You could have done anything you wanted to do, been anything you wanted to be."

"Maybe I wanted to be a fugitive," he said coldly.

"But you weren't a fugitive. You were a fugitive's son. That wasn't as glamorous, surely?"

He remembered now that she had a damn sharp tongue. Annoyed, he said, "If I'd been after glamor, I would have gone to L.A."

"What *were* you after? I've always wondered. Fame wasn't enough? You had to turn it on its head and go for infamy, too?"

"What the hell is that to you?" he countered, amazed at her bluntness.

"I'll tell you what it is to me. I grew up with you, Quinn. I thought we were friends."

"Friends? Isn't that pushing it a little?"

"All right," she said, coloring. "Intellectual comrades, then. Call it what you like. I can't tell you how shocked I was to learn—from the police swarming our grounds, no less!—that you had run off. Without saying boo, without a note, without a hint. I was so dismayed . . . so hurt . . ."

"Christ, it's always about you, isn't it?" he said, remembering that as well. "You know what? I was wrong. *You* haven't changed, either. You—"

"Hiii," Olivia said suddenly to a couple entering the room with their teenage son. "Welcome to Hastings House."

Too late. The group knew they'd strolled into a fight, and no bright smile could hide the fact. The parents walked quickly through the room and then out. Their kid took a little longer, slowing down long enough to steal a burning look at Olivia's breasts.

The boy reminded Quinn of himself just minutes earlier. Quinn had acted like a hormonal jerk then, and for all he knew, he was doing it still. It wasn't Olivia's fault that he had cut and run. And it wasn't her fault that she couldn't understand why. Their lives were night-and-day different. No mother, timid father, nomadic lifestyle, never a mattress to call one's own—these were alien concepts to a woman raised in the lap of luxury by a doting mom and a powerful dad.

Let it go, Quinn. Different worlds. Let it go.

"Look . . . what's done is done. Water under the bridge," he said gruffly. "Maybe we . . . well. Good night." He turned to leave.

No, goddammit. He didn't have to run anymore, least of all from her.

He spun on his heel and faced her again. She looked completely bewildered, which gave him back the advantage. With a smile that he knew women considered disarming, he said, "You're not married, are you?"

"No!"

"Why don't we have dinner? You can fill me in on the last half of your life."

"Dinner? *Huh.* Dinner. That would be rather—"

"Quaint?" he suggested, an edge in his voice.

"I was about to say, that would be rather nice," she said, snapping open her fan, "except that I have to be here tomorrow night."

"Ah," he replied, somewhat sheepishly.

She seemed agitated, fanning herself with quick little strokes. Intrigued, he waited to see what she would do next.

"Why don't we have lunch?" she asked with a brittle smile. "I could get away then."

"Fine," he drawled, making a victory fist in his pocket. "We'll do lunch."

He left, taking most of Olivia's wits with him. The encounter with Quinn Leary had left her completely unnerved. Her heart was hammering, her knees were shaking, and inside she was hot, hot, hot—hot enough that she found herself feeling downright grateful for the cold draft that wended its way from the front door and up her gown, fanning those oddly made drawers of hers.

Oh, wow, this is unreal, she told herself. *This is not normal.* No man had ever affected her the way Quinn had just then. Flirting was one thing, banter another, but this was new, this was completely new. . . .

She began to pace the length of the drawing room, trying to work out the tension she felt. In a reverie of wonder, she tapped her closed fan on the palm of her hand and shook her head as she marched up, then down, the parquet floor, ignoring the visitors who wandered through. The tourists assumed she was playing the role of a character from a Victorian novel, but the tourists were wrong.

I don't have time for someone like him. I don't even have the inclination for someone like him. He's too proud, too prickly, too—much too—controversial. What would Mother and Dad say? They'd be appalled to have a Leary rubbed in their noses again.

Seventeen years. Olivia remembered rushing home after the news of Alison's death and finding her mother sitting alone on the sofa and sobbing. Teresa Bennett, being a Bennett, had quickly wiped her eyes as soon as she saw her daughter. But Olivia, who wanted so badly to hold and be held, had blurted out, "She didn't deserve to die; she never hurt anyone," and burst into tears for her cousin, and then she and her mother had hugged and cried some more, but in secret—because wailing was not allowed in the Bennett household.

The sad thing was, by the time of Alison's murder, Owen Bennett had had little contact with Alison's father Rupert. Olivia didn't know why the brothers had drifted so far apart, and she'd never dared ask. Olivia's father had bought out her Uncle Rupert's interest in the mill, that much she knew. But she'd always had the feeling that there was more to the split than a difference in business philosophies.

In any case, the attendance of Owen and his family at Alison's funeral did nothing to breech the growing rift between brothers. After the murder, the rift became as wide as a canyon and stayed that way.

Olivia pushed away all of the memories; all of them were bad. No, Quinn was out of the question. He was too bound up with the worst period of her family's life for Olivia ever to be able to take him seriously. True, there was that box of stuff she'd been keeping all these years. But after she returned it to Quinn, that was it. The town could deal with him any way it liked; it had nothing to do with her.

"Are these parquet squares the kind you buy at Home Depot?"

Olivia turned to the young couple who were linked arm in arm and studying the drawing room floor. "No," she said with a gracious smile, "they're Burma teak, and their value is priceless."

Quinn drove home in a state of near bliss. He'd gone on the Candlelight Tour for no other reason than to keep a high profile, and he'd come away with a date with the Princess.

Socially speaking, of course, he was a frog. He knew it, and it made the promise of taking her out all the more gratifying. Dating Olivia was something he never would have dared try back in high school, which was undoubtedly the reason he had enjoyed trouncing her in the classroom every chance he got. He had enjoyed it even more than trouncing her brother on the field.

But it was all such kid stuff. What a jerk he used to be. He laughed softly to himself as he drove his repaired rental past St. Swithin's Church, past the bank, past Town Hill with its lit-up tree. *Had* he grown up? He hoped so. He hoped that his reason for wanting to be seen in Keepsake with Olivia on his arm was not because she was a royal and he was a commoner, but because she was smart and funny and, okay, knock-down gorgeous.

But he really wasn't sure.

At three in the morning, Father Tom was lying in bed with a brutal case of heartburn. He shouldn't have done it; shouldn't have had the blessed beer with his pepperoni pizza. He had yielded to temptation, and now the devil was claiming his due. The priest shifted onto his side, prompting an ineffectual burp.

It tasted like popcorn. Another temptation yielded to, but who could watch a videotape of *Mystery!* without popcorn? It wouldn't have been right. The priest sighed and sat up, swinging his legs over the side of his bed. The two antacids he'd popped into his mouth before lying down for the night hadn't done a thing; maybe Pepto would help. He reached for his flannel robe and slipped into his sheepskin slippers, then padded sleepily down the hall in search of relief.

I'm getting old. Old and soft and lazy.

What kind of example was he setting for his parish? He, the driving force behind St. Swithin's soup kitchen, now had a pot of his own. He patted his belly in disgust. Tomorrow he would walk a mile before mass, and no dessert. And it'd be a cold day in hell before he'd order green peppers on a pepperoni pizza again.

By the glow of the acrylic angel night-light—a present from his grandniece—Father Tom took the bottle of pink liquid from the medicine cabinet, then filled the dosing cup. He downed it the way he used to do his bourbon when he was a young man, tossing it to the back of his throat and swallowing hard.

He washed out the plastic cup and inverted it over the bottle, then returned it to its shelf. And then, because he was loath to lie right down again, he stood a moment at the window of his bathroom and stared out at the lighted Christmas tree on Town Hill. It gave him pleasure to see it—one of the perks, he liked to tell everyone, of having his living quarters within spitting distance of the hill. In summer there was the bandstand; in spring, the Easter-egg hunt. Everything nice about Keepsake happened right across the road from where he lived and served God. (The good Lord willing, he would live through this heartburn to serve Him still.)

Father Tom was about to return to his bedroom down the hall when something . . . something caught his eye that wasn't quite right. The priest had a keen eye for pattern and symmetry. If the candlesticks on the altar weren't exactly equidistant from one another, he'd rearrange them before he could even think of saying Mass. So he knew: something was out of whack.

He stared at the town tree. Yes, there it was, on the left side. Something long and shadowy and unlike anything else on the beribboned tree. How odd. He'd have to take a closer look in the morning. He began to head back to his bedroom, but then, because he was Father Tom and quietly obsessed with maintaining some sense of order in a disorderly universe, he detoured into the front hall and took out his overcoat from the closet there.

He slipped the coat over his robe, then stepped out of the rectory, catching his breath in the cold night air. His slippers dragged on the rock salt spread over the brick path to his residence; he began to walk on tiptoe, trying to minimize the damage to the deerskin soles. He stepped to the sidewalk . . . then to the curb . . . then to the middle of the empty road.

Salt-melted slush oozed through the seams of his slippers the minute he paused.

No matter. Father Tom was oblivious to the wet and the cold as he stared in shock at the effigy hanging by its neck on a length of rope tied to the Christmas tree. The effigy was the biggest ornament on it: a life-sized figure roughly shaped from a pair of stuffed pantyhose, a wig of blond hair, and a varsity jacket from the high school. The jacket bulged grotesquely at the stomach. Even Father Tom understood that the effigy was meant to depict a pregnant student at Keepsake High. A hanged, pregnant student at Keepsake High.

With a groan of dismay, the priest resisted an overwhelming impulse to cut down the figure and instead ran back to the rectory, where he had to look up the number of the chief of police before punching it in with a shaking hand.

God in heaven. God in heaven. Don't let this be so.

It was the most fervent prayer Father Tom had ever sent skyward, and the one most doomed to go unanswered.

Five

"*The straw in* the pantyhose came from the manger. That's what offended me most."

Returning from yet another trip to the hardware store, Quinn walked in on that bizarre remark, made by a priest he remembered vividly from the old days: Father Thomas Tomczek, one of Quinn's biggest fans and an ex-quarterback himself.

Mrs. Dewsbury had set a plate of defrosted Danish on the kitchen table and was shaking her head in distress as she poured coffee into a delicate china cup resting in a matching china saucer. Hostess and guest both saw Quinn at the same time; neither offered a welcoming smile.

Quinn, who'd been feeling pretty good about the lunch date looming on his horizon, automatically toned down his spirits to match their mood. He stuck out his hand to the priest and introduced himself as if they'd never met.

"Son, I may have got old, but I haven't gone senile—yet," the priest said with a wink at Mrs. Dewsbury. "How've you been?"

"Pretty good, Father," he said, which was the truth. He added, "Am I interrupting something?"

The burly, bald priest fixed his pale green gaze on Quinn. "Not at all. You're the reason I'm here."

Quinn didn't like the sound of that. He nodded and pulled up a chair.

"I was telling Mrs. Dewsbury that we had a bit of excitement on Town Hill,'' the priest began, taking up the dainty cup with a ham-sized grip. He sipped and gave Mrs. Dewsbury a thumbs-up with his other hand, then continued. ''Someone hung an effigy of Alison on the town's Christmas tree in the middle of the night. They used a basketball to suggest . . . well, a pregnancy. It was crudely done, but effective.''

Quinn bit off the curse before it passed his lips and confined himself to saying mildly, ''Shouldn't any effigy have been of me? I thought the figure was always of someone hated and despised.''

Father Tom smiled grimly and said, ''True. But this made the same point in a much more sickening way.''

''This makes me so *angry*,'' said Mrs. Dewsbury, banging the table with her teaspoon to show how much. ''It will ruin the holiday for sure.''

''Who knows about it?'' Quinn asked the priest.

''Probably everyone, by now. I called Chief Vickers— who told me it wasn't the first expression of someone's displeasure that you're back,'' the priest added in his laconic way.

''It probably won't be the last,'' Quinn conceded. Mrs. Dewsbury was right: The whole town would be demoralized by the vicious act. Oddly, Quinn felt both admiration and contempt for the brazen perpetrator.

But mostly contempt. ''It seems to me that whoever did it took a ridiculous risk,'' he told the priest.

Father Tom shrugged. ''Why? There's no real law against it. And say someone did catch him in the act—''

''He'd just be stating what a lot of people are thinking. That they'd like me out of their town.'' Quinn sucked in air and blew it out again in thoughtful silence.

The priest helped himself to a prune Danish. ''If you can believe it, they stole the straw for the effigy's stockings from the crêche we set up in front of the church. There was poor baby Jesus, lying in the hard wood manger with nothing to keep him warm. I like to cried when I saw that.''

That was the thing about Father Tom: Despite his formidable size, he could weep over a statue left in the cold. It was the reason why everyone loved him.

"I'll say one thing," the priest added. "Whoever did it had b—nerves of steel."

"Do you have any idea who could be doing these things, Quinn?" the widow asked, looking more tentative than he'd seen her before. "Any idea at all?"

Quinn said with a tight smile, "I don't want to brag, but I can think of a dozen people who'd be happy to heat up the tar, and another dozen who'd be thrilled to carry the feathers."

Despite his concern, the priest was amused enough to chuckle. Not Mrs. Dewsbury. "Quinn Leary, you're coming with me to my son's house for Christmas. You will celebrate the holiday with us—with people who like and respect you."

Quinn couldn't resist a smile. "They don't even know me."

"It doesn't matter." The widow gave Quinn a look of pure affection, then turned to the priest and said, "Father, this man is an angel from heaven. You have no idea. My son adores me—but my son is in finance; hammers and screwdrivers frighten him. Gerald wants to pay handymen to do the work, but he knows I won't accept that. With Quinn, it's different. He makes it easy for me to take advantage of him."

Touched by her declaration, Quinn nonetheless stuck to his guns. Though he would never admit it to the widow, he had no intention of leaving her beloved house unguarded and vulnerable while she was away.

Sensing an opportunity, Father Tom jumped in with an offer of his own. "You're welcome to join us at the church for Christmas dinner, Quinn. You can mash the potatoes, serve 'em, eat 'em, or all three; we don't stand on ceremony. Everyone with nowhere special to go is invited."

Quinn accepted at once. "I'll not only serve dessert, I'll bring dessert," he added. "How many pies you need?"

"Oh, that's not—six would be fine."

"Done," he said with a smile.

He had the perfect excuse to remain behind on Christmas.

Quinn replaced a worn-out faucet and corroded trap in the first-floor bath in plenty of time to shower, slap on some aftershave, and head out to his rendezvous. It would be his most provocative gesture so far: having an elegant lunch in town with one of its best-known citizens. Whoever hated— or feared—Quinn enough to hang an effigy on the town Christmas tree was bound to go apoplectic over that one. Quinn felt grimly satisfied that all was going according to plan.

More or less.

He kept coming back to Olivia. She hadn't been part of his original plan, which was to flush out whoever had the most to lose from seeing him return to Keepsake. Over the years, and especially during the last few weeks, he had thought about Olivia, naturally, but mostly it had been in terms of nostalgia: she'd been part and parcel of his youthful drive to excel.

But last night? Last night he'd been much more focused on her laugh and her eyes and her . . . well, not her IQ, in any case. And today as he ditched his rental in the town parking lot behind the bank, he didn't care if her last name was Bennett or Sinkelheinkenschtein. He simply wanted to be with her again.

He had it all worked out. They would have lunch at Entre Nous, an intimate bistro that had caught Quinn's eye. It was the kind of place you took a woman like Olivia Bennett. They'd linger over a bottle of wine, laugh about the spelling bees, and with any luck he'd line up another date—this time at night, by God.

Whistling a soft tune, he made his way down wet sidewalks and slushy streets until he found her shop. The brick building once had been a single-truck fire station, so it had a funky kind of charm. With its slate roof pitching steeply toward the street and its big front window divided by dozens of small square panes, it looked like something out of a children's fairy tale. Quinn was especially glad to see that they'd kept the original door, carved with the initials K.F.D. in elegant Victorian script.

He pulled open the heavy green door, jangling some bells above it, and stamped his hiking shoes on a mat inside the threshold. There were a couple of customers in the shop, and a fresh young thing cutting material from a bolt of cloth, but . . . no Olivia. It rocked Quinn, the wave of disappointment he felt. Then he spotted her hurrying down a narrow open staircase that ran alongside one wall. She grinned and waved, and like a deep-keeled sailboat that's taken a knockdown, Quinn felt himself righting again. The whole thing couldn't have lasted more than five seconds. He found the intensity of it pretty damn scary.

In the bright sun that poured into Miracourt, Olivia looked night-and-day different than she had in the candlelight of a drawing room—not as overtly seductive, and yet no less appealing. Chalk it up to the fuzzy sweater and flowing skirt she wore, but somehow she seemed more . . . straight up-and-down. More normal, more wholesome, more approachable. Or maybe it was her eyes or the way she smiled. Whatever it was, she looked glad and it made him feel good.

"What do you think?" she asked, turning half way round.

"Very nice indeed," he answered under his breath, and then he realized she meant the shop.

The shop was nice, too. He didn't know much about fabric—zip, to be precise—but he knew enough about rich people's taste to know that the stuff around them appealed to it.

"What does the name mean?" he asked, just to have something to say.

"Miracourt? It's an old-style French bobbin lace—similar to *lille* lace." She batted her eyes and added, "I'm sure that makes it all much clearer to you."

He cocked his head and gave her a penetrating look. "Ohhh, yeah."

One thing Quinn did remember about her: She never lost her cool. And yet here she was, for the second time in twenty-four hours, with heightened color in those nicely shaped cheekbones of hers. Feeling suddenly confident about the prospects for that nighttime date, he murmured, "So—are we all set?"

"Let me get my coat," she said, and off they went.

To the drip-drip-drip of melting snow, they strolled past storefronts decked out for the season, with Olivia grading every window display they stopped to view. "Not enough vertical." "Needs a backdrop." "*Great* use of color."

Window shopping, that's what they were doing. Quinn was utterly charmed by the concept; he'd never done it before. He threw a five-dollar bill into a Salvation Army bucket and thought to himself, *I could get used to this*. He was especially pleased that Olivia was inclined to saunter. That wasn't the drive-ahead girl he remembered at all.

In a merry mood, she reached behind him and gave a little yank on his ponytail. "What's *this* thing all about?" she asked.

And then she slipped her arm through his.

She had Quinn on the ropes. He didn't know which of the hits to respond to first; all he knew was that he never saw them coming. He lied about the ponytail, making something up about a centennial celebration back in California, and as for the arm that was looped through his—he decided simply to savor the heat. So bemused by her was he that he hardly registered the occasional glare aimed his way.

They reached the turnoff for the bistro, but Olivia had other ideas. "That Entre Nous is such a pretentious little place," she said, which naturally made Quinn feel pretentious as well. "Let's grab a couple of deli sandwiches and go back to your car. I have a surprise for you that I think you'll really like."

His disappointment fell away, replaced by curiosity, and he agreed to the terms of her counteroffer. They picked up two monster pastramis on rye and a couple of cartons of milk, then doubled back to the parking lot. He wasn't crazy about driving Olivia around in a lowly pickup truck—hence the choice of a restaurant in town—but she didn't seem to mind.

"Is this the one that got the windshield bashed in?" she asked as she climbed into the passenger seat with their food.

Ah, Keepsake.

"The very same," he said, giving her a bland look. The expression on her face was guileless, but he decided that she was simply a damn good actress. "So. Where to?"

"The gardener's cottage," she answered, breaking into a sudden, broad grin. "I think you know the way."

At first he said nothing. Then, quietly, "You can't be serious."

"Of course I'm serious!" she said, laughing, and then she realized that he had no stomach for going there.

"Quinn, it doesn't look anything like when you and your father lived in it," she said in a more earnest tone. "It's a guest house now. My mother has done it *completely* over. Really, you won't make any associations at all."

Annoyed that she seemed to think he was an emotional wimp, Quinn put the truck in gear and said, "You misunderstand my reluctance. What I mean is, do your parents know you're doing this?"

Even worse. Now it sounded as if he were worried about coming over to play without her parents' permission. Frustrated, he said, "Liv, haven't you noticed? I'm public enemy number one in this town. I'm assuming that your parents are on the long list of people who'd like to see me leave, not the short list of people who're glad to renew an old acquaintance."

"I have no idea how my parents feel," she said, dismissing the subject. "They're not in the habit of saying."

He wasn't surprised; they never *were* in the habit of saying. "You heard about the effigy?"

"Yes, I did. I wasn't going to bring it up."

"Then why did you bring up the windshield?"

"I wanted you to know that I knew. It was less painful to do that with the windshield than with the effigy."

Jesus. Definitely *not* a California girl. Dizzy from breathing the rarefied air of her Yankee scruples, Quinn sighed and said, "All right. We will go to the gar—guest house."

The drive out of town was short; upper Main wasn't that far from the quaint shopping district. The street itself took a sharp turn past a rather grand driveway flanked by two massive granite gateposts—the entrance to the Bennett estate. For reasons he couldn't define, Quinn had so far avoided that end of Main. Hastings House, a block or so down the hill, was the nearest he'd gotten, and even there, Quinn had felt edgy.

Olivia punched in a code and the heavy iron gates that blocked the drive swung slowly open. Quinn drove through them, noting with satisfaction that the landscaping had suffered since his father's tenure. It wasn't so much that the big copper beech was gone—over that, he felt genuine sorrow—as that the grounds simply didn't look loved anymore. Not the way his father had loved them. Francis Leary had been devoted to his job as gardener for the Bennetts; he'd loved every hosta, shrub, and ivy leaf as if it were his own. Like a country doctor, he had felt the need always to be there, which is why he rarely went out on his one day off.

And then came the discovery of Alison in the quarry, and the first round of questions from the police, and the humiliating confrontation between his father and Olivia's father immediately afterward. Quinn could still remember every word of it. There had been no presumption of innocence, no strong expression of support by Owen Bennett; only a cold, seething declaration of shock and anger.

After that came the coup de grâce: Francis Leary was fired. Owen Bennett wanted him and Quinn out of the house within twenty-four hours. Quinn could still see his father standing in the small living room of the cottage with his head bowed, just . . . taking it. Quinn had been so frustrated by his father's meekness that he had charged at Bennett with every intention of knocking him down and killing him, but his father had called him back with a single syllable: "*Son.*"

Such memories consumed Quinn as he parked the truck in front of the cottage that had been built expressly for lucky gardeners to live in. Farther up the winding drive was the main house, blessedly obscured from Quinn's view by a massive bank of rhododendrons. With any luck he'd be able to get in and then out of the cottage without the Bennetts being any the wiser.

Maybe to Olivia the house looked different, but not to Quinn. True, the paint scheme had been changed from a drab gray to a pleasing slate blue with ivory trim and ruby-red shutters. But from the gingerbread gables to the diamond-paned casements, the Hansel and Gretel cottage looked like . . . well, like home. Home before the troubles came and forced them to leave it forever.

"You're very quiet, Quinn, and it's making me nervous," Olivia said as he stared at the impossibly charming house.

Quinn tried to lie himself out of his mood. "I thought I heard a mourning dove calling, and it's way too early in the year—that's all."

Olivia seemed relieved. "Come on in, then. You won't believe what I've got for you." She scrambled out of the front seat and by the time Quinn caught up with her, she had fished a key from her bag and was letting herself in.

She was right: The cottage didn't look or feel or even smell the way he remembered. The plain white walls were gone, and so was the vague but pervasive mustiness. All the dark trim had been painted out, and floral wallpaper made the place look both cozier and yet somehow larger than when he lived there. There was more furniture, much of it rattan and wicker. The lighting was warm and discreet, the refinished floors gleamed like spread honey.

And the smell was downright fragrant: Quinn could swear it was coming from the wallpaper. Whereas before the cottage had had a kind of bland, rental quality to it, now it could probably hold its own in the pages of *House Beautiful*.

Quinn gave the poofy, flouncy fabric over the windows a wary nod and asked, "Your work?"

Olivia laughed and said, "No, my tastes run to simpler treatments than that. But my mother's a big fan of Mario Buatta; she made all her decisions based on his gospel. Lucky for her she comes from a family that can snag deep discounts on fabric."

There were miles of it, florals and stripes and plaids everywhere Quinn looked. To him it was overwhelming, but what did he know? "That easy chair looks familiar," he ventured.

"Well, okay, that *is* from before," Olivia confessed. "It's been slipcovered."

"My dad used to like to read in it," Quinn said quietly. He tried to picture his father sitting in the chintz-covered chair with a book about Frederick Law Olmsted on his lap, but he came up empty. The room belonged to women now.

Quinn turned to Olivia, who was watching him with an intensity that surprised him. Again the color sprang to her cheeks. Again he took heart.

"You're right about this place," he mused. "I feel as if we're standing in some parallel universe. Everything's the same—and yet it's not the same at all." On a whim, he stroked her cheek with the back of his fingers and said softly, "Especially you."

She didn't pull away, but her lashes fluttered down in a gesture that struck him as both shy and seductive at the same time. What was it about her? She was driving him quietly crazy.

She said, "And yet you're just the same as I remember."

Quinn shook his head. "No. Not the same at all. Seventeen years ago, I wouldn't have dared done . . . this," he said, lowering his lips to hers in a kiss. It was lightly given, the kind of kiss a very cool quarterback might give a slightly geeky classmate—but it left Quinn's heart pounding wildly in his chest.

He pulled back, as if he'd got a mild shock, and repeated with wonder, "Not the same at all."

Somehow Olivia didn't seem nearly as self-conscious as he was feeling. Those long, thick eyelashes fluttered back up, revealing eyes that were dark, dancing, forthright. She didn't say a word, only lifted her arms around his neck and pulled him back for another kiss—this one hot, hard, and wet.

Sacked!

But not for long. Still reeling, Quinn felt a rush of testosterone and saw a sudden vision of the end zone in his mind's eye as he caught her in his arms. He was determined to score. His mouth claimed hers with a roughness that was not him, and yet when he felt her gasp, then yield to it, he knew that she was as willing as he was able. He backed her against the sofa and she crumpled into it, lying on her back, legs bent at the knees, her feet on the floor. He fell on top of her as if she were a loose ball that he didn't want anyone else, ever, to possess.

"Liv, Liv, where have you *been*?" he said in a muffled voice as he kissed her throat, nipping, tasting, then soothing with more kisses. He was wild to have her, then, there, anywhere. He gave no more thought to her parents up the hill than he once had to fans in the bleachers; he was focused solely, strictly, and very irrationally, on the soft, sweet-smelling body that was arching restlessly beneath his own. His hand ran up the outside of her leg, but outside of her legs was not where he wanted to be.

Good God, son, what are you doing?

Quinn's head shot up. His father's voice was too loud, too clear, to be ignored. He very nearly said "Dad?" but then he realized it was the house. Chintz or no chintz, the gardener's cottage was so bound up with Francis Leary that part of his soul was still drifting through its rooms.

"Oh, damn," Quinn murmured. He lifted his weight from Olivia and propped himself up on one elbow.

"What?" she said. Her eyes, huge, took on a tragic cast.

"Nothing," he murmured, gently raking her hair away from her face. She was so beautiful, so vulnerable just then.

So utterly seducible. "This is not the best place," he said at last.

"It's fine, sure it is," she argued, still breathless.

He could see streaks of green in her eyes. How had he never noticed before? "You're so beautiful."

She gave him a rueful smile. "I can tell."

"If we were anywhere else . . ." He traced her reddened upper lip with the tip of his finger. "I asked you before if you were married, but . . . are you seeing someone?"

"Seeing someone?" she said, a little blankly. "Do I act as if I am?"

He couldn't believe it. For Olivia Bennett not to be claimed, not to be taken—well, he just couldn't believe his good luck. "Plan to see me, then," he whispered to her. "Often."

She snapped back into focus. "You always were a cocky son of a bitch." The palms of her hands were flat against his chest. She used them to push him away, but not so violently that he had to consider it a rejection. It was more like a gesture of miffedness.

She sat up alongside him and raked her fingers through the curls of her hair—which remained exactly the same as before—and then she straightened her sweater and stood up. "I have absolutely no idea why that happened," she announced.

Oh, yes; definitely miffed. Quinn refrained from reminding her that she was the one who had trumped his kiss with one that had left them both senseless. He said with a shrug, "I assume you have to beat men off with a stick every day."

Her response to that was a wry smile, but he could see that her humor had improved. "C'mon," she told him, taking his hands in hers and pulling him up from the sofa. "I promised you a surprise."

"And, boy, I got one."

"Not that, dope." She began pulling him toward the bedroom, the bedroom that used to be his.

Flirt, imp, _femme fatale_—she was all of those and yet none of those. Completely bemused now, Quinn let her drag him along. One thought, and one thought only, possessed him: *If I can just channel all that energy of hers into sex, somewhere safe . . .*

"Surprise!" she cried, gesturing toward a three-board bench at the foot of the bed.

He stared at the bench in a state of amazement. There, polished to sunshine brightness, was arrayed every trophy and citation he'd ever won. His father had cherished them until their nighttime flight out of Keepsake, and Olivia apparently had appointed herself keeper of the flame. Quinn hadn't thought about the awards in seventeen years. Now, here they all were, lined up like golden ghosts to mock his thwarted ambitions:

STATE ALL-STAR FOOTBALL TEAM
CHAMPION DEBATE TEAM
STATE ALL-STAR FOOTBALL TEAM
FOR HIGHEST ACHIEVEMENT IN MATH
MVP, KEEPSAKE COUGARS
MVP, KEEPSAKE COUGARS
DISTINGUISHED ACHIEVEMENT,
LATIN STUDIES

"Pretty impressive," she said, beaming.

"Uh-huh."

Quinn picked up the biggest trophy, an ungainly, gaudy tribute to his prowess in Latin, of all things. He'd taken the course as an extracurricular activity because he thought it would help him in law school. But that was before he became disillusioned with the concept of due process.

He put the trophy back down and glanced at Olivia, who was standing alongside him with a proud look on her face, her arms folded across her chest in a self-satisfied way that he remembered well.

"So," he said, turning his back on the bench, the bed, and her. "Wanna have those sandwiches now?"

Six

"*Exhume her? Are* you insane?"

Quinn Leary sat in Chief Vickers's office with thighs apart, his fingertips making contact across the divide there. His broad shoulders hulked forward in a relaxed, almost insolent way as he contemplated the dumbfounded police chief. Quinn wasn't exactly enjoying the encounter, but he wasn't exactly in pain.

"It seems like the obvious solution. They say my father murdered Alison because she was carrying his baby and had threatened to tell the Bennetts. I say that's horseshit. A DNA test ought to settle the matter once and for all."

He reached into his pocket and came up with a plastic film canister that he tossed on the police chief's desk. "Here. A snip of my father's hair. I can tell you where to find more," he said dryly, "if you need to verify that it's his. The sooner we resolve this, the better. I plan to stay in Keepsake awhile, and—let's face it—you can't afford too many more episodes like those trashed trophies. Sooner or later, someone is going to get hurt."

Vickers barely glanced at the container. "Who told you about the trophy case? We're not letting that out."

Quinn shrugged. "It's a small town."

Someone had broken into Keepsake High and spray-painted all the football trophies in the trophy case. Worse, they'd smashed in all the team photos, many of them signed. Quinn had heard it from Mrs. Dewsbury, who had heard it from the janitor's sister—but Vickers didn't need to know that.

The chief rocked back in his chair. After a thoughtful pause, he said, "What do you really want, Quinn? Why are you here?"

Quinn nodded at the container sitting on the desk blotter. "I told you: to clear my father's name."

"What difference does it make? He's dead."

"It makes a difference," Quinn said, almost wearily. "You're a son. You're a father. How can you not get it?"

"Suppose we leave my family out of this."

The chief's son Kurt had been one of Quinn's teammates: a fullback with good potential but with a chronic need to walk on the wild side. Quinn had heard (again from Mrs. Dewsbury) that after he and his dad left Keepsake, Kurt Vickers had turned from alcohol to serious drugs—another casualty blamed on Quinn. The list kept getting longer.

Quinn said, "How do I make my request official?"

The chief snorted. "Not by bringing it here. Take it to the D.A. if you feel a burning need."

Quinn stood up and took the plastic container back. "Okay. That's what I'll do."

He was halfway out the door when Vickers said, "Francis Leary did it, Quinn. You just can't bring yourself to believe it, that's all. But the evidence is there. Alison confided to a friend that she thought your father was a hunk. He was seen staring at her just a little too keenly. The rope that hanged her came from his potting shed. Fibers from it were found in his truck. No one could corroborate his alibi for the time of death. And last of all, he ran. Innocent men don't run."

"I repeat: *horseshit*. That's not even decent circumstantial evidence, and you know it."

The two men locked gazes. Pete Vickers, lifelong townie, son of a policeman, father of a drug addict, the only active member of a police detail that would never live down the Keystone Kops reputation that Quinn's father had foisted on them—and Quinn himself, first stirring the pot, now lighting the fire beneath it.

Vickers spoke first. "Go to hell."

Quinn's eyebrows lifted in tacit acknowledgment that he might be headed that way. He sighed and said, "See you around, Chief," and walked past the dispatcher's desk and out to his truck.

"I'll never be able to eat pastrami again," Olivia told Eileen over drinks on Saturday. "It was unbearable, sitting on the front seat of his truck and trying to chew."

"And he didn't take his trophies, after all that?"

"No," said Olivia glumly. "I went back yesterday and boxed them all up again."

She was still traumatized by the disastrous date. What had happened? She'd spent the last day and a half trying to figure it out. This much she knew: She was deeply attracted to Quinn, and he had seemed just as interested in her.

"Almost as interested, anyway," she said. "There was incredible electricity. It started at Hastings House . . . the way he just *looked* at me!"

"The corset," Eileen said as she tore Boston lettuce into a salad bowl.

"That's what I thought, too, at the time. I mean, really, what was not to like? He'd have to have been married, buried, or holy not to react. But the next day—you know what I wear to work—he was just as interested, if not more. Eileen, I'm telling you, something clicked. I don't remember ever enjoying myself as much with a man. Or as briefly, dammit."

"I'm telling you, blame it on the corset."

"No; blame it on kismet." Olivia slid off the island stool in her sister-in-law's designer kitchen and ambled over to the Sub-Zero fridge.

"When we were strolling down Main," she said thoughtfully, "something changed in my life. I've never felt it before. It was like . . . what was it like? Like I was a lock, and someone was turning a key in me." She smiled a faraway smile as she poured more tonic over her gin. She could still feel his arm linked through hers, still see the dimple on the right side of his face when he grinned.

Oddly enough, she couldn't remember much about the episode on the sofa. That part she had pretty much blocked out. "Probably because it was Quinn who called a stop to it," she explained, "and not me."

"Men don't normally do stuff like that."

"Well! Consider where we were."

"True. Can you imagine the look on Rand's face if he'd walked in on you? Or your father?"

Olivia shuddered, then bumped the fridge closed with her rear end. "It could easily have happened. I never thought to lock the front door. Thank God one of us had some sense. But I really believe that Quinn had other reasons for backing off—his father, for one."

"They were that close? Here, do the carrots."

"Very close. Which is surprising, considering that—except for being good-looking—they were nothing alike." Olivia rifled through a drawer and came up with a peeler, then pulled a carrot from the plastic bag waiting on the marble-topped island. "Francis Leary was a very quiet, very timid man. He was always hanging back in the shadows, although I think he never missed a thing. Actually, he—"

She decided not to finish the thought, but Eileen knew her too well. "Problem?"

Olivia focused on her peeling. "I feel guilty admitting it, but . . . Mr. Leary used to make me uncomfortable. I suppose it's because I always feel hopelessly overbearing around shy people like him."

"Overbearing—you?" said Eileen, sprinkling raisins like fairy dust over the salad.

Olivia laughed, then threw a carrot peeling at her. "We can't all be the perfect balance of grace and restraint that you are."

Eileen lifted the peeling from the bib of her apron and dropped it on the others. "Which is why I refuse to get into a food fight with you, missy. I could never win."

They laughed together over the prospect of Eileen—Eileen!—hurling food in her immaculate, ultramodern kitchen, then wandered into a discussion of the pros and cons of marble versus granite counters before coming back, inevitably, to Quinn Leary and why he was in Keepsake.

"He's here because of his father, I'm sure of it," Olivia said. "I think he wants to vindicate him."

"And how would he do that?"

"I haven't a clue."

Eileen had heard about the effigy, of course. "I wonder how many shoes can fall before Quinn decides he's had enough and leaves."

"Don't say that! I . . . I don't want him to," Olivia admitted. "Not yet." She took out eight platters from the birch cabinet. "Where are we eating? Dining or kitchen?"

"Dining, I think; those Chinese-red walls are so appropriate this time of year. We'll dress the table with the white poinsettias. Tell me this: What would you do if Quinn did pull up stakes and leave?"

"Hey! Bite your tongue."

"Interesting." Eileen pulled down the oven door of her Viking range. "You know what?" she said, peering at the thermometer stuck in the leg of lamb. "You sound a little desperate."

"Desperate! *Me*?"

Eileen closed the door, stood up, and looked Olivia in the eye. "It's Saturday night and you're eating dinner with us. You do it often. Does that tell you something?"

"Hey! I've been *busy*. Two stores . . . who's got time for the singles—"

"Hi-dee-ho, ladies." It was Rand, entering the kitchen from the adjacent three-bay garage.

Olivia turned to her sister-in-law. "Not a word," she whispered with a fierce look.

It was an unnecessary warning. Insulted, Eileen pinched her arm lightly as she passed on the way to relieve Rand of his cashmere muffler and suede jacket.

Pecking his wife's cheek, Rand said, "Something smells good."

"Tarragon leg of lamb. Because I love you so madly."

He laughed at that and said, "You know you're the only dish for me."

"You're in a good mood," Olivia said on her way out to the dining room. She was relieved to see it; maybe he was finally done sulking over Quinn's return.

"Am I? Why so many plates?" he asked his twin sister as she passed under his nose.

"Mom and Dad."

"Oh, hell. *Why?*"

"You know why," said Eileen, sounding resigned. "To go over the plans, one more time, for the New Year's gala."

"Oh, great. And while you three women are trying to decide which napkins to use, I'll be stuck with Dad in the den. Just what I need. He's bound to grill me about the tax-break negotiations. Don't I get enough of him at the mill all week? Is it too much to ask to spend the weekend in peace? I need a drink," he said, heading for the wet bar.

"Oh, it won't be as bad as all that," said Eileen in her reassuring way. "You have lots of time before the council votes."

"How do you figure? Dad's on the phone with Mexico every day. I think he's as much as made up his mind to move the mill out of Keepsake. The more the council dithers up here, the more likely it is that Dad's going to make a commitment down there. Then what? I don't want to live in Mexico. Do you?"

Eileen smiled and said reassuringly, "He'd never do that."

But Eileen didn't know Owen Bennett, not the way his daughter and son did. Olivia and Rand exchanged one of their shorthand looks. Olivia said, "He wants to keep the mill up here tax-free. Keepsake doesn't feel it can afford to do that."

"Keepsake can't afford *not* to do that," Eileen pointed

out. "Owen's the biggest employer in town. He's the *only* employer in town."

"Let's not forget the superstores," Rand said with obvious irony as he poured scotch over his ice. "Every day more jobs are moving into the area—so the council keeps reminding me."

"Not jobs that can support a family," his wife retorted. "Your father pays twice the wage that they do."

"Which is, of course, the problem," Olivia said. "He needs to stay competitive or he'll go under. I can sympathize with him," she added grudgingly, even though she didn't approve of her father's hardball tactics.

"He's got to demand less from Keepsake," her brother said before slugging down a good part of his drink. "It's no picnic going out there and trying to make his case."

"Of course not," Olivia said. "You're the bad cop. Dad's the good cop. When he thinks the time is right, he'll cut his demand by half and end up a local hero."

"Which leaves me what? The local villain? Sorry," Rand said bitterly. "Been there. Done that."

It was an unmistakable allusion to the stupid, irrelevant, lost championship that seemed so much on everyone's minds again.

For one brilliant year it had all seemed to be coming together, and Keepsake had come down with a case of football fever the likes of which it had never known before or since. Everyone from the busboys at Jasper's to the nuns at St. Swithin's had joined forces and rallied around the Cougars.

But it all fell apart after Quinn ran away and Rand took over and dropped the ball—many times. The plain truth was, Rand had never been a very good quarterback, and after Quinn, he looked even worse. The season had ended up a disaster. There was no point in trying to deny the fact, so Olivia left the soothing to Eileen while she set the dining room table.

Part of her felt genuinely sorry for Rand. He'd never be able to crawl out from under the burden of the town's long memory, and it didn't help his mood lately that her father really did seem to be making Rand the heavy: variance requests, DEM warnings, OSHA inspections—all of was being dumped on the huge walnut desk in Rand's big office.

Poetic justice? Olivia wanted to think so. She had put herself through a year of graduate school in preparation for a job of real responsibility in the mill, and look what had happened: Rand, who coasted to a bachelor's degree from Yale with gentlemen's C's, was made vice president of mill operations while Olivia, who graduated magna cum laude with an MBA from Harvard, was offered nothing at all.

And why? Because her father was convinced that she was going to fall in love, get married, and start nesting, leaving him in the lurch. Olivia was offended, she was angry, and she let her father know it in a way that left the two of them estranged for almost a year.

Her decision to start up Miracourt right under her father's nose had been made mostly out of spite, although she'd ended up truly loving the shop and was planning to open another branch nearer the city. Recently she and her father were getting along well enough to start up the outlet venture together, but even there . . .

We'll never be close, not really. Not as long as he continues to believe the sun rises and sets on his number-one son.

Olivia sighed as she set out the silverware with scientific precision. She was prepared to work twice as hard as her brother to prove herself—but it would be nice if she could do it without getting an ulcer or giving up men.

Her thoughts rushed back to Quinn and were still lingering there when the doorbell rang: Her parents had arrived.

From upstairs she heard her niece shriek, "Grammy, Grampy!" and then the thunderous race down the steps between her and Zack for the front door.

Olivia popped her head around the corner to greet the arrivals, both of them hard-pressed to take off their coats because their grandchildren were hanging on like lemurs.

Kristin wanted hugs and kisses and Zack wanted his grandfather to play Nintendo.

"Not now, Zack!" said Owen Bennett, shooing him away.

Poor Zack was crushed; his grandfather never missed a chance to take him on in friendly, if fierce, competition.

Olivia glanced at her mother, whose hugs were being handed out with less than her usual abandon. She recognized the signs at once: Teresa Bennett was in tiptoe mode.

Uh-oh. Now what?

"Dad?" she said, giving him a quizzical look.

Behind him her mother shook her head in warning, then said to the children, "Well? Isn't anyone going to show me the latest Beanie Babies?"

Zack and Kristin, easily distracted, dragged her upstairs, leaving Olivia to face down her father's wrath.

"I just got off the phone with Pete Vickers," he growled.

"And?"

"For starters, someone's trashed the trophy case in the high school," he said, brushing past her into the kitchen.

Her father wasn't a big man, but wherever he was, he made the room smaller. Even Rand—taller, more hair, three decades younger—seemed diminished by his presence.

Unlike Rand, who was dressed in Paul Stuart elegance from head to tasseled toe, her father preferred more functional wear: polyester pants that kept a crease, a shirt that didn't look stonewashed after half a dozen launderings, and—his one indulgence—a wool sweater from Scotland that would probably last longer than Dolly and all of her clones combined, or he wouldn't have bought it in the first place.

A snappy dresser he was not. And yet no man that Olivia had ever known radiated more authority than Owen Randall Bennett.

Eileen took one look at her father-in-law, spun on her heel, and headed for the wet bar to fix him a drink.

Rand's face was so carefully devoid of expression that

even Olivia couldn't read it. "Did you say someone trashed the trophy case?" he ventured.

"That's exactly what I said. Goddammit, this has gone far enough! I paid for most of those trophies, one way or another. Uniforms, bus trips, the new bleachers—Keepsake wouldn't even *have* a sports program if it weren't for me. I'll have his ass in a sling for this!"

Olivia blinked. "Whose?"

"Leary's, goddammit! None of the vandalism would've happened if *he* hadn't shown up."

Rand was watching his father warily. Eileen was pretending to be in another county. That left Olivia, who was more than willing to carry the banner onto the field.

"That isn't fair, taking out someone's bigotry on Quinn!" she cried, rising up to her full five feet three inches. "I'm tired of—"

"Tired of *what*?" her father interrupted in a dangerous voice.

"Tired of having to repeat the obvious: Quinn didn't break any laws! He was free to stay or to leave back then, and he's free to stay or to—free to stay now. If he wants."

Her father's eyebrows twitched upward, another dangerous sign. "Since when are you his public defender?"

Since he had me flat on my back and I liked it, she thought about saying. But . . . maybe not just then.

"From all I've heard, the man has been been perfectly friendly to everyone he sees," she said. "Mrs. Dewsbury has told half the town that she worships the ground he walks on. He even makes a point of shopping locally for everything. Ask Mike at the hardware store."

Olivia was getting up a head of steam now, and she couldn't resist taking a potshot at her brother. "And another thing that you probably don't know about Quinn: *He* managed to pick himself up by his bootstraps. *He* owns his own business. *He*—"

"Business? He's a stonemason!"

"He's an artist. An architect in stone. You know how much those people make? And anyway, that's beside the point! The point is, he has integrity and ambition and he's the kind of man you'd appreciate if you weren't blinded by the same *stupid* prejudice as whatever idiot is behind these horrible events!''

"I don't care if he owns a fleet of ships and the stars to steer them by," her father said, cutting through the air with the back of his hand. "I want Leary out of Keepsake!"

Olivia planted a fist on each hip. Her chin came up. "Just like that; *you* want Leary out of Keepsake. Who're you, the Sultan of Brunei? Quinn can stay if he wants!"

Too far. She watched her father's face turn a ruddy shade of rage. "Don't even *think* about crossing me on this," he said in a low and dangerous tone.

"Of course I will! You're being ridiculous. This is America. This is *New England*. People here have the freedom to—"

"He wants your cousin exhumed, goddammit!"

He might as well have slapped Olivia in the face. She blinked and shuddered from the blow of his words and then stared speechless as Eileen whispered a pained, "Oh, no," and Rand looked stunned.

"You forced me to this, Olivia," her father said, obviously furious over his own indiscretion. "I haven't said anything to your mother and I don't intend to, so—"

"Oh, he can't *do* that," said his wife from behind him. "It's . . . it's . . . oh, it's *wrong!*"

Everyone turned. Teresa Bennett had come in from the hall and was standing there looking deeply scandalized. Her still-unlined face, so like Olivia's in its expressiveness, was ashen and filled with sympathy for Alison, a niece whom she had loved. Her dark eyes were glazed over with tears, her full lips crumpled with grief and horror.

It's like looking at a medieval painting of Mary mourning her son, Olivia thought, touched by the depth of emotion that she saw in her mother's face.

"It's not going to happen," Owen said gruffly.

"But what if it does? What if it *does*?"

Olivia's father scowled and said, "This is why you

shouldn't have been told." Grudgingly, he went over to his wife and put his arm around her. "Come on. Into the den—where you can compose yourself."

Olivia watched in profound distress as her exasperated father shepherded her mother out of the kitchen.

Teresa Bennett was so unlike her husband that Olivia often wondered how they'd lasted thirty-six years together. Her mother was as soft as her father was hard, as emotional as he was rational, as yielding as he was domineering. It was her mother, never her father, that Olivia ran to when she needed hugs and comfort. If Olivia were ever to find herself in trouble, she could count on her father to find the best lawyer in the country to defend her—but it would be her mother who'd be standing on the other side of the bars with a toothbrush, clean pajamas, and Olivia's favorite pillow.

"Perfect," Rand muttered. He turned around and slammed the flat of his hand on the marble-topped island, sending his wife and his sister jumping back. "That son of a bitch! How *dare* he?"

"You heard Dad," Olivia said, wincing. "Nothing will come of it. And besides—"

"Besides, *what*? What can you possibly have to add to this hideous scenario?"

Olivia stared at the fine blond hairs on the back of Rand's manicured hand. In a bare whisper, she said, "What if Francis Leary *is* innocent? At least we would know that."

She raised her head and looked straight into her brother's piercingly blue eyes, startled, as always, that he could be her twin. Surely he was a changeling. Surely her real twin, dark-eyed like her, was being raised by mistake in a Scandinavian household somewhere in Minnesota.

"Listen to me," he said to her in a controlled fury. "Alison is dead. Whether Leary killed her or the milkman did it, Alison will still be dead. How can you think of putting her through the indignity . . . the desecration . . . on the slim chance that you can disprove a dead man's guilt? *She's* the victim here—not Leary. And it makes me sick to think that you can't seem to understand that.''

But you have an agenda, Olivia couldn't help thinking. *You want Quinn to suffer in any way he can. So how can I be convinced by your all-too-emotional argument?*

Olivia wanted so badly to say that out loud, but she was far too aware that if she hadn't shot off her mouth earlier, she wouldn't have provoked her father into telling them about Quinn's intentions. As it was, her mother was now in a state, her brother was aghast, her father was more outraged than ever, and worst of all—Alison.

''I'm sorry,'' Olivia said humbly, recoiling at the inevitable images induced by the thought of exhumation. To disinter a human being . . . it was something you read about in Gothic novels or in newspaper accounts of mass graves; it wasn't something that happened to a member of your family.

Olivia remembered her cousin—gorgeous, dreamy, naive, and yet so obviously secretive and troubled—and tried to fix a positive image in her mind to blot out thoughts of her grave. Her memory obliged with a snapshot of Alison smiling and happy at the animal shelter. Alison loved animals, and before her father made her quit her job as a volunteer at the Keepsake Kat Shelter, she had lived for Tuesdays and Thursdays when she could groom the animals, clean their cages, and change their water.

A smiling, gentle Alison coaxing an abused, hand-shy cat out of its cage—that was what Olivia wanted to remember.

She kept the mental photo propped up against her wineglass all through dinner, which ended up being a grim affair. The adults said little and the children, picking up on it, were almost scarily well behaved. There was no talk at all of the New Year's gala. Olivia's mother kept her red-rimmed eyes aimed at her plate and every now and then let out a sigh. Much to Rand's chagrin, the sporadic discussion that did take place was all about Mexico.

Olivia's parents left directly after dinner, but Olivia couldn't make herself go. Home was alone. Home was dark.

Home was cold. In contrast, the children seemed to explode with pent-up energy the minute their subdued grandparents walked out the door. Hoping somehow to inhale their high spirits, Olivia volunteered to help Kristin with her bath and then to bed.

The bath was a noisy and splashy affair; both aunt and niece ended up getting scolded for making a mess. After that, Olivia kicked off her shoes and sat on top of the pink-quilted bedcovers with Kristin—all clean-smelling and damp and so astonishingly innocent—nestled under her arm. They read together from *The Book of Dinosaurs* while Olivia absently stroked the child's damp hair, until finally, reluctantly, Olivia said, "Time to go to sleep now."

She hugged her niece—clung to her, really—and said, "I just love you so much I could smoosh you."

Kristin's squeaky giggle was light and rippling and so enchanting that it brought tears to Olivia's eyes.

What happens? What happens between her age and ours?

She buttoned a missed button in Kristin's Madeline pajamas and pulled the cover up to her niece's chin. Then she stole one last kiss, one last hug, to last her through the dark, cold night. On a whim, she reached for the Cabbage Patch doll that sat in a child-sized rocking chair and said, "How about if we let her sleep with you tonight?"

"No, I don't like dolls," Kristin said succinctly.

"Oh! I didn't know that." This was new. "Well . . . your mom can save them until you have babies of your own someday who can play with them."

There was no answer. Olivia turned off the bedroom light and was about to close the door when she heard Kristin say, "No babies."

"No babies?"

The child's voice was very firm. "Babies are messy. Too much work. You hafta change their diapers . . . and they're always crying . . . and pooping some more . . . and you can't even hear the TV sometimes. I want to be like you. No babies. I want to be a doctor. I asked my mom how can I not have babies, but she won't tell me."

Oh boy.

"Well, you won't have to worry about that for a long, long time yet," Olivia said, ducking the hint that had come sailing her way. "You just go to sleep now. Sweet dreams, Kristin. I love you!" she sang out softly.

"I love you, too, Auntie Liv."

Olivia closed the door gently and hightailed it out of the children's wing. No, no, no. Uh-uh. Eileen could handle that one. Wow. Five years old, and she wanted to know about birth control.

I want to be like you. No babies.

Somehow, that stung. Olivia had to wonder whether she gave off such strong vibrations. True, she was obsessed with her business, but that didn't mean she didn't *ever* want children. Necessarily.

Did she? When she came right down to it—did she?

Her mother certainly didn't think so. They'd argued many, many times about the just awful implications of Olivia remaining an old maid. The best furniture would go to the sibling who was married with children, not to the one who lived alone in a townhouse. The folder bulging with recipe clippings would go—naturally—to the daughter-in-law who cooked, not to the daughter who didn't. And as for the estate house at the top of upper Main—that house was meant to stay in the family, which meant that there had to be an actual family in order to stay there. So far, Olivia was a little light on that front.

Because she was nowhere near ready. It would be absurd—immoral—to have children just because her mother's clock was ticking, even *assuming* that Olivia had a sperm donor lined up for herself. Which she did not.

Blame it on the Cabbage Patch doll. Olivia drove home in a mood as dark and brooding as the starless sky that hung overhead.

Seven

On Christmas Eve, Olivia closed Miracourt at noon, gave her employees at Run of the Mill the rest of the day off, and drove her trunkload of trophies, packed as carefully as Dresden china, over to Mrs. Dewsbury's house.

How ironic, she thought. Keepsake's keepsakes were all but ruined, while Quinn's looked good as new. Well, Quinn could do whatever he wanted with his trophies—use them for target practice or eat Cheerios out of them; it made no difference to her. As long as they were out of the cottage and out of her life.

She'd saved those keepsakes for seventeen years. He could have been more grateful. He could have been more pleased. He could have been a lot of things, but mostly he could have *called.* Olivia had just spent five of the most miserable days of her life waiting for the phone to ring.

At first she thought, he doesn't want to seem eager. Then she thought he was visiting his uncle in Old Saybrook. After that she began grasping at straws: He has laryngitis; he's forgotten my name; he's in a coma. But she spotted him, alive and well, driving his rental truck through town that very morning, and that's what had prompted her to close the stores early and load the trunk of her car.

The obvious reason that he might be avoiding her wasn't a reason at all. Olivia had learned from her father that the district attorney, a man indebted to her father for his re-election, had immediately denied Quinn's request to have

Alison's body exhumed, making it a non-issue. Everyone in the family was relieved, especially Olivia. It was _Christmas_, for pity's sake. Did Quinn have no sense of the season at all? He and his father had lived under a cloud for seventeen years. Was it really necessary to go off on a rip right now?

She was wasting her time on him. He wasn't worth defending, and he was an ingrate besides. The hell with him. He was making a shambles of her good will toward men.

Forty-eight, forty-six, forty-four—forty-two Elm. Yes, there it was, a big white house, great bones, needed paint. It looked very much like the home of a pensioned and widowed schoolteacher. Olivia hadn't been down Elm in years; she was surprised to see how tired Mrs. Dewsbury's old house was looking, but she was glad to see an evergreen wreath with a big red bow hanging on the black panelled door. Besides giving the house a much-needed shot of color, it told the world that Mrs. Dewsbury hadn't abandoned _her_ Christmas spirit.

Olivia pulled into the drive, genuinely disappointed that Quinn's truck wasn't there. She would have enjoyed seeing the look on his face when she dumped the box in his arms. Unwilling to leave the trophies at risk on the wraparound veranda, she decided to go around to the back and leave them there instead. With an effort, she slid the heavy box out of the back of her minivan and lugged it up the half dozen steps to the small back porch.

She dropped the box with a thud next to the door, then in an attack of conscience, peeled off the green bow that she had mockingly stuck to the cardboard and stuffed it in her coat pocket. Just because Quinn Leary possessed no apparent Christmas spirit, it didn't mean that _she_ had to go and get snotty about the season. She was halfway down the steps when she realized that music was coming from inside the house. Nuts. Mrs. Dewsbury must be at home. Olivia couldn't very well skulk away like a Keepsake vandal, so she came back up the steps and knocked dutifully at the back door.

"Door's open!"

He *was* home.

Nuts!

Annoyed that he didn't have the courtesy to come to the door for her, Olivia opened it herself and peeked around it into the kitchen. She was prepared for many things—for embarrassed glances, awkward hellos, muttered excuses—but she wasn't prepared for the sight of Quinn Leary up to his elbows in flour, rolling out pie dough on a pastry board.

"Uhhh . . . hi," she said, wracking her brain for an excuse to be there.

"Hey," he said in greeting. He looked surprised, but hardly sheepish.

Quinn Leary was a stonemason. The realization came home to Olivia, big time, when she took in the heavily muscled arms that were working the rolling pin. Quinn's chest, clad in a navy T-shirt dusted with flour, was definitely the chest of a stonemason. His hands, thickly veined and doughy-fingered, were the hands of a stonemason. Even his waist, tucked all around inside his jeans with a big baker's towel, had the taut circumference of a man who didn't sit around on his duff all day.

So why did he give off the irresistibly warm vibrations of a Julia Child?

"Is . . . is Mrs. Dewsbury around?" Olivia asked stupidly, trying not to gawk.

"Nope. She's gone off to New Hampshire with her son for the holidays. You just missed her."

"Are you—?" Olivia fluttered her wrist at the row of empty pie shells waiting on the counter. "Subcontracting, or something?"

Quinn laughed out loud at that, and all of Olivia's hostile resolve slid away on the sound of his mirth. She was ready to fill the pies, sell the pies, buy the pies, eat the pies— whatever it took to hang around him for just a little bit longer.

"I'm baking these for Father Tom's Christmas dinner at the church tomorrow," he explained, still chuckling at the notion of being mistaken for a professional pie man.

God, his teeth were white. It was so nice to just stare at them. "Can I sit down?" she asked. *To stare at your teeth and everything else?*

"I'm sorry—sure, pull up a chair. My hands—"

"Are all sticky." Olivia wondered what it would be like to lick the raw dough off them and immediately blushed down to her ankles. She cleared her throat and said, "You seem pretty good at that."

"Yeah," said Quinn, rolling out a fat edge to match the rest of the circle. "My dad couldn't stand seeing excess harvest go to waste. He was always bringing produce home from the job and doing something or other with it; I guess I learned by osmosis. I also put up a pretty mean jar of preserves," he added with a grin.

He looked unbearably attractive to her. "A stonemason who bakes," she said a little giddily. "You must have to beat off women with a stick."

Aaackk! Wrap your arms around his knees and cling to him, why don't you?

Mercifully, he pretended not to have heard the fawning remark. "So how come you're looking for Mrs. D.?" he asked as he somehow slipped the circle of dough from the floured board to the pie pan, where it lay draped over the sides like ivory Ultrasuede.

"Who?" she asked.

"Mrs. Dewsbury?"

"What about her?"

He brought those terrifically sexy brows down in a squint of puzzlement and simply waited. Clearly he thought that Olivia had purposely removed one of her oars from the water so that she could row her boat in circles for a while.

"Because—your car was gone!" she blurted out, which made absolutely no sense at all, even to her.

"Yep," he said, expertly fitting the dough to the pan. "I gave up the rental and bought myself a new truck. It'll be delivered this afternoon, with any luck."

That made no sense, either, unless . . .

"It sounds as if you plan to stay awhile."

"Yep." He took up a knife and began cutting away the extra crust.

"And that's because—?"

"Yep."

Shit. Because of what?

He gave her an annihilating look that was clearly intended to put her out of her misery. "Because of you," he said matter-of-factly as he crimped the edge with his thumb and forefingers. "Among other reasons."

Because of you.

Among other reasons.

She kicked away the "other" and clung to the "you." "Then why haven't you called?" she demanded, regaining her footing on the slippery slope of their cryptic conversation.

The heartstopping smile turned serious. "I assume you know how I've been spending my spare time?"

She looked away and said, "Yes. Up to no good."

"Mm. I figured you'd hear, sooner or later." He carried the pie shell over to the side counter and laid it next to four other ones waiting for fillings, then came back to the table and scooped another ball of dough from the huge, very old cracked bowl he was using.

"Did you have to go that route, Quinn?" she almost begged to know.

For an answer, he said, "I guess it won't surprise you to hear that I ran smack into a brick wall at the D.A.'s office."

"Well, what did you expect?" she asked, disappointed that he was disappointed. "The courts don't go to lengths like that to prove someone is innocent, not if he's no longer living. Not if he's not in jail. Why *should* the district attorney do anything?"

"How about because it's the right thing to do?" Quinn suggested, sprinkling flour on the pastry board and slamming the ball of dough just a little too hard onto it.

Olivia didn't know what to say to that, especially since part of her agreed with him. But she wanted him to understand all sides of the scenario, so she said, "The thought of

... of doing something like that to Alison hit my parents very hard, Quinn. I can only imagine how my aunt and uncle felt if they heard. I know it's just a scientific procedure—''

"That's all it is," Quinn said flatly.

"—but this is *Alison*," Olivia argued softly. "Someone real. Someone we all knew. The same Alison that you helped out in geometry. The same Alison you played badminton with during our family picnic that time."

"That *one* time."

"But still."

"Obviously I don't see this the way you do, Liv."

She watched in disheartened silence as he worked quickly, almost impatiently, to form the last pie shell. In his haste he tore the circle of dough as he transferred it from the board to the pan. He let out a sound, the barest hint, of exasperation and started over. The second crust went smoothly; she could see that he was focused on the task. It was the Quinn she remembered—cool, deliberate, unflappable. A star at everything he did, even pie crusts.

He broke the awkward silence by saying, "How is it that you don't know how your own aunt and uncle feel?"

"Our families aren't on speaking terms anymore," she said forthrightly. "They were strained even before Alison's death. You didn't know that? I guess we were better at keeping up appearances then. You have to remember, Ricki Lake hadn't been invented yet and people still had a sense of decorum. It was a different age."

"Oh, to have it back again," Quinn said in a wry, musing voice.

"In any case, the rift is an open secret nowadays—and really, what *is* the big deal? Every family has people in it who don't talk to one another," she said, carefully sweeping all the loose flour into a pile with the edge of her hand.

"You don't sound very resigned to it," he said, which she thought was perceptive. He took a pot of filling—pumpkin, by the look of it—from the stove to the counter and began glopping it into the first pie shell.

"To be honest, I don't even know why they're not speaking," Olivia admitted with a sigh. "My parents have always refused to tell me. It's about money, I'm sure. My father's brother went through his inheritance in no time; right there is a cardinal sin."

"Doesn't sound like much of a reason to me," Quinn said, glancing at her between fillings.

She shrugged, uncomfortable with the notion of talking about other people's spending habits. She'd been brought up never to discuss either money or sex, and she was feeling a vague but very definite unease talking about her aunt and uncle. Especially her uncle.

"I do see my aunt in church now and then," Olivia said in her own defense. "I try to get a conversation going, but . . . she never has much to say."

"You go to church?" Quinn asked her.

"Once in a while. Why? Do I strike you as the heathen type?"

He smiled. "Maybe a little."

Heathen apparently meant "nymphomaniac" in his mind. It was the only possible explanation for the look he was giving her.

Dropping her gaze from his, Olivia splayed her hands against the edge of the table and self-consciously studied her neatly trimmed nails. Had she ever had flour under them? She was fairly sure not. She felt a sudden, very bizarre surge of regret. Flour and church and kids—she didn't have time for any of them. What a disaster she was as a woman so far. Her life had been all about the store, the store, the store. She was like her father, with his obsession with the mill, the mill, the mill.

Her head shot up. It was true! She was *exactly* like her father: driven, controlling, and inflexible. It was the most depressing thought she'd had in a long time.

She stared glumly at Quinn, as at ease in the kitchen as he was on a gridiron, and wondered how *he* had managed to turn out so well. "You're amazing," she said, watching as he slid the three pumpkin pies into Mrs. Dewsbury's oven. "I wish I had your . . . your range of interests."

Quinn said dryly, "Oh, yeah—I'm a regular Renaissance man." He set the timer and said, "Three down, three to go."

"More pumpkin?"

"Two apples and a mince."

Now that he said so, she did smell other wonderful aromas wafting from the stove. It shocked her, how oblivious she was to everything but his presence.

She made herself look at something besides him. What she saw was wainscoting nubby from a dozen coats of paint and cupboards that couldn't be more plain. A fridge that was old, a stove that was older. Dotted sheer curtains yellowed with age. A countertop buried under clunky mug racks and jugs jammed with utensils that Mrs. Dewsbury couldn't possibly need, gifts from grandkids, perhaps. A kitchen, in short, that was worn and mussy—a little like Mrs. Dewsbury—but a room that resonated with lifetimes of living. It made Olivia feel lonely somehow.

"Is there anything I can do?" she offered. "Peel apples or anything—?"

Very patiently, he said, "They're peeled. They're cooked. They're ready to go."

. "Oh! Of course. *That's* what smells so good," she said, completely rattled by now. She had the feeling that he wanted to say something, but that he was holding back out of simple politeness.

Let me finish the damn pies. That's what she decided he wanted to say. Well trained, Olivia stood up; she was determined to exit before she was asked.

"I should be going," she said, pushing her chair in and undraping her coat from the back of it. "It's Christmas Eve and I have a million things to do."

"Yeah, me, too," he muttered, taking a bowl from the fridge.

He didn't sound very happy with her. Was it because she had turned away from the burning look he'd given her? *Had* he given her a burning look? Who knew? When she was around him, her instincts bounced around like bullets in a spaghetti western.

She had her hand on the doorknob and was about to wish him a merry Christmas, but instead she turned and blurted out, "What do you plan to do?"

"After the pies?"

"I mean, now that the D.A. has refused your request to reopen the investigation."

He thumped another wad of dough on the board and said, "I guess I'll have to reopen it on my own."

"Oh, Quinn—is that a good idea? You run the risk of alienating everyone in town."

"Including your parents, of course," he said, giving her a level look.

"Obviously. But that's not why I wish you wouldn't pursue this. The reason is—" She bit her lip, unwilling to trust those haphazard instincts of hers. "It's because . . ."

He was waiting for her answer now. His green eyes were alight with curiosity: What dumb thing was she about to say *this* time?

It made Olivia veer away from the truth—that she thought they really might be able to have something together, if only he treaded gingerly and let people get to know him better.

But there was another truth, and it was nearly as compelling to her as the one she was afraid to say out loud. She looked him straight in the eye and said, "There's something unseemly about hurting innocent people to satisfy your own selfish needs."

That got his attention. He wiped his hands on the dish towel that was jammed in his jeans, then tossed it on the table and walked over to her. Without the towel tucked in his waist, he didn't look so warm and friendly anymore. He looked big and strong and way too threatening.

She winced, afraid that he was going to boot her out of his kitchen. But that, apparently, was not on his mind as he caught her upper arm and brought his face within Tic Tac distance of hers.

"Listen to me, Miss Bennett. There was nothing *seemly* about having to skulk off with my father in the middle of the night. There was nothing *seemly* about changing over to my middle name and putting up with an itchy beard to hide my face. There was nothing *seemly* about running like a bat out of hell from a situation when my father could have—should have—been honored as a hero. There was nothing—"

"What do you mean, 'hero'?"

"Just what I said. It's ironic that he's being blamed for taking a life when the opposite is—aw, hell! Never mind."

He let go of her with something like distaste, which was more shocking to Olivia than his diatribe. She blinked and, after an eternity, remembered to exhale. "I guess you've made your intentions pretty clear," she said in lofty tones. "You're going to press your case for an exhumation."

"Bingo."

"Fine." Her lip began to tremble; she refused to let it. "Then let me wish you a merry Christmas and be on my way."

He gave her a look of cool contempt. There was nothing, absolutely nothing, in it that reminded her of Julia Child.

She turned and pulled the door open so quickly that it bumped her knee. *He's obsessed,* she told herself. *I'm out of here.*

On the porch she tripped over the cardboard box filled with his trophies, which she never did get around to telling him she'd brought. She had started down the steps in a flight to her minivan when she stopped, reached into the pocket of her coat, and pulled out the green bow that she'd stuffed there earlier. She crushed the bow in her hand, then tossed it at the brass football sticking out of the box.

"Merry Christmas, my ass," she muttered, and hurried back to her car.

Eight

Two apples and a mince: burnt to a crisp.

Quinn had checked out Mrs. Dewsbury's backup electric stove in the basement before he used it, and the burners worked fine. But it turned out that the oven was another story. Half an hour after he put the pies in, the piercing shrieks of two new smoke alarms brought him hightailing back from the storage shed where he'd been in the process of installing a motion-detecting spotlight to light up the yard.

By the time he aired out the smoke-filled house, found a supermarket still open, and re-peeled, re-cooked, and re-baked replacements for the three casualties, it was marching up on midnight. Lucky for him that his new Dodge Ram had been delivered as promised earlier in the day; it made his mood a lot less foul.

There weren't many relationships in life more intense than that between a man and a brand-new truck, so Quinn searched for and found an excuse to take his sassy Ram out for another spin: to deliver the pies to Father Tom before Midnight Mass. It wasn't the most logical time to drop them off, but what the hell. It was Christmas Eve, and Quinn had just given himself the only present he was going to get.

He loaded the pies into the sparkling clean tool bins of his shiny blue pickup and then all the way to St. Swithin's had to fight an impulse to drive like a wild and stupid teenager. He liked owning his own vehicle outright. Always had, always would. Leasing left him cold, and renting had caused him physical agony. Yup. Buying a truck on the wrong coast of America was the only reasonable thing to do.

Ah, well. At least he hadn't ordered the plow attachment. Yet.

Quinn intercepted Father Tom as he was about to enter the sacristy to don his vestments for the high Mass. The priest's greeting was distracted: The organist hadn't shown, and he should've been warming up the audience by then.

"I don't really see the parishioners muddling through the hymns *a cappella*, he said wryly to Quinn. "We could use someone to give us the pitch. I don't suppose that you—?"

Quinn crisscrossed his hands in front of him as if poor Father Tom were Count Dracula in a cassock. "Not me, Father," he said in something like terror. "I don't have any musical talent at all."

"Then it's the only talent you don't have," the priest said generously. "Okay . . . you may as well take the pies directly down to the hall. See that exit sign? Take the back steps next to it. You got Saran Wrap?"

"I brought a roll, just in case."

"Good man," said Father Tom, slapping him on the back. They broke up their huddle and the priest went off to nourish men's souls while Quinn made arrangements for their stomachs.

The basement was set up not with the usual long tables but with round tables that seated eight, giving the hall the cozy air of a family restaurant. Red checkered tablecloths and centerpieces of holly and winterberry were a nice touch. The ladies' auxiliary had done a great job. In no way, shape, or form did it look like a soup kitchen.

And really, why should it? People down on their luck or with no place to go should be able to spend Christmas in good company like anyone else. Better, actually: At least no one would be feuding in the halls of St. Swithin's.

Quinn saw the folding buffet table that the priest had told him would be for desserts; it was lined up against the far wall, with cups and saucers arranged on it, along with two stacks of dessert plates way higher than Quinn had pieces of pie for. He hoped that Father Tom wasn't kidding about the brownies and the pressed cookies.

He was impressed to see that they were using real cloth napkins, rolled around what must have been silverware and laid out alongside the plates.

Or not. At first puzzled and then with a quickening sense of dread, Quinn approached the table. What looked from across the hall like large rolled napkins were in reality . . . bleached bones, lined up as neatly as any hostess could wish.

The sight of them in the innocent setting was like being kicked in the stomach, and it left Quinn much more breathless than the smashed-in windshield had done. He dumped the two pies he was holding onto another table and returned to the macabre display. *Bones.* Of what, for God's sake?

A dog, most likely. Someone had dug up the family pet, cleaned off the bones, and laid them here. It was a reasonable presumption, and it left Quinn reeling. Disinterment, that's what this was about. Someone was making a statement about Quinn's latest foray down the halls of justice. And if Quinn hadn't stumbled into the basement hall at that unlikely hour, some white-haired volunteers with kind intentions and weak hearts would have had the shock of their lives when they showed up the next day to help serve. News of the prank would have traveled at warp speed, dinner would have been a disaster, and it would have been Quinn's fault and no one else's.

Damn it to hell!

He worked quickly, clearing the table of everything but the bones and then shrouding them in the cloth that they were laid out on. Quinn's sense of liturgy, never very precise, was turned upside down by the grisly prank. This was the season of birth, not of bones. He stuffed the hapless pet's remains, still in the tablecloth, into a black garbage bag and looped the open end of the bag into a tight knot, and then another.

I'll have to stay here the whole blessed night.

It was going to be pointless to stand guard over the hall—no one would be back, he was sure—but if he went home he knew he wouldn't sleep a wink. He looked around for a nice soft La-Z-Boy, but all he saw were metal folding chairs. So, okay, it was going to be not only pointless but painful to spend the night there.

Quinn slung the garbage bag over his shoulder, feeling more like the Grim Reaper than Santa Claus, and carried it out to his truck. After that, he decided to take a quick walk around the white-steepled church, not so much for the cold night air, which he welcomed, but to see if anyone strange and twisted was lurking in the shrubbery.

Who? That was the question. Obviously it had to be someone who knew that Quinn had gone to the D.A. with a request for exhumation.

Hold it. Back up, Doughboy. It could have been somebody who knew from Chief Vickers that Quinn was *planning* to go to the D.A.

Well, that really narrowed it down.

Whoever did it must also have known that Quinn had volunteered to help out with the church dinner. Could the villain of this disgusting little pageant conceivably be a member of the parish? A deacon, a lady on the auxiliary committee, the freaking organist, even?

Where was the organist, anyway?

Quinn peered behind the flat-topped yews and rummaged through the holly bushes, expecting with every poke to see someone's evil, beady eyes staring back at him. Before long, he realized where the organist was when he was yanked from his spooky reverie by the sonorous notes of the church's old Wurlitzer rising up and through the stained glass windows: "Do You Hear What I Hear?"

The Christmas carol was too appropriate, somehow; it gave him chills. What was he listening for? What was he looking for?

Was someone reminded of his own lost promise in life by Quinn's presence in Keepsake and taking it out on Quinn? Or was someone afraid that Quinn was going to prove Francis Leary's innocence—and in the bargain, prove that person's guilt?

Quinn continued his circuit around the church but paused at the life-sized crêche that was set up facing the busier of the two streets that the church abutted. Although Quinn hadn't practiced his faith for many years, he felt obliged to make sure that no one had stolen the straw from baby Jesus' crib again or committed some other wickedness there.

Things looked okay. Baby Jesus looked snug and warm, and nobody had broken off the nose of one of the three kings or moved the donkey into some scandalous position.

Hey guys. You see anyone suspicious go skulking past?

The swarthy kings were silent, but Quinn had the sense that they knew more than they were letting on. He turned his gaze to the illogically blue eyes of the infant lying in the manger and thought, *I know that* you *know. But you're not gonna say, are you?*

Quinn sighed. He was hoping for an offhand miracle, just like in the movies. He swept his gaze from the kings to Mary to Joseph to Jesus again, but no one moved, no one spoke. The only one puffing white breath into the ice-cold night was Quinn. He was warm, he was alive, and he was utterly alone in the universe.

It was his first Christmas without his father, and it was yet another Christmas without a wife and a family of his own. His isolation threw him into a sudden and profound depression.

"It Came Upon a Midnight Clear . . ."

Again Quinn was struck by the irony of the organist's choice of hymns. He looked up at the sky, awash with stars twinkling cold and remote. It was midnight, and it was clear, but what was it that had come? Who? That's what he wanted so desperately to know.

After a last sweeping glance around the crêche, Quinn decided to head back to the basement hall, to spend the night in dreary vigilance. As he passed the double arched doors of the historic New England church, he heard the strains of a carol that was his father's favorite: "Angels We Have Heard on High."

Quinn stopped where he was at the foot of the steps. He could hear his father asking good-naturedly, "Why are all the best songs always about angels?" He could hear his father's voice, a surprisingly rich baritone, singing the refrain:

"Glo-oh-oh-oh-oh-oh-oh-oh-oh-oh-oh-oh-oh-oh-oh-oh-oh-ria, in excelsis Deo . . ."

And he found himself ascending the steps of St. Swithin's and quietly opening the heavy church door, because inside was where he was sure he'd find his father.

"Son, what does that mean, anyway—'*in excelsis Deo*'?" his father had once asked.

Quinn had answered, "It means 'in exultation of God,' Dad," and had turned the page of his novel, secretly annoyed that his father liked to sing along with his Christmas cassettes. What if someone were passing by the gardener's cottage and happened to hear him?

Quinn paused at the back of the crowded church and then slipped into the last pew. Except for his father's funeral, it was the first time he'd been in a church since he ran from Keepsake. His father used to mourn Quinn's obstinate refusal to go, but what could the man do about it? By then Quinn was eighteen—old enough to drink, vote, and be bitter.

Quinn sighed heavily. He wouldn't stay. What was the point, really? He didn't believe. He would just finish out the one carol . . .

At the main altar, Father Tom looked somehow too big, too real, too ordinary to be conducting Mass. A linebacker, yes. But a priest? Quinn smiled. Father Tom was an excellent priest, but he would've made a damn good father, too. Which, come to think of it, he was. And Quinn's father . . . Francis Leary . . . had been a wonderful father. And Quinn, who was so much less worthy than either of the men, was not a father in any sense of the word.

He felt a lump rise and catch in his throat. His thoughts

became blurred in a glaze of tears as he realized somewhere deep in his soul that Francis Leary—the only father he would ever have—was dead and gone forever.

And he was innocent of the crime. He wasn't a taker of lives, but a saver of them. And somehow Quinn had to let everyone know, and then he himself would no longer be an outcast. He felt his spirit aching to join those of the congregation's, and in the middle of that longing, he felt his soul reach just a little bit higher, a little bit closer to his dad.

It was an amazing moment of transcendence for him, and as the carol ended, followed almost at once by another, more poignant one—"O Little Town of Bethlehem"—he was even more amazed to find his thoughts drifting serenely from his father to Olivia Bennett.

Liv! The brainy kid who'd aced him on a math final in their junior year at Keepsake High, the witch who'd once tricked him into confessing that he didn't have a clue what the capital of Montana was—*she* was there, not in person maybe, because the Bennetts were Episcopalian, but . . . there, nonetheless. Her smile, her dark eyes . . . oh, her voice, he could listen to that voice argue with him all day long and not get tired of it. She was warm and kindhearted and she smelled like an angel and no one looked more beautiful in lavender blue. It scared him, how much Olivia was there . . . and it made him feel profoundly awed.

Because somehow, in that church, in that community, he was able to leave all his bitterness and resentment and self-righteousness at the door and join everyone else, if only briefly, in simple praise of the season.

And for that, he was glad.

Nine

Technically speaking, **Olivia** didn't belong in her brother's living room. And yet on Christmas morning there she was, dressed in pajamas like everyone else and plopped on the floor near Rand and Eileen's tree, helping their kids read the to-and-from tags on the mountains of gifts stacked under it.

Olivia had been coming over on Christmas Eve and staying the night since Zack was three—ever since she'd seen the videotape of him making a dash for the presents and tripping onto the pile, sending the presents into the tree and the tree into the fireplace, which luckily was still unlit.

"Oh, what I wouldn't give to have been there!" she'd said through tears of laughter as they watched the tape later that day.

"Come over Christmas Eve next time, and stay overnight," Eileen had suggested on the spot.

"You wouldn't mind?"

"Not a bit."

It was a tremendous intrusion. Olivia knew it, and every year on December 24 she'd call her sister-in-law and best friend and say, "Eileen, are you *sure*?" And Eileen would say, "Yes, I'm sure." There might have been a year or two when Eileen wasn't quite as sure as she sounded, but by now it was a tradition. Olivia looked forward to all of it, from the Christmas Eve service at St. Paul's to the waffles her brother made for them on Christmas morning.

This year, shopping for Kristin's gift had been a challenge. The child was at prime doll-bearing age, which should have made it easy—and yet her position on dolls was depressingly clear. Eileen decided to ignore it, choosing instead to blow away her daughter's resistance with a holiday Barbie and a glittering wardrobe to go with it.

Poor Barbie never made it out of the box.

Olivia, taking seriously her niece's remark about wanting to be a doctor (although obviously not a pediatrician), bought her a precision microscope. Kristin was impressed—for five minutes. How long could you stay worked up about a strand of hair magnified two hundred times?

Kristin was much more enthusiastic about the charming Christmas stocking that Zack had purchased from Olivia's shop for her. That was some consolation. But the biggest hits—surprise, surprise—were the Beanie Babies, around which Kristin and Zack immediately began designing elaborate new skits.

"Oh, well. At least they're using their imagination."

"And the toys aren't violent."

"Or sexist."

"So we should be really glad."

But they weren't. Eileen wanted her daughter to fall in love with holiday Barbie, and Olivia wanted to trump Eileen with the student microscope.

As for Rand, he had his own elaborately worked out theory: "Women don't know what the hell they want."

In short, it was a charming, typical Christmas morning. Olivia had all of the pleasure of seeing the holiday through children's eyes and none of the stress of making dinner for her parents later in the day. She had offered, as she did every year, to help in the kitchen, but her sister-in-law was determined, as she was every year, to stage the event herself.

"Damn it, I want *all* the credit," she told Olivia. "This is serious. This involves in-laws."

So while poor Eileen was fretting about turning out an oyster stuffing that was properly moist and getting all those tiny pearl onions cooked and creamed just so, Olivia was back in her townhouse with her shoes kicked off and a cup of tea on her lap, gathering strength for the second phase of Christmas Day.

The odd thing was, she didn't feel drained in the least by the nonstop morning. Just the opposite, in fact: She was feeling restless and almost unbearably edgy. Her cup of Earl Grey tea and plate of Eileen's Christmas cookies simply weren't going to cut it this year. Olivia wanted something else, something more, something new.

She wanted Quinn.

She told herself that she was being perverse. That Quinn came with too much emotional baggage. That he was arrogant, overly principled, and insensitive. That he might even be cruel—how else to explain his willingness to put her family through such agony over Alison?

And yet part of her, the part that mattered, knew that Quinn Leary had more character, more integrity, and a stronger sense of honor than any man she'd ever met. Did honor even matter any more? She didn't know. All she knew was that it was Christmas and she wanted to be with Quinn, if only to see him smile and hear his voice again.

Abandoning her tea and cookies, Olivia changed from her red corduroy jumper into dinner clothes—a winter white sweater and a black skirt that fell softly to mid-calf—and pinned a whimsical cloisonne-and-rhinestone rocking horse pin to the sweater for a touch of color and sparkle. She kept her makeup to a minimum and ran her fingers through the curls of her hair to tame the bounciest ones, then surveyed herself in the full-length mirror that stood in the corner of her cheerful yellow bedroom.

Is this okay for a soup kitchen?

No. She frowned at herself for being frivolous, then took off the pin and slipped it in the pocket of her skirt.

Olivia arrived at St. Swithin's just as the crowd was beginning to show up in force. She was expecting to see a basic turkey dinner being dished out cafeteria-style, but the scene before her was a real community affair, warm and friendly and relaxed. All manner of people were helping themselves to the buffet—from college kids in jeans and sweats to elderly couples in their churchgoing best. Single mothers were there with their freshly scrubbed children, and unattached men who looked, it was true, both jobless and homeless.

But no Quinn. Olivia expected him to be there and was keenly disappointed that he wasn't. Undaunted, she approached the man who was obviously in charge of the event.

"Father Tom? Hi. I don't know if you remember me—"

The priest started when he saw her. "Of course I do. Olivia Bennett, isn't it?" He stuck out his hand and said, "Merry Christmas," though he clearly wondered what she was doing there.

"I was looking for Quinn."

"Dear God, what now?"

"Well, I—excuse me?"

In a low murmur, the priest urged her to give him a moment of her time. They stepped out into the hall, and in a few frightening sentences, he brought Olivia up-to-date on the most recent of the unnerving pranks that were being inflicted on Keepsake.

"Quinn stayed here all night, bless the man's heart," explained Father Tom. "He's gone home to shower, but he should be back anytime. Please," he added, "don't mention the prank to anyone besides your family."

He glanced around him and dropped his voice even lower. "I'm only confiding this bone business to you because you're so directly involved. Quinn told me about his— ill-advised, if you ask me—attempt to have your cousin exhumed for DNA testing."

Olivia could see that the idea was deeply troublesome to the priest, which wasn't surprising. But she could not see the point of keeping anything secret. "It's better that it all gets out, Father, don't you think? That way everyone can be on guard for whoever it is who's doing these horrible things."

"In theory, maybe," Father Tom said wryly, "but do you think that Mr. and Mrs. Snyder in there would go anywhere near the buffet if they knew it had a dog's bones on it a few hours ago? Never mind that we scrubbed everything down with bleach.''

''No, really, Father,'' said Olivia, digging in her heels, ''I think honesty is always the best policy.''

''Ordinarily, yes, but surely this is an exception—''

Catching himself, the priest shook his head and said, ''Will you listen to me? You're right, of course. Tell the truth, Olivia, and let the chips fall where they may.''

He began to walk away, then turned around and added with a poignant look, ''But don't tell the truth until everyone's had pie, okay?''

Smiling, Olivia nodded her assent and gave him a cheery little wave good-bye.

Now what? She couldn't very well go in there and take food out of somebody's mouth. But she couldn't stand in the hall waiting around for Quinn like some groupie, either. She simply could not stay.

But she sure didn't want to go.

What kind of Christmas was *this?*

She ducked into the ladies' bathroom where she spent some time talking to a tube of lipstick, then came out and scanned the diners one last time. Nope. Still not there. Dismayed by how unhappy it made her feel, she turned abruptly to leave.

And ran smack into Quinn, whacking his chest with her shoulder hard enough to send them both off balance.

''Heyyy,'' he said with a grin as he caught her in his arms, instantly turning her knees to pudding. ''I can't believe Bronsky didn't recruit you for the team back when. He missed a bet there.''

''Oh, you *are* here!'' she said breathlessly. Newly showered, his ponytail still damp, the scent of aftershave still fresh on his high-boned cheeks—oh, yes, he was very much there.

''Were you looking for me?'' he asked her with a hopeful, loopy smile.

Olivia didn't disappoint him. ''As a matter of fact, I was.

I wanted—'' What *did* she want? "To ask you over to Christmas dinner with my family!" she blurted out.

God in heaven! Where did *that* come from?

A veil drifted down between them. "Uhhh, gee . . . it's really nice of you to think of me," he said. "But I'm afraid I'll have to pass."

Praise the Lord.

"Well—what about New Year's Eve, then?" she followed up brightly.

God in heaven! Where did *that* come from?

Still holding her, still puzzled, still smiling, he said, "You make it hard for a guy to say no."

"That's the idea," she whispered on a shaky outflow of breath.

"Okay, then," he said softly. "I'd like that. New Year's Eve it is."

Oh no.

"Great! It'll be fun! My parents throw a really big shindig at the house every year. Just about everyone comes!"

Please don't come. Please, please, please.

"At your parents' house? Ah! Well! Hmm. That'll be a real . . . pleasure. I'm looking forward to seeing them again after all these years."

Are you serious? They hate you. They'll kill me.

She beamed at him and said, "And they'll be looking forward to seeing you, too!"

"Good! That's good."

The conversation had become so surreal that it broke down completely and sat there lost and confused, like a puppy that's wandered too far from home.

Quinn released her at last and nodded sideways toward the gathering inside the church basement. "Are you—?"

"Oh! No, no. I just came to—to invite you! That's all."

"Okay. Well, I'll call you soon."

I might be dead by then, she thought, but she returned his much-too-cheerful smile and said, "I'll be looking forward to it!"

She fled on pudding knees to her minivan, where she sat

and waited for her heart's thumping to die down. Forgotten entirely was the news about the latest dreadful prank; all Olivia wanted was to make sense of her behavior in that hall. There had to be a reason why she had invited Quinn—the one man in the world who could probably make her mother cry on sight—into her parents' home for the biggest party of their social calendar. Everyone would be there: the mayor, the council, doctors, lawyers, her father's peers in the textile industry.

Is that why she did it? To force Keepsake to deal with Quinn head on, instead of whispering and muttering behind his back? Olivia wanted to think so. She wanted to believe that her reason was as simple and noble as that.

If she had any other motive for asking Quinn, it was buried too deep in her subconscious for her to figure it out just now. She put her van in gear and pulled out of the parking lot. Across town, on another planet far from this one, dinner was about to be served.

Her family was in a wonderful mood.

Owen Bennett had just found out from his son that the town council was willing to negotiate a tax break for the mill. Rand was so proud that he'd been up to the challenge that he walked around practically bursting through his paisley vest. Eileen was thrilled with the sapphire earrings her husband had surprised her with after Olivia left at noon. And Teresa Bennett? She was happy simply because everyone else was happy.

It got better. Olivia's father pronounced himself satisfied with the oyster stuffing, pleased with the gift Olivia had given him, a pair of custom gold cuff links in the shape of a loom, and thrilled that he'd finally—finally!—beaten his grandson at Super Mario three games running.

They sang carols together, hopelessly bungling "The Twelve Days of Christmas," and they enjoyed a fabulous whiskey torte with their decaf espresso in front of a crackling fire while a video of *It's a Wonderful Life* played softly on the large-screen TV in the corner. Everyone was feeling sentimental, Olivia's mother, most of all. All she had to do was glance at the movie, and tears flowed freely.

"It's such a magical film," she murmured, wiping her eyes. "If only people lived that way."

Olivia had been watching her mother with a mixture of affection and apprehension all evening long. She knew that her mother offered the one chance she had of sneaking Quinn under the tent on New Year's Eve. The gala was going to be a masked affair, as usual, which meant that at least half of the guests would be thoroughly disguised. That was one point in Olivia's favor. Another was that her mother had never been able to say no to her; not if Olivia was determined to get a yes out of her.

So it was that right after Clarence was awarded his wings, and Olivia's father and Rand strolled off to the study to enjoy their good news and their Macanudos, and Eileen hauled her two sleepy children and their six new Beanie Babies off to bed, Olivia made her move.

"This has been a wonderful Christmas, Mom, don't you think?" she asked, snuggling close to her mother on the sofa.

Sighing happily, Teresa Bennett said, "They all are."

"But this one was better."

"You're just saying that because your father liked your cuff links so well," her mother said, looping her arm around her daughter.

"He did, didn't he?" Olivia agreed. She laid her cheek on her mother's shoulder. "I hope he wears them on New Year's."

"I'm sure he will. He'll want to show them off."

"Mom?" Olivia murmured. "You haven't asked me who I'm bringing this year."

"I imagine it'll be Eric again," her mother said with a sigh. "He's a *nice* young man," she added, "but when are you going to find someone who'll be able to take you seriously, Livvy? Sometimes I despair that I'll ever see you on the arm of a . . . a—"

"You'll be glad to know that there's been big progress

on that front: I've found myself a heterosexual," Olivia said lightly. "He seems very interested in me and he's definitely good breeding stock—smart, strong, a great-looking guy. I'll bet that sperm banks all over the world send him fan mail."

Her mother yanked at her hair and said, "You don't have to be outrageous. Where did you meet someone like that, anyway, working the hours you do?"

"Actually, I knew him years ago," Olivia said softly. She swallowed hard and added, "Actually, so did you."

The hand that had been teasing her hair in idle affection stopped now, and her mother became very still. Olivia opened her eyes. She couldn't see her mother's face—only her neck with its lined skin, the first telltale sign of advancing age. She thought she could see the pulsing of an artery there. She was certain she could hear her mother's heart, pounding in apprehension.

Teresa Bennett sat her daughter up to face her. Her gaze, darker even than Olivia's, searched her face for some hint that she should laugh at the absurdity of the idea of Quinn Leary popping up at a family gathering.

"You can't be serious."

"Mom, I am. I want to bring him on New Year's. I've already asked him," Olivia confessed.

"*Why*, for God's sake?"

"I don't know, I don't know," she said in a baffled wail. "Something made me do it. I think maybe—it's like the Capra film," she said, seized by an idea.

She jumped up and began pacing in front of the fireplace on the Berber carpet. "Ten minutes ago you were wondering why people aren't like the characters in that movie anymore, and you were right: Look how Keepsake is treating Quinn. But we have a chance—"

She stopped midstride and pointed to her mother. "*You* have a chance—to change that."

"*Me!*"

"I know you've never been comfortable in your role as a woman of influence," Olivia said, dropping back down on the pillowed sofa and clutching her mother's hands in hers. "You'd rather be living in a picket-fenced cottage and baby-sitting your grandchildren. But like it or not, you're the wife of the richest man in town. I'm not saying you're Mary Astor; but I *am* saying that if *you* treat Quinn with decency, the rest of Keepsake will follow suit. Most of them, anyway."

Her mother yanked her hands free of Olivia's. "No!" she said sharply. "I can't do that. It wouldn't be right to the family. Think of your Aunt Betty! My God. How can you be so dense?"

"I'm not, I'm not. But, Mom, you know that Frank Leary didn't kill Alison. And even if he did, that's not Quinn's fault. You can't conceivably blame Quinn!"

"Why can't you leave him alone!" her mother said, scrambling to get away from Olivia's grasp. Now it was her turn to pace—less from tension, Olivia thought, than from a desire to be free of her daughter's cajoling influence.

She watched her mother, so self-effacing in quiet beige and a strand of pearls, and wondered for the thousandth time why she didn't stand up for her principles more. Her mother knew that Quinn was being treated unfairly. Why didn't she speak up for him? The emotions were there, the intensity was there, and yet . . .

Olivia understood at last: Everything that Teresa Bennett did was for her family, and only her family. The family came first—her husband and her children and even poor Aunt Betty. Beyond that circle, Olivia's mother rarely ventured.

It was maddening. Teresa Bennett had a true and generous heart and could be the best ally that Quinn could possibly have—except for Olivia herself, of course.

She watched as her mother halted in front of the fire and stared into it. Something about the way she held herself told Olivia that she was beginning to consider and maybe to yield. Eventually she saw her mother's shoulders lift and fall in a silent sigh. Surrender?

Finally her mother turned to her and said in a voice of

obvious mourning, "You have feelings for this man."

"No, of course I don't," Olivia said instantly, and then she remembered her own words, so recently uttered: Honesty is the best policy.

She bowed her head and studied the pearl ring she wore on her left ring finger. Her mother had given it to her on the day she opened Miracourt and had told her, "The world's your oyster now. Congratulations, Livvy. I'm so proud of you."

"Yes, I do have feelings for him," Olivia said at last, twisting the ring around her finger. "There's chemistry between us, Mom, I won't deny it." She looked up and said, "But whether there is or not, I'd still go to bat for Quinn. It's the right thing to do. You *know* that. You're the one who's taught me not to back down from my beliefs."

"And it's a constant balancing act, cheering you on in your independence, yet hoping you won't go too far and do something stupid. You exhaust me," her mother added, and she really did sound tired.

"I know," Olivia admitted with a rueful smile. "Isn't it funny how things work out? Once you were so happy that I was determined to make it on my own," she said, waving the pearl ring in front of her mother to remind her. "And now I don't think a month goes by that you don't say to yourself, 'My poor little girl: one month closer to menopause.'"

"Olivia! How can you say that?"

"Because it's true."

Her mother sighed in tacit acknowledgment. "You're thirty-four, with no children, Livvy. Eileen's a year younger than you and her son is nine years old."

Olivia stood up and whispered in her mother's ear, "Well, hey, there's always Quinn." She stepped back to gauge her mother's reaction and was shocked to see tears spring up in her eyes.

"Please don't joke about that, Olivia. It bothers me in so many different ways."

Too far. She'd gone too far in her teasing again. "I'm

sorry, Mom," she said quickly. "It's just that this whole thing with Quinn has been so *weird*."

Not for anything would she tell her mother about the bones on the buffet. It would simply cause her more agony—and make Olivia's request that much more likely to be refused.

With a purposely downcast face, Olivia said, "So how about it, Mom? Are you willing to set a good example for me and for everyone in Keepsake? Are you willing to let me bring a completely innocent man as my date to your party?"

"Will he wear a mask, at least?"

"Absolutely!"

Teresa Bennett tried to smile, but the effort fell flat and her words came out grim: "Make sure that he does—just in case I lose my nerve when I confront your father."

Ten

A week later, Quinn walked into Tony Assorio's barbershop without an appointment but with a fair amount of confidence that Tony wouldn't turn him away.

"Take it off, Tony. It's time for it to go."

"No kidding?"

"It's all yours."

"How short you want it?"

"You be the judge."

The barber was thrilled. "You know what? I'm not gonna charge. This one's on me."

Obviously Tony believed that the decline of American civilization had just been halted in its tracks. "You're doing the right thing, kid," he said. "How does it look, a grown man in a ponytail? Daniel Boone—maybe. Or that Fabio. But come on."

He kept up a steady stream of banter as he worked with the scissors, then with the clippers. Quinn watched his sun-streaked hair go up, up, and off until he had the look of a GI at boot camp.

When the barber was done, he whipped off the smock with a flourish. "I wasn't thinking buzz cut when I started," he admitted, "but you know, the look suits you. Yeah. You have the face for it. Strong nose, good eyebrows . . . So? What do you think?"

Quinn grinned and said, "I think I should've waited until August. My head's cold."

"You wear a hat. Big deal."

After some back-and-forthing over whether Quinn would be allowed to pay, Tony accepted the money and said good-naturedly, "You always were a good kid." He seemed to hesitate after that before adding, "Take some advice?"

Instantly attentive, Quinn nodded and said, "From you? Sure."

In a low mutter, the barber said, "Watch your back, kid. You go poking around too much, you're bound to piss off some people. Those kinda people you don't want to piss off. You know what I mean?"

He sounded as if he were talking about the Cosa Nostra. Quinn would have laughed off the caution if it weren't for the fact that he himself had begun to feel a real unease about continuing down the road he was on.

"I don't suppose you feel like naming names?"

The barber shook his head. "I gotta live in this town."

Quinn had no fears for himself, but he was feeling more protective than ever about Mrs. Dewsbury. After installing extra fire alarms, he'd sweet-talked her into letting him have a burglar alarm installed as well. But he continued to be concerned about her, so that morning he told her that he planned to move out of her house to a small apartment he'd found on the edge of town.

Basically he wanted Mrs. Dewsbury to have nothing to do with him; she'd be safer that way. He had expected disappointment, but not tears of disappointment. It shook him. His old teacher had argued for him to stay and had almost succeeded in making him change his mind—until this.

"I appreciate the warning, Tony," Quinn said, shaking the barber's hand.

Tony gave him a tight smile and a parting shot. "Never mind about that DNA business, kid. Let it go."

Quinn had a parting shot of his own. "Frankly? That all depends on Alison's parents."

Quinn had gone into the barbershop with two goals in mind: lose the ponytail and launch a rumor that he planned to continue pressing the district attorney. He had scored on both counts, so why was he feeling so crummy?

He wanted to blame it on the weather. After the bright sun of California, he was having trouble with New England gray. The weather was raw and mean, winter at its worst. The blanket of snow that had seemed so pure and magical on the day he first arrived was now dirty and pockmarked, casting an air of impoverishment on all it touched. Everything that could move seemed sluggish and grudging, from Quinn's shoulders and elbows to the door of his truck. As he drove through streets that seemed no longer quaint but merely old, it was easy to understand how snowbirds had come up with the clever concept of Florida.

Did he want to leave California for good and come back to this?

Yes. Quinn was a son of New England, whether he liked it or not. His character had been formed there. The self-reliance, the sense of reserve, the refusal to promise more than he could deliver—all of those traits marked him as a New Englander. They had served him well during his California exile, but he had always felt like a misfit there. Californians were communal. Friendly. Lavish with their promises to help you with anything. And why not? The weather was bound to cooperate when it came time to deliver. No; Quinn was not, and never would be, a California dreamer.

But there was another reason for his desire to come back, and it was playing havoc with his equal and opposite desire for justice: He wanted to be near Olivia. Near her, with her, on her, under her—his desire for her seemed limitless. And yet the more Quinn pressed the case for his father, the more he knew he would drive a wedge between Olivia and himself.

It was that cruel paradox, and not the cruel weather, that had Quinn feeling so damned bummed out.

Mrs. Dewsbury's hands were too arthritic to tie a knot in Quinn's bow tie for him, but she was able to talk him through the process with good results.

"You look as handsome as can be," she said, tweaking the bow just a bit.

"Even though I'm bald?"

"Even so. Why, you could be on your way to your high-school prom."

"Which, by the way, I never did get to go to," he remarked. As a matter of fact, he felt *exactly* like a high-school senior as he checked himself out in the small, weathered mirror of his room. He ran a hand over the bristled remains of his hair and decided again that he must have been mad, giving old Tony carte blanche.

Mrs. Dewsbury was brushing his tux in a final once-over, although she couldn't possibly see the lint. "Do you have the mask that Livvy dropped off?"

"In my pocket," Quinn said, reaching inside his jacket for it. "I just wish I'd been here when Liv stopped by; I might take some getting used to."

"She was all aglow, my dear, trust me. I don't think a haircut is going to change that."

Looking no more substantial in her yellow cardigan than a goldfinch in April, Mrs. Dewsbury perched her tiny frame on the edge of the chenille spread that covered Quinn's bed. She had dragged the coverlet out of the attic, and she had bought—and hung!—new white curtains in his room as well. The needlepoint rug he was standing on was new, and so was the frilly shade on the lamp. She had gone all out for him. Maybe that's what had prompted the tears when he told her that, for her own good, he was going to have to move out.

Quinn fitted the mask over his eyes. It was a plain black affair, but he felt silly wearing it. Thank God Olivia hadn't dropped off something stuck on a stick. He would have felt like an idiot, brandishing it around as he made small talk.

He felt like an idiot anyway.

"I'm not supposed to wear this thing driving, surely. When *do* I put it on?" he muttered as he yanked it back off. "What the hell was I thinking, telling her yes? What am I supposed to say to all those people? We have nothing in common.''

"Stop it right now!" said Mrs. Dewsbury, as if he'd been caught clowning around during study hall. "You have as much right to be there as anyone else. If you have any doubt, think of that box of trophies downstairs. Every one of them is for merit. You didn't buy them, you *earned* them. You're brilliant, you idiot! When will you get that through your thick skull?"

He laughed out loud at her carrot-and-stick approach to getting him out the door. "Boy, I wish you'd married my father," he said, grinning. "We both could have used you to whip us into shape."

"Now that's silly," she said, blushing. "Anyway, if you'd ever attended one of these things, you'd know how completely insipid most of the conversation is."

"Why didn't you say so?" said Quinn, flashing her a rakish grin. "I can do insipid."

"It's the one thing you *can't* do," she said dryly. "But never mind. You are going to have a wonderful time with your Miss Bennett, and then tomorrow morning you are going to give me a complete account of who was there and, more importantly, who was not." With a doleful sigh, she added, "Lord knows, you won't be around much longer for our little tête-à-têtes."

"Now don't start," he warned, still smiling, as he slid the mask back in his jacket pocket. "You know I'm moving out for your sake, not mine. Do you think I want someone terrorizing you with the fat end of a Doberman's thigh-bone?"

"Well, pooh, what do I care? As long as it's not still in the Doberman," she said, hauling herself up from the bed.

She whacked him gently across his knuckles and said, "Do you honestly think that someone's going to break in here and burn my house down just to encourage you to leave town? You have too high an opinion of yourself, Quinn Leary," she said, shaking a finger at him. "You always did."

"I like that! A minute ago, you said I had no confidence."

"Well—never mind. You're a contradiction, that's all," she said, marching past him with a sniff.

Pleased to see that her knees seemed to be working much better nowadays, he said to her retreating figure, "Maybe I should be taking *you* to the ball, Mrs. D. That's a pretty sexy spring you have in your step."

She turned around and gave him an utterly baleful look. "I remember now. You could be *quite* fresh. Will you be back very late?"

"I . . . don't know," he said honestly.

"Will you be back at all?"

"I . . . don't know."

"I suppose I'll have to set that silly alarm, in that case. Well, get moving. It's terrible form to be late on a first date."

Eleven

No bra, sheer stockings, a silver lamé slip dress—it couldn't get more basic than that. It had taken Olivia less than sixty seconds to get dressed, which left her with way too much time to pace the Aubusson rug in her living room as she waited for Quinn to join her in the suicide mission she had planned for them that night.

Her father had no idea that Quinn was going to be one of his guests. At the last minute Olivia's mother had lost her nerve and ditched the assignment. After much agonizing, Olivia had decided simply to wing it. So her father didn't know. So what? He wouldn't make a scene, not with a house full of guests. And if he blew his top after the party, well, it wouldn't be the first time that Olivia had got him to do it.

Currently the plan was for her mother to act surprised when Olivia showed up on the arm of Quinn Leary in the receiving line. It was the only way to spare Teresa Bennett from her husband's inevitable outrage. Olivia and her mother were being completely deceitful, of course, but they were in it too deep to be anything else. Olivia's only concern was that her guileless mother might not be able to pull off the deception.

So much for the honesty-is-the-best-policy route.

Working through her jitters, Olivia fluffed the pillows on her slipcovered sofa and stacked the coffee-table magazines that she had previously fanned, then stacked, then fanned again. She wanted Quinn to be impressed, but she didn't have a clue what impressed a man like him.

If I were Quinn, what would I notice first?

The view, of course. Too bad it was dark.

Her two-bedroom townhouse, one of a dozen on a knoll overlooking the Connecticut River, was pricey for its size. But the mortgage had bought her not only a beautiful view, but such amenities as French doors, a Jenn-Air, a copper hood, and an east-facing kitchen. It was lovely to watch the sun rise over the river as she ate her cereal, and worth every extra nickel. Quinn would think so, too, if . . . if . . .

If.

The chime at the front door sounded as shrill as the steam whistle at the textile mill. Olivia ran to answer it, catching one of her high heels in the fringe of the hall rug and very nearly sending herself sailing through a sidelight. In a fierce effort to compose herself, she took a deep breath and blew it out like a bottlenose dolphin, then put on a smile and swung the door wide.

"Wow."

"Wow."

They stood there, assessing one another in unabashed admiration, until Quinn remembered that he was hiding something behind his back. He whipped out a dozen roses in crinkly cellophane and said, "I sure hope you weren't expecting a wrist corsage."

"Hmm."

"I know; they're not in a box. They're not even fragrant. I'm sorry. It was a last-minute thing."

"No, I mean . . . your *hair*."

"Oh, that. Yeah." He gave her a quirky smile and said, "Aren't you cold, standing there like that?"

Was she? "Oh, I'm sorry. Please. Come in," she said, accepting the roses as if they were gold and frankincense and myrrh.

Looking as grand as her brother ever had in topcoat and tux, Quinn brushed close by her as he passed on his way inside. Olivia's first and only thought was to bolt the door behind them and never let him out again. Ever.

"It's a great haircut," she said, unable not to stare. "You just look so . . . great."

He nodded in embarrassed acknowledgment. His hands were jammed in the pockets of his topcoat, giving him an air so artless that she found it sophisticated.

He said softly, "I can't begin to tell you how beautiful you are."

Her lashes fluttered down. "Thank you. It's the dress."

"That, too." He glanced around, but seemed puzzled why they were still there. "Ready to go?" he asked, gesturing an after-you through his topcoat pockets.

Shy. That's what he seemed. It was their first real date, after all. Olivia found his manner irresistibly intriguing. "We have time," she said, preferring for obvious reasons to arrive with the crush. "Would you like a drink before we leave?"

"Thanks, no," he said with a hapless smile. "I'd better hold on to what's left of my wits."

"Nervous?"

"Uh-huh."

"Me, too." For oh-so-many different reasons.

She looked around them as if she also were seeing everything for the first time. Suddenly, what she saw didn't impress her very much: a small, fireplace living room that fed into an open foyer that fed into a dining area. Two good pieces of cherry furniture from France. A fairly valuable slant-top desk of yew wood. Top-of-the-line fabric, naturally, on all the upholstered surfaces. And the Aubusson. But that was it, the sum total of her nesting instinct so far. It was nothing compared to the loving care that her mother and her sister-in-law had lavished on their respective homes. Olivia hadn't even got around to doing something about the bare walls and windows yet. Except in the bedroom, of course.

"I don't spend much time at home," she said, feeling obliged to confess to that sin. "I've never even used the fancy exhaust hood in the kitchen. I mostly eat cereal."

"You're not domestic. Okay," he said, giving her a puzzled look. "Duly noted."

How mortifying; she sounded as if she were auditioning

for the part of his wife. "I don't know why I'm—we're—so nervous," she said. "We were a lot more relaxed around one another when we were growing up."

He smiled. "You weren't as pretty then."

"And you weren't as debonair. I need a drink," she said, hoping that wine would calm her heart. "Why don't you take off your coat?"

She went into the kitchen and took a bottle of merlot from a cupboard, then handed it to Quinn to open while she slid out a stemmed glass for herself—and then one for him—from a wooden rack above the counter.

Should she warn Quinn that there might be a ruckus in the receiving line? She didn't see how she could. She held out both glasses; dutifully, he filled them.

So there they stood in their fancy duds, searching for something to toast. He touched his glass to hers. "Here's to the modern woman," he said with a look that Olivia somehow took as mocking.

"Because I don't cook? I can cook," she said, bristling. "Anyone can cook. All you have to do is follow a recipe."

Please, please, don't open the fridge. There was nothing there except a carton of skim milk, some yogurt, and some cigar-looking things that used to be bananas. She had put them in the fridge after the fruit flies showed up, thinking—ha-ha—that she'd use them to make some kind of tea bread for her mother for Christmas.

Ha-ha.

"I guess you're right," she said, sipping to his toast after all. "I'm a pathetically modern woman."

He leaned back against the kitchen counter and gave her a thoughtful look. "What did it say under your yearbook mug shot? I was never mailed a copy, needless to say."

"Oh! Would you like to s—?"

Dumb; why remind him of a year he'd never get back? "Y'know, I think it's buried somewhere in a closet," she amended. "Maybe another time. Anyway, as I recall, it said, 'Olivia Bennett—she hasn't got time for the pain.'"

"Carly Simon."

"Mm-hmm," she said, sipping her wine. "I suppose it was as accurate as any of those predictions are. They're a little like horoscopes, aren't they? You see what you want to see in them."

"Liv, I have a confession to make," he said out of the blue. "All those years that I spent in California . . . well, I thought of you more than once. A lot more than once."

Her heart was on the launching pad, ready for liftoff, when he added, "and every damn thought of you was more bitter than the one before it."

"Oh."

He set the wineglass down on her Corian counter and walked up to the bank of windows in the breakfast area, the windows that had a view of a swift-running river he could not see. For a long moment he was lost in his own private reverie, this buzz-cut, cummerbunded stonemason who'd just confessed to harboring bitter thoughts of her.

Olivia waited, baffled, to hear more.

Soon enough, it came rolling out. "I resented you because you had everything I ever wanted in life: stability, a proper family, the admiration and respect of everyone around you.

"Oddly enough," he added with a shrug, "I never resented your brother. I knew I was smarter than Rand, and better on the field. But you! You had everything I had—ambition, brains, discipline—and wealth and status besides. That gave you an unbeatable edge. God, how I hated that. Hated you. Thought I hated you, anyway," he said with a pained glance in her direction.

He turned back to the river that he didn't know was there. "But guess what? It turns out that I was wrong," he said softly. "It turns out that I've been confusing hate with something else. So maybe I'm not so smart, after all."

He got lost in such profound silence that Olivia, type A that she was, felt the need to prompt him. "Something else?"

"Yeah."

He sounded so resigned, so melancholy. But not very specific.

"Something else?"

"Mmm." Turning from the window, hands still in his pockets, he said, "But honest to God, I'm not sure what."

He came back toward her and when he got close he stopped, half-circling her face with his fingertips. "Look at you," he said in a voice of wonder. "There's not a man alive who could resist you. But there are other beautiful women in the world—a lot of them in California—and I've never felt this way about any of them."

He laughed at himself and said, "God, I sound like an arrogant bastard. Am I out of line, telling you this?"

"I'll let you know," she said, hardly daring to breathe. Beautiful? *She* wasn't beautiful.

"Liv, we're not lovers, so how can this be—?" He made a comical face, lifting his eyebrows and compressing his lips.

"Something else?"

"Yeah. That. I spent seventeen years resenting you, and now suddenly it's . . . something else."

Olivia understood completely; she was feeling it herself. She studied his face and marveled that she knew it so well: the hazel eyes, narrowed in self-defense from the sun even when the sun wasn't shining; the eyebrows that were pulled together in determination more often than not; the squared chin with its hint of a cleft; the nose with its bridge more Roman than Celtic; the wide grin with a tiny, endearing overlap in the two front teeth. She knew his face almost as well as she knew her own.

"We grew up together," she said, trying to explain away the comforting sense of familiarity. "That should count for something."

Quinn's response to that was a chuckle. "We grew up together, it's true. But you were a major pain in the butt."

"That's what I thought about you!"

"I never could stand your self-assurance. You were way too cocky for a girl."

"Isn't that funny? I used to think you were rude, refusing to let a girl win."

"I know. You expected me to give up my seat to you, so to speak. And yet *you* always went for the jugular."

"And you always went for the knees."

He nodded in fond recollection. "You remember the day the door of your locker was siliconed shut and you couldn't get at the take-home final you were supposed to hand in? I did that."

"I was sure you did. That's why I stole your term paper from study hall a week later."

"*You* did that?"

"Uh-huh. And then I gave it to Tim Kroft. He got an A."

"You little devil!" Quinn said with a surprised laugh. "If I had known that, I wouldn't have stuck up for you when Jimmy O'Malley wrote that limerick about you and posted it all over school."

"I remember that. You ripped them all down and then you gave Jimmy a black eye. That was really nice of you, Quinn," she said with a sigh, and she meant it. The limerick had been insulting and obscene and she had been completely devastated by it.

She looked up and said, "I was so grateful. I never forgot what you did. I think that's why after you and your father disappeared, I sneaked into the cottage to save your trophies before the police could confiscate them. My parents still don't know that I was hiding them all this time."

"It amazes me that you did that. And even though I reacted like a jerk when I found it out, I have to say, it was a terrific gesture. I should have thanked you properly at the time."

She took a sip of her wine. "Properly?"

Please, please, please.

Quinn smiled, then lifted the glass from her hand, setting it carefully on the counter beside them. He slid his hands behind her head, twining them in the curls of her hair.

"Yeah. Properly," he whispered, bending his face to hers for the kiss. It was tenderly given, a light and yet lingering token that had as much respect in it as it had affection.

She closed her eyes, the better to savor the brush of his mouth against hers, and felt the shiver of his breath as he said, "I want you to know . . . that sometime soon . . . I plan to make love to you, Olivia Bennett."

"Now who's cocky?" she whispered, but the shivers that rippled over her were her own.

Ignoring her challenge, he began to drop feathery kisses on her cheek, her chin, the arc of her throat. She leaned her head back like a cat to savor the strokes and felt his voice rumbling on the surface of her skin as he tested her with tiny, provocative nips and murmured, "I want you to know . . . that I'm not in this . . . for the thrill of it all."

"Oh, gosh, I am," she whispered through a pleasurable haze.

His chuckle echoed close to the beat of her pulse, quickening it. He sounded so sure of himself. "Livvy . . . Liv," he said on a sigh, "you do things to me . . ."

"I can . . . tell," she said as he pressed close to her, signaling unmistakably his arousal.

He brought his mouth back to hers for another kiss, night-and-day different from the first. This one was an expression of raw hunger—rough, ready, a sharp and painful reminder that he meant what he said. Caught off guard by it, Liv made a sound in her throat of surprise and then of surrender as she yielded to the force of it.

His hand caught and cupped her breast through the thin fabric of her dress, sending a surge of desire rocketing through her. He pulled the sparkly string-strap away from her shoulder and ran his tongue in the hollow there, driving her deeper into the ground.

"Christ, how I want you!" he muttered, coming back to cover her mouth greedily with his. He had her pinned against the counter; her hands gripped the smooth Corian in her effort to steady herself against him. His kiss was dark, delicious, an invitation to a steamy netherworld that she rarely had time to visit.

"I'm sorry . . . I'm sorry . . . this isn't what I'd planned," he said hoarsely, but he didn't sound sorry at all.

"I'm sorry, too," she whispered, which also was not true. "The . . . oh, God, the—"

She brought her hands up around his neck and cupped the back of his closely shorn head, pulling him closer, returning his kisses, feeding the fire. It was her one, last, willful indulgence before she broke away and finished her sentence by gasping, "The *timing*. It's awful."

His look seemed blurred and undirected for a second, but he snapped back into focus quickly enough. "The gala?"

She nodded glumly.

He scowled and shook his head, like a boy being offered bad medicine. "I say we stay here instead," he said, bringing his mouth closer to hers again.

"No, wait, stop," she said, laying her fingers against his lips. His face was inches from hers. She stared fiercely into his green eyes, battling the promise of pleasure she found there. She was only a slinky dress and a pair of pantyhose away from saying yes. It would be so easy, so decadent, to hole up with him in her townhouse making love instead of getting on with her campaign to rehabilitate him with the good citizens of Keepsake.

But she had a civic duty.

"We *have* to go, Quinn. They're expecting me. They might think something—"

"Happened to you? Because you were alone with the gardener's son?"

She grimaced and said, "Oh, come on, Quinn. You know that's not what they'd think."

He shrugged. "It was worth a shot." And then he grinned that heart-melting, endearing grin of his and took a big step back from her. "Madame," he said with a deep bow and a graceful flourish of both hands, "your chariot awaits."

She gave him a wary look. "You didn't hire a limo or anything, did you?"

"Are you kidding?" he said as they headed for their coats. "Who's got that kind of dough? High-school seniors, maybe; not grown-ups."

His quip stopped Olivia in her tracks. She turned to him and said softly, "We really are grown-ups now, aren't we?

Where did it go, our youth? It ended so abruptly.''

"No kidding.''

"Oh, definitely for you, but even for me. I worked like a slave through college . . . then graduate school . . . then the shop . . . another shop . . . and where have I gotten? Practically nowhere.''

"Aren't you being a little hard on yourself?'' asked Quinn as he donned his topcoat.

"No. I should be running a company.''

"A textile mill, perchance?'' Quinn ventured shrewdly. "Why aren't you?''

"My father had other plans, all of them spelled 'Rand.' Don't get me started on that one,'' Olivia said flatly. She reached into the back of her closet and took out a floor-length black velvet cape lined in scarlet. It was a ridiculous extravagance she'd bought years ago and had worn only once, but as she slipped it over her shoulders, she knew that on this night, at this gala, with this man, the velvet cape was finally going to fulfill its destiny.

She fastened the ebony-encrusted button and, feeling wildly romantic, turned around in a small circle for him to survey. "Well? What do you think?''

He gave her a look that warmed her down to her silk-covered toes. "I think I'm a damned lucky bastard,'' he said, coming up to her and kissing her softly.

"Hold that thought,'' she said with a sly smile, "for just a few more hours.''

Quinn didn't have a limo and driver waiting for her, but he did have a rented Mercedes. Olivia scolded him for throwing his money around, but secretly she was pleased that he was treating her like a homecoming queen. Yes, their prom days were definitely behind them, and that was too bad. But somehow Olivia couldn't help thinking that the best was yet to come.

Twelve

Quinn was curious to know why, exactly, Olivia *wasn't* working for her father at the mill. It seemed to him that Owen Bennett was wasting the best resource he had.

"Thanks for the vote of confidence," she said as they drove along the river before taking the turn into town. She explained how disappointed she had been when her father hadn't offered her a job.

"I was furious that my father was willing to hand over responsibility to my brother and not to me. Sometimes I think he just wants Rand where he can keep an eye on him—remember when Rand had that summer job at a camp in Maine, and my dad had to go up there to bail him out of jail?"

"When he was arrested for going on that joyride with those guys who stole a car up there? Yeah, I remember. Rand bragged about it to the whole team when he got back."

"Well, I can still hear my dad yelling that Rand was never going to leave Connecticut again, not if my dad had anything to say about it. Which of course he did—and still does.

"Anyway, out of either stubbornness or stupidity, I decided to stick around and beat my father at his own game. I was determined to be a success right under his nose. I don't know what I thought I was going to do. Start a rival textile mill?"

She let out a rueful laugh and continued. "I came up with the idea of Miracourt: high-end fabrics for decorating and for apparel. The store's a success, but I'm not close enough to the city to really take off. So I've begun to import decorator items for the home, mostly from France, and I'm going to branch out into mail order. And in the meantime, I threw in with my father to open Run of the Mill—because outlet stores are where it's at nowadays, I guess."

"You don't sound thrilled."

"I don't like the outlet," she admitted frankly. "It's in a crumbling warehouse with bad lighting and no windows. I get depressed when I go there, but my father is convinced that when the surroundings are dreary, people feel they get more value."

"He's probably right."

"I know that. He reminds me every chance he gets."

Her answer was decidedly tense. Presumably it had something to do with the fact that they were discussing her relationship with her father, which had been problematic for as long as Quinn could remember.

He recalled an April afternoon in seventh grade when Olivia had stopped to talk to him while he and his own father were raking the grounds of the estate. Owen Bennett happened to drive by. He called from the car for his daughter to come back to the house. She refused. He told her again. She refused again. Quinn wondered then—as he wondered still—if Olivia simply regarded him as a handy stick to poke in her father's eye.

He figured he'd soon find out. He drove the Mercedes through the open iron gates and past the cottage he had once called home and headed for the grand house on the hill, obscured from view by carefully placed evergreens growing among the century-old specimen trees that lent the scene such dignity.

"Funny," Quinn mused aloud. "This hill seemed so much steeper when I was a kid."

"Yes. That's how it always is."

He glanced at Olivia and saw that she was as tight as an

overwound clock. "You're not dragging me here over your father's objections, by any chance?" he asked, suddenly suspicious.

"No way," she answered tersely.

He eased into the last turn of the winding driveway, aware of light ahead. His first glimpse of the manor and its immediate grounds was through the grand sweep of branches on a copper beech. Quinn became aware first of brilliance, and then of magic: every tree and shrub between them and the house was strung with tiny white lights. The effect was spectacular, something out of the robber-baron age and wholly befitting a turn-of-the-century mansion like the Bennett house.

Quinn remembered the old days when his father used to climb an extension ladder to decorate two evergreens, one on each side of the portico, with big colored lights. But this! It must have taken a crew of men and a hydraulic lift to get it done. It was beautiful, all right, but it was completely over the top, like something out of Disney World.

"I miss the colored lights," he found himself muttering.

"Hmm? Oh. Those. Yes. They were nice."

She was still somewhere else. He didn't like it. "I'll drop you off and park the—"

"No, they have a valet for that," she said. "Just pull up to the house."

Of course, a valet. He should have known. Thank God for the Mercedes. "Well, this should be fun," he managed to say in a voice not completely grim. He rolled to a stop under the portico of the brightly lit house.

"Quinn! I have a confession to make!" Olivia blurted out as the valet opened her door for her. Scrambling out of the seat, she said in a single breath: "My father doesn't know you're coming or Rand but my mother does but she's not telling so just play along!"

Before he could say, "With what?" the valet was slamming her door in his face. Feeling as if he'd been zapped with a stun gun, Quinn sat where he was.

Now she tells me? Now she freaking tells me?

He snapped back to reality when he noticed the impatient valet, a kid who by the looks of him was a tackle on Keepsake's current team, waiting for him to surrender the wheel. Quinn got out and handed over the Mercedes to him, not without trepidation, and then turned to face the woman he had considered a friend and hoped to have as a lover.

"You evil little witch—this is a setup!" he said, seething.

"It's not! Oh, Quinn, it's not!" she said with an imploring look. "I was going to tell him, really I was, but—oh, what's the difference! Let's just go in and get it over with, can't we, please? All right?"

"No, it's *not* all right, goddammit," he said in a low growl. He tried to grab her arm to lead her out from under the portico, but he couldn't find it in the folds of the goddamned cape. "I'm not going where I'm not invited—not in there! Town Hill is one thing, but—" He swore under his breath and said, "Hell, I'm outta here."

He turned to go, but she caught his sleeve. "Quinn! You're not going to run *again*!"

Bull's-eye. She got him where he lived. He turned back around and blasted her a look filled with pure felony.

How could someone so smart be so incredibly dumb? Was she trying to provoke her father into all-out war? Jesus! Quinn was going to have to count on the Bennetts' good breeding; he sure couldn't count on hers.

"All right," he said. "We go in; we go out. Five minutes, and then I take you home and you'll be free to come back and party on with your peers or sprawl around and watch Guy Lombardo on TV. Just as long as I'm out of it."

Looking chastened and as near to meek as she got, Olivia allowed him to grab a fistful of velvet and haul her up to the double doors, thrown open to a steady flow of incoming guests. Quinn couldn't tell whether she was more afraid of him or of her father at that moment. What the hell had she been thinking, browbeating her mother into going along and then blithely omitting to tell her father? He found himself actually feeling sorry for the Bennetts—something strange and new.

The lofty entrance hall was a cavernous affair floored in marble. Quinn had been in it only a few times before in his life, none of them social. He remembered the most memorable time: Olivia had fallen out of a tree and got knocked unconscious, and he had carried her home in his arms and handed her over, still groggy, to her shocked and hysterical mother.

Ten years old, and in his arms. He should've quit while he was ahead.

"Is this the point when we put on the masks?" he said dryly.

"Oh! I forgot."

She reached inside her silver-beaded bag and took out a narrow slip of silver that wouldn't hide her face at all. Quinn couldn't help feeling that the mask she'd given him to wear made him a lot more incognito. Was that by design? He took the thing out of his inside pocket and slipped it over his eyes.

Hell. It made him feel more like a gate-crasher than ever. Annoyed, he pushed it up to the top of his brow and let it sit there.

Olivia said faintly, "Whatever."

The hall was a noisy, busy place. The line of masked merrymakers waiting to be received by the host and hostess seemed to be moving slowly, possibly because of the trays of hors d'oeuvres and champagne being foisted on them as they greeted one another in shrill, expectant voices. From somewhere inside, Quinn heard an orchestra launch into a swinging rendition of "In the Mood." Suddenly he got why they called it a gala: the atmosphere really was gay.

Except for him and Olivia. His pride was smarting big time; he couldn't stand the thought of being rubbed in her father's nose like month-old bologna. The last time the two were face-to-face was in the gardener's cottage and Quinn had tried to knock him down. Would Owen Bennett remember?

Quinn gave their coats to a hatcheck girl who was set up for the event in a small reception room off the hall. Then, still operating in a chill of silence, he and Olivia took their place in the line of guests.

"How many people are your parents expecting tonight?" he asked, struggling with the small-talk thing.

Olivia shrugged a shoulder—the shoulder he had kissed in hungry abandon half an hour earlier—and said, "Three or four hundred."

"Are you kidding?" he said to her under his breath. "There aren't that many people in Keepsake who can stay up until midnight."

"My father has a lot of different connections," she said without enthusiasm.

"So it would seem."

That was it for his store of party chat. God, how he wanted out of there.

A couple swooped down on them, kissing air all around and waiting gleefully for introductions. Olivia obliged them. The woman, tall, blond, and languid, said, "Quinn Leary—I have heard so *much* about you."

"I wish I could say the same," he said with a smile that was as bland as hers was sly.

The couple moved on, to be replaced by another one equally curious and insinuating. And another. And another. Pretty soon he felt like Errol Flynn, backing up the winding stairs and holding the evil king's forces at bay with only his trusty sword.

And meanwhile they were moving up the receiving line. Before he knew it, he was hearing the dread words, "Mother, you remember Quinn Leary."

He smiled grimly and held out his hand. A woman of sixty, with fearful eyes in an attractive face that reminded him only marginally of Olivia, said faintly, "Of course I do," and laid her hand limply in his.

He remembered a line from *My Fair Lady*, a movie his father had enjoyed. "How kind of you to let me come," he said, even though he knew she hadn't let him come and was feeling anything but kind.

"And, Dad . . . Quinn," murmured Olivia, who seemed to have run out of steam just when her train had the summit in sight.

Back, back she rolled, under the outraged glare of her father, who had obviously been unaware of their presence until then. This wasn't some annoyed father telling his seventh-grader to get along home. This was a man at the top of his game, ready to do whatever it took to have his will enforced.

And he left Quinn cold. "Sir," he said, sticking out his hand. Let the man take it, or not. Quinn didn't really give a damn.

Owen Randall Bennett Senior chose not.

Fine. Quinn turned to Olivia, who looked utterly miserable. In one of those blinding flashes he got occasionally, he realized that she had brought him there not to make her father's life hell but simply to put Quinn back in touch with Keepsake. She was crazy, she was nuts, but her heart was so much in the right place that Quinn found himself wanting to give her old man the same black eye he'd given to Jimmy O'Malley.

He went one better. "Call me crazy," he said, slipping his arm lightly around Olivia's waist, "but I feel like dancin'. Will you excuse us, sir?"

He ushered her past her stupefied father to the sounds of the Stones' driving classic, "Satisfaction." Perfect.

"Did I just get you disinherited?" he asked Olivia as they headed for the ballroom.

Her voice and smile were resigned as she said, "It wouldn't be the first time. I've been in and out of his will so often that his attorneys call me Rainmaker."

"Joke?"

"I got it straight from their secretary; she works at Miracourt on weekends."

"Oh, hey . . . I'm sorry, Liv. Jesus. I didn't think people

actually did stuff like that. Not outside of mystery novels, anyway.''

"Oh, I don't care anymore," she said, waving politely to someone going the other way. "The older he gets, the worse he gets. He tries to control everything and everyone. Rand is completely under his thumb, and so is my mother. I guess I'm the only holdout and it makes him crazy. I can understand why my mother has to put up with him, but I don't understand why Rand doesn't just strike out on his own. He hates working for my father.''

They entered a forty-foot-long room paneled in wood carved in delicate garlands. The room had been designed for dances, but contrary to Quinn's boast to Owen Bennett, he had no desire to dance. For one thing, he didn't know how.

In any case, neither of them felt like rocking to the beat, so they simply stood on the sidelines, watching sexily clad women gyrate with their dates from the pages of *GQ*.

"You know what I think Rand should be doing?" she asked, standing on tiptoe and leaning into Quinn's ear to be heard over the noise of the band. "He should be working with kids—teaching, or maybe even coaching. Of course, there's no money in that. Or status. My brother would rather be vice president of something he hates than be poorly paid doing something he loves.''

Why the hell were they talking about Rand? He wasn't even there. "Got him all figured out, have you?" Quinn asked, without really caring.

"Of course I've got him figured out. He's my brother and I know what's best for him," she insisted. "You remember how he was: very emotional. He has that hot temper—but on the other hand, he can be very devoted. He relates to kids on their level, and they love that. And he gets to be the center of their attention, which *he* loves.''

"I remember the temper," Quinn said, nodding. The day after an injured Rand Bennett found out that Quinn was replacing him as quarterback of the Keepsake Cougars, he went ballistic. Quinn could picture him still, hobbling around the locker room on crutches, ranting and raving about his injury. At the time, Quinn had actually felt guilty for being chosen as his replacement.

No more.

The band slid into a slow number, "Unforgettable," and suddenly Quinn remembered why he'd agreed to come: to be with Olivia. It was true that he wouldn't be outstrutting Mick Jagger or Michael Jackson at the fast stuff anytime soon, but he damn well knew how to hold a woman in his arms and move her slowly to his will.

"C'mon," he said, suddenly tired of her father, her brother, her mother, and every other Bennett on the planet. "Let's dance."

He took Olivia by the hand and led her onto what was now a crowded floor, and he drew her into his arms. Under the cover of a press of couples, he nuzzled her hair and inhaled deeply the sheer, intoxicating scent of her. Her body felt lithe and free and unbelievably well fitted to his, so much so that he knew it when her breasts lifted and fell in a sigh.

She snuggled her head on his shoulder, and he became aware that he'd never felt more content in his life. There was just something about her; it was like coming home. Home at last. He wanted only to hold her, to protect her, to have her forever in his embrace.

He closed his eyes, lost completely in the essence of her. If he were dragged from the Bennetts' house by thugs just then and shipped off to live alone on a rock in the ocean for the rest of his life, it almost wouldn't matter. He knew that he would always, always have that dance.

Live a moment completely and you possess it forever. It was such a simple formula. How had he not thought of it before?

Liv . . . sweet Liv, he thought, kissing the top of her hair. *I'm falling so much in love with you.*

She lifted her face to his. "What did you say?"

He shook his head, not trusting himself to do justice to his feelings. They ran more deeply than words.

She snuggled her cheek back on his shoulder and they

drifted together on the magic carpet of the melody, and when the song ended, they floated down to the dance floor on the sound of their own sighs. Before Quinn could escape with Olivia from the next dance—a driving, pulsing, shake-your-booty number—he felt someone whack him soundly on the back in jovial greeting.

"Quinn Leary, for chrissake! Quinn!" he shouted over the music. "How ya doin'?"

He turned to face Mike Redding, the most irrepressible of his old teammates. More brawn than brain, but with enough personality and charm that no one seemed to mind much, Mike was the kind of guy who used to make the workouts fun and the losses easier to bear. He was just an all-around, uncomplicated, regular . . . guy.

"Hey, Mike," Quinn said loudly over the music as he shook his hand. "Howzit goin'?"

"Never better. I'm a sportswear manufacturer. High-tech stuff—hot-hot-hot. We can't make enough of it. Geez, I'm glad you came," he said, hugging Olivia with one arm as he latched onto Quinn with the other. "I heard you were back, but I didn't expect to see you *here*, for chrissake. This is great!" he said, whacking Quinn on the back again.

"You gotta come over to Buffitt's house tomorrow—not you, Livvy, of course. A bunch of us guys meet every New Year's Day to watch the bowl games. Buffitt lives in a pig-pen and doesn't care when we spill beer on the rug and knock over popcorn. It's great. No wives to hassle you with coasters, no kids running in front of the tube in the middle of a touchdown play.

"Ouch!" he yelped, and turned to a blond woman half his size who had a thumb and forefinger hooked firmly into the back of his arm. "This is my wife, Mitzi."

Mitzi let go of him long enough to shake Quinn's hand. "Pleased to meet you," she said, "and don't you believe him. He doesn't open the door of the rec room during a game unless one of us is showin' blood or guts."

"The first kickoff's at noon. Everyone pitches in twenty

bucks and Buffitt takes care of provisioning. So what do you say?"

Quinn had hoped to spend the day with Olivia, but she was looking way too thrilled that someone was taking pity on him. Come to think of it, she might have set up the whole invitation. But . . . no. She seemed too surprised and too damn pleased about it.

"Sure," he said. "It sounds good."

Another whack on the back and off Mike went with Mitzi, who glanced back at Quinn once or twice from curiosity on their way out of the ballroom.

"Happy now?" he asked Olivia.

"Yes, I am," she answered, preening. "This makes everything worthwhile."

Quinn had to admit, it felt good to be regarded as something more than municipal sewage for once. The plain fact was, he'd lived in half a dozen different cities and towns in his life, and Keepsake was the only place that he had ever considered home. He'd spent the biggest—and the happiest—chunk of his life there, and old memories died hard. It felt good to be back among people his own age with whom he shared a history.

Good enough that he almost forgot why he'd come back to Keepsake in the first place.

Thirteen

Quinn Leary had endured some fairly awful New Year's Eve celebrations in the past seventeen years, but the most dreaded one of all was turning out to be pretty good.

As it turned out, Mike Redding wasn't the only one from Quinn's past who wanted to renew old acquaintance. Over the next hour, a variety of people took the trouble to come over and say hello, and after a while, Quinn detected a pattern: all of them seemed happy with their lot in life. Teacher, nurse, musician, newly adoptive parents . . .

"Obviously they're the kind who look forward, not backward," Quinn told Olivia during a quiet moment alone. They were sitting at a linen-topped table, sampling a plate of sophisticated nibbles that must have cost Owen Bennett a mill worker's annual wage.

Olivia bit into a double-stuffed mushroom and let out a moan of ecstasy that to Quinn's way of thinking was a complete waste of perfectly good passion. "Do you think the reverse is true?" she asked him as she wiped her fingertips on a tiny silver napkin. "Do you think the unhappy ones somehow blame and resent you?"

Quinn shrugged. "Coach Bronsky just walked in and he's spotted me. Check him out—what do you think?"

Olivia glanced up at the coach. "Ouch. He does seem to be sending savage looks our way. Now *there's* someone who should be wearing a mask." She added, "I wonder if he's been drinking."

"Does he have a problem that way?"

"Oh, yes. For years now. It started the year of the murder. He made a fool of himself on local TV after an especially disastrous game, and it's been downhill since. Most of the time he manages to stay sober on the job, but he has a real attitude problem. I have no idea why he's still coaching at the high school. He must know people in high places."

"Speaking of people in high places—here comes your father."

"Oh, no!" cried Olivia, cringing. "Here! Eat one of these! Look impressed! No! Look casual!"

Laughing, Quinn accepted the truffled lobster and then laid it back down on the plate. Sooner or later, this moment had to come. Quinn knew that Owen Bennett was well within his rights to ask him to leave. But the new Quinn, the mellow Quinn, was hoping that he'd be allowed to stay.

Bennett looked—for Owen Bennett—almost pleasant as he came up to their table. "I trust you two are having a good time?" he asked with a fixed smile.

"Very much so," said Quinn, and he, at least, wasn't being wildly ironic.

"Good. Olivia, I wonder if you'd excuse Quinn for a moment? I have something I'd like to discuss with him."

"Oh, Dad, please, don't. Really. Don't. It's my fault—"

"Now, now, you'll have him back in no time. Quinn? Would you do me the honor? I have an excellent collection of antique half hulls in my study," he added, which was relevant to absolutely nothing.

"My pleasure," said Quinn, standing up. He turned to Olivia and said, "Better not go near the shrimp; I remember you broke out in hives at the sophomore dance."

They'd been taking turns pulling out memories, like two kids showing off their baseball cards at camp. The hives reminiscence was new, and Olivia just about clapped her hands with joy at having that memory jogged. Anyone else might have remembered the event with a certain amount of embarrassment. Not Olivia.

Quinn gave her a quick, doting grin and then fell in with Bennett, who, between nods and smiles to his guests, chatted casually about the drive he was spearheading for a new Olympic-sized swimming pool at the high school.

The town of Keepsake, including the high school, belonged to Owen Bennett. That was the message implicit between the lines. Keepsake—and everyone in it—was his. He gave Quinn a sideways look as they walked. Did Quinn understand?

Quinn returned the look. *Yeah, yeah, got it—you're the Big Kahuna.*

Too bad Olivia refused to make it unanimous.

The library was at the end of a roped-off, sentried hall, as far from the merriment as one could get. Bennett took a key from his pocket and slipped it into the keyhole of the massive, paneled door, made from exotic woods that would never again grow on the planet earth.

If Keepsake was Owen Bennett's world, then the library was his sanctum. Everything in it radiated power and prestige: the leatherbound books—all first editions, Quinn had no doubt; the antique spinning globe, roughly the size of a Volkswagen Beetle; framed, fawning thank-you citations tucked like second thoughts on the bookshelves; a fabulous model of a four-masted schooner in its own glass case; and, of course, the ships' hulls. They lined all four walls, a fleet of mastless yachts that weren't going anywhere—except maybe into a list of assets to be probated some day after Bennett sailed off into the Great Beyond.

Geez, Quinn thought, looking around. *If I were his kid and he told me to salute, I'd be damn well tempted to snap my heels and say, "Yessir."* He had to give Olivia credit. It couldn't be easy, resisting the threat of having all those ships' hulls yanked out from under her.

Behind him, he heard a key turn. Owen Bennett was making certain they wouldn't be disturbed. He said to Quinn, "My daughter caught me off guard tonight—she's good at that. It never occurred to me to forbid her from inviting you here. My mistake."

Quinn smiled. "She's a little dickens, all right."

"She's always been a handful," her father agreed with a sigh. He walked over to the leather-topped desk that dominated the middle of the room. "Let's get down to business, shall we?" he asked. He pulled out a side drawer and took out a small white envelope. A small, white, bulging envelope.

"As I say, Quinn, I was caught off guard. I've had to scrape this together from petty cash tonight, but I can no doubt put my hands on more," Bennett said dryly. "Lest you think that those are all twenties in there—they're not." He tossed the envelope on the desk blotter and fanned some of the money out of it. Hundreds, as far as the eye could see, with some McKinleys added for dazzle.

"Door prize?" asked Quinn.

"You've kept your sense of humor. Excellent. I hate to see a grown man whine."

"Au contraire," Quinn said, rocking on the heels of his patent-leather shoes. "Lately it's been nothing but blue skies for me."

Bennett's face, itself a mask of civility, twitched into a sudden scowl. He wasn't a big guy, and that was unfortunate. Quinn was so used to facing a formation of tank-sized brutes on the football field that he found it hard to take a single, smallish, sixty-five-year-old man very seriously, patriarch or no.

Except for the money. The money, Quinn took very seriously indeed. If Owen Bennett could come up with that many thousands just to get Quinn to stop buzzing around him and his family, think what he'd be willing to pay if the stakes were *really* high.

"This money is to buy you a ticket back to California," Bennett said, twitching his lips into a thin smile. "I'll triple the amount if you make it one-way."

"Gee, I dunno," said Quinn with a bland look. "The airlines really penalize for that."

"How much do you want, you son of a bitch?"

The explosion into profanity was just a colorful expression, Quinn knew, but it sent a sharp surge of resentment through him. Who the hell did Bennett think he was talking to?

"Sir," Quinn said, leaning on the desk with the flat of his hands. "I don't think we're communicating real well here. That's my fault, I'm sure. You're a Yale grad, I have a GED. But let me just take another shot at this."

He picked up the envelope and tossed it nearer to Bennett's side of the desk. "I don't want your money. I don't need it, and I don't want it. All I want is to prove my dad's innocence. Now, that strikes me as a mission that any father can endorse. I understand your concern about having Alison exhumed. I understand it. But with the trail to the real murderer paved over and cold, I don't see any other way to exonerate Francis Leary. Can't you comprehend that?"

He stared hard into Owen Bennett's blue eyes, trying to find some hint of who the man was. It was like trying to see water through the ice pack at the North Pole.

Quinn was surprised by Bennett's next remark. "Whoever murdered Alison didn't necessarily get her pregnant. Have you thought of that?"

"I have."

"And?"

"You have to start somewhere."

There was a long, deadly pause. Quinn had the sense that Bennett had played a wild card and was regretting it.

"You're doing this out of respect for your father," Bennett said, taking another tack. "All right. But has it occurred to you that Alison had a father as well? Don't the living deserve some consideration?"

"Your brother Rupert, you mean. In your opposition to the idea of DNA testing, are you speaking for him?"

Quinn knew that he wasn't; the brothers weren't speaking, period.

"Don't underestimate a father's love for his child," Bennett said gruffly, looking away. "Let it go, Quinn," he said, turning back to face him. "I'm telling you, let it go."

Something in his answer touched Quinn. For the first time in seventeen years, he actually felt an inkling of generosity toward the man.

"Look," he said quietly, "I'll go see Alison's parents. I'll explain what I'm doing, why I'm doing it. If they have a problem with it, I'm sure they'll let me know. But I won't see an attorney about pursuing this until I've talked to your brother and his wife. You have my word on that."

It was half a loaf. Bennett, who could buy any bakery he chose, didn't look impressed. Quinn shrugged. It was the best he could do.

"Where does my daughter fit in?"

Quinn shrugged again, but this time he was faking the nonchalance, and he had the flushed cheeks to prove it. "That depends on her," he said.

"Touch her, Quinn, I'll make your life hell."

Lucifer himself couldn't have said it with any more confidence. Quinn nodded slowly, as if he were poring over a menu and couldn't decide between the fish and the chicken. "All righty," he said at last. "That seems clear enough." He gave Owen Bennett a guileless smile and said, "I assume our work here is done?"

"You know the way out."

Presumably he meant out of the library, but Quinn wouldn't have been surprised to find two bouncers on the other side of the door, waiting to lift him by the elbows and chuck him all the way to upper Main.

He turned the key and let himself out, relieved to find the roped-off hall clear except for the security guard at the far end. Nevertheless, he made his way back to the party weighed down by feelings of dread.

I'll make your life hell.

It wouldn't be the first time. If Owen Bennett had rallied to his gardener's defense all those years ago instead of tossing him out on the street without having seen a scintilla of real evidence, then Francis Leary wouldn't have panicked and run, and God only knows how all of their lives would have turned out.

I'll make your life hell. So big deal. There was nothing new in that.

More to the point, though, would he make his daughter's life hell also? If Bennett was as prone to cutting people from his will as Olivia said he was, then . . . Shit. Quinn's Catholic upbringing would never let him handle that kind of guilt. He could sooner mug an old lady than be the direct cause of Olivia's disinheritance. On the other hand, Olivia seemed to be pretty good at getting herself disinherited, so maybe he was worrying about nothing.

There was another aspect that bothered Quinn more than all the rest: He had a strong sense that Owen Bennett was protecting someone. Who it was and why he was doing it—that, Quinn couldn't say. Considering that he was estranged from his brother, Rupert, Owen Bennett seemed pretty damned solicitous of the guy's feelings. Why was he bothering?

That's what Quinn had to find out.

He went back to the table he'd been sharing with Olivia, but she was no longer there. The party had reached critical mass, and the buffet area was filled to overflowing with swarming, hungry guests. There wasn't room to swing a masked cat. The din was horrific. Suddenly Quinn had a headache the size of Rhode Island. It couldn't have been from the champagne, which was anything but cheap; he just wasn't used to this kind of crush. The scene was too contrived and stagy for his laid-back, outdoor tastes. He wanted to get away, to have a moment to puzzle out the nuances of the interview in relative peace and quiet.

Where the hell was Olivia?

He turned and found himself staring into the masked face of a blond aristocrat whom he had once idolized and then overthrown. Rand Bennett—he'd know him anywhere. When they bumped into one another in town the day after Quinn's arrival, Rand had looked both startled and contemptuous. Not tonight. The brilliant blue eyes that gazed through the black mask at Quinn were still contemptuous, but this time they were overlaid with suspicion.

"Evenin', old man," said Quinn in a dead-on imitation of some pompous geezer he'd overheard earlier.

Rand ripped off his mask. Underneath it his fair-skinned face was flushed, not with anger, but from the cold—another fashionably late arrival, apparently.

"What's the deal?" he said in a sneer. "Has my sister got you so whipped that you're letting her use you to get at my dad?"

In a reflex of anger, Quinn started for Rand's throat, then thought better of it.

"I guess I am," he answered with a lazy smile. "Does it show?"

"You—!"

Rand's own lunge ended abruptly when someone pulled him back.

"Are you crazy, Rand? You'll screw up everything!"

Quinn wouldn't have known the man's face behind the big Phantom of the Opera mask, but his booming voice was a dead giveaway: Police Chief Vickers.

Rand twisted his shoulder from the chief's grip and muttered, "Just keep him out of my way, then!"

He stormed off without a backward glance, leaving Quinn to wonder exactly what it was that he was in danger of screwing up.

"Just keep pushing it, Leary," said the chief, and then he, too, walked off—toward the roped-off wing, Quinn noticed with interest.

Quinn watched him swing one leg, then the other, over the velvet rope and then head for the far end of the hall. Reporting for duty? It wouldn't surprise him if the little white envelope ended up finding a home that night, after all.

It was a depressing, disturbing pattern: Everyone around Quinn seemed to be in on something that he was not. He felt a little the way he had back in fifth grade, when Rand and his friends built a tree house on the estate and pulled up the ladder the one time Quinn had ventured to come near.

Rebuffed and embarrassed, he had kept his distance after that. But he didn't embarrass as easily nowadays, not after what he and his father had gone through.

"Oh, Quinn! Oh good, you're alive!"

He turned to see Olivia with a half-ironic, half-sorrowful look on her unmasked face. "I'm sorry, I'm sorry," she said, pressing her hands together in prayerful apology. "Will you ever forgive me?"

He was so happy to see her that he thought, *Forgive you? Oh, yes, and walk to the end of the earth for you besides.*

"Hey," he said in laconic dismissal of the fuss she was making. "No big deal. What do you say we blow off this shindig? I think they're out of party hats, anyway."

"God, yes, let's go."

As they made their way through the guests to retrieve their coats, he found himself wondering why he assumed that Olivia wasn't in on what he now regarded as a conspiracy. Why was it that he suspected everyone of harboring secrets but her?

Because look at her face, you moron. Look at her face.

He did, and what he saw was the face of an angel. Maybe not the best-behaved angel in the universe, but certainly one of the best intentioned. Quinn didn't often trust his instincts, but in this instance, they were far too powerful to ignore. And besides, he was falling for her, and he could never fall for someone he didn't trust.

He handed the hatcheck girl his ticket and they waited as she went off in search of their coats. Olivia explained that her mother had tracked her down and had taken her upstairs not to read her the riot act, but to say how sorry she was that it was never going to work out between Quinn and Olivia.

"She said that?" Quinn said, surprised.

Olivia nodded. "You have to understand, my mother's biological clock is ticking."

"Your *mother's* clock. Uhhh, I don't get that."

"She loves—and I mean, *loves*—babies," Olivia said

with a shrug. "She wants them around while she's young enough to enjoy them."

"Now that's something I never would have considered," he said, trying to seem thoughtful and wise. Holy shit. Considering that he and Olivia hadn't even been to bed yet—were all mothers so Machiavellian? Having been raised without one, Quinn really didn't have a clue.

Olivia smiled and said, "Don't panic. I'm only telling you this so that you know where my mother is coming from."

"Uh-*huh*. Sooo . . . what did you say?"

"What could I say? I told her that clock or no clock, with you or without you, I wasn't ready to—excuse me. Miss?" she said as the hatcheck girl handed them a single wool topcoat. "I had a long black velvet cape?"

The girl, young and bored and no doubt grieving that she had to work on New Year's Eve, shook her head. "Nope. This was it."

Quinn said with a smile, "You can't really miss it. It has a red lining. Why don't you try again?"

Big sigh. Back she went. They waited. She returned. "Nope."

"Do you mind if I look?" Quinn offered.

She had no objection, and he went through every coat on every wheeled rack in the room. He came back out just in time to hear the hatcheck girl say to Olivia, "Now that I think about it, there *was* a guy in here earlier, poking around. I assumed that he came back to put away his gloves or something. Do you think he stole your cape? Why would he steal it?"

"You know," said Quinn, gritting his teeth, "the whole point of a hatcheck girl is to check on the hats."

"I know that, sir," she said with sullen courtesy.

"Oh, never mind, Quinn. It'll show up somewhere. I'll be warm in your car," she said, but she was shivering already as the nearby doors opened and closed.

Something felt very wrong. The cloakroom was filled

with furs, and any thief worth his salt should have gone for one of them, not some funky cape.

"Can you describe the man you saw?" he asked the sulking help.

"No. I only saw him from the back. I couldn't even say if he was wearing a mask, but he was definitely wearing a tux."

"How did he get out of the room without you seeing him?"

"Is this an inquisition?" she huffed.

"Quinn, let it go," Olivia said, clearly anxious to leave.

Fed up himself, Quinn took his coat and wrapped it around Olivia and said, "I'll bring the car around myself."

When he pulled up, Olivia was waiting outside, looking waiflike and lost in his big black coat. Her face brightened when he pulled up, and he felt a surge of odd, unexpected triumph. She was throwing her lot in with him. Olivia Bennett, Princess of Keepsake, was about to take up with Quinn Leary, the gardener's son. Him!

How could he not feel triumphant?

Fourteen

As they drove away from the estate, he could see Olivia's spirits begin to rise noticeably. She didn't ask Quinn about the meeting with her father, and he didn't offer to fill her in. Maybe she knew that Owen Bennett tended to be free and easy with his checkbook whenever things got sticky. If she didn't, then someone else was going to have to tell her. It sure wasn't going to be Quinn.

In any case, by the time the Mercedes began the steep climb up the hill to her townhouse, Olivia seemed to have shaken off her jittery mood and had become, once again, the warm and alluring woman who'd had him going around in circles of lust and longing for the past few hours.

In the hall she dumped his coat over a tall-backed chair and slipped off her shoes, then said, "Turn around."

Puzzled, Quinn did as he was told. When he turned back to her, he saw a pair of gray pantyhose lying on top of his coat. Good news: There wasn't a whole lot of clothing left on her body. Bad news: Why had she made him turn around?

Glancing at a small brass clock on the mantel, Olivia said, "Not long to midnight. I'll make tea."

More bad news. He'd been thinking wine.

"Fine with me," he lied, and he followed her into the kitchen. He watched her put on a kettle, taking satisfaction from the sight of her moving, unbound, in that silvery, clingy dress. She was as fluid as liquid mercury, and probably as tricky to hold.

"Too bad I never got the chance to meet Eileen," he said, trying hard to keep his hands off those hips as she glided barefoot past him. "She sounds like someone I'd like to know."

"Eileen would never come with Zack having a temperature," Olivia said as she took out two mugs. "Frankly, I was surprised to see Rand there; he worries about the kids as much as she does. They're incredibly dear to him."

She added, "I suppose he felt obliged to put in at least a token appearance. New Year's Eve means a lot to my mother. My father proposed on New Year's Eve."

"A time for new beginnings," Quinn agreed, hoping fervently that this was one of them.

She brushed his sleeve as she reached for the tea canister. He turned and brought his arm around her, flattening his hands on the counter on either side of her. Penned in like that, she might have turned skittish, or even hostile.

No siree. "Hey, aren't you cramped in that monkey suit?" she asked, reaching up to his bow tie. With ease she undid the knot, then tossed the strip of black cloth on the counter—and furthermore, went on to undo the top three studs of his shirt.

Good news.

"All better," she said lightly.

"Much better," he said, lowering his mouth to hers.

Their lips met, their tongues touched. Her arms came up around his neck and he found himself sliding his hands along them, simply to savor the soft, smooth surface of her skin. He was used to working with stone—hard, rough, resistant—and she was everything that his work was not.

Liquid mercury she may have been, but she was turning him into a puddle of molten iron as he deepened the kiss, pinning her in his arms, all the while listening to the shriek of his blood roaring through his veins.

"B-boiling," she stammered.

"Oh God . . . you bet," he said in a groan.

"I mean—" She pointed limply toward the stove. The chrome kettle, spouting steam, was doing it with a vengeful screech.

He let her go, reluctantly, and she filled the poppy-red mugs. After that she set them with symmetrical precision on a small wood tray. She put a cobalt blue plate between the mugs. She laid two spoons, like a pair of oars, one on each side of the tray. And then, very carefully, she began carrying the tray out of the room.

"Should we think about tea bags?" he asked at last.

"Oh! Those. Right," she said, frowning into the mugs of boiled water. She looked up at Quinn and the frown remained. "*You.* Into the living room and stay there until I bring the tea."

Quinn smiled and took himself out of her sight, convinced that he was about to experience the best New Year's Eve he'd ever had. He tossed off his jacket—the place was nicely warm—and rolled up his shirtsleeves. Free from the distraction that was Olivia, Quinn was able to focus on the efficient majesty of her townhouse. It wasn't large, but all the glass sure as hell made it look spacious. During the day it probably seemed twice as big, because the floor-to-ceiling windows would bring much of the outside in.

He was standing at one of those bare, oversized windows, looking out into an unnervingly black landscape, when Olivia came in with the tray and set it on a bronze-legged table in front of a sinfully soft-looking couch.

Quinn stayed where he was, thinking now about that blackness and about the missing cape. Who took it, and where was it now? More important, where was *he* now?

"I found some cookies that are hardly soggy at all. Come sit. We don't have much time until they drop the ball," she said, flipping through the networks with her remote.

He walked back to the sofa and sank into a cloud-soft cushion beside her. The TV was broadcasting merriment from Times Square, but his mind was in computer mode now.

Why steal it? Did someone know it was hers? How? Either he had seen her arrive in it, or he had watched the two of them leave the townhouse together earlier. Of course, someone could have known from the get-go that the cape was Olivia's. A friend or a relative. Quinn decided to put that possibility aside for the moment. It didn't make sense, and he didn't want it to make sense.

"Quinn! Really! Where did I lose you?" Olivia asked, waving her hand in front of his face as if she were a hypnotist whose act had gone wrong.

"Hmm? Sorry," he said. "My mind was somewhere else."

"So I see," she said, standing back up. With a look of pure, devilish mischief she hiked her silver slip of a dress to mid-thigh and brought one knee down on each side of him, straddling him. She began working the lower buttons of his shirt.

"Now you're trying to shock me," he said mildly.

"Am I succeeding?"

"Real well." He had a hard-on that felt the size of his forearm. What was it that a great historian had once said? God gave man a brain and a penis, with only enough blood to run one at a time?

Right now, Quinn knew just where all the blood was pooled.

He looked up into Olivia's eyes, dark and dancing and inviting, and he decided, what the heck, first things first. "You're a witch, you know that?" he murmured, slipping his hand behind her dress. He gave a tug at the zipper and listened to the satisfying sound of its effortless slide as the fabric loosed what little hold it had on her body.

He had the sense that he was testing her and she was testing him, but no one flinched. She smiled, and Quinn realized that the smile had been seventeen years in coming.

"Sweet Olivia," he whispered, sliding the thin sparkly strap off her shoulder. He watched with pleasure as her eyes fluttered lower and her lips parted in a sigh. Greedy for her flesh, he nuzzled, then nipped her shoulder, marveling that it was like no other, and peeled her dress lower still, exposing bare breast. With his tongue he tasted its rosy tip, making her moan.

His craving for her was wide and deep, and it left him shaky. "Liv . . . ah, Liv," he said, unable now to utter more than the essence of her. He peeled away the silver fabric like a wrapper from a candy bar, exposing her other breast, sending his own hunger to a new level of anticipation, a boy with a KitKat bar all for his own.

Make it last, he thought, but he couldn't get at her fast enough. He began to devour her, dragging his mouth from one breast to the other, thrilling to the sound of her breaths coming fast, always in fear that, like a candy bar, she would somehow vanish in no time flat.

Her moans became shudders; her shudders, a series of whimpering pants, until she caught his face between her splayed fingers and kissed him hard. Her tongue was everywhere at once, reckless and wanting. He met and circled it with his own, in a dance as predestined as any in the animal kingdom. *Come to me, come to me* was the song on both their lips.

In one easy motion he twisted her up from his lap and onto her back, her left side lost in the seafoam-colored pillows that lined the sofa and tumbled over her like surf. Her face was flushed, her lips puffy and wet; he could not imagine a more desirable countenance.

"Let me love you," he said in a besotted voice.

"Quinn, yes . . . oh yes," she answered, lifting her arms to him. The gesture was so completely without guile that it pierced his heart with its devastating directness. Quinn found himself sitting up and sucking in a lungful of air, simply to get past the blow.

And that was his undoing.

Because as he did it, the beam of a car's lights cut across them like the sweep from a lighthouse. He couldn't believe it. Out there, somewhere below them, was a curving drive where cars were free to roam. Olivia's house was on a knoll and the windows were low enough that the combination provided ringside viewing for the curious as well as the calculating.

"Jesus!" he said. "We're on stage!"

"No, we're not. No one can see us. No one cares," she argued breathlessly, tugging at his sleeve.

An incredulous laugh escaped him. "Olivia—a car just went by. I practically saw the whites of the driver's eyes." He pulled her dress back up, as if he'd been caught doing something wrong, and felt a sudden surge of irritation at his guilty response. Damn it! It was the last feeling he wanted.

He stood up, determined to get past the welter of bad emotions stuck in his craw like lousy pizza. "Hey, kiddo," he said softly, "unless we tape newspapers over those windows, this is not going to happen. Not here, not on this couch."

Her smile was edgy; she was taking it personally. "No problem," she said, sitting up and pulling the sparkly spaghetti straps over her shoulders again.

It was absolutely the wrong time to ask the question, but it came flying out: "Have you ever worn that cape before?"

Obviously the blood had returned to his brain.

She stared at him. "Why are you asking me *that*?"

"Just . . . have you?"

"Yes," she said, clearly annoyed at the shift in his mood. "Once. To the Met, five years ago. Why?" she repeated.

He knew he shouldn't continue to obsess over the cape, but the blood was where it was. "If no one knew that you owned that cape—if it wasn't your trademark, say, during the holidays—then someone must have seen you in it for the first time tonight."

"Your point being?"

"My point being, it couldn't have been stolen for its value, not with all those furs around. Someone wanted it because it was *your* cape, Olivia."

She snorted and said, "I think you're confusing me with Elvis Presley. No one would want a cape because it's mine."

But Quinn was on a mission now, determined to put

some healthy fear in her. She was just too blasé for a beautiful woman living alone and fraternizing with the enemy.

He said, "Indulge me here, please. How could someone have known it was your cape? He could have seen you as we entered the great hall tonight. I admit, that's the likeliest scenario."

He hooked a thumb at the blackness pressing against the bank of windows. "Or he could have seen you as we left here. Which means he could be out there again. If that's the case, I'd just as soon that he didn't see any more of you than he has already," he said dryly.

Her response to that was incredulous laughter. "There's no one out there, Quinn." She stood up and, egging him on with a defiant smile, took hold of the straps of her dress. Apparently she planned to flash the darkness to make her point.

"Oh, for—humor me, would you, goddammit?" he said, reaching her in two long strides. He scooped her up in his arms before she could irritate him any more than she already had and hushed her objections with a hard kiss. Then he began carrying her up the stairs, he didn't know why. To prove how powerless she could be in some man's arms?

She seemed to have mixed emotions about his impulsive act. "Hey! What're you doing?" she cried. "Quinn! Put me down!" But she didn't struggle, and he was grateful for that. He was tired of playing games.

At the top of the stairs, he said, "Which bedroom?" and before she could answer, he toed the right door open and walked through it with her still in his arms.

"Drapes—good," was all he said. She laughed. He laid her on the bed and kissed her again, a wet and hungry promise, and then he began to unbutton his shirt.

Bemused, she said, "I feel like Scarlett O'Hara."

"I never read the book," he said, tossing his shirt on a chair.

"We'll have to rent the video."

He peeled off his undershirt and sent it sailing over to the long-sleeved shirt, then kicked off his shoes and unzipped his trousers. He looked up with a wry smile. "Next thing I know, you'll be wanting to rent *Titanic.*"

"No, I've—"

Off went the trousers, off went the Jockey underwear, and whatever it was that she was going to say about *Titanic,* it never got formed into speech.

That's it, thought Olivia. Spoiled forever. That grin . . . on that body . . . Quinn Leary was the answer to a woman's fantasies. She felt a sudden moment of panic, a stab of inadequacy. He could be in a Calvin Klein ad. She couldn't.

"Almost forgot," he said, reaching into the hip pocket of his pants. He came up with two foil packets and slapped them down on the painted nightstand. "For starters. Now. Where were we?"

He looked and sounded so cocky. If any other man had approached her with such confidence . . . but this was Quinn, the mighty Quinn, and he was definitely entitled.

He sat on the side of the bed and said with a burning look, "Now you."

"Now me," she whispered.

He reached for the sparkly straps with hands that were shaky, and with infinite tenderness he slid the straps from her shoulders. And from that single, tender gesture, she knew: she was in love with him.

"You *have* seen *Gone with the Wind,*" she said in a flash of illumination. "And *Titanic,* too." She knew it, because at that moment she could see straight into his soul. He was a romantic.

But he would never admit it. He gave her a wonderfully wry look and said, "Prove it," then peeled her dress down and down and down.

She felt cool air alight on her bare breasts, her fluttering stomach, her thighs in their high-cut panties. Nearly free.

He knelt on the bed, straddling her lower legs, and slid his hands up the sides of her body, letting them come to rest on her breasts. He kissed and teased and suckled until her nipples ached and she begged for mercy, whimpering *don't, don't*, when she wasn't murmuring *more, more*. Again and again he came back to her mouth, the way a thirsty man goes to the well, and every time, he told her how much he wanted her.

When he had her clawing at his back in frustration, he began a long, slow slide downward with his tongue, building her up, heating her up, making her frantic for release. Her underpants went the way of the rest, and she opened herself to him, welcoming him, and felt his hands, huge, cup her under her buttocks and lift her arching hips to his kisses.

No mercy for her; he kindled her until she was up, up, and nearly over the edge. She was holding back, trying to hold on, when she felt herself slip and begin to fall.

"Not that way, Quinn," she said in a gasp. "In me . . . oh, please . . ."

With a low laugh he said, "For you, anything."

He shifted his position to be even with her and kissed her harder than she'd ever been kissed before. It was new, wanton, rough, and she loved it, loved him. He had complete control over her responses, but she didn't care because she loved him, and if he told her to take a flying leap off a cliff just then, she would do it because he had asked.

She heard a tear of foil and then endured the damnable reassurance of him slipping a condom on himself, and then he slid in easily in one sharp thrust, taking her breath from her, exactly what she wanted, to be left dazed and filled and every nerve ending quivering, and then she cried, *"Wait!"*

"Wait?"

"Yes . . . for me to save up again."

He chuckled, then buried his face in the curve of her neck and said, "Sure," driving her right back up to the edge in no time at all, which amazed her, because she wasn't the type to come quickly or often.

She thought.

And meanwhile, always, always, she was aware of him in her, separated by that barrier, and she thought, what a waste, what a waste to hold back that seed. But the thought went away and she was left with only a mindless drive to completion, a primitive need to drive more deeply into her own pleasure. Wild, she was wild to have him. She sought and found his hands and gripped them in her own on each side of her, pinning herself down with him. Lifting her haunches in a rush to take him all the way in, she matched him thrust for thrust and groan for groan, his equal in everything except her terrifying, deep-seated need to submit, the only way to true equality. It was a profound, completely erotic thought, and it whipped her into a blissful plunge right over that cliff, a freefall into space that must have been very like death, except for the fact that she knew that Quinn was falling with her.

Olivia thought that maybe they'd died, after all.

She had no idea how long they lay in their own dampness on top of the coverlet, wrapped in one another's arms. A minute? An hour? She tried to move, but she didn't have the strength. They could have been lying broken-boned at the bottom of a canyon, the way she felt.

It was Quinn who stirred first. With a groan, he rolled off her and lay flat on his back, shielding his eyes from the light with the back of his forearm. "Tell me the earth moved for you," he said at last. "Because I've just been to Mars and back."

"I think it moved and fell on top of me," she said, staring immobilized at the ceiling.

"This feels like silk," Quinn muttered, sliding his hand over the surface of the bed. "Is it?"

"Uh-huh."

"The condom dripped. Did I just wreck it?"

"Uh-huh."

"Oh, well. In that case . . ."

He trailed the back of his fingers lazily over her knee and up her thigh.

"Oh, Quinn, really, I can't," she said, scandalized at the thought of it. "Honestly. You don't know me. Really. I can't."

His hand slid from the top of her thigh to her warm, wet, still-throbbing cleft.

Amazingly, it turned out that she could.

Fifteen

They lay curled in sleep, Olivia nestled in the curve of Quinn's body, as a sullen drizzle became ugly and turned to icy rain. A nagging northeast wind drove the sleet into the windowpanes, tap-tap-tapping at Quinn's subconscious.

He dreamed fear. It was all around him, a pervasive sense that someone was going to get killed. In his dream he was rushing from house to house, from river to woods, always a frustrating two steps behind a mysterious presence in a black cape. Death? Dracula? He wanted desperately to find out before it was too late.

At the same time, he was afraid. He was convinced that sooner or later he would catch up with the lurking evil, and he wasn't sure that he'd survive the encounter. But he continued to run from hill to hollow anyway, exhausting himself, his breath coming faster and faster until at last he was within reach of the presence. He grabbed at the cape, the way he'd been grabbed by the jersey a thousand different times on the football field, and the presence turned on him, rising up monumentally large and black and powerful and horrifying Quinn.

Quinn started from the nightmare, lifting himself up on one arm, his heart hammering wildly, his eyes wide open to see . . . nothing. Nothing more than the sweet curve of a woman, sleeping peacefully with long, slow breaths, her soul in a happier place than his had been.

He stayed braced on one elbow, waiting for his heartbeat

to calm down, and gazed at the sleeping form next to him. She was so innocent, so vulnerable. He had to protect her—and Mrs. Dewsbury, too—but he couldn't be everywhere at once. Was he deluded? *Were* they at risk? And how could he protect them, when he himself was the reason they were at risk, if they were at risk? Insane paradox!

Olivia . . . sweet Liv. He snuggled into the softness of her pillow, breathing her scent, restoring his baffled and battered spirit with the simple nearness of her. Oh, to wake up every day next to her . . . no man could ask for more. He slid his arm around her waist and snuggled her to him. Olivia sighed in her sleep and burrowed her hips into his crotch; and in the space of that single movement, his desire to protect her became transformed into a hunger to have her. Earlier that night he had wanted her desperately. Now he needed her, just as desperately.

He lifted his arm and brought it back to her buttocks, then slipped his hand between her thighs from behind. He had one goal in mind: to arouse her. If only he could make her want him . . . if only she would deign to receive him . . . he would consider it an honor of the highest magnitude. He had no rubies for her, no pearls. He had only his ability to give her pleasure.

Please let it be enough.

He began a slow, gentle caress, separating her soft, warm flesh, and then with feathery strokes he began to coax her back from her dreamworld and into the waking one where he lay alone and bereft.

She stirred, and then she stirred a little more. Her sigh, half moan, told him what he needed to know. He was coming to her, hat in hand, and she was willing to hear him out.

He quickened the pace of his strokes, focusing on the hard nub he found there, marveling that a thing so small could contain power so vast. Her moans were no longer sighs. She was inhaling deep, long draughts of air, letting them out on the sound of his name: "Quinn . . . oh, Quinn . . . oh, Quinn . . ."

She rolled over on her stomach and brought herself partially up on her knees, inviting him in, unmistakably. In a waking dream he swung his knee over her calves and brought himself in an easy slide deep inside of her. He was reaching into her, reaching out to her. She was the one, the only one, who could make his life whole again. His movements became a pumping scramble for oneness with her, a defiant stand against caped villainy and murdered dreams.

With one hand he gripped a spoke of the headboard, with the other he braced himself on the bed as he plunged over and over into her, hanging on for dear life, waiting for he didn't know what. And then she cried out, and he knew at once what it was: her. He was waiting for her. Had been waiting, for seventeen indistinct years. He felt an explosive, tremendous release into her, and his body collapsed on hers, but by then he was somewhere else altogether—on some other plane, in some other realm.

But with her.

Olivia Bennett, so-called morning person, opened one eye and was amazed to see that it was eight-thirty. She never slept past six.

She was alone in her bed. With a stab of disappointment she rolled over, and then she saw Quinn, dressed in shorts and T-shirt and sitting in the tub chair, watching her. His face was a study in serenity. He looked exactly like what he was: a man who acted with purpose and a sense of commitment. It gave her a rush to know that he couldn't be involved with her just for the thrill of it.

Through the window behind him, she saw scudding clouds being bumped out of view by brilliant sunshine. As with everything else in her life just then, it promised a new beginning.

"Happy New Year," she said to him softly. She stretched luxuriously and sighed, then jabbed an index finger playfully into the rumpled covers beside her. "How come you're over there instead of over here?"

"I wouldn't have been able to let you sleep if I were lying awake next to you," he said simply. He stood up and elbowed his shoulders back as if he'd been sitting in one position for too long, then slapped his flat stomach. "And— I was afraid you'd hear my stomach growling and think a wild boar had got into the room."

Smiling, she said, "Breakfast sounds great. Where should we go?"

"On New Year's Day? Unless you have a thing for Egg McMuffins, I think we should stay right here and scrounge up something," he said, walking over to the bed and sitting on it beside her.

"Here? Hmm. You know, I might be a little low on supplies. I didn't have a chance to go food shopping this week."

Or last. Or the one before that.

"No problem. I'll rustle up some pancakes," he said, taking her hand in his. "You have mix?"

"I . . . had to throw it out last summer. Moths," she said, feeling desperately ashamed.

"Got any eggs?"

"Egg Beaters. I think. No, wait. I defrosted the carton for a cat I was watching. That was dumb. She hardly went near it. I should've refrozen it."

"Bread?"

"A couple of ends. They might be a teeny bit green," she admitted.

He cocked his head and said, "You're not one of those anorexic types, are you?"

"*No*! Bring me one of your pies and see for yourself," Olivia said with spirit. She sat up but—intensely aware of the wantonness of their middle-of-the-night coupling—she was feeling suddenly shy, so she kept the sheet tucked demurely around her breasts and under her arms.

He noticed it, of course. "You shower first," he said, chastely kissing the top of her head. "I'll see what's down there. I can always run out to a Store 24."

"In your tuxedo?"

"Oh, hell—right. Boy. Those McMuffins are sounding better and better," he muttered on his way out of the room.

It rankled. "Hey!" she shouted after him. "If I wanted to, I could be a *great* cook. As it is, I'm a . . . perfectly respectable one. Perfectly!"

She had to do it—she just had to tell that lie.

He backed into the room. "Oh, yeah? Pop quiz: how do you make crêpes?"

"Crêpes? What's the big deal? Some flour and . . . and eggs and you mix it up," she said, waving her arms in a wild stirring gesture, "and you bake it and you're done."

He poked his tongue in his cheek and nodded. "Uh-huh," he said with a lazy, knowing smile.

It was only after he was gone that Olivia realized that the sheet had fallen down to her lap and that he had been, in fact, enjoying the view. With anyone else, anytime else, she would have been half annoyed, half embarrassed, but now she felt brazenly flattered.

You shameless little hussy, she told herself, smiling as she threw back the covers. She headed for the shower in a blissful, sated mood and turned on the water. How long had it been since she'd felt this good?

Get real. You've never felt this good.

And now that she had discovered this new and sexy self of hers, was her life about to become richer and fuller at last?

Not without Quinn, dimwit. Not without Quinn.

It was a scary thought: She was never going to be All That She Could Be without Quinn around to make it happen. It had always been true on an intellectual level, and now it was true on the physical. She was doomed, unless she could come up with a plan to keep Quinn in Keepsake. Her mind wandered through a dozen scenarios, all of them equally stupid, before coming back to the only one that made any sense to her.

We have to get married. Obviously. I'm just going to have to propose.

Olivia Bennett was a type A, independent, take-charge kind of woman; but even she could see that Quinn Leary might think she was possibly jumping the gun by proposing. Still, if the time and place were right . . .

She was wrapping a towel around herself, relieved to have a plan—no matter how whimsical—when Quinn walked in.

Right time? Right place?

"Chief Vickers is walking up your front steps."

"*What?*"

As if on cue, the doorbell rang. "Don't answer it!" she cried.

"The man isn't blind, Liv. He looked straight at the Mercedes as he walked past it."

"That could be anyone's. We don't have to open the door—I've seen the cop shows—not unless he has a warrant."

"If that's what you want to do."

Olivia could see that Quinn was convinced she was afraid to be caught with him. Could anything be further from the truth? "On second thought, we have nothing to apologize for," she said, tossing aside the towel and pulling the sweatshirt over her head. She jabbed her foot into one of the legs of her sweatpants. "We're consenting adults. Let's hear what the man has to say."

If this is Dad's doing, I swear I'll kill him.

"Fine with me," Quinn said with a shrug. "I'll put on my trousers and meet you downstairs."

Olivia dashed down the stairs and swung the door open to the dour-faced chief.

"Got a minute, Livvy?" he asked her.

"It's not the best time, Chief," she said loftily. "I assume it's important?"

"You tell me," he answered, and marched past her. In the sunlit entry hall he looked more official and misplaced than ever. He glanced pointedly up the stairs, then said, "You're missing a black velvet cape?"

"Oh, good. Someone turned it in. But you didn't have to make a special trip."

Unless you're looking for an excuse to spy on me and report to my father, that is.

The chief dumped the duffel he was carrying onto the varnished hall table, making Olivia wince. He unzipped the bag, reached in, and pulled out her sodden cape.

Dismayed, she cried, "Someone threw it in a ditch!"

"Not exactly," he said, holding the cape by the shoulders and letting it drip onto the slate floor of the hall. "Someone hoisted it up the flagpole on Town Hill. It stayed there most of the night until—wouldn't you know it?—poor Father Tom saw it early this morning. But here's the interesting thing," he remarked, spreading the front panels outward for her to see.

The satin lining had been slashed to shreds. Long, frayed ribbons of red hung like thirsty tongues from someone's private hell. Instinctively Olivia stepped back, trying to distance herself from the display of violence she saw there.

Quinn was now behind her. He said quietly to the chief, "I guess we don't have to ask if Father Tom saw anybody hoisting this. Might he have *heard* someone doing it, somewhere in the back of his mind? The wind was blowing like stink from the northeast, which means that the flag halyard would have been slapping hard against the flagpole all night. But that would have changed over to silence as the cape was hoisted and a load put on the halyard. It would give us a time of occurrence. Father Tom might even have seen a car go by sometime around then—if he could remember when it became quiet."

The chief snorted and said, "What're you, a junior detective now?"

Quinn didn't rise to the bait. Olivia wasn't even sure he heard the crack, so focused was he on the discovery. He took the cape from the police chief with a "May I?" and laid it out on the slate floor.

"It would be good if you could come up with a list of early departures from the gala," he told the chief as he crouched beside the cape, studying the gashes in its scarlet lining. "Or anyone who left and then came back. But I don't have to tell *you* that."

Apparently he did. Vickers aimed a scowl at the top of

Quinn's head and said, "You're implying it was one of Mr. Bennett's guests?"

Quinn didn't bother to look up. "I'm not implying. I'm saying."

Olivia, feeling queasy, stuck in her two cents. "My father doesn't know anybody who hates me that much."

"Not you, Liv," said Quinn. This time he did look up. His brow was raked over with concern and in his eyes she saw something she'd never seen before: fear. For her. Because of him.

She shivered. The chief saw it and said, "Your hair is all wet. You'll catch cold, Livvy."

She tried to be flippant and brave. "Probably someone just walked over my grave, that's all," she said with a tight smile at Quinn.

"Cut it out!" Quinn said.

"Oh, all right," she answered, deflated by the sharp tone of his voice. "But really—I mean, how can a guy in a *tuxedo*, no less, stroll in dress shoes through mud and snow and dog poop to the top of Town Hill, then hook up a cape to a halyard and hoist it to the highest point in town, without ever being seen? How?"

"We don't know that he wasn't seen," said the chief. "It's early days yet."

"He might not have been wearing a tuxedo," Quinn pointed out. "Not everyone at the gala came in black tie."

Olivia chewed on her thumbnail. "That's true." She turned to Quinn and said, "Was Coach Bronsky wearing a tux? I can't remember."

The chief exploded. "What the hell are you asking about *him* for?"

"I . . . I don't know," Olivia said, faltering before his wrath. "I suppose because he gave us such an evil look."

"I doubt he was the only one."

"*I* didn't notice anyone else. Did you?" she asked Quinn.

Quinn was about to say something but stopped himself.

"I suspect the chief is right," he said calmly. "We tended only to notice the good guys."

"Don't go characterizing people around here as good or bad, Quinn. You don't know shit about who's either."

"I guess we'll find out, won't we?" Quinn said as he got to his feet again.

The two men were the same height and standing eye to eye. All that separated them were twenty years and a beer belly. During all of those years and all of those beers, Chief Vickers had nourished a keen grudge; Olivia couldn't remember him ever saying a positive thing about either Quinn or his father, and she could see why. He blamed Francis Leary for getting away, and Quinn for the fact that his own son had never done much with his life.

It was hard to say which of the men standing there resented the other one more just then, but Olivia had no intention of finding out. "Does my father know about this yet?" she asked, tossing out the question like a biscuit between two growling dogs.

Chief Vickers turned and snapped it up first. "Mr. Bennett had a long night; I didn't want to barge in on him too early. And I wanted to make sure this was yours. I thought I saw you arrive in it last night," he said, crouching down to roll up the cape. "If you don't mind, I'll keep it for a little while."

"By all means," Olivia said, glad to see it go.

He stuffed the rolled cape back into the green-and-white duffel bag—a Keepsake Cougars team bag—and then he gave the visor of his hat a yank.

"Enjoy your day," he said with one last glance at Quinn. It was meant to be insinuating, and Olivia took it that way.

She closed the door after he left and leaned against it, mostly for support and partly to keep the man from coming back in. "Well, that was exciting," she said. "And I thought last night couldn't be topped."

Quinn shook his head. "It's not a joke, Liv. These attacks are too choreographed. Whoever is doing it is nuts and he's fearless; it can't get more dangerous than that."

Olivia used the sleeve of her sweatshirt to blot a small puddle on the glossy surface of the hall table. "Do you really think so?" she asked, angling her head to see that she'd got all the water. "I don't. I mean, they're pranks, that's all. Vicious, maybe, but they're still pranks."

"The effigy was a prank. Slashing the lining, that was an act of terror."

She looked up from her task at him. "I wish you wouldn't look like that, Quinn," she said softly. "You're scaring me."

"I want you to be scared, dammit! We don't have a clue what we're dealing with here. You may be the Princess of Keepsake, but trust me, that's just a figure of speech. You saw the cape. That could've been—"

The unfinished thought hung in the air between them like a half-spun web.

Quinn let out a sigh of exasperation and took her in his arms. He held her tight. "This thing is so damned frustrating—I can't think straight."

"Because you're hungry," she said in a muffled voice as she buried her head in his shoulder. "C'mon, let's go to McDonald's. They have a drive-through."

Olivia pulled a hooded sweatshirt over her head while Quinn donned his topcoat; they made a comically incongruous pair.

"All set?" he asked, holding the door for her.

"Starving," Olivia said. She stepped around the wet image on the floor as if it were a chalked-in body at a crime scene, and let Quinn lead the way to his car.

Sixteen

Ray Buffitt was the same amiable slob he'd always been, only now he was able to convert his bad habits into a social asset: The rented house in which he dwelled was considered a paradise by every one of his wife-fearing pals.

Quinn was given a quick tour of the place before the six men who were gathered there hunkered down for their marathon of football viewing. Since Quinn had never had the chance to go away to college, what he saw was an eye-opener.

Half-full beer cans, empty Doritos bags, crumpled Ding Dongs wrappers, and dried-out bean dip floated throughout the house like water lilies on a pond. There were exotic waterfalls, two of them: one from the leaking sink in the kitchen, and one from the sink in the downstairs (no one in his right mind would call it a guest) bathroom. There was white sand from a litterbox tucked in a corner of the kitchen, its gritty contents half kicked out and grinding underfoot. There were tropical fish (four guppies swimming in a tank) and tropical snakes (a boa constrictor in another tank, waiting perhaps to be fed the fish). All in all, it was a paradise, a fantasy.

A pigpen, just as Mike Redding had said.

As for the media equipment, it was all state of the art and thoughtfully arranged. The big-screen TV was hooked up through the stereo and jammed against a window to block the sun from washing out one's viewing pleasure. The CDs, many hundreds of them, were arranged on the eye-level shelves of two bookcases for easy selection (the *Sports Illustrated*s, except for the dog-eared swimsuit issues, were confined to the lower shelves and were harder to peruse, but it couldn't be helped). A pair of speakers as tall as Quinn were situated for excellent sound separation on each side of the non-working fireplace, which itself was being used to house part of Ray's vast and valuable collection of beer bottles.

"He had 'em appraised once," Mike explained to Quinn as they slugged down their Coors before the first game. "They're worth a fortune. Take that Blow Hole from Wyoming, Rhode Island," he said, pointing to an unopened bottle with a pristine label. "That one alone is worth two hundred bucks—extremely limited edition," Mike said in a voice of envy.

"I'd love to have an awesome hobby like that," Mike added with a sigh. "But Mitzi says beer caps only, no bottles." He shrugged and dropped his empty Coors can into a bamboo magazine rack. "What're you gonna do?"

Quinn made sympathetic noises, but the whole scene was beyond him. He had been raised by his father to be both methodical and thorough, and acts of domestic defiance left him unimpressed. Besides, seventeen years of exile had made him something of a loner; it was unlikely that he could ever feel like one of the guys the way he once did.

And yet they had welcomed him into their haven easily enough. Mike, Ray, Neal, Cutter, Todd—all of them were friendly and accepting in an offhand way. As far as they were concerned, Quinn was just another fist pumping in the air after a kick-ass play.

Quinn settled into a plaid easy chair whose arms had been shredded by the cat he now knew was called Digger, and began munching his way through a bag of Ruffles as Tennessee kicked off against Nebraska in the Cotton Bowl. His interest in the game was minimal; he was there strictly to keep his eyes and ears open for useful scuttlebutt.

In fact, he hadn't wanted to come at all, not after the

cape episode. But Olivia had refused to let him stay behind just to stand guard over her. She was bound for the outlet malls with Eileen, she had told him, while Rand stayed home with the kids. Eileen would have her head if Olivia begged out of their annual foraging expedition.

In any case, Olivia was far too independent to be watched over. It was both her great strength and her maddening flaw.

"Bronsky said the guy couldn't run—hah! Look at 'im go!" crowed Neal. "Bronsky don't know from squat!"

They watched the replay and then Cutter turned to Ray and said, "You ever gonna let Coach back in your house, Buffitt-man?"

"No way," Ray said. "Not after that."

Quinn's ears pricked up. "What'd he do?"

Ray said, "Ah, the asshole got drunk and smashed up some of my beer bottles. I like a drinker as well as the next guy, but I hate a mean drunk. If he—way to go, Dejuan! How many yards was Dejuan good for this year, Todd?"

Whenever anyone needed to know something, he asked Todd. An accountant by trade, Todd had an encyclopedic memory. Not to mention, he'd once won a pair of tickets to the Superbowl in a bar-sponsored trivia contest.

The game was pretty good. After a scoreless first quarter, the lead moved back and forth between the two archrivals. Quinn made sure that he hooted and hollered with the rest of them, but his mind was fixed firmly on the torn-up cape that Chief Vickers had recovered early that morning.

While the others gnawed on beef jerky, Quinn chewed on the ongoing mystery. Was he the only one who believed that each of the "pranks" was more ominous than the one before it? The goal was obvious—to get Quinn out of Keepsake—but how far was some creep willing to go to achieve it?

By halftime, the score was tied and everyone in the room was beered up and pumped. They switched to another game, but it was laughably uneven. Ray Buffitt, ever the perfect host, had anticipated the dread possibility and had programmed the best of two dozen CDs into a nonstop blitz of rock and roll.

"Don't wanna lose momentum, right?" was his explanation as he cranked up the volume.

Between the music and the two or three conversations being shouted back and forth over one another as the game played on the giant screen, there was a real danger of sensory meltdown. Quinn, used to the serenity of the outdoors, was going nuts. It was probably quieter in the commodities pit the day after Oprah told her audience that hamburgers scared her.

Quinn was about to rip the CD player out of its perch in the bookcase and throw it into the fireplace when Cutter shouted to him, "Hey, I forgot! Guess who asked me about you the other day?"

Quinn shrugged and shouted, "You got me. Who?"

"Alison's old man, that's who! I guess he recognized me from the old days when he used to bring in his truck for a tune-up; I don't know where he takes it now. Anyway, we were at the same self-serve island at the Shell—near the IHOP? I haven't seen him in years. Man, the old bastard is as ornery as ever. I don't know how Alison ever put up with him."

"She didn't," Neal said, flattening a beer can with his shoe. "She got herself her very own knight in shining armor."

"Oh, yeah—Sir Lancelot," Cutter said with a snort. "A lotta help *he* was."

"What did you expect? What did Randy Lancelot ever end up doing for any of us?"

"Not take us all the way, that's for sure. Sixth place, that he could do. Whoopee."

They laughed contemptuously and turned to other talk, leaving Quinn sitting there stunned. The exchange had come and gone in the crunch of a potato chip, but it left no doubt in Quinn's mind that Rand Bennett had been deeply involved with his cousin Alison. The question was, what kind of involvement? Quinn had never seen any evidence that the two had been close. Did that itself point to a secret involvement of a sexual nature? Or had Rand simply and quietly been acting like the big brother that Alison never had?

Quinn felt as if he'd been staring into a kaleidoscope and someone had given it a giant turn.

"Hey, Cutter!" he said, trying to get the talk back on track. "You never told me what Alison's old man said."

"Oh, yeah. He said, 'Is that punk still hangin' around town?' And I said, 'Which punk would that be, Rupert?' And he goes, 'It's Mr. Bennett to you, you little punk.' And I go, 'Not if your truck ain't in my boss's garage.' "

"Good one, Cutter," said Neal. "What'd he say then?"

Cutter popped a tab on another can and said, "His exact words were 'Tell Quinn I know where he lives.' That was it. Then he went inside to pay for his gas and leer at this chick behind the counter who was young enough to be his daughter, naturally."

"He's had plenty of practice at *that*," said Todd, sneering into his beer.

"Todd, put a lid on it, would you?" Mike Redding snapped. "It's ancient history. Ray, turn that damn thing down! The game's starting, for chrissake." He glanced at Quinn apologetically, as if he could no longer be responsible for the juvenile behavior of their old teammates now that they were grown.

It was another wild turn on that kaleidoscope. Quinn sat back in his plaid chair, mesmerized by all the new pieces he saw. A mere ten percent of his brain was needed for following the game and keeping up with the score; the rest was focused on the shocking innuendo that had been run past him in the last few minutes.

Rand. Alison. Rupert. It was a triangle of involvement that Quinn couldn't have imagined in his wildest dreams. Immediately his mind, like a computer, began mulling the possible combinations. The more he mulled, the queasier he got. He pushed away the half-eaten jerky; he couldn't stand even to look at it.

Someone impregnated Alison, and someone killed her.

Those were facts. Alison hating her father, Rand becoming her knight, Rupert leering at girls—that was all gossip. Quinn knew all about the downside of gossip. It wrecked dreams and it ruined lives.

But assuming that there was some kernel of truth in the guys' drunken remarks—what then? Quinn couldn't think about Rupert without picturing his niece. He couldn't think about Rand without picturing his twin sister. And he couldn't think about Alison without picturing her cousin. Olivia was everywhere in his thoughts, slinky in silver, soft in wool sweaters. Olivia—idealistic . . . loving . . . defiantly loyal to family and friends, including outcasts like him.

Oh, damn. Oh, hell. Please . . . let it have been someone with no connection to her. A bum. A teacher. The mayor of Keepsake.

By the end of the first game, Quinn resolved to corner Mike Redding in the next couple of days and find out what he knew. If Mike wouldn't talk, Quinn would go to Cutter, then to Neal, and on down the line. Someone had to be willing to pass on the full dirt—which was all Quinn believed it was. If there had been anything truthful to it, Mrs. Dewsbury or Father Tom would have heard about it over the years.

Yes. Idle gossip between horny teammates who'd lusted after the mysterious Alison themselves. Quinn remembered well their locker-room talk about the girl. Everyone wanted her; none of them had had her.

The Cotton Bowl ended in overtime. Quinn groaned inwardly as he cheered outwardly. Eventually Tennessee beat Nebraska and they all moved on to the Sugar Bowl. From the first pass, run all the way in for the touchdown, the Sugar Bowl was a blowout—boring, interminable, and embarrassing, at least to Quinn. The rest of the guys loved it, of course. As with sex, they didn't care who scored, as long as it was often.

By halftime Quinn had had all he could take. Over everyone's protests, he stood up to leave. His excuse was lame—

he told them he'd promised to bring back a prescription for Mrs. Dewsbury. It was the best he could do.

"Y'know—you may as well be married," said Neal with more than a hint of condescension.

Quinn laughed it off, but Mike was feeling his beer. "You should talk, Neal," he said with a burp. "You're gonna have to install a freaking dishwasher for having today off."

"Oh, like you're here free and clear? Who's in charge of the sleepover at your house next Friday? Huh? Who?"

"You guys are pathetic," said their bachelor host. "Tell you what. I'll give you eight bucks an hour if you come and clean this dump on your next day off," he teased. "I'll even supply all the rags."

"Hey, here's a thought," said Cutter, also single. "You can call yourselves the Merry Mates. Get it? Merry *Mates*?"

"*Haw-haw-haw.*"

Their pissing contest was still in full swing when Quinn waved them all a genial good-bye and took off.

Somewhere during the second quarter of the Cotton Bowl, he'd had a premonition. He didn't like to think of it that way; he was more comfortable calling it a hunch. Either way, he wanted to act on it.

Before heading back to Mrs. Dewsbury's house, he drove downtown, parked his car on one of the deserted streets there, and strolled around the corner to check out Miracourt. He was relieved to see that it looked the same: sophisticated and warm and inviting, and all in one piece. He strolled up to the window and peered inside, checking out the interior to make sure that everything was okay. Several glass-shaded lamps threw a soft glow over the fabrics and bric-a-brac scattered around the shop. It all reminded him of Olivia. He liked that.

Reassured, Quinn turned and headed back for his truck. And then, because he was brought up to be thorough and because he wanted to clear his head and because he could not shake his hunch of a premonition, he detoured and walked around to the alley that ran behind the shops.

The alley was narrow, deserted, and dark, with bleary lights standing guard over dark brown Dumpsters and cardboard boxes flattened for recycling. Patches of cobblestones peeking through asphalt echoed under his footsteps as he tried to figure out which back exit belonged to Miracourt. A stack of wooden crates, obviously from citrus fruits, told him that he'd reached the juicerie next to Olivia's shop.

He wasn't surprised to see that Miracourt's backside looked as trim and neat as its front. The metal door, painted a deep shade of green, was decorated with a handpainted wreath of twigs and flowers; the light that shone down on it looked like an old ship's lantern, another anticommercial touch. Quinn smiled. Leave it to Olivia to bring charm and whimsy to the most workaday site.

The door was closed, but Quinn tried the doorknob anyway. He winced as he did it, fearing that he would set something off, and was surprised when the knob turned easily. *Shit.*

He stepped cautiously inside a stockroom filled with boxes and bolts of fabric. The room itself was unlit, but a rectangle of amber told him that the shop lay directly ahead. He was in the cutout of light with no place to hide, so he stood and just listened. It was eerily quiet. Whoever had been in the shop had come and gone, of that he felt sure.

He walked into the warm glow of the shop itself and went immediately up the stairs to the second-floor loft. That's where Olivia's desk was, and her personal effects. Quinn decided that if anyone had gone amuck, he would do it upstairs, out of the view of window-shoppers.

And he was right. At the top of the stairs he saw her desk, a big wooden antique in great shape and set squarely in the middle of the loft. He could see that papers were strewn across the desk and all over the planked floor around it. As he got closer, he discovered something else: a humongous rat, bloody and eviscerated, lying sprawled across a stack of invoices and packing receipts on the desk.

Quinn stared with disgust at the mauled rodent. It was déjà vu all over again, except that this latest punch to the gut—maybe combined with all that beef jerky—was a little more strident, a little more vicious. The thought that Olivia was intended to stumble sleepy-eyed onto this scene the next morning was chilling.

As for the rat, Quinn actually found himself feeling sorry for it. There it had been, sniffing around for crumbs and minding its own business, when . . . *whack*. How exactly had the critter been dispatched? Surely not with a knife. Quinn turned the three-way lamp up to its brightest light and, flopping the carcass over with a pencil and a ruler, gave it a closer look.

As he suspected: a bullet hole, right through the middle. So the rat was a country rat and the prankster, an expert marksman. Surprise, surprise. Hunters were common in Keepsake: Some hunted for food, most for sport. It didn't much matter to Quinn why the guy had acquired the skill. The important thing was that he possessed it.

Automatically he reached for the phone to call Chief Vickers, then thought better of it. Olivia would want to be in on the loop. She might be home. Clutching a nearby sample of fabric, he used it to pick up the phone, then punched in Olivia's number with a pencil point.

She answered on the first ring. She sounded relaxed and happy. It made him sick to have to be the one to tell her what had happened, but there were no better options. The first words out of his mouth were, "Does Miracourt have an alarm?"

"Of course. My insurance requires it. Why?"

Shit—an expert marksman who was bright enough to cut the right wire. "The alarm's been disabled," he said. In a few terse sentences he explained where he was and what he'd found.

"I'll be right over," she said in a wobbly voice, and she slammed down the phone before he could ask about Vickers.

While Quinn waited, he looked around more carefully. Nothing seemed to have been stolen. There was only the rat and the papers strewn like flower petals in a path to the carnage. At the last minute Quinn thought, to hell with Vickers and proper procedure, and he rolled the rat up in a Miracourt bag like a gourmet cheese head, then tied it around for good measure with twine. He didn't want fearless Olivia taking a peek; he really didn't.

Olivia had no intention of looking in the bag.

"Take it out to the Dumpster—please!" she said, trying not to picture its contents. "If Chief Vickers needs the rat for an autopsy, he's welcome to retrieve it."

She forced herself to become all business. Snapping open a shopping bag, she said to Quinn, "Would you hand me the pinking shears?"

"The—?"

"Those scissors with the zigzag blades," she explained. Quinn gave them to her on his way out to the Dumpster, and she began to pick through the wreckage of her paperwork, using the scissors like tongs to retrieve the invoices and dispose of the packing slips.

Her hands were shaking as she did it. She told herself that it was with indignation, but that didn't account for her skyhigh jump when Quinn came back into the loft and started to say something behind her. "I'm sorry," she said, as if she'd done something to be ashamed of. "I'm just—"

She threw down the shears and said, "Scared. Quinn, I'm a little scared now. This is two in a row. Why is he suddenly targeting me?"

Quinn took her into his arms and immediately she felt safe. If she could only stay that way, she'd be ready to take on the world. Once upon a time, she thought she *could* take on the world. Not anymore. This was not a world she either knew or understood.

Quinn held her close, caressing the back of her hair. "He's figured out how much I . . . I care for you," he said softly, "and he's sending me messages—"

"*Is* he a he?" she asked, hoping somehow he was not.

"I'm pretty sure of it," Quinn said. "Although, none of these stunts took exceptional strength—just a strong stomach."

"Which I don't happen to have," she said, shuddering.

Quinn sighed and said, "Anyway, the text of the messages seems to be, 'Go away and I'll leave her alone.' "

"I know," she admitted in a faltering voice. "I've read them that way, too. But . . . you're not going away. I don't want you to go away, so what will we do?"

He said nothing. For much too long, he said nothing. Olivia felt her heart plunge like a cannonball into her admittedly weak stomach. "Quinn?" she said, looking up at him. "Say something?"

She knew him well enough to know when he was picking and choosing his words with care. This was one of those times. She laid her head back on his shoulder and waited.

"Olivia," he said softly, "we have to wonder whether whoever is doing these things got your cousin pregnant, or murdered her, or both."

He was telling her that he thought the prankster was the killer. But that couldn't be. Not after all these years. It would mean that the killer had lived among them all these years.

"No. I don't see it," she said, shaking her head. "Killing a woman is different from killing a rat. *This*," she said, waving her hand at the bloody mess, "was disgusting and mean, but that's all. People kill rats all the time. They hire hit men; we call them exterminators. Or they use them for target practice—you remember how kids in school did that with their BB guns."

"I understand that, but—"

"No," she said, cutting him off. "I really do not see it. You're overreacting." She preferred her version of events to his, so much.

"I wish I could agree with you, Liv."

Olivia glanced at the papers that remained to be cleaned up. She wanted to wave a wand over them and make them go away. But no one else knew which things to keep and what to toss, not even Quinn. It was up to her.

She picked up the pinking shears and went back to work. "After this, I want cocoa. A Hershey bar won't do. We have to find cocoa. And marshmallows, too. We'll make a nice fire in my fireplace, and I'll make the cocoa extra rich and sweet—''

''Olivia, do you have a gun?'' he asked, interrupting her ramble.

She stopped and stared, more distressed now than before and more determined not to let him know it. In a weird way, it was flattering. He thought she could handle a gun.

''No. I don't.''

''Does anyone in your family? Does Rand?''

''Well, yes, I'm sure he does. For skeet shooting. You remember that he was always pretty good, don't you?''

Quinn shrugged. ''I suppose. Sometimes you move on. But you're saying he's . . . kept up with it?''

''There's a range not far from here. It's what some men do in the country. Why are you asking? Do you think I'd actually tell Rand that I need his guns to protect myself? My God, he'd have my mother in hysterics.''

''Yeah, you're right,'' Quinn said abruptly. ''Forget I mentioned it.''

''Now that I think about it,'' Olivia added, ''I'd rather not have Chief Vickers know about this disgusting episode.''

She raised her hand over Quinn's objections and said, ''Wait, wait, hear me out. Vickers hasn't been able to do a thing so far about these pranks. And you know what? I don't think he wants to. We both know he'd rather you just went away. So what will we accomplish by telling him? He'll go straight to my father, upsetting him needlessly and making things even harder between you and me.''

''That's not a good idea, Liv.''

''Well . . . that's how I feel. It's bad enough that my father knows about the cape.''

''Are you sure that he does?''

''Yes. He told Rand about it—in strictest confidence. Naturally Rand immediately told Eileen, also in confidence; she called me as soon as she heard. My mother, as usual, hasn't been told anything. Eventually she'll find out and then she'll be angry at all of us. But that's the way my family operates. I can't even keep track of all our confidences anymore; after a while, they begin to blur." She plucked the last bloody paper with the pinking shears and dumped it in the wastebasket.

Quinn pulled out the plastic liner. "I always thought honesty was the best policy," he said, glancing up at her as he knotted the bag tight.

"Nobody lies," she said with a shrug. "Just . . . nobody tells."

Quinn smiled wryly at the distinction, then said, "Are you missing anything from your desk—a knife, a letter opener, a pair of scissors?"

Olivia glanced at a small ceramic vase that she kept filled with pens and pencils, rulers and openers. "Yes. I keep an X-Acto Knife right there. Why? Is it the murder weapon?"

"Not exactly. The rat was shot. The knife was used to draw and quarter it."

Olivia took a deep, slow breath, then let it out just as deliberately. With a lift of her eyebrows, she said, "Well! I hope he has the courtesy to replace the blade before he brings it back."

She was dismayed to see that Quinn neither laughed nor smiled.

A little later on, they found the bloodied knife after all, lying on a bolt of winter-white silk.

Seventeen

The only night that Mike Redding was home and available for buttonholing by Quinn happened to be Mitzi's Bunco night.

Mike had to baby-sit, so Quinn found himself in Mike's basement workshop, trying to carry on a conversation with his old friend as he alternated between sawing wood for a new set of kitchen cabinets and yelling up the stairs at his three kids, who sounded bound and determined to tear the house down as fast as Mike could build it up again.

"God, I hate January," Mike growled. "At least in the summer they're outside."

He marked off a dimension with a carpenter's pencil on a sheet of lumbercore and carried it over to the table saw. "Hold that end up while I rip this, would you? Thanks."

The sound of bodies rolling and thumping on the floor above them made Quinn glance involuntarily at the ceiling to see if it was coming down.

Mike sighed. "I hate January," he repeated. "I hate Bunco. But most of all I hate being responsible for breakage when Mitzi's out for the night. You're a lucky sonofabitch you never married, Quinn."

"Yeah, well, the right one just never—"

The rest of Quinn's sentence got drowned out by the whine of the saw as Mike split the sheet into halves, then quarters. It was fairly obvious that Mike didn't care nearly as much about Quinn's love life as he did about woodworking. Mike was a hard-driving, extremely successful businessman, the owner of his own import-export firm, but his real passion in life was wood. Right now he looked overjoyed to be traipsing around in piles of sawdust, despite all the macho griping about being forced to baby-sit.

A bloodcurdling scream followed by a horrific *thunk* sent Mike back to the foot of the basement stairs. "Hey! Guys! You sound like a herd of elephants up there! I'm not gonna tell you again!"

He returned to his cabinetry and to Quinn. "So what's on your mind?" he asked as he took a sip of tea from a World's Greatest Dad mug.

Quinn put down his own mug and said, "When we were at Ray's, some of the guys were throwing rumors around about Alison. You tried to shut 'em up, and I appreciate the spirit in which you did it—but I'd like to hear what you know that I don't."

Mike looked suddenly uncomfortable. He shrugged and said, "Hey, it's nothing we *know*, exactly. It's just what we heard."

"I understand that they're just rumors," Quinn reassured him. "But I'd like to hear them anyway."

After a long pause, Mike said, "All right, I guess it's only fair. But it's pretty sleazy stuff. Don't ever tell Mitzi I told you. She's too much of a parent to believe it can happen."

Quinn nodded his agreement and waited.

"Look, it's just talk, but . . . after you and your dad left Keepsake, Myra Lupidnick got drunk one night with Monty Johnson and got a little blabby. She told MoJo that Alison once confided that her father used to like to feel her up. Later Myra took it all back. She said it wasn't Alison's father at all who used to cop the feels, but the owner of the dress shop where Alison worked after school."

"What, that shop on Main?"

"Yeah, it's not there anymore. Casual Shop? Something like that. The owner had already died of a stroke by the time

Myra ran off at the mouth to MoJo, so, you know, that was that.''

"Did anyone ever tell Vickers this?"

Mike picked up a sanding block. "You'd have to ask him," he said, gently hitting the raw edges of the sawn wood. "Anyway, no one really believed Myra. You know how she was. Hell, she went around bragging to anyone who'd listen that she took your cherry."

"Huh?"

"Did she?"

"No."

"See? She was a lotta talk. I'll say this for her, though. She gave pretty good—" Mike glanced upstairs and lowered his voice. "You know."

He chuckled in fond reminiscence and said, "You remember the time she sneaked into our locker room and— oh, no, wait, you were gone by then. Well, anyway, back then we figured Myra was just trying to puff herself up by spouting so-called inside knowledge. She was always trying to be somebody. That's the thing about going to a really good public high. The parking lot is filled with Jeeps and Corvettes, and the kids who take the bus have to walk right past them on their way to class. One way or another Myra managed to hitch a ride, every once in a while."

"Where does Rand fit in all of this?"

"That's a good question," Mike said. He pondered a vague spot in the air as he formed his answer.

Suddenly he moaned, "Oh, geez, I forgot to close the lid on the washing machine," and hustled over to the appliance. "Mitzi is gonna have a fit," he muttered, blowing sawdust off the agitator cap and out of the bleach dispenser. He dropped the lid and wiped off the top of the machine with the sleeve of his flannel shirt, then came back to the workbench where Quinn was waiting with arms folded casually across his chest.

For the rest of his life, Quinn remembered exactly what the scene looked and sounded and smelled like at that moment: the fine mist of sawdust swirling under the long fluorescent light, itself swaying lightly on its chains as the boys tore through the house; the pungent bite of newly cut wood tickling his nostrils; the giggly bickering of the kids some- where distant. Everything seemed so right, so ordinary, so utterly benign.

Until Mike spoke. "Look, it's obvious that you and Livvy have something going, so I don't even know why I'm telling you this. I need your word that you'll forget that I'm the one who said it."

"You have it."

"Okay. Here's the deal: Rand Bennett apparently had a heavy-duty thing for his cousin Alison. Again, the source for all this was MoJo, and he's dead as a doornail after wrapping himself around that tree in the Alps, so believe as much of it as you want."

Quinn was listening so intently that he could hear the rasp of Mike's beard as he rubbed the palm of his hand along his jawline.

"You know what a hound MoJo was," Mike went on. "Before he settled for easy sex with Myra, he made a big move on Alison. She rebuffed him and must have told Rand, because Rand confronted him about it and beat the crap out of him. Now, the way MoJo told it to us, all he did was make an everyday, garden-variety pass. So why did Rand react like MoJo tried to rape Alison or something? That's what you naturally wonder."

Quinn was thinking that Alison's father had sexually abused her; that she had run to Rand for comfort; and that Rand had overreacted by taking it out on somebody else. That's all that Quinn was thinking.

"There's more," Mike said quietly.

Quinn didn't want to hear it. He did not want to hear it.

"MoJo said that when Rand had him pinned to the ground with his hands around his throat, Rand said to him, 'No one touches her but one man. Got it? One man. And you're not that man.' "

It was as bad as Quinn had feared.

"So MoJo somehow gets the courage to croak, 'Oh,

yeah? I suppose you are?' And Rand says 'That's for me to know and you to find out.' ''

Quinn's relief came out in a snort of laughter. " 'For me to know and you to find out'? Come on, Mike, get real. MoJo made that up. No adult talks that way.''

"We were barely seventeen," Mike pointed out. "And it was a—slightly—more innocent age.''

"It's still not conclusive.''

"There's more.''

"Christ. *What*?" Quinn snapped, annoyed at Mike for parceling out the revelation.

"The next day, when MoJo showed up in school with a black eye and a busted nose—remember? He told us he got in a fight with some biker?—Alison supposedly said to him, 'I'm glad you wouldn't take no for an answer. Because of you I just got engaged.' 'To who?' says MoJo. She answers, 'To someone I'm not supposed to marry, according to the Church.' ''

Quinn let out a long, low whistle. "Ho-ly shit.''

"Exactly. I never was as smart as you," Mike said without irony, "but it doesn't take Scholar of the Year to figure out that marriage between first cousins is forbidden in the Catholic Church.''

"So is a marriage to someone divorced," Quinn shot back.

Mike gave him a skeptical look. "Put it all together, man. She was talking about Rand. I don't know who got her pregnant, her father or Rand, but the promise to marry her—that had to be Rand.''

"It looks that way," Quinn conceded, but all the while he was shaking his head in denial.

Mike added, "You remember how Ray and a couple of the guys got real quiet when the talk turned to Alison over at his house on New Year's Day? They're still scared shitless that someday this will all get back to Rand, and their asses will end up in a sling. The Bennetts own this town—you know that. Rand could pull some strings and have them fired from their jobs in the blink of an eye—and probably me as well if I were still working at the mill, never mind that I was their top-grossing salesman. As it is, Owen Bennett and his son have to make nice-nice to *me*. They know I'd rather buy Polartec from Malden Mills than Artica from him for my shop in the Philippines.''

Mike Redding was a bear of a man with a thick head of hair that was graying way too fast. Maybe it was the three boys; maybe it was his concern for his old teammates; maybe it was the time he was spending in the air between Keepsake and the Philippines, away from his family and table saw. Whatever it was that was stressing him out, Quinn did not want to add to his burden.

''Understood,'' he said simply. ''I won't drag your names into anything. Tell me one thing, though. When did MoJo tell you all this?''

''It was during our first New Year's Day reunion, four or five years after you and your dad split. We all got good and ripped and vowed to meet faithfully every year, wives and girlfriends be damned. Someone mentioned that we should've invited Rand, but you know how it is. We blamed him for that lousy season even more than we blamed you,'' he said with a wry smile. ''Anyway, that's when MoJo told us the stuff about Alison.''

''Was Coach at that first reunion?''

''Yeah. Why do you ask?''

''Just wondering.''

There was more thumping upstairs—this time, followed by a loud crash of something heavy onto the floor.

Mike cocked his ear. ''I didn't hear actual breakage, did you? Sounds like they just knocked over a bookcase or something.'' He went back to the foot of the stairs.

''Hey, up there!'' he bellowed. He listened for a response and got silence. ''Ah, the hell with it,'' he said, and went back to his tea.

There was stoic acceptance in Quinn's voice as he said, ''I appreciate this, Mike.''

''Hey, c'mon,'' Mike said, waving away Quinn's gratitude. ''We go way back. I owe you for all kinds of stuff, including the time you stepped in between me and the coach; he could have had me up for assault. Besides, I always thought your dad really got screwed. The way they jumped on him was criminal.''

Quinn left Mike to his sawing and hammering and headed back to Mrs. Dewsbury's to check on her before going on to Olivia's. He mulled over Mike's revelations, looking for an interpretation that he could live with, but he came up empty. The Bennetts—one or more of them—seemed to be up to their ears in the tragedy that was Alison.

The thought absolutely paralyzed Quinn.

He kept veering away from his suspicions, preferring to focus on his old coach. How did Bronsky fit in? He had been present when MoJo blabbed to everyone about Alison, and he had done nothing.

Quinn could understand why his old teammates had been too intimidated to expose the Bennett family to an investigation, but he couldn't understand how the coach, a close friend of Chief Vickers, could keep such incriminating information from him. Vickers had been a sergeant back then. You would think a pal would want to give a low-ranking officer his big break.

On the other hand, maybe Coach Bronsky was being bought off; maybe that's how he was managing to hold on to his job despite his drinking problem. Ironic that it was Olivia who'd suggested the coach might have friends in high places.

For that matter, maybe Chief Vickers had been bought off as well. He *was* the chief of police, after all. Maybe all of Keepsake was in on a conspiracy of silence. At the very least, it looked as if a lot of people had been turning a blind eye to the whole affair. It pissed Quinn off more than he could say.

Money and sex: They were powerful motives, and completely entwined in this case. Olivia believed that the rift between her father and her Uncle Rupert was over money— how they had handled their inheritances. What if it were over Rupert Bennett's sexual abuse of Alison instead? That would account for the genteel break between Owen and Rupert; Olivia's father didn't seem like the type to turn in his brother for being a child molester, no matter how appalling the crime.

Say that Alison *had* become pregnant by her father. In that case, it was possible that Rand had acted out of chivalry and had offered to marry his cousin simply to get her away from her abusive father. But would Alison keep a baby conceived in those heartbreaking conditions, and would Rand take over the fathering of it? It was hard for Quinn, knowing Rand, to believe that.

On the other hand, if Rand *was* the father, maybe he decided to step up to the plate and take responsibility for the baby. It was easy to picture Rand in love with his cousin: She was good-looking and personable—just like him. He was the Montague to her Capulet. The idea of love between first cousins of a feuding family would have appealed to Rand's emotional, tragic side.

There was a third possibility. Maybe Rand got Alison pregnant and regretted it. Maybe he wanted her to get an abortion and she refused. Maybe she began living some fantasy, hearing a proposal where none had been made.

And maybe Rand decided to murder her.

Quinn slammed his hand in frustration on the wheel of his truck. The two top suspects in his investigation so far were Rupert Bennett and his nephew Rand. Somehow Quinn had got himself in the bizarre position of actually *hoping* that it was Alison's father who had made her pregnant and then murdered her. It was the less horrifying of two horrific scenarios.

Quinn's mood was utterly black as he let himself in through the front door of Mrs. Dewsbury's big white house on Elm. He found his old mentor at a makeshift desk in the dining room, seated in front of her brand-new toy: a twenty-inch closed-circuit TV that magnified printed material a huge amount and made it possible for her to read again with ease.

Mrs. Dewsbury looked up from the screen at him and her face creased into a county roadmap of wrinkled joy. "Quinn, I *love* this CCTV thing," she said in a young girl's voice. "I had just about stopped reading, and look at me now!"

She motioned him over. She had placed a list of recent books acquired by the Keepsake Library under the camera, and the list was being magnified twenty times on the screen.

"See all the books I've checked off on this list? I'm going to reserve every one of them, from the biographies to the sexy historicals. This is—*truly*—a miracle! Thank you so much for buying it on the spot when you came across it. Two hundred dollars seems awfully reasonable for something so sophisticated."

It had cost Quinn two thousand dollars, but she never would have accepted a gift like that from him, so he had made up a story about finding the vision aid in the Granny's Attic shop of his uncle's retirement home in Old Saybrook. Even at that, she had insisted on reimbursing him for it.

"All it is is a camera and a TV box," he explained to defend the apparently low price. "The concept is actually very simple."

"It doesn't look that way to me," she said. She added, "How do I know it isn't stolen?"

He pretended to be scandalized. "Mrs. D.! What do you take me for?"

"Well . . . all right. Just be sure to cash my check, you hear? I don't want you carrying it around in your wallet for a month the way you do. It throws off my bank balance."

"Yes, ma'am," he said, delighted to see her so pleased.

She cocked her head at him. "I see you're not taking off your jacket. I assume this means that you won't be back tonight?"

"Nope. I just stopped by to activate the alarm, because the chances are good that you will not."

"Yes I will. But not right away. Helen next door is coming over to see this thing. Her mother has macular."

"But you'll set it after she leaves?"

"Mm-hmm," the schoolteacher said absently. It was clear that her mind was on something else, and it wasn't the library list.

Out of the blue, she said, "May I ask you what your intentions are toward Olivia Bennett?"

His intentions. Now there was the sixty-four-thousand-dollar question. He wanted to say, "Entirely honorable." But it was hard to reconcile that answer with his ongoing campaign to investigate Olivia's family.

"We're enjoying one another's company," he settled for saying.

"So are you and I. That doesn't mean that we'll be marrying anytime soon."

He laughed, then raised one eyebrow and said, "Just because I haven't asked you yet . . ."

"Quinn, I'm serious. Sleeping over is what teenagers do at slumber parties. You are thirty-four years old. You should be a father by now. If the attraction between you and Olivia is that deep . . . that irresistible . . . well, don't you think you ought to be backing it up with a commitment of some sort?"

Feeling cornered, he said, "I'd give her a fraternity pin, but you know how it is—I'd have to go to college first."

"Don't be flip. Besides, you're only a few night courses away from a degree, so stop trying to sound underprivileged. It will not work with me."

He shifted tactics and went on the offensive. "The 'attraction,' as you term it, has only been going on for a couple of weeks or so."

"The attraction has been going on all of your lives! Why do you suppose neither of you has ever married? Can't you see that you've been waiting for one another? My goodness—I thought *I* was blind."

"It's not as simple as that," he said, looking away. How could he possibly explain that his love for Olivia was now at odds with his love for his father?

Mrs. Dewsbury picked up on the torment he thought he was concealing. "*Quinn.* Look at you! What's going on?"

Now he did feel cornered. "The pranks," he said, hedging the truth. "They're demoralizing."

"Oh, those. Of course they are. But sooner or later, this man is going to do something stupid. He'll be caught in the act and made to feel ashamed. Or else he'll see that you're determined to stay in Keepsake, and he'll simply give up. That's what I predict. He'll simply give up and fade away."

It wasn't *what* Mrs. Dewsbury said, exactly; it was more the way she said it. Here she was, an eighty-something woman with limited means and failing eyesight, and she was bucking *him* up.

Quinn smiled and said, "I bow to your indomitable spirit, Mrs. D. You are one in a million." He bent down to kiss the top of her head and said on his way out, "Don't forget the alarm."

"The alarm ... right," she said, off in a world of her own.

Quinn made love to Olivia with exquisite tenderness, even sadness, after he returned from seeing Mike Redding and Mrs. Dewsbury. Olivia was surprised by his melancholy, which seemed to run deep.

Afterward, they lay in bed under the covers. Olivia was propped on an elbow with her leg thrown over Quinn's as she twisted the hairs on his chest idly around her finger.

"Take me with you," she said.

He stared at the ceiling. "Not on your life."

"Quinn, why not? They won't open the door if you show up alone. Believe me about that. My uncle is eccentric, a recluse. If I'm with you, at least you'll get inside the house."

Quinn rolled his head in her direction and smiled wearily. "You never give up, do you?"

"I've never learned how to."

Nor had she ever learned how to stick out her lower lip and pout prettily to get what she wanted. Or how to use tears. Or, God forbid, the silent treatment. Olivia's basic philosophy in life was that if you had logic on your side—

especially if you were talking to a man—then you would prevail.

So why wouldn't Quinn let her prevail? That's what had her so stumped.

"Come on, work with me here," she said lightly, taking a tiny yank on his chest hairs.

"Ouch. Stop. No. You're not coming with me."

"Qui-inn," she wailed, trying to win by whining after all. "You're being irrational, and it isn't like you. I think I've made my case. I've come around completely to your side. I believe that you *should* propose the DNA testing to my aunt and uncle. I know that you'll be delicate about it, and I know how much it means to you to vindicate your father. I know how much you loved him. Much more," she confessed, "than I love my own father, ashamed as I am to admit it."

Quinn looked startled by the remark, and very interested. Oddly, she would have called his look hopeful. "You don't love your father?" he asked.

"Of course I do. But there's love . . . and there's love. And let's face it: I've never forgiven my dad for not offering me a job in the mill and generally for favoring Rand over me."

She sighed and said, "My feelings for my dad are based more on respect and—I wouldn't go so far as to call it a sense of obligation; more a sense of rightness. It's *right* that you should love your family. It's really sad if you don't, or can't. I'm not saying that people don't have valid reasons for being estranged from members of their families," she added thoughtfully. "I'm just saying that you lose some of who you are when that happens, and it's too bad."

Quinn said, "Do you feel that way about your mother?"

"Mom? Oh, no. I love her unconditionally. It's so easy."

"What about your brother?" he said softly. "What about Rand?"

"Ah—that one's more complicated. As you know, Rand gets under my skin a lot. And there are things about him that—I have to admit—I don't admire. He's hot-tempered.

He's egotistical. He sulks. He has no ambition. But deep down he's . . . all right. And more than that, he's my *twin*. There's a bond there that I can't explain. You really have to be a twin to understand.''

''Whereas I don't even have siblings.''

''Which is really too bad, because I'm doing a lousy job of explaining this, aren't I?'' Olivia said, laughing softly and flopping over on her back. ''I think I'm more visual than I am verbal.''

Quinn took advantage of the remark to murmur, ''You're a sight for sore eyes, I agree.'' Bracing himself on his elbow, he lowered his head to hers for a kiss.

''Wait, wait,'' she said, slipping her fingers between his lips and hers.

He sighed. ''Who says you're not verbal?''

''Before you wipe out my short-term memory with a kiss, I really, really would like to get this business of my aunt and uncle resolved.''

He didn't look melancholy anymore. He didn't even look surprised. He looked annoyed.

''It *is* resolved. I go. You don't.''

''That's a bad decision. I must urge you to reconsider, sir,'' she said, trying to keep her tone charming.

''No! And you know what? You can be a real pain in the butt.'' Scowling, he opened his mouth to say something more, then thought better of it and rolled away from her.

It stung. She had never seen him so tense, so dark. It was disheartening. They'd grown up together and she thought she knew him inside out. True, he could be fierce and competitive. But this—she didn't know what to call it: Hostility? Bitterness?—this was new.

She was completely convinced that she was right and he was wrong. How could he not see that if she went with him to her Aunt Betty and Uncle Rupert, his job would be easier? All she could do was hope that he'd come to his senses and change his mind before lunchtime tomorrow, which was when he implied that he was going to try seeing her aunt and uncle again.

Olivia sighed, loud and mournfully. When she got no response, she switched off the brass lamp on her nightstand and curled up, facing away from him. The second sigh that escaped her was much more private and much more painful than the one she'd let out for his benefit. The second sigh hurt. She lay curled alone for a long time, with that sigh stuck in her throat, before dropping off to sleep.

Mrs. Dewsbury was upstairs, tired and happy and soaking her dentures, when a thundering crash sent her jumping through her woolen bathrobe.

The mirror! was her single, dismayed thought. *I knew it was too heavy to hang on that hook. He should have listened to me.*

Convinced that the heavy gilded frame had fallen on her Portuguese soup tureen and had left a hideous dent in her mahogany sideboard, she left her teeth fizzing in their glass and made her way down the stairs by the light of the bathroom to assess the damage.

He seemed so sure about hanging it that way. Why didn't the boy listen to me?

At the foot of the stairs she turned on the light, expecting the worst. She was surprised to see the mirror still hanging peacefully above the sideboard, just where Quinn had hung it.

That's odd. That's very odd. What else could it have been?

Instinctively she swung her gaze toward the next breakable object in the room. Her wonderful high-tech miracle, the bright new window into her old world of books, had been smashed to atoms. She stared in shock at the gaping hole that used to be a closed-circuit television. The pain was as sharp as if someone had driven a stake through her own eye.

And then came a sudden pain at the back of her head, and it was far more sharp and far more real than anything she could ever have imagined. After that, her sensations were neither sharp nor real. She felt nothing. Nothing at all.

Eighteen

The jangle of the phone ripped Olivia from her troubled dreams. She groped for the light, then for the receiver. It was nearly midnight.

A faint moan on the other end seemed to be some kid's version of fun. It was creaky, trembly, a pale specter of real speech—a little prankster's idea of a ghost.

"I'm sorry, you have the wrong number," Olivia said, irritated that her heart had been sent careening for nothing. She was in the process of hanging up when she heard, or thought she heard, the name "Quinn."

She brought the receiver back to her ear. "Who is this?" she asked sharply.

"Miz . . . Dewsbuh . . . Qui . . ."

"Mrs. Dewsbury? What's wrong?"

Quinn tore the phone from Olivia's grip. "I'll be right there," he said after listening for a scant second or two. He hung up and dialed 911 and in a few terse phrases directed an ambulance to the widow's house on Elm.

By the time he got off the phone, Olivia was dressed. "I'll start your truck and bring it around," she said, grabbing his keys from the dresser.

She was through the bedroom door before he could object. Outside, she brought the truck to a screeching halt alongside him and slid over to the passenger side as he climbed in, pushed the seat back and took off.

You should belt, she wanted to insist, because now she

was thinking thoughts of death. Instead she forced herself to say calmly, "What happened?"

"Someone hit her from behind. God, I'm going to get you all killed," Quinn muttered through clenched teeth.

Was that a promise? He was driving like a fiend. Bracing herself with a furtive grip on the door, Olivia said, "Why did Mrs. Dewsbury call me instead of 911?"

"I programmed your number on her speed dial. All she had to do was hit the number one."

That was the entire conversation en route to Mrs. Dewsbury's house.

By the time they reached Elm Street, the ambulance had arrived and the paramedics were trying the front and back doors. Olivia ran instinctively to the side of the house that she saw was sheltered from its neighbors by a row of towering hedges. Yes—an open window.

She climbed through the narrow window, one of the side openings of a walk-out bay, and found herself standing in the dining room across from Mrs. Dewsbury, who was sitting in a chair by the phone with her head drooped forward over her chest. Quinn had apparently let in the paramedics with his key. One of the them was tending to the widow while the other was laying out the stretcher.

Olivia was dismayed to see that the old woman didn't seem able to speak. Dazed and shaking her head, she kept waving the three men away. Her gaze was glassy-eyed— until she saw Olivia standing across from her. Then she seemed to snap into focus.

Weakly, she beckoned Olivia to her side as the paramedics continued to hover over her, trying to take her vital signs. She clutched feebly at Olivia's jacket and pulled her closer.

Olivia rested her hand lightly on the stricken woman's back as she bent down to hear. "Yes, Mrs. Dewsbury?"

"My teesh," said the widow. She pointed a finger straight up.

"Your—? Ah. I'll get them and bring them to the hospital," said Olivia, divining the widow's concern.

Mrs. Dewsbury gave her a trembling smile that started

tears rolling down her withered, pale cheeks. Olivia left her to Quinn and the paramedics and ran up the stairs and into the bathroom. She grabbed the glass with the dentures in it, intending to turn it upside down to drain.

That's when she saw that her hand was smeared with blood.

They were keeping Mrs. Dewsbury, despite her objections, overnight for observation. The staff physician at Eastwood Community Hospital seemed more impressed with the widow's iron skull than with her iron will.

"I doubt that there's a concussion, but I want to be sure; she seems a little disoriented," Dr. Tann told Quinn. "I don't know whether that's in character or not."

"It's not," said Quinn.

"She's not very happy about staying here, which isn't unusual with the elderly," the physician explained. "They like to be in familiar surroundings."

"Who doesn't?" Quinn snapped. He was incredibly tense. "What about all the blood?"

"It looked worse than it was; she didn't even need stitches. Any idea what was used for the blow?"

"Yes," said Olivia. "A dictionary. We found it on the floor at the foot of the stairs. Mrs. Dewsbury is a retired English teacher; she'll be amused."

The physician smiled wryly and said, "I doubt it. She's too upset about some television that got smashed."

"Can we see her?"

"No. Tomorrow's soon enough. I understand that she has a son in New Hampshire—but he's on vacation in Curacao with his family?"

"That's right," said Quinn. "He's due back at the end of the week. Should I try to get in touch with him now?"

"She's already said that she'd rather call him in the morning, which is reasonable. However, assuming there are no complications and she gets discharged, I'd still prefer that someone keep an eye on her for a while. When her family returns, maybe she can stay with her son, since his wife is available during the day. It's too bad," he added, "that Mrs. Dewsbury lives alone. She's at an age—"

"When her independence means everything to her," Quinn finished up. "She needs to hold on to the house; she was born in it."

"Be that as it may, she's eighty-one years old. She's in reasonable health but her vision is poor," Dr. Tann said, shaking his head. "Her days of living alone are winding down."

"We'll see," Quinn said coolly.

Olivia was touched by Quinn's fierce loyalty to his old teacher. For someone who'd had virtually no family of his own—but maybe that was why.

Quinn seemed more tight-lipped than ever as he said, "When exactly will she be released?"

"If her signs are stable she can go home tomorrow mid-morning."

"I'll be here."

The physician left Quinn and Olivia alone in the tiny visitors' room, a dreary cubicle with a small TV mounted on a wall above a bistro table that held an assortment of ragged, outdated magazines.

Suddenly the long night caught up with Olivia: the midnight dash through deserted streets, the shock of seeing an elderly woman assaulted in her own dining room, the lingering tension between Quinn and Olivia over something as trivial as whether or not she should go with him to her Uncle Rupert's house.

"Quinn," she said, humbled by circumstances, "I'm so sorry."

"For what?" he said bitterly. "*You* didn't knock her down."

The barely repressed rage in his voice didn't surprise Olivia. "You think it's the same man," she said, aware of the new burden of guilt he was feeling.

"Gee. I wonder why," Quinn answered. He walked up to the double window that looked out at a parking lot. His hands were jammed in the back of his jeans as he stared, not at the boring view, but at the windowsill, working through his wretchedness.

"We'll *get* this creep," she said. "This isn't about torn capes and dead rats anymore. Chief Vickers will take the case seriously, now that someone's been hurt. I wish I hadn't come in through the window, though," she added, aware that she'd trampled over the crime scene in her zeal to reach Mrs. Dewsbury.

There was no response. After a pause, Olivia began to get frustrated. "You act so paralyzed. You act as if everything's hopeless," she said, trying to get a rise out of him.

His response was surprisingly subdued, and that alarmed her even more than it frustrated her. "You don't have the whole picture," he said without turning around.

"What parts of it don't I have, Quinn?"

He shook his head.

Weary of his continued refusal to confide in her, she glared at his broad back and said, "Sooner or later I'm going to figure it all out for myself, you know."

"God help us, then," he said softly.

"*Damn* it, Quinn!" She said it so sharply that a passing nurse stuck her head in the room and shushed her.

Embarrassed that she had had to be reprimanded, Olivia said in a well-mannered hiss, "This is all your fault. You're acting as covert as a double agent."

"I'm sorry."

"Well, what do we do now? Sit here reading *Time* and *People* till morning? I already know who won the last election."

He turned. She was shocked to see his face. There was agony there, and guilt, but also a sense of menace. He was ready to annihilate someone.

"I'll take you home," he said, scooping up his jacket.

She folded her arms across her sweatshirt. "Absolutely not. I'm going back with you to Mrs. Dewsbury's house. I want to be there when you call the police."

"That's nuts. It's the middle of the night."

"I'm a witness—and maybe even an accessory," she

said, digging in. "I stepped all over any footprints under the bay window when I climbed inside the house. It's better that they get my statement now than have to chase me down later."

He sighed and said, "Fine. At least I'll be able to keep my eye on you. Let's go."

She grabbed her parka and fell in step beside him as he headed for the elevator. "And then tomorrow we'll tackle the other problem," she announced as they passed the nurses' station. "Our visit to my aunt and uncle."

"*No*, Olivia! Jesus! How many times do I have to tell you!"

"*Shhhh!*"

The good news was that Mrs. Dewsbury did not seem intimidated by the attack of the night before, despite a morning interrogation by Chief Vickers. The bad news was, she had developed a distressing tendency to lose her train of thought somewhere in the middle of a sentence.

"They're keeping me in this blessed place another whole day," said Mrs. Dewsbury, and Dr. Tann was right: She wasn't very happy about it.

"Did they say why?" asked Olivia. They knew of the delay, of course, which explained the small travel bag that Olivia was unpacking.

"Oh, I don't know. Something about my blood press— is it cold in here?"

Quinn, who was already half prostrate from the heat in the room, said, "I'll have a nurse turn up the thermostat." He ducked outside and when he returned, Olivia was helping Mrs. Dewsbury into a chenille bedjacket that she had found on the bedpost in the widow's bedroom. Olivia had grabbed other things, too, odd little luxuries: a brush, soft tissues, lotions, a bag of lozenges from the nightstand, and—for the doctor to see—medication for high blood pressure. Quinn was afraid that Mrs. Dewsbury would take offense at Olivia's liberties.

Not in the least.

"You're such a dear . . . so thoughtful . . . this is exactly what I needed."

Olivia threw Quinn a superior look and said, "Men simply don't understand that these things matter."

"What was I doing with this?" the widow said, staring at the brush in her hand as if it were a garden rake.

"You wanted me to run it through your hair for you," Olivia answered without missing a beat.

She took the brush and combed Mrs. Dewsbury's white hair, which looked to Quinn just about the same afterward as it did when they walked in, but the women seemed to think it was an improvement. After that, Olivia freshened the water in the drinking pitcher and moved Quinn's flowers to a more prominent spot.

Finally, when Mrs. Dewsbury looked reasonably comfortable and at ease with them, Quinn got down to business.

"How did your son take the news of all this?" was the first thing on his mind.

"I . . . haven't called him," Mrs. Dewsbury admitted sheepishly.

"The nurse didn't give you the number of the Windward Hotel? I called it in."

"She gave it to me."

"And you're having trouble getting an international call through the hospital's phone system? It can be confusing. Why don't I—?"

"It's silly to ruin Gerald's vacation," she said, fussing nervously with the sheet laid over her lap. "He gets so little time away. I don't want to be a bother."

They went round and round on that for a while, but Mrs. Dewsbury was adamant. Quinn didn't want to upset her, so he dropped the matter for the moment. That brought him to the delicate business of asking her what she remembered about the attack. He knew Vickers wouldn't tell him squat, so any information was going to have to come from the victim herself, and she was old and fragile and traumatized.

"Mrs. Dewsbury—guess what?" said Olivia before Quinn got the chance to bring up the subject. "When we were poking around under your bay window, we found a navy blue watch cap!''

Oh, perfect. *"Olivia—"*

"It's not Quinn's and I'm willing to bet hard cash it's not yours. We think it belonged to the guy who broke in."

The widow got a blank look on her face, as if she'd just remembered that she'd left the oven on.

"I never set the alarm!" she said, apparently realizing it for the first time. "I heard this tremendous crash and I came downstairs. And right before I was hit, I think I caught a whiff of bourbon. I know, because my Larry was partial to bourbon for his nightcap."

"Bourbon, huh?" said Olivia, obviously intrigued by the information. "Did you tell Chief Vickers that?"

"No. When he was here I wasn't quite . . . I wasn't . . . what was I saying?"

"We were coming up with a profile of the jerk who did this to you," said Olivia, and even Quinn had to admit that she made the discussion seem matter-of-fact. How did she do it?

Mrs. Dewsbury suddenly winced, and immediately Olivia was all solicitousness. She jumped up and said, "What hurts? Tell me."

Mrs. Dewsbury touched the back of her head gingerly and gave her a tremulous smile. "It doesn't hurt, exactly. I think I was reliving the blow just then."

"He hit you with your dictionary, you know," said Olivia with a wonderfully sympathetic smile.

"He did *not*," said the widow, bristling.

"But . . . we found the book on the floor by the stairs."

"Because I knocked it over when I was trying to reach a chair. Oh, no. It wasn't a dictionary, my dear. It was something hard and I think metal."

"A candlestick, maybe?" said Quinn. "That's what he used for smashing in the television."

"Yes, it could have been a candlestick," Mrs. Dewsbury decided.

Quinn said, "Chief Vickers will check the one lying in

the television for prints, but he didn't sound hopeful. In any case, the intruder wouldn't have smashed in the screen, then walked over to the stairs and . . . and . . .''

"Bopped me on the head."

"Bopped you on the head," said Quinn with a wry smile, "and then returned the candlestick to the TV screen."

"Was the other one on the table? I kept them placed on each side of the bowl of wax fruit that's on the table runner."

"I don't recall," said Quinn, but Olivia did. She said that the mate was on the table, just where it was supposed to be. Hell.

He mentally ran though a list of possible weapons: lamp, poker, knickknacks . . . Suddenly a light bulb turned on in the closet of his mind and he had a pretty good hunch about what the intruder *did* use for a weapon.

He turned back to Mrs. Dewsbury to say something and was dismayed to see a tear rolling down over her quivering lip.

"I could understand how someone would want to rob me," she said, sucking in her breath in a shuddering effort to gain control over her emotions, "but why did he have to smash in the monitor? I was so excited to have it. Ask anyone."

So that's why the son of a bitch sadist did it, thought Quinn. *Because you shouted your joy from the rooftops.*

The blow to the head, that was more difficult to account for. The act seemed motivated not as much by cruelty or sadism as by simple panic. Then again, Alison had been murdered by a blow to the back of the head. Was it mere coincidence, or a pattern?

There was nothing more to be learned. Mrs. Dewsbury was too weary to be cheered by Quinn's reassurance that he would find her another monitor. When they walked out of the hospital, it was with a fair amount of trepidation.

"I'm going to call her son," Quinn said as he and Olivia got out their car keys. "Obviously he has to know about this."

"I agree. Well, I guess I'll see you . . . ?"

"Tonight. Should we meet here?" he suggested.

"Yes. She needs to have visitors often, but in brief spurts. All right . . . well . . . bye," Olivia murmured, gazing at him with those fathomless dark eyes. Her look cut him up like a chainsaw, leaving a jagged streak of pain in its wake.

She turned to leave, but he caught her by the arm. "Olivia," he said, "I know I've been a shit. I'm, uh, having a real hard time with something right now. I hope . . . I hope that . . ."

What he was hoping was that she would understand. Blindly, without questioning, that she would somehow smile and say, *It's all right. Go wherever the path of justice leads you. I don't mind. Indict my uncle. Arrest my brother. Lock my dad in a small room and beat him until he howls. Break my mother's heart completely. Do whatever you have to, as long as you find out the truth. That's what counts.*

But her smile was sad and baffled, and worse, the spark that he loved seeing in her eyes was fading fast. She wanted him to share what he knew, and he couldn't. Not yet, and maybe not ever.

"I hope that we can work this through," he said at last in a voice wrung dry of emotion.

It wasn't much, but she seemed to take comfort from it. "I know we can, Quinn," she said earnestly. "We have so much going when we're together—as long as we *are* together, we can work anything through."

They kissed, a tender, hurried kiss that felt almost painful to him, and then they got in their cars and drove off in opposite directions—Quinn, with murder on his mind.

Olivia ducked into Miracourt just long enough to ask the help to hold down the fort until mid-afternoon, and then she got back in her car and headed for her parents' grand house at the end of upper Main. Her father would be at the mill, of course, which was fine with her. It was her mother she wanted to see.

The morning was gray but mild. Winter was easing its

grip on Keepsake, at least for the moment: It was the January thaw, right on time. Olivia rolled her window part of the way down, sniffing the gentleness in the air. What would it be like, she mused, if every day were as kind as this?

She daydreamed, again, about moving to California but decided, again, that she'd make a crummy Californian. How could she stand all that fine weather? When you lived in New England, moments like these—when Mother Nature stopped screaming at you long enough to give you a hug—seemed to make life all the more worthwhile.

How pathetic, she realized. *I'm thinking like an abused child.*

She was right about the weather, though: At the head of the drive she saw her mother wearing no coat, only her camel-hair blazer.

She tooted twice on her horn in reply to her mother's surprised wave, then pulled under the portico and left her minivan there. She'd dressed with special care and had left her coat unbuttoned so that her mother could see the olive-green silk dress she wore. With its autumnal scarf cinched by a pin, the outfit was a little on the fancy side for Olivia, but Teresa Bennett loved to see her little girl all decked out.

"Don't you look nice, honey," her mother commented predictably as Olivia bussed her cheek. "I've always liked that dress."

"Hi, Mr. Thurber," said Olivia to the gardener, who took himself off to the side to peruse his notes. "Mom, we have to talk."

"I'm afraid not now, Olivia," her mother said in mild reproach. "You can see that I'm busy with Mr. Thurber."

"But it's important. It's got to do with Quinn."

Anyone would think that Olivia had just let out a string of four-letter words. Her mother silenced her with a scandalized look and said, "Put on some coffee, then; I'll meet you inside when I'm done here."

"Mom, I don't have much time—"

"Olivia," her mother warned with a dangerous smile. "You'll have to wait your *turn.*"

Chastised, Olivia said, "Okay, I'll wait, but I don't really want coffee. This'll only take sixty seconds."

She paced the length of the redone kitchen for twenty minutes as she waited for her mother to finish her business with the gardener. It was dumb to have tried cutting ahead of Mr. Thurber. Teresa Bennett had always treated the help with at least as much civility as she treated her friends and relations; it was the reason people liked to do business with her.

Olivia sighed and put on the pot of coffee after all.

Eventually her mother came inside, and Olivia meekly set a steaming cup in its saucer on the granite-topped island where her mother liked to sit and read her morning paper.

"I'm sorry I interrupted you and Mr. Thurber," said Olivia before being handed an official reprimand. "By now I should know better. And I was indiscreet. About Quinn, I mean."

"I *know* what you mean," said her mother. "What's this all about? You come flying up the drive like a sparrow two steps ahead of a hawk, and you start flapping on about Quinn. What's wrong with you, Olivia? Do you understand the word discretion at *all*?"

"Not by this family's definition, that's for sure," Olivia shot back. She slipped onto the high stool opposite her mother's. "But listen to me, Mom. Something's happened. Mrs. Dewsbury was attacked in her house last night. She's in the hospital now."

Olivia related the few details she knew to her shocked mother, then said, "In a way, the attack just shows that Quinn is right. He has to prove his father's innocence—otherwise, whoever is doing these things will just keep on upping the ante. *I* could be next," she threw out, trying to alarm her mother into endorsing the logic of the plan she was about to announce.

So much for psychology. Her mother went directly past logic into a state of high anxiety. "Quinn has got to leave Keepsake!" she said, slapping the dark granite with the palm of her hand. "He's putting everyone around him in peril. Everyone!"

"Don't you think he knows that? That's why he's going out to see Uncle Rupert this afternoon."

"What . . . do you mean?" asked her mother. Her face had turned a deathly shade of pale.

"Well . . . *you* know. He's going to ask them about agreeing to have Alison's body exhumed for DNA testing. If she wasn't pregnant by Mr. Leary, then there would have been no real reason for him to have murdered her. That's pretty obvious."

Her mother simply stared. "But I thought that was all done with. I thought the district attorney refused to do anything about Alison. Why *would* he? Francis Leary is dead. I thought . . . that was all done with," she repeated numbly.

"I know it's upsetting to think about, but we have to be rational about this. Eliminating his father as a suspect is the only way that Quinn can stay in town without having to worry constantly that people he . . . he cares about are in danger. I mean, let's face it," Olivia said lightly, "he can't go installing a burglar alarm in the house of everyone whose hand he shakes. As soon as the test results become known—"

"They can't become known!" her mother cried. "That's nobody's business!"

Olivia stood up. "Of course it is, if there's a crime involved. That's why I'm going over to Uncle Rupert's now," she said, slipping into her long wool coat. "To help Quinn talk them into cooperating."

"What! Are you *insane*?"

"Why does everyone keep asking me that?" Olivia said with a laugh, determined to seem unconcerned. If she showed the least bit of empathy at her mother's distress, she'd never make it out the front door.

"Olivia, you cannot go there!"

"Of course I can, Mom," she said. She kissed her mother's cheek in farewell. "I know it's painful, dragging the whole thing up after all these years. But people have Alison on their minds anyway, with all these horrible acts going on. The whole town's on edge—except for Mrs. Dewsbury, of course. You can't believe how unflappable she is."

She glanced at her watch. "Shoot! Look at the time!" Snatching up her butter-soft bag from the back of the chair, she hooked it over her shoulder and said, "I still have to stop at the bakery for something sweet to bring Aunt Betty. Gotta run. If Quinn beats me there, he won't have a prayer of getting inside the house, though he'd be the last to admit it."

"Don't go!" her mother said in a sharp cry of agony, grabbing her arm. "Olivia, I'm begging you—don't!"

"I have to," Olivia said, unsettled by the depth of her mother's distress. "I'm only telling you beforehand because I don't want to do anything behind your back. Please, Mom," she said, freeing her mother's hand from her sleeve. "I've thought this all out. Aunt Betty was always fond of me. I used to stay over when I was a kid; she won't have forgotten that. She'll listen to me, even if she won't listen to Quinn. I promise I'll let you know how it goes. I'll even offer to tell Dad, if you don't want to."

Her mother grabbed her by the shoulders. Swaths of emotion were splashed across the tawny skin of her cheeks. Above her burning cheekbones, her dark eyebrows, heavier than was strictly fashionable, were pulled down in pain. Her look was as tortured, and as fierce, as the grip she had on her daughter.

"If you go," she said in a choked and agonized voice, "then don't bother coming back to tell me. *Ever!*"

Olivia blinked. "You don't mean that, Mom," she said, amazed and almost annoyed by her mother's melodramatic tone. "You're just saying that."

"I do mean it!" Teresa Bennett cried, and she burst into sobs. Tears rolled over her cheeks as she said over and over between hiccups of pain, "Don't, honey . . . don't . . . please don't . . ."

Now it was Olivia's turn to stare. Her mother had always been emotional—but this! She had always been kind to poor Aunt Betty—but this!

"Mom, it's no big deal," Olivia said, engulfing her mother as if she were a five-year-old with a scraped knee.

"You're getting way too upset for Aunt Betty's sake, honestly."

Her mother would not be consoled. Finally, in wonder and exasperation at her hysterics, Olivia stepped back and blurted out, "I have to do this, Mom! I love him!"

"You don't love him!" her mother shrieked, slapping Olivia's shoulder in her frustration. "You only think you do! You just want to fly in the face of your father! This is all about getting back at your father, Olivia, and nothing else!"

"But I do love Quinn!" Olivia cried, stunned by her mother's response. "My God—how can you say I don't love him? How can you possibly know how I feel?"

"You've never had time to love any man! They're annoyances to you, distractions from your career. Why would you suddenly think you love this one, unless it were to hurt us all?"

Olivia's purse had slid down to her wrist. Frustrated and infuriated, she looped the strap around her hand and slammed the bag in a vicious arc onto a counter. "Damn it! No matter what I do, it's not good enough for you! Dad wouldn't let me work at the mill. Now you won't let me love Quinn. What does it take around here? *You're* the one who always told me to follow my heart. *You're* the one who always told me to make my own dreams happen. Well, that's what I'm doing! I love him, Mother! *I love Quinn.*"

Three little words. They silenced as efficiently as a sword plunged directly through the heart.

Teresa Bennett became very still. Without another word, she moved away from her daughter and slipped back onto the woven seat of the wrought-iron chair at her new granite-topped island. Without another word, she moved her cup and saucer carefully to one side, then folded her arms in front of her on the dark green stone. Without another word, she bowed her head and pressed her brow against the soft ivory cashmere cocooning her arms.

Olivia stared at her mother for a long moment. And then she left, without another word.

Nineteen

Quinn went directly from the hospital to the police station and told Vickers where he could find the weapon that was used on Mrs. Dewsbury.

The chief laughed in his face. "You're completely paranoid, you know that? Too many years brooding in exile, if you ask me."

"Get a warrant," Quinn said. "Go to his house. Hell, stop by for a beer. You're a pal of his. Check the place out for yourself."

"I *am* a pal, Leary," he growled, "which isn't the only reason I'm telling you to get the hell out of my office. You've given me no cause to search the man's home. A dirty look on New Year's Eve and some psychological claptrap about—what?—sour grapes or something? That don't qualify as cause. Stop wasting my time. I'm late for a meeting already."

And that was that.

Seething, Quinn decided to retrieve the weapon himself. Maybe Vickers would call and warn his old friend, but maybe he wouldn't have the chance. It was worth a shot.

Quinn left his truck parked at the end of the block and headed for the bland little bungalow where Coach Bronsky had lived alone all of his life. He found it at the middle of a tree-lined street, looking—like its owner—saggier, baggier, somehow more mean.

A beat-up truck sat parked next to the house. As Quinn

suspected, Bronsky was home. It was the lunch period at Keepsake High. It didn't take a rocket scientist to figure out where a boozing coach who lived nearby would spend the free time.

The house itself presented a surly facade. The shades of the four windows that faced the street were pulled completely down, just the way they used to be. One of them had a big rip near the roller. For all Quinn knew, it was the same torn shade that had hung there two decades ago.

Even then, Coach Bronsky used to scare the kids. Not scare, exactly; more like thrill them. He was tough and mean and called them unspeakably insulting names, and underneath all their terror, they loved it. He was a role model for them, mostly because no one had a father with a repertoire of insults as vast as his. But the allure wore thin by sophomore year, and by their senior year, most of·the guys despised him.

The coach was a bully and a browbeater, a grown-up version of the kind of boy who pulled wings off insects in the name of science. He had a meanness of spirit, a pettiness of emotion. He blamed everyone for everything. Quinn could not remember a single instance when Coach Bronsky admitted to a mistake or said he was sorry. He intimidated the younger kids with his size and the older ones with his authority. Single women shunned him. Mothers resented him. Fathers felt guilty that he had charge of their sons.

He was a thug.

A BEWARE OF DOG sign, rusted and hanging from only one of its holes, was wired to the chest-high chain-link fence. Quinn opened the gate without bewaring. The dog was dead, Quinn had no doubt—he knew where the bones were.

Quinn walked up the five cracked concrete steps. Ignoring the bell, which was missing its button, he knocked and then waited. Three rectangles of glass in the door, stepping down from upper left to lower right, had been shaded with blue-lined pages of looseleaf paper, and one of the sheets had been pried from its tape to make a peephole. At six-foot-three, Quinn was able to see through the hole into the house.

The view inside was dismal: an end table piled high with

magazines and dirty dishes and topped with a chartreuse ceramic lamp whose shade was akilter. A dirt-colored couch with lumpy, torn cushions. A carpet that was matted and gray and littered with bits of food and scraps of paper. And over everything, a pall of grime and grease, rage and despair.

Quinn stepped out of view through the pulled-away sheet in the window. Eventually the door swung open a few inches. The smell of whiskey—bourbon, Quinn assumed— added one more layer of sourness in the air between Bronsky and him.

"What do *you* want?"

"A word," said Quinn, slamming the door clear of the coach's grip. It hit the wall with a bounce as Quinn pushed his way inside and grabbed the coach by the throat with one hand, pinning him against the stairwell as he kicked the door shut behind them.

The warm, flabby flesh of the coach's neck felt irresistible to Quinn. He got a death grip on the man's windpipe, then loosened his hold just enough for the coach's head to slump back into position on his shoulders. Before the coach could catch his breath, Quinn tightened his grip and slammed him back into the wall again. This time he squeezed harder.

Bronsky's round face turned florid; his eyes were no more than slits above puffy bags and a foul-smelling mouthhole gaping for air. Just before the coach passed out, Quinn relaxed his hold on his throat, then tightened it and slammed him up against the wall another time.

Bronsky couldn't speak, and Quinn didn't want him to. Not yet. Quinn positively needed these dribs and drabs of release; the alternative would have been to kill his old coach with a single blow. He eased his grip just enough for a trickle of air to flow down Bronsky's throat. The gurgling sound he made, so like a death rattle, was deeply satisfying to Quinn's ears.

"Listen to me, you sorry sonofabitch," Quinn said, his face within inches of the loathsome one he knew so well. "You want to knock out little old ladies, you ask me first.

You want to terrorize single women, you ask me first. You want to panic a bunch of churchgoers, you ask me first. Got that?''

The coach was in no position either to shake or to nod his head. He squawked what sounded like a denial. It infuriated Quinn. He slammed the man's head against the wall again. This time the answer he got was more to his liking.

''Ayight . . . ayight.''

Quinn let him go. ''Where's the trophy you stole from the box in Mrs. Dewsbury's front room?''

Coughing and sucking in air as he massaged his throat, the coach croaked, ''I don't . . . have any trophy.''

''The hell you don't,'' said Quinn, sending the coach stumbling before him with a shove to his back. He scanned the living room, then said, ''Where's your bedroom?''

Since Coach looked like a man who didn't climb steps if he didn't have to, Quinn looked for and found a sleeping hovel on the first floor. It was at the end of the hall, next to the kitchen. He shoved Bronsky into the room and flipped on a light. The tiny bedroom smelled rank, a stale mix of booze and b.o. Quinn glanced around and saw the stolen trophy—a brass-plated football mounted on a wood base—sitting on a dresser whose drawers were hanging half out. He pulled a hanky from his hip pocket and used it to pick up the football by its stem. If the weapon still had fingerprints, it would have forensic traces of Mrs. Dewsbury as well.

The coach glared at him. He looked almost indignant. ''You're going to jail for this.''

Quinn snorted. ''I don't think so. Not unless I follow through on the yen I have to bash in your head with this thing. And even there, I'm pretty sure the town would thank me.''

He walked past the coach out of the room, but then turned back for one last warning. ''If I ever hear of another attempt by you to frighten someone—if you so much as whisper an unsettling word in anyone's ear—then I'll hunt you down and kill you. You know me well, Coach. You know I will. Are you sober enough to understand me?''

The coach's glare of defiance quickly turned sullen. He

let his gaze slither away from Quinn and hide in some laundry lying on the floor.

"Yeah, I get it."

Quinn muttered, "You asshole."

As he walked out of the foul-smelling house with his recovered trophy, Quinn glanced through the broken blinds of a filthy window that looked out on a small, overgrown yard. It didn't surprise him to see a mound of soil piled next to a dug-up hole in the ground.

Poor dog. His mortal remains were now in a plastic bag lying somewhere in the town dump. God only knows what kind of life and death the animal had suffered as the pet of this brute.

All things considered, Quinn figured the dog was better off in the landfill.

It was a fact that Coach Bronsky had an alibi for the time of Alison's murder—it was an unacceptable fact, but an undeniable one. Quinn would gladly have given all the money he possessed to prove that Coach had done the deed, but everyone knew that he and then-Sergeant Vickers had played poker with two other buddies all night long.

Besides, Bronsky had never been linked, even as tenuously as Quinn's father had, to Alison Bennett. No gossip, no anecdotes, *nada*. Quinn's old coach might have been a scumbag, but apparently he wasn't a murdering scumbag—although he'd just come damned close with Mrs. Dewsbury.

In the meantime, Quinn was approaching the house of Olivia's uncle with dread. His mind had locked onto three scenarios, all of them involving Bennetts. In one of them, Rupert Bennett impregnated his daughter and later murdered her. In another, Rand got her pregnant and Rupert murdered her. In the third, Rand did both. It was like juggling three hand grenades with the pins pulled out.

The house where Rupert Bennett lived, like his brother Owen's, was not visible from the road, but that was all that the two houses had in common. Rupert lived in a simple saltbox Colonial that dated from maybe the early 1800s. It had a classic, uncluttered look to it that appealed to Quinn; if he were to settle down in the east, such a house would be his choice.

It was built on a clearing in the middle of a second-growth forest. Someone had once farmed the land, but not for a generation or two. It wasn't hard to see the writing on the wall. The land around the house would be sold off, if it hadn't been already, for a shot of income. Evidence of poverty—more likely, of a money-sucking habit—was staring Quinn in the face. Rupert's house was as shabby as his brother's mansion was pristine.

Simply put, the Colonial structure was falling down in place. The roof was sagging, shingles were missing, the leaky wood gutters were doing much more harm than good. The windows needed glazing, the foundation needed tucking, and as for the sills . . . Quinn could almost hear the powder-post beetles munching away as he drove up. The craftsman in Quinn wanted to buy out the Bennetts then and there and save the house, but that was not why he had come.

The winding, rutted drive continued on behind the house, but Quinn took the spur and parked his truck directly astride the front door, which apparently was little used. He stepped out of the truck and—because the weather was mild—right into mud. He should have known better than to approach through the formal entrance, but he didn't want the Bennetts to feel that he had presumed by driving around to the back.

Would Rupert be in? Quinn almost hoped not. Betty Bennett didn't sound like the type of woman to say boo without her husband's permission. On the other hand, it was Rupert whose measure Quinn wanted to take. If he seemed nervous or panicky or anything other than predictably hostile, then that would be significant.

Quinn cleaned the mud from his workboots on a metal bootscraper set into a chunk of concrete, then gave a rusted hand-cranked doorbell a turn or two. Its loud, shrill ring was enough to wake up the dead. In a sense, it was what Quinn had come to do.

Eventually the door was opened by a churchmouse. Betty

Bennett was a hundred pounds of fearful impulse bundled in gray sweats. Under a wisp of graying hair, her eyes, washed by too many tears to the color of faded jeans, seemed incapable of returning his direct gaze. A quick, scared glance was all he got from her. He felt like Godzilla trying to sell Girl Scout cookies.

"Mrs. Bennett?" he said gently as he took off his baseball cap. "You probably don't remember me—I'm Quinn Leary. I wonder if I might have just a moment of your time."

To his amazement, she said, "Yes, all right," and opened the door wide.

Well, hell, that was easy enough, Quinn thought, stepping over the threshold. He followed her across wide-planked floors through a neat, cozily furnished parlor and then through a fireplaced keeping room, all the while wondering whether she wasn't leading him straight into an ambush. It didn't help his morale that a rifle seemed to be missing from an otherwise well-stocked gun case that they passed along the way.

The expected ambush took place in the kitchen: Olivia Bennett, wearing olive silk and a fancy bandanna and looking wildly sophisticated in the austere pilgrim setting, was sitting demurely at a big pine table by a massive hearth with a cup of tea and a giant muffin set in front of her.

Son of a bitch. Now what? Son of a bitch.

He looked at the niece. He looked at the aunt. He looked at the niece again.

"Now why am I surprised by this?"

"I can't imagine," Olivia said, forcing herself to seem offhand. "Didn't I mention that I might be stopping by my aunt's? I thought I had."

Quinn had arrived before Olivia had had a chance to prepare her aunt for his request. She'd barely got out the heads-up that Quinn Leary was going to be stopping by when they heard the crank on the bell. Her aunt, predictably, wanted to run and hide under the couch; Olivia had to reassure her that she would stay by her side and give her moral support. And meanwhile, Olivia's Uncle Rupert was due back from town at any moment.

Betty Bennett didn't know what to do with Quinn, that was plain to see, so Olivia took over as hostess. "Can I get your . . . something?" she asked, stumbling over the sentence. God, he had a look. Even she was nervous.

"I'm all right," he said in a perfectly even tone.

Ah, that tone. It spoke volumes.

He turned to Olivia's aunt and said in a much more gentle way, "I know it's distressing for you to see me after all these years, Mrs. Bennett. You suffered a terrible tragedy, and I'm a reminder of that time. I know that. I wish I could be someone else right now. I wish I could be someone you knew and trusted—but there's no one else who can make this request of you except me."

He added softly, "I'm here because no one else cares enough about my father to prove that he had nothing to do with your loss of Alison."

Once he put it that way, Olivia understood things much more clearly. He was right. She had no business being there. This was between him and Alison's parents. He *was* right. And so was her mother. What on earth had she been thinking?

Something about Quinn's soft, sympathetic tone made her Aunt Betty murmur, "Please. Sit down."

She pulled out a chair for herself so meekly, it broke Olivia's heart to watch her. Here was a woman as fragile as the butterflies she had raised in her greenhouse before a storm knocked it down. It seemed cruel that sweet Aunt Betty had had to suffer the loss even of a single butterfly. But to have her only *child* murdered, and then to have no one with whom to share her grief except a brooding, remote husband—that was unbearably cruel.

Quinn hooked his jacket over the back of the ladderback chair and sat down. For a big man with solid biceps and a tough-looking haircut, he seemed amazingly unthreatening. Olivia knew how tender he could be in bed; that had a lot to do with her impression. But there was more to it than that. Women responded to Quinn because he empathized with them. Because he was gentle and tough and kind and interesting and curious and chivalrous and, okay, super-confident, not to mention because he made pies. You could trust such a man. All you had to do was look into his eyes and listen to his voice.

And her aunt was doing just that. Perched almost primly on the rush-seated chair, Betty Bennett folded her hands in her lap and listened intently to Quinn as he presented the reasons that his father had fled in the night so very long ago.

"My father was a shy man, and gentle," Quinn said, without making it sound like a character flaw. "He was appalled at the thought of having to fight to defend himself. He was even more appalled at the threat of being locked in prison, away from his gardens. All my father ever wanted to do was to nurture growing things. He lived very simply. He didn't want money; he didn't need fame. But he needed—truly needed—to be taking care of things."

Quinn might have been describing the woman who was listening to him so raptly. Olivia watched as her aunt nodded sympathetically at one statement after another that Quinn was laying out before her. It occurred to Olivia, really for the first time, that Quinn's father and Betty Bennett would have been a match made in heaven.

How sad, she thought. What a waste of love. She let her gaze wander around the well-kept kitchen. From the gleaming finish of the pine table to the homey, hand-braided rug that her aunt had made from fabric scraps, everything around them spoke of nurturing impulses that had nowhere to go.

How truly sad.

"I'm not sure how familiar you are with forensic science, Mrs. Bennett," Quinn said, easing into his painful request, "but nowadays there are methods to prove someone's innocence that weren't around seventeen years ago."

"What kind of methods?"

"Well . . . have you heard of DNA testing?" he asked her softly.

"I do have some idea, yes, from watching news about the O. J. Simpson trial. But I didn't watch the trial itself," she added with a troubled shake of her head. "It was too awful to see."

"You were better off," Quinn agreed with a sympathetic smile.

Olivia began a major project of rearranging crumbs into a circle around the edge of her plate and didn't look up during the painful pause that followed.

"A DNA test means that they would take just a few cells of tissue to determine the genetic makeup of the . . . unborn child," Quinn explained while Olivia held her breath. "And they would compare them to a DNA profile which they would get from analyzing strands of my father's hair. The two won't match, you see, and that will clear my—"

"Oh! Your father wants to return to Keepsake, then?"

Her aunt did not want to understand the implications of what Quinn was saying; Olivia was sure of it. She was re-routing her attention from her dead daughter and unborn grandchild to Quinn's father and where he should live. That, she could handle.

Quinn said softly, "My father died just before Thanksgiving."

"Oh, I'm . . . sorry."

Olivia glanced at Quinn and then at her aunt. They were sharing a moment of hurt, an awareness of loss, that drove home how wrong it was for her to be sitting at the table with them. She'd give anything to be able to leave them alone. But she couldn't just stand up and go; she'd be trampling all over their fragile connection. She went back to arranging her crumbs with renewed intensity, as though the fate of the free world depended on having a perfect crumb wreath on the rim of her cake plate.

"The thing is, Mrs. Bennett, he was a really good man and he deserves to have his good name back. I've never known anyone more steadfast . . . more loyal . . . more heroic.''

"Heroic?"

Olivia was curious about that, too. It was the second time that Quinn had referred to his father that way. She saw color rise on Quinn's neck as he said, "After he left Keepsake, my father did some good things."

"So you want to do this DNA test and clear his name,'' Betty said. "I can't blame you, Mr. Leary, but . . . well . . . I'm not sure. I think it would be very"—she took a deep breath and blew it out—"hard."

Catching a lock of hair at the back of her neck, she tugged at it nervously as she stared at the clean-swept hearth. "Hard on my husband, you see. People would—they'd start talking again. Rumors . . . they can be *so* hurtful."

She returned her hands to her lap and forced herself to look Quinn in the eye. It didn't last long. She dropped her gaze and studied the butter crock on the table instead. She said apologetically, "I think maybe we should just leave things be. I don't think my husband will agree to this at all."

Olivia looked from her aunt to Quinn. She expected to see his jaw set the way it did when he was opposed. Instead he said softly, "Those rumors have already surfaced, ma'am. There's only one way to lay them to rest now."

Olivia blinked. What rumors? They weren't talking about Francis Leary any longer. What rumors?

Her aunt had turned as pale as the whitewashed walls of her kitchen. She stood up and seemed to shake herself free of Quinn's spell, like a child who's lingered too long in the park and knows she's going to catch hell at home. "You really should go now. My husband could be back anytime. I'm sorry we can't help you. I'm sorry," she said with something like urgency. "Your father sounds like a nice man."

But she was too late. They all heard the door to the mud shed slam loudly, and they all turned at the same time to behold Olivia's Uncle Rupert letting himself through it to the kitchen. Olivia hadn't seen him in over half a year. When she stopped by for her Aunt Betty's birthday in August he'd been asleep, and when she dropped off her Christmas presents in December he hadn't been home.

He looked much the same: lean and leathery and dour.

He sneered at Quinn and said, "Well, well, well. Look what the cat dragged in." He didn't seem surprised, and Olivia wanted to know why. Would he really know Quinn's truck?

Earlier Olivia had wanted to be invisible. Apparently she'd got her wish; her uncle didn't seem to be aware of her at all. "Hello, Uncle Rupert," she said rather loudly, as if he were not only blind but hard of hearing. "I haven't seen you for a while. How are you?"

He was watching Quinn the way a tom regards a stray who's wandered through his territory. Without taking his eyes away from him, he said to Olivia, "Since when do you care?"

He was right, of course. Olivia had never cared for him, not for as long as she could remember.

When she was a little girl and he was still part-owner of the mill and their families were closer, Olivia used to sleep over occasionally. He always came into Alison's bedroom to kiss them both good night, and Olivia had never liked it. His mouth was too wet, and he often smelled of old beer. After a while, she began to insist that Alison come over to *her* house for sleepovers. But her uncle had nixed the idea, and that was that. She and Alison stopped having sleepovers.

But now, what had seemed like an irrational childish aversion to a grown-up suddenly took on another meaning altogether. Something deep inside of Olivia seemed to shift and move, like ice over a pond in the January thaw. She felt her cheeks turn hot and her heart take off on a sickening run.

Quinn, still seated, broke the brutal silence. "I don't pretend to be here out of anything beyond self-interest," he said in a much more steely voice than he had used so far. "I've come back to Keepsake for one reason only: to prove my father's innocence."

"If you want my blessing, you're in the wrong place," her uncle growled. "Go see Father Tom."

"No," Quinn said coolly as he leaned into his forearms on the table. "It's the district attorney whose blessing I'll need. I'm here to say that the only way to clear my father's name—and yours—is for us to throw in our forces together."

"What are you talking about?"

"I think you know."

"Suppose you tell me."

Olivia saw Quinn glance at Betty Bennett, who looked ready to burst into tears. She realized in a blinding flash that her uncle was banking on Quinn's natural reluctance to inflict pain on downtrodden women. It was a game of psychological poker, and Uncle Rupert was calling Quinn's bluff.

The men remained locked in a standoff for a brutal moment, and then Quinn shrugged and said, "Okay. Since you want it spelled out."

Olivia held her breath. Her aunt gasped.

"There are rumors around Keepsake that your relationship with your daughter was—"

"No more than it should have been, goddammit!" Rupert said, refusing to look at the cards that Quinn was about to lay out. He turned to his wife and said, "Leave us! This isn't for a woman to hear."

Apparently Olivia didn't fall into the woman category. Either that, or she truly was invisible, because her uncle completely disregarded her as he waited for his wife to scurry up the stairs and out of earshot.

Olivia watched him with a feeling of dismay that was rapidly imploding into one of disgust. Was it possible? Those vague and uncomfortable feelings that she'd had as a child . . . the squirmy reluctance to be left, with Alison, in her uncle's care . . . the sinking feeling when he walked into a room, any room, where she and Alison happened to be.

Was it *possible*?

She stared fiercely at his face, willing her memory to dredge up some clues, any clues, as to what kind of man he was behind that domineering sneer. But as hard as she tried, all she could see was a truly awful version of her father. A taller, lazier, more irresponsible version of her father, a man who preferred to wear plaid instead of pinstripes. The same instinct to control was present in both brothers, but her Uncle Rupert was lording it over a much smaller empire: one shy woman, to be exact.

No. He might have been domineering and he might have been awkward—even repulsive—in social situations. But he was not the father of his unborn grandchild. Olivia was absolutely convinced of it.

He had been leaning his weight on one leg, one shoulder higher than the other as he watched his wife leave the room. Now he swung around fully to face Quinn. It was the posture of confrontation. Olivia had a sudden urge to duck under the table.

"I never touched her, not in that way," he said with a burning look. "She was my *daughter*, for God's sake."

His face, so like her father's and yet so utterly unlike it, was contorted with emotions that Olivia couldn't begin to understand. Rage? Grief? Horror? Frustration? They went so far beyond Olivia's limited palette of experience that she found herself groping for terms to describe them. The one thing she recognized, the one thing she knew, was that he was telling the truth.

She turned to Quinn to gauge his reaction. She was sure he'd look relieved; that he'd believe her uncle. But what she saw on Quinn's face was a look of surprise and, oddly, dismay. It left her completely bewildered.

"Agree to the DNA testing, then," Quinn said, ignoring her as thoroughly as her uncle was doing. "I'll pay for the attorneys, I'll pay for the test. The results won't tell anyone who the father is. But at least they'll tell everyone who he isn't."

Her uncle bent his head and squeezed his temples with the fingers of one hand as he tried to come up with a response to that. When he looked up, his eyes were glazed over with tears. Olivia gaped at him, astonished at the display of emotion.

His answer was choked, halting. "I went to the D.A. . . . I wanted them to do something. I wanted them to go after your father, go after someone. I got *nothing*. A cup of coffee, a pat on the back. They seemed perfectly happy to have your father on the loose and the murder unsolved. Christ, where was the justice? Where was the law? I hired a P.I. He didn't do shit."

He dropped his chin to his chest. "Ah, damn it to hell. The rumors won't end . . . they'll never end. Keepsake is obsessed with them. My God. My great-grandfather built this town up from a general store and a post office. Keepsake wouldn't *exist* if it weren't for the mill, if it weren't for the Bennetts."

He shook his head and sighed heavily. He looked resigned, even defeated, as he said, "Go ahead. Do whatever you have to do. Tell me what I need to sign. But leave me alone until then, do you hear? Both of you."

He turned away from them and left the room, his own private demons nipping at his heels with every step.

Olivia stood respectful and silent until she knew that he was well up the stairs, then turned to Quinn and murmured, "I think we're on our own as far as finding the door."

Quinn's face had a stony expression that left her feeling desperately uneasy. It didn't make sense; he should be happy that they were finally on the way to clearing the air. He *couldn't* be angry that she'd shown up despite his warning not to. It would be far too small-minded a response for someone like him.

"All's well that ends well—right?" she ventured with a tentative smile as they left the kitchen together.

His look stayed grim. "It's barely begun."

Twenty

"*All Wools, Forty* Percent Off."

Olivia placed the small sign, done in a calligrapher's exquisite hand, on a pretty brass stand and positioned it in a puddle of blue worsted spilling from its bolt in the window of Miracourt. Advertising a winter sale in her York Street shop didn't take much more than that. Her clientele was strictly local, and they knew that come January, all wools would be forty percent off.

The customers who flocked to her mill outlet from all over the region, however, were another matter. Olivia was targeting her Run of the Mill audience with a big, flashy flyer about to be included in a weekly newspaper that served the whole county.

GIANT WINTER SALE! OVER ONE MILLION YARDS OF FABRIC! DESIGNER WOOLS AT FIFTY PERCENT OFF LIST AND MORE! CLEARANCE ON ALL CORDS, WOOLS, AND VELVETS! SHEERS, LACES, LININGS, HOLIDAY PRINTS AND TRIMMINGS, SEVENTY-FIVE PERCENT OFF! SUPPLIES LIMITED! HURRY FOR BEST SELECTION! DOORS OPEN 6 AM! FREE 9 FT. GARLAND TO FIRST 100 CUSTOMERS!

The asterisk warned in small print that the designer wools were seconds, that the sale could not be combined with any other offer, that all sales were final, that previous markdowns were not applicable, and that the sale ended February tenth.

Olivia proofread the ad with a certain amount of distaste. She hated having to grab people's attention by shouting at their eyes. But her father was right—this was how it was done in the outlet trade. Still, she found the flyer embarrassing. The thing was not only tacky, but sounded paranoid. How much nicer it was to know her customers personally, and to take back the fabric if they changed their minds, and to ask them how their kids were doing at hockey this season.

I'm a village shopkeeper, not an outlet entrepreneur; that's all there is to it.

It was an ongoing revelation to her, this softer, gentler side of herself. Was it because she had fallen in love? And if that was true, then why wasn't the same thing happening to Quinn? She wanted to believe that he had fallen as hard for her as she had for him, and yet every time they were together lately, he seemed a little more edgy, a little more . . . remote.

That was it: remote. She didn't like even to *think* the word, and yet there was no other way to describe the look that she now saw routinely on his face. He would be with her, talking and listening, and yet . . . somehow . . . not with her at all.

And I can pinpoint exactly when and where he began to act that way: New Year's Day, after Ray Buffitt's football bash.

Obviously that was where he had heard the rumor about Rupert Bennett being the father of his daughter's child. Armed with that knowledge, Quinn had taken a huge gamble with Olivia's uncle, and it had paid off. With Rupert Bennett's cooperation, Quinn would now be able to clear his father's name and—something Olivia hadn't even known was necessary—clear her uncle's in the bargain.

Hooray. Three cheers. Shouldn't they be drinking champagne?

"Beth, I'm going out," Olivia said to her assistant as she faxed her approval of the sale flyer. "I should be back in an hour. If I'm not, just close up here, would you?''

"Sure thing.''

"Thanks. You're a doll.''

Olivia grabbed her coat and blew Beth a kiss on her way out of the shop, then got back in her car to head back up the hill to her parents' house, aware that she had got absolutely nothing done all day.

This couldn't go on. Being in love and walking around with your head in a cloud was one thing, but this wasn't that kind of cloud. This one was filled with rain and fog and, worse, the occasional thunderbolt. All things considered, Olivia preferred to do her strolling in rose-tinted sunglasses.

She drove in deepening twilight through deserted streets toward her parents' estate, clinging psychologically to the thin streak of orange that slashed the cloud bank above the dropping sun. A cold front was pushing through, which meant that tomorrow would be bright and sunny. But the day would still be cold and short; so who cared, really, whether the sun came out or not?

I do, she decided. Anything to banish the sense of gloom that was plaguing her lately.

At that hour, she expected to find her father home from the mill, but finding Rand at her parents' house was an unexpected bonus. He was sitting in his Lexus parked under the portico. Was he coming or going? Going, apparently. He waved a hello–good-bye to her and started to drive off, but Olivia flagged him down. She wanted him to stay. For one thing, her mother was much more likely to let go of her anger at Olivia if he were around. And with Rand there, Olivia would be able to grill all of them at the same time about the appalling rumors concerning her Uncle Rupert. That way, they wouldn't have a chance to coordinate their stories.

By now Olivia was reasonably sure that she had been the only one among them who had lived so happily clueless for seventeen years. It pained her to think that her family had conspired to keep her in the dark like some rainforest flower that would wilt and die if put out in the sun. Damn it! Why was *she* always the odd one out in the family?

Rand buzzed his window down and said, "Run while you can. She's in one hell of a mood." He gave Olivia his trademark bemused smile, the one that always left women's hearts aflutter, and said, "That's the last time *I* offer to drop off Eileen's leftover borscht."

"Did Mom say what was bothering her?"

"Nope. She just took one look at me and burst into tears. I said, 'What'd I do now?' and she shook her head and moaned, 'Not you, not you.' That was good enough for me. As soon as I could, I cut and ran."

Still angry! "Uh-oh."

Rand gave her a sharp look and said, "So you're the 'you' she was talking about? Oh, great. Is this about Quinn?"

"It's more complicated than that, Rand."

She hurried around to the passenger side of the Lexus and dropped into the leather bucket seat, then brought her brother quickly up to date on the hair-raising showdown earlier in the day between Quinn and their Uncle Rupert.

Her brother's reaction was concise. "Oh, shit."

"You knew all along, didn't you, Rand? You knew that people suspected Uncle Rupert," she said, convinced of it now. "Why didn't you ever tell me?"

"Why bother?" he asked, staring straight ahead. "There's no truth to it."

"Still! It concerns us all."

He turned and challenged her in a sneering voice. "What would you have done if you did know?"

"Well . . . for one thing, I wouldn't have fought the idea of DNA testing when Quinn first suggested it. On the contrary, I would have pushed for it. I don't know why Uncle Rupert didn't do that himself when the rumors first surfaced."

"The test wasn't invented, for one thing."

"Oh. Right. Well, then Uncle Rupert should have just . . . I don't know, issued a statement of some kind."

"Oh, *there's* a plan. Send a letter to the local editor saying, 'Just so you know, I'm not the one who knocked up my daughter.' Olivia, do you have *any* idea how rumors work? Don't you see how counterproductive it is even to bring them up? You're the Shakespeare expert. Do the words 'Methinks he doth protest too much' mean anything to you?''

"That's not the actual quote," Olivia couldn't help saying. "The actual quote is, 'The lady doth pro—' ''

"Stuff it!" Rand said, out of patience with her. "The point is, after seventeen years, people's minds are set. The best thing is to let those opinions stay sunk in the mire where they belong. Why dredge everything back up? Why foul the air?"

"The point is to *clear* the air, Rand, once and for all. Maybe you can't do that without making a stink first."

"How easy for you to say."

"But it would be so much better if this were all resolved," she said, pleading with him to rally around to her view. "The truth is always better. Always. I agree with Quinn completely on that one. And I'm not just promoting that agenda for my sake."

Her brother let out a short, bitter laugh, but his voice turned almost wistful as he said, "You honestly believe that, Livvy? That you don't have an agenda in all this?"

"Well . . . yes."

When they were young, Rand had a little thing he did when he wanted to make a point: He would give her earlobe a gentle yank and say, "Listen up, little sister."

With a sad, sweet smile, he gave her left ear that gentle yank. But he didn't have to tell her to listen now; she was rapt with attention.

"Olivia, walk inside that house. Take a good, long look at our mother right now. Then come back out," he said softly, "and tell me that you believe this is all for the best."

Olivia shook her head. "That's not fair, Rand. Mom has always been an extremely emotional woman. She overreacts to everything."

"You say that about most women."

"Maybe most women overreact."

He sighed. "You're the brains of the family, Olivia. As by now we all know. But I wonder if you have the emotional smarts to back up all that theorizing."

This was new. "Meaning what?" she said testily.

"Meaning sometimes you have to hide the truth from someone you love *because* you love them."

"But then your whole relationship is based on a lie. No, I can't buy into that, Rand," she said, shaking her head emphatically. "I've never done that in a relationship, and I never will."

He shrugged and said, "You don't have relationships."

The point was offhandedly made, and yet it practically blasted Olivia out of the seat of his car. *You don't have relationships.* Is that how her family viewed her? As an uninvolved, ambitious, hard-driving witch?

"I do have relationships," she said, devastated by his remark.

"None that matter, Liv."

"I have Quinn Leary," she insisted, near tears now.

"Quinn? How do you figure you have Quinn? Are you married? The mother of his child? How do you have him? Where's the commitment?"

She bowed her head. "Quinn matters to me," was all she could say.

"Assume that he does," Rand allowed. "Would you lie to spare him pain?"

"Never!" she said with a fierce look at her brother. "Quinn wouldn't want that. And neither would I. And he knows it," she insisted. "We tell each other everything!"

But even as she said it, she could hear the Bard whispering in her ear. *The lady doth protest too much, methinks.*

Letting his head fall back on the headrest, Rand stared at the folded-up visor before him. "Yeah, well, you two have an unusual relationship. To say the least."

"It's true," she murmured, leaning back and staring in the mirror of her own visor, which had been flipped down;

but she looked and sounded as if she was trying to convince herself now. Quinn was so obviously *not* being truthful with her. The only question was, was he simply holding something back, or was he out-and-out lying to her?

Sighing heavily, Olivia rolled her head in Rand's direction and said, "I assume Mom and Dad are both aware that some people think Uncle Rupert had an incestuous relationship with Alison?"

She watched him close his eyes and mutter an oath. "We haven't chatted about it specifically," he said without opening his eyes. "But, yes, you can assume they've heard the worst."

"Then why did Mom get so upset after I told her that I was going to help Quinn persuade Uncle Rupert to agree to an exhumation? You would think she'd be happy to have the scandal cleared up."

She saw her brother's brow furrow, as if he'd been hit with a sudden, blinding headache. For a moment he was silent. Then, "Resolving the issue of paternity doesn't do much about the rumor that Uncle Rupert murdered Alison."

"Oh, but it does!" Olivia said. She sat up straight and turned to her brother. She was bursting with theories, some of them years old, some of them hours old.

"It's more than likely that whoever got Alison pregnant was the one who murdered her," she speculated. "Maybe to keep her from exposing him, because—who knows? It could be that he was married. Or in love with someone else. He could have been an older man. Someone prominent— the mayor, the coach, her doctor, anyone. And Alison was a minor, don't forget. It would have destroyed the career of anyone of any importance."

Rand sighed and said, "You've worked it all out, have you, Sherlock? Take some advice. Don't run all your brilliant theories past Mom just now. I doubt that she'll be as impressed as you are with them. If I were you, I wouldn't bring up Uncle Rupert at all."

"See, that's another thing I don't understand. Why is she so concerned for the sake of Uncle Rupert? Or even Aunt

Betty, if that's who she's worried about. It's not as if they're still close. Or do you think it's just the Bennett name in general that's concerning her? That makes sense, although I still say she overreacted this morning. Did she tell you about our confrontation? I mean, she really freaked. She—''

"I gotta go," Rand said, cutting her off.

"Well—all right. If you're in *that* much of a hurry," Olivia said, hurt, as she swung her door open.

She had one foot on the macadam drive when he said her name with that apologetic, melancholy smile that somehow always made things okay again between them.

"Look," he told her, "maybe it's just that time of year. You know how intense Mom gets about the holidays. Afterward, she invariably feels let down. Statistically, this is when people are most depressed and anxious, you know— when they're most likely to kill themselves or, if they're sick, just give up and die. Did you ever think that maybe Mom just has a case of the January blues?''

"Oh, come on, Rand," said Olivia. "You're not blind. Has she ever looked at you and burst into tears before in January?''

"I gotta go," he said doggedly.

They were twins. Olivia may not have possessed her brother's emotional acumen, but she knew when he was being less than candid. He was refusing to look her in the eye; obviously he was far more upset than he was letting on.

"Bye," she said, puzzled by his response. "Tell Eileen I'll call her tonight.''

He drove off. Olivia decided, after all, that she did not want to face her mother just then. She told herself that she wasn't being cowardly, exactly, but that she and her mother needed a little time away from one another to calm down. Fortunately her parents lived in the back rooms of the house except when they entertained. They wouldn't even know that she had come and gone.

A cold blast of wind cut through her, making her decision

suddenly easier. Better to be with Quinn, snuggled in front of a fire.

She glanced at the main-floor windows in the front of the house before she turned to go back to her car. As she did so, a figure retreated behind the drapes and out of her view, but not quite far enough to be undetected by her.

In the soft light of the reception room, the same room that had been converted to a cloakroom for the New Year's Eve gala, Olivia recognized her father. He had been watching as she sat in the car with Rand. She was sure of it.

Quinn Leary felt like a man being sawn down the middle as he sat alone at a table at Vincent's, a small and nearly deserted Italian restaurant three miles outside of Keepsake. He nursed his beer, despite the waitress's efforts to replace it with a new one, as he watched twilight deepen into night. Myra Lupidnick Lancaster was late.

He was about to blow out the sputtering candle in the chianti bottle when she came in, looking different than she had at the tree lighting on Town Hill. Was it the big hair? She looped her coat on a peg near the register and turned to him with a self-conscious smile.

Holy cats, she was decked out for a prom: the dress, red and shiny and drifting somewhere above her ankles, was not exactly business as usual. On the other hand, spaghetti sauce wouldn't show on it, so maybe that was why she wore it. Quinn stood up with a hapless smile and pulled out a chair for her. The woman was married and the mother of four children; he hoped she remembered that.

"I'm really glad you agreed to meet me, Quinn," she said as she let him angle her chair for her. "I've been in such agony ever since I saw you on Town Hill."

Quinn didn't like the sound of that at all. He took in her red, red lips and black, black mascara, and then he motioned for a waitress just so he'd have somewhere else to look. "What'll you have?" he asked.

"Oh, a beer is fine." Myra looked up at the approaching waitress and ordered it herself: Miller draft, if they had it.

She turned back to Quinn and said, "When I called and you said that you had been thinking of calling *me*, that's when I knew. I told myself, this is definitely an act of God."

She made a small, quick sign of the cross which was so completely at odds with her getup that Quinn sat back in his chair, partly relieved but completely confused. "It must have been hard for you to get away," he said. "You have a big family."

Remind her, remind her.

"You're right about that," she said, rolling her eyes at him. "But George is home. Actually, he's been home all week on vacation. Well, not vacation, actually. Not in the regular sense. He's helping me and the kids pack. We're moving to Albuquerque. On Monday."

"Ah." Okay, so Quinn was a jerk who couldn't read women. He relaxed his guard and said more congenially, "It'll be a big change from New England."

"We're hoping. Two of our kids have asthma. And the living is so much cheaper there. George's people are out there—his father is a plumber, too, and George is taking over the business. Another good thing is that we'll have help with the kids when I go back to work."

"Oh?" He shouldn't ask, but he did anyway. "And what is it that you do?"

She said, "You'll laugh. I'm a nail stylist."

"Why is that funny?"

She wiggled her slender, pretty hands in front his face. The nails, once red, were broken and peeled. "I've been packing frantically all week, and seeing you was definitely a last-minute decision, so I didn't have time to—"

"Oh, that's all right," he said, aghast at the possibility that she'd primp any more for him than she had already. "I won't tell if you won't."

Something in what he said sent the gaiety in her face plunging into a free fall. "That's why I called you, Quinn," she said. "That's exactly why."

Trying not to act mystified, he nodded and said, "I see. Because—?"

"I can't take the responsibility any more. It's just too much. And now that we're leaving, I was going to just throw them out or give them to I don't know who. But then you came—really, it *was* an act of God, your showing up in Keepsake and then George's father getting that heart attack out in Albuquerque. An incredible coincidence, don't you think?"

"I don't know what else you can call it," he deadpanned.

She plunged one hand into the sack of a purse she had on her lap and fished something out. "Well—here," she said, holding a fist toward Quinn. He extended his hand and she opened hers, dropping a heavy class ring into his outstretched palm. "Look at the initials."

O.R.B. All that was missing was the *Jr.*, which Rand had always despised. Heart hammering, Quinn tried to seem sage. "Yep. The senior ring," he said, turning its faceted burgundy stone this way and that to catch the candle's light. Quinn had thrown his own ring away in disgust many years ago. "Probably only two men in town have those initials, and I guess the date tells us which of them lost this."

"Lost it!" She snorted and said, "Rand gave it to Alison just before she was murdered. It was instead of an engagement ring. She told me so herself."

They were first cousins. Not second, not third. First. The ring was a token of his promise to take care of her, no more than that.

But that wasn't what Quinn said to Myra. "I'd heard rumors around town about the two of them," he admitted, feeling a sick obligation to let her run. "How did you come by this, anyway?"

Quinn tried not to sound accusing; the last thing he wanted was to imply that he thought she was a thief.

"Well, *obviously* she couldn't wear his ring out in the open," said Myra, a little testily, "so she wore it on a chain around her neck, under her sweaters and things. She was afraid if she took it off and left it in her purse, her father might go rummaging around and find it. He didn't want her seeing boys; he was always looking for evidence of it. You remember that, don't you, Quinn? How Alison never got to date?''

He remembered it all too well. It had only added to Alison's allure, as far as the guys were concerned. "Something like that," he said, trying to ward off the sinking feeling in his gut. If Myra was making all of this up, she was as good a storyteller as Ulysses.

The waitress came with Myra's beer and she took a sip before resuming her tale. "Sometimes I think that's why Alison liked me," she mused. "Because I dated so much. I knew about, you know, psychology and stuff between guys and girls," she said, lowering those big, black lashes and batting them once or twice. She was Myra Lupidnick, after all; she truly could not help herself.

"Did she talk about Rand much?"

"Oh, not at all, at first. He was always 'this guy I like.' But I couldn't figure out where she'd get the chance even to meet a guy, much less develop some kind of relationship. I started watching her in school, I saw her talking to Rand in the hall once, and from the way she looked at him—from their body language—I knew."

She shrugged and took a good long swallow of beer this time. "So I confronted her about it, and after a few times of denying it, she said, yeah, it was Rand. And then she opened up. I think, because she'd bottled it up so long and she had absolutely no one to talk to, and really, she was in love with him. It was . . . she really loved him. You know?''

Myra's face got a thoughtful, faraway look; she was back in her parents' split-level, advising the most beautiful and mysterious girl in town in matters of the heart.

"It was the real thing," she murmured at last, shaking her head. "I felt so bad after they found her."

"And yet you didn't say anything."

"No. I didn't," Myra acknowledged.

"Did the police ever question you?"

"Hardly at all."

She folded one hand meekly over the other and lifted the fingertips back a little, staring at her messed-up nails. She sighed, then looked up and said, "I was scared, Quinn. Don't forget, my dad was a foreman at the mill. He would have lost his job for sure. And after a while, when they didn't arrest anyone and the whole thing seemed to fade away, well, it didn't really make any difference anymore, did it?"

It was all he could do not to pop her over the head with the chianti bottle. *Idiot! You could have done the right thing and come forward and my entire life would have been different!*

But he knew better than to go down that road. He'd been down it so many times before, and it always ended smack in the same brick wall. He reminded himself for the thousandth time that a dozen lives had been saved because a crime, this crime, had gone unsolved. It was enough. In the grand, chaotic scheme of things, it was enough.

A thought occurred to him. "Does your husband—does George—know about any of this?"

"Oh, no. I could *never*. That's just what I mean. That's why it's been eating a hole through me all these years. Right here," she said, pointing a chipped red fingernail at her heart. "And I'm just . . . ready to start over. I really want to start over," she repeated, this time with a trembling lip.

A big tear rolled out and sat on her thickly caked lower lashes, unable to break through and run. Quinn waited, mesmerized, for the tear to fall, but she blinked and it flattened into a saline line in the rim above her lashes.

"I'm sorry," she said, dabbing at her eye with the back of her wrist and leaving a smudge on the skin there. "I didn't think I'd cry."

Considering the amount of mascara she wore, that was Quinn's assumption, too. Her sincerity and good intentions touched him—much more at that moment than they ever had in high school. Somewhere under all that makeup was the still-pretty face of an ordinary girl who had always wanted simply to please.

He reached across the table and squeezed her hand. "Hey, now, Myra . . . you've carried this ring around for a long time. You didn't have to do that. You could have just chucked it and forgotten about the whole thing, but you didn't. I think Alison would appreciate that you stayed loyal to her memory.''

''Really?'' she asked, doing more dabbing, this time with a napkin.

''Absolutely.''

He picked up Rand's ring and circled his thumb absently over the chiseled surface of its stone, sobered by the awareness that Alison Bennett had once slipped it over her finger and dreamed of setting up house with its owner.

But had she really? The ring wasn't proof of anything. Thank God, it wasn't proof—even of paternity, much less of a murder. Quinn could rationalize that much. He could live with the responsibility that Myra was handing over to him. For entirely different reasons, he would do exactly what Myra had done: nothing. And if the ongoing silence ended up boring a tiny hole in his heart, so be it—because this time, finally, it was his turn for happiness.

The waitress came over and asked to take their order, but neither of them was hungry, so they settled for splitting a side order of calamari. Quinn realized that he did not have even an appetizer's worth of small talk left in him, but he needn't have worried.

Myra, looking more relieved and brighter by the minute, suddenly said in a much perkier voice, ''I almost forgot!''

She fished around in her purse again, and this time she came up with something more lethal. ''The letter!''

Twenty-one

"*What letter?*"

"From Rand. Oh. I guess I haven't filled you in. Do you want me to start from the beginning?"

"*Please.*"

Quinn accepted the letter from Myra, not daring to glance at it until he got his emotions under control. *A letter from Rand.* What next? A notarized confession? This was turning into the probe from hell.

Myra took a deep breath and said, "Okay, this is what I know firsthand. Alison and Rand had been . . . uh, well, doing it, since July in the summer after our junior year. Their first time was in the backseat of his—you remember the red Pontiac? God, I loved that car. It happened after he took her home early from a wake at his parent's house. Alison made up a story about how she thought she was coming down with something; that's how she got out of going home with her parents. Even Rand believed her. But I guess she knew what she wanted.

"After that, it was whenever and wherever they could. I remember she said they did it once in the gardener's cottage when you and your father were off buying some fancy trees for Mrs. Bennett. I'll bet you never knew that," Myra said, smiling behind her next sip of beer.

"How right you would be," Quinn said faintly.

Myra put down her glass with a grin; she was relaxed

and in her element now. "Anyway, that's pretty much how the summer went," she said. "Alison was happy, all things considered, and no one was the wiser."

"Except you?"

"Not me! I didn't know any of this at the time; those two were amazing at keeping it secret. And besides, Alison and I didn't really become close until after we went back to school for senior year. I remember I told her how pretty her hair was, but that it would look fantastic if it was highlighted. I've always had a professional interest in hair, you know. She said she couldn't afford highlighting, so I offered to do it for her. They have kits. Anyway, that was in early September. I didn't learn about Rand until late September, and by October I knew she was pregnant."

"She told you she was?"

"Not in so many words. She said, 'I think maybe we were careless a few times.' Well, what else could that mean? Later, of course, I knew. Eventually, so did everyone."

He nodded. "How did she seem about it?"

"Not depressed or scared, if that's what you're thinking. I remember she just looked . . . well, you know what they say about a pregnant woman's glow."

Quinn didn't have all that much experience with glowing pregnant women—none, to be exact—so he settled for a vague nod of recognition. "She had that glow?"

"Oh, yes. She was radiant. No morning sickness, nothing. And don't forget, she had Rand's ring. She had his promise that they'd get married as soon as they got their parents' permission. *Plus*, she also had his word in writing."

She pointed to the pale blue sheet that lay on the table in front of Quinn. It was his cue. He picked up the letter and began dutifully unfolding it.

Myra rested her cheek on her fist and said dreamily, "He bought that stationery special, you know. He told Alison that he wanted something permanent that wouldn't fade or tear. He wanted her to know how serious he was. I remember thinking, that was so sweet."

Dearest Alison,
I need you to know that their will never be another
girl in my life. You are the best thing that has ever
happened to me. I can't stop thinking of you, no mat-
ter where I am. In study hall, on the field, and driving
around. I drive around a lot, thinking of you. I wish
we could be together more. Nothing really matters to
me except you. You know, I'm glad you're pregnant.
Maybe I shouldn't be but I am. It's a sign that our
love was meant to be. And also, since your pregnant
our parents can't say no. I know my mother would
never want you to have an abortion no matter what.
And your mother wouldn't either. So I think we're o.k.
on that. Know this, Alison—I love you. I love you. I
love you.

> *Yours,*
> *Rand*

Misspellings and bobbled punctuation aside, the letter
was still powerful in its naive sincerity. Quinn felt like a
voyeur reading it, and yet he couldn't help himself. It was
like staring at a videotape of his past.

At least one mystery was now solved: Rand's embarrassing collapse as an athlete in the fall of their senior year.
It wasn't a poor recovery from his injury that had taken him
out of the competition with Quinn to be quarterback; it was
his obsession with Alison.

Quinn refolded the letter and laid it gently beside the
class ring—two such ordinary items, and yet so resonant
with power. He stared at them while the candle's flame sput-
tered and fretted in the chianti bottle, dropping bits of light
in a random pattern over the poignant still life.

Stilled life, he realized. Alison was dead. What did these
keepsakes matter now? Tokens of love, proof of malfea-
sance—what did they matter?

Quinn said wearily, "His feelings do seem straightforward."

"Guys always are," said Myra, still with her cheek on her fist.

She was watching Quinn for his reaction, and he was determined not to give her one. He said without emotion, "He wanted to marry her."

"At first," said Myra.

She made herself sit up straight again, like a witness at a trial. "But then suddenly he asked for the letter back. He said she could keep the ring, but she had to give him the letter back. They had a *huge* argument over it. It was on a Sunday afternoon, late. Alison and I were working on the homecoming float that Coach and a couple of teachers had rolled onto the athletic field behind the goalposts temporarily.

"Alison's father was supposed to be picking her up any minute when suddenly Rand showed up on the field, I don't know from where. I saw him before Alison did. He looked grim. He didn't say boo to me, just marched right up to Alison and said, 'We have to talk.'

"They walked way over to the far end of the field. You couldn't possibly hear them, try as I might. It was getting dark, but I could see she was upset. She folded her hands across her jacket—body language, right?—while she watched him walk back and forth, back and forth, throwing his hands up every once in a while. He was more upset than she was, I think. Then Alison's father showed up and whistled her back and Rand cut across the field and disappeared. Her father was really pissed. He said, 'What did I tell you?' and gave her a kind of a shove on her shoulder. Not a *shove* shove, exactly, but a little less than a shove."

Quinn listened intently to her precise recounting of the event. No question, Myra was the perfect witness, not calculating enough to put undue spin on events, just an alert, keen observer. Shit. Quinn didn't like where this was going at all.

"I assume that Alison talked about it afterward with you?" he asked, hoping against hope that she had not.

"Oh, yes. She didn't say very much, but I could see that

something was going on inside her head. All she told me was, 'He wants the letter back . . . How *could* he? . . . I'm not giving it to him . . . The only way he's going to get it is over my dead body. Or yours.' Then she laughed—but she wasn't really amused, you know the kind of laugh I mean? She was hurt and angry. That's when she handed me the ring and the letter for safekeeping. I was supposed to hold on to them just until homecoming. She was going to tell both their parents about her and Rand that weekend— when they came to school for the big game. She didn't want the meeting to be in anyone's house. I thought that was really good thinking. It made a lot of sense, when you came right down to it."

Quinn, still stunned, had absolutely no response to that.

"That's the last thing Alison ever said to me; I never saw her again," Myra said, gliding to a halt on a glaze of new tears. "And that's all I know. I don't know who killed Alison. I hope it wasn't Rand. But I know who was the father of that baby." She sighed deeply; her long ordeal of silence was over.

Just in time for the calamari. The waitress laid an oval platter between them with a careful-it's-hot warning, and then a smaller plate in front of each of them. Quinn stared at the deep-fried loops with revulsion. He might as well have been looking at his own intestines, breaded and served to him piping hot.

Myra, meanwhile, was calling the waitress back with the apologetic courtesy that everyone in the service industry uses with everyone else in the service industry. "Miss? If it's not too much of a bother, could I possibly have some ketchup, please? Thank you."

Olivia paced the living room of her townhouse in a state of wretched anxiety. It was now clear to her that everyone in her family—everyone in Keepsake!—knew more about Alison's death than she did.

Maybe if she hadn't been so busy with school and then with her career . . . maybe if she had taken the time to actually listen to gossip, instead of always nipping it in the bud . . . if she had just sat back silently once in a while and watched, instead of always trying to run the show . . .

But she hadn't done that, and probably never would. Her brother was right. Her emotional IQ was down in the single digits. Could you raise your own IQ? Could you learn from your mistakes? She wasn't sure it was possible, but from now on, she was going to try.

And meanwhile, no Quinn. She glanced at the brass carriage clock that sat on the mantel mocking the time she was wasting just . . . pacing. She should be doing something! She had a million yards of fabric at Run of the Mill to mark down; she couldn't expect her young assistant, no matter how willing and enthusiastic, to make those decisions herself.

Oh—right. The stickers.

Before she forgot, she went straight to the closet in the second bedroom and fished out two rolls of bright orange circles from among her extra supplies, then tossed them in her leather carryall. There. Something accomplished. As soon as Quinn got in—if he ever got in—she'd grab a bite to eat with him and then race down to the outlet. It was going to be a long, long night there.

Couldn't the man have the simple decency to carry a cell phone? It was making her crazy not to be able to contact him. They might just as well be living in the Stone Age. Smoke signals, Morse code, carrier pigeons—*anything* was better than this. Inconsiderate man! She should just leave him a memo the way any business person would do. Yes. A curt note, damn it. If he wasn't going to call her, then that's all that he deserved.

She began scribbling an explanation to leave under her door knocker, but almost at once she tore it up. Quinn would have called if he could. Surely he would have called. Something must have happened to him. Oh, God, surely something awful. The ratslayer, the bonelayer, the twisted, evil sicko that had nearly killed Mrs. Dewsbury, had now come after Quinn. Of course he had! For whatever reason, it was

Quinn that he wanted, not anyone else. Everyone else was incidental.

Olivia felt a surge of fear for Quinn. What if he were lying in a ditch somewhere, stabbed or shot and bleeding to death? What if he'd been in an accident? He could have been in an accident. The roads were dark, winding, the intersections unmarked in a lot of places. What if he were dead? How could she go on living without him?

Don't let him be dead. Please, please don't let him be dead.

She felt hot tears spring up; her body began to shake. What could she do? There must be something. Call the hospital. She ran to the phone book to look up the number and then realized that because of Mrs. Dewsbury, she'd already punched it into her electronic notepad. Altering course, she ran for her carryall instead to retrieve the notepad. The entire time, she was aware that she wasn't being rational, that Quinn wasn't dead and he wasn't injured. What were the odds, after all?

I'm going out of my mind. This aimless, free-floating anxiety is taking its toll . . . I'm losing my grip . . .

She heard a truck pull up and ran to the window, her heart lifting to the sound of the engine she knew by now. *Yes!* Yes, yes, yes! Alive and well and all in one piece and she was going to kill the man the minute he walked through the door. She ran to open it before he had a chance to ring the bell; she wanted him to know how worried she was before she actually went and strangled him.

She opened the door to see Quinn dragging himself up the six steps that led straight to her. He was acting like a man climbing a gallows. It was a shock to her to hear the strain in his voice as he glanced up and forced out a greeting.

She stepped aside to let him in; he walked past without meeting her baffled gaze. Uppermost in her mind was her fierce resolve to be the new, the improved, the emotionally intelligent Olivia Deborah Bennett.

"Where the *hell* have you been?" she blurted out. "I've been worried sick."

"Yeah."

"*Yeah*? That's your explanation? I thought we agreed to meet at the hospital," she said, closing the door after him.

She watched him stop in his tracks as his head dropped back in realization. "Jesus," he muttered. "I forgot all about it. How is she doing?" he asked without turning around.

He took out a wood hanger from the hall closet and hung his jacket over it with care, squaring the shoulders before he looped the hanger back on the rod. Olivia took the gesture to be symbolic. She had the sense that he was stalling— again, as if he'd rather be facing some hangman than her.

A queasiness rolled over her, but she shrugged it off and said, "Mrs. D. is fine. As antsy as can be, of course; she wants to go home. The nurses are all threatening to roll her out into the parking lot and let her go anywhere she wants. You won't forget about her again, will you?" she added in an acid tone. "Or would you rather that *I* drove her home tomorrow?"

"No, of course not," he murmured, turning around at last. He held out his arms to her and whispered in an agonized voice, "I'm so sorry, Livvy. Oh, God ... I'm so sorry."

Surprised, she let herself be drawn into his embrace. With a smile of confusion, she said, "You don't have to be *that* sorry, Quinn. I forgive you." She snuggled as close as she could to him and sighed deeply. "I was in a panic about you, though," she confessed. "It came on me in such a rush. I began to be terrified that I might be psychic or something awful like that. And I realized—you know what I realized?"

She pulled a little away from him so that she could look up at his face. "I realized how much I love you," she said simply. "I had been imagining all kinds of horrible ends—if you only knew!—and I'm just so happy ... so *happy* ... that you're here, and safe, and with your arms around me," she said, fitting herself almost shyly back in his arms. "I love you."

Olivia had been planning to make that confession for a while now, but she was probably more surprised than he was that she had chosen that exact moment in which to do it.

So! Wouldn't it be nice if Quinn felt the same urge?

If he did, he was suppressing it. She waited in his arms with her cheek against his shirt for as long as she reasonably could and then, disappointed, said, "I was going to order a pizza for us. Are you in the mood for one?"

"I'm not hungry," he murmured.

"Actually," she said, sniffing his shirt, "you already smell like a pizza. Or something. That's definitely garlic." She looked up at him again, this time with eyes slanted in comical suspicion. "Hey, you're not cheating on me, are you?"

He let out an incredulous snort, then held her so tightly it took her breath away. "Livvy, Livvy," he said suddenly, "let's make love. Now. Please . . . right now."

He caught her chin in the cup of his hand and brought his mouth down on hers in a fierce, deep kiss that sent her nerve ends humming, her brain cells spinning, and her knees and ankles crumbling beneath her. The suddenness of his desire rocked her; but she righted quickly, matching his kiss and meeting his hunger.

"Quinn, Quinn, let's agree never . . . ever . . . to argue," she said between kisses. "Over *anything* . . . ever . . ."

"Don't talk, don't talk . . ."

Still locked in their embrace, they bumped against the wall as they fumbled and tore at buttons and zippers. She was wearing tights under her wool skirt—the warehouse was drafty, she had to dress warmly—and he muttered an oath as he struggled to find the waistband. He yanked one legging part of the way down; she stepped out of the rest of it, trailing it like a kite tail behind her as they half groped, half stumbled their way to the wrought-iron bed.

They tumbled onto the down comforter—no more silk

for them—with Olivia underneath him, overwhelmed and unresisting.

He brought his hand up under her skirt, fanning his fingers, stroking her flesh, bringing down wetness. Electric, that's how it felt, electric to the point of pain. "Too much, too much," she cried, clamping her legs together. He hooked his hand on the inside of her thigh and pulled it away from her other one, exposing her again to his rough caress.

She was hungry, but not like this. There was a desperation, an urgency in him that intimidated. "Quinn . . . we have all night," she said, gasping.

"You're right . . . I know . . . all night . . . yes . . ."

He stopped and raised himself by his arms, staring down at her with a look she could only describe as demented.

"What's wrong? Why are you looking at me that way? All I meant was for you to be more gentle," she said in confusion.

He said nothing, only stared at her, his face twisted in contours of agony. "Why are you *acting* like this?" she cried.

"I don't know, I don't know, oh, God, I don't know." With a tormented look, he pushed her back down on the bed and said, "I hate this. I *hate* this!"

It left her flabbergasted. "Then why did you start—?".

He squelched the rest of her sentence with a kiss that was so brutal it hurt. She tried to push him away, a pointless exercise; he was so much more powerful than she. He caught her wrists. Her protests were muffled by his mouth bearing down on hers, drowned out by the anguished sounds coming from his throat. He sounded tormented, a beast in pain, and he was frightening her.

She broke away from his hold and dug her nails into his ribs, using all of her strength as she tried to push him away. It seemed to snap him out of it. With a cry of frustration he rolled off and away from her in one fluid motion, ending up sitting on the side of the bed with his back to her.

Olivia scrambled out of the bed and began tucking herself back in her bra and untwisting her skirt.

"I have to go to work," she said, in a seething rage. "I have . . . *stickers* to stick!"

Quinn propped his elbows on his thighs and dropped his forehead to the palms of his hands.

"Oh, God," he mumbled in misery. "Oh, God." He was a portrait of remorse.

Olivia stared at him the way she would at a drunk coming off a bender. And then she turned on her heel and walked out.

She spent the next two hours in a state of shock, stickering any bolt or remnant that displeased her. And they all displeased her. Suddenly the colors seemed too dull, too bright, too busy, too plain, too irrelevant to possibly matter. She stickered them all, a compulsive personality gone amuck, until her assistant came up timidly and said, "Is it all right if I go home now?"

Olivia pulled out of her daze long enough to stare at her watch: ten o'clock. It was half an hour past closing time at Run of the Mill. She looked around and blinked, trying to clear the cotton from her head, trying to focus on the reality of her night so far.

She was able to remember it perfectly well. After the debacle in her bedroom, she had actually got into her van and driven the two and a half miles to the row of shabby old warehouses, some of them empty, that lined the banks of the Connecticut River. She had marched into the outlet, greeted the help, taken out her stickers, and got to work. She was here, wasn't she? All in one piece? With her stickers mostly stuck? Obviously she was fine. Obviously time had passed.

The fact that she couldn't remember the two hours that she had spent in this dreary hole—that, she could attribute to the numbing monotony of marking down merchandise. She scanned the cavernous room. Yes, there it was, all around her: merchandise. Mountains of it. More bolts and

remnants than she could possibly sell, more than her customers could possibly sew, in a lifetime. In ten lifetimes.

As for the customers themselves, she was fairly certain
that there had been quite a few of them rummaging through
the piles, but now they were nowhere to be seen.

"You closed up?"

"Um . . . you told me to?"

"I did, didn't I. Okay. Thank you, Sharon. And I'm sorry
for keeping you late," she added in a dull voice. "I guess
I just got carried away."

Energetic Sharon, Olivia's most valuable asset by far,
giggled and said, "Oh, that's all right. My friends don't get
off work until one-thirty. This way, I'll have one less drink
to nurse while I wait for them."

They left together, Olivia, reluctantly. Her world seemed
to be collapsing around her; she was afraid to go out in it
anymore.

All the way home, anxiety gnawed at the pit of her stomach, making her sick. As she careened down the road under
bright stars flung across a clear black sky, wave after wave
of nausea washed over her. More than once she was tempted
to pull over, open her door, and throw up. She was deathly
ill, deathly tired.

And unprepared for the sight of Quinn sitting on the bottom step in front of her townhouse.

Twenty-two

It was eleven at night and twenty degrees out; what was he doing there?

Olivia had the obvious option of driving right past him and entering her house through the garage that was built into the berm on the side. But he was Quinn, and he was there, and she couldn't quite make herself reach up to press the garage door opener on her visor. Instead, she parked alongside his truck. Better to get it over with.

Quinn got to his feet as she approached; she could see that he was stiff from waiting in the cold. "Still here?" she asked unnecessarily. For once, she didn't know what to say.

"I left," he said. "I drove around. I came back."

His hands were in his pockets, his cap pulled down low, his collar flipped up against the sharp wind that hacked at them both. Huddled into himself, he said, "I have nowhere to go, Olivia; nowhere to be, except with you."

Haloed in the haze of their frozen breath, they faced off for the second time that night. Olivia's mohair muffler lifted and fell in the wind, marking time as she searched his face, looking for answers to all of her questions. What did she know about him, really? Seventeen years apart: It was half a lifetime.

"All right," she said at last, too exhausted and cold to stand there. "Come inside."

She led the way, aware that he had a key to her place

but had declined to use it. Why? Was it mere courtesy—or was there something deeper at play?

"We have to talk," she said tiredly as she slipped out of her coat and draped it across the nearest chair. "Whatever is going on with you, it's scaring me, Quinn. We have to—"

"I know . . . I know," he said. He sounded deep in melancholy.

He threw his jacket over hers and surprised her by taking her into his arms.

She was too tired to resist, too tired to respond, too tired to do anything but repeat dully, "We have to talk."

"Shh," he said, holding her close and kissing her hair. "Shh. Just . . . let me hold you."

His body felt cold against hers. She wanted to bundle him, warm him, make him hot tea; she wanted to slap his face.

And yet there she was, too tired to do any of them. All she could do was negotiate. "Quinn, I want some answers. Before anything else can happen, I want you to expla—"

"Shh. Let me make it up to you . . . for before. Shh. I won't insult you by saying I'm sorry. The words aren't adequate for what I've done."

He let out an odd little laugh, as if he were indulging in his own private joke. And then he said in an aching voice, "I love you, Olivia. I love you so much . . . so much . . . you're everything to me." Holding her close, he caressed the back of her hair and whispered, "I love you more with each breath I take. Please believe that. No matter what happens, please believe that."

She nearly broke down in tears. *Now* he had to tell her? Now, when she felt as drained as a pool in January? She had been waiting to hear those words from him for seventeen years. Perhaps not consciously—but somewhere buried deep in her psyche, there had always been an awareness that other men were a waste of time. Only one was a match, more than a match, for her. And now she knew, beyond a doubt, that Quinn Leary loved her.

So why wasn't she jumping with joy?

She didn't know what to say to him—he seemed to want her to say nothing—so she snuggled against him and murmured innocently, "Are you hungry for that pizza yet?"

"Nope," he said, lifting her face to his. "You?"

She wasn't queasy anymore, but: "No pizza for me."

"I've got a better idea," he said, lifting her effortlessly in his arms.

"What? Lasagna?" she asked with a tired smile.

"Not exactly," he said, headed for the stairs.

"Fisherman's Platter?"

"Keep babbling, woman; it'll make the climb easier."

"Quinn, *no*," she said, laughing despite her exhaustion. "You can't keep doing this! I'm too heavy!"

"Granite is heavy. You're a basket of laundry."

"You say that now, at the bottom of the stairs; what happens when we both go tumbling ass over teakettle from the top?"

"Then we'll die in one another's arms."

"You say that now, at the bottom of the stairs."

"Shh."

He carried her up and no one fell, and then he carried her into her bedroom, just as he had their first time, and laid her on the bed, just as he had their first time. On New Year's Eve they had been wild and hungry and just a little bit drunk. Tonight they were tired and sorry and just a little too sober. But what they lacked in fire, they made up for in tenderness. Quinn loved her, and she loved him, and every touch, every kiss, every caress as they made love was wrapped in that declaration, one for the other.

I love you, Quinn. I love you. When Rand wouldn't let me in his treehouse and you built me my own, I loved you for that.

I did it because I loved you, although at the time I thought it was just to spit in your brother's eye.

And when you left those bright red roses in the Maxwell House can on the table in my treehouse? I loved you for that.

You knew it was me?

Who else? Not my brother!

That time you fell out of the treehouse, my heart stopped.

My mother told me you were a hero, carrying me home. I was always too embarrassed to thank you. Thank you. I love you.

And I was always too embarrassed to thank you for defending me when Old Man Ryckhart accused me of stealing his power saw.

One of Rand's friends framed you, but I have no proof. Rand defended you, too, Quinn. You probably don't know that.

Shh. What's past is past. I love you. I love you.

They fell asleep in one another's arms, two lovers who agreed, if only for the night, to spend it in that treehouse of theirs.

Olivia awoke before Quinn did. It was early, but she knew that he'd be spending the morning getting Mrs. Dewsbury settled in from the hospital, and she wanted to do something lovely and domestic for him first: make breakfast. After the mortifying empty-cupboard episode on New Year's Day, Olivia had made a point of stockpiling every breakfast item she could think of. She wasn't in such great shape for throwing together a lunch, and God forbid she should have to make dinner—but she could do breakfast in style now.

She eased the comforter back, leaving an exhausted-looking Quinn quietly snoring on his side of the bed, and went downstairs to take sausages and a can of OJ out of her freezer. After starting the meat defrosting in the microwave, she made up a pitcher of the juice, which she left on the counter to breathe. After that she got the coffee going. She was thinking omelettes. How hard could they be? For some reason she was truly enjoying puttering about in her kitchen.

The reason was sleeping upstairs in her bed.

It was chilly in the house; she needed her robe. Back up the stairs she went. The robe was in her bedroom, hanging on a funky clothes tree that she'd found while cruising the

Brimfield flea market with Eileen one fine day in May. In the glow of the hall light, she tiptoed across the room and was in the process of wrapping herself in floral flannel when the timer on the microwave sounded.

Beep, beep, beep, beep. Not especially loud—but Quinn shot up in bed as if four different cannons had blasted. He looked disoriented, even spooked. Olivia knew the look from the day before; she had hoped never to see it again. But then he spotted her standing near the bed, and his demeanor relaxed.

It felt so very good to see that happen. She grinned and whispered, "Good morning, pizza man."

"It can't be morning," he said with a moan as he dropped back on his pillow. "I feel as if I've been shoveling snow all night."

"Then go back to sleep." She pulled the covers over him and kissed his brow. "I'll let you know when breakfast is ready."

"Mmm." He yawned heavily and said, "Who's cooking it?"

"Hey! *I* am," she said, sending an accent pillow sailing over his head.

He chuckled; it was sweet music to her ears. She was on her way out to the kitchen to cook up her first storm ever when she spied something shiny on the white carpet beneath the chair over which Quinn had folded his pants.

"Huh." Like a trout after a bright, shiny lure, she swooped down on it. "Quinn? Look what I found on the floor. Is this a class ring?"

His head came up. Propping himself on his elbows, he said in a surprisingly tense voice, "Yes. It's . . . mine."

"But you told me you'd thrown your ring off a bridge," she said, moving toward a lamp in the hall.

"I—that was a figure of speech, that's all," he said. He threw back the covers and got out of bed.

"This isn't your ring. It couldn't possibly fit your finger—now *or* then." She stuck it under the light for a closer look.

"Jesus Christ, Liv! Do you have any concept of personal property?" he said, coming after her.

"It's from our year," she said, reading the date on the side of the stone. She began rotating the band, looking for initials. Quinn snatched the ring angrily away from her, but not before she had a chance to read them.

"*O.R.B.* Owen Randall Bennett," she said with a puzzled look at Quinn.

"Oscar Reginald Baxter. Orville Raymond Bonaparte. Obadiah Rufus Blackw—"

"Very funny," she said, trying to snatch it back without success. "There were no Oscars, Orvilles, or Obadiahs in our class. This is Rand's ring. But Rand told everyone he lost it swimming at the quarry. How did *you* end up with it? Quinn?"

Her voice had been edging higher with each succeeding sentence. By the time she got to Quinn's name it sounded shrill, even to her.

He looked so determined not to tell her anything. His eyebrows were drawn together, his mouth was clamped shut, his breathing was labored. His eyes glared at her through a curtain of suspicion. Prisoners of war must look that way all the time. The rising panic she felt was balanced by rising anger, and both were overwhelmed by plunging hopes. What kind of relationship could they possibly have if he regarded her as his number-one enemy?

"*Damn* you, Quinn!" she cried, hurling the words at him like dinner plates. "How can you treat me this way? It's offensive. It's insulting. It's—you said that you loved me!" she cried, because for her, it all came down to that. "I would never do this to you! I would never shut you out from something that was eating at me!"

He stood there, shirtless and in his drawstring pajama bottoms, looking more than ever like someone in shackles. Oh, how she dreaded that look, that posture.

"Quinn, Quinn, we can't go on this way," she said, shivering despite the robe she wore. She wrapped her arms around herself, trying to steady her nerves. "Please—if you love me, tell me: *Where did you get that ring?*"

Quinn tightened his fist around the ring and wondered why the floor didn't just open up and let him drop straight into hell. Apparently it was someone's plan that he should writhe on earth for a while first. He stared at the face of the only woman he would ever love, stared at her dark mop of curls and her blazing look of hurt and the way she bit her lip, trying not to cry, and he thought, this is the way to make me burn alive: force me to watch her suffer.

"I can't tell you," he said at last, in excruciating agony himself. "Please, Liv, don't ask."

Her sigh was quick and frustrated. "*You* would want to know!" she cried. "You would demand an answer!" She turned away, unable to look at him anymore. He saw her clamp her hand over her mouth and bow her head, as if she were going to be sick.

The worst of it was, she was right. He *would* want to know. He *would* demand an answer. Did she deserve anything less than he himself would expect? He had grown up with her; he had watched her struggle every day to be accepted as the equal of the males around her. The town princess she might have been, but he had never known either girl or woman who wanted less to be sheltered, less to be coddled. *Just give it to me straight.* It was her credo in life.

But still he couldn't tell her. Some instinct in him that ran deeper than logic told him it was better not to disillusion her.

He saw her shoulders lift with the huge, deep breath she took before hauling out the last big weapon in her armory: the ultimatum.

She turned slowly around to face him. Her chin was high, her gaze steady and true as she said, "This all has to do with Alison. Tell me where you got the ring, Quinn," she said gravely. "Tell me, or it has to be over between us. You *know* that it has to be."

It was over between them whether he told her or not; that

was the agony of it. The only question was, should he let her continue living in blissful ignorance? If—when—she found out about her brother someday, would she hate Quinn still more for not having told her?

It was a measure of how much Quinn respected her that he thought she would.

"Myra gave it to me," he said at last.

It took her aback, but not for long. "Myra! Then she stole it!"

"Alison gave it to her."

"Alison! Then Alison stole it!"

"Your brother gave it to Alison."

Her head was spinning now. "*What*? That doesn't make sense. Why would Rand give his ring to my cousin?"

"He loved her."

"Of course he did. We all did. But not to give her his class ring."

"He loved her. He loved her the way a man loves a woman. The way I love you."

The emotional body slam sent Olivia staggering. Her mouth fell open in shock and anger; she clutched at her lapels in a huddle of denial. "How can you *dare* say that?"

"Ask Myra."

"Myra lies! Everyone knows that! You can't believe Myra. She lies! Look what she said about being the one to take your . . . take your—she'll say anything to be the center of attention. You said so yourself!"

"I believe her," he made himself admit. "She knew too many details."

"You're naive, Quinn! She made them all up!"

"*I'm* naive?" he said with gentle anguish.

"All right, fine!" Olivia conceded. "I'm naive! At least I'm aware of it. But *you*! You'll believe any—" She stopped and sucked in her breath, stunned by yet another thought. "When did she tell you this?"

"Last evening."

More shock, new fury. "And you went from hearing that vile slander straight to my *bed*? How *could* you?" she cried.

"When you knew what this would do to you and me . . . to me and my family. My God . . . I can't *believe* this! You go dragging your feet through a muck of lies and then you march right in and make *love* to me?"

In his black despair, Quinn saw black humor. "That's not quite true. I didn't have any luck the first time I tried, remember?"

He was all too aware that he had felt miserably unable to make anything happen then. He had tried to bully himself into potency, which was absurd; he couldn't have made love to her in that frame of mind in a million years.

And meanwhile, Olivia was staring at him with a look that transcended shock: It burned with loathing and contempt. Maybe it was better that way. If he was forced to back away from her, bowing and scraping and with cap in hand, at least he'd have an excuse to resent her. It wasn't much, hanging that old princess label on her again, but it would have to do.

"Get out," she said in a shaking voice. "Just please get dressed and get out."

It was time to do just that. He had overestimated her. He shouldn't have been surprised by that, and yet he was. Surprised—and bitter. She should have respected *him* enough to know that he wouldn't tell her something so appalling without knowing it was true. As it was, Rand's letter was burning a hole in his pocket. He had no idea what he was going to do with it.

Olivia tailed after him into the bedroom and stood there as Quinn pulled on his trousers right over his PJs. He was in a hurry. He wanted to sail out of there on a wave of resentment; he knew it would be easier that way.

But Olivia had never been one to make things easy.

"You have no proof, you know," she said, practically taunting him about it. "Only one woman's word, and a ring that could have come from anywhere. Maybe Rand just *thought* he lost it. It could have fallen off his finger onto the blanket before he went swimming at the senior picnic. How would he know? He's a guy; they're always losing things. Then *she* picked it up and worked out a whole fantasy for herself. Myra had a thing for Rand; everyone knew that. She probably resented that he hardly looked at her, and she made up the story. Made it all up! It's the obvious, logical interpretation of events.''

In self-imposed silence, Quinn pulled on his undershirt and shot one arm, then the other, into the blue sand-washed shirt that Olivia had liked so well on him.

She circled him the way a country lawyer would, pointing out his flaws for an imaginary jury. ''You know I'm right, Quinn. If this were about anyone else, you'd use your formidable powers of logic to figure out the most likely, the most logical scenario. You'd reach the same conclusions I just did.''

He tucked his shirt into his pants and tightened his belt, all without looking at her.

''But no-oo. You're determined to clear your father's name at any cost. What's wrong? You couldn't wait for the exhumation? You had to jump at this outrageous, sordid version of events? It doesn't bother you that you're being irrational?''

Wallet? Pen? Comb? He patted his pockets.

''How unlike you, Quinn, to be irrational. You, the finest thinker at Keepsake High.''

He looked around the room. Anything left? Nope. He traveled light. The razor, the toothbrush, the roll-on—to hell with 'em.

She stopped her pacing and pointed an accusing finger at him. ''You know what I think? I think you're looking to sabotage my family in any way you can. It bothers you— doesn't it?—that they're well regarded around here. You think that by tearing them down, you can somehow build your father back up. It doesn't work that way, Quinn. I hate to keep harping, but again—illogical.''

Should he say good-bye? Interrupt her harangue? Probably not. She wouldn't hear him, anyway. He glanced at the door, ready to make his break.

''Myra's a liar,'' she said, faltering a little. ''If not a liar, then . . . then at least an exaggerator of the first order. You probably just misunderstood her, Quinn,'' she said with an anguished look. ''Men don't speak the same language as women. Haven't you read Deborah Tannen?''

Tannen. As if.

He sighed.

For whatever reason, that got Olivia going again. ''At least admit you could be wrong!'' she cried. ''Is that so much to ask? You're being so *irrational*, Quinn. Think about it! Someone would have picked up on the two of them. Some old biddy would have got wind of it and gone straight to my mother—or my aunt. You can't keep a love affair secret—not around here. Look at us! The whole town knows!''

He allowed himself to respond, not to what she said, but to the pleading tone in her voice as she said it. ''You could have had enough faith in me to believe me, Liv,'' he murmured.

One little opening. That's all he gave her. One tiny opening. It ended up being the perfect place to drive the last nail into the coffin of their relationship.

''Believe you? Why should I? Myra's a known liar. The story's incredible. And there is no proof! *You. Have. No. Proof.* Show me the damned *proof*!'' she shrieked, rushing at him with a shove of frustration as her rage came crashing through her veneer of reason.

Caught off guard by her ferocity, he staggered back. Something in him snapped, a seventeen-year-old rubber band wound a little too tight. ''You want your proof so goddamned much? *Here*,'' he said, reaching into his back pocket. He pulled out the folded blue sheet and flung it at her. ''Here's your goddamned proof!''

He walked away. She could read it or she could flush it, he didn't care. In the hall, he stopped long enough to slap Rand's ring down on the table. Let her deep-six it in the quarry if she wanted to. Anything to bring this sorry adventure to an end.

He was outside, five steps from his truck, when he heard

a window above him being thrown open. Despite himself, he looked up at it.

"You couldn't let well enough alone!" she screamed, obviously ready to break down altogether. "You couldn't just prove someone's innocence. Not you! Not the mighty Quinn! You had to take it one step further! You had to prove someone else was guilty! I hope you're happy now! Damn you, Quinn! I hope you're happy!"

He felt as if he'd been shot between the eyes. His last words to her were: "I didn't call Myra, so help me God. She called me."

But Olivia couldn't hear him, not above her own heart-rending wails.

Twenty-three

It wasn't definite that Rand killed Alison. There was no proof.

After a morning of emotional devastation, that single uncertainty was all that Olivia had left to cling to. So many other horrors were certain now. It was certain that Rand was the father of Alison's baby. That Olivia's relationship with her family was changed forever. That she and Quinn were through.

She spent hours of heart-wrenching tears and unbearable agony holed up in her townhouse before being thrown into a sudden, violent panic.

The ring . . . the letter. They're evidence that could be used to indict Rand.

It was the most obvious danger in the world, and it had taken her most of the day to see it.

She scooped up the letter and the ring from her bed and began rushing around her townhouse looking for a hiding place. A closet? A vase? A bag of A & P coffee? Her jewelry box! Yes, somewhere obvious like that; the police would never look there. Of course they would! Somewhere else. The box of Kleenex on her nightstand? No one would ever look there. No, too risky! What if she threw the box in the recycle bin by mistake when the Kleenex were gone?

What if she did? That would be the best thing—to get rid of the evidence. She didn't even know if the letter was real. She was assuming it had come from Myra, along with the ring. Maybe Myra had forged it!

She studied the letter through swollen eyes. It was Rand's handwriting, all right, as distinctive as a thumbprint. She ran to the cupboard and grabbed a box of matches, then lit one and held a corner of the letter in the flame. It caught.

What was she doing? She couldn't do that! It was destroying evidence, against the law! She smacked the letter on the countertop and, even more panicky now, put out the smoldering flame with the sleeve of her robe. The last *I love you* was scorched, but not Rand's signature. So deep was Olivia's despair that she didn't know whether she should feel happy or tragic about it.

She burst into tears again, amazing herself. She wanted to be done with all that. She wanted to be completely adult about the whole affair. Her basic problem in life was that she had never been touched by tragedy, that was her basic problem in life. Alison, yes, her death *was* a tragedy; but other than that, Olivia's life had gone smoothly. Very smoothly. Too smoothly. That was the basic problem. One little setback like this, and—

Who was she kidding? An old gas oven that poofs and singes your eyebrows, that was a setback. One that blows up your house with you in it, that was a tragedy.

And I don't know how . . . I don't know how . . . I'm ever going to crawl out from under the rubble, she told herself, bowing her head in tears.

The doorbell rang, sending shock waves anew through her. She yanked the silverware drawer open and threw the scorched letter and the ring into it, then ran to see who it was. She peeped through the keyhole. *Shit.* Eileen.

Olivia stood without breathing, waiting for her sister-in-law to leave.

Not Eileen.

"Livvy? Livvy, are you in there? Olivia!" Eileen began knocking, then banging, on the door. She peeked through the sidelights while Olivia flattened herself from view.

The phone had been ringing on and off all morning and

Olivia had ignored it. Big mistake. And she had left her car parked outside for all the world to see, for God's sake. What a stellar fugitive she'd make.

Desperate to ward off a call to the paramedics by Eileen on her cell phone, Olivia took a deep breath, wiped her eyes, and opened the door. Smiling wanly, she tried to look ill.

She was a grand success. Eileen took one look at her and crumbled into motherly sympathy. "Oh, Livvy—you've come down with something," she cried, rushing inside to embrace Olivia.

"No, no . . . you'd better not," said Olivia, keeping her distance. "You're bound to catch it."

"Don't be silly; I never get sick. You poor thing . . . all alone here . . . you didn't hear the phone? The girls at Miracourt have been calling all morning, they told me."

"I just didn't feel like answering the phone," Olivia mumbled, which was true enough.

"I stopped by the shop, and when they told me they couldn't reach you, I made excuses for you—but I was worried, Liv. With all these things that have been going on . . . Well, forget about that now. Have you taken your temperature?" she asked, putting her hand to Olivia's brow. "You feel all right. Have you been *crying*?" she asked, scrutinizing Olivia up close.

Olivia drifted out of the sunlight and into the shadows of the living room. "No. Why would I be crying? I . . . was petting the neighbor's cat. My eyes got itchy. You know how allergic I am."

"Then why let the cat in your house, for pity's sake? Especially when you're not feeling well."

"I was looking for sympathy, I guess," said Olivia, managing a wry smile.

"But what about Quinn? He doesn't have to be anywhere."

"Oh, but he does. Mrs. Dewsbury gets out of the hospital this morning," Olivia explained, grateful to have something true to say. She had to get Eileen out of there!

But Eileen, in maternal overdrive now, was heading for

the kitchen. "You just go right upstairs to bed and I'll make you some lemon tea."

In the kitchen she glanced around and said, "You must have been right in the middle of making breakfast when you got hit with this thing."

"Sort of, yes."

"Poor baby. I'll straighten up," she said, heading for the eggs and juice and opened loaf of bread.

"No! No, that's all right," said Olivia. "I just need to lie down, that's all."

"Yes, do that, Livvy," said Eileen, clearly concerned now. "You look a little green."

"I think I'm going to throw up," Olivia blurted out, and this time she was telling the truth.

"Go, go," said Eileen.

Olivia turned and made a sprint for the guest bath, while behind her she heard Eileen call out, "My God, what happened to your sleeve? It has a big hole burned in it."

Olivia threw up in what was probably record time, rinsed out quickly, and raced back to the kitchen. "It passed," she said grimly.

Eileen had put away the eggs and bread and juice and was sponging off the ashes of Rand's letter from the Corian counter.

Olivia became faint with fear simply from the sight of it.

"How on earth did you manage to set your robe on fire? And this Corian is going to need repair," her sister-in-law said, scooping the ashes into her free hand. "You're in no state to be playing with matches."

"So . . . true," said Olivia.

"I'm going to heat myself a cup of this coffee. You have a whole pot of it untouched," said Eileen, opening the microwave door.

She discovered the half-nuked sausages and took them out, holding them toward Olivia for her inspection. "I think we'd better toss these, don't you?"

The meaty smell of the gray, greasy links sent a new surge of nausea through Olivia. "Haftathrup," she gasped.

Off she went, back she came, more terrified than before that Eileen had found Rand's letter. But Eileen was opening lower cupboards, not the drawers, looking for the garbage can in which to dump the sausages.

"Don't . . . don't, Eileen. Please. Go home," said Olivia, taking her by the hand and coaxing her toward the door. Weaker by the minute, Olivia felt as if she was dragging a bolt of corduroy behind her.

Eileen protested, but faced with the opened door, she had no choice but to go through it. "Well . . . all right. But please—answer your phone. When will Quinn be back?"

"Oh . . . not today."

"Oh, right—Mrs. Dewsbury. In that case, I'll stop by tonight. Flu is nothing to fool with, Livvy. You could become dehydrated and end up in a hospital. You never pay enough attention to your health. You don't exercise, you don't eat right . . . you think you're so invincible."

"Please, Eileen—not now."

"Okay, okay, no more lectures," she said, kissing Olivia quickly on her cheek. "I love you and I worry about you, that's all. See you tonight. Now go back to bed, and drink plenty of fluids."

Smiling dutifully, Olivia closed the door after her sister-in-law and sank exhausted to the floor. More tears, an endless supply of them; where were they coming from?

Eileen, her oldest friend . . . oh, God, and the *children* . . . Kristin and Zack would never recover from this. Look at Quinn, the scars he bore—and *his* father was innocent. And Olivia's mother and father—what would they say, what would they do, if they knew about their son? Her mind veered away from the thought; it was too appalling.

Gradually, inevitably, the tears stopped. And in place of the crushing sorrow that Olivia felt, something new came creeping in, as stealthy as a cat on the hunt: suspicion.

Did her parents already know? Bits and pieces of odd recollections flashed briefly across Olivia's mind like the Pleiades across a winter sky: her mother, a little too hysterical at the thought of testing the DNA of Alison's unborn baby . . . her father, taking Quinn aside on New Year's Eve . . . her brother, warning her that she didn't have all the facts . . . her father again, hiding behind those curtains.

Myra knew. Quinn knew. Was it such a stretch, after all, to assume that her parents knew? And if they knew that Rand was the baby's father, did they know even more about him besides? The thought was far more appalling than any that had preceded it.

Why couldn't it have been some stranger who did it? Or the coach . . . Francis Leary . . . even, horrific as the situation would have been, her Uncle Rupert. Anyone but her brother.

Her need to keep her immediate family intact was primal, desperate—and a revelation. Up until this day she had not known how much they mattered to her. Now she did—and it was too late.

She sat on the floor for a dreary eternity, unable for once to get up and go. The tears kept rolling down. Poor Eileen . . . Poor Kristin . . . poor Zack . . . poor everyone.

God help them all.

Quinn had ordered a new monitor for Mrs. Dewsbury to be delivered via air freight; it arrived half an hour after he brought the widow home from the hospital. She was furious at him for his extravagance, ecstatic at the speedy replacement. She did love her CCTV.

That evening, when they were sipping tea in the parlor after one of Quinn's pot roast dinners—like most bachelors, he was on intimate terms with aluminum foil and onion soup mix—Mrs. Dewsbury kicked back in her La-Z-Boy and said out of the blue, "I was thinking, maybe we should invite Olivia here for dinner one night."

The chocolate chip cookie that Quinn was eating turned into mulch. He swallowed hard, then said quietly, "Sure. Maybe when you get back from your stay with Gerald."

"I do like that girl," the widow said with obvious fondness. "I had no idea that she could be so warm and charming, so really delightful."

She nibbled at her fancy bakery cookie and said, "I remember her as being very different in high school. *You* remember her then: She was always so very—hmm, how can I put this nicely?—determined."

"She still is," Quinn said with a grim smile. He was thinking of Olivia as she hung out the second-floor window that morning, willing and able to pull out his hair.

"Yes, but I see a softer side to her now. She's grown as a person. You know what I think? I think she's very much in love with you. You've done her a world of good. I'm assuming, by the way, that you feel the same about her," Mrs. Dewsbury added with a gently probing smile.

For a hundred-pound octogenarian, she was flattening Quinn as well as any steamroller could do. He found it impossible to peel himself off the floor and skip around like a man in love. He mustered all the strength that he had left to say, "There will never be anyone else."

Two cookies later, Quinn excused himself and went to bed. It was seven-thirty. Mrs. Dewsbury laughed at him. Even hundred-pound octogenarians stayed up later than that.

Four days later, a package arrived at the big white house on Elm.

Quinn had been working feverishly to complete his long list of projects before climbing into his truck and driving off into the sunset. He was intensely aware that he had done massive damage to one woman's life. Somehow he hoped to make up for it by doing extensive repairs to another woman's life. It didn't make much sense, but in his present state of meltdown, it was all that his brain could manage.

"Wash your hands and sit down," the widow said, flipping two grilled cheese sandwiches. "The soup is getting cold. I don't see why you have to obsess over that work list, Quinn. Surely the flashing can wait until you get back from California; the weather will only get nicer."

True enough, but he wouldn't be around to enjoy it.

"Now that I know where the leak is coming from, it would drive me nuts to leave it the way it is," he said, more or less telling the truth. "I can't believe a smart lady like you let some con artists rip you off with those replacement windows," he added. "They're garbage."

"Well, at least I had enough sense to contract only for one side. Once I saw how flimsy they were—anyway, you needn't be so snippy about it," she said, obviously hurt by his tone. "What's the matter with you, anyway? You've been this way for days."

"Sorry." He didn't even try to come up with an excuse. Nothing short of terminal disease would explain a mood as foul as his had been—another good reason for having thrown himself into his chores.

"What was in the package?"

"I don't know; I haven't opened it yet."

"How can you not open a package?"

When it has Olivia's handwriting on it, he thought, but aloud he said, "Haven't had a chance, I guess."

"I'll get it for you," said Mrs. Dewsbury, a catalogue shopper from back in the days of the Wells Fargo wagon. "You eat."

He dumped half a box of oyster crackers into his Campbell's tomato soup, just to convince her that his appetite was normal and his mood jim-dandy. And meanwhile he wanted to tear at his clothes and howl at the moon with rage and frustration.

Four days without holding Olivia, hearing her voice, inhaling the scent of her hair. So this was what it would be like. Four days. Four lifetimes.

Olivia, he thought, shutting his eyes from the vision of her. Oh, God, please . . . Olivia.

He was having a hard time breathing, much less eating, but he plowed away at his soup and crackers, wondering how he could have considered it a treat when he was a boy, and why he had ever made the mistake of admitting that to his hostess.

He was rescuing the grilled cheese sandwiches from their

overlong stay on the griddle when Mrs. Dewsbury shuffled into the kitchen. She was managing to get around without her walker nowadays; it was one of the few bright spots in the black void that Quinn was currently calling a life.

"I'll do that, I'll do that," she said, waving the package at him. "Here. Open it. I'm so curious. There's no return address, did you notice?"

"Yeah." He took out his Swiss Army knife and sliced through the wide clear tape that sealed every edge shut— Olivia was nothing if not thorough.

He found it hard to believe that she was returning the ring and the letter to him, but if she was, he had an explanation ready for the curious old lady who was hovering near: the ring was his, the letter, an old note from his dad. Mrs. D. couldn't possibly read Rand's handwriting, much less recognize it.

That was the general theory, anyway.

He opened the flaps of the shallow box and stared at the contents. Olivia was not re-burdening him with the care and protection of the critical—and possibly criminal—evidence. She was merely returning, in order of importance, his pajama tops, Mennen deodorant, Bic razor, and Oral-B toothbrush.

"Well, that's odd," said Mrs. Dewsbury. "What are *those* all about?"

Quinn went blank. He was clean out of lies, excuses, and stories to tell. "Um," he said.

"Olivia sent these, didn't she?" asked the savvy widow. Without waiting for an answer, she said, "You two have had a fight. Well, that explains your mood, and why you've been hanging around the house and fixing everything in sight."

In silence, Quinn went back to the grilled cheese sandwiches, cutting each of them diagonally and allocating three halves for him, one for the widow.

"For heaven's sake, Quinn—how long are you going to let this go on? Whatever you do, don't turn it into a competition between you. Just say you're sorry and get on with your lives. It's so much simpler in the long run.''

"It runs a little deeper than that," he said quietly.

"How deep?"

"Too deep."

"You mean you two have broken it off?"

"It looks that way."

"That's ridiculous! Pardon the cliché, but you two *are* meant for each other."

"Thanks," he said tersely, taking his seat again. "That makes me feel better."

"Don't play the sullen teenager with *me*, young man," she said, tapping the table with the tip of her forefinger. "I want you to march right down to that little shop of hers and take her out to lunch and make things up with her."

Quinn was completely at a loss over how to deal with his old teacher. He'd never been mothered before, and he could feel his impatience waiting to spring.

He tried disarming her with humor. "What? And walk out in the middle of this fine repast?"

"Oh, please. I'm sick of tomato soup and grilled cheese sandwiches; you must be, too," she said, snatching away his plate and sliding the meal into the garbage can.

"Mrs. D.—!"

"Right now. You don't want to be going off to California for two weeks and leaving her so upset. Life is too short to waste time in anger. Quinn, believe me. No one ever listens to the old, but we know better than anyone: Life is *short*."

"Don't you think I'm aware of that?" he said through gritted teeth.

"Obviously you're not, or you wouldn't be doing this. Not only that, but you don't seem to understand how hard it will be to reconcile by telephone."

"Oh, for chrissake! There's not going to *be* a reconciliation!" he said, standing up so abruptly that he knocked his chair over. "And I'm not going off for two weeks!"

Right now, all he wanted was to get away from the widow's well-intentioned kindness. He'd made it just fine so far without a mother and without a wife. Obviously nothing was going to change.

The old woman searched his face and must have found the answer she was looking for in the misery that was etched there. "Oh, no. Oh, Quinn, no. You're not going to run *again*?"

"I didn't run," he said with an utterly grim smile. "I accompanied my father."

"Whatever! This time it's running!"

"This time, I don't care," he said, and he left to go off to McDonald's.

Twenty-four

A crooked heart. How fitting.

Olivia caressed the smooth surface of the red glass paperweight, a quirky Elsa Peretti design that so enchanted her when she came across it in a Tiffany catalogue that she had ordered six of them for the Valentine's Day window of Miracourt.

But that was a month ago, when the world made sense and her own heart was still in good shape. Now she rued the extravagance.

Still, Keepsake's shoppers looked forward to Olivia's window displays, and she did not want to disappoint them. Against a backdrop of discreet gray, she began to arrange tiers of classic French ribbons that she had painstakingly rewrapped around antique wooden spools—exquisite ribbons of velvet and organdy, passementerie and jacquard, in silk and cotton and wool.

Except for a single spool of red grosgrain, the colors were rich, muted, and subtle: earthy greens and old-world mustards, royal burgundies and not-quite-blues, and a shade of rose that hinted of the spring that must surely come, easing the pain of winter.

Olivia laid the glass hearts among the spools, refocused the halogen spotlights, and then stepped outside onto a deserted sidewalk to gauge the effect. She was unhappy with it. The left side seemed more harmonious than the right. Now what? Rearrange the whole thing?

She looked at her watch. It was nearly seven. Eileen and Rand were having a dinner party to celebrate their twelfth anniversary. Olivia had promised the children that she'd come over early to play with them; she hadn't seen them in weeks. Obviously that wasn't going to happen. If she hurried, she could just catch the end of the cocktail hour before having to sit through a meal she couldn't taste while smiling at chitchat she didn't want to hear.

The window would have to do.

February 5

Dear Mrs. D.,

So far, so good. Made it to Philadelphia, but then detoured to Harrisburg, PA on a whim (went that route out west with Dad the first time, and wanted to see if I could touch base with old ghosts there. I could. Made me feel better, somehow.) Anyway, heading south again. Hope you can read this tiny print on your CCTV.

Love, Quinn

On February 15, Olivia removed the Elsa Peretti hearts, but she left the spools of ribbon in place. She had no real inspiration for a new display. Anyway, why bother? The spools looked all right.

March 1

Dear Mrs. D.,

Forgot to put a stamp on my last postcard to you. Did you get the one from Cape Hatteras? Don't know where my mind has gone. I stayed there longer than planned. Liked the wild, windy beaches. Did a lot of walking. Hope all is well with you. Is the new window flashing doing the trick?

> *Love, Quinn*

On March 3, Olivia bought three paper shamrocks from the Hallmark shop on Main and tossed them on the spools of ribbon. Green was green.

> *March 18*

Dear Mrs. D.,

> *Good talking to you last week. Glad to hear that things are quiet up your way. Spent yesterday at a bar in Lubbock called O'Toole's. Meant to grab a sandwich and ended up staying till last call. I'd forgotten what it means to be Irish. Yesterday I was reminded. Hope the squirrels are leaving your crocuses alone.*

> *Love, Quinn*

On March 18, Olivia sat on the edge of her bed staring at a little stick that she held in her shaking hand. She was fighting back not only nausea but terror as she watched the pink color move across the top.

After weeks of on-and-off vomiting, Olivia had decided that simple stress could not be the cause. And since as far as she knew there was no such thing as two-month flu, she had bought a guide to medical symptoms and looked up potential causes. Tumors, gallbladder problems, ulcers—all were possibilities. Bulimia was not. That left morning sickness associated with pregnancy.

It couldn't be that, she knew. She and Quinn had always used condoms. Besides, she was getting sick at all different times of the day. They didn't call it afternoon sickness, after all, or nighttime sickness. She had been looking up ulcers, thinking that they were to blame, when suddenly it had dawned on her: She couldn't remember her last period.

With a pounding heart she had tried to clear her brain of every other thought but her monthly flow. December, yes, December was easy to remember. It came before Christmas. She had been wearing a pale knit dress and the onset was sudden and heavy; she had had to go home to change the stained dress.

Okay, January. January, January. She couldn't remember most of the damned month. When would she have been due? Sometime in the middle. The middle was the wrenching breakup with Quinn. No, definitely: no period. But was that so surprising? She had skipped periods before in times of stress, and it didn't get more stressed than the middle of January.

February. When had it come in February? Obviously not at all. February was the darkest, the dreariest, the most depressing month she'd ever known. Much of her body and all of her mind—everything that wasn't absolutely essential to life—had shut down during the month of February. That explained the lack of a period in February. Surely that explained it.

But it was heading for the end of March; something should be flowing by now. Olivia hadn't the excuse of being frantic, as she had been in January, or desperately depressed, as she had been in February. Nowadays she wasn't happy, wasn't sad, wasn't anything at all. She was numb. Which was fine with her. Numb let her get on with her day and sleep through the night and get through the occasional visit with her family.

Her life was normal—almost abnormally normal. Her family, relieved that Quinn was gone, was being excruciatingly kind to her. Her mother seemed to have forgotten their blowup, her father had gone back to being preoccupied with getting his tax break from town, and her brother had begun again to exhale. On the professional front, both the shop and the outlet were making money.

So where was the blood?

She watched in horror as two lines showed up in the little window. *Two!* Her cheeks turned hot, her pulse knocked around violently in her head. *Pregnant. Pregnant?* Impossible! They had been so—

Oh, my God. New Year's Eve. In the middle of the night on New Year's Eve. She and Quinn had engaged in sex that was uncalculated, uninhibited, unbelievable—and unprotected. Would that have been her fertile time?

Fool! Idiot! Of course it had been her fertile time. That's what created the drive that made the babies! And yet the next day neither of them had alluded to the possibility of her getting pregnant. Not even a simple "Gee, we should be more careful next time." Their lovemaking had been somehow more sacred than that; she remembered well her reluctance even to bring it up the next morning.

Pregnant. For a long time, Olivia sat on the edge of her bed holding the stick. From there she could see the box from the testing kit, still half nestled in its bag from a Wal-Mart far away, sitting on the bathroom sink.

Of all the half-formed thoughts that took turns fighting for stage center of her brain, only one kept coming back: Thank God she hadn't gone to the drugstore on Main.

Punchy from his long drive, Quinn dropped his duffel bag next to the door and headed straight for the cordless.

The feeling of impending doom that hit him after he sent off the postcard from Lubbock was so strong that he had chucked his plans to knock around southern Arizona and had driven straight home instead. He arrived to find that his house hadn't burned down (though the plants had all died) and his business hadn't gone bankrupt (though it might be on the way), so his premonition must have had something to do with out east.

His first thought was for Mrs. Dewsbury, he told himself. She was old, she was frail, anything could have happened to her. But the darker thought, the more hidden thought, was that something had befallen Olivia.

It was ten in the morning out there, a good time to call. He waited impatiently through at least half a dozen rings, opening windows as he wandered through his rambling, one-story house on his way to the bedroom. As soon as he threw open the patio doors, he got hit with the scent of roses. Damn, if he didn't prefer this to March in New England.

"*Hel*-lo," came the cheerful, upbeat voice.

Immediately Quinn knew that nothing was wrong. "Hey,

Mrs. D.," he said, relieved. "Just thought I'd call and let you know that I made it back safe and sound."

"For goodness' sakes! What happened to panning for gold in Arizona?"

"I bought a few lottery tickets instead. How's your weather?"

"Oh, don't ask. It's been raining ever since you last called. I might as well be living in Oregon. Every joint in my body is killing me, including my two new fake ones. I'm not sure I can manage these stairs much longer."

"Baloney. You're just looking for an excuse to move in with your son."

She laughed out loud at that; she had told Quinn a hundred times how much she wanted to die in her own home. "Oh, I do miss you, dear. Every time Gerald and Kathy come over, they treat me like a helpless, doddering thing— or worse, a child. I really do not like being condescended to. You've spoiled me that way, treating me as a friend the way you do."

"Well . . . that's because you are," said Quinn, swallowing down a ridiculous surge of self-consciousness. No, damn it! He was done with emotional commitments of any kind. Been there, done that, got burned good.

"And Olivia stopped by," she added, giving the knife a little twist.

"How nice." His tone was dangerously polite.

Accepting the rebuff, she turned quickly to another subject. "I'm working to clear up a little mystery about you, by the way."

"Oh?" He didn't like the sound of that. "What mystery would that be?"

"I'm not saying. In case I'm wrong, I don't want to look like an old fool. But I'm willing to bet my Social Security check that I'm right. I'll know more tomorrow, after Judy Damian drops by."

"Ah, Miss Damian the librarian. Is she driving the library van nowadays?"

"She's doing a little research as a personal favor to me. We're in cahoots. How do you like *that*, Mr. Leary?"

He laughed politely, puzzled by her smug tone. He was in the kitchen now, holding open the fridge door and staring at its lone contents, a six-pack of Coors. His idle mind was computing that it had cost him about five bucks a bottle to keep them cold for the past three months.

"So . . . I take it that all's quiet on the eastern front?" he asked, knowing she'd understand what he meant.

"Oh, yes. No tricks, no pranks, no random acts of violence. The town has been absolutely quiet since—"

"I left," he said, helping her over her embarrassment.

"It *was* Coach Bronsky behind it all, wasn't it?" she said. "He's the one who bashed in my monitor."

Quinn sighed. He had bought a forensics kit and dusted the trophy weapon for fingerprints himself; it had been wiped clean. "It's nothing we'll ever be able to prove, I'm afraid."

The widow snorted and said, "I'd like to bash *him* one. But never mind, I've had my vengeance: Coach Bronsky has been fired. He showed up drunk once too many times for the school committee's taste. Of course he's filed a grievance, but I'm not worried. He's finished at Keepsake High, and good riddance to him."

"Well, well."

Immediately Quinn began to work out the ramifications. All in all, he'd rather have the coach staggering drunk around the field than sitting home drunk with time to brood. "Look, I want you to make absolutely sure that you—"

"Yes, yes, I know. Keep the alarm set at all times, even when I'm pruning roses ten feet from my door."

"Even then." They chatted another minute or two before Quinn, dog-tired and still nursing a headache from his St. Paddy's Day hangover, hung up with promises to keep in touch.

Now what? Threaten the coach again for good measure? It would be so much simpler if the man would just drink himself into a stupor every day. But Bronsky wasn't a worst-case wino, and it made him all the more dangerous. Hell!

Consumed by guilt with no hope of absolution, Quinn headed for the medicine cabinet in search of aspirin. His stomach let out a sullen, hungry growl, like some beast in a cage who could care less if his handler wasn't up to speed. *Feed me.* Quinn popped the aspirin and, rubbing his stomach, went foraging through the cupboards. He hoped the beast liked Dinty Moore.

Rubbing her belly surreptitiously under her coat, Olivia stood in line at the Book Bay, the biggest, most anonymous bookstore in the area, clutching a Dorothy Sayers mystery and a Fodor's Guide to Bermuda with a copy of *Pregnancy and You* sandwiched discreetly between them.

Don't get sick, don't get sick, this is a bad time; don't get sick. Think about something else.

But the book on babies might just as well have been a real live toddler bouncing on her arm. She could think of nothing *but* the baby she apparently was carrying—at least, if the three pregnancy kits were to be believed. She had made an appointment with a gynecologist (in the next county) to make the results official, but in the meantime, she wanted to learn all she could before deciding what to do.

She knew virtually nothing about pregnancy. Because it had little to do with running a business, Olivia hadn't paid much attention whenever her friends—even Eileen—became pregnant. The women all got bigger and bigger, and then they went into a hospital and when they came out, they were smaller and had a baby in their arms. Olivia was only slightly more knowledgeable about the whole process than the child who's been handed a bill of goods about the stork.

A tap on her shoulder sent her jumping. She whirled around.

"Mrs. Hyart! What a surprise! Well, how do you like that! Gosh. Shouldn't you be in your quilting class?"

The sixty-ish woman smiled and shook her head. "Tonight's my reading group. I'm here to pick up our copies of *Rebecca* so that I can pass them out for next week's discussion. We're doing three months of classics."

"Ah! What an interesting life you lead!" said Olivia with revolting cheerfulness. She sounded unhinged; truly, she was scaring herself.

"What about you?" asked Mrs. Hyart, tilting her head

to read the spines. Before Olivia could react, the appallingly curious woman said archly, "*Pregnancy and You*?"

"It's a shower present."

"Oh, trust me, then; she probably has it."

"Bridal shower! I'm moving along."

"Do you think that's—? Well, all right," said the woman, straightening back up with an apologetic smile. She acted as if she'd just stepped on Olivia's newly planted pansies.

Olivia whipped out her Visa, paid for the books, and got out of the Book Bay as fast as she could. She was thinking about the doctor she'd signed up to see; obviously she should have chosen one in the next state, not merely the next county. Damn all small towns! Suddenly the charm of them eluded her completely.

She drove home and read until midnight, trying to devour every fact, every nuance, every clinical detail of what it meant to be pregnant. By the time she closed the book and went to bed, Olivia understood many things, including her craving for cheese and her aversion to fish, but she didn't know the answer to her most burning question: What should she do about this incredibly unexpected development?

Her dreams that night were muddled and terrifying. Old college chums with sophisticated attitudes about unwanted pregnancies drifted in and out of them, and her cousin Alison was screaming at them all, and Quinn was racing to catch Alison before she dropped into the quarry and drowned. Only Alison wasn't drowning, she was hanging by her neck, and Olivia was crying and trying to cut down the rope and pull her cousin to safety. But Alison was too heavy; Olivia needed Quinn.

In her last dream, Olivia had the horrifying sense that she was going to fail; that Alison wasn't going to make it and it was going to be Olivia's fault. Just before it happened, she woke herself up. And after that she kept herself up, propped in a sitting position against two pillows, one of them Quinn's, until the first glimmer of light appeared and a robin began its absurdly cheerful refrain from a branch of a maple outside Olivia's bedroom window.

It was the first day of spring.

Twenty-five

Judy Damian was all aflutter.

"You were right, Mrs. Dewsbury! It *had* to have been Quinn and his father. The timing was right, the place was right—and you have the postcard to corroborate it all!" The librarian collapsed her umbrella and untied her rain bonnet, then unbuckled her trench coat as Mrs. Dewsbury tried to rush her along.

"What a wonderful memory you have! How many people can recall news from seventeen years ago? Certainly not me. Oh, this is *so* exciting! I'm so happy for Quinn, really I am! I always knew he was special. And now look—I was right!" she said, pulling a couple of Xeroxed sheets out of her carrier and waving them in front of the widow's failing eyes.

"Judy, please calm down; you're going to have a heart attack," said Mrs. Dewsbury. She herself was far more tense than giddy. "Give it to me, would you? I'd like to read it for myself."

She laid the first sheet of the seventeen-year-old newspaper article on the moveable platform under the camera of her CCTV and adjusted the focus, then selected the white-on-black exposure to make the print jump-out clear for herself.

She caught her breath at the date, magnified twenty-five times so that she wouldn't mistake it. "I knew it! October twenty-third—less than two days after they took off from

Keepsake. That's about how long it would take to travel on a bus as far as Harrisburg, don't you think?''

"Absolutely," said Miss Damian. Biting her lip and shaking her head with emotion, she added, "Why didn't Quinn *say* something after he came back?''

"Quinn? He would never bring up something like this, not until later, after he'd proved his father's innocence.''

"And now he's gone again!''

"Shh! I'm trying to concentrate.''

Mrs. Dewsbury kept her focus locked on the monitor as she moved the platform where the news piece from the *Pittsburgh Courier* lay. Slowly and methodically, she read the information being flashed so large on the television screen before her.

HARRISBURG, OCT. 23—A BUS TRAVELING WEST ON INTERSTATE 76 BETWEEN NEW YORK AND PITTSBURGH AND CARRYING THIRTY-SIX PASSENGERS OVERTURNED AND CAUGHT FIRE ON AN EXIT RAMP NEAR HARRISBURG EARLY THIS MORNING. TWO UNIDENTIFIED MEN ABOARD THE BUS ARE CREDITED WITH SAVING THE LIVES OF AT LEAST A DOZEN PASSENGERS WHO WERE OVERCOME BY SMOKE. TWO OTHER PASSENGERS DIED IN THE IMPACT.

WITNESSES SAY THAT THE YOUNGER MAN, STRONGLY BUILT AND IN HIS EARLY TWENTIES, PULLED THE DAZED AND SOMETIMES UNCONSCIOUS PASSENGERS, MOST OF THEM ELDERLY OR WOMEN WITH CHILDREN, FROM THE CONFINES OF THE SMOKE-FILLED BUS. THE OLDER OF THE RESCUERS, A MIDDLE-AGED MAN, WAS SEEN TO CARRY TWO CHILDREN FROM THE BUS AND ADMINISTER CARDIOPULMONARY RESUSCITATION TO ONE OF THEM UNTIL THE FIRST OF A DOZEN EMERGENCY VEHICLES ARRIVED ON THE SCENE.

FIREFIGHTERS QUICKLY PUT OUT THE BLAZE, BUT THE EXIT RAMP REMAINS CLOSED UNTIL AN INVESTIGATION CAN BE COMPLETED. THE DRIVER HAS NOT BEEN CHARGED.

THE IDENTITIES OF THE RESCUERS ARE NOT KNOWN AT THIS TIME. RHYANNA WHITE, A PASSENGER ABOARD THE BUS, STATED TO POLICE THAT AFTER THE ARRIVAL OF THE

PARAMEDICS, THE TWO RESCUERS, WHO ARE BELIEVED TO
BE A FATHER AND HIS SON, FLAGGED DOWN A PASSING
VEHICLE AND LEFT IN IT. THE CAR WAS A TWO- OR THREE-
YEAR-OLD GOLD COUPE, POSSIBLY A CHEVROLET CAMARO,
WITH ONE OCCUPANT. ANYONE WITH INFORMATION IS
ASKED TO CONTACT EITHER STATE OR LOCAL POLICE.

"Oh, Quinn," murmured Mrs. Dewsbury after she finished. "Oh, Quinn."

"Quinn was seventeen at the time, but you know how
mature he looked. And he was a big guy, even then. He
could easily have passed for someone in his twenties."

"This is awful, this is tragic. This is so unfair."

"But . . . I thought you'd be happy," the librarian said.

"So did I."

After a moment the younger woman said hesitantly,
"What do we do now?"

"I wish I knew," said Mrs. Dewsbury, slumping in front
of her CCTV. "I wish I knew."

Quinn parked his truck in the cemetery lot and made his
way on foot to his father's grave, dreading the moment as
much as if his father were alive and anxiously awaiting news
of Quinn's adventure out east.

But he wasn't. Francis Leary was dead and buried, and
the grass growing over his grave was well established. A
patch of clover had sprouted near the middle of the mound.
It drew a mournful smile from Quinn. His dad loved to see
clover growing in grass he maintained; it was proof that the
soil was herbicide-free.

Quinn dropped down into a catcher's crouch, with his
hands dangling loose between his thighs. In his state of despair, it was the nearest position to prayer that he could
swing.

"I blew it, Dad," he murmured, "I blew it big time. I
went charging off to Connecticut like a stoned Crusader,
convinced that I could unmask the villain in the piece and
set your reputation right once and for all.

"Well, guess what? The villain in the piece turned out to be me. You got it—your number-one, overachieving, underwhelming, self-destructive, star-crossed son.

"I did manage to win one tiny little skirmish: at least three people are now convinced that you're innocent. The rest of the time I spent sacking and plundering an innocent woman's relationships with everyone she's ever loved. I was *real* thorough, Dad, even for me. By the time I left, there was nothing left standing, emotionally speaking, except her white-hot hatred for yours truly."

He plucked some of the strands of grass that had escaped the caretaker's weed whacker and were growing tall beside the new headstone. "So here's where we stand," he continued, convinced he had to say it aloud. "Olivia's brother—or even worse, her father—killed Alison to keep her quiet. You remember her brother Rand: nice guy, bit of a charmer, family man now, active volunteer in town events. And Owen Bennett—still a ballbuster, to be sure, but holding Keepsake together single-handedly by keeping the mill in operation there. As I say, I make a hell of a better villain than either of 'em.

"Did I mention that Rand has two great kids and a dynamite wife? She's Olivia's best friend. And Livvy adores the kids. Well, she used to be able to, anyway."

Quinn ran his hand tenderly over the patch of soft clover. "Think there's a four-leaf version in there for me?" he whispered. "I could use a little of that vaunted luck o' the Irish."

A puffy cloud scudded between the sun and the grave, subduing hope. The silence was overwhelming.

Quinn sighed and said, "So! Heard any good undertaker jokes lately?" He laughed softly at his own lame idiocy, then stood up.

"I'm sorry, Dad," he said, looking down at the grassy mound at his feet. "I'm sorry. I wanted to get this one thing—this one fucking thing—right. And I blew it. Oh, God, how I blew it."

He felt a hard lump in his throat, and then tears. He

closed his eyes, overwhelmed by the crushingly bleak life that lay ahead of him, and then suddenly he dropped to his knees and bent prostrate over the grave. His forearms prickled from the newly cut grass; he grabbed clumps of it in his fists and pulled, trying to open the door to eternity.

He wanted advice; he wanted love; he wanted, in this most despairing moment of his life, to connect again with humanity.

"Oh, Christ, Dad, I blew it," he said, his body riven with sobs. "I blew it . . . I blew it . . . I blew it . . ."

Olivia was sitting in front of her computer in the loft of Miracourt and grinding out numbers for her accountant when she heard sharp tapping on the storefront window below her. Determined not to lose her train of thought, she kept plugging away at her column of numbers. The shop was closed and tax day was looming. A sale wasn't worth it.

The rapping continued, more urgent than before. Olivia stood up and peeked out the Palladian window. No UPS truck was parked below, but it was pouring out, which she hadn't realized, so she went downstairs to answer the summons. Whoever was there must be desperate.

She was amazed to see Mrs. Dewsbury under the shop awning, peering through the door as she rapped on the window with the handle of her black umbrella.

Olivia rushed to unlock the shop and let the old woman in, chiding her for being out in such awful weather.

"I take my rides when I can get them," Mrs. Dewsbury said, using the umbrella as she would a cane. "Father Tom stopped by for tea, and he offered to give me a lift downtown. He's waiting in his car now, so I have to be brief." She glanced around her and said, "Where can I sit down?"

Olivia ran for an old armchair that she liked to update every once in a while in a new fabric and keep handy for the weary, and she settled her old teacher in it. True to her word, Mrs. Dewsbury got right to the point.

"I've agonized over this long enough. I know very well that Quinn wouldn't want me meddling between you two—

don't look at me that way, my dear; I'm older and wiser than both of you put together—and up until now I've respected what I know would be his wishes. How*ever*."

She unzipped her black purse and took out two sheets of paper that were folded in half and handed them to Olivia. "This is the man you're throwing away. If you read the article and can still do that, you're a lot less smart than I've always assumed. All right. I've spoken my piece," she said, using the armrests to push herself up with an effort from the chair. "Do you remember what I told you on the day before you took your SATs?"

In a daze, Olivia stared at the silver-haired teacher in the porkpie rainhat. She shook her head.

"I said, 'Don't disappoint us.' I'm repeating it now, Olivia. This is the most important decision you'll ever make. All *this*," she added, waving a hand at the shop, "is nothing. Not by comparison. Good night."

She turned and began limping toward the door. Olivia rushed to hold it open.

"I don't know—thank you," she mumbled in confusion. She had no idea what she was supposed to be grateful for.

She waved at Father Tom as he emerged from his black sedan under another umbrella to get the door for Mrs. Dewsbury. The car drove off, puffing steamy exhaust into the wet, cold night, and Olivia locked up shop again. She sat in the tapestry-covered armchair and, with more dread than curiosity, she unfolded the pages.

Harrisburg, Oct. 23—A bus traveling west . . .

Olivia read the article through, and then she went right back to the dateline and read it through again. She remembered Quinn's words when he was reading her the riot act back on pie day: *a situation where my father could have—should have—been honored as a hero.*

This was that situation, without a doubt.

With a deep sigh, made even more profound by the hormonal swings she was daily enduring, Olivia folded the pages and laid them on her lap. It didn't seem possible that one man could be so good, so brave, and so wronged all in one lifetime. And to have lived his life in hiding . . . and then to die without having been vindicated—it was almost unbearably sad. No wonder Quinn had been so determined to clear his father's name.

No wonder.

After a long and mournful moment, Olivia stood up and drifted over to the storefront window. She had replaced the spools of ribbon—finally—with bolts of frothy spring fabrics: pink organdy, pale lime chiffon, and white netting bunched in makeshift tutus for all those sewing mothers whose little girls had dance recitals coming up.

It hit her: Francis Leary had never lived to see a granddaughter in a tutu.

She fingered an edge from the bolt of chiffon. It was such a delicate fabric. It would take a number-nine needle; anything bigger would leave holes. Her mother had sewn her a tutu once. Pink, of course; there was no other color for a six-year-old ballerina with dark curls, an attitude, and legs just a little too short ever to be called lithe.

Mom, that was a really nice thing you did. You weren't very good with a Singer. Even I remember the seams you had to tear apart and resew. It was a labor of love, I know that now. Thank you.

She sighed. Everyone around her seemed to labor from love. Even her father . . . why else did he drive himself so hard, if not for the mill workers? He would never admit it, of course, but he felt a tremendous responsibility to every one of them. He wasn't fighting for that tax break to enhance his own wealth; he could easily move the mill to Mexico and make a lot more money. *Keep it in Keepsake*: It was the creed he lived by.

And Eileen—Eileen had love to spare for everyone. She handed it out like candy. Rand? No father loved his children more than Rand did. That's what was so hard: to reconcile this Rand with . . . that Rand.

She couldn't destroy her family by turning Rand in. She couldn't. She was going to have to live in misery with the secret for the rest of her life.

Which brought her back to Quinn. Everything that he had done, he had done for love. Olivia knew that. It was the most heart-wrenching fact of all. But it didn't change the impossible situation that the two of them were in.

Oddly soothed by the steadily falling rain, she wandered back through the softly lit shop, looking at it with Mrs. Dewsbury's eyes. Did it have any worth? Any meaning at all? Olivia wasn't sure of the answer to that anymore. She paused at a bolt of Ultrasuede and slid her hand over the fabric: soft . . . smooth . . . like a baby's bottom.

Quinn's baby. Francis Leary's grandchild. She was carrying good and honorable and heroic instincts, passed to yet another generation. She couldn't have Quinn. But she *could* have the best of him to love and to care for.

Poor Mrs. Dewsbury. She had shown up with her black umbrella on Miracourt's doorstep like an elderly Mary Poppins, convinced that she could make things right between Quinn and Olivia. She hadn't done that; no one could.

But she had made Olivia feel so much better about having the baby alone.

After weeks of wet spring weather, the sun rushed in full of apologies and determined to make amends: The day was bright, benign, and deliciously warm, a perfect spring bouquet offered to sullen and sodden New England.

Sometime during Saturday's downpour, Olivia had learned that Rand would be home with the kids all day on Sunday. She had made up her mind to see him then—but her mission would have been so much more fitting in rain.

She drove with extra care to his house, which was built, like hers, high above the Connecticut River, upstream of the mill. That upstream view of the water was all that her house and his had in common, however. Olivia had opted for a place she could afford. Rand's reproduction Colonial was sited on a rolling lawn with mature trees, a guest house, a greenhouse, a chicken coop, a barn, a paddock in the making—and a mortgage that was mind-boggling.

But on a day like today, who cared? Certainly not

Olivia's brother. She found him running around with his children on the flat part of the lawn, engaged in a game of Frisbee made a little more tricky by the fact that Zack couldn't throw a Frisbee and Kristin couldn't catch one.

The real star of the show was Samantha, their golden retriever. Sam caught the plastic disk perfectly in her mouth every time—whether it was whizzed to her or not—and then she ran down to the river with it, and the kids ran after her, and invariably someone slipped and fell and got even more muddy, which apparently was the real point of the game.

It all looked a little too frisky for Olivia, who was still getting used to the idea of being pregnant, so she declined to play. Since she was wearing jeans, she dropped down on the damp ground and watched them go at it. Pretty soon Samantha ran up to her and knocked her over, and Olivia ended up just as muddy as everyone else.

"Sorry about that, sis," her brother said, laughing, as he stuck out a hand to pull her up. "Sammy can't believe you're not playing. Frankly, neither can I. How're you doing?" he asked her as they walked back to the house over the children's howls of protest. It was obvious that he thought Olivia was still brooding over her breakup with Quinn.

Right now, he couldn't have been further off the mark. "I'm fine, really," she said, rolling up her sleeves above the wet and muddy elbows of her white shirt.

"You *look* good," he said with a quick sideways glance. "I guess your appetite's back, anyway."

Automatically she sucked in her stomach. Not that it did any good.

Rand kicked off his muddy moccasins in the mudroom and proceeded barefoot to the fridge. "Beer?" he asked her.

"Oh, that sounds—"

Alcoholic. She declined and said she'd rather have water.

"Water? At least have a Coke."

Olivia shrugged and said, "I don't need the caffeine." For whatever reason, she threw up less when she avoided it. The baby knew more about nutrition than she did, it seemed. She poured herself a glass of water and sipped while her brother took a long, satisfying slug of beer and then washed up at the sink, keeping an eye out the window at his kids as they romped in the yard.

He was wiping his hands on a towel. His fair skin had great color from the sun and the exercise. He was smiling, relaxed, in a wonderful mood. He looked as happy as she'd seen him in half a year.

Could she do this?

"You know, it's no accident that I'm here today," she said, mustering every bit of her formidable resolve.

"I figured," he said, cocking his head at her. "Normally I don't rate. What's on your mind, Livvy?"

Most of the smile and all of the ease had gone out of his face. He knew, more than anyone else, when it was serious between them.

Olivia looked away, then made herself look into her brother's eyes. She had rehearsed her opening line so many times, and now she couldn't remember a word of it.

"I have some things of yours," she blurted out.

Twenty-six

Rand's laugh was tight as he said, "Oh? You finally gonna return my Abba tapes?"

She said, "These go back to almost as long."

Olivia had tucked the ring in the front pocket of her jeans, the folded letter in the back. She hadn't dared risk being knocked unconscious in a car accident and having some rescuer find them as he went through her handbag looking for names of next of kin.

Fishing the ring out first, she handed it to her brother.

He looked at it and nodded. There was no shock, no dismay, no panic: only the simple, eloquent nod of recognition. She remembered it for the rest of her life.

"You got this from—?"

"Quinn. Who got it from Myra."

"And you're wondering how Myra came to have it?" There was a glimmer almost of hope in her brother's eyes as he asked her. He so clearly wanted her answer to be yes.

Olivia dashed that hope when she reached into her hip pocket and brought out the pale blue sheet with its charred edge. With downcast eyes she handed it to him. "This too."

"Oh, Jesus."

There went her forgery theory. She thought he would read it, or maybe rush to his big Viking stove, turn on a burner, and set it afire. Instead he stuffed the letter in the front pocket of his grass-stained khakis. He looked ashamed and embarrassed, as if it were a note from the principal.

He didn't seem to know what to do about the ring. The ring was different. The ring was okay to have. He held it between his thumb and forefinger, thinking of—what? Alison? The big game? The path not taken? He surprised Olivia by slipping off his wedding band and slipping his class ring on that finger. Making a fist with his left hand, he rubbed the surface of the ring with the palm of his right.

All the while, he was in some other place, during some other time. Olivia had no idea how to get to where he was, so she waited.

After a while, he looked up and said, "Why give these to me?"

She shrugged and said, "Too law-abiding to destroy them myself, I guess."

"Why not give them to Vickers?"

She blinked. "You don't know? You honestly can't figure it out?"

"Zack? Kristin?"

"And Eileen. Mom. Dad. Why do you *think*, you idiot?" She could feel all the horror come rushing up like acid bile. There it was, that sudden urge to be sick. Convinced despite her doctor's assurances that she was harming the baby every time she threw up, she made an intense effort to control the nausea.

"I have to go," she said coldly, and she turned to leave.

"Livvy, wait!" Rand called. Now there was anguish in his voice.

She whirled around. "*What?* What can you possibly say in your defense?"

"I didn't kill her. You have to believe me, Liv. I loved her—I thought I loved her, anyway. I was seventeen, for God's sake!" he said, raking both hands through his hair.

Olivia studied him as closely as she ever had in her life. The stakes were high; his answer mattered.

"I don't know how it happened," he said. "One minute I was her cousin, someone for her to vent to, and the next, we were . . . But I didn't kill her, I'm telling you. I was all set to marry her, to raise the child—well, you saw the letter,'' he said with a smile that was bitterly wry. ''I was just your average teenage doofus. God only knows how I thought I'd support us or where we'd live. Certainly not in Keepsake.''

Olivia had only one question: ''Does either Mom or Dad know?''

He shook his head. ''Eventually reality set in and I started having second thoughts. I wanted Alison to put the baby up for adoption. She got angry; we had a fight over it. But before anything got resolved, she disappeared. Then they found her hanged at the quarry. I was as shocked as anyone. Livvy, I'm telling you the truth,'' he said with a look of burning desperation. ''I've never lied to you—not when it counted.''

Olivia had expected her brother to deny murdering Alison, but she hadn't expected to believe him. The emerging agony she felt was because she had absolutely no acceptable fallback scenario to him being the murderer.

Her next question came out in a whisper. ''Who do you think killed her, then?''

Grimacing, Rand rubbed his brow with his middle finger and said, ''Uncle Rupert? I've always assumed that she told him about us. You know how possessive he was—''

''No, no, it wasn't Uncle Rupert,'' Olivia said, feeling a new wave of nausea kick in. ''When Quinn and I went over there, he told us that he had pushed hard for the investigation to go forward back then. With no results. Didn't I tell you that part?''

''No,'' he said with a blank stare.

''It wasn't Uncle Rupert. Someone else.'' Her heart was beginning to feel as cold and glassy as an Elsa Peretti paperweight.

Rand looked frightened now. ''Oh, man . . .''

Their thoughts were locked on exactly the same plane. Neither spoke. The only sounds were of children screeching and a big dog barking.

And then the deep, resonant chime of the front doorbell.

"Oh, hell," Rand said. "I'm going to have to get that. Your car's out front, the kids are outside."

"I'm going, then," she said. "I've got to get out of here."

That didn't happen. The visitor was their father, and he was in a fury of indignation.

"Those sons of bitches on the council aren't going for the tax break," Owen Bennett said, waving his briefcase at both of his children.

Rand was stunned. "Dad, no way! The whole point of this last postponement was to get Murphy in line."

"Murphy! Murphy managed to turn everybody *else* around! You know what you can do with Murphy!"

"How'd he do that? It's impossible!"

"Is that so? Tell it to the mayor. I just had lunch with him. He gave me the heads-up: The plan will be shot down five to two at Tuesday's council meeting. All right, let's get to work," he said, heading for Rand's study. "I want to have dates, I want to have profit projections, I want to have numbers to rub in their smug, short-sighted faces. I want that mill shut down *mañana*!"

"Oh, Dad, not that," cried Olivia, following him into the small office. "You're not really going to move the mill to *Mexico*?"

"Oh no?" he said grimly. "Watch me. Three god-damned generations of Bennetts have busted their humps to keep this town afloat. I've watched my profit margin tighten like wool in a hot dryer. No more! Keepsake can go the way of every other mill town in New England. See if I give a damn."

Dismayed to see that he wasn't just posturing, Olivia said, "That's not even true! Look at Aaron Feuerstein at Malden Mills! Three generations in Lawrence have busted *their* humps, and Feuerstein is still committed enough to have rebuilt a burned-down mill from scratch!"

Owen Bennett leveled his daughter a look as calculated, as cold, as any she had ever seen. "We can't all be heroes,

Olivia; I'm sorry to disappoint you. Now run along. Rand and I have work to do."

Brother and sister exchanged one quick glance, and then Olivia walked out in a state of shock.

It wasn't her uncle . . . it wasn't her brother.

Who was the adult that Alison would have gone to first? Of course. Who was the one who would have tried hardest to make her pregnancy go away? Of course. Who would have tried, first, to buy Alison's compliance, and failing that, taken more drastic measures? Who had the most to lose in reputation and prestige, and the money and the will to see that that didn't happen?

Who else?

Sickened still further by this latest turn of events, Olivia detoured to a clump of forsythia and threw up behind it, then rinsed with a bottle of soda water she carried everywhere now.

Suddenly she heard her niece cry, "Auntie Livvy, Auntie Livvy, I see you!"

Kristin was peering at her through the yellow shrubs, obviously assuming a game was afoot. "Now it's our turn! You count to a hundred, and Zack and me will hide. No fair peeking!"

"Oh, wait, sweetie, no, that isn't—"

Her niece, muddy from her Mary Janes to her nose, halted and turned for further instructions. Were there other, more special rules to be followed? She was ready! She was willing! Her eyes were huge with expectation, her mouth opened and ready to swallow everything that her beloved aunt was willing to tell her. Hop on one leg? Run away backward? Just say the word.

With a laugh that was half sob, Olivia dropped into a crouch and held her arms out wide. "Hug first. Then we'll play. And make it a *big* hug."

Kristin broke into a wide, gap-toothed grin and ran full speed into her aunt's arms, then squeezed as tightly as a five-year-old could. Anything for love.

Olivia breathed the child's innocence deep into her lungs

the way a firefighter would suck in air after escaping a smoke-filled building. It was all for the women and children now, her silence.

The men in her family were tainted.

Quinn Leary was in the last few days of building a stone wall for a well-heeled cosmetic surgeon in Santa Barbara. He enjoyed the work, enjoyed not having to make any decision more earth-shattering than which stones would lie flattest on top of which other stones. When his beeper sounded, his first impulse was not to respond. He had taken very few commissions since his return to California, and he liked it that way. For now, he was going to continue to pick and choose.

But that's not why he had the beeper. Thanks to the marvel of caller ID, he knew that it was Mrs. Dewsbury trying to get in touch with him. The widow was strictly A-list, so he grabbed a bottle of water from the cooler in his truck and found himself a shade tree.

He was concerned—Mrs. Dewsbury would never call before the rates changed unless it was important. Presumably it had nothing to do with her recent discovery about the burning bus. He never should have sent that provocative postcard about Harrisburg, not to a woman as shrewd and well-informed as she was.

He sighed. She looked like such a little old lady. Why the hell couldn't she *behave* like a little old lady?

He dialed her number. She answered at once.

After gliding through opening pleasantries, she said, "My dear, I have some very interesting news for you."

"Don't be coy, madame," he said, sitting back against the tree. "It's not your style."

He was slugging water from the bottle when she said, "All right, then. Olivia is pregnant."

Out came the water through his nose and down the wrong pipe, giving him a choking fit that ended in tears.

"How do you know this?" he managed to croak.

"Promise you'll keep it a secret until the day you die?"

"Yeah, yeah—*who*?"

"Father Tom. He did *not* hear it in the confessional," the widow hastened to say. "He heard it as gossip. There's a difference, you know. He's not bound—"

"I don't care, I don't *care*," said Quinn. "Just tell me how reliable the rumor is."

"On a scale of one to ten, I would say eight. Father Tom heard it from his housekeeper who heard it from her niece, who works in the billing department of an ob-gyn in Middletown. Apparently Olivia didn't want to put in a claim to her insurance and insisted on paying cash. Well! Even though she'd gone to a clinic outside of Keepsake, the girl in billing still recognized the name. I mean, really. Bennett Milled Goods. It's like being a Hershey in Pennsylvania. Olivia should have used an assumed name if she really wanted it kept secret. Of course, in that case I wouldn't be calling you now."

Quinn let her roll to a complete stop before his next question. "Who else knows about this?"

"I imagine it's just a matter of time before everyone does. Father Tom may have been one of the first; I doubt he'll be the last," Mrs. Dewsbury said dryly.

"When did Liv make that initial visit?"

"Early April, I believe."

"Has she gone since?"

"Oh, yes. More than once."

She was keeping the baby, then.

"And why did it take the blabbermouth so long to blab?"

"It's ironic. She was pregnant herself, and went out on maternity leave right after Olivia's initial visit. Father Tom's housekeeper eventually went to see her new grandniece, and that's when she got the scoop. Since then, of course, the housekeeper has made it a point to keep herself informed."

Just as well that Quinn was sitting down; he was reeling. He thought of asking, "Is Olivia seeing some other man?" but the question seemed absurd. He knew she wasn't. The conviction came from the same place deep down in his soul as the belief that the baby was his, conceived on New Year's

Eve. It had felt, on New Year's Eve, as if they were reaching for the stars. Now he knew that they'd managed to snatch one and bring it down to earth.

It was going to be a girl.

"I'll be on the next plane," he said.

"I knew you would. Hurry home, dear."

Olivia's mother had created charming hanging baskets of annuals for every shop on the cobblestoned court.

"At first I just made one for you—to hang from the lamp in front of Miracourt," Teresa Bennett said. "But then I thought, why stop there? Is it really so much of an effort to make up ten of them? I hope the other shopkeepers won't think I'm being presumptuous."

Olivia flattened her hands against the rear window of her mother's Explorer as it sat in the street with its engine running and its air conditioning on. The cargo area was filled with magic: green-glazed pots that would hang where they were told, tumbling over with bright pink ivy geraniums and silver-green lamium and exploding with compact daisies in the middle.

Olivia straightened up and gave her mother an enthusiastic squeeze. "They will *love* them. Do you want me to take them around to the shops for you, or would you rather do it yourself?"

"Oh, honey, would you? I'd feel a bit funny."

"I'll be glad to—but let's hang this one first."

She was standing on the second rung of her stepladder, reaching up to hang the pot from a cast-iron hook on the antique lamppost, when her mother smiled and said, "Speaking of pots . . . ," and patted Olivia's stomach.

"Mother!" Olivia said, shocked to the core. She scrambled down the ladder.

"Livvy, I was only teasing," her mother said, taken aback by her daughter's vehemence.

Olivia folded the stepladder with a smack and said primly, "It's *not* very polite."

"I'm *sorry*."

"Well . . . never mind. I'm just self-conscious about it, that's all."

To say the least. She was going to have to tell her mother, and soon. But, oh God, she didn't know how. One thing was apparent: The charm of the moment was gone. "I'll unload the car," Olivia said stiffly.

"I'll help you," offered her mother, much more subdued than before.

It was so awkward. Quinn was everywhere in those pauses between them, which seemed to come more frequently now. It was Olivia's fault, of course; she was the one who had pulled back from her whole family. But her mother obviously was assuming that it was because she had objected so violently to Quinn, and now that he was gone, she was always trying to bridge the gap between Olivia and her with little gestures of affection. With no more success than today.

For the past few months Olivia couldn't help wondering whether her mother had known about Rand and Alison's affair. Now she had begun to wonder whether her mother might not know even more than that. If Owen Bennett had acted true to form and had tried to clean up the scandalous mess that his son had got into, then how could his wife not know it?

All in all, better to stay estranged.

Olivia spent the next hour passing out hanging baskets to pleased and grateful shopkeepers. It was such a beautiful day, and she enjoyed wandering around the cobblestoned court. She came back to Miracourt with real reluctance, which surprised her; the shop had always been her first love and her paramount joy.

But today she was drawn to flowers. If she owned a garden, she'd be home in it. She watered the dusty miller and ruby-red impatiens that were just getting started in the long box beneath her shop window, and then she dragged out the stepladder again; she wanted to rehang her mother's pot so that the sun-loving daisies faced south. Small gestures, perhaps, but they appealed to her newly discovered nurturing instincts.

She was standing on the ladder, gazing with pleasure at the flower baskets that hung from every lamppost in the court, when something propelled her to look toward Main. Whether it was a car horn or loud music or just plain magnetism, she never afterward knew, but the first thing to pop into focus was Quinn Francis Leary, striding toward Miracourt as if he were late to pick her up for dinner.

She hadn't seen him since January 14: four months. Long enough for his hair to grow out and hers to be cut short. Long enough for him to lose weight and her to put it on. Long enough for her to forget how tall he was, how rugged, how head-turning handsome.

Long enough for her to have lost touch completely with deep, abiding joy.

Twenty-seven

"*Hello,*" *she said,* gazing down at him.

"Should you be climbing ladders?"

He knew.

"I'm eighteen inches above the sidewalk, Quinn. I think I can handle it." *I love you, I missed you. How could you leave me?*

"It was a question, Liv; I didn't come back to tell you what to do."

"Good." *Why did you come back at all? Nothing has changed.*

"I understand that there's been a . . . development."

Oh. Right. That one thing. "You heard it from Mrs. Dewsbury, I take it?"

He smiled. It was such a sad and melancholy smile. "I'm not allowed to say."

"I don't know why people bothered inventing the Internet," Olivia said, climbing down the two rungs. "A few Mrs. D.'s strategically placed could do the job just as well for a lot less money."

He had been appraising her figure, Olivia knew, deciding for himself if the rumors were true. For one vindictive moment she wished she owned a muumuu.

She tried to close the ladder, but for some stupid reason the metal spreader wouldn't fold. "Here, I'll do that," Quinn said, moving in to help.

"No, really, I can do it myself. I—ow!"

He'd closed the spreader on the edge of her little finger, hardly a tragic event. But Olivia was feeling tragic, and her cry reflected the sharp pain in her heart more than the little pinch on her hand. Again Quinn apologized, this time profusely.

"It's nothing," she said, sucking the spot. She glanced at it and added, "A little blood blister, that's all."

With a shaky laugh he said, "Before I maim you for life, will you agree to see me somewhere? Livvy, my God, we *have* to talk."

How odd. Not so long ago, Olivia was begging him for the very same mercy.

She glanced around the court. There was Ella, spying on them over the checkered café curtains of her bakery. Burt was outside his antique shop next door, feeling a sudden need to resweep his sidewalk. Mark—no discretion there; he just stood in front of his music shop with his arms folded, watching the show. Any minute now someone was bound to pop out of the sewer with a manhole cover on his head and snap a photo of Quinn and her for the bulletin board at the foot of Town Hill.

She crossed her arms and hugged her sides, mostly to cover her stomach, and said, "Okay. I suppose I owe you that much. Where do you want to meet?"

"Your place?"

"Are you crazy? No!" she shouted. "You can't just waltz back into my life!"

She was overreacting; even she could see that. "Somewhere else," she said, lowering her voice, "but nowhere public. I don't want to be hashing this out in a restaurant or, for that matter, where we're standing. God, I'm *sick* of this town and its gossip," she added. She felt like taking all of the hanging baskets back.

She stared at the sidewalk while she chewed her lower lip. Finally she looked up and said, "I know where: the gardener's cottage. My father is in Mexico—yes, Mexico," she snapped when Quinn did a double take. "He won't be home until after midnight, and my mother always stays near a phone when he's away. We won't be bothered at the cottage.''

It was the perfect place: private, but too haunted by memories of Quinn's father for Quinn to try any funny business.

"Miracourt is open late tonight," she added. "I won't be able to meet you there until ten. Park off the estate somewhere and then walk in."

"All right, I'll see you then," Quinn said, searching her features for some sign of welcome.

He didn't find it.

By the time nine-thirty rolled around, Olivia had already made a quick trip home to change from her slacks—obviously too tight—to a denim jumper with an empire waist, which she slipped over a black top and tights. It was the kind of outfit she'd wear on a cool night in front of a fire with someone she loved.

The night was cool, anyway.

She drove to the cottage second-guessing herself the whole way. What if her mother had guests? What if she decided to drag them down after dinner to ooh and ahh over some new antique in her charming guest house? Olivia thought about it and decided that if that were the case, she would simply introduce Quinn to everyone as the father of her forthcoming baby, say good night, and the hell with them all.

I will not put this baby through any more stress. This baby comes first. It was such a new priority in Olivia's life, and it was all the more fierce for being new.

She drove through spitting rain to the entrance of the estate, then punched in the security code that activated the low iron gates, closing them again after she let herself in. The Hansel-and-Gretel cottage was enveloped in blackness; she had forgotten how dark that part of the estate could be. With neither flashlight nor umbrella, she had to pick her way carefully to the front door. Angry, tense, made more jumpy by the swaying moans of the trees around her, she rooted through her bag for her key, then fumbled for the lock on the darkened stoop. To the west, thunder rumbled behind flashes of light.

Getting closer.

In her hurry, she dropped her keys.

"Shit!"

"Liv—?"

"Yah!" She jumped half a foot before whirling around to face the looming shadow that was Quinn. "What're you *doing*, sneaking up on me like that?"

His voice was bran-muffin dry as he said, "Sorry. I was trying to be discreet. I guess I should have shouted your name from a hundred yards away."

"Oh, never mind. Let's just get inside."

She picked up the keys, plucked the cottage key from among them, and unlocked the door. Pushing it open, she let Quinn precede her; presumably he remembered his way around.

"Shall I turn on a light?" he asked from inside the dark hall.

"I'll do it."

Olivia stepped over the threshold in a state of high alert. That wasn't just some burglar or serial killer waiting for her; it was Quinn Leary. Her heart was pounding loud enough to be heard up at her parents' house. Olivia took a deep breath to calm herself, but all she accomplished was to inhale the scent of Quinn. It rocketed her back to dark and intimate times; she felt a spasm of hatred for him, hard on the heels of her lust.

How could he do that to her? How could he whip her around emotionally like that? Just . . . just standing there!

It's not him, it's the hormones, stupid. Try to remember that.

There was a fifteen-watt lamp on a semicircular hall table that stood under an oval mirror just inside the door. Olivia turned it on and Quinn stepped back from her with what she took to be exaggerated, ironic courtesy.

Immediately Olivia went around and closed the shutters, top and bottom, in the two sitting rooms that fed into the hall. She didn't bother turning on any other lights.

"We can talk in here," she said, beckoning him to have a seat in the parlor.

He declined her choice of a chair for him—too late, she remembered that it had been his father's favorite—and sat on the love seat instead. It was Olivia who took the easy chair, covered now in unmanly chintz.

The moment had the feel of a summit meeting between warring allies. If there was some way to ease the tension—a joke, a pleasantry—Olivia couldn't think of it. She was like a wader trying to get her footing in shifting sands and roiling surf. She didn't have energy for anything except to keep from getting knocked down and sucked out to sea.

"The baby is due September thirtieth," she announced, no doubt unnecessarily. "Everything looks fine so far. And by the way, I do not plan to find out its sex beforehand."

"It's a girl."

"Is that so?" she said. "Well, gee, now you've ruined the surprise for me."

"Sorry," he said. He drummed his fingertips on the rolled arm of the loveseat. "It's just that I know."

"September thirtieth," she repeated, looking around for the thread of her thought. "Naturally I don't expect you to contribute to his support. You know as well as anyone that I'm perfectly capable of earning all we'll need. And, of course, I have expectations."

"Do your parents know that you're pregnant?"

"They do not. Yet."

"Then I don't think you should be so quick to count on those expectations."

"And I don't think you should be so quick to judge my parents. They would never let their granddau—son starve, or go to any college that wasn't Yale."

"I'm sure you're right," he said, taking the hit. "But as I've seen firsthand how fickle life can be, I'd feel more comfortable if my daughter had a little something in the bank."

"Stop it, Quinn. Stop calling h . . . it . . . your daughter."

He looked at her with edgy surprise. "But the baby is mine. And the baby's a girl. I believe that makes her my daughter."

Another wave washed over Olivia, this one of resentment. How dare he stroll back to Keepsake and begin lording it over her? She had been brought up by an authoritarian. One in a lifetime was one more than she needed.

She stood up. "I know how tenacious you can be, Quinn, and frankly, I'm not prepared to fight you. I don't need any more stress. So, yes, you can set up a trust fund at the appropriate time. Our attorneys will be in touch. In the meantime, I would very much appreciate it if you'd leave Keepsake as quickly and quietly as you came," she said, turning away.

She was being ironic, of course; by now everyone in town knew Quinn had returned. As for leaving quickly, she had no hope at all that he would do it, but that didn't stop her from trying. With her arms folded across her chest and her back to him, she said to him for the second time in her life, "Please? Would you please just go?"

A mistake, to turn your back on an enemy that was once an ally.

She felt his hands touch her shoulders lightly as he said her name, and she reacted explosively, whirling out of his reach and shouting "No! *No!*" at him the way she'd been taught to do at an attacker.

After their formal, civilized exchange, her eruption seemed all the more shocking. Quinn looked stunned, then offended, by turns. He put his palms face out to her, reassuring her in a scathing way that he meant no harm.

"Listen to me," he said. "Just . . . listen. I came back because you and I, the two smartest kids in school—and, I'm sure we thought, on the planet—have managed, either accidentally or on purpose, to get you pregnant. That is a fact. You are carrying our child. I can see it in your face . . . in the way you carry yourself . . . in the way the wheels of your mind turn in a different way now.

"Which means that I am part of your life whether you

like it or not. I wish you liked it, Liv. God knows, I wish you did," he said in a husky plea. "Just . . . say the word . . . one simple 'yes' . . ."

Her icy silence was far more final than any shouted "No, goddammit!" could be.

"All right, all right. I understand. I do. But in the meantime, I am *here*. I'm not going to California before the baby is born, and—truth?—not after. I'm here. I'm here for you, and I'm here for her. This child is going to have a mother *and* a father in her life. Not like me. I'm here, Olivia," he said, watching her warily. "Deal with it."

Her plan for dealing with it was not to deal with it at all. Compared to everything else that had rolled over her so far, he was a tsunami. She didn't dare try standing up to him. Her only chance—and it was slim—was to run.

Which was what she did. "Do what you want," she told him. "But don't plan ever to see me again. Whatever you have to say, it will have to be through an attorney."

All of his composure, all of his confidence, suddenly dissolved. In a voice thick with emotion he said, "Livvy . . . Livvy, don't do this! You were entitled to cut out my heart and hurl it to the winds, but this . . . Liv, it's a *baby*, for God's sake . . . yours and mine, conceived in love . . . more love than we'll ever have for anyone else but her . . . for other babies of ours . . . Liv, can't you see that? Don't, don't do this. Don't cut yourself off from me."

"What do you expect me to do?" she cried. "You've made my life completely unbearable. I'm going to have to get through it as best as I can. The baby is my biggest complication—and my only consolation. And if I—"

What was she doing? She wasn't fleeing anymore; like a fool, she was trying to face him down. Run. *Run.*

"Go away, Quinn. *Please*? So that I can lock up here and get on with my life?" She was losing her footing, slipping in the shifting sands of her loyalties. Tears welled up. She wiped away one that spilled over.

Quinn, who had not dared to touch her during his impassioned plea, took her hand and dropped a feathery kiss on the wet spot, and then, even more tenderly, kissed the tiny red blister on the edge of her little finger.

Closing her eyes to hold back other tears, rivers of them, she let him have his way this one, this last, time. She could feel his warm breath on her fingers, hear his voice whisper, "I love you," as he relinquished her hand. But she didn't see him leave, because she couldn't bear to watch.

She kept her eyes closed until she heard the door of the cottage shut behind him, and then she collapsed on the love seat that he had vacated. In misery, she slid her hand over the soft brushed cotton of the upholstery, searching for his leftover warmth. But Quinn had been out of it too long; all traces of him were gone.

Olivia allowed him time to walk down the hill and off the estate, and then she went out into the hall where she took one last look around at the flowered walls, overstuffed chairs and well-worn antiques of the cozy cottage. She would not come here again.

A clap of thunder made her jump. She wanted to get home, to hide under the covers, to put this latest and most searing trauma behind her. She wanted to sing soothing songs to her baby and think happy thoughts of impending motherhood.

Instead she turned off the lamp, opened the door, and stepped over the threshold into the arms of a living nightmare.

Twenty-eight

"*Inside, bitch!*"

It was his voice more than his hold on her that terrified Olivia. It was crazed and singsong and out of touch. If only she didn't know it so well!

She tore loose from his grip, surprising him with her strength. Her mind shut down in denial as her body reacted on automatic: *No, this can't be happening. To the car, to the car.*

She made it to the car, made it to the door, made it to the handle on the door.

And then he had her again.

He yanked her by her arm hard enough to pull her off her feet. She stumbled, fell to the ground on one knee, felt something tear and heard something crack, and then she was being dragged back in agony to the cottage she had just disavowed. She got out a single cry for help before he slapped her with his free hand, slapped some stars into her, and then got a firmer grip around her, muffling her mouth and dragging her the rest of the way easily. She tried to bite. No good; he held her too tightly for that.

What, what—what could she do? Kicking, screaming, biting, all those tricks—useless! She cursed her small size . . . karate . . . why hadn't she learned? Her heart was thundering, her lungs laboring, as he kicked open the door and threw her inside.

He lunged after her, an easy prey: his eyes were adjusted,

his own strength intact. But she eluded him again and staggered from sofa to table to chair to table, overturning whatever she could in his path. Eventually he tripped, swore, reached out, grabbed her ankle and caused new and more wrenching pain as she went nose down on a musty oriental carpet. She should scream—but who had the time? She was too busy trying to claw out of his grip.

She pulled her ankle free of his hold but he caught her other one, and this time he had her. He mounted her from behind, crushing her under his weight and straddling her the way he would a horse. "Make a sound . . . and I'll break your neck," he said, even more out of breath than she was. He grabbed one of her hands, then the other, and twisted them behind her back. In two quick seconds she was handcuffed. Handcuffed!

He rolled her over, then dragged her by her armpits to the love seat and propped her up against the back of it. Dazed, bruised, and in wrenching pain, Olivia fought back waves of nausea as she waited in fearful silence for his next move. Think, think! she told herself. But she tasted blood in her mouth, surely an omen, and her mind kept shutting down in terror.

Nudged by a rising wind, Quinn walked against traffic, away from the cottage and toward the rental that he had dutifully parked far from the estate, two blocks away on Pine. Behind him the sky lit up repeatedly and rolled with thunder . . . but still no real rain. He was sick with heartache, and angry as well. He wanted the rain, would welcome a downpour. Anything to wash away the dread misgivings which clung to him like sweat on a clammy night.

Olivia watched him crawl around on all fours, searching for a turned-over lamp that still worked. In the dark he seemed bigger and more powerful than he had on the field: There, he had paled in size and strength next to the kids he tyrannized. Olivia had always been surprised that they could be afraid of him, this middle-aged man with a gut who often slurred his orders and paced the sidelines with an unsteady gait.

She wasn't surprised anymore.

Finally the coach found a lamp in working order which he righted on the floor. With a grunt he rolled onto his right hip, sitting across from Olivia.

Wide-eyed and still panting with fear, Olivia studied his cruel, weather-beaten face and tried to gauge the depth of his psychosis. Could she pierce through it with logic, with threats, with pleas for pity? Or was he too far gone to be reached?

His own breathing was deep but even now as he said, "You got a lotta fight for a girl. 'Course, I'm not as young as I used to be." He leaned back on his left elbow, stretched out his right leg and, with a grunt, reached into his front pocket.

The knife that he brought out and opened was enormous. Olivia could see that it wasn't new; the blade that gleamed under the lightbulb had been sharpened so many times that it had a hollow.

"Oh, Coach . . . why are you doing this?" she said in a low wail.

His laugh was no more than an explosion of phlegm. "Why-why-why. I remember that's how you were in school. Always with the why-why-why."

He ran the blade appraisingly across the flat of his thumb and said, "Believe it or not, this wasn't planned. Everything else, oh, yeah; but not this. This was—hmm, what's the word I want? You would know," he said, glancing slyly at her from under bushy brows. "Serendipity! That's it." He grinned, flashing a set of big yellow teeth that she found especially repulsive.

"Talk about luck. There I was, poking around the potting shed for a can of gasoline, when in you drive. I figure you're going up to see your mommy—lonely tonight with your dad in Meh-hee-ko, poor doll—so naturally I'm surprised when you pull in front of the gardener's house instead. And even more surprised when the fugitive quarterback comes strolling up behind you.''

He gave her leg a little nudge with his foot. Leering, he said, ''I figure you two are here for a little slap and tickle, hey? Quinn sneaks in on foot, you close all the shutters, and then you go at it. Because you like it a little on the dangerous side,'' he added, jiggling the knife in her face. ''Am I right?''

Gazing fixedly at the blade, she said, ''No, that . . . that's not how it was.''

''If you're talkin' about that dustup you two had in front of your shop this afternoon, I heard all about it. But weren't you here to kiss and make up?''

She bowed her head and he said, ''Oh, well, so I was wrong. Whatever. You know what I'm thinking? This might work out even better than Plan A, burning your mommy's house down. Tell me what you think. Pay attention now. I know you'll find any flaws in this scenario.

''You told Quinn to fu—excuse me—buzz off in front of half the town today. Okay, that much, everyone knows. After that, he follows you here. You fight again and he storms out, maybe after doing a little damage to you. Since he hates this house and all it stands for, he decides to do something about you *and* it. He has an inspiration. The potting shed is right next door. It has gas cans for all the mowers and tools stored there. He thinks to himself, 'Now here's a simple, straightforward solution to my problem.' Or rather, he doesn't think at all. He just acts. Call it a crime of passion. With a good enough lawyer, he might even get off.''

Scraping the blade against his chin stubble, the coach said musingly, ''It could fly.'' He remembered that Olivia was there. ''Think?''

Oh, God. She wracked her brain searching for a hole in that all-too-plausible scenario. ''Why would I risk meeting him under my mother's nose?'' she said, grasping at straws.

''Ooh, good one. Thank you. Why, indeed? Uhh-h-h . . . okay, how's this? You're here because you didn't want to make a scene at your place. You have neighbors. This house don't." He shrugged in apology. "I know it's a little dumb. I'm not as smart as you."

Dumb it was, but it was true. Her heart sank.

"Quinn and I aren't together anymore, Coach," she pleaded in a last-ditch effort to reason with him. "If you're trying to get back at him by hurting me, it won't work . . . truly, it won't!"

"Sure it'll work. Besides, this gets back at everyone, not just Quinn. Oh, yeah. Plan B is lookin' better all the time. No kidding; talk about luck!" He looked genuinely happy as he scrambled to his feet and began looking around the room.

While he was distracted, Olivia made a desperate attempt to stand and make a run for it. But the handcuffs hindered her and all she got for her trouble was a brutal kick in the thigh above her injured knee. She nearly passed out from the pain.

"I *said* . . . sit." He stood over her. "You're beginning to piss me off, you know that? I guess you're a Bennett after all. Your mother spurns me . . . your brother loses me the job of a lifetime at Notre Dame . . . your father gets me fired from this shitty one . . . and now you're being a real pain in the ass."

All of it was news to Olivia, but one claim stood out more than the others. "Spurned you?"

"She never said? I tried to take her out. More than once. Thirty-seven years ago come June. She wouldn't have no part of me. I guess she'd set her sights higher than the likes of a high-school coach," he said in a sneer. "Her! A baker's daughter!"

His voice dropped into a sudden, savage growl. "The bitch—it all started with her! I could have been someone . . . done something with myself!"

"You killed Alison!" Olivia said suddenly. "You killed her to try to frame my brother and hurt my mother. You knew Rand was boycotting the senior party that night and didn't have a decent alibi. But you didn't count on my father to line up doctors to testify that Rand wasn't strong enough yet to stage the crime. You hate us all,'' she cried, "and you killed Alison!''

"Ah, what're you talkin' about? I didn't kill shit.''

Disappointed, Olivia seemed to collapse in place: she would not even have the small comfort of knowing he was the murderer.

She closed her eyes, blinking back tears of defeat, and then forced herself to engage him again. Anything to stall for time.

"So . . . so it's not Quinn that you've had the grudge against all this time?''

"Him, too, goddammit! Him more than your brother! Leaving me with my thumb up my ass just when scouts are swarming the field, when I've had my first interview, when we're *that* close to a championship. So *yeah*, Quinn, too! All of 'em! It's all their faults! Nobody's had the shitty breaks I've had! Nobody! My whole life . . . one after another—''

He stopped abruptly. "Ah, what the hell. I'm wasting my time here.''

He grabbed the fringed silk shawl that Olivia's mother had draped so artfully over a chair, and he tied it tightly around Olivia's mouth. She shook her head and tried to mumble a protest as Bronsky walked away; the scarf was making her gag. In seconds he was back, this time with a tieback tassel from one of the drapes. He bound her feet with it.

"Okay, that should do it,'' he said, almost bemused as he looked down at her. "Sorry we don't have a railroad track handy to tie you to. You stay here, now. I'll be right back.''

When the rain came, it came suddenly and horizontally, raking Quinn's back like shotgun spray and plastering his clothes to his shoulders and legs. He sprinted toward the rental that he'd parked on Pine, confused for a second by an empty space where a van had been. The white Camry— that was his, right? Grateful that he hadn't locked it, he made a dive for the front seat and slammed the door after him. He slicked back his hair and started his engine, then turned on the lights and glanced in the rearview mirror as he got ready to pull out.

His soul turned to ice.

The car parked on the other side of the empty space behind Quinn—surely he'd seen it before. A pickup with a headlight bashed in . . . surely he'd seen it. . . .

Parked in front of a chain-link fence that had a BEWARE OF DOG sign half hanging on it. *Jesus Christ. Oh, Jesus Christ.*

He swept every thought aside except one: Get to the cottage *now*. His mind, his hands, the feet that pushed the pedals, all were locked on a single, imperative goal: *Get to the cottage now!* He peeled out of the parking space and turned down Main, bound for the cottage that was a block away in the next galaxy.

Olivia shook her head at the coach so violently that she became dizzy. He misinterpreted her as he tipped the gas can and carefully trickled its foul-smelling contents on the rug, over the love seat, and across Olivia's black tights.

"I know what you're thinking," he said, "and you don't have to worry. I'll knock you out before I light the match. What do you take me for, an animal?"

But Olivia wasn't thinking as far ahead as the match. It was the smell she was focused on; the smell of gasoline made her sick, so sick that she always tried to breathe through her mouth when she filled up her car. And she didn't want to throw up—oh, God, not now, she couldn't. If she did, she would choke and die. *And the baby—oh, she is a girl, she is—and her name will be Jessica . . . Jessica would die with me . . . don't throw up, don't throw up, don't . . .*

"Oh. One other thing. I need your key. I'm going to have to lock you in, naturally, to slow people down." He went out into the hall where she had dropped her handbag in the initial scuffle.

In a profound state of disbelief, Olivia watched him fish

out the keys and try several different ones in the deadlock before finding the one that fit.

She continued to take shallow breaths. She was about to be immolated, and yet the number-one problem she faced was nausea. If she could beat the nausea, if she could just hold on . . .

As it turned out, she got a little help in that regard. Coach Bronsky came back into the parlor, stood over her, and said, "Have to leave this lamp on, I'm afraid. I don't want to risk a spark, turning it off. I'd blow myself up—and how much fun would that be? 'Course, you won't know if the light's on or not," he said.

And he was right. After the sharp blow to the back of her head, Olivia's world became all black, all white, all the time.

The iron gates were still locked. Quinn turned wide and gunned the Camry, crashing through them and setting off a pompous alarm. Forget the element of surprise. If Bronsky was around, Quinn wanted him scared and running. He roared up to the house that once had been home and slammed on the brakes in front of it.

The wind and most of the rain had eased off now, and he was able to make out the coach, standing outside in front of a single square of light—an open parlor window. Quinn jumped from the car and was instantly wrapped in the reek of gasoline, which solved the puzzle of why the coach was poised by the window.

Jesus.

Too late. Quinn saw the single, tiny flame erupt at the end of the matchstick . . . saw the match arc, in seeming slow motion, through the open window . . . and then the *whoomp* . . . and then the horror of flames everywhere, reaching out and clawing at the coach, who let out a howl of pain and began slapping wildly at himself, then dropped shrieking and rolling onto the wet grass.

Olivia! In the house or not? Quinn hardly had time to spare the coach a glance before lifting a huge pot of geraniums and smashing it through a second window in the back of the parlor, sending the inside shutters flying open. He climbed through the window, ignoring the shards stuck in the glazing, mentally thanking God that a lamp was lit in the room, making a search possible.

He found Olivia unconscious behind the love seat, a few feet away from approaching flames. Holding his breath, he scooped her up and ran, desperately aware that she had been turned into a human wick by the psycho outside. He carried her through the dark bedroom that used to be his, stumbling into furnishings set in unaccustomed places, his mind reeling from the horrific possibility that Olivia could burst into flames in his arms.

And then came heaven: The two big windows that used to look out at the grounds were now a pair of French doors. With one savage kick, Quinn sent them flying open and escaped with Olivia into the safe embrace of damp night air, far from the house. He laid her on the grass and undid her gag.

Breathing? He lifted her chin and tilted her head back, then turned his head with his ear over her mouth and listened for the sound of her breath and tried to feel the warmth of it on his cheek as he watched her chest for movement. _Please, please, breathe, Livvy._ Convinced that she had broken ribs, knowing that she was pregnant, he dreaded the thought of CPR.

Yes—breathing! She regained consciousness with a fit of coughing, and the sound was music to his ears. Reassuring her with motherly, mindless words, he cut through the cord around her ankles with his pocket knife and cursed the handcuffs; he hoped her captor suffered extra agony for those.

"Sweetheart . . . Liv . . . I've got to get you to a hospital," he said, lifting her in his arms. "Maybe I can get the key to the cuffs—"

She said hoarsely, "No . . . never mind . . . only the baby . . ."

Her head fell forward and her shoulders hunched in sudden pain, and he knew, despite never having seen it before, that she was in labor. ·

God in heaven—what more?

He carried her around to the front of the cottage, astonished to see that it was still in flames; that three police cars, lights flashing and radios chattering, crowded the area; and that a hook and ladder was heading up the drive through the chaos to fight the fire. He hadn't been aware of anything except the injured bundle of life that he held in his arms.

The first one to speak through the din was the police chief, and he had a gun drawn. Quinn looked around: they all had guns drawn. What were they, crazy?

"Hand over the girl, Quinn. Nice and easy, now."

"Don't be a fool, Vickers! We have to get her to the hospital. She's hurt!"

"Fine, we'll do that," he said, cautiously holstering his gun. "Just . . . hand her over. I'll take care of it."

"No, goddammit, let me through!" Quinn said, moving toward his car. "I'm not the one who did this—Coach is!"

"That's not what he said," Vickers answered. "We'll have to straighten this all out. But Olivia comes first. Hand her over to us, Quinn. You're wasting time!"

Even as Vickers negotiated, Quinn was aware of the sound of a siren fading down Main. The coach was being hauled off in an ambulance! The coach, getting care before Liv!

"Yes . . . all right," he said in a confusion of agony.

"No, Quinn," Olivia moaned, pressing her cheek close to his chest. "Stay with me!"

"Oh, sweetheart—" Quinn turned to the chief. "Which car, goddammit?" he said savagely.

"Give her to me, Quinn."

"No, Quinn, don't do it . . . stay with me!" She buckled inward with another contraction, unable because of the handcuffs even to satisfy the instinct to clutch her belly.

The scene bordered on the surreal. By the light of leaping, dancing flames, he scanned the faces of half a dozen hostile police officers and their chief, a lifelong friend of the psychotic villain who had been bent on destroying all that Quinn held dear.

"We're going to the hospital *now*," he growled. He turned and began carrying Olivia toward one of the squad cars, ignoring Vickers, ignoring the guns. "Someone get in that last car and drive; this woman is in labor," he shouted over his shoulder, throwing Olivia's ill-kept secret into the flames with everything else.

The standoff dissolved altogether when Olivia's mother suddenly burst from the shadows behind the police officers. "Oh, my baby, oh my God, Livvy!" she shrieked, throwing the scene into even more chaos.

After that, it became a blur. Everything happened in slow motion, or maybe it didn't happen at all; Quinn was never able to recall. Bits and pieces, those he remembered: someone freeing Olivia from the handcuffs; Olivia's urgent, anguished ramblings and Quinn's own fury at the unnerving noise of the sirens; her mother, a ghostly image in the rear window of the squad car riding ahead; a pair of latex gloves, but on whose hands? All of it was a jumble.

In the hospital they took Olivia away from him and treated him for his cuts. He gave a terse statement to Vickers, bitterly aware that it was only because of Olivia's intercession that he hadn't been hauled off to jail. After that he went to the visitors' room, and there he sat like one of the stones in one of his walls, in a state of total inertia.

Across the room, Olivia's mother waited with her head tipped back for support on the wall behind her, a trail of tears rolling out intermittently from under her closed eyelids.

So far she and Quinn had exchanged no conversation. What could he say to her? "By the way, the baby that Olivia is in danger of losing—that's mine"? The chances were good that Teresa Bennett had figured that out. She had probably also figured out that Quinn was responsible for Olivia's self-imposed estrangement from the rest of her family. And finally, although it paled by comparison, she was probably chalking up the loss of her beloved guest cottage to him as well.

All in all, it was hardly surprising that she was so quiet.

Rand's arrival changed all that. His mother jumped up from her chair and flew to embrace him, and Quinn became aware, as he never had been before, of how instinctively families circled their wagons in times of crisis. With Quinn it had only been his father and him. It was hard to make a circle with just two wagons.

He got up to leave, to make it easier for them to rail at him in his absence. He didn't care. He was too sick at heart to think of anything else but the woman who was fighting for their child's life in there.

He was on his way out of the room when Rand grabbed him roughly by the arm. "Where do you get off playing God? Coming back the first time to demand justice, then coming back again—for what? She doesn't want any part of you. The whole *town* heard her say that today!"

Quinn shook his head. "Cool it, Rand," he said, fighting an impulse to knock him down. "We're all wound up a little tight right now."

"Rand, you don't know everything—" his mother began.

"I know one thing: Livvy wouldn't be in there now if it wasn't for him." He swung back to face Quinn and said, "Do you deny that?"

Quinn got the word out through clenched teeth: "No."

"Rand, stop . . . I didn't tell you everything on the phone. I didn't—she's pregnant by him!"

"What?" Again he turned back to Quinn. His face was flushed with a complex of emotions; Quinn couldn't begin to guess which ones.

"Nice going, ace," Rand said in a voice tight with contempt. "Anything else that you'd like us to know?"

"I'm not the one with the secrets."

The cut drew blood, but not enough to bring Rand down. "Why can't we get it through your thick head that you and you alone are responsible for everything that's happened so far? We were all fine before you showed up. There was no problem before you showed up!"

Quinn exploded. "Get real, Rand!" he said, fed up with his refusal to accept responsibility for himself. "Myra had your ring, your letter. She was moving to the other end of the country. She would have given them to someone else if I hadn't been around. Would you rather it were Vickers?"

"What ring? What letter?" Teresa wanted to know. Her voice was high and shrill, the voice of a mother who's out of the loop.

"Shut up, Quinn. Shut the hell up!" Rand growled.

But Quinn had been pushed over the edge one time too many. He was tired of hanging by his fingernails and having to claw his way back to their level.

"Listen to me, you fool," he said. "Some of what happened *was* because I came back, but not all of it. The coach has been planning bloody vengeance for years; Olivia told me that on the way over. It was your father's decision to move the plant to Mexico that pushed him over the edge; time was running out for him to make good on his paranoid delusions. He was after your mother tonight. Would that have been any better?"

"Bullshit! Why should we believe you?"

"Ask your sister. Jesus, you don't deserve her! Tonight she was dragged, beaten, doused with gas, and in premature labor, and still all she could think about was that Coach didn't kill Alison. She desperately wanted him to be the one who did. How does that make you feel, pal? Your sister's hanging by a thread and all she can worry about is you and whether you were the one who killed Alison to cover up your affair gone wrong."

"Rand—then it was true!" Teresa cried. "You *were* the father! Oh, God, how I hoped that you weren't. All these years, I hoped, I prayed, I wanted it to be—God forgive me, I wanted it to be Rupert. Oh, Rand, Rand . . . then it was *true*," she wailed.

Rand, battered from both sides, said in a daze, "I'm sorry, Mom. I am. No one regrets it more. But I didn't kill Alison, you have to believe me." He whirled around on Quinn and said, "Don't you dare try to tell me I did!"

Hotly, Quinn said, "If you didn't, who did? Your father? Your father, who's gone behind you your whole life long with a shovel and pan, cleaning up your messes?"

"The answer to that is, yes," came a voice from behind Quinn.

It was Owen Bennett, looking every one of his sixty-five years and carrying an overnighter in one hand. "So you can stop the shouting match right now. I was able to hear you all the way back at the nurses' station." He put down his bag and came over to his wife to embrace her. "How is she?" he asked Teresa softly.

"Livvy will be all right. They don't know yet about the . . . about the baby."

He held his wife close and rocked her in his arms. "Shh . . . everything's going to be fine, honey. Everything is going to be fine."

Quinn stared at them in disbelief. "You're all living a fantasy, you know that? Everything's *not* going to be fine. It hasn't *been* fine! Understand this: When Vickers comes back to grill me again as he's promised to do, I'm not holding anything back. Not a thing!"

"You don't *know* anything," Owen Bennett said calmly over his wife's head.

"Maybe not enough to satisfy Vickers; nothing I tell him ever does. But I'm damned if I'm going to continue to be part of this conspiracy of secrets and lies. Christ! How can you live with yourselves?"

Teresa Bennett broke away from her husband's embrace and made an imploring dash for Quinn. "You can't do that, Quinn. You can't! Think of Olivia! Think of that child!"

"That's exactly what I'm doing," he said coldly, disengaging himself from her grip. "Excuse me, will you?"

He turned and began walking away, desperate to be breathing clean, rain-washed air. But he wasn't out of the room before he heard Teresa Bennett's voice, clear and surprisingly calm, say, "My husband didn't do it, Quinn. And neither did my son."

Twenty-nine

Quinn stopped and turned to see husband and son with the same wary and baffled expression on their faces. As for the object of their stares, Teresa Bennett looked as convinced as they looked confused.

"Please don't tell me that you're the one who killed Alison and then strung her up beside the quarry," Quinn said wearily, unwilling to suffer through some heroic attempt by her to shield either of the men standing beside her. He'd seen enough Bennett-style loyalty to last him a lifetime.

Owen Bennett took a step closer to his wife. "Teresa, don't say another—"

"I did not kill Alison, Owen," she told him with remarkable dignity.

Owen looked relieved, but Quinn did a double take. It was hard to believe that this was the same woman who a minute ago had been an emotional wreck. "But you know who did?" he asked her, almost politely.

"No one killed Alison."

"Ah, we're back to the old suicide theory," Quinn said with a sigh.

"No. Alison died accidentally."

Quinn snorted and said, "I wonder why the police didn't think of that. She was just playing around with a rope, practicing how to tie her bowlines, when something went terribly wrong?"

"She fell," said Teresa, unimpressed by Quinn's dry wit.

"She came to the house in the afternoon; no one was home except me. She told me that . . . that Rand was in love with her," she explained, faltering for the first time. "And that she was pregnant. I was horrified, outraged; I went for her, I admit. I was going to, I guess, shove her or something. Maybe slap her. I don't know. She was quick, she jumped out of my reach. But she caught her foot on a table leg and fell backward. She hit her head on the marble hearth. I think she died instantly—certainly within seconds."

She paused. No one moved or spoke. Quinn felt instinctively that he was in the presence of a truth teller. Her gaze, dark and beautiful still, swept over each one of them, compelling them to continue with her on her melancholy journey into the past. Quinn understood what a powerful presence she had once been, would always be, among those of the opposite sex. The atmosphere in the small room was electric, rolling from one to the other and leaving the hairs on the back of Quinn's neck standing on end.

All of the men believed her, of that there was no doubt.

She wasn't looking at any of them now, but seemed to be peering into some dark and forgotten corner of her mind. Peering so hard that she squinted, as if there were no hope of getting any real light there, so she was just going to have to do the best that she could.

"I didn't know what to do. She had no pulse, she wasn't breathing. I ran to the phone to call an ambulance, but I knew she was dead. What could they do? They would ask questions. There would be an inquest, an autopsy perhaps. My mind went completely blank. I hung up."

She sighed and said, "And then I ran to the gardener's cottage."

It was a megawatt jolt to Quinn's system. His head snapped back and his knees went limp. It was all he could do to keep standing.

"I knew that Francis Leary had . . . feelings for me. I'm sorry, Quinn, this will be hard for you, but you wanted the truth. He had spoken of how he felt—obliquely, of course— one afternoon when we had been working a long day in the

garden and I invited him in for iced tea. He was so sweet,"
she added with a smile that wasn't at all self-conscious.
"Another day, he reciprocated with tea in the cottage, and
I could see that he had made an effort to lay out a pretty
table. But he never hinted at those feelings again. I think
. . . well, I think he understood that I loved my husband. But
he wanted me to know, that's all."

She seemed embarrassed by the recollection. Holding
herself close, she walked away from them all and up to the
window that overlooked the parking lot, the same window
that Quinn had stared through as he and Olivia had waited
for news about Mrs. Dewsbury.

"I knew, in any case, that I could trust him completely.
So I ran straight to him and told him what had happened,
why Alison had come to see me. I told him that she had
said she was pregnant, but—and this is the truth—that I
thought the baby might be Rupert's. Rupert was always so
possessive about her . . . jealous, even. And Rand and Alison
were always such good friends; Rand *would* do something
silly and chivalrous like offer to marry her," she said,
throwing a mournful smile over her shoulder at her son.

"And who could believe Alison? She was always such
a hard girl to know. I would have confronted you about it,
Rand, but I never got the chance.

"Anyway, I told Francis everything. I told him that the
scandal would destroy our family. That it would make it
impossible for us to stay in Keepsake and for Owen to keep
the mill . . . everything that was in my heart, I told him."

She turned around and said with a painful laugh, "I
wasn't so composed in the cottage as I am now. The truth
was, I was hysterical. But Francis managed eventually to
calm me down, and then he came up with a plan. He would
stage it to look as if Alison had committed suicide. The blow
to the back of her head, that would be from hitting the
quarry wall when she threw herself over the edge with . . .
with the rope around her neck. He—"

She turned slowly away from them again.

"He took care of everything."

She sighed, and except for the vague hum of hospital machinery, there was no other sound. Three men, none of them shy, and there was no other sound.

Quinn was reeling. In a daze, he said, "My father? He took care of everything?"

Teresa Bennett turned back to face him. "He did it for me, Quinn. And when the police began to close in on him, he ran. Not because he was afraid for himself, but because he thought they might figure out what really happened. By running, he was drawing suspicion away from me, from my family. I'm sure that's why he did it."

"For you. For your family," Quinn repeated, trying to get it into his head. All he could think was: Once again, aced by the Bennetts. Two lives, shot to hell, all for the Bennetts.

Almost automatically, he reached back for his single best defense against self-pity: Twelve lives were saved because of his father's misbegotten chivalry. Children's lives and mothers' lives. In the great, twisted revolution of force and matter that made up the cosmos, everything had somehow worked out.

He had labored through that reasoning so often before, but now, with a creation of his own struggling to survive, he understood it in a profound and almost religious way. *It all works out. Somehow, some way, it all works out. Believe that.*

He bowed his head, humbled at last into acceptance.

After a long eternity Teresa Bennett said to her son, "Quinn is right, Rand. You will have to tell Eileen. She loves you so much. I think you'll be all right . . . but give her time."

To her husband she turned and said, "I'm sorry, dear. I know you were afraid that it was Rand who killed her, all these years. I should have told you, but I couldn't bear to see the look in your eyes that I'm seeing now," she whispered.

She reached up to touch his cheek where a tear had rolled down. "I'm sorry."

Last of all, she turned to Quinn. "Your father was the kindest man I've ever met, and the truest gentleman. I didn't know that men like him existed outside of women's imaginations. I can't ask you to forgive me," she said softly. "And it's too late to ask him."

She sighed and looked longingly at the door, contemplating flight herself, Quinn supposed. Or maybe she was simply willing someone to come through it and give her, just once, some good news.

In any case, that's what happened. Dr. Jack Whiteman, the physician in attendance, had a cautious smile on his face as he said, "The news is encouraging. There was no bleeding, the membranes are intact, the cervix hasn't dilated. She's stronger than she looks. We're going to keep her here for a bit, and after that, she'll need to limit her activities and get plenty of bed rest. If Miss Bennett is conscientious about restricting herself, then the chances are very good that she'll carry to term."

Teresa Bennett said calmly, "Thank you so much, Doctor," and burst into tears.

Her husband rushed to her side. She threw herself into his arms, and between heartrending, uncontrollable sobs, Quinn heard her say over and over, "Oh, thank you, thank you, God . . . oh, thank you, God."

Quinn had trouble speaking with the hard knot in his throat, but he said to the physician as he was about to leave, "Can I see her?"

"You're—?"

"The baby's father."

"Two minutes."

"You bet."

Pale and shaken, Rand said, "Mom . . . Dad . . . I'm going home. I, ah . . ." His sigh was a long, shuddering effort to get his own emotions under control. "I'm going home."

He and Quinn exchanged one brief glance, and then Rand walked quickly out of the visitors' room ahead of him, perhaps in a hurry to make up for lost time.

Quinn never could recall how he got himself from the

visitors' room to the side of Olivia's bed. Possibly with wings; maybe on a magic carpet—but there he was, still knocking back that lump in his throat and wishing he could will away the tubes and the black-and-blue marks and the cast on her leg.

Olivia gave him a trembly smile. "We made it . . . she and I made it, Quinn . . . thanks to you." Her smile firmed up as she said, "I'm glad you had experience saving people from fires."

She was so beautiful, an angel booted down to earth expressly to dazzle him through the remaining years he had to live there. Pray God they were many.

He brushed aside a curl that had flopped over a bandage on her forehead. "I love you," he said.

He was surprised to see a flush in her cheeks. "And I love you, but you'd never know it the way I acted today. Oh, Quinn, I'm sorry," she said in a soft wail. "This whole thing wouldn't have happened if I hadn't sent you away."

Quinn shook his head and said, "We're not going down that road—ever again. We're not going to look back anymore, Liv; too much wonder lies ahead."

But Olivia wasn't quite ready to turn around and face happiness square in the eye.

Plucking nervously at the sheet, she said, "I have to keep looking over my shoulder, Quinn. My family's past is like some big, horrible crow, flying low behind me and waiting to peck me to pieces if I trip and fall."

"Not anymore," he told her.

Perhaps it was her mother's place to explain—Quinn had no doubt that she would be doing that—but he wasn't willing to let this one, this great love of his life suffer a single new moment of anxiety over someone else's mistakes.

"It was an accident," he said, and he went on to explain how good people with good intentions had ended up doing a horrible deed.

When he was done, she murmured, "Will you ever forgive him, do you think?"

"I already have." He couldn't help adding, "What about you, Liv? Can you forgive your mother?"

"I don't . . . know." She frowned in confusion, and yawned, and then closed her eyes. "They've given me . . . just a little something . . . for the pain," she explained with a sigh. "I wonder . . . what my mother can take . . . for the . . ."

She was gone. Asleep, whether she wanted to be or not.

Quinn got up quietly and turned off the light above her bed. In the dim glow of the nightlight, he studied her bruised and scraped face, aching to make it all better.

Almost without an effort, he was able to picture her in the same bed with color in her cheeks and their daughter in her arms.

I wonder how she feels about the name Jessica.

Smiling, he stepped quietly from the room. He would ask her first thing in the morning.

Epilogue

"*No, no, no,* Jessie! No, no, sweetie. Come here. Sit by me. Sit by Mommy."

Olivia held out her arms over her impossibly bulging stomach, but Jessie had other ideas. Off she ran, charging out of the conference room and down the halls of Sayles & McCromber, fully prepared to be chased, caught, and swung in the air. Wasn't that Daddy's favorite game?

"Quinn—!"

"Say no more—I'm on the case," said her husband ahead of her. "That's a little lawyer humor, get it?" he said with a wink on his way out.

Eyeing the sticky handprints on his glass-doored bookcases, Albert Sayles sighed and said, "Children rarely manage to sit through real-estate closings."

He was kind enough not to mention that this one hadn't started yet.

"I'm so sorry, Mr. Sayles," Olivia said for the fourteenth time since their arrival fourteen minutes earlier. "The sitter didn't show, and I couldn't reach my sister-in-law. Maybe if *I* hold Jessie . . ."

She began the massive effort of lifting her unwieldy body out of the wooden-armed chair, but that sent the elderly bachelor into total panic. "Please, Olivia, it's no trouble," he hastened to say, gesturing her to keep her seat. "I'm sure Quinn has the tot in hand."

The joyful shrieks of the tot in question bounced loudly

down the hall and into the conference room, causing Mr. Sayles to suck much air through his nose.

"Oh, dear," said Olivia, trying to look dismayed. "I hope no one's reading a will just now."

"She seems a handful," he said on the exhale.

"My mother says she's just like me."

"I don't recall that they ever brought you into the offices."

Fifteenth time: "I'm so sorry."

"When are you expecting your—?" He nodded vaguely at her stomach.

"A week?" Olivia hazarded. "It's a surprisingly inexact science. It's been a wonderful pregnancy," she added, although he couldn't possibly care. "Whereas with Jessie . . . So I'm hoping that this child will be a little more laid back."

"That *would* be nice. For you, I mean. Naturally."

And there they left it until the arrival of the seller of the big white Victorian that Quinn and Olivia had contracted to buy. Mrs. Dewsbury, dressed in burgundy twill and walking with the help of her Sunday cane, came stepping in smartly ahead of Quinn and Jessie.

Relieved, Olivia greeted the widow with a big grin. "Ah, you're here—and don't you look nice, Mrs. D."

"My dear, *you* look *enormous!*"

"*Nur*-mus," said Jessie, holding on to her father's hair with lollipop hands. Her vocabulary was getting better every day, even if her hygiene wasn't.

The elderly woman took a seat, and Mr. Sayles popped out of the room to see how long it would be before her own attorney showed. Clearly he wanted to get the show on the road.

The widow was in a state. "I was up all night, fretting," she confessed to Quinn and Olivia. "I ought to have made up my mind sooner about selling you the house. I feel just terrible. How will you handle a move and a new baby, not to mention that one up there?" she asked, pointing to the dark-eyed monkey who seemed to be enjoying the view from atop Quinn's shoulders.

"Don't be silly. It's not as if we're moving right in," said Olivia, handing Quinn a wet wipe for Jessie. "We'll need to get the workmen into the kitchen and—"

"That's another thing. You're paying me far too much for the house; it's falling down."

Quinn laughed and said, "Are you kidding? We practically stole it out from under you. I just hope the AARP doesn't hear about this."

"Oh, you stop that," the widow said gaily.

"You stop that!" mocked Jessie as Quinn reached up over his head to clean her hands.

Olivia was glad to see that Mrs. Dewsbury was exhilarated at the prospect of moving into a retirement community and passing the house on to someone she loved. Quinn had been very careful about approaching her, checking first with her son and afterward insisting on three separate appraisals before he made an offer over and above the highest of them. Everyone was happy, Olivia, most of all. It was much too quiet outside of town, and besides, they were bursting their seams in the townhouse.

Mr. Sayles returned with Mrs. Dewsbury's attorney, a man even more bent and white-haired than he was, and they began the numbing process of handing over a venerable piece of Americana from one generation to another. Olivia signed wherever they pointed, but—her advisor at Harvard would have been ashamed of her—her mind wasn't focused on the numbers at all.

Her mind was where her heart was: in a big white house on a wide street in a nice neighborhood in the center of Keepsake, where an old porch swing had been left hanging on its chains especially for her. She planned to spend a lot of time there, nursing her newborn baby while Jessie ran around on the lawn. When the children were in school, maybe she would go back full time to Miracourt. But not now . . . not yet. Now was the time for porch swings.

She glanced sympathetically at her husband, stuck with the job of deciphering dust-dry legalese while he rubbed sleepy Jessie's back.

Poor Quinn. What a long list of projects she had lined up for him: a lamppost at the turn into the drive . . . a pergola in the backyard, leading to a small, stone-walled, and very secret garden . . . a fountain like the one he had carved from granite for her mother, with a tiered waterfall tumbling soothingly into a tiny hollowed pool . . .

All in his spare time, of course.

"What're you smiling at?" he murmured, echoing hers with one of his own.

"Oh . . . nothing. Just happy, I guess."

Poor, poor Quinn.

The Memorial Day dedication didn't begin until six. There had been plenty of time after the closing on their new house for Jessie to nap and Olivia to put up her feet and rest. Quinn, still traumatized from her difficult first pregnancy, hadn't wanted her to go to the dedication at all, but Olivia had insisted.

"Quinn! You volunteered to build the memorial wall, stone by stone and with your own hands. How could I not go to this?"

And so she put on a maternity dress of pale blue floral linen and dressed Jessie in buttercup yellow, and they picked up Mrs. Dewsbury and drove to Town Hill to wander the grounds before the official ceremony to honor Keepsake's fallen.

It was a wonderful afternoon, sunny and warm and mild. Mrs. Dewsbury went off to the penny sale tent in search of bargains, and Quinn and Olivia pushed Jessie in her stroller past the bake sale table, emerging at the other end with a gooey cupcake for Jessie and brownies for themselves.

Nibbling their treats, they stopped to buy a dozen tickets from Betty Bennett, who was manning the booth for the Sewing Club's charity raffle of a wedding quilt.

"My aunt seems happy, don't you think?" asked Olivia as they wandered out of earshot.

"Very. Sad to say, but the divorce is the best thing that could have happened to her."

"She didn't think so at the time."

"Even before it, she was happier than your Uncle Rupert will ever be. She has the capacity for joy. He doesn't."

As usual, Quinn's understanding of people Olivia had known all of her life was better than her own. She was too close to them, she had long ago decided; she couldn't see them as clearly as he could from the sidelines.

They were resting near the gazebo in chairs set up for the band concert when Rand came by in search of Mrs. Dewsbury.

"Try the penny sale tent," Olivia told her brother. "What's up?"

Rand sighed and said, "She left a message with my office that she wants to bring her old Kenmore stove to the new place when she moves in on Monday. I've explained to her that her stove is gas and that there's no gas available on that side of town yet. She says she'll wait."

"She will, too," Quinn said with a laugh.

"Is she your most difficult buyer?"

Rand shrugged. "Average. It's a retirement community; the elderly tend to know what they like." He leveraged himself out of his chair by pushing hard on his thighs. "Frankly, I admire that generation. Their credit is perfect and they understand the value of a dollar. But—I can't produce gas where there is no pipeline. Has Eileen showed up with the kids yet?"

"Haven't seen them."

"Tell her I'll be in the tent with Mrs. D."

He walked away, a man with a mission.

Smiling, Olivia said to Quinn, "Getting out of the mill— and from under my father's thumb—was the best thing that's ever happened to him. Look at him hustle. He really wants to succeed. It's an amazement to me."

"He's just a late bloomer, that's all. Some people are like that. Look at you," Quinn said, slipping his arm around her shoulder and sneaking a kiss. "Getting better every day."

"I feel like an elephant at a tea party," she grumped. "I want this baby born. *Now.*"

"Yikes, watch what you're saying," said Quinn. He leaned over Olivia's stomach and said through cupped hands, "She didn't mean that. There's no hurry. Anytime after the weekend is fine."

"Oh, stop," said Olivia, laughing, as she batted him on the head. "Ah, there's Eileen. Over here!" she cried, but she needn't have. Kristin had spotted her cousin and was speeding like a cheetah toward the stroller.

Olivia got out her wet wipes and went to work, handing over a less sticky but still chocolate-covered little girl to her bigger-girl cousin. She watched with pleasure as the two of them went romping on the green, with Zack on the sidelines trying to look cool but itching to join the fun.

Yes. This is as it should be.

Eileen had the same thought. "Thank God we all toughed it out."

"I think of that every single day," Olivia said, turning in surprise to her sister-in-law. "Every single day."

Quinn could see girl talk coming; he excused himself and wandered off toward the book sale table.

"Is your father here yet?" asked Eileen.

"He will be. I don't think he's ever missed a Memorial Day ceremony. And this year there's Quinn's stone wall. He'll feel obligated."

"He does have a way of soldiering on. Who would have thought he'd keep the mill in Keepsake this long?"

"Oh, he won't relocate the mill anymore."

"Too old to do it?"

"My father, too old? Hardly. I think keeping it here is his way of compensating Keepsake for the . . . inconvenience . . . our family has caused people," Olivia said with a dry smile. "Even if he *is* going slowly broke doing it."

"Mm." Eileen sipped her Snapple through a straw and sat back with a thoughtful sigh. "Any chance that your mother will show?"

Olivia shook her head. "Once you become a recluse, it

becomes harder and harder to go anywhere. Mom has scarcely been out to buy a quart of milk in the past couple of years; I can't imagine she'd suddenly show up at a town event like this. In fact—''

A grating screech from the sound system being tested brought everyone to attention: The memorial was about to be dedicated. The two women gathered up their children and their men, and they joined Father Tom and Mrs. Dewsbury and Chief Vickers and the rest of the townspeople assembling in front of the low fieldstone wall that Quinn had built behind the flagpole on Town Hill—the same flagpole from which Olivia's velvet cape had hung in scarlet ribbons, one sleet-driven night.

But that was in another lifetime, as far as Olivia was concerned. Quinn had said it best: All's well that ends well. She slipped her arm through his, and they stood with Eileen and Rand and their children in the front of the crowd, on the left side of the memorial.

"I guess my dad's not coming," Olivia said, scanning the assembly. She was both surprised and disappointed.

Mayor Mike Macoun, newly re-elected and on his last term, began a long and heartfelt speech about patriotism. It was the Memorial Day weekend, after all, and the stone wall was being dedicated to men and women from Keepsake who had died in service to their country. Everyone stood respectfully, trying to reconcile thoughts of war with the wonderfully fine evening and friendly gathering.

They nodded when the mayor effused over Quinn's generous contribution of time and material in the creation of the fieldstone memorial that would grace Town Hill for centuries. The low V-shaped wall was beautifully made with no visible mortar and had been the talk of the town for weeks. Quinn had built it as a labor of love, but ironically, everyone who could afford one suddenly wanted one: He had been turning down commissions left and right.

After a round of grateful applause, the mayor cleared his throat and added, ''We're here today to honor Keepsake's fallen heroes, but there are two of ours whose heroism has never been properly acknowledged, and now seems like the proper time to do it.

"Twenty years ago come October," he said, "Francis Leary and his son—the man who built this wall—were instrumental in saving the lives of a dozen women and children and elderly in a terrible bus accident near Harrisburg, Pennsylvania."

His words were electrifying. Olivia didn't dare look at Quinn. She didn't have to, to know the surge of emotion he was experiencing. She could feel it in the hand that was holding hers, hear it in his quickened breath.

"A lot of us have heard about the incident," the mayor continued, "but we haven't rightly figured out how to acknowledge it. Well, due to the hard work and generosity of a prominent citizen who wishes to remain anonymous, the Keepsake Memorial Commission has been able to locate and fly in several of the survivors from that terrible time. They're here with us today, and I would like to introduce them to you now. Here are: Rhyanna White Johnson, Martin Lindsey, and Christy Ptak."

The mayor motioned for the three to join him at the speaker's podium, and they came shyly forward. Then he turned to Quinn and said with a smile, "Quinn? I think these folks have something they'd like to say to you."

The mayor stepped back. For an awful second, Olivia was afraid that Quinn might refuse to step out from the crowd. But he was acting on behalf of his father now; he had no choice. Flushing deeply, he walked up to the podium.

Rhyanna White Johnson, a beautifully poised black woman in her thirties, recognized Quinn instantly. She let out a cry and opened her arms wide as he approached, engulfing him in a bear hug. Martin Lindsey, two generations older and obviously frail, hung back until it was safe, and then he took Quinn's hand in both of his and thanked him quietly and repeatedly.

Christy Ptak, who could not have been more than Jessie's age when Quinn and his father pulled her from the bus, was the last to come forward. She couldn't have understood in any profound way that she was standing there because of the heroism of a father and his son; possibly she was there because it was a free trip out east, a lark with meals and lodging thrown in. But she was the one of the three who seemed to have moved Quinn most deeply. His mouth compressed in a tight line of emotion as he nodded and accepted her tentative hug.

He's thinking like a father . . . he's thinking of Jessie . . . Oh, Quinn . . . how I love you.

Tears were running freely now; Olivia hardly heard the mayor's announcement that a memorial plaque would be installed at the base of the flagpole to honor Francis Leary. She lifted her hands to wipe her eyes, because she didn't want to miss any of it, not a look, not a smile.

But letting go of Jessie's hand had an inevitable result: The child, set free, took off at a gallop, heading not for her father at the podium, but for the opposite side of the semi-circled crowd.

"Oh, Jessie, wait—!"

And then Olivia saw where she was headed. Owen Bennett was standing soldier-straight in the space behind where the survivors had been waiting.

And next to him, his wife.

"Gammy, Gammy, Gammy!"

Teresa Bennett turned from the podium to the fat-legged child making a beeline for her. She dropped down low and held out her arms, and some of the old joy, and all of the old radiance, returned to her face as she hugged her granddaughter tight.

Survey

TELL US WHAT YOU THINK AND YOU COULD WIN

A YEAR OF ROMANCE!
(That's 12 books!)

Fill out the survey below, send it back to us, and you'll be eligible to win a year's worth of romance novels. That's one book a month for a year—from St. Martin's Paperbacks.

Name _____

Street Address _____

City, State, Zip Code _____

Email address _____

1. How many romance books have you bought in the last year?
   (Check one.)
   __0-3
   __4-7
   __8-12
   __13-20
   __20 or more

2. Where do you MOST often buy books? *(limit to two choices)*
   __Independent bookstore
   __Chain stores *(Please specify)*
         __Barnes and Noble
         __B. Dalton
         __Books-a-Million
         __Borders
         __Crown
         __Lauriat's
         __Media Play
         __Waldenbooks
   __Supermarket
   __Department store *(Please specify)*
         __Caldor
         __Target
         __Kmart
         __Walmart
   __Pharmacy/Drug store
   __Warehouse Club
   __Airport

3. Which of the following promotions would MOST influence your decision to purchase a ROMANCE paperback? *(Check one.)*
         __Discount coupon

       __Free preview of the first chapter
       __Second book at half price
       __Contribution to charity
       __Sweepstakes or contest

4. Which promotions would LEAST influence your decision to purchase a ROMANCE book? (Check one.)
       __Discount coupon
       __Free preview of the first chapter
       __Second book at half price
       __Contribution to charity
       __Sweepstakes or contest

5. When a new ROMANCE paperback is released, what is MOST influential in your finding out about the book and in helping you to decide to buy the book? (Check one.)
       __TV advertisement
       __Radio advertisement
       __Print advertising in newspaper or magazine
       __Book review in newspaper or magazine
       __Author interview in newspaper or magazine
       __Author interview on radio
       __Author appearance on TV
       __Personal appearance by author at bookstore
       __In-store publicity (poster, flyer, floor display, etc.)
       __Online promotion (author feature, banner advertising, giveaway)
       __Word of Mouth
       __Other (please specify)_____

6. Have you ever purchased a book online?
       __Yes
       __No

7. Have you visited our website?
       __Yes
       __No

8. Would you visit our website in the future to find out about new releases or author interviews?
       __Yes
       __No

9. What publication do you read most?
       __Newspapers *(check one)*
         __*USA Today*
         __*New York Times*
         __Your local newspaper
       __Magazines *(check one)*

  __*People*
  __*Entertainment Weekly*
  __Women's magazine *(Please specify:_____)*
  __*Romantic Times*
  __Romance newsletters

10. What type of TV program do you watch most? *(Check one.)*
  __Morning News Programs (ie. "Today Show")
   (Please specify:_____)
  __Afternoon Talk Shows (ie. "Oprah")
   (Please specify: _____)
  __All news (such as CNN)
  __Soap operas *(Please specify: _____)*
  __Lifetime cable station
  __E! cable station
  __Evening magazine programs (ie. "Entertainment Tonight")
   (Please specify: _____)
  __Your local news

11. What radio stations do you listen to most? *(Check one.)*
  __Talk Radio
  __Easy Listening/Classical
  __Top 40
  __Country
  __Rock
  __Lite rock/Adult contemporary
  __CBS radio network
  __National Public Radio
  __WESTWOOD ONE radio network

12. What time of day do you listen to the radio MOST?
  __6am-10am
  __10am-noon
  __Noon-4pm
  __4pm-7pm
  __7pm-10pm
  __10pm-midnight
  __Midnight-6am

13. Would you like to receive email announcing new releases and special promotions?
  __Yes
  __No

14. Would you like to receive postcards announcing new releases and special promotions?
  __Yes
  __No

15. Who is your favorite romance author? _____

WIN A YEAR OF ROMANCE FROM SMP
(That's 12 Books!)
No Purchase Necessary

OFFICIAL RULES

1. To Enter: Complete the Official Entry Form and Survey and mail it to: Win a Year of Romance from SMP Sweepstakes, c/o St. Martin's Paperbacks, 175 Fifth Avenue, Suite 1615, New York, NY 10010-7848, Attention JP. For a copy of the Official Entry Form and Survey, send a self-addressed, stamped envelope to: Entry Form/Survey, c/o St. Martin's Paperbacks at the address stated above. Entries with the completed surveys must be received by February 1, 2000 (February 22, 2000 for entry forms requested by mail). Limit one entry per person. No mechanically reproduced or illegible entries accepted. Not responsible for lost, misdirected, mutilated or late entries.

2. Random Drawing. Winner will be determined in a random drawing to be held on or about March 1, 2000 from all eligible entries received. Odds of winning depend on the number of eligible entries received. Potential winner will be notified by mail on or about March 22, 2000 and will be asked to execute and return an Affidavit of Eligibility/Release/Prize Acceptance Form within fourteen (14) days of attempted notification. Non-compliance within this time may result in disqualification and the selection of an alternate winner. Return of any prize/prize notification as undeliverable will result in disqualification and an alternate winner will be selected.

3. Prize and approximate Retail Value: Winner will receive a copy of a different romance novel each month from April 2000 through March 2001. Approximate retail value $84.00 (U.S. dollars).

4. Eligibility. Open to U.S. and Canadian residents (excluding residents of the province of Quebec) who are 18 at the time of entry. Employees of St. Martin's and its parent, affiliates and subsidiaries, its and their directors, officers and agents, and their immediate families or those living in the same household, are ineligible to enter. Potential Canadian winners will be required to correctly answer a time-limited arithmetic skill question by mail. Void in Puerto Rico and wherever else prohibited by law.

5. General Conditions: Winner is responsible for all federal, state and local taxes. No substitution or cash redemption of prize permitted by winner. Prize is not transferable. Acceptance of prize constitutes permission to use the winner's name, photograph and likeness for purposes of advertising and promotion without additional compensation or permission, unless prohibited by law.

6. All entries become the property of sponsor, and will not be returned. By participating in this sweepstakes, entrants agree to be bound by these official rules and the decision of the judges, which are final in all respects.

7. For the name of the winner, available after March 22, 2000, send by May 1, 2000 a stamped, self-addressed envelope to Winner's List, Win a Year of Romance from SMP Sweepstakes, St. Martin's Paperbacks, 175 Fifth Avenue, Suite 1615, New York, NY 10010-7848, Attention JP.